This one has been a long time coming. Originally written when I was made redundant in 2003, it had been left alone for a very long time after my laptop died and I lost the editing. So for any of you that buy this, I hope you enjoy. In my opinion the writing is far superior to the first book. With the fact that this has been seven years in the making, I have numerous names to mention. I would like to dedicate this to my family: My wife Tricia, my boys Ben and Scotty, and my two beautiful daughters Samantha and Jessica. Mum, Dad, David Farland (always an inspiration) and Juliet E McKenna for making me want to write at all, and very importantly, Pauline for continually badgering me into getting this released.

Cover art has been adapted by David McElroy and completed by Andrew Thomas

www.jrdf.org.uk – get involved, donate money, help save my sons life.

M

Prologue

The icy wind blew for several cycles of the moon at this time of the season. It was born in the far north, nurtured between the costal glacier and the polar glacier until it grew strong enough to roam upon its own. From there it crawled across the frozen wastes of the Uporan Steppes, tasting the lives of the tribes that dwelt there, and moving on. The mountain chain of the central continent deflected the wind, twisting it around the tip to be drawn down across the grassy plains of Ciaharr - home to farmers, small villages, and the occasional traveller. There was no moisture in this great expanse of land, and the wind remained bitter, pursuing its intractable goal of touching everything with frozen fingers. From the plains it slashed down the Ardican estuary, the easiest way for the wind to travel unhindered. After the estuary, it was anybody's guess as to where the wind went. It seemed to spend itself amongst the island chain of Qua'Clira, amidst a mass of storms caused by the clash of frigid, polar air with the moist sea breezes.

On the plains of Ciaharr, a man stood shivering, bound captive by several others. He was of medium build, with hair that had greyed before its time, and many days of unshaved stubble on his wind-battered face. He was dressed in a tunic and hose of good brown country leather, clothes that were common amongst the villagers in the region. His half-boots were of good thick leather with cloth sewn inside to protect his ailing feet from bunions, inexpensive to most but precious to him. These clothes he had worn for so very long now. His only other possessions were a bottle of drink, and a knife, both taken by the man who now glared at him. His captor wore a face he wished he had never chanced upon. The man staring at him was much bigger than he, dressed from head to toe in black, and sporting long dark hair, and a complexion equally as dark. The only contrast was his icy-white skin. The rest of the group were likewise attired. His captor measured him without comment, an eagle's predatory gaze at a rabbit that could do no more than struggle weakly against the iron clasps of the men that held him. He refused to whimper. He wouldn't even give them even that much. "I know you for what you are. Murderers and cowards to a man. You will not get anything from me, no matter the cost." He should never have been in this position, and would never give a sign that he was almost dead from starvation.

The stranger chuckled, amused at this show of defiance. "You have a lot of spirit in you, I'll give you that. In the end it will make no difference. You are still going to die."

Cursing inwardly, he considered the events that had led him into folly, and regretted them as quickly.

In his life he had been called 'miller' by everybody, for that had been his trade, but the name used by his wife had been Vero. In his younger days, he was always strong, full of life and surrounded by friends and family. He had been successful, and merchants travelled from far and wide to buy his flour. He had given away as much as he had sold though, the tenets of the Old Law stating that no person was above any other when it came to helping your fellow man. For this too he had known fame as Vero, a man who could be trusted, and had a very generous heart. He had enjoyed nothing more in life than a nice tankard of frosty ale at the end of the day, and the company of his wife and children. His life had been complete; at least it had until just over a season ago. A season was twelve turnings of the Moon in the countryside. They preferred to live by the natural methods as befitted their lifestyles. The farmlands of the central plains relied on weather and good soil for their incomes, and not the gold that was so important to city folk, who had adopted the term 'Month' in defiance of the Old Law. Twelve moons had passed since he had been shocked into a flight of numbing terror over the grasslands of Ciaharr. He had been on a trip to a nearby farmstead, bartering and dispensing his flour for other farm goods that his mill and his family had needed. It had been a successful trip, the flour netting him cheeses, sides of meat, and staples that would last his family for a long while. His flour in return would make bread and all manner of baked goods that would provide a little bit of cheer and a lot of sustenance. He had given almost as much away to the workers of the farm. If flour could be construed as a gift, then the farm workers treated it as such.

In the early morning he had returned to his village and mill full of good cheer and looking forward to seeing his family, as the round trip had taken him several days. "Soon, boy. Soon we will get you into the stable and you can have a nice well-earned rest." Vero had spoken gently to his horse, his old travelling companion. The horse, who had never had a name, nickered back eagerly, and got a reassuring pat to the neck as a result.

"There, you see? Home awaits us both." He looked with a smile at his mill on the skyline, the sails rotating in the chill breeze. It was always the last thing he saw upon leaving, always the first sight that appeared on his return. The cart rumbled up the rutted track to the village, the wheels creaking and grinding over the stones knocked loose by many previous trips. He remembered staring at his only home from on his cart, and thinking something was amiss. The village normally radiated daily noises, even this early in the morning, but there was absolute silence. No hammers of the blacksmiths at the forge, no children playing in the streets. Just the creaking of his cart and the blowing of the wind. Even the air around him seemed oppressively silent. The houses nearby were lifeless with doors and windows shut, and many had the drapes pulled behind them as if they were shutting out something. "This is most unusual. Not a soul awake," he observed to his horse. "Ah well, perhaps they are still abed. It is rather early." Vero passed, apparently unnoticed. This was unusual, for he never made this journey without a friendly face popping up to wish him well. He did not expect it of course, but his neighbours were practically family. The cart trundled over the recently repaired bridge in front of the mill, and the light of the sun became hidden by the squat tower that was the working part of his business. He entered the yard, climbing wearily down from the cart to look for his two sons to help him with his wares. The horse snorted as he walked past, and he laid a hand on his old friend's nose. "We will get to the source of this soon enough, old boy."

The horse snorted back, less than impressed by being left attached to the cart. Vero grinned at the indifference and turned to the house. Something was odd, or maybe he was just bemused by the quiet in his tired state. He wanted nothing more now than sleep.

Entering the house behind the mill, he noticed that the quiet extended even to here. "I'm home, love," he called. "Come help me lads!"

The only reply was the creak of the wind in the sails of the mill. His house had never been empty. Never. Curious now, and a little worried, he moved quickly through his demesne. It had not been disturbed. Everything was in its proper place. The beds lay untouched, the

kitchen clean and tidy, a sign of his wife's sure touch. "Carlyon?" Vero shouted the name of his wife, not able to understand where she would have gone. The mystery deepened. His only answer was that the playful family of his could be hiding in the mill itself. With a smile to reassure himself, he went outside, around to the mill. His pride and joy had recently been whitewashed, and had earned it the name 'The Ivory Tower' from the rest of the village. It meant everything to him, as was clear to anybody that saw it. He entered through the sturdy oak door in the yard, and climbed the spiral stairs up to where the meal was ground to flour. He noted that the machinery needed greasing,

and promised himself to complete the task as soon as he had had some rest and could get a hold of some decent rendered fat.

"Jo, Bess, are you two fools in here?" Vero demanded, growing rather irate at the lack of anybody to greet him after his long trip. He threw the door open, and was met by carnage. His face dropped, and he fell gasping to his knees. The stale metallic odour was ripe, and burst past him down the stairs. He would never forget that stench. Death had visited him in the vilest of ways. Tears streamed from his eyes, and a racked sob came from deep within as he beheld his wife and two sons. Stakes had been nailed to the woodwork, and his family thrust upon them. Stunned, he stared unseeing around the grinding room. With a detached look, as if he was not in his body, he had looked around at the blood pooled between the wooden floorboards and on the benches at the side of the room. The metallic reek violated him to his very core. What made it most unreal was the sunshine glowing softly in from the window, as if beams of light were trying to comfort his family, or to free their souls for the next life. He dared not look at their faces. He knew well enough the warm smiles and looks of contentment his family used to give him, and he did not want to see the inhuman masks of agony they now wore. His legs felt like quivering stumps of jelly; he propped himself up using the banister of the stairway, and left the room, pausing long enough to close the door. His mouth hanging open, and his head shaking slightly in uttermost denial, he made it to the bottom of the stairs before he fainted.

He remembered coming to, and going out into the light. He had thanked the Seven Gods that it was still in fact day. He was so scared, so overcome with grief, that he could not have bared to have gone anywhere in the dark. His village was not big by any standard, and it did not take him long to search it. It was the same in every building. The doors had been shut but not locked, and everyone had been butchered in grotesque mockery of a night twenty seasons before, almost a generation in the past. His friends, and his relatives, all skewered like boars in the woods. He had quickly given up any hope of finding anyone alive. By the end, he had but to open a door and taste the metallic reek of blood on the air, and he never even bothered going any farther. He had trudged back through the village in a daze. It was surreal to be the only person alive. In the end he had just gotten back in his cart, driven it out of the yard, and onto the road heading east. He kept riding for several days at least, though he lost count. All he knew was the care of his horse, and that he had to keep going. Something evil had happened to all that he had known and loved, something from a nightmare. He could not even face the direction he had come from, let alone consider going back. With tears streaming down

4

his numbed cheeks he faced the north wind, begging it to wash him clean of the memories that plagued him. At length he came to a crossroads, and found the wood nearby that had been his home ever since. He made do with what he had, storing spirits and food, water and provisions for the horse in a rude shelter deep in the wood, out of the continual breeze. That was when he had discovered the stumps. Coincidence or not, the discovery shook him to his core. The number of stumps in the woodland glade were just about the same as the people in his village. The thought, the very implication that the place he had decided to make his refuge could be the same place that they took the stakes from was too much for him. Confused, and unable to strike out at the invisible foe that had destroyed his life, he began to drink. Vero had had a winter's worth of brandy to last his family through the cold moons ahead, but he managed to drain it down to nothing in almost the course of just one passing. The numbness was not pleasant, but it was a far cry from the hideous memories that attempted to rise to the surface like a bubble in water. In the end they could not be contained. He woke one day to discover that his horse had been taken, but even that fact failed to rouse him from misery. The only word he could utter for a long time was "Why?" and he uttered it seldom.

He wandered the forest for days on end, eating when he could, using the herb-lore that had been his pride to keep himself alive. Then the strangers had come. A group of them, wizards and warriors all, asked him about his woods and about the area. He had helped them. He felt somewhat more like himself for a while. The human contact reminded him that although he had lost a lot, he was still alive. At least he had felt more alive after he recovered from the blinding hangover, a direct result of what one of the wizards had given him – spiced brandy, some fancy name. He reasoned that although he could never go back there again, at least he could divert anybody else from going there too. He prayed that they would not find the village, that the tomb of his past would go undisturbed. He should have known better really, and not said anything to them. Vero would make it his mission to start again, and to prevent anybody from desecrating the tomb of his friends and family. His mood reflected the bleak skies above him, and the forbidding wind around him. He had come back out to this point every day to persuade travellers to go aside, to take another path. Any path but this one. His warnings of doom and death were enough for many of the dark-haired travellers that seemed to be abroad, but not for the men he stared at now. They had come out of the East, as had many of the others, but instead of heeding his warnings they had laughed at them, and grabbed him.

"So you are the miller who escaped, are you?" demanded one huge man with a scar down one cheek and a variety of weapons. "Tell us of those you have spoken to from here. Who has passed you?"

Suspicion overcame his grief and distress. "What do you mean, the miller who escaped?" The man loomed closer, and he could smell the acrid stink of strong drink on his breath. He wondered if this was what he smelled like, and felt an instant of guilt; His wife would never have forgiven him if she had seen him like this. He vowed that he would never be in such a state again.

"Was there a group, with guildsmen and thin warriors?" the man pressed. Suspicion dawned into realisation as the miller comprehended who these people were. "You. You killed my Carlyon, my Jo and Bess, my friends." Animal rage overcame him as he attempted to break free and exact his vengeance upon the man closest to him. He lashed out with a foot and caught the man square between the legs, but he was so weak and undernourished that he managed only a moment of this fight back. The killers regained control of him, and the man he had kicked stood and punched him solidly in the stomach. Vero would have doubled over. Instead he retched, and spat blood in the face of the man, his only method of defiance. It made him feel better for a moment, until the brute wiped his face and delivered a backhand blow that would have felled him had he not been gripped by the other two.

"Come on, be done with it," called a voice from behind, someone sitting up on a horse. "He won't tell you a thing, not now he knows who we are."

"He has that much right. I would die before I tell you a thing, you filth." Vero the miller glared right at the man he was facing, who surprised him with a response of utter dispassion. He shrugged and turned away. "So be it, let us go. We can learn nothing more."

For the briefest of moments he felt the grip of his captors loosen, and prepared to strike one blow at the man who had his back now turned to him. The Old Law prohibited violence of any kind, but what did he have left to care about? The Old Law had not protected his family; they were no more alive for following the tenets of the Law. He balled his fist, and then to his dismay realised that they were only shifting their grips on his arms. Before he knew what they were doing, he had been hoisted up in the air, and they were moving him backwards. "Whatever you do with me, you will get your comeuppance." He kicked feebly but it did no good.

The big man turned around and watched, eyes wide with his tongue licking around his teeth in a grotesque expression of pleasure and anticipation. "This is what happens to you pitiful followers of the pathetic Old Law." The man who intended to be his end spat on the ground. "There is no place in the new

6

world for it, or for you." He flicked his hand in some kind of gesture, and the miller was thrust back. In one of the most lucid moments of his life, the miller swore that he was again looking down at himself, as he screamed in mortal agony. He was certain that he could feel the bark of the stake passing through his back, and out the front between his splintered
ribs. He looked down on the shell that was him, and felt him scream himself hoarse. The blood erupted from the wound, and from his mouth. The band of mercenaries around him just stood and laughed, as if this was all some grand jest. He looked away, and as darkness passed over him like the embrace of nightfall, he swore for a moment that he saw his wife coming to greet him, bringing his two sons with her. There was contentment on her face, and a rapturous joy at seeing him again. It felt to as if he were finally home.

From a vantage point on a hill protecting a small wood, another old man sat watching in the lee of a boulder. His cloak was the colour of the surrounding grass, so he was camouflaged well. He cursed the fact that the drunkard who had stumbled upon his home had decided now was the point to flee. He grimaced and closed his eyes, opening them only to shed tears when he heard the animal scream of the man's death cry. "The Gods bless the poor bastard," he said quietly, in reverence to the passing soul. He looked down at his feet, and shook his head. Turning around, he regarded the dozen or so strangers hidden in the path behind. They were of a dark complexion, with a strange tattoo on their throats. He shook his head slightly, and they too bowed their heads in grief for the stranger. Nobody should suffer as he had done.

Chapter One

The old man, known as the Witch Finder for deeds accomplished in times long past, watched through a scrying focus as his creature apprehended some of those he felt sure would lead him to the girl. His thoughts turned sour as he reminded himself that he could no longer trust anybody not directly under his control to accomplish a task for him. His former underling Maolsechlan had shown him that. Despite his years of service and unswerving loyalty, indecision had proven his downfall, and he had been sent to the eternity of torment that awaited any of those unlucky enough to be taken by the Golem, a creature of stone and darkest magic. He should have taken the chance when it presented itself, and captured the girl he was sent to look for, not return with assurances that they would not get far. His chance had now passed to another though, as he had been enveloped by the dark magic of the old man's greatest achievement to date, the binding of a mortal by use of the darkest focus ever conceived into the creature of stone that now filled the vision in his focus. It had always been a means to an end, and the souls of countless mortals had been used to keep the ever-increasing hunger of his creature at bay.

"Will it ever reach a point that there are not enough people left for the magic to consume?" Armen, his long time aide, watched the focus from behind.

"It matters not. By the time that ever becomes a possibility, I will be the owner of the book, and the source of a stronger magic." He frowned again, twisting parchment with meaningless scribble from one of his scribes into a tight knot. "I walked the land ere most of these lower beings were born. I have waited long enough, but I am patient." In the highest tower of Raessa, where he could view the world with a magical eye, he was as impotent as a mule when it came to controlling the destinies of mortals. He had captured the tribe that harboured the Tome of Law – the book of the Gods, but that had yielded nothing to him. Even though he had not been successful, his reputation had spread far and wide, and rapidly so. It was this that kept the ways to Raessa clear of any traffic, and it was this that had allowed him to gain knowledge surpassing that of any being in the world.

"One day soon we will no longer need these rocks to cast a spell. The time is at hand when emotions will rule. Heavy, useless rocks. They will be obsolete."

"How?"

"You will see, if you live that long. The Golem grows ever hungrier." No matter what his servants tried; no matter what magic they employed through other means, it did not work. The cold rock was still the source of all magic. Something had garnered his interest somewhat more just now. "Look, Armen, what do you see beyond them in the focus."

Garias shifted so Armen could get a better view. "I see nothing beyond them, master."

"Exactly. That is what you are supposed to see. There is a distortion there, much like that of the Forest people. It is something the focus can not penetrate, and something that the Golem and that fool O'Bellah will not notice by being there. There is a distortion in the focus, designed to divert the eye." As he had watched the capture of the tinkers through the eyes of the Golem and the focus generated by what was left of the Earth guilds pitiful circle, it dawned on him that there was something special about this valley. There were differences to the forest. The distortion concentrated on a single point whereas the great forest had generally encouraged one to look elsewhere. None of it fooled him. Weak in power though he may be, the wisdom of countless years showed him what he needed to see. "There is something of great importance there, and I will have the answers." If he had to travel for years to get them then he would do so, but there were other ways.

"Get out, wizards." He dismissed the few old men that had survived the backlash of the explosion. Once young and full of vitality, they had had nearly all of their ability to focus taken away from them in the harshest possible manner. They scuttled out, fearfully avoiding his gaze. He looked out of his tower, full of contempt. Once he would have gained pleasure from watching lesser creatures timidly stepping around him, looking down, scared to tempt his wrath. He had lost all pleasure in such entertainments as he had gained wisdom. They were no more than a distraction to him. The book that he quested for consumed his thoughts. His zealots were enough to keep the public scared that he should ever pay them a visit in person. He could do without all that, but he would never let on to anybody of that fact. Even as he stared out over the mountain range to the South, so close to his window that he could almost touch the nearest peaks, he pondered the conundrum. In a rare moment of reflection, Garias spoke normally to Armen, as he guessed others might do. "Twenty seasons back or thereabouts, the book was on its way to me, courtesy of that lowlife thief from Dupodi's Tail. All of a sudden, the book and the thief disappeared. Not a word, not a clue as to where it had been. I had people set in place everywhere. The plan to bring the book in secrecy to my hands had been executed perfectly, but not to fruition. What went wrong?"

"I... uh... don't know."

"Spoken like the true commoner you once were. I swear to this very day that those forest rats had hidden my book in an attempt to call on their pathetic Old-Law Gods, but they too escaped my plans."

"Well what else is there to do?"

"There has been time enough to try stealth and clever ideas. Now it is time for me to try something more straightforward. The armies I have created with the taint of the Golem's evil will do the grunt work. They will drive out the scattered tribe from their temporary hiding places in the lowlands, and scare the villagers into believing that they are coming for them as well. There will be no place for them to hide in the flat grasslands of Ardicum and Ciaharr. He will see them rounded up and dealt with, and I will have my Tome! But that was not for now, no. I have waited for so long, I can wait another year or two. The Tome will be mine!"

A stray breath of wind whispered around him from the open window, reminding him that while he felt little for humanity, he was still human. "I have stood here long enough. Go about your duties, Armen. The mountains are not as inspiring as once they were. I will seek my inspiration elsewhere." Not waiting for a response, The Witch Finder opened a side door into the wall of his chamber. He climbed down the polished stone steps from his tower into the halls that comprised most of his citadel. Enough gold to pay for a country shined back at him as he walked past, unaware of the splendour. As with the lives of humans, the meaning and worth of gold meant less to him than to most. He existed, he wanted. That was enough. What it took to get it was immaterial, but failure would not be tolerated.

A timely reminder of this appeared in the silent form of Maolmordha. Tall and lithe, the striking woman fell in behind him, following to wherever his feet led them. From the corner of his eye he noted her blonde hair, tied back in a horsetail with a band of silver. That was all she needed. She was far more than the beautiful woman most perceived her to be. If he had had any feeling at all about her predecessor, Maolsechlan, it was anger over his failure to deliver up the girl who would one day touch the Tome of Law. That was unforgivable. That they had at least brought somebody with them was small consolation.

"The training progresses?"

"At a rate unheard of."

The girl, now clad in darkness, was maybe a few years older then the age that Maolmordha had been when she had been dragged screaming into his tower. The Golem had cowed her soon enough, its very presence scaring her to silence. He glanced aside as they walked through one of the towers' long maze of corridors. The woman was striking, intelligent, and very useful as a tool through her total and utter dedication to him. She had not turned out bad in the end. "Excellent. She will have a chance at completing before you did perhaps." The thought that chafed at him most, like the continual rub of manacles on one of his captives wrists, was that it had taken nigh on twenty years or seasons or whatever the commoners called it for her to become as she was now. "There must be a faster way to subvert the minds of the young, and speed their development."

"You would know if there was, master."

"Perhaps. There are many ways, some more successful than others. My experiment with binding farmers to the Golems aura was not a total success. It is true that nearly all of them are now under my sway, whether they knew it or not. Come the gathering in the springtime, I will have an army at my disposal the likes of which have never been seen before. The coastal Dukes in their fine mansions care not a whit for what happens leagues inland from their pretty women and fine wines. Gold sees to that. As long as they have their sea trade and their great vessels, they are content. A well-placed bribe in certain places ensures that the inland Dukes are always distracted. My web of followers is placed all over the land, so why can nobody find my Tome?" This, more than anything else frustrated him. He had been giddy with anticipation as he felt Maolmordha and the lackadaisical Maolsechlan nearing Raessa such a short time ago. The rug had well and truly been pulled out from under his feet in that respect. "Still, with a little training and a lot of reconditioning, the tinker girl might end up being our most prized asset, if for no other reason than she might be a good bargaining tool with the fools hiding the girl I am truly after."

"She will be found."

"I know. You will find her for me." The portents had been read, and every one had stated that she was destined to find the Tome of Law. It should only be a matter of tracking her, but it seemed that he could trust nobody else to do that for him. He would have unleashed the Golem but for the fact that the very aura that kept it in that form and enabled it to contain the magic it did gave it away. He was immune, as he just did not care any more, but it was easy to spot that the aura of evil that was the very essence of the creature quailed most people. Even Maolmordha looked uneasy, and that was despite her years of conditioning. So he was reduced to searching by stealth.

"There are many deeds to be accomplished ere this is over. We need more tools. It is time to call in some of my allies. There are not enough wizards in the tower, and I need their talents."

"What about your greater focus?"

Maolmordha knew of many of his secrets, so this comment was unsurprising. "Useful if one is within range, but we need a more direct approach. That is not your concern. There is a new mystery, one I wish you to see to personally. In the valley where the Golem stands is something of great importance to me. Seek it out, and discover the meaning. No focus can scry there. Perhaps you will find other means." He was sure there was a significant meaning, never previously considered, and Garias realized now where he had intended to go. "I will start at once."

Pondering his thoughts, he came back to himself for a second to find that Maolmordha and the girl were still accompanying him. He stopped.

"Take the girl, and train her in the arts of the assassin," Garias commanded with a smile of malicious glee.

"Is it not too soon, master?" Queried Maolmordha.

"Maybe, maybe not," he replied, his mind already elsewhere. "Try her with it and see what you can accomplish. Be persuasive if you need to, but I think she will be tractable."

Maolmordha immediately stopped following him and set off for a side door in the corridor.

"Of course, it is on your head for her to succeed," Garias added, his tone frosty with clearly implied meaning.

Maolmordha stopped, turning to face him, her face an unreadable mask.

"Remember what brought you to the fore, my dear. Nobody in my domain is immune. If she should not prove useful, you had better pray that you are beyond my reach."

Maolmordhas eyes narrowed ever so slightly. "She shall succeed." She pivoted with a flick of her blonde mane, and exited through the door, her protégé right on her heels.

The door slammed, and Garias relished the anger that had emanated from her. "Still an echo of the resentful girl she had been as a child, so much the better," He chuckled as he strolled along. This day had its positive moments despite all that had happened.

One of the benefits of power and influence was that the wielder often had the opportunity to gather a significant amount of information, should one but have the desire to. Garias dismissed the pathetic Dukes, more concerned with their gold coins and pretty wenches. True power came through research and carefully laid plans, and for seasons had been gathering information on any event of significance, right back to the alleged forming of the world, which lesser beings believed to be the truth. Garias knew that if the world was formed in the way the stories told, that there would be some evidence of their tampering. The discovery of the focus in Ciaharr now had him wondering if this was the proof he sought, and whether or not it was related to the cavern in the forest that he could not penetrate. He knew that he would find the answer in his library, perhaps the largest single collection of scripts, tomes and scrolls outside any ducal collection. They collected books to impress others with their wealth and large, imposing rooms. He collected them because he valued the information.

The library was nearly the size of his beloved grand hall, but there was an obvious difference. The hall was grand in every respect, golden, bright and spacey, with the air of a throne room. The library was the complete opposite. Shelves crammed every conceivable space, some reaching twice as high as a man. If there was knowledge to be gained here, he knew it was merely a matter of time before he found the answers.

At length, he reached the doors of the library, monoliths looming over him guarding a treasure of information. It was ostentatious of him, but he loved the huge doors everywhere, even when they were not practical. With a lack of wizards, Garias did not open the main doors, but chose instead a side entrance through the servant's quarters. It amused him to sometimes come upon his servants unawares and find them not performing as they should. It often meant an object lesson involving the Golem, but then the Golem could always do with another soul to tap. That in itself would be a problem he would have to deal with, and he was sure that in the library he could track down the information that could at least lead him to somebody that he could use to control the destructive magic inherent in the Golems aura. Slipping quietly in through the door meant he had to pass through an antechamber which was packed full with useless rubbish. It was amazing to him the amount of pointless detritus humans could accumulate. Why a dried up orange would bring so much amusement to one of the menials he never knew, but to have a whole series of them, each one in a different stage of desiccation was beyond him. Still, he was not petty, and as long as the library was orderly, he was not the least bit bothered about one small antechamber. Emerging into the repository of his accumulated intellect, he was struck by the aroma that threatened to take him back to his youth, before he had had any aspirations. The musty smell was overpowering, and it took a bit of getting used to. Fortunately for them, the menials who maintained his great collection were hard at work cataloguing and arranging new additions to his growing base of knowledge. He may have had to rely on capturing wizards for their use of focusing, but he paid these people to look after his library, and they did their job well.

The sun filtered down from windows high up in the lofty ceiling, highlighting specks of dust in the air as it shone down to land on the rows of parchment below. The warmth glowed from the wood of the many shelves as the sunshine landed on them. It was almost enough to make Garias forget that he was the most feared man in the Duchies, and just another scholar. But not quite.

He approached one of the librarians. "Show me the listing of rare works from the southeast Duchies."

The librarian turned away, a rare breach of respect, but one Garias was willing to forgo. "Would that be rural editions, or Ducal collections?"

"Collections, but of rural origin."

"Here." The librarian handed him a list.

"Take me to them." Garias found himself being guided through the honeycomb of shelves. There was a raised walkway along one side of the library where new shelves had been added. From there it was possible to see the entire lower section of his collection. It was more like one of the mazes that the Dukes wasted a fortune on in construction, so that empty-headed ladies could wander and get lost, pursued by over-ardent suitors for a hidden tryst. But he had selected every one of the librarians personally from the Order of Knowledge; one of the Guilds noted for their affiliation to the God Jettiba, the God of life. They had memories like no other people, and were among the few beings tolerated. They served their purpose splendidly, and led him right to the book he had been hoping he would find. "The prophecies of Eimaj."

"Would you like to know a little about it?"

"No. Leave me."

Grasping the leather-bound tome tightly, he moved to one of the nearby tables and brushed away the paraphernalia from its surface, unmindful of the fact that the very same person that had brought him here and found his book had been working for several days cataloguing everything in this section. He never heard the small pleasantries tinged with extreme annoyance at what he had just done; he was a thousand leagues away, already digesting the text that had been scrawled on the pages contained therein. This tome was not the original, but a scribe had been paid a fortune to spend his life making copies of the original text, as the orders prized them highly. Some madman in the southeastern Duchy of Pahrain had scrawled the original. Now this Duchy was barely known for anything save its imports of rare material from far-off countries to the East. It was fortunate that a merchant had been travelling near

14

the headwaters of the river Todya, and had discovered the tome. Some madman living at the base of Mount Eimaj, one of three extinct volcanoes, had been yelling for years at anybody who would pass near him about the Gods' methods of talking to mortals, and how they were not really gone, just waiting to be contacted. Most people dismissed the lunatic as insane, and left him well alone, but for some reason the merchant stayed and listened. Something in the manner of the madman made sense to the merchant, and he sat there for a full month writing the ravings down. At the end of the month he looked through what he had written, and found that it was more than a passable tale. The Lord of the small Duchy, a fat Duke that lived in the coastal backwater of Cuc decided to take a copy with him on a visit to one of the other Duchies, and the fame of the tome spread from the squabble that ensued for nearly a generation over possession of the piece. Now Garias had found all this out by means of another tome, one that described rare works of great potential, and he had demanded a copy. Of course, events had transpired to keep him away from his books until now; the discovery of the girl destined to wield the Tome of Law had consumed his every thought. He considered that maybe he was going about this the wrong way.

The tome in front of him consumed his interest now, and by the time he had read every last page the sun had passed from the lofty windows and far beyond the mountains to the West. The library was filled with the steady yellow glow of the focus stones used by the order of knowledge. One of the few focuses they believed in utilizing regularly, it meant that they could get more done. The night was a good time for study and contemplation, and Garias did not need sleep any more. He rose, leaving the tome he had been studying to the ministrations of the librarian, and exited the library. The book had given him an insight into his present issues that he could have got from no other place. He headed straight for his tower, whispering through the corridors like some pale wraith. He needed to be where he could contemplate his thoughts with no chance of being disturbed. Even the quietest librarian was a distraction at his age.

Reaching his private rooms, Garias bolted his door, only finding after he had done so that Armen was already present. "How do things progress?" he asked, his surprise masked with a cold stare.

"Word has been sent. Your allies, whoever they are, approach even as we speak."

Garias reclined in his a seat with the company of a goblet of Ardican wine and the focus stones he kept to hand. It was enjoyable to revel in his underling's discomfort; Armen had no idea of who he spoke. "They will come in very useful."

"Is that the book?"

"It is a book." As Armen stewed, Garias continued. "The Eimaj prophecies were indeed a revelation to me, assuming they are accurate. The madman believed that each of the Gods had His or Her own special place; a shrine one could almost call it. In that place they had what the madman, who was convinced that one could communicate with the Gods, had called a Grand Focus."

"Does it say where?"

There was no record of the locations despite the words. He had to ask himself why there would be a source of power in such a place as he had seen. It did not fit the surroundings. He had long suspected that there was something of that ilk in the forest chamber, hence the reason he had tried to invade it with magic and manpower. All that had proved to him was that force would yield him nothing.

"It does not matter. I am not after contacting Old Law Gods. My goal is the Tome, and anything beyond that is my providence alone."

"But this distortion. It is open and unprotected, and ripe to be explored, if not abused."

Armen made sense. "So be it. I will send Maolmordha and the girl. It would take them a while to get there because they lacked the equilibrium gained by three running together, but they would get there eventually."

"O'Bellah is closer."

"You would have me trust that fool? The Golem is not an intelligent being, its lust for souls becoming an overpowering hunger that it cannot see beyond, but it is a genius compared to that one. Besides, if it went, the reek of evil would never aid me in doing anything constructive, so I am forced to use the one person I can trust." Sipping his wine, and appreciating its subtle qualities, his eyes roamed over the collection of stones in his study. There was something else that he had read in the book that eluded him for a second. It was the briefest of passages, read at a point when he was skimming through the book. What was it? He thought back through his period of reading, trying to recall what exactly he had been doing when he read the particular passage. He had noted that the library could benefit from focus lights on the desk he was reading at, and then he had been annoyed at a page that had had to be prized apart from the next. Then it came to him. It was not the page after the page that was stuck, because that contained gibberish about some focus the gods used. It was the page after that.

"The gates aligned focus the mind to cross the bridge. That was what it had read, and had no reason to be on the page."

"What does that mean?"

"It means that there is now a link between the forest and the valley. We have two of the seven Shrines of the Gods, I would bet your soul on it. I need proof from one of these places, and the valley is the most obvious place. Maolmordha shall go there since I need to actually be able to learn something about the distortion." There had to be something that would tell him that this was a focus for the Gods. Of all the people he could trust, she was the most dedicated. In truth he had already made up his mind to send her there the instant he had seen the stone. Again Garias cursed the fact that he could not move swifter himself. Having long ago given up counting the years he knew that utilizing the greatest focus only would relieve him of the ravages of age. That, or the Tome of Law. One way or another, he would accomplish his goals.

In a much more relaxed frame of mind now, Garias became aware of a timid tapping at his study door. Aware that the burdens of ruling a city the size of Raessa meant he would never seem to get a moments peace, Garias unbolted the door. On the other side stood a guild runner, one of the few people that the Witch Finder would allow in his private study without good cause, Armen watched in silence as the messenger followed him into the study. Garias took position on his seat, and resumed contemplation.

"Wine, Armen?" Garias indicated with a tilt of his head that if Armen wanted a goblet, he needed to fill two. Armen complied. One did not decline an invitation from the ruler of Raessa, no matter what the option.

"So what have you to report about tonight then?" Garias asked in a tone hovering on utter boredom.

"The wizards are nearly here, master. Nothing else seems to change. The commons still hang nightshadow over their doors and windows, convinced it will keep them from being sighted by 'the evil eye', as they put it. I have no idea if it is successful, but it gives the city a distinct aroma."

"I don't recall the last time I went down there."

"The focuses still hold on the walls, and the greater focus draws people from as far away as the headwaters of the Hotiari, leagues to the East. The city is packed. People will have their diversions, I guess."

Those that did not have the privilege to live behind the insurmountable city walls were forced to make do outside, and over the past twenty seasons or so, the city had grown considerably. Why they felt drawn here, they never knew,

17

but Garias had it all in hand. The misbegotten souls were drawn by the addictive power of the city itself.

"Excellent. So the thousands that now flocked inside and out are ripe for use in the defence of the city should the need arise, and to feed such dark magic as the Golem." It was a useful focus, and had added benefits. On top of the fodder down in the city, the focus also drew those with similar abilities from the nomadic tribes that Garias loved to hate. They had provided him with a steady supply of humans with the ability to focus all sorts of magic, and had taught him a lot. The fact that he despised the use of such magic was a side issue. The knowledge was locked away safely in his library, and he had proven time and time again to himself that it was not what you knew that was the key to success, but where to find the answers. The answer to one question, the question of what the commoners believed, was a simple answer.

"Nightshadow will not help them at all, Armen. The simplest focus could scry into any house from this tower. There is not a secret that I could not find should I have but the need." Garias closed his eyes and breathed deeply, his body on the verge of a new discovery. As the Golem grew, so did he.

"The question I would like you to answer though is why they would be doing such a thing. The focus around this city ensures that an original thought from any of this chattel is erased as soon as they think it. They do, they exist, completely unawares that they are as a fly in a spiders web."

"Could it be the focus itself?"

Garias looked at his underling with a dismissive glare of contempt.

"Stupid imbecile. Were that to happen do you not think every focus wielder in this entire tower would not come running? Even those who give us the delightful feeling of hate would know."

Armen bowed his head in supplication. "I will keep my ears open for any stray comment, master."

"You do that," sneered Garias. Annoyed by Armen's implication that the focus that he spent over thirty years and used countless lives to perfect would have a flaw, Garias turned his back on the underling in an all too obvious gesture of dismissal. "What do you have for me?" he asked of the messenger, who stood holding an empty wine cup.

"The wizards have arrived, my Lord."

"How are they here so quick?" Armen burst out, a lack of thought in his sentence.

"There are other methods than walking. Go see to them. You, messenger, go to Nejait and bring me the head of the Guild of Fire." With that dismissal, Garias studied his wine. The aroma was thick, full of wild fruit and a robustness that

18

matched his own desires. Armen had his uses after all, but he had to constantly remind Garias that he was as dense as the rest. If Armen had not proved so useful as the public face of the overzealous 'Witch Finder', Garias would have had him removed permanently.

Hearing the door close, Garias decided to walk down to the prison. His entertainments had been few and far between in recent times, and he had missed revelling in the stink of fear and misery that reeked from the very walls. He used the door in the lower chambers of his tower now, for it provided a much easier route. The windows showed that it was completely dark, not just the false twilight provided by the receding sun. This was the right time of day for visiting such a place. It looked too hygienic and airy during daylight hours, for Garias preferred space for his minions to work on their victims. He had one man in mind as he walked down the passage that squeezed through false walls along the edge of the fortress and down into the bedrock beneath. The old man from the guild in Eskenberg. This was a particular source of irritation, as he had been on the verge of taking not one, but three wizards of great potential. One of his informants had come across one of the three one day, and had witnessed him demonstrating and selling a focus stone to some fat merchant. From that point on the informant had followed the man, and his two close friends, noting points of interest and passing them via the network to Armen, whom he believed to be in charge of everything in Raessa. The informant had it on good authority that these three had found something that would allow them to break the conventional boundaries of focusing, that most of the Law Guild used. That was a wasted community if ever there was one; wrinkled old men harping on about their sacred old law while all they did was use the occasional focus to prolong their sorry lives. It was not even worth plundering that useless pot, not unless he had truly desperate need. The only danger was the relative proximity to Raessa, but he had seen to that. These three, they could have been such a find, such a source of knowledge for him, to the point that he entrusted the Golem to retrieve them from their warren. The plan had seemed so simple. In order to research in relative peace they apparently had isolated themselves from the rest of their order. It should have just been a case of swooping in there and removing them with nobody the wiser. As luck typically had it, an of explosion ripped through their demesne just as the Golem entered. The reason he knewe this was the state of the only survivor of the debacle, this one old man. Garias had literally hit the roof when all that had returned was this. The survivor had borne the brunt of his anger for days on end. Garias was nothing if not vicious and thorough. It has been nearly a full pass of the moon since Garias had seen the man, and tonight he intended to get answers to his questions.

Reaching the remarkably well-lit chambers, Garias paused to savour the raw emotion in the air. It had helped to have the dwelling of the Golem so close. Every being in this wing of the city was afraid, almost to the point of outright panic. They all knew what walked within these walls, and that it hungered. Many a torturer had been lost because the Golem needed to absorb souls and became impatient. That was just a fact that Garias had to live with. The three he had hoped to catch would have been a huge stepping-stone to discovering a way to contain the hunger of the creature's aura, but that moment had passed. He had to make do with what was in front of him, and this old man would tell him tonight what he wished to know. As he passed like a wraith down the corridor, a succubus intent upon feeding off of the emotions of men, he heard one feeble voice crying out:

"Water, please, whomever you are," came a croak-like whisper from behind the door as he passed it. Garias closed his eyes and reached out with his mind. It was one of the green men, the sole survivor of his massive focus used to attack the forest. The desperation was like an elixir to Garias, who knew the Golem would benefit greatly from this soul. But power did have its uses, and this remaining guildsman was strong to have survived the blast that had shattered so many of his brethren into limp bundles of flesh and bone. "Do what he asks. Give him some. . . water." Nodding to one of the guards stationed outside the door, Garias moved on, sure in the knowledge that the man would get water, if not a little beating as well. The room he had been seeking was three cells down. This room was no different to the others, except for its contents. The rest of the chambers had a bed and a bucket, but on the night that this particular prisoner had been captured he had been in such a rage that he had had him manacled to the wall, and had left him in that state. As he opened the door the results were there to show. The gnarled shell of a man hung from the chains by his arms, his wrists chafed and scarred from never being released. A sense of defeat and hopelessness permeated the air, and this thrilled Garias. The stink of excrement was enough to make any lesser being gag, but Garias barely noticed it. He just stood there and watched. Presently, the prisoner trembled, coming out of a dream into a nightmare. The old man, hair lank and greasy, beard tattered and grey, looked up with a tremendous effort. He was unable to hold his head up for long, and soon it dropped back down to hang limp in front of his body.

"Still some fight left in you, Obrett? Or have you decided to give in." A widening of eyes was enough reaction to tell him that there was understanding. "Yes, I know exactly who you are." His words made the room all the more stark, the walls colder and the emotions much more negative as his intended victim suffered. "I could end it you know. It would be so easy to let go." Garias tried to sound compassionate, but the tone of his voice was alien to him, and he could not manage it. Instead it came out more like a sarcastic statement.

It did not have the desired effect. The limp figure in front of him started to shake, wheezing, until Garias leaned in closer to discover that it was a harsh dry laugh the man was trying to bark out. The laugh became a racking cough, and Garias endured the delicious sight of the man in agony as he tried to master the pitiful excuse that was his own body. The cough passed, and the old man looked up, tears in his eyes from the effort.

"You. . .could. . .end it?" He rasped, his voice dripping with irony. Obrett trembled once more, but his head never dropped back down. With a Herculean effort, Obrett looked at him and Garias found his gaze being held by someone who should not have had that much will left in him.

"You could never end anything if you tried, not if your life depended on it. And it will be your downfall. I have seen your work from within this room, and you are already out of your depth." Obrett was quiet for a time, but he never dropped his gaze. Garias stepped closer, and let fly with a slap to the old mans' face, hard enough to rock his head back against the cobbles in the wall and off again. The prisoner shivered, wincing at the new pain, but he still held his gaze.

"You will not get anything out of me, so called Witch Finder." The anger coming from this husk of a man spoke of untapped resources; he was becoming more animated by the moment. "You are right though, master of lies, scum of the earth. I can let go, and if I chose to do so, there will be not a thing you can do about it."

This time it was Garias who chuckled. A chill forbidding sound that came from deep within him. The grin across his face was filled with the tinted insanity of a maniac. *This* old man had the temerity to try and match wills with *him*? Garias, the master of Raessa?

"I think my friend that there is a lot I can do about it. You are in no position to tell me what I can and cannot do. You know very well that I have the means at my disposal to make your life last a very long time, every moment in agony. You have seen my creature, for I have seen it watching ever since it captured you. It hungers for your soul. It knows, as I now do, that you are stronger than

21

you seem even in this state. If it could speak it would beg me to give you to it, to feed its life force. You would live for a very long time, wailing out your bitter pain as part of its spell." Garias reached down suddenly, pulling Obrett taut against the chains by his face, and breathed the words to him.

"You can die in peace, quickly, but if you do not tell me what I wish to know, you will regret having ever looked upon me."

The prisoner edged his face around, and spat at him. Garias jumped back, wiping his face clean. Nobody had ever dared such a thing, not in the centuries of his existence.

The prisoner sneered at him, defiant eyes wide in hollowed sockets. "You do not want answers you piece of filth," he hissed, "You want me to fear you. You want a supplicant that you can draw from in order to bolster your own measly attempts at focusing." He turned his face away, contorting, as if he were reaching with his teeth at something inside his mouth. He turned back and spat a tooth at Garias. "Well you shall have neither."

Garias burned with a barely contained fury, to the point that he would have stabbed the prisoner, had he but had some kind of blade to use. Unfortunately there was not even a spoon in this cell, as the old man had barely eaten since his capture. Refusing to lose his temper and give the prisoner a sorely fought after victory, Garias calmed the stab of fury in his belly enough to whisper quietly in his ear. "You will rue this, forever." He then turned, and in a flash of robes, left the room, not even bothering to shut the door.

In the hallway, Garias stopped one of the guards. See to it that the prisoner is fed and watered. I want that cell in a fitter state when next I see it."

"It will be done, my Lord." The guard stood to attention.

"What good will that do?" Said a voice from within the shadows. "His life is all but spent. He is too weak to survive much longer. Why prolong it?"

"For exactly that reason. For the sensation."

"Then why do you need us if all you are going to do is sit in a torture chamber living off of other men's wretchedness."

"You are here at my bidding, to serve me. Always remember that. Question the motives of anyone with more wit than you again, and you shall find yourself a permanent resident down here. You have been summoned to bear witness to the re-emergence of another type of magic. The days of sifting through rocks will soon be gone.

Caldar stopped. "You have found the secret to emotive magic?"

Garias smiled. "Prepare to say goodbye to your Old Law Gods, Law wizard. They are about to be handed their notice."

Chapter Two

Keldron watched Raoul hurtle across the road and behind some bushes where he noisily threw up. "What's he doing that for?"

"Don't know," Belyn shouted back. "He opened the door of that cottage, took one look inside, and then ran for the bushes."

Coughing now, Raoul stood back up, his narrow frame towering over the bushes that had previously concealed him. "I've never seen anything so horrific in my life. I wasn't prepared for it, that's all." Raoul remained where he was, trembling.

Keldron opened the door of the cottage and peered inside. "Oh good Gods above!" Keldron was amazed with the reaction he had shown. His own hands felt cold. He was surprised that the blood still ran in them, as the cold had spread all the way up to his arms. His feet were cold too, but the breeze was unforgiving. Back in Eskenberg, he would have just thrown more wood on the fire, but here he had to make do with extra clothing that still seemed not to help. Clenched up as he tried to control himself, he felt shivers running through him, and he was sure that they were not all physical. Seeing that bloody mess had rocked him to his very core.

"What?" Belyn shouldered past him and came to an abrupt halt. "Oh."

"It stands against everything that the Old Law and therefore we stand for. Murder, and on such a scale. How can people do this?" The mere thought of such a contravention, and the agony that must have been involved set his own stomach to clenching, and he tried to heave, but Keldron had not eaten, and he just concentrated on the pain in his ribs until he calmed down once more.

Moving a few paces away from the site of the bush, Raoul stood up, pale and weak. He held onto one of the stubby trees that grew in defiance of the weather, and forced calm breaths of the frigid North air. "That wind is penetrating." He observed.

"Well it would be if you gulp it down like last orders, Raoul." Belyn tried to sound jovial, but it had little effect.

"It is the only way I can concentrate."

"Breathe through your nose. It will seem easier."

After one final breath, the Guildsman, until recently of the Order of Law in Eskenberg, sighed and opened his eyes to the picturesque village once again. "Is this all we are here for now, to traverse the land and stumble across horrors?"

The time had long passed when Raoul had accepted the arguments of his two closest friends, Belyn Stroddick and Keldron Vass, that they had in fact

suffered a *de facto* expulsion from the order that had been their home for so
many years. Middle aged, they still looked young, a bi-product of the magic
produced by the focus stones which wizards used to sharpen their abilities and
perform feats that while everyday occurrences to them, were viewed as
spectacular and wondrous by those not of their orders. Many commoners were
afraid of the magic, but most, especially those who held to the tenets of the Old
Law, accepted it as just another facet of the seven Gods' blessings upon the
land. As for Raoul, he had proven that he was no mean practitioner of the art,
but Keldron knew it was not the reason he had joined the guild. A childish
ambition of being a wizard often amounted to nothing in most cases. Raoul
was more interested in preserving the law that so many seemed to be
forgetting. He himself was not above bending the rules occasionally, but at
heart he stuck to what he believed in.
"Are you going to stand there all day Raoul, you skinny son of a goat,"
Boomed Belyn, the words aimed to repel the feeling of dread.
"I am over it brother," he called, moving out from behind the tree. Belyn, as
visually loud as his voice, stumped over to him. The big man had flame-red
hair, and possessed one of those great bushy beards that made a face come
alive with comic effect. He was a man who enjoyed his food, and it showed in
his girth. His dark red cloak just set the colour of the man off perfectly;
Keldron could not help but feel better when he saw his friend. Belyn was the
man responsible for them not starving on this little venture. In fact, he had
saved their lives several times with his extended knowledge of the properties
of focus stones and which suited different situations best. His friend had come
across a book, unsigned, that contained extensive research into what most had
considered a lost topic. He was the only member of the Guild prepared to
experiment with focus stones. Keldron remembered with regret and not a little
disgust how all the old farts in their guild had stared down their noses at the
three of them when sending them on a 'pilgrimage' to restore the temple in
Caighgard. He would prove them wrong, and actually do it. The bonus for
him was that somewhere in this great expanse of bitter cold land there was
about a third of the Merdonese forest tribe wandering around willing to aid
him.
Belyn strode up to Raoul, and peered at what Raoul had left under the bush.
"That much, eh?" he observed. Receiving a nod from Raoul he grunted. "Well I
can't say that I blame you my brother, it is one sticky mess in there."
Keldron opened the door to the cottage.
"You actually intend to go inside that building?"

"I try not to think about the agony they went through. That I bet is what got you, much though you would think it to be a smell or a sight. I need to go in there. It is not a case of choice. I am searching for the reason behind this all, so I have to be objective." Raoul remained where he was, leaning against the tree shaking his head. "It just doesn't make sense. I tell you what though; the Merdonese won't even go near the buildings. Joleen is all freaked out and Yerdu will not come any closer to the cottages than she has to. It was all she could do to actually stay inside the village. I tell you, this place reeks of evil. Something bad happened here, and not something obvious."

Keldron thought about this for a second. "They are much more sensitive to the aura of events that transpire around them, are they not?"

"Perhaps. It may be that the focus they lived under for so long has made them sensitive to certain aspects of nature."

Raoul shrugged. "You have a good point, Bel, but forgive me if I do not go into any of those buildings again. I cannot face it."

This brought a chuckle from his large friend. "Brother, I thought your face could not actually get much paler in this wind, but I swear that after your little episode your skin has actually gone grey. I do not think that anybody would begrudge you staying out here. Besides, Keldron could do enough work for all of us the state he is in. There has been murder here on a scale unheard of in twenty years."

"I have to go in there, Raoul. You do not have to stay. Belyn, would you scout around and see if our worst fears are actually true?"

"You do what you have to Kel, I'll survey the graveyard."

Keldron knelt close, examining the wood. He was careful to crouch down without actually kneeling on the floor as much out of respect for the spilt lifeblood of the poor soul that had perished in tortuous agony here as the fact that he didn't want to risk soiling himself in the blood of another. The result left him in what would have been a comical squatting pose, but for the gravity of the situation. "The blood poured from this person as they half stood, half hung here on the stake," he said as Belyn entered the grisly scene. "I take it there were more cases."

"I have never seen the like, old friend. Is that all blood?"

"Indeed. It's all dry. One good sweep of a broom would remove all the evidence, but this has been left for a reason. There is much of importance here, not the least being the fact that the body is still on the stake. Nobody has been here since this happened. The back of this poor person had arched and twisted so much when it was impaled that it had become wedged against a table."

Keldron judiciously avoided looking at the face of the corpse. Agony and death-encompassing pain were things that he really preferred to stay apart from, and he was here to do a job. Instead he concentrated on the wood, which was much more likely to give away a clue about the attackers. He carefully peered around. The stake was covered in blood in all but a few places. "Anything?"

"Perhaps. Where the wood is clear, it reveals that it has been scraped free of bark." The once-shiny wood was now dark in places, mostly around the knots. "It is chipped too, where somebody had obviously been in a hurry to finish the job." Cracks rose from the knots along the shaft of the spear where the moisture of the blood had gotten into the wood, giving the spear the impression that it too had been bleeding. Keldron picked at one of the knots with a knife that had been left on the table. The wood from the knot crackled and popped out as easily as if it were paper. The stake was rotten, but it was also bone dry. He decided to poke around no more, for fear of disturbing the garish scene. Avoiding the stiffened limbs of the corpse, Keldron untangled himself from the mess and looked around the house.

"All in all, I am uncertain as to my conclusions. I need to think upon this some more. Aside from the leavings of small animals, nothing has been touched." It surprised him that no predator or scavenging animal had come near any of the corpses in the village. Perhaps the animals too had sensed the enormous wrong that Keldron was feeling. He had not managed to convince anybody other than Belyn to enter the houses, and he had doubted from the look on his skinny friend's face that Raoul would even last long in the village. "I don't think we need to look any more in here, or the other houses for that matter. It will be pretty much the same."

"Good. I am out of here."

Keldron stood up, stretching limbs that had been bent at awkward angles, and scribbled a few notes in a journal he kept about the whole affair of the Night of Spears. As he made to follow his friend out of the cottage an impulse stuck him as he felt the lump of his focus stone in his pocket, and he grabbed it, pulling in his concentration and focussing on the stone. Immediately the room became animated. Keldron found that he was witnessing the bloody rite. He had no idea who the men were that held this poor soul in front of the spear. The victim struggled like a rat in a trap, but he was hoisted as if he were a child up into the air and then literally thrown onto the spear. Blood erupted from his chest, and his head sagged backwards and to the side, causing his body to twist. The men were gone. Keldron watched in shock as the blood ran in rivulets away from the body, pooling on the stones of the floor. Then his vision shifted. There were still cobbles, but instead of the blood, he saw a cell. An old man hung huddled up against a wall, trying to speak to someone. Trying to speak to him. The old man widened his eyes and mouthed a name in question. "Keldron?" There had been no noise to the voice, and yet he heard it as clearly as if he were there. Thrown back to himself for just a moment, Keldron lurched out of the building and into the slate-grey afternoon light of the Ardican winter.

He saw Joleen in the distance, but couldn't control his own movements. The yellow-haired member of the Merdonese tribe, for a while now Keldron's closest companion, came running over to him, her eyes full of concern. She ran her hand over his face and cupped his chin.

"Keldron what is it? You look like you have seen a ghost."

Keldron could not speak. Even to respond to the honeyed tones of one that he had to admit was beloved to him was a greater challenge than he could accomplish. A man of strong moral stature, and hardy endurance as a result of their extended journey thus far, Keldron could do no more than stare at her, breathing shallowly. The cold of the wind was as nothing to the piercing cold that cored into his soul.

Joleen was not prepared to wait for an answer. "Belyn!" The powerful voice seemed too loud for her lithe woodlander frame. "Come over here now!" He watched her staring into his eyes, several of the tribesmen hurried over in the background. "It is Keldron. He has done something. What did he do in there?"

"He was right behind me, just writing some notes." Keldron saw the face of his long-time friend stare at him for a moment before moving out of the way. Malcolm, the near-giant of a man who had been the landlord of the only inn of the Forest of Merdon and had been a rock so many times, peered closely at him. Keldron saw Malcolm up close, but as with Joleen, he could not respond. The pain of the memory he had experienced was too great. Malcolm lifted Keldron's arm with one huge paw. "He is as cold as ice."

"He witnessed a sacrifice," replied Aynel Deeproot, one of the warriors that had accompanied them. "It has affected his mind. Do something quickly, or you might lose him."

"What do you mean witnessed a sacrifice?"

Aynel spread his arms around him. "You feel the emotions that surround this village. Hate, woe, fear, agonising pain. There is a reason that we did not want to come into this village and the seeker of Truth has discovered it to his detriment. Only the biggest of shocks can bring someone around from a spell such as this. Emotion has too great a hold on the human soul."

"A shock, is it?" she answered. "Let us see what we can do." Joleen grabbed Keldron and shook him, trying to make him come awake. "Keldron! Wake up! Snap out of it!" From the point where consciousness was held in check by the icy haze that had fallen on him as he had exited the house, Keldron fought to say something, but he could not. It was as if ice had frozen his jaws shut, and his face was numb. He felt himself descending away from consciousness, into an abyss within his mind that he was afraid that he would not rise back up from. The light faded to a point far above him, and he clawed at it, grasping, seeking to widen that point. Then a shock of red-hot pain flooded his senses, and the light came shooting back towards him, slamming into him with a violence of colour and noise.

Keldron dropped to his knees, and looked up. The first thing he felt was joy at the relief evident on Joleen's face. The next thing he felt was agonising pain on his arm. He grabbed around with his left hand to his right arm, and instantly regretted the reflex that had made him do it. "Ow! What did you do to me?" He pulled away from his arm and looked at it. A great crimson burn covered most of his upper right arm on the sensitive flesh underneath. As Keldron peered over his shoulder at the crisped wound, he heard a familiar voice.

"Sorry I had to do that brother," came Belyn's sombre and regretful tone, "but we were losing you there. You had to be shocked out of it according to our tribal friends, and it looked like our timing was just right." Belyn was clearly abashed at what he had just done, his face was a conflicting mix of morose guilt and relief. His head dropped for a moment, and then Belyn faced him. "If there was any other way, I would have chosen it."

"What did you do to cause this?" Keldron held his arm up, causing the pain to spread and his close friend to wince at the sight of the huge burn. The wound stood out like an accusation, though everybody was relieved at the fact that Keldron had recovered from his shock in the house.

In return, Belyn brought out one of the muddy red stones that he had carried with him from Eskenberg. "The focus power of flame, Kel. You needed a shock to return from whatever was holding you. It seemed that something hot was exactly the tonic needed to bring you round."

"Well have you learned anything about focussing on the power of healing?" Belyn looked abashed. "No my brother I have not, though you raise a very good point there. It seems that the easiest focuses to accomplish all end up with a destructive result. The more we try to learn of the different properties of rock, the wider our ability to do damage can be utilised."

"Almost as if the base focussing skills are a direct affront to the Old Law," chipped in Raoul, frowning at this sudden realisation. In contrast, Belyn's face was alight, as he revelled in the increased understanding of his chosen aspect of study.

"Well before you boys get into one more argument, how about we bandage Keldron's arm?" Interrupted Yerdu, the dark haired and very diminutive tribal woman who was as close to Belyn as Joleen was to Keldron. Despite her size she could hold her own, and had repeatedly proven this. She was the perfect foil for Belyn, constantly taking the wind out of his sails and reducing his overburdened pride to a more humble level. He appreciated this, despite his bristling beard and narrow eyes whenever she brought him back down to her level. It was an unspoken feeling of affection for each other that this pair, mismatched to the casual observer, held for each other. Their relationship was very private, but when the situation required it, Yerdu took control.

Taking Keldron by his good arm, she pulled him away from the gathered crowd and took him to the horses to get some bandages from her pack. Joleen trailed behind closely.

Raoul chuckled as he followed behind. "It seems our arguments are becoming legendary for their bad timing, old friend."

Belyn grinned in response and clapped Raoul on the shoulder. "That they are, brother. And before you say it again, I agree with you. It makes me wonder why all of this hasn't been previously studied. Every explosion we make, every person that gets hurt is a contravention of the Old Law, but it seems that in recent times we have had to exist that way, or we would have probably found ourselves ending up like these people."

"So what would you do, give up this studying of focus stones?" Keldron responded, his reply becoming a key question.

Belyn laughed out loud, in stark contrast with the ghostly silence of the village. "Absolutely not Kel. We are on the verge of discovering something big here, I can almost put my finger on it."

Raoul looked around him at the bleak, slightly overgrown verges on the side of the track. "Here?"

"No!" Belyn exclaimed, cuffing his friend around the back of the head to emphasise his point. "I mean this situation, coupled with what we are learning about the stones. There is something looming over the horizon, metaphorically speaking. We just need to walk in the right direction, using the right knowledge, and we will find it."

Raoul frowned. "I just want to get to Caighgard."

"All in good time, my friend. It wouldn't surprise me if Caighgard was wrapped up in this mess as well, but I am sure that we will get there in due course. We have been following events ever since the night we left the Order, and we have barely stopped for breath." Belyn looked skywards, his face full of a mock humility. "If I were a betting man, I would say that we have not seen the last of whomever was behind the disaster in the forest." He looked around at the gathered tribesmen and grinned. "Thank the Law I am a guildsman, and not a betting man."

Malcolm approached them from the horses, where he had been gathering ointments. "Will these do?"

Yerdu poked around at the various jars in his immense hands. "You have most of what I need. What's the rush?"

Seeing Keldron's arm as if for the first time, Malcolm grimaced. "It would be better on my brothers if they went out of the village. I think this is disturbing them a bit more than they would care to admit."

Keldron glanced over at the tribesmen. They appeared as they always did, straight-faced, ready to move quickly if needed, but there was the slightest tightening around their eyes, as if they were ready to shift uneasily. "By all means, do so," he replied. "I know exactly what you mean. I am not altogether comfortable here either.

"I will join you." Raoul strode off behind the tribesmen.

"Well the colour has returned to his face at least, cold wind or not." Belyn spoke aloud to nobody in particular. Keldron saw it as a need to fill the void in this village.

As he watched Raoul stride out of the village, Keldron let the ladies administer his arm.

Belyn kept his distance. "I'm ashamed at what I had to do, that there was no better solution to snapping you out of it."

"Don't be."

"How is it?" He asked, looking at Keldron's arm.

"Hurts like hell, but thanks for doing that to me," Keldron replied. "Why did you have to be so thorough?"

"My friend, you were gone from us." Belyn admitted. "I let the smallest of flames sear your skin for but a moment, thinking that would bring you round, but it had no effect. I had to increase the power of the focus tenfold, and even then I was afraid to let it touch you for more than the briefest of moments. If I had left it any longer, you would have use of your arm no more."

Keldron flexed his arm, wincing as he did so. "Well the bandages and ointment my nurses found for me seem to be helping somewhat. It feels more comfortable already."

"Aye, and it will only stay that way if the bandage is redressed and ointment applied regularly, wizard," replied Yerdu, eyeing her work. Then she winked at him. "I think I will leave that in the capable hands of my sister."

Joleen had the grace to blush, before giving Keldron a sly glance and a small smile. He grinned in response. Joleen always looked lovely to him, but she could stop his heart if she so wanted.

"So come on then Kel," said Belyn, suddenly assuming a businesslike manner. "A problem shared is a problem halved or some such statement. Tell us what you saw."

Keldron looked at the ladies. "You do not have to stay to listen should you feel the need."

Yerdu let out a loud 'Harrumph'. "We share the same beliefs as our fellow tribesmen Belyn, but we will listen to your story. Wild horses couldn't drag us away, not out to that cold wind beyond the edge of the village."

"Okay then," he replied. "First off, I do not believe that this has been done by those responsible for the Night of Spears twenty seasons ago. There are just too many things that ring false about the whole situation." Keldron shivered in the slight breeze, and Joleen led them into the lee of one of the houses, one attached to a large mill whose sails now barely moved in the breeze. They sat down on the porch, leaning against some of their bags, and Keldron continued. "The spears are the most important part. The records show that twenty seasons past, witnesses saw spears heavily etched with runes and other engraved symbols. The spears that have impaled this poor lot have none of those. The spears from before had crosspieces. There were none this time. I think the biggest difference was the selection of those that were killed. Random or not, the numbers were far fewer. It is my opinion that whomever did this was again trying to make it look like a repetition, but they had none of the skill, or even the beliefs of the murderers from yesteryear."

"Could they not have been in a hurry to complete their work?" Queried Belyn.

"I do not think so, my friend," Keldron replied, absently reaching for his arm only to have his hand slapped away by Joleen. "If they went so far to get stakes, assuming that was the same people that took the trees in that woodland we visited, then they knew their purpose, and were in no hurry. Consider what you would do if haste were an issue." Keldron pointed around him. "If you were going to do something so violent to so many people, there would be plenty of wood locally to use in such a crime." They looked where Keldron pointed. The house had wood on the porch, wooden poles holding it up, and piles of wood to be used in the fires that held off the deep chill of the wind. "See? They made a point of going afar to get the wood. They, whoever these people are, made a point of trying to make this seem like something it wasn't. I think that they were uninformed. I would say that they have only heard what talk people have said on the streets and tried to replicate the Night of Spears." "But that is not entirely the point of this massacre, is it?" Belyn said quietly. Suddenly to Keldron the air seemed that much colder, and the sense of ill-feeling seemed that much more palpable. He shook his head, looking into the distance as if trying to understand something beyond his comprehension, something that was just out of sight. "When I had finished looking at the spear, I stood up and made a few notes in my journal. As I put it away, I felt that I had to grasp my focus stone. I know not why, but it was a compulsion." Keldron furrowed his eyebrows, and pursed his lips. "Well not really a compulsion. I didn't force myself to do it. If that had been the case then I am sure that you would have had the same need to focus on the grisly scene. No, I think it was more like something in that room triggered an impulse in me. I just reacted to it without thinking."

"What did you see?" Yerdu urged, caught up with his tale. Despite the fact that their very nature made the tribeswomen uncomfortable, it seemed that the Wizards' understanding of events was rubbing off on those of the tribe that were close with them. At one time Joleen and Yerdu would never have come into this village, relying on instinct to keep them away from anything as evil as this.

"It was amazing, and terrifying to behold. I have never witnessed anything like it. I saw the men, for men they definitely were by their large menacing stature. They manhandled the victim, picking him up like a toy, and throwing him with contempt onto the stake, which they had wedged against the table." Keldron sat down, and Joleen unconsciously put her arm about his shoulders, being careful to avoid his burn. "The man screamed as I have never seen anyone scream before. The suffering was on a scale greater than the broken heart of a lover. Imagine you had had your entire family killed, and everyone you know stabbed before your very eyes. I think this was the level of pain experienced by this man. I saw his ribs part as the stake slid through him. Belyn, I could see his ribs! I could feel the stake moving through him as if it were me! Blood fountained everywhere from the wound, splashing the men responsible for this. . .this evil. I watched as the man died twitching on the stake, as he twisted and injured himself more than I thought possible. His name was Dessoc. He was a carpenter. I saw the blood pool on the stone floor as the murderers left."

Keldron sat there for a while, quietly. It was obvious that this experience had affected him in a way more profound than any experience of his life so far.

After a time he found that he could speak again. "Then I was taken somewhere else. I saw somebody I recognised chained to a wall. In a prison cell."

"Who was it?" Belyn spoke quietly as the gloom around them deepened.

"Belyn, it was Obrett. Our master has been taken captive. He was just hanging there. I think he was trying to use a rock in the prison wall to focus to somebody. Perhaps us, maybe somebody else. He was surprised to see me, I could guess that much."

Belyn stood and started to pace. "Any idea where?"

"Sorry, there was nothing. Wait, there was a feeling. It was in the distance but altogether evil, and quite overpowering. I have felt it only once before, when we were hiding out the back of an Inn, in the Forest of Merdon. The nameless evil that appears all to often."

"That creature can only have been conjured in one place, Kel. That means our master is prisoner in Raessa. Damn it, we are so far away."

"Then don't worry about something you have no control over, foolish man." Yerdu tutted after she spoke. "Continue, Keldron."

"I think that I managed to get myself out of the house before I lost track of my actions. It felt as if I were falling down a freezing abyss. I could see you all as if through a far-off window, but there was nothing I could do, no action that I could take to bring myself back, however hard I fought. I just went deeper and deeper, further away from the light until it slammed back with a force that rocked my very soul. The next thing I knew, you were standing by me and my arm was fried to a crisp." Keldron glared with mock anger at Belyn, who cowered, if such a thing were possible for the big red man. Keldron would milk this for all it was worth. He rarely got one over on either Belyn or Raoul and despite the pain, he was enjoying that part of his experience. "But there was something more to it, I am sure. I got the impression from the murderers that they were not satisfied, and I am certain that this feeling was not that they hadn't finished off the village. They were in a rush, but they were far from satiated. It was as if this village was not enough for them. The feeling extends to something more." Keldron shuddered, as if he was afraid of prophesising a doom he could not escape from. "I believe this is not the only village that we will find like this. I believe that there is somebody out there with a massive ill intent to this land and it's inhabitants." His companions reflected his mood: pale, sober faces.

"What you say is chilling, Kel. I have never heard you speak so before. You are analytical, and driven in pursuit of your goals, but never like this. Belyn's sombre tone left them all with nothing to say. Yerdu clutched at Belyn, and Joleen hugged Keldron's good side as hard as she could. The need for words was set aside as they heard the rapid thump of heavy footsteps running through the village. Out of breath, Raoul thundered up to them, and then leaned on the post at one edge of the porch, panting as he tried to master the angry protests of his body in order to speak. His eyebrows rose as he comprehended that all was not well. His tongue hung out like a hunting hound as he breathed in deeply to calm himself, and then doubled over as he realised his mistake.

"Yes Raoul, the air is still cold." Keldron's comment brought a rustle of laughter from the rest, to which Raoul shook his head violently.

"Here, wipe the sweat off of you before it freezes to your skin." Yerdu handed Raoul a cloth, getting a nod of thanks.

"There is a group of horse riders heading this way out of the East, following the same track we did towards the village."

This prompted Keldron to stand and look in the direction from which Raoul had run. There was a different look in his friend's eyes to any Keldron had ever seen before, as if Raoul had suddenly discovered some kind of unavoidable fate, and was intending to rush headlong to meet it. He decided that he had to keep a close watch on his friend, as he would never be prepared to lose him.

"Our tracks, will they be noticed?"

"No. The tribesmen will make sure that the road to the village looks untouched, and Malcolm is checking around the village to conceal our signs." In the breeze, doors swung on rusty hinges, and shutters clacked against window frames. "I don't think Malcolm will find concealing our tracks here a problem, my friend. This village was an unkempt tomb before we arrived, and I don't think we have done enough to make it look any different." Raoul said this with confidence, as much for the benefit of his friends as for himself.

"True, we have not been in many buildings, and even then not for long."

"Who would want to?" Belyn added, his voice sombre.

Shortly, Malcolm joined them, and not long after that, the reminder of the tribesmen passed quietly but quickly through the village.

"That mill looks to be a good place to conceal ourselves. It has an empty stable and plenty of defendable space to hide ourselves in."

"Defendable?" Queried Raoul. "We don't even know who they are. They could be merchants, villagers responding to this massacre, who knows what?"

"And they could also be those responsible for this, or even worse," asserted Malcolm, his squeaky high voice sounding belligerent as he tried to lower it. "Would you risk that? From the mill we will be able to see who they are and whether or not they bear us any ill will. If you are right then all the better, but would you risk it?"

At this, Raoul acquiesced. They moved quickly and quietly into the yard of the mill, and stabled the horses. The tribesmen, Aynel, Arden Silverbark, Handel Broadbough and the fourth member, Seren Willowonce, accompanied the horses, as did Malcolm. Raoul remained in the yard with Joleen and Yerdu; there was not a chance of any of them entering the house. Belyn led the way into the miller's home.

"The reek of wafted evil is not as strong here."

"I guess that had there been any occupants, the miasma of woe resulting from their agonizing deaths would have touched us by now, judging by what we have seen. I think we are safe in this place. Nobody was murdered in here, Bel."

A reassuring nod from his fellow wizard reassured him. "Go and get the ladies."

"Raoul too?"

Belynn smirked, and then broke into a grin, showing that he still maintained his sense of humour. "Did I not say go get the ladies?"

Belyn let out a short guffaw, and Keldron received a rough pat to the shoulder. He turned quickly to protect his wounded arm, and Belyn grimaced at nearly having caused more pain to his friend.

Leaving Belyn to find a spot where they could watch and yet remain sheltered, Keldron returned through the parlour to the yard. He found Raoul shivering just inside the gate that had been left ajar, just as they had found it. Raoul stood there with his arms wrapped close, hugging himself against the cold. Joleen and Yerdu had prudently seated themselves out of the breeze.

"L. . .l. . .l. . .lookout." Raoul managed to chatter.

"Lookout my behind," Keldron replied, "come inside." Raoul began to protest, as Keldron well knew that he would, he added, "There was no murder in this house, brother. Do you think that I would allow you all in there after what happened to me?" This mollified his friend, who followed him in. At the discovery that the house was clean of the foul aura that clouded the rest of the village, Joleen and Yerdu also accompanied them in. Malcolm and the tribesmen remained with the horses to keep their steeds silent as only people so in tune with nature could do.

Inside the house, the four of them made their way around the building until they found where Belyn had secreted himself. It was a study with an open window, and drapes that had never been closed. The dust on the windowsill was deep and grey, further evidence that nothing had been touched. Belyn had taken a seat in one of the sturdy but comfortable looking chairs. The study did not look like it had been used much. A few books, a pot of quills and a couple of ledgers were all the room contained aside from the larger furniture.

"The miller had either been a man who loved order, or he had not been one for letters and numbers." Belyn peered at the ledger and nodded in approval. Keldron took his eyes away from the slit in the drapes to take note of what Belyn was doing.

"Something you like?"

Belyn smiled with a tinge of regret. "This miller was one with the Old Law. He made flour and gave away as much as he sold. In fact, he hardly made any profit, just enough to keep everyone happy. The ledger shows what he did with the flour. It looks like he gave it away as gifts to the workers both here and on other farmsteads." Belyn shook his head in disbelief. "Why would someone want to kill a generous people like this?"

"That is one question to which I would like to find the answer. I think that my quest has gone beyond the old Night of Spears."

"You think there is more to this than just a coincidence?" Asked Raoul, who had gone to stand by the window, and looked out as he spoke.

"I am sure of it now, old friend." Keldron replied. "There is too much coincidence. First off, we set out to find the Merdonese, just to get knowledge. We almost get trapped in a lake of evil, and end up in a different reality in the chamber of what may well be one of the Gods. Then we get chased over countless leagues, as somebody just happens to destroy a greater focus that has stood over the forest for generations. Once we do gain a measure of relative safety in the mountains, we find ourselves pursued by horsemen. Then we happen to find a village where everybody has been slaughtered in a poor imitation of the original massacre. Coincidence?" Keldron asked of his friends. "I think not. Something is going on here, something sinister." He pointed out of the window. "Why is it that we have not seen a single Merdonese tribesman aside from those that accompanied us on our quest? Where are they? There were surely enough that escaped the forest and I am worried about them."

"Keldron, calm down." Spoke Joleen's soothing voice. "I am sure that our tribe would find many ways to exist peacefully out of the forest, and hide also if the situation requires of it. Besides, this is a big land, and they could have gone in any direction once they came down out of the pass."

"You be confidant, Jo. I will worry." Keldron frowned, and clamped his mouth shut. Joleen and Yerdu exchanged a look that was a cross between exasperation at the fact that a man didn't know his place in the scheme of things, and a concern that maybe he was not quite as recovered as they had previously thought. To take the frosty atmosphere away from the room, Yerdu busied herself with bustling Keldron to the opposite side of the room, far from the windows, and checking on his bandages. Everybody was now clearly subdued.

Raoul left the drapes and went to the doorway. "I am going to find a vantage point from which to view these horsemen as well as hear them." Shortly they could hear the creak of the stairs betraying his progress to the upper level of the house.

"Could be a good idea," Keldron said thoughtfully, his sense of futility somewhat mollified by the urgent need of his burnt arm. Looking around to see if anybody was going to follow him, he left the study and climbed to the top of the house. The stairs creaked for him as they had for Raoul, and he found his friend in one of two bedrooms situated at the front. Keldron nodded a silent greeting, and went to the other room. It was cosy, some might say small, but the pallet inside was close to the window, and packed full enough for him to sit and still have a good view of the track out the front. Opening a window, he winced as the hinges shrieked in protest. The cold chill swept through the room, probing, as if it had to touch everything. Keldron shivered; his arm was particularly sensitive in its raw and burned state, even under the bandages and ointment he had been given. Trembling slightly from both the cold and the expectancy of the situation, he waited for the horsemen to show. A noise interrupted his concentration. It was not the horsemen, but the door opening behind him. Expecting Joleen, Keldron was surprised when Yerdu popped her head around the door. She came and sat next to him on the bed, peering out of the window.

"You wizards always find levity in situations, I have seen it in your faces often since we left the forest many moons ago. Things have changed, no?"

Keldron smiled, regretting the actions that had led from them searching for simple answers to questions to hiding in a village full of people murdered in the most heinous of ways. "Things have changed. Would that it were all simpler, and the answers I sought were available to anybody."

"Are the answers you seek so special that you alone can find them? Is that not arrogance and presumption showing in your argument?"

Keldron missed her jest, caught up in the moment. "Yerdu, nobody else knows what we know. Nobody else has seen what we have seen. How many times have we escaped with our very lives, and we have travelled the merest fraction of our journey." He sighed, too caught up in his own emotional turmoil to think completely rationally. "I just hate not being in control of my life." "Welcome to the world we live in, brother Keldron." The sarcasm brought him back to his senses. "Stop wallowing in self-pity. There is more out there than your quest, and this experience should teach you that. What happened here was terrible, and what happened to you was but a fraction of that. Do you not think that the amount of suffering that came out of this village was for you alone? We *all* feel it, every one of us. I can tell you that no other member of my tribe would have even dared to come near here. This much evil was felt ten leagues off, but we came here with you three because we believe it is in the best interests of our tribe to do so. We did not even stop to consider the emotional anguish it would cause us should we actually come to the middle of this evil nest of snakes, we just followed you because you represent the chance to save our splintered tribe from extinction." Yerdu gestured out of the window. "This is exactly what will happen to our tribe should we fail. This, or something like this."

Keldron expanded his senses, trying to pick up a vibe from the surrounding walls. "How do you sense evil?" he asked.

"How do you not? Our elders always taught us to sense the air around us. As children we learned to sense the merest imperfection in the flows of the forest. Such flows exist everywhere, and we feel them all the time."

Less than satisfied with this evasive answer, Keldron leaned back. What Yerdu said made sense in a twisted way. He had had an experience that had chilled his very soul, but there was more out there than his self-pity. "You are right, Yerdu. I have been so self-absorbed because of what happened to me that I did not see that the answers are still out there and I need to be the one to find them."

Yerdu smiled gently. "Well, you are only a man, and you do need someone around to do the thinking for you."

"Will you two please hush?" Whispered Raoul from the passageway. "If you look out of the window you will see that we are about to have company."

Instantly, their conversation ceased. Along the track through the main part of the village came a band of five horsemen. The horses were in a wretched condition, from what could be seen. They were lathered and gasping, driven to their limit.

"Thank the Gods Malcolm can't see this. He would be out there in an instant."

The men were heavily armed, although they did not look like the band that the wizards and tribesmen had met on the route down from the pass out of the mountains. They were similarly attired though, and their weapons brought that familiar gleam from the flashes of sunlight. These men were not merchants or tinkers. They were out to perform a much more grizzly task. Keldron leaned towards the window, as he was sure that his friends were all doing at that moment. The voices were quiet but as the men rode through the village and closer to the mill where everybody was secreted, their chatter became more distinct.

"I told you, Bob. This place is a ghost town. It has already been cleared."

"And I told you Seth to mind your own. We have been given orders by his mighty lordship that we are to double and triple check the villages that have been cleared. I am sure that I heard something from far off."

A deeper voice interrupted the two. "If you two idiots would just shut it fer a second, we would be right able to 'ear if there's anybody about."

"Oh roight, yer hoigh and moightyness," mocked the first voice they had heard. This was followed shortly by a thump, and a louder crash to the ground as somebody was taught a painful lesson. A raucous cackle followed, as the rest of them enjoyed the moment.

"That'll learn ya," said a fourth voice. "Now shut it, so we can hear what there is to hear." The horsemen stopped outside of the mill, within touching distance of the porch, and the windows behind which three men and two women were trying hard to not even breathe, lest they give themselves away. The moments passed, and Keldron found that as he held his breath, his heart pumped steadily stronger to compensate. He closed his eyes and willed himself to breathe, calmly, slowly. He moved through the exceptional skills of concentration he possessed to relax. It worked, and as he opened his eyes, one of the men outside grunted in disgust.

"Bah, nuffin," came the voice of the fifth and until now only unheard horseman. "If there's a soul alive in this village they are either exceptionally quiet, or a damned fool."

"Why don't you go ask one of the corpses if they are harbouring anybody, Daercy?" the horseman who had been called Seth asked sarcastically. "Perhaps they would give you a clearer answer than you have already got."

"You would probably look better with a stake through you, just like all those backward followers of the Old Law," Daercy replied. "Now go do a sweep of the outer village, and take Bob with you. Perhaps with your exceptional skills in tracking you might actually find something to prove the usefulness of your continued existence." Silence followed as Seth glared at the man in charge, and then with kicks to the flanks of their already beleaguered horses, two of the horsemen went charging off into the distance.

"Are you sure this is going to work?" The voice they had heard fourth said quietly.

"Apparently so, Daan." Daercy replied. "We were told that they would be loyal and follow orders without question. They have done that."

"Couldn't that wizard have done a little trick to shut them up?" said the voice that had spoken last of all.

"The way I hear it, Jaerger, that was not part of the deal," Daercy replied. "You have to remember, that these volunteers are not part of our trained force, but are mostly these very people. Villagers, like these saps. They are expendable, and in the end we are expected to lose them one way or another. They are fodder, and they are to be given every chance to expend their miserable lives. In the end, it doesn't even matter how hard they try. If they make it through this, they will be taken anyway."

Jaerger cackled, an evil sound. "Don't let that on to them though, eh. It will be all the richer for us at the end when we are there and this land is empty of this type."

"Where are they?" said the voice that belonged to Daan. "They should have been back by now. This is a village, not a Gods be damned city."

"We were told that they were loyal,." replied Daercy. "We were not told if they would be of any use to us. They probably couldn't track a fire through a forest. They serve their purpose though. They are the manpower we need to fulfil this grand plan that those in charge seem hell bent upon seeing through to fruition. We just need to hit the right villages to keep those miscreants from across the mountains heading the right way. There is no need for a tribe of beggars and whores to come here and infest our land with their presence. Let them be dealt with the way the master sees fit. We will herd them on like cattle and then rape these villages for what they are worth. They might say that they do not make a profit, but I bet you that all of these houses are loaded down with gold, hidden away in some secret place."

Inwardly, Keldron groaned. He had heard enough to know that even those in charge of fooling the others were being fooled. The promise of gold, taken from those who had little. He could not believe that people were being killed for that purpose alone.

"What about the ghosts?" asked Daan.

"Don't be a fool, Daan. There are no such things. This village is completely dead. All you have to worry about is falling over a corpse with a great big stake sticking out of it."

Presently, the sound of horses straining to a gallop echoed through the village.

"Here comes the fodder," announced Jaerger.

"Shut it. Don't be more of an idiot than you already are." Daercy growled, authority strong in his voice. "Anything?" he yelled at the returning Bob and Seth.

"Nothing," Seth yelled back. "Nobody has been here in days. There are no tracks on any of the surrounding paths. Now where do we go?" The two of them dismounted, and Keldron saw from the edge of the window that they were near the bushes that Raoul had been near when he had entered the house. He ducked back through the doorway and looked into the next room. Raoul was frozen in place, stricken as he watched the two men standing mere footsteps away from where he had thrown up. Keldron edged up behind his friend to see that he was trembling. He placed a gentle hand on Raoul's shoulder, making the wizard jump, but not enough to give them away to the horsemen.

"They are going to find it, and us." Raoul looked around, his blue eyes flashing in recognition and disphoria all at once. He blinked slowly, evidence that he knew he was perilously close to having given them away. "All it would take was one stray glance, one sniff of the air in the right place."

"Stay quiet, my friend. We may get out of this yet."

Outside, the jibes and banter had degenerated into an argument over where they were to go next. The smell that should have made things fairly evident that someone had recently been here was obviously not as rancid as it had been. Maybe the wind was just blowing in the right direction, or maybe these men were as inattentive to the more obvious signs as they were to the fact that this village reeked of evil. These men were obviously not chosen for their intelligence. The argument seemed to centre on two choices; going West to where the action had evidently been more recent, or going East to another village nearer the mountains where they might plunder.

Daercy ended it with a thumping blow to the side of Jaerger's head. The horseman fell out of his saddle, and slumped to the ground. Daercy dismounted and stood over him. "You will go where I tell you, unless you want to make an enemy of the wizard, and just about everybody else with the sense to see how incompetent you would be as a commander of even a troupe as small as this. Now mount up. We will head North and West to the next settlement, and check on that."

Daercy mounted, and led the other three out of the opposite end of the village to which they had entered.

Jaerger mounted quickly, grumbling. "You see who comes out of this better, you son of a motherless whore." He snarled at his rapidly disappearing commander's back, and then followed as fast as his horse would allow him.

41

Raoul's shoulders slumped as he sighed in relief at the fact that his weakness had almost given them away. "A close one." He said quietly to Keldron, who was watching as the dust from the last rider settled back to the ground.

"It would never have been your fault if they had seen that Raoul." He answered, sympathy strong for his friend's guilt. "Nor would any of us have blamed you." Keldron looked out on the village, seemingly lost in his own thoughts. "None of us knew how we would react to seeing so much bloody carnage. It took guts for anybody to enter this village, let alone take a look in the houses. I myself know the consequences of that, and I am glad that Belyn did not have to burn any more of us." Keldron absently touched his arm, feeling the tender burn beneath the bandages and ointment.

"You aren't the only one, my friend." Raoul chuckled. "I think we should go back to the others, see what we can make of that commotion." They left the room, joining a silent Yerdu on the stairs.

Joleen and Belyn were already in the parlour, and not long after they had all gathered there, Malcolm, Aynel, Arden, Seren and Handel joined them shortly.

"The horses are eating," Handel Broadbough spoke in a whisper, as was his way.

"They did get a bit jittery when those other horses were near. They wanted to neigh out a greeting, but we managed to keep them quiet. Good horses those," added Malcolm in his high-pitched voice, "so did you learn anything?"

The two women kept silent during the recital of the facts that had been unwittingly revealed by the horsemen. They had been stunned by the callous lack of regard for the lives of innocents in this land, and even the normally forthright Yerdu had been shocked into silence. The three wizards combined their opinions with the facts to relate a macabre tale to the tribesmen. The normally reserved men came as close to losing their calm exterior as Raoul had ever seen them. As he watched and as they listened to Belyn, he swore that he could see the colour drain out of their faces. It was as if someone had broached a metaphorical keg in their faces with a tap, and had turned it on. The change of colour was visible. The story of the fate of these and so many other innocent people left them helpless with frustration for the first time that they could remember.

When they had finished relating the facts, Malcolm was the first to respond, as the other members of the tribe were beside themselves with emotions that they were frankly unused to. "You were right. If I had heard what that scum had had to say, I would have been right out there and to hell with the consequences." Malcolm frowned, bursting at the seams with repressed rage. "I would have ensured that there would be five less maniacs out there dealing blows to innocents."

"That would have made no difference, except it may have been detrimental to you, my friend," Belyn answered. "It looks like there is more to this than just a bunch of killings. They made repeated references to higher authorities, and especially at least one wizard." Belyn stood, and paced the room. "Now I shudder to think who would involve themselves in such a dire scheme, but I cannot think beyond the Witch Finder. He is reputed to be a wizard of great power. Someone of his stature and reputation would be the sort of person that would be able to inflict damage on the scale we have been seeing. The fact that it is so far from Raessa, his stronghold, is no never mind to him. The question is what can ten of us do here and now to prevent this going any further?"

"Kel, what can we do when he has stretched out his arm and taken our mentor?" This fact hurt Belyn, it was clear from his words. "If I could I would tear down the walls to set him free."

Raoul jumped forward in his seat. "Whoa there, brother. Enough with the heroic talk. There is nothing that we can do about events that have already occurred here and you know it. We can't go rushing off without looking at the bigger picture. We are not insignificant, especially with the experiences we have had and the knowledge we have gained. But I think that going after something as widespread as this is getting extremely sidetracked."

Belyn glared at his long-time friend, on the verge of yet another rowdy argument, but ever the mediator, Keldron decided this was the best point to step in. "What are you getting at, Raoul? What exactly is your point?"

Raoul stood up, facing his nine companions, and for once his face was not full of his trademark zeal for the joys of the Old Law, which was what they were all expecting. "Remember what happened in the chamber of Ilia, back there in the forest. The old man charged us to search for the Tome of Law, as our answers would lie therein."

"That's not what he said," Belyn snapped, in a grumpy mood now that he had had the impetus taken away from him.

"It is close enough," Raoul continued without missing a beat. "The point is that while we are out here, saving the world from all of it's ailments, we are devoting less and less time to that."

"Do you find these events to be insignificant?" questioned Handel in a cold, low voice. He had been impressed by Raoul's knowledge and utter dedication to the tenets of the Old Law time and time again on their journey, but even he had a frosty edge as he spoke.

"Absolutely not," Raoul replied with a hint of self-mockery. "I would hardly have done what I did out there had this all been a walk in the woods for me, Handel Broadbough. I just think that these events are part of a greater whole than we are looking at by coming to one instance of this..." He looked to grope for a word, shaking his head as he searched for the right one. "This evil," he said after a brief pause. He implored each one of them. "Feel the emotion around you. This is not something that we can prevent by means of an action that ten people are capable of. If what we heard is true, then ten tens of our number would be insignificant. We just have to look at this another way."

"The temple," Belyn prompted through tight lips.

"The temple," Raoul replied, a serious mien to his face. "I know what you would say Belyn, and you may well be right. But I believe that we are looking at this the wrong way. You may say that it is my zealous heart, and the Gods know even I can see when I am being a bit overdriven when it comes to the Old Law, but I think, no I know that we will find more than just the shell of a building that needs a good clean to make people come back to it. We need to find answers that we are capable of using to our advantage, otherwise we will just be swept to the side when whatever evil this is that is massing for a strike comes to the fore."

"What about the other Merdonese, Raoul?" asked Keldron of his friend. "They are still out there, and from what we have heard they could well be driven like a herd by these instances of evil towards some point with who knows what waiting for them at the end of it."

Raoul glanced at Handel, who spoke now. "My brethren are stout and adaptable, seeker of the answers. They will not be overcome so easily, and always remember there are other fractions of the tribe beyond the mountains. If we can find enough of them, mayhap we can mount some sort of resistance against this evil from right under their noses."

"If anybody can do something to ward off this potential catastrophe, it is the Merdonese." Raoul said on the end of Handel's comments. "But how will you contact them?"

Handel shrugged, as if it were of no matter to him. "We have methods, and there are signs that can be read to tell us their whereabouts. There are many tribesmen nearby. They feel the trees as they felt a connection with the great forest. You could say that we are drawn to them, that we know where to look. There will be enough of us to start something. I swear my soul to the green cave of the forest, we will save lives."

"One thing vexes me about this," Belyn said. "We are all followers of the Old Law, more or less. How do you propose to go about this if fighting is the only resort?"

Handel narrowed his stare at the large man. "We will win."

At the sight of Belyn's raised eyebrows, Raoul stepped in. "There is nothing in the Old Law that says one cannot fight, just that the cause should be true. We are not talking about an aggressive strike against innocent people my friend. We are talking about saving a way of life should it come to that. Why should any one of us be the person who stands aside while entire villages are butchered?"

Belyn relented. "You are right of course, Raoul. I could never beat you in discussions of the Old Law, and for that I am glad." Belyn stood and addressed everybody, his bulk making his forthright stance imposing. "My friends. As my brother has quoted the Law, so let it be done. I for one say that we should attempt both quests discussed here today. This evil aura shows that we need to do *something* about this situation. If the tribe is willing, go against these mercenaries using the way of stealth that is your legacy to the world, but stay safe, that we may meet again." As Belyn said this, he looked across the table at Yerdu as if it was going to be the last time he ever laid his eyes upon her. Nobody else was in his sights. Keldron pretended not to notice, but Joleen was gazing at him in exactly the same way, and that was something he could not ignore. "We will continue our long journey towards Caighgard under the advice of my brother Raoul, and should we find nothing to aid you, we will make use of the information and somehow get it to you." Finally Belyn tore his gaze away from Yerdu, and looked at the other tribesmen. "Is there anything we can do to help you now?"

Handel, Aynel and Arden spoke almost in unison as they said, "Please, let us out of this village now, we can not stand it for much longer." Despite his reticence, Seren's eyes betrayed the fact that he was obviously in agreement with his fellows.

Belyn smiled, full of compassion for the tribesmen. "Thy will be done. May the leaf shelter you and the trunk protect."

"May the trunk protect." They intoned in solemn departure, and the four tribesmen hurried out into the yard. The horses had not been unsaddled due to the hasty nature that they had entered the miller's grounds, and the tribesmen were gone in moments. Belyn, Raoul, Malcolm and Yerdu went out to see the tribesmen ride through the village and out back to the East, leaving Keldron and Joleen alone together in the parlour. Keldron looked at the person that had become without a shadow of a doubt the focus of his existence. She totally captivated him. Her wealth of luxurious blonde hair and the curve of her neck. Her bright eyes and radiant glow of vitality. It was almost too much for him. He had regretted this moment as soon as Raoul had started talking about their options.

"Do you need much from me before you go?" he asked, unsure of what she would say. Joleen just looked back at him, shaking her head slightly. At length she spoke. "Maybe once I would have left with them, but things within me have altered." Joleen looked down at her hands and snorted a small laugh. "You know, I should be out there, riding for my life and my sanity, as far away from this village as I can possibly get. But I am not. That is enough to know that things have changed." Joleen then looked up at him with that gaze that was so penetrating, he felt as if he had nowhere in the world that he could run that she would not find him. "I will run nowhere, and hide under no stone that you are not under, Keldron." He looked at her, uncomprehending, still thinking that she was going to leave. "You stupid fool, I love you. I would not be parted from you by tide nor storm, by root nor branch. My life is with you Keldron, now and for ever."

Keldron could not believe what he was hearing. A lopsided grin came over his face, as if he had just discovered some secret that would forever be his. Joleen stood, and with her very presence lighting up the room, leaned towards him and kissed him lingeringly. Keldron returned the kiss, and before they knew it, they were holding each other in utter contentment, enjoying the peace.

"Ahem, when you two are quite finished. . ." came the jolly voice of Belyn. "We have some things to discuss."

As the rest returned from the yard Keldron leaned towards his friend. "She loves me." He said with a small smile, never taking his eyes off of Joleen, who sat demurely at the table, looking down at her hands, the hands that had touched him so softly.

"And I assume you love her." Belyn replied, with mirth in his voice.

"Why, yes. I suppose I do," Keldron replied lightly, as if this had suddenly come to him in a moment of pure revelation."

Belyn clapped his friend on the back. "Good. It's about bloody time you came to that conclusion. Now you can stop mooncalfing around and find some proper answers to your self-imposed riddles." He turned to address everybody else in the room. "This is it then. We move out of this forsaken place, and hopefully never set our eyes on its like again. But steel yourselves, my friends, for I am sure that this is not over. We have some hard decisions to make, and the least of those is whether or not we forage for supplies in this village. Anybody have any thoughts?"

Raoul spoke up. "Let us look around this miller's house for anything that we might use. He was immersed in the Old Law to say the least, and I am sure that were he here, he would not begrudge us some aid. As for the rest of the village, I am not going near any building that has had somebody murdered in it, not for anything." He sat there in silence, daring them all to defy him with his arms folded across his chest.

"That may be a prudent choice, considering all that has happened in this dreadful place so far." Malcolm agreed, looking at Raoul as if to reassure the thin man. "I for one would like to respect the dead and leave them in peace, if that is at all possible. But let us not disturb their slumber any more than we must." This brought a general murmur of agreement from the rest of the group, and without another word, they got up to explore the house and yard. The search yielded a few things of use for them, but they were loath to probe too deeply, for to do so would come dangerously close to breaking the tenets that prohibited stealing. The guilt that they suffered was bad enough, and made many hard choices for them. In the end, they only had enough items to cover the table around which they had been sitting. A few clothes, and a few bags of well-preserved staples were all they were willing to take.

Belyn looked over the table, taking note. "Not bad." This received a huff of disagreement from Raoul, despite his feelings about the idea of taking from another person's possessions. Belyn smiled broadly, and reached inside his pocket. His face dimmed for a moment as he concentrated, and the other wizards could feel the subtle touch of Belyn's concentration as he focussed. Then it was gone, and Belyn stood there eating an apple. "Remember, my brother." He said around a mouthful of apple, "We do not really need all that much." He then tossed more apples to the others.

Raouls deft catch betrayed his quick reflexes. "As I have said before, brother mine, that is all well and good as long as your luck does not run out. There are people back in Eskenberg who I am sure were far from happy to see us leave. It is only a matter of time until safe houses such as yours are discovered." To this, Belyn smiled smugly. "They will never find it Raoul. It is hidden within the depths of the labyrinth at the centre of Eskenberg."

Raoul looked impressed. "How in the name of all that is good and right did you find anybody who knows their way into the middle of that place?" At looks from those who knew nothing of Eskenberg, Raoul explained about the labyrinthine district that filled the centre of their former home city. "The centre of Eskenberg had grown from the very beginnings of the city, houses and corridors merging on many levels into what could only be described as a several story cube where the majority of the poor lived. It opened out onto the harbour of Lake Eskebeth, and there the fishers and tanners did their work, but nobody of sound mind dared enter the place. The culture within was a completely different way of life to that outside, in the rest of the city. Gangs ruled under the stern discipline of one man, known as the Illeist, who ruled with an iron fist. No authority even contemplated an assault on the labyrinth, for they knew not where to start looking. The mare fact that Belyn had gotten somebody inside, and had even managed to keep them alive is what astounds me. Well?" He pressed.

"One day, you might know the answer, my friend." Belyn replied evasively. "But today is not that day. All you need to know is that as long as you have got a good hold on your focus stone, you will not go hungry." To prevent further questioning, Belyn changed the subject. "If this is all we are taking, then I feel that we should make a move."

Malcolm looked out of the parlour window. "It is going to grow dark soon. It is not my place to suggest this, especially considering what has happened here today, and also considering the feeling we all still feel about this village..." Malcolm looked down as he faltered.

"What is it, Malcolm?" Asked Keldron, concern etched on his face. "You think we should make use of this house for the night, don't you?" Malcolm nodded without passing comment. "You know what that means? It means we have a whole night of this ill-feeling, this evil." Again Malcolm nodded, obviously content to remain silent.

"It makes sense," Raoul said quietly. "This is probably the only decent shelter for leagues around, and we have the only building that is not filled with the taste of foul murder." Raoul looked at Malcolm. "It makes sense," he repeated.

"You may be right," Belyn conceded, "but I think Keldron should decide our fate this night. He after all has been the one most affected by today's events." They looked at Keldron, and he looked back at each one of them.

"We will stay."

Chapter Three

Relief emanated from around the table. It was clear that nobody wished to spend yet another night wrapped in blankets under the questionable shelter of a set of bushes. "The horses seem to be content with a nosebag of feed and a good rubdown, but their human counterparts are a lot less hardy." "Speak for yourself," Malcolm replied.

"Yes, I know. You are the sole exception. For a man that used to the woods and wilderness you seem to be comfortable in any other place." Many the time had been when they stopped for the evening under the frigid sky to find him with a twine-bent stick wrapped around another as he whirled it in apparent magic, resulting in smoke and eventually flame.

"Well with you around, one could grow lazy. I refuse to let you wizards use your magic to do anything that I can do with my hands and the natural materials around me."

"In a way, Malcolm typifies the type of person that had belonged to this village. They were all devotees of the Old Law, living with the land in it's natural element where they could use it without harming it, and benefit from what it had to offer them. In the miller's case it had been grain for his flour, and in turn for the bread that fed so many. In Malcolm's case, it is the deadwood that feeds the campfires he seemingly makes out of nothing, and the small game that he traps to feed us every night."

"It makes sense," Belyn agreed, "but tonight, after witnessing the horror that we have, and despite the fact that we are still under the shadow of the aura of evil that permeates the very ground like a frost, I bet even Malcolm is glad of the four walls around him and the roof over his head."

Twilight beckoned from the East, creeping out from the mountains and on to the plains of northern Ardicum. Keldron left Joleen and walked out into the late afternoon, feeling the need for fresh air. He strolled around the yard, listening intently for any sounds of approaching horsemen, be they tribesmen or others. Not a sound approached his ears though, not until he walked near the stable. The quiet nickering of the horses greeted him as he stuck his head around the stable door. The horses for their part were indifferent to the ill feeling that was so thick in the air that Keldron felt he could almost reach out and grab it. They were content in their stalls, either asleep with one leg half-cocked, or just content to munch on hay. It had obviously been a good year for the village, until the fatal event had happened. The hayloft was full, and this had the added benefit of shielding the horses from the persistent breeze that had been dogging them for months. It was a wise choice. From what Keldron knew about this side of the continent, the breeze struck down from a point between two of the glaciers that pushed out like icy monoliths from the North. It did this as autumn arrived; in fact it was responsible for the harvest season. Otherwise they would have at least a couple more moons of good weather to enjoy. The stable was much warmer than the yard, and Keldron tarried, trying to forget the horrendous experience from earlier that day. He felt secure here, in fact he had not felt as secure in a place since the last time he had looked out at the sunshine over Lake Eskebeth, shortly before Raoul had taken him to the council that had altered his life. The light gradually dimmed as the afternoon became evening, and Keldron remained with the horses, brushing them down in meaningless work that was designed to take his mind off of the days events. The moment left him sour, and he rose to leave. As he reached to open the door, it was unlatched from the other side. As the door swung silently towards him, he decided to hide behind it out of a sense of pure impishness. The door opened wider, admitting the bulky form of Malcolm. The innkeeper closed the door quietly behind him as he looked into the cosy gloom that filled the stalls. The horses, docile and warm, nickered a greeting to him, but none betrayed the fact that Keldron was standing quietly behind him. Malcolm peered into the darkness of the hayloft. "Keldron?" He spoke quietly, but loud enough for anybody within the stable to hear him. Silence answered the former innkeeper. Keldron, still possessed by this impish state of mind, whispered under his breath. "Boo." The effect was instantaneous. In one motion, Malcolm turned mid-air and managed to land with his sword drawn and pointing at Keldron. That such a large man was so incredibly agile took some comprehending, but he had seen it all before, and relied on it in many cases. Malcolm took one look, and then let his guard down with a sigh of relief. He did not like fighting. The line between self-defence as defined by the Old Law, and outright aggression was very slim, and Malcolm was obviously afraid of breaching the miniscule gap that turned defence into offence. Sheathing his sword, he nodded with a rueful grin. "You made me jump." This simple statement diffused the atmosphere, and soon both men were laughing out loud, something that Keldron had been sorely missing. They sat down on two bales of hay across from the horses, and wiped their eyes clear of tears.

"I must admit, I was glad that you had moved a step or two into the stable," Keldron admitted. "I knew that you were fast, my friend. Obviously I underestimated you."

"Keep it quiet, you might ruin my reputation as a huge lumbering giant."
Malcolm replied through a grin. "You might want to also keep quiet that you
scared me nearly out of my skin with but a word."
"Ha. It was my skin that I was more worried about for a moment," Keldron
conceded. "I must remember to frighten you when you aren't armed."
"The horses seem content. "Their heat and closeness in the stalls are relaxing.
I'm not surprised you are in here."
Keldron located several candles, and a series of lanterns. He used one of his
focus stones, for Belyn had given out several, to create a small flame that he
used to light the candles in the lamps. These he placed on hooks hanging down
from the roof, and went on about his work, brushing down the bay mare that
always nickered in greeting whenever he came near. The horse took his
ministrations in its stride, shifting around the stall as Keldron moved around
with the brush and handfuls of straw he was using. It munched away at its
food completely unconcerned. Eventually tiring, Keldron selected himself a
nice spot between three bales of hay, fallen from the hayloft, and sat down.
The straw poked at his skin through his clothes, and seemed to make him itch
in just about every place. He remembered then that he would need the
dressing on his arm changed again. As this thought struck him, the arm in
question started to throb, as though the very nerves had been waiting for him
to give them attention. It did seem a little better for all of the fuss being made
over it. He chuckled, leaning back into the straw in blatant defiance of both
reason and the aforementioned nerves. He had been so busy with the horses
that he had not even noticed whether or not his arm had been giving him pain.
In fact, it seemed like the pain was a manifestation of the evil that rose from
the village, for not a moment had passed after his thoughts about his arm, than
he was worrying about the village again. The moment ruined, Keldron decided
to go back into the house. "I can feel it more now."
Malcolm examined Keldron's arm. " You have been working it hard. We must
get you back inside, my friend. All this work has begun to unravel the
bandaging, and I doubt not that the pain is returning."
"It is okay," Keldron replied, though Malcolm was indeed correct. "I have
lived through worse. This is not as bad as broken ribs."
"But I hazard that it is almost as painful. That is some burn that brought you
back to us. Let us go and sort it out." They left the stable with a comforting
goodbye to some of the horses, ensuring that they had snuffed out the candles
in the lamps first.
"Dark in here." Only then did Keldron realise how late it had actually gotten.

Malcolm opened the door to the stable, and barely anything was visible. "You were in here a long time. That's why I came after you."

As Keldron ventured cautiously out into the whispering breeze and its eternal promise of winter, he walked carefully sideways to avoid knocking his arm and aggravating the injury. He tried to make out the yard as he had remembered it, but the drums, and other tools that were stacked neatly only showed up as yet more darkness amongst the shadows that his eyes just could not penetrate. There was the merest slip of twilight in the West, where the blue-black cloud had parted to show the darkness mingling with a hint of dark red to create a vivid violet as Matsandrau, the Sun god, sped his creature on its never-ending journey around the earth. Above, a bank of cloud sealed the moon and stars from him.

"Here, in the absolute blackness of a village that died before its time, one can finally understand what absolute night feels like."

"Does it worry you?"

Keldron turned towards the voice in the dark. "No Malcolm, it feels somehow comforting."

"It would be too much for many city folk, existing under such vastness."

Keldron shivered unconsciously, holding his elbows with the opposite hands. They had seen the night sky clouded over and dark when they had been travelling, but here it felt right that there should be light, and yet there was none. "It is the feeling of absence that gives the darkness its edge of despair. There are no people here. This former beacon of light at the end of the day, this gathering place for travellers, has become a darker hole than many would ever be able to comprehend. The worst part of it all is that there is no way to bring significant respite to the dark horror that is this village."

"True. It is quite possible, even with a few too many candles, to make a beacon of ourselves in the great blackness of the rural night. We might be seen from anything up to a league away if those looking know what to spy for, and there is nothing to say that the horsemen are anything like that far away. For all we know, the horsemen are right outside of the village, just waiting for us to give ourselves away."

"Let us get inside then." So it was that as Keldron approached the parlour, only through experience was he able to tell that there were a couple of carefully shielded candles alight within. The drapes were all drawn, as he guessed that they would be. They would not give themselves away without good cause. Opening the door, he entered with Malcolm close behind to see that things had changed a considerable amount in the time that he had been.

The packs had been distributed around the room, and the table had been moved respectfully to one side of the parlour in order to give them somewhere to lie down. Cushions and blankets from the bedrooms draped the floor.

"It is a shame that the miller would never again see the house that he once called home." Keldron touched the furnishings with respect. The miller had dwelled here in domestic tranquillity, but that was all past. A shock event had seen to the end of his existence in this place, and now all that was left were bad memories to be carried into eternity, forgotten to all.

"Sit down." Keldron was brought out of his contemplation of the foibles of life by Yerdu, who silently motioned for him to sit to the left of the table, balm and bandages at the ready. "Let me see to that wound of yours."

"I'm fine."

"Of course you are. That's why you went and spent an age in the stables with horses instead of in here in the warm, because you are fine."

As Yerdu unwrapped the bandage, it felt to Keldron as if he were having his very skin unwrapped from his body, so sore was his arm. Malcolm motioned to them that he was heading outside to watch and would leave Yerdu to it. Yerdu tutted as she looked at the state of the wound, weeping with pus because of the stress he had put himself under whilst tending the horses. "You men really do not know how to take care of yourselves. Still, it is looking somewhat improved already."

Joleen entered the parlour with another lamp, setting it down on the table. "It is lucky that you have us here to look after you, or you would end up with bits dropping off, and would never even notice."

Yerdu smiled at that comment, and added, "We couldn't have men without their bits now could we." This brought a chuckle from Joleen, and Keldron remained seated, his face in mock anguish. "Oh woe is me, and woe for us men, to be so helpless as to be mere babes in your care." He tried to add a flourish as he said this, but Yerdu had his arm in an iron grip as she applied the soothing balm, and would not let him move an inch.

"This is a torrid injury, and sums up your day, wizard. You would do well to remain still as I apply this balm, and stop acting like such a blatherskite." Noting that Yerdu was now being serious, Keldron became contrite, allowing Yerdu to finish her work. As she tied off the bandage, Keldron admitted that his arm was feeling much better. "What is in that balm?" he asked as she was replacing the pot in her pack.

"Herbs, soothing creams and a little bit of forest magic." She replied with a hint of evasion. "It will heal your arm quicker than your body can naturally, and judging by the severity of that burn, you need it."

Keldron leaned back into the cushions he was resting on. The parlour, in it's dim light and subtle warmth, was restful and quiet. "It seems as though anything associated with the Merdon forest has an amazing healing property." Yerdu nodded in agreement. "Does it surprise you that we regret nearly every moment that we are not there? The forest, aside from being our home, is a miraculous place, evidence of which you have seen first hand."

"I recall the very first image I saw as I left the tent. I looked out upon a valley shaped in a perfect bowl, full of magnificently old trees. Amongst the trees small campfires produced streams of smoke that went straight up into the sky where they mingled and danced as if at play. There was an absolute lack of a breeze, and like so few places, I felt quite at rest there. It had been clear when first I emerged from the tent that there was something eldritch about the valley, but it was a good thing, and the tribe prospered under it's protection." Keldron tried to forget that somebody was responsible for destroying that peace, and attacking the tribe in their one point of contact with outsiders. He regretted that such a rash move by whoever was responsible, Witch Finder or other.

"You have seen but a little of our lives, wizard, but you see to the heart of what we miss."

"Should the Merdonese recover from the assault upon their home, I regret that they may never again trust to contact with outsiders, a fact that would detriment both them, and those who relied upon their contact."

"There is nothing to say that there is no other avenue open to us, Keldron."

"Well when the time comes, I will do my utmost to ensure that the entire tribe is safe and yet not hidden. There is too much hate and distrust in the world already. One day we shall see the forest restored to the peaceful haven that it was before we came. I think that I speak for all of my brothers when I say that I am glad you decided to come with us." He spoke the words to Yerdu, but again his eyes met with Joleen, who smiled back at him.

"I will hold you to that, wizard," Yerdu said as if she had not noticed Keldron looking away. "I think that a great many moons will pass ere we return to our forest in peace. We should make the most of what we have tonight, even if it is in this village of evil under a sky with no moon. These are ill times indeed when such coincidence happens."

That was what had made it so dark outside. Keldron had been so overtaken by events that he had missed completely the fact that the moon had been gradually waning over the past several days, and had appeared to them only two nights previous as the merest of slivers in the night sky. He found all of a suddenly that he missed the long cloudless nights of Eskenberg his home where the moon shone like a beacon over the waters of Lake Eskebeth, turning the night into a vista of silvered magic and silent contemplation. The near-constant cloud cover almost made him lose his sense of direction. To console himself, Keldron decided that he would pick up a little something from the room back in Eskenberg. "If I can not actually go home, I can return there in spirit, if but for a moment. Thank you for being patient with me, Yerdu." Keldron moved to a part of the parlour where he was unencumbered by the relative crowding of bodies and furniture. He reached for his favourite focus stone, the old marble that he had possessed for so long now, and fed all of his concentration into it as he focussed.

Instantly, the pain from his arm reduced. In a split second he remembered the old cantankerous man that supposedly headed up his former guild; they spent their entire lives performing the most miserable of focuses so that they could live beyond their years. If the focus could lengthen their lives, then why could it not heal a wound? The very act of focussing benefited him in a way that those old men would never conceive. As he poured his awareness into the stone, he felt much better, and by the time his awareness was in that room hundreds of leagues away, he had forgotten that he had ever been injured. In his spirit form, he was a new person, hale and full of vigour. Even the woes and the ill feeling that emanated from the very air of the village his body was resting in seemed as if it was on another world, though as he looked back, there was something that nagged at him. It had never occurred to him that he would not bring his ills onto this plane of existence. Here and only here, he was as strong as his spirit allowed him to be, and that was the only limit. The revelation that came to him seemed suddenly a great deal more important than a mere object, and he hastened to accomplish his task. Locating what he needed from the hidden room, Keldron propelled himself by force of will back to his body, excited by the prospect of what his discovery could mean to him and his friends, but found himself going in a different direction. Keldron arrived in the cell of his master, to find him waiting there patiently.

"How did you do that?"

"Simple, if you know how."

"You look better," Keldron observed.

"I feel well again, my son. Hearken to me, and keep the knowledge safe until you feel the time is right to impart it unto others. You are about to make a grand discovery, Keldron, one that has implications beyond anything you have previously learned. You were onto the secret just before you came here. Look at your arm when you get back: It will be healed."

"What do you mean, master? Are you all right?"

"I am fine, now go."

Keldron's eyes snapped open, and he fumbled with bandages in one hand, and a bottle of their very own-spiced brandy that they had at some time in the past called 'orit' in the hand of his injured arm. Yerdu saw what he was suddenly doing, and lurched towards him, her face full of concern. "Do not do that, Keldron! You will only injure yourself further. The burn must be left alone or it will not heal."

"Take it off, quckly." Keldron was so excited he nearly dropped the bottle.

"Don't be stupid, wizard. You will damage your arm beyond all repair."

"Take the bandage off." The authority in his voice was slow and deliberate. Confused by this sudden change, Yerdu complied with not a comment. Her frown and pursed lips clearly said that she was less than pleased with this course of action, though she undid the bandage as gently as she was able to. As she unwrapped the final strip, Yerdu let out a gasp that showed she was clearly not expecting what she saw. "Sweet Ilia." She swore, invoking the name of the Earth Goddess that watched over them in the forest of Merdon. Keldron knew what had happened, but still he turned his arm to look at the results. The red angry burn with its weeping edges and cracks had diminished considerably, leaving a healed scab with scarred skin around it.

"The pain is all gone." The skin bore clear evidence of a recent wound, but from the difficult view that he had of his twisted arm, Keldron saw that it looked freshly healed. All of a sudden, Keldron found himself twisted and bent over so that Yerdu and Joleen could get a look at the until-recently wounded arm. They were thorough in their examination, and Keldron felt more then uncomfortable bent in an awkward position with his head almost down by his knee.

"What is this?" Came the quiet exclamation of Belyn's voice as he entered the parlour. "A threesome? Why wasn't I invited?" Even bent nearly double, Keldron still managed to laugh as Yerdu leapt up and punched Belyn in the stomach as a response, almost doubling the big man over.

Her dark eyes flashing, Yerdu directed Belyn towards the place in the parlour where Keldron was now acutely aware of how ridiculous he looked, and also of how much his back was going to need straightening out. "Look at that, you comedian, and tell us what you think."

Belyn peered at Keldron's arm, forcing him to endure more moments of agony. "Oh my." Was all his big friend managed to get out before Keldron stood up, rubbing at one now-uncomfortable side of his ribs. "Ahhhhhh," he sighed in clearly evident relief. Keldron glared at the other three in the room. "Next time you lot can stand and look where it suits me."

"Looks like we might not have a next time judging by your little miracle." The normally strepitant Belyn replied. "Care to tell us about how you preformed your little act of healing?"

Keldron bent his arm. Whereas earlier the burn had almost prevented him from being able to move his arm through pain and stiffness, now there was most definitely a lissome quality. He revelled in having the use of his arm back, and reached almost without thinking to scratch at the edges of the scab. "Well you know how all the old politicians spent their best days striving to merely exist within the dusty halls of our old home?" Belyn nodded, eager to hear any findings associated with a focus. "Well I found that. . .Ow!" Keldron stopped scratching at the scab as Yerdu firmly smacked his hand away.

"It is not healed yet, wizard, and spell or no spell, you will let me treat this arm, if not quite as often as earlier."

Keldron laughed. "Yes ma'am," he replied. "Anyway, the old codgers used the power of focussing to prolong their lives. I focussed to Eskenberg for a little light relief." At this, he held up a flask of the brandy, bringing a smile to his friend's face. "When I returned, I felt different, and my arm confirmed this." He stood up, and grabbed his friend by the shoulders, to the annoyance of Yerdu, who was in the process of trying to re-tie the bandage. "Belyn, the very process of the focus aided my body in healing my arm. It was if there was some sort of positive residual feedback into my body from the focus."

Belyn took one look at Keldron, and then did something completely unexpected. He raised his hands to his face in anguish "Ah! How could it have ever been so blindingly obvious and yet so impossible?" He crouched, bending his body in an almost foetal position, and then before anybody could react, he drove himself at the door towards the yard. He hit it head first, with predictable results. Slumping semi-conscious to the ground with a cut along his brow the width of one hand dripping blood down his face, Belyn wheezed a chuckle. " I have a bit of a headache," he said to nobody in particular. Then he grabbed at a focus stone from one of the many pockets secreted about his robes, and concentrated. Keldron felt the enormous will of Belyn building, magnified by the stone in his hand, one of the same ilk that Keldron had just utilised. The pressure in the room was immense, though only Keldron could feel it. The two women looked on in horror, and then dawning amazement as the blood stopped dripping. The cut sealed itself up from left to right; the flesh of his forehead disappearing under newly repaired skin. Soon the scab reduced to a thin white line, and eventually that too disappeared. A flask of orit popped into existence next to Keldron as he felt the power of Belyn's focus dissipate. Belyn sat up with a start. He moved his head slightly, tilting it from side to side in inquisitive movements that were more akin to a small wild bird, and which looked oddly comical to be seen coming from a big man with a red beard. "Amazing." He breathed in wonder. "I would never have guessed that it would be so simple." He looked at Keldron, who leaned forwards to offer an arm to his friend. Pulling himself up, he continued to scan inside himself for some injury. "I hit that door frame as hard as I could, and yet I am fine. Who would have thought it? Those old fogies sitting there in their musty den, holding the secret to eternal life in their pockets."

"I don't think you can quite call it that." Keldron disagreed. "It looks as though you have to be holding the stone for it to work any sort of benefit on you. How do you use a focus stone if you are already dead?"

That brought Belyn up short. "There must be a way." The determination was strong in his voice. "If we can understand this, then we can learn. This could benefit everybody. I will strive to figure out a way, but I must meditate upon this. I will fid a way to release Lothan from the cave, and I will find a way to ensure we can heal others." Belyn made to leave the room, and paused in mid-stride. "Hang on, when you told us that you had injured yourself in the forest, how come you hadn't healed yourself when you prevented the army from chasing you?"

"Simple." Keldron answered. "I created the wall to block them before I fell. Afterwards, I had not much cause to use a focus stone, as we were too busy trying to evade them. I never healed myself then because I never had cause to."

"What about when you slept?"

"That was the forest, whose eaves we were still under when the army passed by us. I had nothing to do with that enchantment, but I bet you wish you knew how it was performed."

Keldron chuckled as Belyn strode from the room, seeking solace. Yerdu charged after him. Joleen giggled. "I don't think that Belyn is going to get the peace and quiet he desires, Keldron."

"No? He can be pretty dogged when he needs to be."

Joleen came to him, wrapping herself in his arms. "That is not what I mean. Did you see my sister's face when he ran at the door like that? Yerdu does not like surprises, and it will take her a long time to get over that shock."

Keldron squeezed her tight against him; the summer smell of her hair was a comfort in this perilous place. "I know what you mean, Jo. I had no idea he was going to do that either, and I have known him for more years than anybody but Raoul. Crazy stunts do not usually come from him, but at least it proved my point."

Joleen snuggled closer. "Do you think that he will be able to heal people?"

Keldron shrugged, and revelled in the sensation that he was able to do so. "He might well find a way. Mind you, he might as well find a way to restore the great focus over the forest, and he might find a way to bring this village back to life as well."

Joleen untangled herself, searching his face to see if he was mocking. What she saw both surprised and heartened her. Keldron was deadly serious. "He could do that?" she asked, clearly in awe of powers she did not fully comprehend.

"Who is to say what he could do." Keldron replied diffidently, aware now that there was someone close to them who knew more about focussing than Belyn. "The point is that there is so much that we don't know about our art. So much has been lost. Belyn possesses the knowledge of one that we like to call our 'benefactor', though we know not who he was, or even when he set his ideas down on parchment. But he gave ideas that led Belyn to believe that the order of Law was once more than a bunch of old men sat around telling merchants how to behave. He believes that the order of Law was once the paramount guild in the land, presiding over the rest."

Joleen frowned at this. "So you are saying that you want supremacy over everyone else? And this makes you better than those mercenaries how."

Keldron shook his head firmly. "No Jo, that is the last thing that we want. But what we *do* want is to give people the power to chose. We want to balance the equilibrium and help everybody. We most certainly want to save anybody that might be in trouble from these riders." He shook his head slowly, watching her. "The Gods alone know what we can not do. We can only try what we know."

Their quiet moment together was broken by Raoul, who came into the near-silent room like a thunderstorm. "What is this I was told about injuries and magical healings before I was bundled out of the room I was using?"

Keldron outlined what they had learned as a result of the focuses they had performed, and then finished by unwrapping his freshly wrapped wound to show his friend.

"Well blow me down." Was all Raoul could say, and he went looking around the parlour. Pretty soon he found what he was looking for in the form of a large knife. Grinning up at Joleen and Keldron in the crazed look of his zealous Old Law faith, Raoul slashed the knife across his arm, drawing blood. "Ow, that hurts," he grimaced, staring at the cut, and then reached inside his pocket for his own focus stone. Pretty soon Raoul's unique blend of zealot's concentration and his marble stone throbbed through the air in time with the blood from his arm, but that did not last long. It seemed only moments until he was stood there eyes open, gazing in wonder at his healed arm, with a flask of orit in the other hand. "Well I never. Who would have thought that it would be that easy?" He turned his arm over, checking for any sort of a scar, but there was none. "I don't believe it."

Joleen had moved apart from Raoul and Keldron during this, and looked from one face to the other. "You are all mad!" she exclaimed, pulling away from them. "Was there no other way for you to test this healing?"

Keldron grinned at Raoul, who grinned right back. "I guess not." Joleen just shook her head, her face pale and drained, and left the parlour, letting the door swing ajar behind her as if it could not care who passed through.

"What was wrong with her?" Raoul asked with mild curiosity.

"I know not, my friend." Keldron replied as he hefted his flask. "But I am sure that I will find out at some point soon." Keldron hefted his flask and raised it towards Raoul. "To you and your miraculous recovery, my friend."

A broad smile lit up Raoul's narrow face. "I'll drink to that!"

After repeated toasts to various happenings, and several quick swallows of the brandy, both men felt a little better, but the situation had not become any less grave. Raoul put his flask down with a sigh. "It is not the same without Belyn." He conceded ruefully.

"I know what you mean." Keldron agreed. "This place does not help. It makes me feel so on edge."

Raoul's gaze dropped to the floor. "The cushions and blankets suddenly seem so inviting. I think I am going to take a nap. Might as well make the use of this place while we are here."

Suddenly Keldron felt drained, the events of the day catching up with him. With not a word more, he dropped to his pack, and fell asleep. If Keldron had hoped for peace, his wishes were not heard. The moment he dropped off, his dreams were plagued with darkness and death. He felt constricted by an unending abyss of evil, grabbing at him and drawing him ever deeper into its depths. Keldron beheld a mass uprising of people in a city with high walls, while his master ran through tunnels. He realised that he was seeing Obrett and three men as yet unknown to him escaping the Witch Finder. His master had found a way out of Raessa. The evil was great, a pulsing mass of blackness that permeated the very rocks. People were dying there. As Keldron watched, helplessly held in the thrall of his subconscious mind, faceless people were impaled on stakes as they were held hand and foot by tangible ropes of darkness. As each one was pierced, the man or woman looked straight at him, mouthing obscenities as they were pierced by wood that was too blunt to pass through them, but did so nonetheless. The wounds did not bleed, but pulsed black viscous fluid in his direction, filling his vision. He screamed, and the corpses laughed back at him, waving and jeering as if their souls had been damned and they enjoyed the sensation. They filled his vision to the widest periphery, all waving at him and welcoming him as if they would embrace him given a chance. He fell further into the abyss, but could not look down. Whatever was holding him in this veritable nightmare was preventing him from seeing what he was being dragged down towards. The corpses hung off of their stakes, grinning with madness. They moved away from him but at the same time there were more of them. He realised that the black abyss had become the top of a yawning cavern. He stared about himself and realised that the cave was alight with evil and darkness. Thousands of mad corpses gibbered at him in dark ecstasy, waving their arms and spouting curses. The noise was deafening, every voice shrieking at him in some mad language. He found himself accelerating to the pool of black liquid at the bottom of the chamber, while all around him the frantic waving of arms became rippling as if the corpses were spiralling down towards the liquid. He realised as he looked that they were. The chamber of his nightmare was feeding the dead and the dying into the pool, increasing its potency. His arms were thrown forward as he was thrust towards the pool and he found his chin upon his chest. The noise became deafening. The bodies disappeared in a blur of pain and nausea as he hurtled backwards towards the pool, and then it all stopped. The voices silenced, and all he could hear was a drip. He hung from something, something that made the sound. He was on an islet within the middle of the black pool separated from it by not much more that a stride or two of rock. Everything was upside down. The bodies off in the distance stared expectantly, awaiting a stigma to set off their insane gibbering once more. They looked much more human from the funny angle Keldron was resting at. He pushed his arms behind himself for support so that he could raise himself up, and found that he could not move. Something prevented him by pinning him to the ground. He moved in a gentle rocking motion, and determined that whatever it was had a hold of his chest. Straining his already injured neck, he tried to look up and across himself, but something long and dark prevented him. With a Herculean effort, he raised his head, and found that an immense stake had thrust through his chest, and was almost as long as he was tall. The girth of the stake was impossibly wide, and his blood dripped from it onto his own body, the drips making the gentle patting sound that echoed all around the cavern. The corpses looked on, expectancy falling from them to the base of the cavern like blood. Unable to keep his head up any more, he let it drop back, and the liquid at the edge of the island bubbled and frothed. Something raised the surface of the liquid nearest to the point on the island where he was pinned. A voice whispered to him.

'Find me, unbind me. Before they do.'

The bulge in the pool sank back down, and molten pain seared his chest. Blood started to spurt out in huge gushes, and he screamed the scream of the damned. Upon hearing the scream, every corpse in the cavern reacted as if this was the sign they had been waiting for. They threw back their heads and screamed, and black blood gushed out of the wounds in their chests as it did from him, and poured straight to the point at his head where the liquid had bulged. The screaming increased to a pitch so high it felt as if his ears were in as much agony as his chest, and Keldron clenched his eyes shut, willing the cacophony of evil away. Waves of pain thrust towards him, and into him through the wound that now pulsed with his heartbeat in the middle of his chest. Somehow, Keldron willed himself to twist around, and as he concentrated he felt that it might actually happen. With strength he never knew he possessed, he wrenched his shoulders, bringing his body around with him, and hit his head on the stone.

Abruptly, everything went silent. Keldron kept his eyes screwed tight, lest the cauldron of noise come back. He realised that the smooth surface he could feel against his face was not that of the rock. He reached to his chest with his arm, and patted it all over, feeling for the wound. His clothes were intact, not a rent, not a loose hem of a stitch. He led there for a moment longer, trying to absorb his surroundings. He could hear breathing, the breathing of more than one person in close proximity. He knew where he was. Opening his eyes, Keldron found that he had twisted himself over onto his front. Joleen was nearby, her face close to his. An angel asleep in the dim lamplight of the parlour, he dared not disturb her. Keldron was comforted by the warmth of the room, relief flooding into him as his awareness came fully back to the present, and out of his nightmare state. He levered himself quietly up, and saw that everybody else was spread out around the room, aside from Malcolm, who was nowhere to be seen. He sat there on the cushions for a while, just enjoying the fact that he was awake and not in a cavern full of gibbering corpses. Closing his eyes again with a deep sigh, he revelled in the close company of friends, but something nagged at him as he sat there. It was an echo of the feelings he had until so recently been experiencing. Then it came back to him. This room might be comforting, but it was the thinnest shell against the very reason they had come to the village in the first place. Keldron remembered the face of the corpse he had seen in the house the afternoon before, and suddenly a connection hit him, as if prescience had inspired him to make a connection that

had just been waiting to occur. Ensuring he did not disturb anybody, Joleen
especially, he rose on legs made shaky by his unconscious experience.
Stepping over and around his friends, Keldron made his way to the hallway,
and then to the upper floor of the house. Aware of the dangers of moving in
complete darkness, he stretched out his hands to catch himself should he hit
anything. Fortunately the house was not full of the clutter that marred so many
of the town houses in Eskenberg. They apparently believed in order in this
part of the Nine Duchies, which was as much as any follower of the Old Law
would do. Remembering what was on the floor from his sojourn up to the
bedrooms from before, Keldron stepped into the bedroom with the larger
window. He guessed that Malcolm would be keeping watch from there as it
had a better view of the village. He had guessed right. The big man was a
shadow almost one with the dark blackness of the drapes at the side of the
room, but still Keldron spotted him.
Malcolm turned in the darkness, rippling the shadows as if a breath of wind
had caused the drapes to shift. "Keldron," he said by way of greeting.
"Malcolm. How goes the watch?"
"Peaceful," came the reply, ghosting out if the darkness like an owl given
sibilant voice. "There is nothing out there, or at least nothing living."
Keldron detected the unease that lay behind Malcolm's words. "I know
nobody will feel right until we have moved on from this place, and had put
some great distance, and not a few memories between ourselves and this
experience, but this house was too good an opportunity to miss. Why don't
you go downstairs and get some sleep? I will keep watch on the world while
you slumber."
"You don't mind?" came the high-pitched reply.
"Not at all, my friend." Keldron replied as he shuddered at the thought of
sleep. At this point he felt as if he would never do so again. "Bad dreams," he
added by way of explanation, moving into the room so that Malcolm would
not trip over him. "But I suppose some sleep is better than none at all."
"No," came Malcolm's sorrowful reply. "I think that no sleep is sometimes
preferable when the situation demands it. Yet I am weary, and I will try to
sleep if I may. You are a good friend, wizard, and it gladdens me that you are
as hale as when you began this quest of Keldron settled into the niche at the
side of the window, feeling the need to stand tall and face the darkness. His
standing there was a small gesture of defiance in the very face of this evil. He
knew that should he fail in his duty to seek out the answer as to the source of
this catacomb of nightmares, that he would fail every free person in the Nine
Duchies. His own emotions could not get in the way of his duty to people he

knew that he would never meet. The Old Law taught selflessness, not selfishness, and he would see his journey through to whatever end. As Keldron's eyes adjusted to the pitch black, he was able to pick out details with increasing clarity. The road became the houses of the village, packed together and filled with their sorrowful contents. The houses eventually became the road beyond, and small hedgerows, fences and gates. The cloud overhead was visible, not as the result of any light, but because its depth of black was different to that of the land beneath. The houses should have had lights, and warmth, but they just stood there, bleak and empty as if they were mourning for their former occupants, yearning to be lit up with the gay exuberance of children running around and filled with the warmth of the mothers at the stoves and the wisdom of the old folk with their many tales. No, that was all gone, replaced by empty husks filled with bad memories and wooden stakes. These people would never even be afforded the dignity of a simple burial; for nobody would come near the place once they had heard about what had transpired here. Nobody but mercenaries on the loot. This event was beyond ordinary folk, and they left it well alone, exactly as they should do. Keldron surmised that whomever had the greater plan behind this would effectively do a great job of sealing off entire areas of the countryside. People only went so far to visit other villages in this region, and once a village such as this blocked their route, they would gradually retreat into themselves until the countryside became a collection of hermits. He made a mental note to remind the tribesmen to ensure this did not happen. His thoughts changed then, as he recognised an aroma in the air. It was the scent of summer woodland that always accompanied Joleen wherever she walked. It assaulted his senses in this dark place, bringing a relaxing relief. He smiled, not even turning. He knew that she was sat down on the bed behind him, and he revelled in her presence. The village clear to him, he looked out upon the various shades of black. Nothing moved as he watched the various hues of deepest night.

Joleen's presence moved closer, and he became more aware of her. She reached up and put one hand over his shoulder, joining him in contemplation of the night's vista. "Anything?" she said softly in his ear.

Keldron shook his head, a movement that was barely perceptible, but was enough for her to feel. He did not want to give anything away to anyone that might be watching. "Excuse the pun, but it is dead quiet out there," he replied, leaning his head back and tilting it to one side as he spoke so as not to lose his view of the village.

"So why are you up here when you could be sleeping. This is not like you."

"Bad dreams," Keldron admitted. "This village does not give one much cause to sleep." They stood there for a while then in silence, sharing their communion with the village via the pane of glass in front of them. Keldron felt something in the way Joleen was stood by him. She had a need that had to be fulfilled, some question that had to be answered. As the night wore on, still nothing came from her as she shared his watch, and so he decided to take the initiative. "What is it, Jo? What ails you?"

A pregnant silence followed, in which Keldron sensed that Joleen was trying to formulate a way she could communicate to him her feelings. "When you found that you could heal your wounds with your magic. . . You wizards didn't seem to think straight. Do you know how frightening that looked to see people I always knew to be in complete control acting like they did not have a rational thought in their heads? Injuring themselves to prove a point?"

Keldron swallowed, he knew he had a part in this as much as his two friends." Jo, I. . ."

"You nothing, Keldron Vass,." she replied, her whisper carrying tones that brooked no argument. "I know from what you have said that being able to heal yourselves with your magic was something special that you have yearned for despite years of searching. How come you have never found this out before?"

Keldron smiled, making sure she couldn't see him; the answer to that was simple. "Jo, when you first met me, us, how did we appear to you?"

"Strong, confidant." Was her immediate answer. "You looked like you could tackle any problem you set your minds to."

Keldron turned so that he could see Joleen's outline in the darkness. "That's not quite what I meant. Let me rephrase what I said. Physically, how did we look to you?"

This took Joleen longer to answer, but not much longer. "You looked as though you had embarked upon a journey that you were not ready and really capable of undertaking. You weren't physically fit." She snuggled against him. "But I believe that has changed."

"But what you said before was exactly my point," Keldron replied, determined to press his point home despite the comfortable situation he was now in. "Before we came to your forest, we had barely set foot outside the guild since our initiate. We might go to the marketplace, or to a tavern nearby, but the secular nature of the guild kept us separated from most goings on in our very own city. Even with our studies, we were not too different to the old men who sat around trying to remember what they had been doing the day before, vegetating and existing just for the sake of existence itself. We were not fit

Joleen, and we were not travellers. How do you think that we could have ever been in a position to injure ourselves and then cast a focus straight after? I can promise you that nobody in my guild ever suffered anything worse than a skin cut from parchment. They were never in a position to."

This mollified Joleen somewhat, but she was still not herself. "But why did you all have to go to such extremes to prove it earlier? You looked like masochistic madmen downstairs. I could not believe people could act with such disregard."

Keldron now felt a tinge of shame on behalf of his brothers. "Oh Jo, I am so sorry for that. We were caught up in the euphoria of what will be a major discovery in the lost arts of focussing. I guess that that was the best way for Belyn and Raoul to prove to themselves that it actually worked."

"Would you have done the same?" Joleen asked warily.

Keldron had to think for a moment, but his mind came up with nothing. "I can't say for sure." He felt the bandage over his upper right arm. "The burn would be gone if I focussed once more, but it makes me think. What if we became addicted to using the stones just in case anything was wrong? We would lose all ambition of other goals in a selfish circle of self-healing."

"No, I don't think so, Keldron. You are not like those others from your guild. You are beyond that, hence why you shocked me so."

"Well I think I had better bring that up with the others in the morning, just in case. I can't say what I would have done. However, I am glad I did not do it, for I would not want to suffer the same roasting I am sure that Belyn got from Yerdu"

This time the quiet chuckle came from Joleen. "He will not be doing such a stupid act again in a hurry, Yerdu made sure of that."

Keldron winced for his friend. He had seen a tongue-lashing from Yerdu first hand, and wished that not upon anybody. "Good." He replied. "For all of us. I. . ." Something caught Keldron's attention out in the village. He turned to follow it, but it disappeared.

"What is it?" Joleen asked, noting the change in his stance.

He peered out into the dark, his eyes attuned to the night. " I don't know. I thought I saw something." Still, nothing else seemed out of the ordinary. He shook his head, looking down at the road beneath the house. "Maybe it was just me." He turned to say something to Joleen, and there was a flicker of light once again, right in the extremity of his view. "There it is again."

"There is what? I can see nothing out there."

"I just saw it. Something off over the other side of the village."

Joleen stared past him, looking for a sign of what he had seen. "There is nothing out there, Keldron." Joleen continued staring for a few moments. "There is something wrong though."

"What do you mean?"

"That feeling. The feeling of ill we have all been having since we got here. It has changed."

Keldron concentrated on that feeling of dread that had pursued him tirelessly since he had come to this village. Joleen was right. The sensation was there, but there was a distinct difference, as if it were awaiting something. Such expectancy worried Keldron. Instinct made him reach for his focus stone. Pulling his concentration in, he sent his thought out to the village. "There is an impression, almost an intelligence out there, but I can't quite grasp the nature of it.

"I can't feel anything now."

"It is elusive. Every time I get close it slips away, as if I am not concentrating on quite the right thing. Oh. Joleen, get Belyn and Raoul. Now."

"Is everything all right?"

"Wake the others. Get them outside the front of the house, for that is where I will be. I need to get a better view of the sky. This window is too limited."

Keldron gave Joleen a quick squeeze of the hand, and slipped past her, vanishing into the shadows of the house. He hurried down the stairs, and wrenched the door open, stealing out into the night like the sole ghostly occupant of the entire village. The chill wind caught at his breath as he hurried out over the porch and into the road. There was nothing obvious to behold, but as his thoughts gained pace and consumed the night around him, he knew that something important was occurring. There was a tingle when he focussed on the night sky again, but nothing was clear to him. He clenched his eyes shut as he forced himself to explore every aspect of the sky through his stone, and then it hit him. The thought attracted his concentration like a flower attracted a butterfly. He opened his eyes, pocketing his stone, and licked one finger, holding it up to the feathery breeze. The wind blew as steadily as it had done before, but it was coming from the opposite end of the village. Amazed that he had not noticed it the second he had emerged from the porch, he walked slowly around in circles, trying to get some idea of what was going on. A pain from a weight in another pocket that pressed to his chest reminded Keldron that he had several different stones with him. He pulled out a lump of what could only be granite, and brought his concentration to bear. He searched the sky for the answers that anybody alive in this place could sense were out there. "Movement. This stone confirms it, but whatever it is seems to be indistinct and determined to remain that way." The temperature had dropped on this moonless night, and Keldron was convinced that it was not wholly due to the breeze and the time of season. Something eldritch was at work here, and the bad feeling he had experienced was as strong as ever, stronger perhaps where he was nearer other buildings. He heard footsteps, and turned to see everybody else joining him in the darkness.

They moved quietly, even Belyn, for who it was an admirable feat. "Ok Kel, what is it that is so important that you have dragged us from our beds? What can't wait until the morning?"

Keldron hushed them with a wave of his hands, and raised his head, listening to the air around him. "Can't you feel it? There is something at work here, something that we all can sense in different ways.

"What is it?" Raoul asked, still half asleep and best known for being surly when woken.

"Dark magic," came the answer from Belyn.

"No," disagreed Joleen, "this is not dark magic. You can feel it in the air if you but stand and open yourself to it. It is a magic born of desperation."

"Raoul shivered, and held himself to keep warm. "Is there any aspect of this village that isn't desperate?"

Keldron tried to explain. "When I was watching over the village, I could sense things that were just beyond my sight, as if I was not quite meant to see them. I focussed using a couple of my stones, but I could only get impressions of something moving around outside here."

"So why don't we see if any other stones give us a result?" Suggested Belyn.

"How many different stones do you have?" They emptied their pockets of the various focus stones Belyn had deposited with them, and it turned out that all three had four of the same type.

"Well we can forget these two," Keldron said, holding up his marble stone and the granite. "That leaves these other two."

"Why don't we all try the same stone at the same time, in case we miss something?" Raoul suggested. The other two nodded in assent. Standing with their backs to each other, the three wizards formed a rough triangle, with the tribes people in the middle. Holding onto black cubes of volcanic rock, they threw their concentration into the stones. Each wizard pushed out with his mind.

"It is the same. I can feel the brushing of something close, but there is nothing to see."

"Agreed, Kel. I can see vague shapes in the air, dashing around them as if they are caught in some sort of vortex."

Keldron withdrew the focus, to see Raoul clearly as perplexed as he was. "That was as far I could see."

Belyn pocketed his stone. "Nothing more is available to us from this type of rock. The shapes faded into the background as soon as they came into range." Keldron hefted the last stone in his possession. It contained streaks that seemed to give off phosphorescence in the utter dark, and was strangely pyramidal. "Well it's this or nothing." He raised his hand with the stone balanced on his palm. Feeding his concentration through the stone and out into the night sky, Keldron was faced with a vision at once so delightful and yet so full of despair that he did not know whether to laugh or cry.

"Sweet Ilia," swore Raoul, and as Keldron watched, he heard a similar utterance from Belyn. He gaped about him. It was as if the night sky had come alive through different eyes than his own. Phosphorescent light gleamed over the village as beings swirled about him, dodging around them all randomly. "They are spirits, and from what I can judge, they are the spirits of the village." They had tears flowing in continuous streams, and they looked abject and miserable. Yet they glowed in such splendour that they were magnificent to behold, and he felt tears flowing from his own face. In the pitch black of the night, they danced and cavorted through the air, now that gravity had no hold on them. But they were not released. Something capped the air over the village. Now and again a spirit would rise to the height of one of the buildings, and rebounded off of something, swirling with the grace of a butterfly back to the ground, to attempt another escape moments later. The spirits had no comprehension of the watchers, and passed through and around them as if they were the ones that did not exist. Keldron wished that they did not appear so normal. The ghastliest thing about them was that behind the glow and the otherworldly appearance, they had normal clothes on, the clothes they were most likely wearing when they had been so needlessly murdered. The speed with which the spirits rose to hit the barrier increased somewhat.

"Kel, look over the middle of the village." Raoul directed the focus inwards. Keldron turned his augmented sight to look up and across at the behest of Raoul's asking, and saw something that amazed him further. Something flashed as every spirit hit the barrier, and seemed to feed an umbilical that arched off into the distance, as far as the horizon. It defied comprehension. The spirits calmed, and only a couple continued to hit the barrier. The rest went back to swirling in misery around the village, leaving luminous traces of their passing.

"Is there something wrong?" Yerdu asked, her timid voice frightened.

"Of course there is," Raoul replied without turning. "This was not meant to be. This is not right."

Almost on cue, the wraiths that had once been villagers started in a crescendo of light without sound to arise once again, hitting the barrier and deflecting off it to skid in a cascade of phosphorescent beauty back to the ground.

"They are trapped in a cycle; Whatever is holding them in is feeding off of their anguish. Can you not feel it?" Nobody replied. Keldron broke off his focus and turned around. Joleen and Yerdu were in tears, and Malcolm had his eyes screwed shut. Raoul and Belyn also stopped, having felt Keldron break contact. "What is it?" he asked in the darkness.

Joleen practically jumped into his arms. She was cold and he could feel her trembling. "We could see them," she whispered, her voice only an inflection higher than the surrounding breeze. "When the three of you cast your focus outwards they were revealed to us, beautiful, and yet in such utter pain." Joleen turned in towards him and he could feel the heat of her tears through his clothes.

"This is not right," Malcolm said quietly. "Souls should not be damned in a trap like this, they should be able to depart for the next life. Something is very wrong."

"Might we be able to help?" Suggested Raoul.

Keldron shook his head. "This is beyond anything we can comprehend, my friend. The answers lie elsewhere, and certainly not in this village. There is nothing we can do but watch them in their sorrow and torment. Let us go back into the house, and try to get what rest we can."

The remainder of the night passed slowly. Whatever they did to ease their discomfort at the sights revealed to them that night, nobody could sleep. Keldron spent the night gazing out at the village, and as the darkness receded with the first promise of dawn in the Eastern sky, he felt nothing but relief. Daylight would soon push back the fear, the misery that they had all suffered. As the sun rose behind the mountains far to the east, a mist formed through the village, sweeping slowly around the houses as if the village suffered a sequela of the night before. The mist clung to the ground, rising no higher than the fences, and Keldron realised that this meant only one thing. There was no breeze. For the second time he rushed downstairs, but instead of going out onto the porch, he crept back to the parlour. Edging around the door, he found that everybody else had finally fallen asleep. He smiled in gratification that somebody had managed to find some peace. He knew that he would not while he stayed in this place. Making his way out of the house, Keldron passed the porch, and walked through the light of earliest morning to a point just beyond the small wooden bridge that crossed the stream. He followed the path of the stream with his eyes. It led down to the main river, which itself could not be called much more than a stream. The mist clung thickest where the water flowed, like a shroud trying to cover the events that had happened only moments ago, or so it seemed. He found that from this point he could behold the sunrise, and he willed it to speed to him with every fibre of his being. Black turned to inky blue, and the cloud became more visible. It had holes in it that allowed him to watch the sky change colour. The dawn crept towards him with the gradual creep of arctic permafrost. It could not come quick enough. Blue became lighter blue, and then the mountains lit up with the flames of heaven as Matsandrau sent his creature full circle around the earth. Even without actually seeing the sun, Keldron felt better. The glow of a sky borne hearth made the spiny teeth of the grating so appealing in the distance. He would have held his hands out towards it but for the obvious fact that it was cold here. He had been right though. The breeze had dropped in between them witnessing the wraiths and the coming of morning. It was a completely different world now. Almost as he watched the cloud receded, and broke apart. The last stars were visible as he looked to the heavens and watched light blue in the distance now become yellow with the promise of the sun. Dark shadows of the mountains stretched hungrily towards him across the vast expanse of the grassland, and were then obliterated as the sun made it's blazing entrance between two of the far-off peaks. Keldron winced and looked to one side, unprepared as he was for the entrance of the sun, and nearly jumped out of his skin as he found Raoul standing next to him. "It really makes you think, doesn't it brother," he said philosophically. "How can there be so many bad things in the world when there are sights such as this to behold?"

Recovered slightly, Keldron stammered to agree with him, still frightened half witless by his friend. "They will never take it from us." He finally managed to get out.

The two friends stood and watched as the sun rose with the grace of a swan, gliding up beyond the mountains into the sky above. It had not gotten a hands-span above the mountain line when they heard a gravely voice shouting for them. "Heh. Old Stroddick is hoping we aren't caught in a dream out here." Raoul surmised. "He hates missing out." Smiling at Raoul's remarks, Keldron followed his friend back into the house, hoping beyond hope that whoever those riders were, they had gotten far enough away to have not heard his large friend's early morning bellows.

Inside the house, the mood was sombre. Everybody worked with efficiency in order to get his or her belongings packed. In thanks to the household, they also cleaned it as best they could. It would always be obvious that someone had been in this house, but they were not prepared to leave their temporary refuge in any state of disarray. The horses reflected their mood by acting skittish and playing up as Malcolm tried to feed, groom and saddle them for the next stage of their journey. They too knew that something had happened, and even stuck in the stable they were able to sense it. Still, a calm hand and sure touch settled most of them down, though they still rolled their eyes at the door. The time came when they were ready to leave, and Keldron shut the gate of the miller's house respectfully, thanking the departed soul for one night of respite from the physical elements at least. Dawn had now passed, and they rode through the village following the last traces of the mist along the side of the stream, which bubbled away joyfully, as if no spirit or emotion could quell its simple needs. They rode back towards the East, as by general consensus they wanted to head in the other direction than the horsemen had gone, at least for a while. The border of the village passed away, and with each retreating step they felt better. The horses calmed, and the day even warmed a bit, if it were at all possible to call the lack of a freezing breeze in winter 'warm'. At length they had reached a point far enough from the village that they were no longer troubled by the miasmic aura of the place, and it was only visible if one were to peer closely. The land was not completely flat, even here and the ever-so gentle roll of the slopes had hidden the terrible place from body and mind. Keldron decided that it was as good a time as any to turn North and West. And so they rode for the best part of the day, until a feeling started to nag at him.

As Keldron stopped his horse, Belyn came riding up beside him. "What is it, brother?" he asked, still toying with the stone that gave out a glow and enabled them to see the spectres the night before.

Keldron looked around them, for nothing seemed amiss. "I have a nagging feeling. We are being watched as we travel."

Belyn looked around them, causing the others to stare blankly at the slopes around which they travelled. "I can't see anything, are you sure?"

"I am," Keldron said after a moment's thought. "Belyn, lend me that stone if you will." Belyn didn't hesitate in handing over his stone. Keldron examined it for a second, wondering if it would do as he wanted, and then pulled in his concentration and became one with the stone. Belyn watched as his friend performed whatever focus it was that he was attempting. "Anything?" he asked.

Keldron's smile was all the answer they needed. "There is a large group of them beyond that rise to the east. There must be thirty or forty of them."

"How do you know that?"

Raoul smiled as if enraptured. "Belyn I can see them, I can see their auras. Belyn, they are tribesmen."

The look of surprise on Belyn's face was repeated on the faces of the four other riders. Quickly he turned and looked at Malcolm, who nodded briefly, and dismounted, striding off to the low hill with a great amount of urgency. The air cleared as Keldron relinquished his focus. "May I?" Belyn indicated the stone. Keldron nodded, still at peace with himself, and watched as Belyn attempted the same thing. "Look for what we sought last night, and you shall see something entirely different."

A moment passed before Belyn inhaled sharply. "Oh my," the big man said. "I see what you mean. You can tell it's them by their very auras."

"Or is it their souls?" Raoul suggested.

Belyn altered his focus. Keldron could feel Belyn as if he were in two places at once. Something touched them on a spiritual level. Belyn grinned, and opened his eyes. "Amazing. It's like seeing all of you in a new light." Belyn looked around at them all. "You look so pure."

"What do you see?" Yerdu asked him, not sure what to make of herself.

"You glow. Green if it is any colour, but it is an ethereal light. It shines from you all, right out through your skin and clothes. It accompanies you, and a trail is left when you move." Belyn's eyes glazed, and Keldron felt the subtle magic of the focus dissipate. Belyn leered at Yerdu. "But you look much better in the flesh."

"Flatterer," harrumphed Yerdu, letting Belyn enfold her in a hug.

Belyn squeezed her momentarily, and let go, looking towards the rise. "They are on the way. They were moving when I viewed them." He looked at the stone in his hand, and let out a laugh of pure delight. "What a little treasure we have there," he said, smiling at everyone around him, and pocketed his stone. Keldron hoped that it always showed the better side of people, but wondered nonetheless if it could be used to determine a person's aura if they had not been touched by a forest's spirit. He did not voice that openly, for he wanted to give the thought more consideration. A flicker in the distance caught his attention, and Keldron looked on approvingly as Malcolm led a band of the tribesmen towards them. Unable to restrain themselves, Yerdu and Joleen jumped down from their horses and ran to the warriors, bestowing hugs and kisses to their extended family. The warriors reacted in their usual reserved way. As more and more of them rounded the rise, Keldron commented. "You were right, Belyn. And I am overjoyed to see this many of them in one place." Belyn grunted in agreement, as if his focus-sight had never been in doubt. Malcolm approached, with none other than Seren and Handel, who greeted them with bows and the ritual greeting of the tribe.

Returning the pleasantries, Raoul asked, "How did you find them all?" Handel shrugged, as if the question was pointless. "They were there, and we knew how to find them. They left signs." He turned to look at the men and women with him. "There are more," he volunteered.

"What will you do?" Raoul asked.

"What would you have us do, Law Wizard?" Handel asked in return. "We are yours to command, and we know of your wishes."

Raoul turned in his seat to his companions. The burden of responsibility was lying very heavily on his shoulders, and Keldron well knew it. Were he or Belyn to offer anything in the way of advice, that the burden would be passed to them, and it would do their friend some good to learn something new. This was Raoul's task. Sensing nobody was going to say anything to him, Raoul turned back to the questioning eyes of Handel. "Can you survive out here?"

"It is not the forest." It was not Handel, but Seren who replied, "But we were not always forest dwellers. We were once travellers of the land you call the Nine Duchies. We gave it a different name." Seren looked off into the distance, as if he were searching for an answer in the sky above.

"What was the name?" Raoul asked, ignorant of any other name that had been given to the countryside that he lived in.

Seren turned back to him. The dark features of the warrior gave nothing away to indicate his thoughts. "We do not know. We cannot remember, else so much more of our past would we know. The name was lost in our history, but we are hoping that association with you, with all of you." He indicated the three of them with a broad sweep of his arm. "We hope that we may find an answer, but for now we will do what is needed."

The answer was easy. They had discussed it at length the previous day. Raoul straightened in his saddle. "Search out villages in this region, and save their people. The feeling we encountered yesterday is so much more than an aura of ill, it was the spirits of the past, forced towards the next life, but struck in between by magic dark in nature. Something has left them there, stranded. It is our thought that whoever did this intends to do this to everybody, and wipe out the rural folk in this Duchy, and perhaps in others. Now I know that you suffer as greatly as we from the woe and agony that has left its imprint in the very Earth. I urge you to steel yourselves against it, for defy it you must. It may be that you have needs to enter such a place, and do not hesitate if the need is there. We cannot help those who have passed beyond, at least not for now. Ilia knows that if we find a method of healing their eternal torment, we shall use it. But we have to search, and that means that we have to seek out the island temple."

Seren glowed with pride as he listened to the words of Raoul, the Law Wizard. "It will be as you have commanded."

"No," Raoul cut in sharply, "I have never presumed to command you, and I never shall. The Old Law runs as true in this as in any of its tenets. Commanding implies dominion of one over another, and I adhere to the Old Law. I have no dominion over you."

"But we give our service freely," Seren insisted, reinforced by nods and murmurs of assent from the gathered tribe.

"Hearken to my advice," Raoul replied, determination written all over his face, "For advice it is only. There are those out here who may need you more than we will. Be true to them, for they are innocent, their only flaw being in the eyes of others. Be true to yourselves, for only in faith and devotion to the Gods and the Law will you prevail." Keldron looked across at Raoul. The religious zeal with which he spoke these words was beyond the comprehension of the man who was speaking them. He talked as if augmented by some higher power. "Be true to the land, for it will aid you when you need it, as once the forest did. Be true to each other, for you will prevail as a group, even if not all of you do as individuals. Finally, be true to the forest and the memory of Merdon, for it shall always dwell in your hearts, and we shall be able to see you from afar. We shall always be watching."

At that, Raoul closed his eyes, and turned his horse to the West, riding off slowly. Keldron looked at the others. "Shall we?" he invited. A few brief hugs were all that there was time for, as Raoul already grew small in the distance. "You are ok with this?" Belyn asked of Seren.

"We are," Seren replied as Handel exchanged a few quiet words with Joleen and Malcolm. Seren reached up and clasped Belyn's hand, and then Keldron's. "You find the island, and solve your riddles. We will preserve the mainland while you are gone. They will not reduce these people to cowering slaves. The forest tribe shall see to that. Would you hearken unto a word of advice to you before you depart."

"Oh?" Keldron said, suddenly interested.

"Look for our people along the way. Some of us have gone ahead, and do not know what the rest of us plan. Advise them, and let them make their own choices. There is more now at stake than the finding of an island and the upholding of our ancient traditions. Something new seeks to disturb the balance of the very land we walk upon. We can tell that much as we walk the turf and touch the leaves."

Keldron watched the tribe as it departed. Already there were but ten of them left. "We will do our part, as I am sure that you will do yours," he said gravely, "until we meet again under Merdon's green boughs."

"Until then, wizard." Said Seren, and they departed, merging with the grass and bushes as if they were born to become one with all around them.

Keldron looked back to their own path. Raoul had already disappeared completely. "We should catch him."

Belyn grinned, exhilaration showing behind his ruddy beard, as if he were a mirror of the sun beating back its magnificence at the glow in the cerulean sky. "We have a long way to go, my companions. There is no time like the present!" And filled with anticipation of what they had to do, the five of them rode after Raoul at a joyous gallop.

Chapter Four

Bay's Point had begun its existence as a smugglers port, base to only the pirates that were desperate enough to endure the frigid winds and ripping tides that scoured the coast on their way down from the arctic North. For generations it had been nothing more than an undisturbed ramshackle of warehouses, piers and hovels with not even a tavern to keep them warm. Instead pirates and bandits infested what was no bigger than a coastal hamlet sought their ale and treasures by a different method. They would quest out in their sleek corsairs, and raid the more substantial settlements to the South and East, sometimes travelling as far as the other side of the great bay, or even, when times were desperate, across the sea to the great forest villages of the distant island to the West. Always too late, the authorities of these various targets would send their own fleets after the brigands, but they would never find them. Countless vengeance raids by the authorities on the settlement would reduce it to cinders an almost infinite number of times over the seasons, but the colony endured. Always within a couple of turns of the moon, there would be a fresh raid, and the furious and frustrated crews would arrive at the mouth of the Boarsrushflow to bear witness to the fact that not only had the settlement reappeared, but it had prospered. The regenerative power of both Bay's Point was incredible. It stood defiantly in the face of the logic that dictated to the surrounding villages that once they destroyed the place, it would no longer grow back. The area was simply too deserted and the surrounding land sparse. Not much more than a thin acidic soil clung to the coastal rocks to each side of the river, so crops could not grow, and herds could not graze. Therefore there were no farms to sustain the populace. Even so, the other coastal villages had not reckoned on two things. Firstly the resourcefulness of the brigands, and secondly that the river had to lead from somewhere. The stupefying fact was that every time Bay's Point was raided in revenge for an act of piracy, they never once saw or found any trace of the ships. The buildings were always empty, and were ransacked out of sheer frustration. They never found out until much later on that there was actually a thriving village to the North, just up around the point of the coast from which the pirates took the name. In fact, the true Bay's point had always been a small cove, protected by a magnificent natural breakwater, where weak rock had been eroded away and left a gap two ships wide through a deep vertical cleft in the cliff. One could have sailed straight past it for seasons unending and never noticed the entrance, so great was the natural concealment. The pirates enjoyed a life of luxury and protection in their true home, while the decoy settlement took repeated damage. It was a simple case of making the crossing overland and rebuilding the settlement with wood harvested far upstream. This was their other secret. Many of the coastal towns and villages were very provincial, preferring their own company, and only visiting to other towns on the rarest of occasions. That preferred isolation also spread to the interior of the land, and rural folk rarely ever saw a 'squab', or 'coast-hugger', as they were called in suspicious derision on the occasions such folk met. The Bay's Point brigands, aside from the crimes they were responsible for on the coasts and high seas, were also merchants, negotiators and adventurers. They revelled in the exploration of the land behind them, and had very early on made contact with the settlements along the river not for plundering, but for trade. In this time, generations before the Nine Duchies, the rivers were where farmers and rural folk gravitated towards, and the early merchants made the most of this. The Boarsrushflow danced and ebbed along what would eventually become the natural boundary between the Lower Uporan Steppes, and the northernmost reaches of an embryonic Ciaharr. If folk wanted to trade, they came to the river. In its early days, the only use the brigands had for the village at the river's mouth was as a store point for goods to be transported by boat upstream to various markets. It was true that the merchants knew what they were, but they never questioned the motives or the source for the goods. Rarities were novel to the rural folk, and the brigands were the primary source. For their part, they traded honestly. They had no need to bargain outrageously, for they were in as desperate a need for the staple goods the farm folk had on offer as the farmers were for their bolts of cloth or rare gemstones. All in all, a wary but gradually burgeoning friendship grew between the two communities. The farming spread down the river, and eventually, the two communities became one. The natural midpoint was the false village, and this became a place of business. The brigands still raided across the great bay, but their secret was safe. The farm folk adopted the village at the mouth of the river as their own, and soon it became a prosperous town. This was mainly due to the amount of traffic that passed down river bearing goods of all sorts. Food, sundries, rarities, all came to the main focal point through the smaller villages upriver. Word eventually spread that Bay's Point was not just a pirates' hovel, and the other coastal villages began to take note. The pirates still raided, and every small armada that sailed towards the town in revenge had to turn back when they realised that they could no longer raze to the ground what had once been a ramshackle collection of warehouses. This became final when out of nowhere within the space of a moon, an immense breakwater sprang out to either side of the river mouth, creating a massive harbour. This was the time when Bay's Point really became a city in its own right. It was also the time of the formation of the Nine Duchies, and while other more foolish men were leading campaigns to the ice plains, the pirates installed their own self-styled 'Duke', a rather unsavoury fellow called Skull. This man did nothing much for the city, but the men behind him knew about the power a city-state held over a region, and the canny brigands also knew that a city at the mouth of a river bisecting two major regions would also become a key focal point. So they planned ahead. They erected two great walls of stone a ways out from the settlement, to allow for the expansion they were sure would happen. The North wall was not a great deal, for there was nobody from whom the citizens needed protection, and the pirates' own village was the only real settlement up the coast. The Southern wall, though East would be a more accurate direction, was a different matter. The pirates employed stonemasons to erect a mighty fortification ten times as high as a man, and three times as thick as a house. This protected the city from the coast to the river in a gradual arc. It had immense wooden gates, and was considered impenetrable, mostly because rarely anybody had the resources to mount an attack on it. Only once did this happen, and the man behind it was hung on a gibbet outside the city to show others what would happen to them if they tried.

From then on the city prospered, becoming the centre of trade for the neighbouring duchies. As predicted, the city filled out until it touched the walls, and then expanded beyond them, but not far. There was always a wariness about the folk that lived within. Rumours abounded about the pirates, but they were never seen within the city, only on the high seas, or in raids far and wide, but never within a few days sailing of the Bay's Point. The merchants ignored this though, many forgetting their humble origins, shunning the ancient law of the rural folk in their greed for profit. So it became that Bay's Point was a prosperous city, but somewhat of an outcast. The folk there were regarded as hostile, though they would have merely seen it as high-spirited. The city attracted more of its like, and became a major port, full of the roughest sailors, and the slyest merchants. But those that risked their lives to exist alongside them usually ended up prospering.

        Zya could well believe it as she walked with Lorn through the streets of the prospering city. Everywhere that she looked were the signs of prosperity. Three storied houses crowded the streets, leaning over protectively like ancient old crones trying to stay standing. In places, the roads even spread out to show far off estates and the crystalline splendour of the far-off and rarely glimpsed Ducal Palace rising on the hill near the coast. "It would take most of the day to walk to the palace from here."

"Rumour has it that mercenary guards spring as if from nowhere, if anybody should actually get that close. If you were to approach the palace, you had better have a good excuse, or watch your back. Bay's Point is that sort of a city. Every person has a weapon of some kind. Old ladies peddle a splendid variety of knives on street corners. From the sturdiest dagger to the daintiest poniard, everything is on sale."

"So I see. They all walk around as if they own the place."

Hulking pirates swaggered up streets, cursing merrily, great falchions and cutlasses swinging precariously from their scabbards, though not too many of them made it as far as the area of the city they were now in. Children played with dogs in the street, unafraid of anybody that might pass by.

"Bay's Point is their heritage. If they exude a sense of ownership, they have every right to. The children are bold and courageous, pirate's children from birth. They are born knowing that their fathers have ridden the waves for generations, and are brought up to appreciate what they fought for."

"I hear they can curse as colourfully as the pirates. You know this rubbed off on Ju."

"Zya, Ju is only a little older than most of these street urchins, and he has settled in at home in this city as though he had been born here. I would not be surprised if he could curse like that before you knew him. Now do we cross the river today?"

They had been in Bay's Point for just over one turn of the moon, or month as the city folk called it, and the place still seemed unfamiliar to her. She had not even attempted to cross the river on one of the many ferries to discover the eastern half of the city, though Ju and Lorn had crossed over there regularly. The western City was a mix of docks, merchant houses and wealthy estates. From the talk they had shared in taverns, the estates were apparently the homes of the descendants of the original Bay's Point pirates, who had raided the coast so many generations ago. Zya wished to see the buildings, the palace especially, for she had never been anywhere near anything bigger than a small town. Until arriving at the city, the biggest building she had encountered was the Town Hall in the unfortunate village of Hoebridge. Even now, as she turned and looked back to the East, unconscious thoughts rose to do the bidding of the part of her that worried. Zya knew that something was wrong back where they had turned aside from the rest of their travelling companions. "I can't cross it, Lorn. Something is wrong with it, and I feel queasy even thinking about doing such. It is as if the wrongness flows down out of the East, from where we came." The river that split Bay's Point like an arrow split a target in a tourney. Thinking of arrows, she looked back across at Lorn, who was contemplating her as she mulled over her thoughts. He smiled as he noticed her coming back to herself amidst the rubbish-filled streets of the pirate city. That was enough for Zya. Lorn's dark features were so similar to her own, and yet to subtly different. The tilt of his eyes, the confidence in his ability betrayed by his sure stance. Lithe as her father, Zya appreciated the slightly stockier appearance of the nomad from the Uporan Steppes. Walking down the street together, their dark features and their height served to make people think that they were family, married or brother and sister. Zya had never really considered how similar they actually did look. Their only real difference was in their style of dress. Zya had managed to combine her leather riding gear with the woollen tribal material favoured by the wise women, the tribal seers of the steppes. Lorn stuck to his traditional warriors garb, leather and skins with his bow slung across his back in its oilskin. It was well that he had come with them. Although this city was not half the size of granite Raessa, it was the main trading outpost for the Uporan tribes, and they had their own section of the city, near the northern wall. Making contacts quickly due to his status within his own tribe, Lorn soon had a roof over their heads, and jobs for them all. The house they had been granted from the elder tribesmen in the city was not big, but it too was unsettling. Zya could not bring herself to stay confined within the stone walls. She needed to move, to see different things. The boxed nature of the house made her feel trapped.

"Well there is plenty of the city for us to see yet. I just appreciate being back in such a place. Being a traveller of sorts is nice, but the hustle and bustle of a city reminds one that there is no cause to be lonely in this world."

"Strange. My father and Ju are not like that. When I asked him about it, he said to me that he had had cause to live in a house a long time ago, but would offer no more." Her father was busy this day, employed in the job that had made him his living. He had been a wandering carpenter with the travellers, or tinkers, as they were more commonly known. He was now installed in a carpentry that was rapidly gaining renown for his deft touch with the plane and the lathe, even after this short amount of time. Lorn had been placed with a weapon smith, for he was an adept at the making of arrows and the other weapons that the nomads had need of. "Should you not be getting back to your work?"

"I have finished for the day. I am only going to make so many arrows for that man. Weapons I put my touch to should be for hunting, but these will be used in less than noble contests, resulting in the spilling of blood in anger rather than for survival. This does not concern the weaponsmith, so long as the customers are happy." Fletchers were few and far between in a city dominated by the sword, and many a pirate had been caught trying to entice Lorn to join them on a ship bound for some mysterious place, for archers of quality were even rarer.

"Well at least Ju is happy," Zya countered. Ju had amusingly been given the child's job of a message runner, and they rarely saw him. "He has found his niche in life for the present, and from what I hear he revels in it," Lorn agreed. Ju's quick wit and fast legs gave him a tremendous advantage, for the local children might be hardy, but they were not always the cleverest of people. He also gained access to many of the larger houses, which caused Zya pangs of jealousy.

"He gets to visit the places I can only gaze at from afar. I have not even seen the halls of the guild I am working in."

"Which guild is that?"

"I have no idea, Lorn. I never get beyond the kitchen, and nobody will tell me. They wont even talk unless it is to order me around." The irony of it was that Zya had been put in a guild house doing menial chores, as befitted one of her 'station', though the guildsmen themselves had descended from pirate stock. She was in a large, almost palatial building, but she never got to see any of it because the seamstresses and cooks only entered through a half-rotten mouldy door on the corner of a street off of one of the main thoroughfares. The guild was protected within its own walls, but she could never see any of the splendour, and was barred from most of the building. She was never one to hold a grudge though. She worked hard, and was rewarded with pay. This was one bonus, though she kept very little for herself. The tenets of the Old Law were strong in her blood, and as a result of her until recent life Zya really did not crave for very much. Her belted dagger and her necklace were all that she wanted, and neither was obvious to behold.

"How far until the market?"

"We are almost there."

Today they were out shopping for food. Zya had never needed money, or possessions, but Gren had instilled in her a love of food that went beyond passionate. Though she would never be comfortable here, the markets took that worry away from her for at least a little while, and she anticipated every visit. Merchants brought in produce from the farmsteads upriver, many of which she had passed by in person. They also brought in all manner of delicacy from different parts of the Nine Duchies, and it was these that she had gawked at in stupefied wonder every time they had passed by. There was no need to buy them, but the pleasure of discovery was ever strong in her mind, and the scented fruits and spiced meats that the vendors did their best to sell were worth a long walk into the middle of the town. The marketplace they were headed for was right in the middle of the exquisitely decorated western side of the city, in amongst the guilds. Tales had it that the guildsmen of old did not want to have to move far to purchase their luxuries, and so the merchants had moved to where the money was, and there was plenty of that. The greed and avarice that Zya saw on a daily basis had literally turned her stomach. If these people had ever followed the tenets of the Old Law, they had clearly forgotten them. Thievery was rife, but only because the fat merchants and dim nobles swaggered through the town with their pockets dripping gold, and their fingers and ears decorated with a years wage to a farmer. The thieves were almost as gaudily attired, and Zya was sure that on many occasions she had seen a thief end up as the victim. She felt a need to speak to them, about what she saw, but she had the common sense to see that it would do no good. 'Keep your head down, keep your wits about you, and stay busy' was what Tarim had told her when as a child she had asked about why not everybody followed their way of life. It had been a cryptic remark to make, but it was only in situations like this that his words rang true. Zya thanked her father silently as she looked away from the gaudiness of the busy citizens, and up at the sky, a steadfast companion that had been with her on the road for all of her life, and was resolute in its winter grey.

"You okay?"

Zya came back to herself, withdrawing her perceptions from the purity of the sky, and looked across at Lorn. He watched her strangely from under the dark locks that had loosened themselves from his warrior's tail. Zya noted once again how fathomless his eyes were, and felt that were they a lake, she would dive in and willingly drown in their midnight perfection. "You okay?" he repeated. "You were looking up at the sky, and you just stopped, right there in the middle of the street."

Already people were milling around as the street blocked up, a result of them stopping in such a narrow place. Over to the side, a door crashed open and a huge baker in less than pristine white hat and apron leaned out, his red, sweaty face looking for the cause of the blockage. His eyes found the two of them. "Move along you two!" he bawled, spittle flying from his mouth, "you are blocking my customers!"

"Yah, like anybody would buy bread made from the filth you get a hold of," bellowed a man, equally as large, and attired in garish purple and yellow, with a blue-steeled falchion strapped to his back. Zya tensed, feeling there was going to be some sort of conflict, but the two men stood to one side of the milling crowds, bellowing and exchanging such a vile series of epithets and curses that Zya felt the beginnings of a flush start to creep up her neck. Then she looked around. Nobody cared, and those that did pass by chuckled at the exchange. This was obviously something that had become common between the two men, as both were grinning, and laughing out louder the worse the insults became. Lorn beamed back, a flash of white teeth, and led Zya out of the flood of humanity and up a shortcut through a side street. Zya glanced around as she walked. "The people bustle on as if nothing had happened there."

"Of course they do. This is a city. They are too preoccupied with their own business to care about a couple of locals." Lorn led her on slowly, walking under tar-smeared wooden buttresses. Tar was evident everywhere they looked, and the trade was a major source of income. The houses leaned in even closer above them, and it looked as if the only things supporting some residences were the adjacent buildings. Arches and doorways loomed, turning the morning into a suspicious twilight. "Be careful, "Lorn warned." These sorts of alleys are where lurkers prey on the unwary."

As they walked warily along the cobbles, slippery with filth and the Gods only knew what else, Zya was careful to not look down. She had been down this alleyway before, and knew it to be a shortcut. Nevertheless, Zya had her hand on her dagger, for one never knew when one would suddenly become a potential mark. They had been accosted but once before, Zya's dagger singing as it whistled out of its sheath to be bared alongside Lorn's longer and much heavier Borad dagger, a sturdy knife reputedly used by a tribe far to the South. The pair of thieves had reconsidered, and ever since they had been left alone in this part of the city, their threat of violent self-defence showing that they were obviously not to be trifled with. "So are you feeling okay?" Lorn persisted.

"I don't know, to be honest." Zya replied with a dumbfounded scratch to the back of the head. "I found myself contemplating the clouds, and then all of a sudden it was as if I was not standing there next to you any more. I was much closer to the clouds, or they were closer to me." She shook her head as the memory stayed with her, fuzzy and indistinct.

Lorn studied her, straight faced. She felt somewhat lost. "Our wise women would say that your head in the clouds is not the best place for it to be."

The irony in the statement made Zya smile, and she saw that Lorn was joking with her. "Fool."

He smiled back, eventually breaking into a grin. She felt much better for it, her spirits rising as they rarely did in this place. They turned and walked on, their company enough to make them oblivious to their surroundings.

"In truth, I find all the twists and turns of the dirt-filled alleyways rather intriguing. There is always a new path to follow, a new nook to discover."

"The fact that it was so close to the rich estates is what truly amazes me. No, perhaps close isn't the right word." Zya mused. "On top of is more like it."

"That is the nature of cities. You never know when you are likely to get surprised." One moment they were twisting through a veritable maze tar-topped stone buildings, with rotting little wooden porches and a small dog barking out of every shadow, and the next they were in a wide-open space, where a large mansion dominated the scenery, its grey stone walls and columns magnificent in spite of their dreary colour.

"That is hideous." Zya looked over the building.

"It happens that rock was in great abundance, but those with money aren't always blessed with sense. Fortunately for the citizens of Bay's Point the stone was also cheap, hence the height of houses and the stark splendour of the great buildings. If any building in the region was made of stone, the chances were that the stone had come from the quarries. Because of this, the stonemasons' guild has always been a close second in size to the fishers' guild, the official name for the pirates. They operate out of separate ends of the city, the fishers having a large collection of dockside warehouses, and the stonemasons being situated closer to the walls."

"Proximity is of great value to these people, isn't it." Zya saw this every time that she turned from one scene to another.

"Absolutely. When one lives in such a climate, proximity is necessity. Consider my tribe. We move to where we can find food. The same can be said metaphorically for these people. Fortunately for the stonemasons, the rock is easily accessible, and they had created huge pits in which they toiled to excavate rock on the Southern side of the city. Your father remarked on this when we first arrived, saying that it was not defence that was the reason for the smaller wall in the North, though the bluffs and sharp drops did their job very well, it was money. Moving all that rock across the river would have taken a massive chunk out of the profits of such an endeavour as building the city walls, and the effort of crossing it over the river to the other side even more so. Therefore it was only the rich that had built their massive mansions, for most others could not afford the ferry price. The rich here were the same as the rich any place else. They were the guilds and the nobles. The commons were left to fend for themselves in most places, although it did appear that

Bay's Point has been very well constructed. The houses are well built, and in most cases the proximity of so many huddled demesnes served to protect them from the cold that was perpetual all year round as the Arctic's deep cold struggled to spread down and beat back the warmer conditions that threatened its absolute grip on the Northern climes. Only a noble is able to afford to pay the woodcutters and merchants that continually ferry in stacks of felled lumber from any number of places, and for that reason the woodcutters' guild has grown considerably."

Zya looked over the giant shell of a building with its iron-grey pillars, it was as imposing as anything she could remember. Walking past it seemed to take an age. Zya gradually became oblivious to Lorn's commentary. Most houses paled back into the dusky shadows after but a few steps, but the grey bulk with its spiked iron gates, covered in pitted rusty holes, left more than a shadow of an impression. Zya closed her eyes, as she trusted Lorn to lead them through the crowds of merchants and pirates and many others that thronged in the streets, and still she could feel the impenetrable bulk of stone around her. In a way, it was similar to the experience she had had with the clouds but moments earlier. She could feel the way the rock had been pressured into its current state, heat altering it, making the crystalline structure melt into something else. She could feel as the picks and chisels bit into the rock, shaping it into something other than its intended shape, and she wondered why they would do that; to her it was as plain as daylight that this was not its intended shape. Surely they too had seen this, for they could not have possibly ignored it. Zya never thought to consider why she was so worried about the fate of a stone building; all she felt was the ill structure of the stones that were a part of its whole. Gradually a new feeling crept its way into her mind as she expanded her consciousness to include the whole structure. In her mind's eye the bulding was different. She felt that she could see into the stone, and as she did, she was hit by a wave of nausea. "That building radiates wrong." There was no other word for it. The emanations from the rocks combined into a whole that was just so ill. And now that it comprehended her, it understood her, and tried to use her compassion to aid itself, to shape itself to her intended form. Zya did not know what was happening, but she regained enough control to open her eyes. It did no good. With a gasp of an inhaled breath, and her eyes staring wide into nothingness, she looked around, graping to focus on her surroundings.

The only person taking any notice of her was Lorn. "What is it?" he asked, his face alive with concern. She stared at him, understanding his words, but prevented from replying by wave after wave of nausea hitting her right in the stomach, reaching to every part of her body. Her mind was alive with images as if seen through a crystal, superimposed over the reality that she could see. It was coming at her in flashes, faster and faster. Crystalline structure turned at many different angles hit her through her eyes and seared their impressions into her very soul. "Zya? Zya!" Lorn grabbed her shoulders roughly, and shaking her, tried to snap her out of it, but Zya knew she was too far immersed in the ill that was not just this building, but seemed to be coming from beneath her very feet too. She suddenly was not sure if she was floating, falling, soaring in the sky. It seemed like all of the impressions rounded up into one cacophony of emotion, and she was floating in it like a bottle upon the sea, resisting the pull of forever, the sucking of the depths beneath with its fragile buoyancy. Her rock was Lorn, and she concentrated on him as he tried to bring her back. She rolled her eyes, which were still wide open, and her mouth opened slightly, as she breathed fast and deep, trying to will the passionate wrong that had taken a hold of her out by sheer brute force. It did no good. There was a pressure on her forehead, and there was nothing she could do to shift it. Her arms dropped to her side, and she saw Lorn's face, justified concern betraying his normally stolid features. She retched, trying to force words from her throat. Somehow Zya managed to get control of herself long enough to turn and grasp the iron bars that separated the great mansion from the pathway. She stared at the building momentarily, and then turned back to Lorn. Grabbing him by the arms, she fought to hold herself upright, which took a gargantuan effort, for she was blacking out with the sensation the stone of the building was emitting. She managed a mere two words as she dropped to the floor.

"It's wrong," she gasped, and as unconsciousness beckoned, she realised with a truth as crystalline as the stone that was beating her under that the wrong was exactly the same as the wrong she had felt so far back in that distant village by the river. It was the briefest of feelings, but she understood it clearly as she spiralled out of reality down through a vortex of crystal images.

Zya felt herself hit the floor, despite Lorn's attempts to hold her. As she did so, her eyes popped open.

"Lorn."

"Its okay, I've got you." Lorn held her close. Clearly afraid he was going to lose her, he checked her pulse from the wrist he had grasped hold of as she had slumped against him. Lorn risked a glance up and around, but people were ignoring him, or if they were paying any attention to him they were making a good show of hiding it.

"What happened?"

"It's the mansion. Lorn, we need to go."

"Can you stand?"

Zya attempted to, but her legs gave way.

"Well that answers that question." Seeing no other option, Lorn moved slowly along the street, with Zya clasping for her life to him. Her lithe body was no significant weight if there was even the merest of responses, but the near-deadweight would be a test for his endurance. Lorn had not made it much further than a dozen steps before he was forced to stop and take an extensive breather. "I always thought you were lighter than that, "he gasped."

"Well thank you very much." Zya replied.

"No, I . . . I mean."

"Lorn, it's okay. I'm just joking. I'm grateful for your help."

He wiped the sweat that had formed on his brow despite the frigid atmosphere. "This is not proving easy. I have newfound respect for the predators that live on the steppes. The mountain lions are reputed to take a kill up to a league from their den in order to hide it from scavengers. We normally gut our kills to make carrying it easier."

"I prefer my guts where they are." Zya put her hand protectively over her midriff and smiled.

"Well maybe if I don't try so hard to make us look like we are locked in some sort of embrace, it will be easier."

The bustling crowd continued by, for the sight of two people so intimate was nothing uncommon. This people had a very open and emotional nature to them, and lovers were so often seen in a tryst that they were respected and politely ignored. Fortunately for Lorn, help arrived in a very familiar form.

"Ho lad!" boomed a voice from behind him as a meaty hand clapped down upon his shoulder. "Looks like you have fed your lass a few to many shots of rum there! Let me help you get her home." The hand lifted, and Lorn felt Zya's deadweight lessen. The large man that had diverted the baker with his violent cascade of insults stood next to him, and looked around the crowd, and then broke into a grin. His purple waistcoat hung unbuttoned, for it could not have been done up anyway due to his barrel chest. His yellow silk shirt stretched at the buttons that by some miracle held it together, and it was literally bursting at the seams wherever else it showed through. His hair was heavily oiled, and hung down his back, waterproofing him with it's excess, but he did not notice. The man buried his shoulder under one of Zya's arms and draped her arm about his neck.

"Is this necessary?" Zya asked the pirate.

"Just close your mouth, lass, drop your head and keep quiet."

Taking the cue without missing a beat, Lorn did the same on the other side, and they moved off into the crowd. As Zya was part lifted and part dragged across the cobbles of the road, the brightly attired man kept up a diatribe of beration, calling Lorn every name under the sun, and demanding continually as to why he had let her get into this state. Zya recognised something forced in the man's way of speaking, and understood that this was a show for anybody that might care to listen. For his part, Lorn acted contritely, cursing back at the man whenever he deemed it appropriate, but he let the pirate do most of the talking, and let the man lead them away from their intended destination, the market, to a completely different part of the city. They were shuffling towards the warehouse district, where it was rumoured the pirates stored their booty. The smells of the river ahead wafted up towards them from time to time, and judging by the strength of the aromas Zya could tell that they were pretty close. If the proximity of the houses was great in the places he had already walked, the dwellings of those that lived in this district were positively tangled. There was an abruptness about the place, as if Zya expected to turn a corner and not be able to find her way back. That would worry Lorn, but then he was not experienced in urban surroundings. The houses were rickety in appearance, but seemed sturdy enough. Zya recognised good craftsmanship when she saw it, courtesy of her father's craft, and these houses were deceptively well made. She kept this revelation to himself, as the stranger at his side was just that. She was grateful for the help though. By the time Zya had become thoroughly confused, the pirate stopped cursing at Lorn, and became more alert. The crowds of people had thinned to the point that they had hardly seen more than a glimpse of a person in a good long while. It was easier to think that they had disappeared by coincidence, but knowing what she did of this city, Zya was more convinced that it was by active choice that the city folk did not come into this area. The paths were as dirty as in any other part of the crowded areas, but no more than a few tracks were visible.

"Where are we going?" she mumbled, attempting to sound drowsy and not really faking it.

"Somewhere safe. You can stop your acting now if you wish."

"She isn't acting, pirate," Lorn defended her.

The area they were passing through now seemed a bit warmer, and lighter. There was an inner glow from the houses that set them at ease. Chickens pecked and clawed at the dirt, searching for a meal, ignoring the passers by. Wooden gateways and fences sprung up for no other obvious purpose than to just block the way, and the pirate, for that was surely what he was, dodged surely around them, following the track where the cobbles were shown underneath the dirt and refuse. They stepped over a pile of clothes and were presented with a light wooden door that was obviously intended to look shabbier than it actually was.

"This place is not as it appears to be," Lorn commented.

"Oh?"

"I have watched carpentry, pirate. This door is much more secure than it is made out to look like. This is one elaborate deception, but to what ends I do not know. Zya knew that Lorn could protect her if the occasion arose, but he would have wanted to get her somewhere safe. Before Lorn could voice any more concerns, the pirate stepped away, leaving Zya in Lorn's arms. The pirate blocked the view of the door with his large frame, and fumbled with something for a moment. A couple of clicks later, and the door swung inward on hinges that were well oiled; they did not make a sound, which was normally the sign of a carefully kept house, but not in such surroundings. The door opened fully, and the gaudy man passed into the house, beckoning towards Lorn urgently. Seeing no need to pretend any more, and understanding that the man knew Zya was not simply drunk, he discarded all propriety and lifted Zya into his arms, carrying her gently into the house. The interior of the house matched the pirate's clothes. Bright colours were overly abundant, and very ostentatious. Purples and yellows brightened up the walls in the form of silks and drapes. Oranges and greens were all over the floor. The change was so radical, so incredibly blatant that Lorn stood there gaping for a moment. Then his senses recovered from the rainbow onslaught, and he looked for a place to put Zya. The house stretched in several directions, again adding to disperse the preconception that Zya had already decided about the house. It was far bigger than it was made out to be. Off to their right there was a parlour of sorts, where an immense cauldron stood with clothes steaming away inside. Stood to one side was a tiny little woman, dressed in a plain blue dress with her hands on her hips and an astonished look on her face. Zya had seen the look on her face before, on the faces of the wise-women of his tribe. It spoke a volume about who was in charge here, and as she looked back to the man, there was supplication on his face. "Oh my," she said, approaching them with quick, little steps. "Whatever has happened here?" The small lady said in not so small mothering tones.

"This little darlin' has had a turn for the worse, and it was safest to bring her here."

"I am fine," Zya protested, trying to stand and failing miserably.

The little woman looked up at the pirate under a mop of light brown hair, greyed at the temples, and the slightest raising of one of her eyebrows was all that she had to say about that decision. Then her face became the epitome of concern, as she studied Zya, still in Lorn's arms. "Oh the poor dear, bring her in here." She indicated a room that was to the left of the parlour entrance that contained a small bedroom. Lorn brought Zya quickly to the bed that was contained therein, along with a desk and a small wooden chest that was locked, and placed her gently on the bed. He brushed her hair back softly, looking with concern at the woman before him. "Okay?"

"I hope so." Zya smiled at him, feeling genuinely safe for the first time in what seemed like an age. The big man entered, having shed his grisly purple waistcoat, and having donned a much less garish and much more serviceable leather jerkin. The woman entered behind him, with a bowl of warm water and a cloth. She quickly shooed the two men outside and pulled up a seat, dabbing at Zya's forehead with a great deal of care. "Whatever happened to you, my dear?"

"I passed out," Zya admitted, willing to allow that much of the truth to be heard.

"Well you were lucky my man was there to bring you home. Bay's Point is not a safe city to lie unconscious in for long. You stay there and rest."

"No, honestly I am all right."

"Lie there and rest." The mothering tones became that of a matron, one who was used to being obeyed, and Zya lay still.

Moments passed, and then Lorn and the pirate returned, carrying tankards brimming with foamy ale.

"Get this down you, lass. You will be right as rain in no time at all."

The woman took a tankard and tipped some of the contents down Zya's throat before she could protest. It tasted nutty, and wholesome.

Lorn raised his tankard to their hosts. "Your good health, whoever you may be."

"And yours also, young archer." The pirate replied amiably. They both drained a good swig of their ale, and the pirate leaned back, stretched expansively, and let out a thunderous belch. "Ah, by Panishwa's arse, 'tis a good brew, don't you think?" Zya could not help but agree. She wanted answers though. "What is your intention concerning us?"

The man became all business at Zya's direct approach, his jolly face replaced by one of uttermost seriousness. "Do you not think that we could at least make our introductions before we get down to all that?" He said, sounding slightly hurt.

Lorn nodded. "Very well. I am Lorn, son of Hern, of a tribe in the Uporan steppes."

"I am Zya, of the East country travellers."

The man stood, and offered a hand that Lorn felt obliged to shake, and did so to relieved the tension after his previous statement. "Well met Lorn, son of Hern. I know of your father, an honourable gentleman and a shrewd bargainer." At the look of surprise on Lorn's face, the man continued. "You were not expecting that, young Lorn. Well suffice it to say that your father and I have done business on occasion, and that I knew of your coming long before you arrived. I am Darrow, an inhabitant of these parts, and oft time merchant, though I dabble only a little." He knocked one ham of a fist against his forehead. "Not much of a head for figures, me. Just good knacks for a deal and a lot of luck have seen me through is all."

"And the lady?"

"My woman, Yneris. She is as good a lady as I have known. She will look after your girl, if that is what is needed." Darrow looked slyly at her. "Welcome to my home, lass. That was some seizure you took there, lass. Care to share your thoughts?"

Lorn sipped at his ale. "Let me first ask you a question. You have been gracious enough to someone who has offered you not much more than suspicion and caution, but we do need to know that we can trust you."

Darrow considered this for a second while he wiped foam off of his stubbled face with his sleeve. "Okay, how can I prove that I am who I am? I know your father well, and we have even hunted together once, when I met him with goods from the city. He showed me the trophy that he has carried with him since his ascension to the status of hunter. The antlers of a deer, with points sharpened and tipped with dyes of several hues. They can be found mounted on his seat in the tent that he uses for tribal meetings."

"You have quite a memory, to remember all that." Lorn complemented.

"Does that mean you trust me?" Darrow asked, his look intent.

Lorn clasped his hands together, with his elbows on the arms of the seat, his index fingers pointing up as he pursed his lips and rested his chin on them. "What would my father say in a situation like this?"

Without missing a beat, Darrow replied. "He would say that your Old Law states that one should judge a man by his actions and intent, rather than by preconceptions."

Lorn nodded. "That is exactly what my father would say. You appear to know him well."

"Are you one with the Old Law?" Zya interrupted.

"Probably not as much as you would like, lass, but that is the nature of things in this Port." Darrow leaned back in his chair. "Like I said, son. I have known your father for many years. He and I. . . well we understand each other, even if we never always see eye to eye. I am, as you may have guessed, not strictly a merchant. Now, to your friend here, what is your story?"

Lorn related the tale of how he had met Zya while she had been entranced by the far-flung magic of Raessa, and how he had met her father and the young boy, Juatin, known to his friends simply as Ju. As he mentioned these names he was met with a chuckle from Darrow. "I know the boy. Been running messages for the guilds and merchants almost since you first got here. Making quite a nuisance of himself too. He is a nimble little creature. None of the pickpockets can get near him."

Zya did not know quite what to make of Darrow's knowledge of either Ju's doings, or of pickpockets; she just let the comment pass her by. Lorn told the tale of how Ju had accompanied him into the chilly northern wastes and had proclaimed himself a hunter by his hunting down of a deer, and carrying it back.

"Impressive." Was Darrow's only comment. "Now I know somewhat of a carpenter named Tarim s'Vedai. He would be known to you both.

"He is my father. How do you know him?"

"Who do you think made the door on the front of this house?" The only person Darrow did not seem to know much about was Zya. Lorn concluded with their arrival in Bay's Point, and what they had been doing since.

"I know of your comings and goings in the city," Darrow stated.

Lorn shifted uneasily, not enjoying the prospect that he had been continually watched for the passing of a moon. "Then why did you wait until now to speak to me, if you knew my father so well?"

Darrow shrugged, a mountainous movement for a man so big. "I wanted to see what you were about, what sort of man you were, and what your companions were up to. I wanted to see if you were trustworthy. It does well to have those as you can trust at your side in a city full of brigands and mercenaries."

"I have seen no real evidence of such people."

Darrow laughed out loud at this. "That my young friend is because I have been keeping them off of your back. This city is not the people infested, litter plagued marketplace you believe it to be. There are thugs on every street corner, swords ready and willing to fight at the drop of a hat, and sometimes that is all it takes. This is Bay's Point, the roughest toughest city in the Nine Duchies, the scourge of the seas and the name that puts fear into those little country Dukes that hide up in their mountains. The people are true, but they are of a stock descended from the very bottom of the sea I say. Brine for blood and daggers for teeth, one and all. If I had not kept a watch on you, you would have had as much chance of ending up in a gutter as you did of getting to a marketplace, being an outsider."

Zya considered this. "It is true that people had almost been desperate to avoid us at times, circling around whenever they had the chance. The people were more than happy enough to barge into each other. What about the alleyway that we were attacked in?"

"Tests, to see if those weapons that you carry are just for show. I could see plainly that they were not. Now my own questions. What *are* you doing here in this city?"

"I can not say with complete certainly." Zya replied, receiving a frown from Darrow. "Honestly, I tell you the truth. We decided to come here, but to what ends I cannot say. I felt that it was the best place to come for information." Zya knew that she was only telling a half-truth, for she did not want to give anything away without justification.

To give himself time to think, she took a long pull of her ale. It was cold, and extremely fruity. Quite the best ale she had ever had. She sighed with gusto. "This truly is magnificent."

Darrow laughed out loud. "It is called Autumn Berry, and is brewed far to the South. They say that they add wild berries to the vats to give it that unique flavour."

"So how come you by it so far up here?"

Darrow looked around conspiratorially. "We, have our methods," he said vaguely, not looking like he was really willing to say any more on the subject. It was clear that the man was going to give nothing away. Instead, he returned to the subject of them. "So you, Zya. Are you prone to collapsing in the middle of the street?"

Zya knew she was going to get away with no less than an honest answer, but Lorn spoke for her. "Not since I have ever known her, but she has an air about her. It reminds me of our wise women, but is somehow different. She had received training from one such person for a long time while they stayed with the tribe on its southern migration."

"Really?"

"But of what passed in the tent, only myself and the teacher shall ever know." Zya gazed around the room as she spoke. Paintings of the sea struck out at her, great ships battling the elements forever in a world of canvas and oils. It reminded Zya that she had only seen the sea for the first time recently. She wondered what it was like to ride the crest of a wave on a great dromond, living only for the thrill of life without the thought of setting one's foot on the land again.

"I think that Zya feels there is something to wait for in this city, and nothing will force the event upon us. We must be patient."

"Is that why you are reluctant to join any of the numerous crews that have asked for your services?"

Lorn had spoken to her about this only once. The man truly seemed to know everything, and Lorn wondered if he was more than he made himself out to be. "That, and I find a great distaste in making arrows to be used as weapons against one's fellow man."

"Oh come now." Darrow returned. "You cannot say that your Old Law does not allow you to kill. How do you survive?"

Darrow was trying to bait them. "There is a difference, sir, in killing a deer for survival, and the senseless slaughter of people for vengeance and enjoyment. I abhor the fact that I must kill those magnificent creatures for food and warmth, but I will never for a second shirk from my duty to my people. The same applies to the boy, Zya and her father."

Darrow leaned back into his seat and laughed out loud.

"I can see little to laugh about in that. Zya was on he verge of getting offended."

"I mean no disrespect, lass. Lorn is just like his father. I could never draw him into an argument over that sort of thing. Let me guess, you carry on working as a fletcher because it is all you know how to do."

"I fletch because I enjoy it, and because I am good at it." Lorn replied. "If you know my father then you know that we are adept at many things. It passes the time for me while I dwell here, though I will never enjoy the prospect that my work would go into battle. The Old Law decrees that violence is only just in self-defence."

"Well said." Darrow finished his ale, setting the tankard on a table.

Yneris returned to dabbing at Zya's face with the warm cloth.

"She is so terribly cold." Yneris stroked back Zya's hair, as a mother would do. Lorn leaned forward, placing his hand on her brow. "There is a distinct chill there. It does not feel right. They say that the tribal wise-women go into death-like trances when they have a vision. Mayhap this is a similar circumstance."

"When I first saw you today, she was looking a bit peaky." Darrow observed as he took his jerkin off and hung it on a chair. The room was warm, and the presence of four bodies combined with the proximity of the steam-filled parlour set the air to heating, and Zya felt herself becoming drowsy. She was content to let Lorn do the talking. "What happened to her?"

"I do not know," Lorn replied simply. "One moment we were walking along the streets, minding our way and then she stopped, looking up at the clouds. Her face was indescribable. She was not there at all, within her own mind I mean. Then the baker shouted, as did you, and we left. From that point on she was agitated by something, and it reached a peak when we walked past that huge building. Zya became rooted to the spot, and the only time she moved, she looked at the building then at me and just said 'it's wrong'. That was it, nothing more." Lorn looked up at Darrow, his hair falling loose to cover Zya like a human shroud. "The rest you know, as you arrived soon after that, thankfully."

Darrow put his hand to his chin, as he frowned in serious thought. "That was a bad place for her to be acting up like that. There are eyes in that building that are unfriendly to people with the best intentions. Even the locals try to stay clear."

Yneris looked from Lorn to Zya, and finally to her husband. "The mercenary guild?"

He blinked slowly, his tongue in one cheek as he thought of implications that were possibly to come. "Aye, lass. And there's nothing that we can do about it. Those mercenaries are an enigma, a law unto themselves, and they say nothing of what goes on in that building. Even the highest authorities in the city have no idea what occurs in there." He shook his head regretfully, with the reluctant anticipation of somebody who knew that something was bound to come of the situation. "No, somebody will have seen what happened. You must be careful, though I will do what I can for you, it might not be enough."

"We need to get word to her father. He will become concerned if neither of us return."

"Not a problem," Darrow replied with a flick of his hand. "I have just the person to send a message, your sneak-thief little friend."

As Lorn looked up, Yneris interrupted his question. "O-ho, not this time, Darrow. You do not have the solution to every problem. That boy is run off of his feet, and he is asleep. You are not going to disturb him." Her answer was final, and Darrow seemed to know better than to argue with her. Given a chance for his question, he voiced one querying word. "Ju?"

"Aye, that's the one." Darrow replied, still staring his wife down, to no effect. "A nimble little sprite, that kid. I would have no other message-runner."

"Where is he?" Lorn asked.

"Up the stairs, on a pallet." Yneris replied. "Don't either of you dare disturb him."

Lorn flashed a grin, easing her stern demeanour into a softening smile. "I would not dare to go against the word of somebody so caring." Lorn left the room, and Zya could hear the creak of the stairs as Lorn and Darrow climbed them.

"Are you all right now?"

"You are called Yneris?"

"Yes."

"I am tired. My head is fuzzy."

"Well by all accounts, you have had a rough day. Don't worry, you are safe here until you get better."

Something nagged at Zya. "No, I need to get home."

"Young lady, you are in no fit state to move around, let alone travel halfway across the city. Is the boy sleeping?" Yneris directed her question to the returning men, confusing Zya more as she mumbled a reply.

"Out like a lantern." Lorn replied. "I need to get a message to Tarim, Zya's father. He needs to know of this, and be brought here."

"That is not wise lad," Darrow warned. "You must understand that we took a risk bringing you here at all. If it were not for your woman's misfortune, I would have caught up with you elsewhere and introduced myself."

"I insist," Lorn replied forcefully. "Her father needs to know of this. There is more happening here than just a faint."

Darrow looked at his wife. "We must wake the boy, he is nimble and will be there a lot quicker than the lad here."

"Ju won't wake." Zya said through half-closed eyes.

"He will if we shake him hard enough."

"No. Lorn knows."

"I do not think that Ju will wake until Zya does, sir." Lorn replied, looking seriously at Darrow. "Ma'am, when did he fall asleep?"

"A while ago, now."

"Long enough for two people to slowly drag a third back from that mercenary building you mentioned?" Lorn asked, hopefully.

Yneris thought about it, concentration furrowing her smooth brow. "Why yes, I think that would be about right. He had been running an errand while my lump of a husband was out chasing you two around the city streets and arguing with his friends. The boy came back and fell asleep on the bed, almost collapsed onto it as he was talking to me."

97

Lorn turned to Darrow. "I need to go. I am almost as fleet of foot as your nimble message boy. Her father needs to see this."

Darrow looked at his wife, who stared him down, a look of agreement clear in her eyes. She was certainly a figure to match the bulk of her husband. "Very well, lad." Darrow said in defeat. "But be careful. One of my crew is waiting outside, and will escort you to a place that you know of. He will wait for three soundings of the palace bell. If you are not back by the time the third watch has changed, you had better remember your way here."

"I will be back," Lorn said with a grave face. "You have my thanks for all you have done." He bowed to both of them in the tribal manner, doing them what they knew to be a great honour, for tribal leaders seldom bowed, and he had been next in line. With a smile and a wave he shut the door behind him.

"Do you think he will have any problems?" Yneris asked her big husband.

Darrow sat down and began to polish his falchion with a whetstone and cloth, paying particular attention to the inside of the blue-steeled blade. "I think that the lad will find his way back if he has a need, and he truly does have a need. If he wants to see them again he will have to be quick, and if he wants to make it out of Bay's Point alive, he had better be quicker. If he does not join a ship's crew as an archer, he had better have eyes in the back of his head, for somebody will surely hunt him down and drag him in chains to the bottom of the bay."

"They will come for me." Zya defied the previous statement, not caring what anybody thought of her opinion.

During the afternoon Zya drowsed, but never fell fully asleep. She was too worried about being vulnerable in the deep sleep to let it claim her, as it had already claimed Ju. He was surely waiting for her on the other side. In what seemed but moments, Zya could hear her father, his voice full of concern.

"I would get to know you better, Darrow, but I would like to see my daughter."

"That is to be expected, Tarim S'Vedai. Please, come this way."

Then her father was there, kneeling down at her side. "Zya?"

"Father," she whispered.

"What happened?"

"It is okay. It is part of my training."

Tarim turned from his daughter for a moment. "I need to see Ju."

"Come with me." Yneris led him out of the room. Moments later, they returned, her father's face drained.

Yneris closed the doors to the room, and then joined them around the bed.
"I must thank you for the care you have shown by looking after my family like
this." Tarim said, his face grave, made all the more so by his unbound hair
reaching down across his chest. "You did not have to do this for strangers, and
I am in your debt. If there is any way I can repay you for your kindness, you
have but to name it."

"Can you shoot an arrow through a target a fingers width wide, like the lad
here can?" Asked Darrow.

"Oh hush, you huge fool," snapped Yneris. "Stop thinking about your ships
for a change." At a warning glance from Darrow, she persisted. "You are not
as clever as you think, my husband. I can tell from his face that our guest has
already got you sussed, isn't that right?" Yneris looked at Tarim, her left
eyebrow raised in query."

He smiled, the smallest of smiles, but an affirmation nonetheless. "I would say
that your husband has been a pirate so long that it is ingrained into his very
being, ma'am. His walk has the rolling gait of one used to living on water, and
he is used to being obeyed without question. Am I not right?"

"What does a wandering carpenter know about the life of seafaring folk?"
Demanded Darrow.

"I wasn't always a carpenter," Tarim replied, "and I have been around cities
enough to recognize the defensive layout of buildings that have been
constructed with the dual intention of confusing and trapping the unwary, or
unwanted. Am I not right?"

Lorn was looking perplexed, trying to figure out just whom he was actually
sitting with. "A pirate captain?" he said, looking at Darrow. "And who exactly
are you?" He said to Tarim.

"I am Tarim S'Vedai, father to Zya, onetime a traveller and often a carpenter,
as you have seen, Lorn. Anything else is my business, and my business alone.
How about you?" Tarim looked at Darrow, who still couldn't believe what he
had considered to be an elaborate ploy showing domestic felicity had been
shattered by the straight talking and clear logic of an outsider. "I am Captain
Darrow, of the pirate ship Nightsnake." He said simply. My wife Yneris is in
truth my wife, and is it seems, far cleverer than me. Of course, now you know
this, I am going to have to kill you."

Before Tarim or Lorn could do anything, Darrow let out a bellow of a laugh,
and downed his tankard of ale.

"Fool man." His wife said in a manner that spoke volumes about her having to
put up with his stylised sense of humour for many a season. "One day your
rash jokes will rub somebody up the wrong way and you will end up filleted

like a fish." She turned to Tarim. "What we mean is that we would rather you not mention to anybody what we have talked about here."

"Consider it done," Tarim said simply, grinning at Darrow. "I like a joke, and Darrow's sense of humour is very infectious. Nobody shall hear from my lips that Yneris the captain of the Nightsnake, and her husband the first mate are masquerading as a couple intent upon domestic bliss." At the shocked look from the two, Tarim continued. "It is more than obvious who is in charge here, but your secret is safe with me."

Yneris looked shocked. "Who are you?" she asked mysteriously.

"Nobody of consequence," Tarim replied. "Now Lorn, why don't you tell us what is going on with my daughter and Juatin, and why we should only be mildly concerned, and not worried to death over their fates?"

"I can speak for myself," Zya tried to protest, though her eyelids were growing heavier and heavier.

Lorn took a swig of the fruity ale, and used the time to gather his thoughts. "It is conjecture, not a lot more than hear say, but I think that it is the key to the unusual behaviour. In the tribal history, the wise women have never ruled the tribes, but have held their own council and have heavily influenced tribal politics. They all have one thing in common, the ability to read the future through dreams, the ability of a seer."

"You mean your little woman is going to be able to dream the future?" interrupted Darrow. "You are a strange and valuable bounty, the lot of you." Darrow sat back, smiling smugly, as if he had just uncovered a treasure. He had the confidant air of one who knew how to turn a situation to his advantage.

"No, that is not necessarily the case and not necessarily what is happening," Lorn said pointedly to Darrow, leaving the man crestfallen. "Like I said, we are not sure of the society of the tribal seers. They do not allow information to escape their society willingly, as they value privacy above all else. Outside interference distracts them from what they believe to be their prime calling, using their seer's gift to aid the tribes. One thing we have learned from seeing tribal daughters that have gone on to become seers in later life is the initial reaction to a vision: They drop into a trance, seen to the unskilled as the deepest of sleep, grow cold, and can remain this way for an indefinite period."

"What do you mean indefinite?" asked Tarim. I don't want Zya to lie comatose for the God's only knew how long until she recovers from her affliction. Jettiba grant that my only daughter will be up and about in a few days, rather than miss out on the prime season of her life because of something that may or may not happen."

"Again, I do not know," Lorn replied, aware of all the gazes settled on him. "It is only a rough guess, but most of those that have been recorded outside of the society of the wise women have been seen up and about sometimes ten days or more after the wise women take them. They seem to be able to sense when one of their blood is undergoing the change, and are there almost as soon as it happens. This of course does not mean that it always takes that amount of time for them to wake, but again I can say no more on the matter because I do not know it."

"I never knew that you nomads had such a complex society," said Darrow, who was just about taking it all on board. "To me, it seemed like you were just following the herds, hunting and existing, but this is a whole level more."

"It might run deeper." Lorn said with a hint of mystery in his voice. "It is said that the wise women are also adept at magic in various forms, but there has never been a sighting, there has never been any proof of this. It is all just rumour."

"Well there are certain advantages to a society run by women, whatever you may think." Said Yneris from the chair in which she was so ill suited to sit because of its size; she looked like a child's doll. "You will never go hungry, and all the decisions made are wise and well thought out." If she was expecting any argument, she got none, and the men all burst out laughing.

"You will get no argument from me there, my love," said Darrow fondly. "Nor any of the crew."

"Me either." Tarim agreed. "You know about the travellers and how they are led by a woman. I would have it no other way."

"So how is the boy involved in this?" It was Yneris who asked Lorn, Tarim and Darrow ready to reminisce over tales of the past.

"That is where I can only guess, ma'am." Lorn replied evasively but politely. He was hiding something, but Tarim suspected that he would never tell Darrow and his wife. "The boy is suffering exactly the same symptoms as Zya. He has the deep sleep, the cold touch of the skin, and the same pallid demeanour. If I were in a wager, as I believe is the custom, I would say that the boy is in the same pre-seer trance as I think Zya is falling into. Though why he would do that at exactly the same time as her is beyond my comprehension. One thing more. I think that this is a first. Either that or they have kept any rumours extremely quiet to the point that tribal chiefs have never heard about any case. This worries me, but I believe that all we can do is wait until they both wake up, and see what they have to say."

"The weapons. They link us." Zya felt herself being drawn deeper and deeper, despite everything she could do to fight.

Outside the bell toll echoed across the late afternoon from within the Ducal Palace. It was the last bell of the day watch, and soon a quieter, softer bell would be heard as the night watch took over at the Southern Gate, the impenetrable defence against the rest of the Nine Duchies.

"Well all we can do then is wait," Darrow decided out loud. "I offer you all the hospitality of my house, while the girl and the child sleep on. It seems the most prudent course, as moving them would surely not be good."

Tarim offered his hand, receiving a hearty shake and a comradely slap on the back.

"What say you to getting drunk together?" Darrow asked, receiving a groan of dismay from his wife.

"I would," Tarim replied, "but I do not feel in the mood for it presently. I would rather wait by my daughter's bedside if you will excuse me."

Darrow nodded. "You care for her greatly."

"She is the centre of my life, there is no doubt. There is something special about her, but what it is I don't know. Mayhap this is the beginning of the unravelling process for us all." Zya stared across the room as Darrow rambled on, her eyes lost in the picture of a painting about a ship, its prow breaching the crest of a wave, as if it were alive and dancing of its own free will on the surface of the ocean.

Chapter Five

She swayed with the momentum, swinging gently from side to side with the rhythmic movements as the ship quartered, waves hitting it from an angle, and forcing it to endure a subtle impact. The waves were not big, not any more than a leg's length from crest to trough. They were just little things that decorated the surface of the sea, driving monotony away, and brought the ship to life in a gentle manner as opposed to the lurching panic of wood strained while forced to endure a storm surge. The sky was blue, that light blue that spoke a promise of distant cloud that never intruded on the horizon any more than it dared. The wisps that did pass them by were accompanied by small gulls for the most part, and the very rare sighting of an albatross if one was lucky. The wind was a tentative touch on her face, as if it feared to intrude, but it was enough to catch the sails higher up, and make them crack and boom as the helmsman attempted to squeeze every drop of speed out of the ship on this sunny day. Everything was quiet. Even if the ship was not becalmed, it seemed as if the crew were. They stared out from their posts, transfixed by their surroundings. Crewmen hung from ropes, leaning out, with the taut sinews of their arms the only things holding them from falling to a watery grave. They were all completely silent, even their breathing did not intrude on the slow creak of the hull and the masts as they yielded to the feathery presence of the breeze.

The only noise was the rumbling curse of the pirate captain, called Halitosis by his crew in mock affection of his habit for eating the foulest of foods and as a result having the worst breath in history, or so it seemed when the crew told their stories. The tales she had heard of the man eating meats so spicy one could not actually describe what animal the flesh had originally come from, and foul vegetables from far-away cities that had the one redeeming feature that they did not smell as bad as they looked, were countless. His breath was safely out of range up on the wheel deck, where he was inflicting its aroma on the poor helmsman, who could do no more about the wind than anybody could.

Behind her and to her left, her young companion lounged on a pile of ropes as he enjoyed the quiet and the warmth of the sun. Something intruded upon her consciousness as she looked up to the cerulean ceiling of the world and felt warmth but saw no sun, but she disregarded it and concentrated on becoming as relaxed as her companion. The wood was warm at her back, as only wood heated by half a day's exposure could be. It had been scrubbed clean, and the lack of polish meant that it absorbed heat as readily as it absorbed water in a storm. It had that smooth grainy feeling that only worn wood could give, catching slightly upon the skin of her hands as she moved her palms up and down the imperfections in the wooden floorboards. No splinters here. Everything had been scrubbed with sand, and was as smooth as could be. She tapped her fingernails as she closed her eyes, enjoying the mellow tones of dull wood containing musical tendencies that only made the feeling more right. She rested as she would as if asleep, but no sleep came. The birds cried overhead as they circled. Some even dared to land on the rigging, but kept well away from the crewmen. Not that it would have mattered. They all stared out into the ocean as if expecting something to happen, but events were moving too slowly for anything of significance to occur. Something nagged at her. The entire situation was not right. The gentle rocking of the ship seemed surreal, as if it existed, and yet was only a figment of her imagination. Climbing the steps of the ship to the aft deck, she gained a better view of the surroundings. Her companions now were the helmsman and captain. The helmsman, his calloused hands a solid grip of iron on a wheel that needed barely a touch to turn it in the quiet breeze, was nothing out of the ordinary on a ship such as this. He wore a black bandanna and a flaring white shirt that tapered to his waist. The black trousers that he wore were cut short at the knee as was the style, and she looked down at her own legs, noting the frayed edges where she had cut her own breeches in order to fit in. Looking back up, she saw her companion drop down lightly beside her from the rigging. He had taken to the rigging like a squirrel to a tree, and was as at home in the ropes as he was on the deck, or in the bilges, or in any part of the ship for that matter. His rapidly growing hair was tied back pirate fashion, and he looked quite the part, in a brown waistcoat and matching short trousers. Even her hands had become calloused from work; though he had worked much harder on this trip, so agile was he. The pirate captain stared at them from the other side of the helmsman. Halitosis had one of those faces that made him look decidedly feline. His nose was too small for the size of his face, and his eyes were big and round, but also had that piercing gaze that spoke of intelligence, as if he had a way of seeing through everything around him. His demeanour had earned him the title of 'Halitosis, captain cat face' amongst the land-based, but amongst the community of pirates, he was well respected. He stared slyly at her, with not a word, as if he was expecting something to happen. She ignored him, and gazed off into the distance, searching for whatever it was that was worrying her. She glanced off to the starboard side of the ship, and there it was. An inky smudge on the distant horizon, different in aspect to the wispy clouds that seemed too frightfully polite to intrude upon them. This band of cloud was a bullyboy in contrast. It ploughed its way North at a terrific pace, too fast for normal cloud. It was a great angry black blob of turmoil, there was no other word for it, as it was bulbous in countenance. It seethed as it moved, and was soon joined by what could have passed as its twin. It looked to be passing the ship far off in the distance, but she looked back behind her, and the same distance behind, another bulbous band of cloud seethed up from the south. The strangest thing was that the sailors were still immobile, aside from the helmsman, who continued to struggle against a non-existent wind, and the captain who continued to growl and snarl at nothing in particular.

The cloud, so very black, and pierced with the occasional spark that had to be lightning, swept on, oblivious of their tiny bobbing presence on the sea. Ahead of them and to the right, the cloud merged with the distant hilltops to become one angry mass of cloud and land. The rain was so dense that it was possible for one to observe sheets of it drenching down on the distant hills, rendering them dark and barely visible. All that was left to see was darkness, where the smudge in front was maintaining its assault on the land. Behind, the cloud had passed on, leaving nothing but a sense of foreboding in its wake. From the distance, guttural rumbles were the obvious signs that the weather was as abrasive as it looked. From the cloud there issued white streaks, where the rain was so dense and sudden that it had become visible from this distance. Once more, a streak of cloud passed by them to the stern, and she felt as if she were the only one watching it. It growled from close behind the ship, and the density of the cloud seemed to push the wind out in front and to the sides of the cloud mass. A rush of wind became a gale, and then a roar as the cloud touched the sea, sending waterspouts spinning off in all directions as the vortices from the cloud drew up anything they touched. The wind pushed the ship into a hurtling race with waves that had erupted out of nowhere, heading straight towards the distant shore that was now not so distant. The storm in front was a mirror of the storm behind, and was ravaging the headlands with such savage, naked force that the cliffs were beginning to crumble from the onslaught of the waves. This should not have been obvious to her, for they were still too far away, but nevertheless, she could see all that was happening, from the way the trees bent under the desolation of the wind, right down to how small creatures buried deeper into the ground as if to escape what was happening at the surface. The landmass was shrouded by the storm, enduring it as only it could. She was not so sure that she could endure such animosity from the natural elements, but it looked like she was the only one that cared about what was happening. Her companion still smiled amiably, leaning on the rail as if nothing were amiss. The helmsman looked more in his place now, as if he were truly attempting to strain against the wind and waves that were now pushing them ever faster, ever closer to land. This was of course a mixed blessing. Land meant safety, and she had no desire to drown, but at the speed they were moving, they would crash into the rocks before they had a chance to disembark. The captain stared around him, grumbling at everything, seeing nothing. The crew were still at ease in the rigging, seemingly oblivious to everything going on around them. The ship turned as it was caught by a wave that approached them at an angle that should not have been possible, and it went dark and she knew no more.

He stared out at the ocean, with his companion by his side. How they had reached this place he did not know, but he felt the memory of climbing rigging as strong as an aftershock to the turmoil that was his mind. He knew that he should fear for something had happened to him, but he was safe on land, with the ebbing wind pulling at his clothes. Evidence of a storm lay all around him. On the rocks out in front lay the carcass of a ship, split asunder by constant pounding of the stormy sea. The mast was rent in two, and lay in defeat almost to his feet, which were dry when he was sure that they should have been wet. His companion stared out into the distance, and he did not know what held her attention. She was absorbed by some distant spectacle. Flickers of light as remote as the memory of his mother were in the direction that she stared, but it was something only she could see. Boxes and barrels floated in the shallow pools that were almost an afterthought of the storm. The sand under his feet was strewn with weeds and other flotsam that had been washed as far as he could see. He found himself suddenly knee-deep in the pools, dragging the crates and barrels out of the way of another rising tide. His companion was at his side, and together, they made short work of the barrels, all of them watertight but varying in weight. He did not pause to consider what was within. His only thought was to get them as far away from the ever-hungry yawning maw of the ocean, that would reclaim them too readily given favourable winds and the merest sliver of time. The rest of the wreckage they ignored, even though it shrieked and groaned at them as it protested at its manhandling by its twin captors, the sea and the rocks. The great spikes thrust out of the water in such a fashion that the ship seemed impaled upon them, as if it had been lifted by an immense wave, and thrust to lie hanging limply on it's death bed of stone. The word 'impaled' stuck in his mind as he paused to look. If the ship had been a person, it would have been in agony, but it was an empty husk, its contents already spilled. Torn sails fluttered in the breeze from the West, like the heartbeat of a man who had given up on any hope of survival, and lay in his deathbed awaiting the inevitable. They were the only tenuous link to the life of the ship, the only defiant movement it had left to make. They seemed to stick out at the wind, daring it to tear them from their fastenings and settle them on the small but persistent waves that caused the ship to settle further. He looked around the cove. There were similar outcroppings all around, and if he was not mistaken, and he so seldom was, at least one more wreck, abandoned to the elements, and already covered with barnacles where it was submerged. Time had ravaged that, so that all that was left of another wooden behemoth were the ribs of its underbelly, and the rusting metal that stained the blackened wood with a shade of bloody red, as if there were a wound that could never be closed. This cove was a death trap for ships.

Not long after his thoughts, they completed the rescue of all of the barrels. It had still not occurred to them to take a look inside one. His only thought was to get them to a town and sell them as salvage that he could make a little money from, enough to survive. The light was not good, as the clouds from the storm still weighed heavy overhead, boiling and seething in their surge towards the North. The light that there was came as a dark grey, as if there was a concealing mist all around them. It was obvious that it was morning, but the almost total lack of clear visibility made it seem as if it were about to be extinguished for good. The moisture hung heavy in the air, ready to erupt into rain at a moments notice, but none ever came. The two of them loaded the barrels and crates up onto the back of the cart, straining in an effort to raise the bulky objects almost as high as their heads at times. It never occurred to him to question the origin of the cart, or the horse that stood dutifully in front, attached to the harness. He knew that they would be there, and here they were. His companion showed a total lack of surprise as events unfolded, and therefore he was not in the least bit concerned. With a regretful last glance for the ship that had landed so badly in the cove, they set off on the track that led away from it, and on towards the village that lay half way to the city. As they climbed the hill to the cliffs that overlooked the bay to the North, they saw the real extent of what had happened. Trees were blown flat, and the grass had yielded in an effort to stay rooted in the ground. It looked as if something had tried to suck the very marrow out of the earth. Waves still rushed up the bay towards its terminus, cresting and plunging every so often. Where there should be seabirds, there were none. The gulls and other flying inhabitants had long since departed ahead of the winds that must have done all of the damage to the coast. The lack of avian forms was somewhat disconcerting, but it did not bother him as much as it should. Normally a coast without birds was as bad as meat without gravy, or a merchant without gold. All he felt was apathy, as if his goal was more important to him. The cart trundled along, but he did not notice, as his eyes were on his companion. She sat there placid and content, unaware of the extensive damage done by the storm, rocking slightly as if she were aboard a ship, floating along on the waves that now battered the cliffs and sent spray much further. He could taste the finest salt crystals in the air as he breathed deeply in the gale. By all rights, he should have been cowering in the shelter of rocks or trees, not riding along a coastal path towards the village in the face of a full gale. This fact concerned him just as little as all the other things that were wrong with his situation. He could still not remember how he had got there, and the missing link of his memory seemed important, but still, he did not care. Neither did his companion, and if she had any fear of getting blown off of the cart, for by all rights they should have ended flat on their backs several times already, she did not show it. His attention turned back to the track in front of them. The horse, a white stallion with bunching muscles that belied its apparent career as a draught horse, plodded placidly along in front of them paying little heed to the bushes that bounced around elastically in the wind, or the grass that showed streaks of colour as it yielded *en masse* to any direction the wind chose to take it. The horse knew its path, and it plodded forward resolutely. At length, the track swerved perilously close to the headland, and they came in full view of the bay, and more importantly, the cove that they had climbed up from. The track was pure rock where the soil had been eroded away, and it was difficult going for both horse and cart. That concerned him less than the group of people already on the headland. Several turned at their approach. One in particular he thought that he recognised. The man was dressed as a corsair, and had the strangest feline face, with large eyes, and a button-tiny nose. The man walked up to them as the horse heaved the cart over a rut in the stony track, and walked right past them to look at their cargo. The man paused as he eyed every barrel, and every crate with great detail. Then with not a word or a glance, the man walked back to the edge of the cliff, and resumed his vigil with the others. Sat motionless on the cart, for he knew not what was going on, he looked at his companion. She was still at ease, apparently finding nothing unusual about their situation. He looked instead at the others on the cliff's edge. There were a group of them that looked extremely relaxed, as if they were enjoying something that only they could see. One of their kind stood there, blood dripping from his hands as he clenched at the remnants of something wooden. Huge spokes stuck out from between his fingers, forcing them apart, but he seemed not to notice, caught as he was in his own private torment. He climbed down from the cart, running his hands over the horse and feeling the surge of blood in the creature's veins, despite its appearance of apparent lassitude. He approached the edge to behold the massive seascape beneath. It felt as if they were on a pinpoint on the top of the world, so sharply did the cliff fall away. If a thousand men stood on each other's shoulders, they could not reach this height, and yet he could see down to the sea floor, as the sea was transparent to his young eyes. This did not concern him overmuch, for he was looking at the ship. The tide had risen, and the ship was bucking on its deathbed as bigger waves threatened to move it. Barrels that had until now had remained unseen were afloat in the shallow cove that they had emerged from, and this was what interested the others. A look of glee rose from every man there, and without a word, they turned to trudge back to the cove in euphoric hope of finding something more there. Very suddenly he found himself alone, except for his companion and the horse, which was chewing contentedly on a mouthful of lush grass that had escaped the teeth of the wind. Alone in his contemplation of this unimaginable vista, he watched the ship free itself of the stone spikes that had held it prisoner. He watched in disbelief as the ship turned and floated out of the cove, and into the West. Water did not enter the gaping wounds that bled cargo, and the scraps of sails that had escaped the beating the ship had taken were catching a breeze that seemed from the waves to be blowing in the opposite direction. He swore that if the scenery did not feel so real, he could have been dreaming. Watching the ship disappear off over the horizon, he climbed back into his seat at the front of the cart. His companion set the horse into hesitant motion as it was still enjoying the grass, and was reluctant to move on.

Something had changed, and this time they both realised it, looking at each other in alarm.
"How did we get here?" they both asked at the same time. "I don't know." they also replied simultaneously.
Zya held up her hand to silence him. "Where were you?"
She looked past him. The scenery had changed once more, the cliffs and wind having disappeared, being replaced with lowlands and the sea beyond. She had no doubt they were further along the road, but Ju was unsettled nonetheless. "I was at a cove collecting barrels, and then on a cliff with some pirates, and then here with you." He shuddered as he looked around. How

could the scenery just change instantly? "You have been with me all of the way, haven't you?"

"Not as far as I can recall," Zya replied, nervously eyeing the land around them. The sea was a lot calmer than she remembered it, the waves barely lapping against the shore. There was a village ahead in the distance, its rooftops visible above the nearby horizon created by low hills. The track bent around to the left, almost onto the narrow strip of beach, and the to the right around a hill. "I was on a ship, on the sea, and then in a storm, except that I was the only one concerned. You were with me, Ju, and I could not understand why you were so at ease." She looked at him, and spoke words that scared him for some reason. "I was with a group of pirates too." That was the last that either of them spoke, for they started to hear noises that sounded nothing less than violent. Something was smashing wood and glass with such apparent ease that it could be heard though they were yet a mile off. They rode on in mute apprehension. The cloud piled over them as they reached the village, passing as fast as the wind. The light dimmed, and the clouds brought dark shadows sweeping by as they crawled to a stop at the outermost point of the village.

"The horse senses something."

"I know," Zya replied in a whisper. "Something dark is in this place, something that belies the very substance of nature."

Emanations of darkness flew out in waves that knocked them back with their ferocity.

"We have to move on," Ju shouted above the force of the darkness.

Zya cajoled the horse with a firm shake of the reins. The stallion hesitated, and the started forward as slow as it could possibly go. They inched through the town, the noise becoming deafening as they did so. All of a sudden, the source was revealed in horrific splendour. A group of what could only be called monsters was attacking a large building in the centre of the village. The creatures had all manner of sharp protuberances coming out at every direction, but if the spikes, for spikes they surely were, inhibited their movement, it was not obvious. In fact the creatures seemed all the more comfortable leaning on these spikes. They were huge, twice the size of the horse and cart combined, and they stood on hind legs, smashing at the walls and windows with their forelegs. If the creatures had any mouths, they were hidden under the mop of fur that covered their faces, all except for the glowing red eyes that oozed malice. The horse was moving slowly enough behind the smaller houses that they got a good enough look at the creatures to see that they almost acted like a family group. Two of them were much larger, and one was dominant, growling and warding the others off. It was as if part of the building was a territory, and sole property of each creature. Baffled by this, they glanced at each other, and prayed the horse would take them away from this scene of madness. Of course it was naturally that at this point the horse decided to stop, fear making it tremble to a halt.

"Come on," Zya urged, trying to shake the reins without making any noise. The very moment the horse halted, one of the creatures looked around, seeking them out. Finding them, the creature barked a warning to its family, a bubbling rumble from deep within its stomach. The noise was terrifying, and echoed off of all of the buildings within earshot, magnifying the sound. They realised that that was most of the noise that they had been hearing during their approach to the village. As the creature barked the others dropped to the ground. She had a leap of intuition. "They seem to be listening with their feet rather than with any sensory organs on their head."

"How do you know?"

"I feel sick from the vibrations coming up through the ground. They are magnified. I think that has something to do with it. They are talking through the ground."

The monsters started to edge away from the building they had been molesting, leaving it open for view. It was a guild house, seen by the crest above the door, the only part of it still intact and undamaged. Which guild it belonged to was a mystery, as the crest was in a state of flux, constantly blurred. One of the creatures began to lope towards them, the smaller of the adults. Ju shook the reins violently, trying not to look at the approaching creature, almost as big as the houses around which it stepped. The horse was unresponsive at first, resigned to the ending that fate had decided for it, but then it responded with a single step. This had the effect of halting the creature, less than two houses distance away from them. The creature seemed to sniff at the air, and cock its head to one side. Then the horse took another step, and another, and the creature rumbled a deafening call to the group. As if this was the key to unlock the hesitant behaviour of the horse, now the poor creature began to pull at the wagon in a nervous attempt to get out of the village.

Strangely enough, this resulted in the monster nearest them, a collection of spikes and claws all over it's body as revealed to them by it's proximity, turning and rejoining it's group and attacking the guild house with renewed vigour. She shook her head slightly, as if doubting to believe that any of this was real, and looked back at him. He was biting his upper lip with his lower teeth, struggling to say nothing, eyes wide with fright and relief.

"Don't worry Ju."

"Easy for you to say."

"It seems that as long as we keep moving, we are protected from these creatures."

"Weird."

"Well consider where we are, Ju. We are plainly not where we should be."

They continued through the village on a side track, avoiding the monsters that had become considerably quieter, and yet were still clearly in evidence.

"The houses were all empty," Ju observed.

"I don't really think that's much of a surprise, do you?"

Doors were open, and belongings were scattered on the ground. They came to a place where the horse stopped once more, and this time no amount of cajoling could move it. The horse appeared to have reached it's destination, and would move for nothing.

"Come on!" Ju shook the reins. The horse remained still.

"I don't think he is going anywhere, Ju."

"Well we should hide."

Zya looked back towards the centre of the village. "No I don't think we are going to be followed. Nothing is forthcoming. They would be on top of us by now and there is neither noise or vibration."

Climbing down from the cart, they entered the nearest building which was revealed to be a store. It had shelves filled with rusted tankards, and barrels full of seemingly random bits of metal. Everything was covered in spider webs, and many of the scuttling creatures could be seen in the windows, spinning their traps thicker and thicker in the hope of catching a meal. This looked the sort of shop that if they had still intended to sell their cargo, they would have found ideal.

"This place has been deserted for seasons."

"So it would seem. Ju, I have a feeling about this place. Don't touch anything. Be extremely careful."

They explored the shop, afraid to touch anything lest it be disturbed. There was a serenity about the whole shop, as if they would reduce the dusty perfection of the place with their touch. Implements and gadgets adorned the walls, obviously used in all manner of household chores. They made an unconscious decision at exactly the same time. This room was not meant to be touched, though they did not know why. There was a feeling, well more the potential for a feeling of wrong should they handle anything, so with a glance at each other, they left it to its dusty infinity. Returning to the sky that moved with rapid bursts of cloud, as if time was speeding ahead of them, they found a small girl stood next to the cart, stroking the horse's head. She was about eight or nine seasons old, with long dark hair, and a serious demeanour. She wore a brown homespun dress, not unlike the type favoured by many of the travellers, and she was barefoot, though she seemed unconcerned about the muddy track. As they approached her, she smiled. "He's my dad," she said softly, indicating a man wrapped in rags that until now had been hidden behind the horse. The old man, for wrinkled and gnarled he was, with his hands curling inwards and his arms clutched to his chest, could not have been the girl's father, so maybe it was a metaphor.

They looked at each other, not more than a single stolen glance. This place had no people. Why were there suddenly two more here? "What is your name?" she asked of the girl.

"He is two," the girl replied, indicating her father and showing no recognisable sign of having even heard the question. The girl looked calmly up at her. "He is two," she repeated insistently. "He needs to be one."

She thought back to her childhood, recalling memories that seemed so distant and difficult to obtain in this place. The girl in front of her reminded her of someone familiar, and she thought about the two girls that she shared her childhood with, though they were younger than her. They were fairer of hair and face than this girl. The thought struck her, and she cursed herself a fool for not having thought of it before. The girl reminded her of herself as a child. The face showed the simple signs that would develop into the young woman that she had become. The tilt of the eyes, with their intelligence and stubborn streak firmly entrenched behind them. The small pout of the lips, and the lustrous black hair grown so long already. All were reminiscent of the child she had once been. She knelt down to the height of the little girl. "Is he injured?"

This seemed to bring a discomfort to the child. The little girl squirmed, and shifted, trying to avoid eye contact. "He needs to be one," she said firmly, as if this were the answer to all of the questions pointed her way. "You can make him one. He needs to be one." With this, the child looked up, and then across at her companion. She hissed in recognition. "He should not be here. This is unjust, and not the way of things!" The childish voice had changed, and sounded much older, and wiser."

For his part, her companion looked around at her in complete amazement. "I didn't want to be here in the first place, I'd have you know." He retorted, upset by the sudden change of character, and drawn into a defensive stance.

The child hissed all the louder. "This is how it never should have been! This is a blasphemy, and should never happen again! Wrong, you are. Wrong!" Then a change of character came over the girl, as the child within her reasserted itself. "Are you here to help my father? He needs your help." She looked imploringly at them both, and the back to the old man, wretched and twisted in his own private agony that nobody could share. "He needs both your help." Leaving them stunned, and unsure what to say as a reply, the girl took the old man by one of his twisted hands, and led him into the doorway of the shop. "The beach calls you, you should respond," the child said to them as the door closed on whispered hinges.

"The beach calls us?" Ju echoed, perplexed.

She looked out towards the sea. A strip of yellow was visible as the hills closed in on the coast. "There is a beach over there, if only a sliver of one. Let's go have a look." They walked warily across to the sand, a distance that was perhaps a mile, though it seemed less. When they reached the edge of the sand, they looked back, and saw the village in the extreme distance, almost an impression on the horizon. They had walked much further than they thought. Turning back to the sea, they looked out on the waves to find that it had calmed to almost mirror sheen. If there had been any breeze before, it had disappeared now. Where the beach ended, the hills began, and there was a jumbled mess of wood everywhere. Crates and pallets stacked up in piles on the low slopes, and on them were growing many plants. If they realised that such a mess could have a purpose, they had no idea as to what that purpose was. All manner of plants grew out of pots, pans, helmets; anything in fact that could be used as a container had a plant in it. Fruit trees, vegetables in stunted terracotta vases. Flowers grew in patches, their blooms looking so out of place in such a surreal situation. But everything was on top of wooden pallets, as if each person had been allotted a space. The manic scene extended as far as the eye could see, all across the cove. The sand had not been touched by anything other than the sea, and this line of demarcation stood to separate the water from the line of plants that appeared to form a defensive wall against the water.

"This is strange," she said, as they walked the edge of the beach, looking at the plants, and the copious amounts of wrecked wood beneath.

"Strange? That is this season's understatement. This is downright weird, and it is not right. What did the girl mean that the beach calls us?" They stood and listened for a moment, expecting to hear the sound of the sea, or the wind. They heard nothing. "I don't like this." He said, looking her in the eye with the defiance of his youth. "I want to leave here."

She nodded her head in agreement, though he did not need that indication to start walking back. "Wait for me," she called, though she overtook him with merely a step. Their journey back to the village took them in many directions, and at different speeds. They could not keep together no matter what they tried. It was as if some entity was seeking to separate them by an act of force. However it could not complete the job, and they arrived, severely shaken and very confused back at the wagon, where the horse regarded them with the lack of interest that a draft horse was so apt to show. As one they turned and looked back towards the distant beach, which now did not seem nearly as far away as it once had. They looked at each other, stunned to muteness by the strange events happening to them. She looked down at him, mouth slightly open, and her head shaking as if she could not believe that she had been flung over the nearby countryside like some lost rag doll. Her hands shook as she raised them to lean herself on the cart, which was still full of the salvaged barrels and crates. She paid them no attention as she looked towards the shop they had entered before. There was a change. The spiders still filled the glass like a collection of angry old widows in their shawls, and the ledges outside looked ready to drop off from rot. "There is a difference, a character almost, or a consciousness." A feeling she had sensed in places before assailed her senses. It was a feeling both very recent, and brought back to her from a place long since visited. She did not know what it meant, but intended to find out. "Where did the girl and the old man go?" he mused, looking around, and instantly Zya knew what the shop was about.

"In the shop," she replied, "that is where he went, him and the girl both. We need to go in there also."

He looked a bit nervous, as he bravely said. "Let's get in there, and then maybe we will find a way out of this place." Leading the way, he opened the door, and nearly jumped out of his skin as the door yielded with a protesting shriek, clamouring to be left alone. Things had certainly changed. Forcing the door open wide enough to admit them both, he left it wedged amongst the rust of hinges that had not been oiled in a lifetime of use. The shop was as they had left it, but it was warmer, against the bleak cold of the day that had seemed to penetrate through its very walls when they had been in there before. They traversed the network of shelves, until they reached the dust-covered counter at the back of the shop. This had evidence of more recent doings. There were hand marks in the dust where somebody small had made a pattern with their fingers, and there were footmarks leading behind. He peered around the counter, and for his efforts was sent sprawling as a small fist connected with his jaw. The girl jumped out from behind the counter, and instantly she could see that the girl was the source of the difference. She was the same as before, but her eyes were rolled up in her head, giving her the semblance of some wild and unnatural creature. There was nothing unnatural about the way the girl moved though, for she was balanced on the balls of her feet with catlike agility, ready to spring. The feeling, the distant memories. They were all centred on this small character that appeared before them. "You should not be here!" The girl screamed, and then looked directly at her. "The gates aligned focus the mind to cross the bridge," she hissed in a low menacing voice. "Set me free. I must be set free!"

"I don't understand," Zya replied, though the girl barely seemed to be listening, so intent was the girl on her companion, who led there stunned. "How can I set you free? What must I do?"

"Free!" screeched the girl, and then preceded to do a silly little dance, wiggling her head about. "Free free free free free. Free us! Fulfil your destiny. Freeee us!" The girl pulsed, for there was no other word for it, and a wave of energy sent them both back to the doorway, skidding along the floor. The girl raised her face to the ceiling, and a purple glow erupted from within her. The girl yelled and the two companions let out a scream at the same instant. The light dropped outside, and the only thing that could be seen was the eerie glow of the light from far within the shop. A laugh was heard, and the ground rumbled beneath them. "The beach calls you." Said a sinister voice, and the floor beneath them liquefied. They felt it sucking at them, and they were drawn down into it, slowly, gradually. Then they were on the beach, but still sinking into the quicksand. As they watched, a river shaped itself about them, avoiding the quicksand as if it were anathema. The river actually seemed shaped by the presence of the sand. They clawed and pushed, but it only served to make them sink quicker. She panicked, letting out a yell, and he did the same. The sand closed up around her neck with the cold tingle of snow, and the pressure of mountains. Her last sight as she went under was of the girl running straight for her, purple light streaming from her eyes, and a maniacal laugh issuing from her mouth.

Zya coughed, retching imagined sand as she lurched upright, and then inhaled the deepest, sweetest breath of air that she could remember. Afraid to open her eyes, she felt around her. She was on a bed of some description, with a mattress underneath, and a comforter gently pressing down over her legs. She checked herself over with her hands. She felt cold, and numb somehow, but the warmth was returning rapidly, which came as a relief. "Welcome back to the world of the living, lass," said a voice that she did not recognise, though it had a familiar quality about it.

Risking her other senses, Zya opened her eyes, to be assaulted by sunlight from a distant window. Flinching, and protecting her eyes with her hand, she tried to get a look at the man that had spoken to her. She peered out past her fingers. The man was big; not fat-big, but muscle-big. As her eyes came into focus, she saw that he had a pair of the gaudiest green trousers she had ever laid eyes on, mismatched with a blue jerkin that sparkled, and was edged in lace. "Darrow? Where am I?" She asked, her normally smooth voice coming out of her mouth as a gravely croak.

"You are in my house, young lady, where you fell asleep an age ago."

"I must have lost it for a while. I don't remember coming to this place. What has happened to me?"

The large man sat down, exposing her to more sunlight. As Zya winced, and almost dived back under the covers, he realised the nature of her discomfort and closed the door firmly. "Do you not remember?" At a shake of her head he continued. "You collapsed outside the mercenary guild after uttering some pretty strange things, so I have heard. Your man and I dragged you back here and you have been asleep ever since. Your young friend has been here too, and he has been in exactly the same state as you. Your man hints that it may all be connected."

The memories and feelings hit her all at once. The boy, her 'man', the uneasy feeling she had been having. It all centred upon the rock of that building. "Ju? Lorn? Oh Gods, O'Bellah!" She screamed as the realisation hit her. "He is in this city! We must get out of here!"

Chapter Six

Darrow put his meaty hands on her shoulders, preventing Zya from getting up. "No lass, you aren't going anywhere yet. Not until you are fully recovered from your ordeal, and your man says you have to stay abed for a while after you wake, to recover your strength."

"He isn't my man," Zya said absently, though the phrase brought a warm feeling.

"Whatever," he replied. "You still can't get up, you are too weak."

"Nonsense, I feel as well rested as ever I have." Zya tried to reply with a defiant look in her eyes, but failed.

He shrugged. "I have no time to argue with you, girl. So be it, but don't say that I didn't warn you." He turned, and leaving the door ajar, left the room. Outside, Zya saw a glimpse of Yneris. Darrow passed her with a lingering touch to her arm. "She won't listen."

Yneris chuckled. "Just as they said that she wouldn't. Is she well?"

Darrow shrugged noncommittally. "Well enough to try and get up, but not well enough I think to be able to move more than a couple of steps, if she is strong and extremely fortunate."

Zya climbed out of bed in an attempt to prove them wrong, and abruptly proved them right by crashing to the floor as her legs gave way.

"Come, dear. Lets get you back into bed." Yneris cooed in her most mothering voice.

"I can't. I need to. . . you know. . ." Came her weak reply.

"Oh, yes I suppose you would."

The surprised look on Darrow's face was enough to tell a story as his wife came out of the room with Zya's arm draped around her shoulder.

"Move it you lump," Yneris ordered, and Darrow obeyed without hesitation. "What are you doing?"

"What do you think," she answered. "This girl has been asleep for the Gods only know how long and is weak as a kitten. She can't stand on her own, so what in the name of the ocean do you think I am doing? Help me take Zya upstairs, and while we are about it, go and check on the boy."

Darrow helped Yneris bundle Zya up the stairs and into the room. Ju lay there, motionless, although his visitors caused quite the reaction. "Zya is here?" he called.

"Yes I am here too, Ju." Her voice echoed around the halls.

"Well blow me down,." he said, a smile erupting like a sunrise on his face.

"Did not expect her, eh lad?" Asked Darrow. Zya sensed his obvious surprise, now mixed with relief.

In response, Ju shook his head absently, his eyes widening as he saw Zya. She frowned, implying that nothing was different.

"So how are we doing, my little sneak-thief?" Darrow said in a guffawing display of camaraderie.

"If I don't get out of this bed and to a privy, I'm gonna wet me britches, Captain Sir." He replied in his typical forthright manner.

"Well lets get you ship shape then, boy." Darrow scooped Ju up and carried him.

After their ablutions, Zya and Ju found themselves in the large room they had previously eaten in. Balancing ale, meats, cheeses, bread and a variety of sauces on several trays, Darrow and Yneris soon joined them with enough food to feed a family for a week.

"Ready for some food, me little darlin'?" Darrow asked of Ju. "Would you like me to feed you?"

"I can do it myself," the boy announced, full of insult and belligerence.

Levering himself up, Ju wobbled as he made his way to the table, beads of sweat standing out on his forehead. He made it though, and reached straight for the ale tankard. Taking a huge gulp, his face screwed up. "Pah. Eww."

"Too strong for you, young scamp?"

Ju looked up with a glance that would have put a child in its place. "No, Mr Captain sir, the ale has been watered down. How do you expect me to get better with this watery excuse?"

Darrow burst out laughing, slapping his hand on his thigh in mirth. "By the Gods you are a handful! One of your age should not be sampling strong ale!"

Ju stared steadily at him, showing tremendous patience and making Darrow think that he was missing something. "I grew up around an Inn. Do you think I would have spent all of that time there and not sampled ale? I could match you in a drinking contest."

"No you could not, whelp. Not in this house, not even in this city." Yneris was in the doorway, and had been watching this exchange. "You are lucky that you were not given goat's milk, and should be thankful for what you have got. Many go with much less, as you well know."

Darrow watched as his wife's words sunk in. Before the boy could retort, he added a comment of his own. "The lad was only jesting, go easy on him."

Yneris gave him a look that spoke as plain as daylight that she did not believe either of them for a second, and then left, her heels thumping on the steps as she walked downstairs. "I have sent for the father and the tribesman," she called from the kitchen, "they will be here presently."

Darrow sat down on a chair bed while Ju and Zya tucked into the food with an appetite that had been growing for a long time. "So what do you think of my beds and my house?" he asked, more for conversation than anything else.

"This is not your house." Ju answered around a mouthful of cheese. "You do not live here. It is not big enough for you. I would say that this is a front for something more."

"What makes you say that?"

"The size of the house." Ju mumbled as he stuffed a crust into his mouth, leaving barely any room for more food. "I went around the outside, and the rooms in here are much too small for the size of this building. I would say that you are not a trader, but a pirate, and this is your storehouse, nothing more."

"And I would say that you are a bit too clever for your boots lad, to be making wild accusations of me like that. Darrow replied, feigning insult. "Whatever I may be, I am certainly one to thank for keeping you here this long, and also, I will have you know, for helping to keep your lady friend here safe."

Ju attacked the remaining crusts and rinds. All in all, he ate just about everything that was put before him, and drank even more. "You look different." He observed of Zya as he pushed his plate away. "Yneris braided my hair to keep it tidy, which is a new look for me. I have never done this before."

"Keep it that way, dear. It suits you, and will not mark you out of place in this city." At a silent command, they were helped back into the bedroom by this oddest of couples. Ju was placed upon the foot of the bed, his bow still behind him, and apparently causing him no concern at all. He barely seemed to notice that it was there.

"I must thank you for all you have done for strangers, ma'am." Zya said with a respectful nod of the head. "I would ask one further boon of you if I may."

Yneris smiled. "Anybody who speaks so politely will surely be granted all the boons they like, my dear."

"I am most grateful. May young Ju and I be left alone to talk quietly until my father and Lorn arrive?"

"Absolutely," Yneris replied, "I am sure you have a lot of catching up to do. She prodded her husband out of the room before he was given a chance to leave. As the door was closed firmly, they listened to the ensuing conversation.

"When are you going to start wearing decent clothes again?"

"I am Darrow the pirate, and everybody expects me to wear the most outrageous finery there is available." Darrow sounded hurt.

120

"But do you have to wear it in such confined spaces, my love? There is enough of you as it is, and all this colour is giving me a headache. Go on with you, go and pack for the journey we must make. Return when our guests arrive and mayhap we can make more out of this situation than you have managed to make so far."

Watching the door as the couple left, Zya bade Ju be silent for a long while until she was sure that nobody was near them. She looked from the door to him, bidding him to ask the question.

He did not disappoint. "Where were we?"

"I have no idea," she replied. "Honestly, if I have ever been there, it was not in this life. I have never been in the sight of the sea until I came to this city, and we saw a lot of sea. I have certainly never been aboard a ship before. How much do you remember?"

Ju sighed. "I'm confused. I know that we salvaged a wrecked ship, and almost drowned in quicksand." He looked hesitant. "I know more than that, and you know exactly what I know, more or less."

"I think that I do, Ju. It is like we stumbled into the same dream from different perspectives. Do you remember anything about a storm?"

"No, do you of the barrels and crates we spent half a day heaving up?"

"No I do not, Ju. But I will never forget the girl. She reminded me of me."

Ju looked prophetic as he said, "The gates aligned focus the mind... Or something like that."

Zya paled as the words came back to hit her. "The beach calls you. Oh Ju, who was the old man?"

Ju looked angry for a second. "Forget the old man, the pirate captain that looked like a cat and smelled like its rear end. What were we doing? And what was I doing there?"

Zya looked into space for a moment, trying to comprehend what had started the chain of events that had brought her to this place, abed in a stranger's house, in an unknown place in the city. "O'Bellah is here."

"What? How can you be sure?"

"I just am. Something tells me so. He is here, now, in this very city. I don't know whether or not that is a coincidence. I am sure that he had been in or is currently in the large stone building that I had been passing by when the very rock had spoken out at me, causing what surely must have been a seizure."

No, it was not a seizure, she thought to herself. It was an opening of the mind, leading to events that she could recall. She thought back to all of the things she had learned from the old woman in the tribe. Listen to her feelings; trust her instinct above all else for it surely was right. Suddenly it all became clear. "I am becoming a seer!" Zya gasped, almost whispering the words reverently in the moment of her discovery.

"Congratulations." Ju said with a profound lack of respect. "Why was I dragged in there? I don't want to be part of dreams like that."

Selfish as he sounded, Zya could not help but feel sorry for the boy. She could well understand that such events could frighten him greatly, and he looked pale from the experience despite all the food and drink he had swallowed down. "I do not know, Ju. In all the history of the tribe, there has never been a male seer. I cannot believe that this will suddenly change, but every fibre in my being says that you were there for a reason, that there was a tie between us that even prophecy cannot cut. Ju, I was glad you were there." Zya stared so intently at him as she said this, that he was forced to avert his face from her dark-eyed gaze.

"What do we tell them?" He asked. "Do we tell them everything?"

Something warned Zya against this. "No. I have to keep some of this to myself."

"Don't you mean to *ourselves*?"

"You don't know all of the answers, Ju. That is for me to find out. The wise women of the tribes never gave out all the information. I am suspicious of those that keep their motives hidden. They serve the tribes, and aide them, but to what extent?" If what she had learned during her tenure with the wise woman in the tent of herbs and signs was correct, then this instinct came as naturally to her as it did to them. There was something more that eluded her senses, a feeling that there was something else that she needed to learn. It was not the embryonic power of a seer that warned her against telling all, but something else. Ju had shared her dreams, and despite it all would do whatever she asked of him. The boy was still visibly shaken, and would remain so for a very long time. "No, we need not tell them everything. There are issues that we need to work out for ourselves. Meanings we need to try and understand. We can tell them about the dream, and what we saw, for they will be interested. Even more so if you tell it, for something unusual has happened here, and I do not know how to deal with it as of yet."

"You mean to keep the words of the girl between us?" said Ju as he shifted his bow without conscious thought.

Zya looked down at her own dagger, knowing it to have an addictive magical quality. Were the weapons connected? Was there a link? She had been made aware that her dagger had some dangerous quality; perhaps the same was for the bow. Her father had never given her anything other than stories about where he got them from, and she had yet to hear a plausible explanation. "The words of the girl, yes. If what is happening here is as I think, they will listen to every word we say, and make a lot out of it." Zya realised that the words she spoke were overlaid with what could only be termed the conscious thoughts of the woman whose tent she had entered what seemed like an age ago. It was as if the seer were speaking through her mouth. Zya suddenly had the forewarning to realise that they would come for her, as they had come for many other girls that had become seers and wise women. She would not let them take her. "We need to figure out what it means."

"What it means? I'll tell you what it means. It means we have to get out of here before we drown, or get stabbed, or sucked into an abyss prepared for us by some cat faced pirate fish on a ship that will sink and then float off again." As Ju spoke of the dream, Zya could see every image as clearly as if it had already happened. "We do not know that any of that will ever happen, Ju, just that it might. I think this dream means a lot of things, but it does not mean that we are going to experience it at all. The Old Law says that we must listen to our hearts in this, and the ways of the wise women echo that, whatever their motives."

Ju looked unconvinced. He slipped his bow from his shoulder and shook it in his fist. "This is what I want to be, a hunter, not a seer. Even a thief in this city would be more fun."

"No it wouldn't." Zya's firm hand reached across to sit Ju down. "That is against everything the Old Law teaches us. To steal is one of the worst possible acts against another person, and the Old Law forbids it."

"The Old Law does not exist in this city." Ju argued, and Zya could feel the boy's frustration. "Merchants hold the sway here, merchants with money, and reason will gain you nothing without force."

Zya could see that the experiences that the boy had been having in this city were very different from her own. "Those things are what you should be concerned about, unless you want to stay here. Ju, we will leave this city eventually, and you know that well. Will you fall under the sway of the greedy and corrupt? I think not, and I know that you have the feeling you will move on because we shared that experience in our dreams. There is a higher power involved, I swear it. We were not meant to stay here." She leaned forward, taking one of his hands in her own, and implored him. "Please, Ju. Be a warrior some other day. Be my friend today. I am as scared of what is happening as you are, and I need somebody to help me through this. You are the only one that knows what this is like. Help me. Help me to find the answers."

Ju looked torn as he struggled with himself. "I have settled the most of all of us in Bay's Point, and would be prepared to call this place home after the waxing and waning of only one moon."

"You are young, and really the most adaptable. I am envious of the fact that you have had only had a few places to call home. I myself have been on the move around the central and western Duchies for as long as I can remember. I have never had a place to call my own. My home has been a collection of people rather than a house or a town. I am definitely not comfortable in the city, but can appreciate that you are definitely not the same as me." There was a kindred spirit, and both of them knew it. Something bound them together. Something indefinable that had drawn them into an unconscious reality on more than one occasion, showing them wonders, and scaring them beyond the capacity for rational thought, leaving them running with nothing other than the basal instinct for self-preservation driving their flight. That something had also kept them together and alive, and it was that indefinable quality that she hoped would influence Ju enough to help him make the right decision. He looked calmer, as if something within the boy becoming a man had been decided. "I will always be your friend, Zya. And I will always go with you." He said the last with regret on his face, but he had said it, and she knew that he would hold to it no matter what the cost. Zya reached forward and hugged him in relief. It was good that they had reached this decision without outside influence. "So what do we do now? Do we leave the city?" So resigned to his fate. "I assume that we will leave as soon as is safe."

Zya shook her head. "No. There is something that we need to find out here. When I first met you, back in Hoebridge, we had gone to the councillors and spoken to them about many things. One was the so-called 'Mayor', O'Bellah. They said that from time to time he disappeared, leaving lackeys spying on them. I am wondering if this is the place he visited, and if so, why. It may be that this is the reason for coming here, to find out what is up, or it may just be me. This is not a coincidence."

Ju looked up with disinterest. "I had heard people in the inn talk of him, but I did not know the man. I had never even seen him. Was he bad?" The innocent look on Ju's face served to remind Zya that he was still a boy, and it had not been more than three quarters of a season since they had first met. So much had happened to them all during that time that it was hard sometimes to remember that not that much time had actually passed.

In answer to his question, Zya responded tactfully. "I felt something about him, a feeling that was not right. It began in the council hall of Hoebridge, and as we travelled away, I felt it spreading through the very land. It was not what could be called bad, or evil, but it was wrong. I felt the very same thing when I beheld that building before I collapsed. It triggered something in me I think. Did you feel anything before you fell asleep?"

"I don't know," Ju shrugged. "I may have felt funny, but I was tired, and so I slept. How long did I sleep for?"

"I cannot say." She replied. "Let us wait for my father and Lorn to arrive, and then I am sure that we will get more answers."

It did not take long for Tarim to arrive once he heard the news. As true as he typically was, Tarim took Darrow at his word and left Zya alone, knowing that as far as Lorn was concerned they could do nothing. That did not mean that he was worried, but he threw himself into a frenzy of work, leaving himself exhausted at the end of each day. The commoners were appreciative, for he always finished each piece to perfection, be it the most intricate carving or the tiniest spoon handle. Work was the only way that he could channel his energies. Lorn on the other hand, skulked and brooded around the smithy he fletched arrows in. He was afraid for Zya. Not only did she have the mark of the seer on her, bringing the strange dreams and all that followed, but also he was afraid that the wise women, with their strange connections, would appear and whisk her off without him even being able to say goodbye. Thus did he abide by his own advice to stay away, but he would forever find himself tasks that involved passing through that area of the city, so that he could at least feel that he was near her. But upon receiving the news that the two had awoken, both men near-ran to the bakery, from which the same man guided them. Once Tarim had asked the guide why they still needed him when they knew the way.

The man had looked at him steadily, pausing in his stride. "Fir yer own safety." He had said in a coarse accent that spoke with the voice of another region entirely. "Iff'n ye try and go there alone, ye will be shot down afore taking two steps." The man had said nothing more, but had guided them faithfully to the house. Lorn judged that so many of the twists in the warehouse district were just rat-traps, designed with the sole purpose of baffling an enemy while archers took them out from the copious metal-reinforced windows that were shuttered around above them. He suspected that the roofs were flat also, but the streets were so narrow and the houses loomed so close that it was impossible to tell from down in the murk. Tarim meanwhile was just intent on one thing. Zya was the core of his life, and his sole reason for being. He just wanted to get to her, and see that she was recovered. Upon entering the house, he uncharacteristically bypassed all

125

welcome from Darrow and Yneris, forgoing their greeting understandably, and charging to the room that contained his daughter. When he entered, he found the room to be empty.

"If you would just wait a second and hear what we had to say, you would know that your daughter is elsewhere." Said Darrow from the hallway. The pirate then indicated the room that they had previously sat in with a nod of his head.

"My apologies, to both of you." Tarim replied with a bow. "It is most unseemly for a guest to abuse the polite intentions of his hosts and I beg your forgiveness."

"Think nothing of it," Yneris replied. "It is well that you think of your daughter in such a way. Much that has happened we know little of, and we would be as worried as you are."

Tarim smiled a silent thank you at her, and hurried to the room.

"Are you not going in there too, lad?" Darrow asked Lorn, who had edged closer, but not actually stepped in.

"I don't want to crowd them," he said by way of explanation.

"Go on, there is plenty of space."

As Lorn entered, Tarim was checking over Juatin. Zya looked radiant, visions of prophecy filling her eyes, and exuding an air of untapped power, raw authority in the making. She smiled at him when he looked at her, and he approached, relieved. The young woman he had known before was still there, but augmented in some way by a power that was hundreds of generations in the making. He dropped to one knee, and looked up into her eyes. "If I had known that this would happen. . . " Lorn was lost for words.

"You would have never brought me here in the first place," she finished for him, and he was not sure if that was the thing he had meant to say, but it seemed to fit his sentence. "That would not do," she continued. "I would have come here anyway. This was destined to happen, I can see it now."

"But. . ."

"Lorn, it would have happened whether we had come here or not. The place was a coincidence, but the time would not have changed. That much I can see from my experience."

"So it is true then?" her father asked. "You have become a seer?"

Zya thought for a moment, seeking the answers inside. "No, not by a long shot. I am on the path, but it does not feel right with me. There is something else that needs to temper the visions. Something that I need to seek with in this city. I still do not know what it is."

This concerned Lorn. "You know that you will not be able to remain here. The wise women will come for you."

"They will not." Zya countered, her voice full of authority. "They have already taken me in, back in the tribal gathering."

"But. . . that only happens." Lorn could only think of one thing. "That only happens to girls that have already had a vision."

"This was not your first, was it my daughter?" Tarim saw straight to the heart of the matter.

Zya shook her head. "No, nor was it my second. This was the third time this has happened to me, and the second time that Ju has been involved."

This was news to Lorn, who was ignorant of any of these facts until now. "But how. . . when. . ?"

"The first time I had a dream of this magnitude it scared me half to death." Zya admitted. "That was the dream that I had before we left the caravan, and met you. The second dream was while I was in the tent of the seer, the first time that I shared a dream with Ju." Zya looked over at her young friend with sympathy for his plight and admiration for his grown-up way of dealing with it. "We have no idea why he has begun to share the visions, but we have hope. The point is that no wise women are coming to whisk me off because if you recall I was gone for quite a while."

"And you were vastly changed when you came out of that, I noticed." Tarim observed.

"Yes, and though things were different, I managed to find my way back to myself," Zya said with a smile. "If I was born to be a seer then that is where I would be right now, though I think that my path of dreams is different to the others. There is something that needs to be done, and yet I do not know what."

"Do the dreams show the way?" It was Darrow, who entered with a tray loaded with food, Yneris following closely behind with tankards and a huge jug of ale.

"Maybe, if I could find the right road to tread," Zya answered. "So far, they have had little obvious meaning."

"But I had heard that the seers of the North were able to predict events." Darrow persisted.

"Maybe the dreams show future events," Zya responded vaguely. "I can tell you that from the dreams that I have had recently, little is meaningful. Whether or not the dreams have a purpose has yet to be decided." Zya looked over at Ju, who stood up bravely, becoming the focus of the room.

"We were on a pirate ship, and it became wrecked. The captain stank, and had a face like a cat. We salvaged goods and took them to a village with no people in it and monsters attacking a guildhall." Ju's description of the dream was accurate, but it left out many key facts. Zya smiled in approval. She wanted time to digest the meaning, to understand what it was she was supposed to take from such a vision with her into the world of waking.

"A face like a cat." Said Darrow, deep in thought. "I have never heard of such a man, if one exists." He looked at Yneris, who shook her head doubtfully. "Are you sure that was what was in the dream?"

"I am sure, but who is to say that the fact has any truth? I am new to this, and a mere fledgling in the art of picking out the meaning from a dream. It could be that the point of the dream was obscure, and had nothing to do with a pirate at all."

Darrow looked unconvinced. "I think there was more to that than you let on."

"Perhaps, but why would you care? You have been kind to us, but I don't even know you. Who are you, and what does piracy have to do with you?" Once more, introductions were made, but this time nothing was left out. At some unspoken command from Yneris, she was introduced as the captain and Darrow as her subordinate. They held no obvious information back, and Darrow concluded with the one statement that Ju had known all along. "This is not actually our house, but the front for a warehouse."

"I knew it!" Ju nearly jumped out of his chair.

Darrow laughed, as did the others. "Well I suppose that we should show you what we mean by this being only the front. Are you two up to a walk yet?"

Zya stood, expecting to have little strength, but the food and drink she had taken had worked wonders on her. She felt as fit and alive as ever she had. "I think I am better, how about you Ju?"

The boy jumped to his feet, almost unable to contain himself. "I can't wait to see this."

"All right then," Darrow said in response. "Now bear in mind I do what I do because I think that we have some mutual interest here, and this will hopefully show an element of trust from our side. You have done well to trust us on the mere fact that I know Lorn's father, now we shall trust you to that same measure." Darrow opened the door from whence he had brought the ale, and beckoned them in. The room was not large, but there was space enough for all six of them. Closing the door and locking it from within, Darrow pressed against a section of the wall. With a click and a rumble, the wall detached and rolled to one side, opening up a passage for them.

"Come on, in you lot." Ordered Yneris. "Time and tides wait for no man."

They entered the corridor, which was lit periodically with lanterns. On both sides of the passage were doors at intervals. They bypassed many of the doors as they walked.

"What is behind these?" asked Tarim, peering closely at one door etched in gold.

"Death traps." Yneris replied. "Behind every door there is something, and they are enabled or disabled on different days, so that the true entrance is only known to a few. I would not touch *that* particular door if I were you. Not today." She led them to a drab wooden door with a faded brass handle, and twisted the handle one way and then the other. The door creaked open slowly, resisting her push. They stepped inside. A series of counterweights hung behind the door, and off to one side, a selection of the cruellest looking spears were primed to burst out of what could only be described as an immense crossbow.

"Ouch," said Ju, referring to the spears.

"Ouch indeed, lad," agreed Darrow. "Only once have I ever seen these things used, and it was not a pretty sight. The poor soul took a short while to die, but was in the most extreme agony. Most of his guts were back in the hallway, on the end of the spears. It was an accident that did this to him, as the fool did not know the right door."

"Thus do we make sure we know the right path before we set our feet upon it," concluded Yneris.

"A wise move indeed," agreed Lorn, who had been content until now to watch and listen. "But is it such a wise move on your part to take us any further? You and my father had good reason to disagree. What you may show us here is exactly the sort of thing frowned on by the rules that we live by."

"Truer words have never been spoken, young archer." Yneris conceded, getting echoes of agreement from her husband. "We do have good cause to show you this, despite your concerns. If you will be patient with us, we will try to explain it. Mayhap you will look upon us differently in a while." Yneris spoke no more then, but led them through the room and down a set of stairs to another hallway, this one lit much more brightly by chandeliers. It was an oddly ostentatious touch in an otherwise drab building. Down one more set of stairs, and then they reached a doorway.

Darrow reached for the handle, and turned. "They will see you enter with us, so you will be safe. Come through here on your own, and you would be dead before you had a chance to cry out." Opening the door, he added, "Welcome to the real warehouse district." They all stepped through, and exclaimed astonished gasps at what faced them. If it could be called a room, then it was an understatement. A cavern was closer to the mark, a great dark maw that seemed to stretch out to infinity, shadows endlessly chasing the smoky lights used to keep the place lit. Every so often pillars buttressed the ceiling, and stacked everywhere were crates. Some were so large that they themselves held crates, like a great wooden anthill the place stretched out, making a maze of pathways.

"You will not be able to see far, for we are still at ground level. Climb these stairs for a better look." Darrow led them up a staircase onto a gantry that crisscrossed the room, and from this point they could see that everything was organised. Off to the east, daylight spilled in, and two huge gates could be seen. Just in front of them a couple of ships were moored. The ships looked more like merchantmen than anything a pirate would use.

"You have an underground marina?" Said Tarim in an astonished voice.

"That is not all," said Darrow, proud as a father of everything that he surveyed. "We have another room almost the same size on the far shore."

"And all this." Lorn waved his hand around, indicating the countless crates. "This is your plunder, gathered and collected over the years?"

"No." Darrow said this with a lot of emphasis, but it appeared to Zya he was bordering on the insulted. "I will admit that a small portion of this has been claimed and stored as a result of piracy, but most of what you see here has come from honest traders, both within the city, and from inland. It goes from here by night to places all over the Nine Duchies, from as close as villages down the coast to Caighgard and as far away as coastal Pahrain, away down south. This is where the real trading goes on, not up there in the city. The real rulers of Bay's Point are down here, amongst the crates, sitting on a throne of wood. Come, let me take you amongst them."

They made their way back down the stairs, and wound gradually through the enormous cavern. Water, and the God's only knew what else dripped down from the ceiling, but most of the crates were proofed with tar, so that their contents would not be spoiled. As they walked, various people called out to Darrow and Yneris, introducing themselves with friendly handshakes and back slaps to all.

Lorn dropped back beside Zya as they followed this strange path.

"I was afraid of what I would see in your eyes when I entered the room."

"That why you held back?"

"I have seen it before, too many times. If what I have guessed is correct, then you will inevitably be taken away from me one way or another."

"Lorn, the wise women will not arrive. I won't seek to join them."

So strong was her destiny, she knew this would never happen.

"I will just have to make the best of the time that we do have." He was not listening. Zya ignored his moping and watched the scenery unfold. This was a side of the city that Zya would never have known about, and the closeness of the community only served to remind her that she should never judge a book by its cover, or indeed a city by its inhabitants. From the tales she had been told about the history of the city, it seemed that Bay's Point was still in some ways a decoy. The rough and tumble surface hid well the thriving community beneath. Eventually they reached an office that had been built near the centre, a 'throne-room' of wood and tar, where the Lords of the underworld could look out on their empire of goods. Here they entered, Darrow providing refreshment by grabbing a cask of ale on the way up, and broaching it with his fist. This time, Ju managed to get himself a full tankard of proper ale, a fact that caused him no end of joy.

After they had settled, Tarim started talking. "So you are in effect merchants."
Darrow made a conciliatory gesture with his ale tankard. "More or less."
"And you obviously make a profit from your endeavours."
"Always, though not as much as you might think, not recently."
Tarim raised an eyebrow. "How so?" He asked this cautiously. Zya felt that they were reaching a sensitive subject.
"Okay, so you would realise that we do not follow the Old Law here in the city, yes? Things are different in this world, names we give things, opinions we have. A moon to you is a month to us for example."
"There is never a problem with having an opinion." Tarim conceded, leaning forward with interest, his chin resting on his fist as he tried to guess where this was going.
"Right," Darrow replied. "See the thing is, there are some amongst this population, those living above, that will not demean themselves by coming down here and working 'honestly' with the rest of us. They seek to change things. They seek to make everybody pay their prices, for a protection, or so they call it."
Now Zya's interest was piqued. "Who are these people?"
"The current Duke, and his cronies. They believe that because they are descended from the original pirates, that they have every right to call the shots around here. We do not see it that way, but they are making moves in the city to try and force not just us, but the farmers and villagers inland to accede to their wishes, and it looks like they are using force."
"O'Bellah." Zya said out loud.
"What? Here?" Her father turned to her. "How do you know?"
"It all ties in, father."

131

Tarim held up his hands, begging the pace of the conversation to slow. "What do you mean, it all ties in. We seem to have leaped to a conclusion without any meaning."

Zya smiled. She loved to confuse her father. "When I passed out, we were looking at a building, a huge, grey building like a monster built out of rock. I felt something there, and the sensation was exactly the same as the feeling that I got when we were in Hoebridge, of the wrongness that we connected with this man and his doings. The very same feeling that I could sense spreading, and crossing the countryside behind us."

"That is right." Darrow agreed. "The building that your daughter collapsed beside, aside from being the worst possible place for her to cause an outcry, is the mercenary guild. But who is this O'Bellah? Zya you screamed his name once before, care to enlighten us?"

Zya sighed, remembering the ill feeling she got from even hearing the man's name. "He is somebody we have heard of, but never met. He had all but enslaved a town back in the foothills of Ciaharr, by the headwaters of one of the tributaries to your great river. He might be a wizard; we are not sure on that one. He does have some kind of power, and a lot of influence, for I have seen evidence. There is a great wrongness associated with anything that he does, and even now I can feel it permeating the land, stretching forth like mystical fingers through the mud and stone." Zya had lapsed into a dreamy state, almost whispering as she spread her consciousness further afield. She was not even aware that she was doing this, and nothing was obvious to anyone else in the room, except that Zya was acting strangely. "The wrongness has followed us, sometimes at a distance, sometimes closer. The closest that I have been to his machinations was when we stood outside that great stone building, that monolith of dark stone, your mercenary guild."

Darrow snorted at the mention of them. "Man they are like a private army in there, and it is nigh on impossible to get anybody inside to find out what they are up to. But that does not mean that they are without resource. Any other place than where we brought Zya would have resulted in certain death. They are very wary of outsiders."

"Outsiders? But I thought that everybody in your city knew each other?"

"For the most part we do, but more recently there have been those coming in that nobody knows, and nobody has had a chance to talk to," Darrow admitted, looking at his wife for reassurance.

She gave it. "Mercenaries. The building that Zya collapsed beside is the mercenary guild, and nobody gets in there unless they are trusted completely by the guild heads. They are up to something though, and while we may not follow your Old Law of the countryside, we know that it is conducive to business that we appreciate those that do. Which brings us to the heart of the matter."

"You want us to help you." Said Zya, cutting through the preamble. "You want us to defend your ships with arrow and sword, and the same for the villages inland. But you don't want anybody to know about it. Why?"

The pirate couple looked at each other, knocked by the fact that Zya had seen straight to the heart of it, bypassing any subtle words they could have possibly used to make it sound more ambiguous than they had already.

Yneris raised her hands briefly in defeat. "Your perception does you credit, young woman. We are trying to keep this quiet because we don't know whom to trust. For generations the entire population of the city was trustworthy; we knew all of the merchants, and all of their families. But as trade routes improve, there are merchants coming in that we have never encountered before, charging outrageous prices, and demanding that we match them. They are trying to bleed the Duchy dry. Any merchant with sense knows that there is a fine line between making a profit, and reducing a person to poverty. We are merchants, not thieves. These merchants hire the mercenaries to bully the countryfolk, but that is only the half of it. There are too many in the mercenary halls now. Something is up and we are looking to protect our interests. You are the best hope of doing that. Anything that might give us an advantage should be grabbed with both hands, and held on to for dear life. Do you not agree?"

Zya nodded. She could not argue with their logic, followers of the Old Law or not. "So was I right? Is that what you want of us?"

Darrow nodded cautiously. "Yes, that is what we want."

"You know that the Old Law forbids violence of this sort."

"We are not in Old Law country any more, my dear Zya. Different rules apply in the city, and you should follow the local customs should you not?"

This brought a frown to her face. "No, I do not believe that we should. The Law that we follow is more than a set of rules, ready to be cast aside at the first convenient time. It is a way of life, living in harmony with those around you, and respecting the laws of nature. Violence in this form is prohibited."

"Ah, but is it not also true that you can use violence to defend yourselves when attacked?" Darrow replied, showing evidence of his insight into the very tenets that she defended. "Are we not protecting our ships and wagons in the very same way that you would protect your own?" He had her there, and she knew it. Her face flushed as she thought of a response, but none was forthcoming. "So what do you say?" Darrow's question was aimed at Tarim, identified by the pirate as the leader of their unusual little group, and to a lesser extent Lorn, who obviously would have the archers' skills of his tribe to call upon, or so Darrow supposed. To their surprise, Tarim deferred to his daughter.

"No, not at this time. Something tells me that we cannot do this, for it will alter our path, and the road that we tread is very precarious." A funny feeling passed over Zya. She shook her head to clear it and found Ju to be speaking. He had spoken as if possessed, but his words came out as if they were her own. Pausing for a second, he jumped visibly, and then his eyes focussed and he came back to himself. He looked around at them. "What?"

"What did you just say, lad?"

"I didn't say anything. I fell asleep listening to you lot arguing over archers and wagons. Why? What did I miss?"

"You just told us that you could not help us."

"And he was right, we can't," interjected Zya,. "at least not for now. There is something that we need to do, and we need to be topside in the city to do it. I do not know what it is, but I have to trust my feelings on this."

"Here, in the middle of our kingdom, you would deny us?" He bellowed.

Zya remained resolute in response. "You cannot decide what has already been decided. You cannot force a nomadic tribe that follows the Old Law to wage war on mercenaries with no cause but protecting goods for profit. The same stands with us. There is something that I need to do here, and I do not know what it is. All that I do know is I will not be able to do it acting as a guard on a caravan. If I had wanted that I would have remained with Venla."

"You may yet, Zya. They are in the region."

"What?" Zya, her father and Ju said the same word almost together. "How do you know?"

"I received word from acquaintances in the quarter."

Zya spared a thought for the motherly matriarch of the caravan her father; Ju and herself had rode away from back in earliest autumn, hoping that she fared well. "Chances are that things may yet change, and we will be able to ride one of your great ships, using our skills to make it safely to the end of its journey, but that time is not now. You must let us continue with our lives until that has passed." Zya glared at Darrow, and let her gaze fall on Yneris, dripping with sincerity. Every fibre of her being cried out to fulfil tasks that she had no idea about. Something needed releasing, something was chasing them, something awaited them, nothing was clear.

"What makes you so sure that we could help you anyway?" Piped up Ju, who had been content until now to absorb the surroundings, evidently much more at home in the shadows below than the street-gloom above.

"Lad, you are the four most unique and interesting characters to enter this city in years. Pirates, merchants, guildsmen. That is all anybody seems to be. And here you lot come, with your archery, nomad tracking, psychic abilities and magic, and I have already told you that people will sit up and take notice." Zya met her father's eyes as Darrow mentioned the word 'psychic', and he returned a glance that spoke volumes. His face read like a book. *He does not know what he means, but attempts to impress with grand words and flowery descriptions.* He had always said that their family had a broad streak of cynicism, and it had saved their skin on many occasions. Zya was sure that her father's description of the gaudily dressed mate and his unassuming and exquisitely polite pirate captain wife were the same as hers: They were honest for their part, but as with most people, they had a hidden agenda. Mayhap the unmasking of that agenda was what they were here for, she just did not know. "Well what is past will be left there," Tarim answered. "We don't want to disappoint you, and you have my eternal thanks for all you have done, but we need to find the answers in our own way, in our own time. However, if there is anything that we can do for you in the meanwhile you have but to name it." Darrow sighed, as if defeated, though Yneris looked as stolid as always she did. "Never mind. We can but try. Well if you are offering, my friend, then I would ask that you keep a line of communication open between yourself and me via the lad here. He has the quickest set of feet I have ever seen." "And getting quicker every day, now I know of your massive warehouse." Ju answered with a knowing grin. "I bet there are many other exits from this place, all of which would make transversing the city a hell of a lot easier than running twisted streets." "Damn the boy *is* good." Darrow exclaimed. "This was not an entirely wasted effort. I am sure that we can find someone to show you the ways around the underground." Ju jumped up at this. "How soon? There's no time like the present." This caused Zya to laugh out loud. When she had gathered a breath she spoke. "You are becoming more like my father every day, my foster brother. Now you are even talking like him." Ju looked around at Tarim, finding a rare smile on the man's face. So stern in demeanour, it was a rare thing that broke that façade. At this time, he looked less like the warrior Zya suspected that he was, and more like a proud father. Darrow's answer to Ju's request was much more direct. At an approving nod from his wife, he stepped to the door of the office and opened it. "JENNI!" Zya was sure that the doorframe rattled as he bellowed. Shortly, soft feet were heard on the steps up to the room, and a slight girl with red hair in curls entered. She had a face like a little mouse; shy and yet inquisitive with brown eyes that were framed by her hair like a portrait. She wore a dark brown dress with green patches, all earthy colours that made her seem to fit in just fine under the city. She was older than Ju, but not by much. It was her height that gave her away, as it was common that girls sprouted before the boys, especially in the North. She had that fresh-faced look of youth, but there was no naive gaze of a cozened girl about her. She radiated an aura of self-confidence. Zya knew that nobody else would be able to pick up on the characteristics of the girl, but Ju had already taken to her. They had struck up a conversation almost as soon as she had entered the room, and had to be interrupted by Yneris.

"Jenni, would you please be so kind as to show Ju the hidden entrances to the underground, as he will be doing a little work for us."

"A little work, eh," Jenni spoke, and instantly revealed maturity beyond her years, and a strength that belied her slender frame. Zya was amazed that she could deduce all of that from just a few words, but she was sure of it, just as she was sure that she could read the character of every person in that room. The fact that she could actually do that at all dawned much more slowly on her, and she had to grip the window ledge to steady herself. Nobody seemed to notice, their attention taken by Jenni, but Ju glanced across at her, a look of concern in his eyes. He knew. How did he know? Zya returned a barely perceptible shake of the head, and he turned his attention to the red-haired girl by his side.

"Is that all?" Jenni clearly expected something else, but nothing was forthcoming. Jenni glanced around the room, her eyes lingering on Zya for a moment longer than anybody else, or rather on the dagger at her side. As the girl exited with a wave and a 'come on then' noise to Ju, Zya's hand went protectively to her hip. The dagger felt reassuring, despite the fact that it carried a curse of addiction. Zya had been trained to see though the illusion of addiction, but the dagger was still a gift from her father and therefore immensely precious to her. The fact that somebody so young could covet something that belonged to her was unnerving. Then Zya came to her senses. She gave herself a mental slap as she reminded herself of who she was. Not a city-dweller with possessions, but a traveller at heart, a nomad whose only worldly goods were the clothes on her back and the shoes on her feet. As Ju exited the room behind the girl, he gave the bow on his back a touch, and this simple act reminded Zya that although she had been given the opportunity to see through the curse that masked her weapon, the boy had not. Soon she would find time to try and make him see this, and to question her father on where he had gotten the weapons. It may be that there were more of them, and others shared this compulsion too. There was only one thing that she wanted right now though, and that was fresh air. "Can we go back above ground?" She asked, desperation creeping into her voice.

"Don't you like it under here?" Yneris asked. At a puzzled look from Zya she continued. "A fear of confined spaces, especially the underground, and you would definitely have that in such a place as this, even if it is wide open."

"I have never gotten used to this city." Zya admitted.

"Ah don't worry lass, it all takes time," Darrow reassured her. "We will get you out of here and back to the city if that is what you wish."

Zya caught Lorn's eye, and she could see from his face that he shared her sentiment. She turned to face Yneris and her husband. "I know our paths will cross again, sooner than we may think perhaps, but for now, I would ask that you grant us the freedom to find the answers that we still seek."

Tarim and Lorn agreed with nodding heads. "When the time comes, we will do for you what we can." Tarim said with a handshake to the pirate.

"I will ask my father, if I can get word to him." Lorn promised. "But you know him well, and the tribe is his main concern."

"That is all we ask of you, lad," Darrow replied. "The Gods willing we are wrong, and overcautious. Something is not right here."

"If I may suggest something." Interjected Yneris. "I feel that it might be useful to pool information from time to time. We know this city better than anybody, and you seem to be dragging incident after incident wherever you go. It might help us."

"That it might," affirmed Tarim. "We would want to know about that guild at the very least, and how we could get somebody inside."

"Leave that to us," Darrow replied. "There are many ways to gut a fish, as they say over the water. We will find out if there is indeed a problem. It may turn out that we need nobody's help at all."

"And where would that leave us?" Lorn asked.

Darrow boomed a laugh out loud. "Lad, I really need to speak to your father, get him to tell you a few things. I owe your family more than a dozen lifetimes could repay. This is the least that I could do, isn't it my lovely?" With that he looked at his wife, who just smiled. Zya just could not accept that she was the captain and he the first mate.

They left the pirate couple to their business, finding themselves escorted back to the surface by the same man that had guided Tarim and Lorn already. They skirted through the house, and the warren of narrow streets that

137

guarded it. This was all new to Zya, who felt unease at walking so fast so quickly after her enforced slumber. They eventually ended back up in the bakers, and from the view onto the street Zya recalled exactly where she was, and shuddered at the thought of the alleyway and what it led to. There were tables and chairs in the bakery, despite its lack of room, and some of these were free. "Will you take a hot cup of something with us?" Tarim asked of their escort.

"Ahm, sorry pal, but I cannae stop fer pleasantries." The man replied with a grin that was more toothless than anything else. "Ahv got work tae do. But iffn ye come back to the boss, I'll be here tae guide ya's." And with a brief shake of hands the man disappeared out the back of the bakery.

"The strangest accent." Lorn observed as he sat down with cakes and the hot bitter drink preferred by the city folk. "I just can't place it."

"It's Qua'Cliran." Tarim replied.

"You have been there?"

Tarim sipped at his drink, giving nothing away. This was one of those times when Zya saw her father at his most evasive. "Let's just say that I have known a few of the islanders in my time, and leave it at that." He clearly did not want to be probed any more on the subject, and Lorn was too honourable to pursue the matter.

Zya had her own questions. "Try this one then, father. How long was I asleep for?"

"Ten long days, my daughter." Tarim replied, his dark eyes piercing hers, as if to search for answers in the hidden depths of her mind. "I hope that it will not always be like this."

Zya shrugged, considering the time well worth it if it would give them any sort of an advantage, even if she could not yet see the path. "No, I do not think that it will ever last that long again. The worst is over."

"Is that what they told you during your teaching?" Lorn popped the question suddenly.

"I could not answer that question Lorn, as you well know. You will not get an answer out of me with clever timing." She looked at him, a challenge in her eyes. He would accept that challenge without a doubt. There were interesting times ahead. Biting into her cake, she was pleasantly surprised to find honey dripping out amongst the sesame seeds that were contained therein. "Oh my favourite, thank you both."

Tarim smiled, the first unforced smile of pure pleasure she had seen from him since her awakening. It was a reassurance to say the least.

"We had them made for you. We have had cause to be in and out of this bakery a fair bit of late, and we have come to know the baker." At the word 'baker', a huge man turned around from behind a counter. It was the same man that had bellowed at them when they blocked the street. He gave a grin and a wave to Tarim and Lorn and continued about his business. "He has certain ah... 'enterprises' that are common with our pirate friend shall we say." Her father looked around in case anybody was listening, but they were alone as they could be in a crowded shop. People minded their own business when in this place.

"Right. Tell me what we are going to do about Venla and the others." Zya's tone of voice changed and her face took on a serious mien.

"I don't know too much, except that they are nearby."

"Nearby where? A league? A hundred?"

"To the south of the river, maybe ten or twenty leagues. They have been spotted by tribal trackers."

"Are they safe?"

"They are moving in funny directions, as if they are looking for something. That is all I know. Do you want to go to them?"

"No, I think not. The time is not right. At least they are near should we need to find them. That is a comfort."

They finished up, and after quickly thanking the baker, and accepting a basket full of the cakes, which incidentally had begun a new craze in that part of the city, they made their way very indirectly back to the tribal quarter of the city.

"Will your father help Darrow?" Zya asked of Lorn as they passed down a boulevard that was far too sparsely populated for anyone to overhear them. "It is hard to say," he admitted, "since I do not have the slightest clue as to why he would suddenly want members of a nomadic tribe that spends their life in a climate ten times as cold as this to up roots and aid merchant wagons. It may be that there is a hidden message in there somewhere, and if so, that is between him and my father. He has done enough to convince me that he is genuine, and he knows things about the tribal chief that only the closest of friends could have known."

"The problem seems to stem from that mercenary guild." Tarim mused as he walked. "If what you say about O'Bellah is correct, and he has had dealings with mercenaries, this could spell trouble."

Zya snorted and shook her head, hair flying out behind her in the breeze. "All this trouble from a man that we have never met."

"And do not ever want to meet, judging by your reactions," Lorn observed.

"Well that is just wishful thinking," she replied, her voice full of disdain, unwilling to admit to them that she was sure a meeting was in the offing. "Our paths have almost crossed too many times already."

"Do not worry yourself needlessly, Zya." Said her father from in front. "If it is meant to be then it will happen."

"It is the nature of such a meeting that worries me, father." She admitted. "Would we rather come upon such a man in the middle of a city, or in the wilds, where we could not escape him?"

"I think that the wilds would be an easier place for us to escape, unless he has my level of tracker's knowledge," Lorn replied.

"It won't help." Zya said ruefully. "Either he is a magician, or he has access to one for I can feel his passing in the very rock beneath our feet."

"The stories never told of any wise woman feeling the travelling of any one person before." Lorn said this after a pause, showing he had been giving it careful consideration.

"Maybe you just never heard the right stories," Zya replied, knowing that he was fishing for information. She had been taught that the wise women held themselves apart from the tribe more or less, but only now was she realising just how different first hand access to such a person, albeit a novice was for Lorn. "Look I will tell you this. Tribal seers dream to see their way. None have ever seen what I see. That is why I think there is more to be learned. That much is safe to say because it has never happened before."

Lorn stopped in his tracks. The street loomed around them, closing in towards one end as the boulevard narrowed to a point where the houses crowded together once again. Tarim walked on, and then realising that there was nobody beside him, also stopped and turned around. "What is it?"

"We must be very careful in guiding your daughter, Tarim," Lorn said quietly. "She may be more than just a novice seer."

"What do you mean?" Zya asked, curious, and not a little afraid by Lorn's ominous tones.

"We heard a story once of a seer who could do more than just dream. She was the one that led a portion of the tribe to their doom inside the boundary that marks the edge of the Raessan enchantment. They were all lost, because they believed in her dreams."

"You seem to have heard a lot of stories. Hang on a second," Zya argued, "how do you know that I am anything like that? What does this all have to do with me?"

Lorn walked to the side of the street, away from any passers by. Zya and her father followed closely. "She claimed to have followed the path of somebody she could sense. A man that had been plaguing our tribe, trying to remove any that claimed a magic of sorts. The man they long ago called the Witch Finder. He lived in Raessa, and claimed every man and woman that was caught in his trap. Some say that he feasts upon their powers, and not just a parent warning off a naughty child. It was the very reason that I caught you before you strayed too far beyond the boundary. It is the same reason that I counsel you now. Do not follow the trails of this O'Bellah too closely, Zya. It is perilous."

Zya smiled with confidence born of one who was beginning to understand her fate. "Well I will try to stay away from his snares if at all possible. I value my freedom too much. But it seems that him and those like him are everywhere."

"Vigilance never hurt anyone," Tarim offered in the way of advice. "Now I think a vigilant person would want to get out of the public eye with such a conversation. Even in the shadows voices can be heard." Zya and Lorn both realised that he was right, and not a word more was said. They returned to the tribal quarter, and once they were within the area, a calm settled over all of them. It was the feeling that spread throughout the nomads of the north, and was indescribable. "Much more like home." Lorn stated in approval of their surroundings.

"You miss it, don't you?" Zya saw the feeling behind his eyes.

"It is enough to know that my own kind are around. I have nothing against the city folk of Bay's Point, nothing against any man for that matter, but since living in the city, the feeling of the tribal quarter is what keeps many of us from bolting for the gates every single day."

"We all need that sense of security, son." Tarim was speaking to all of them. "It is because you know that we can trust every single tribesman around us."

Of course the tribal quarter was not exclusive, and many other merchants and peddlers hawked their wares here as much as anywhere, but here the population was concentrated more towards the tribes, many of them coming and going through the gates that while not as imposing as the Southern gates, were still an ominous prospect for an assaulting enemy. They made their way through the side streets rather than the middle of this part of town now, for they wanted to attract as little attention as possible. The usual sneak thieves and pickpockets did not tend to hang around in the tribal quarter, so it was generally considered safe to wander in the gloom of the dank streets with their rubbish and dirt paths. Eventually they had no choice but to brave the wider streets of town, as they began to run out of shadows to hide in. The three of them emerged onto the main street to the North gate from the East, and made their way towards the carpentry, passing taverns and armourers, both of whose owners were known to them, and shouted greetings that were heard dimly amongst the noise of the general populace, and responded to in kind. The blood was different, but the habits of the people were the same. Bay's Point was a good-natured place for the most part.

Zya stopped, and turned to Lorn. "So what are you holding back from me?"

"Excuse me?"

"When you mentioned our companions, you did not tell all."

Lorn looked slightly offended. "I am no liar."

"I did not say you were, but nonetheless, you held back something. Lorn, you couldn't fool me before, and you certainly can't now. What is it?"

Lorn took a couple of slow breaths before continuing. "They said that some of them had been taken to a camp, that they had been captured by mercenaries."

"Do they know who?"

"A couple of women and a man were all that they said. There were others that joined them not long after. That is as detailed as it gets."

"Women. . ." Zya mused aloud. "There were only Venla, Anita and Ramaji. Mavra is too young. As for the men it could be any one of them but I would guess not Cahal or Jaden."

"They would go down fighting rather than be captured alive." Tarim agreed.

"Not if ordered by Venla." Zya countered.

"Perhaps. Remember they are only paid mercenaries themselves."

"No they stopped being that a long time ago. The question is what are we going to do about them?"

"Well what would you have us do?" Lorn asked. "We are here at your behest. Will leaving here mean that you will miss out on whatever you came here to find out?"

Zya thought about it. "Nothing tells me that I shouldn't. I have no feeling against it."

"So should the three of us just up sticks and head out again?"

"That wouldn't be wise," Tarim cautioned. "Let me look into the state of things before we move. Lorn, you find out anything else you can."

It did not take long for them to reach the carpentry, and as they did so, the scribe from the next shop but one hailed Tarim, and approached him.

"How goes it with you, friend?" Tarim asked with a bow

"It goes well, good carpenter," he replied amiably, the brown robes of his trade folding out with the exertion of the stranger's own bow. He stood, and held his hands in front of him, the fingers interlocked. "I happened to be walking by when I saw a man sneak into your carpentry around the back entrance. I just thought that you should know."

"This man, was he armed?" Asked Lorn, already suspicious at what had happened to them in the city."

The scribe looked skyward as he recalled the person. "Not that I could recall. He was slight of build, with dark robes, but nothing obvious. Is he known to you?"

"We will see when we get in there," he answered ambiguously. "But my thanks for the warning."

"My pleasure neighbour." The scribe hurried off, with the huddled gait of somebody perpetually in a rush to be about places.

"I don't know why the scribe would be interested in our goings on, but I see no problem in answering such as him." He said by way of explanation. Tarim leaned close to the door, listening for any obvious signs of noise within. Hearing nothing, he opened the door almost silently, while Zya and Lorn looked on. Without knowing it, Zya had her dagger in her hand, and Lorn had also drawn a knife. With a flash, Tarim swung the door open, lunged in, and in one swift movement had reached and unsheathed his sword, bringing it to bear against whoever their mystery opponent might be. Zya jumped in next, and Lorn followed, closing the door behind them and bolting it. Zya felt stronger waves as soon as she entered. She closed her eyes, rubbing at her forehead. Something seemed to be pressing at her, but what was causing it was unclear.

"What is it?" Lorn asked, obviously aware that something was affecting her.

"I don't know," she replied, unable to look up. "It is as if the feeling I had outside the mercenary guild has returned, but it has none of the ill-feeling that stank of O'Bellah."

"It is as if something speaks to you, is it not," said a light and yet gravely voice from a shadow in the corner of the room.

"Yes, that is exactly it," Zya replied without thinking.

In an instant, so much happened. Tarim and Lorn both whistled their blades towards the voice, light flared into the room, and Zya let out a scream as the pressure in her head bordered on pain. Something tested her. As the shutters flew open, a man was revealed from the shadows. He was not a big man. His eyes were no higher than Zya's shoulder. He was balding, and had the wisps of hair that were left brushed forwards and sideways to hide the shiny reflection of light from his skin. He was attired in the dark clothes the scribe had described, making his pale skin ghostly in comparison. He looked up at them, and the one thing that struck all three simultaneously was the fact that he looked straight at them with one eye, and the other looked off to one side.

"Please gentlemen," the man said quietly, raising his hands in a gesture of placation. "Let's not be hasty with those swords."

"Answer us then, quick," Tarim replied, his voice cold and deadly as a man who had dropped back into the calm stance of a trained fighter. "Who are you, and what do you want, sneaking around into our home?"

The man lowered his hands, popping what looked to be a small stone from his right hand into a pocket. "My name is Ralnor Scott, and I am of the Earthen Cleric's Guild in this city. We are an order devoted to preserving that which was created by the Gods of land and sea." He pointed at Zya. "I have come for you."

Chapter Seven

"What do the Earthen Clerics want with my daughter?" Her father maintained his posture, eyes sharp, arm rock-still.

"It. . . it came to our attention that she was attempting a focus, and she is strongly biased towards the ground in her skills. I have come as a tutor of new students to train her."

"What if I don't want to join your guild?"

"You already have, Zya. You work in the kitchens. We only allow those with an aspect of focussing already in their nature to enter our guild house, member or otherwise."

This took Zya by surprise. She had not forseen this turn of events. "I cannot go with you."

"But. . ."

"I cannot go with you right away. I have an errand to run first."

Obviously not used to being rebuffed, Ralnor stepped forward, only for blades to be raised once more. "There is no need for violence."

"Wizard or not, you have broken into my home. I see it as nothing less than prudent to protect my family." Behind his blade, Tarim was a picture of cold finality

"If you are who you say you are, then I shall return to you presently. I have a matter outside of the city that needs my attention."

"Do not tarry, young Zya. Your skills may cause someone damage if they reign unchecked."

"I will be as long as I need to be, Master Scott."

The wizard moved between Tarim and Lorn, and then turned at the doorway. "You do know that I could destroy those blades."

Tarim's face was grim. "Let us pray you never see the day you want to try."

Tarim closed the door behind the wizard and then turned to his daughter. "You have changed your tune all of a sudden."

"I didn't expect that. For all that my seer's skills have been any use to me, I never thought we would get here to find a wizard waiting in our house.

"I doubt he will be the only one," Lorn warned. "Give it a few days and expect a visit from every Guild in Bay's Point."

"That settles it then. We go now. Lorn, find Ju and grab him back from his tour of the city. Father, are the horses well enough to ride?"

"They are recovered from the chill of the Steppes if you mean that."

"Good. Get them hitched and we ride tonight."

A fortnight they were on the road. During this period, Zya became unduly reticent, spending increasingly long periods by herself, wrapped up in thoughts about her possible position within a guild, the seers and especially her dreams. Where did all this fit in? There was no ill-feeling in the guildsman approaching her, not like any other situation that had led her to make a decision based on instinct.

"So care to share?" Lorn had ridden up alongside her, and she hadn't even noticed. It was enough to surprise her to speak.

"Not really."

"Oh, okay." Suitably miffed, Lorn made to drop back to where Tarim and Ju were practicing fencing with whittled sticks, but Zya reached out.

"No, stay. I didn't mean it."

Lorn resumed his place. "Look, I know you must have a lot on your mind."

"More than you could imagine, Lorn."

"You do know that you could talk to me about it?"

"No actually, I could not. My thoughts are my own, and have to stay that way. I can only say that my reason for leaving was purely personal, and not a reaction. I don't want to be a pawn in some power shift, not when I am unsure of my own skills."

"Then I would say that your greatest power is common sense." Lorn approved of people that could take care of themselves. Zya had been striving to show him that side for many moons.

"So my common sense tells me you should be looking for tracks in the road."

"Your common sense would be right. We have been following their tracks for the last day or so."

"Really? How close are we?"

Lorn peered in front of him. What he was looking at was beyond Zya's examination of the dirt. "I would say we are a day behind them at most. The tracks are still fresh enough to tell. We shall be with them by tomorrow."

"And they are following somebody else?"

"Yes. If they had gone through here first we would never have seen their tracks. A great many men and horses have been here recently, doubtless the band of mercenaries that hold captive those that were lost. Evidently somebody has tracking skill amongst your friends."

"That would be Cahal and Jaden, if either of them are still there." Tarim and Ju had finished with swordplay and now rode close behind. Her father's face showed relief that she was finally talking.

146

"Let us hope they both are, father. We can't take on a mercenary band with a cart and a herd of draft horses."

"Are they reliable swordsmen?" Lorn asked.

"You wouldn't want to bet against either of them in a one on one, or even worse odds." Tarim replied. "They have proven themselves countless times over the seasons."

Lorn looked less than convinced. Zya didn't doubt that he wanted to test the mettle of such strangers.

"What about the rest of them?"

"They are followers of the Old Law, like you and I. They have never known violence. The mere thought would be abhorrent."

"There is knowing how to defend yourself, and that comes a long way short of the boundary where it becomes senseless violence. Let's get a move on, we need to catch them sooner rather than later."

By the time the day ended, they had not gained on the travellers, so reluctantly in the gloom, Lorn and Tarim made camp. They were up at the crack of dawn the next day, light barely over the mountains to the distant east.

"Why the rush?" Ju asked as they began to ride once more.

"Your friends have taken a different direction to the mercenaries. Their tracks lead off to the South while the wagons continue to roll south-west. The sooner we find them the better."

"When did the tracks diverge?" Tarim dismounted and studied the ground."

"We camped at the point last night, so however far they have gone, they will be twice the distance behind by the time they return here, and losing time if they are still in wagons."

"Let's make best time then."

They rode for most of the morning, passing from the level grasslands into a low range of hills that were dotted with a series of large copses.

"Nice to see a change from all that grass." Zya commented as they rode towards one particularly dense area of woodland.

"You will see more in a moment." Lorn replied. "They turned here into those woods."

"How in the world did they get wagons in there? I don't see any way in." Ju walked to the edge of the trees, and laughed.

"What's so funny?" Zya called, still astride Red, her mount for many seasons now.

Ju tugged at some branches, and a whole section fell away, revealing an artfully hidden track.

"Good, but not quite perfect. Well found." Lorn approved of Ju's actions. "He is doing well as a tracker. Might be able to hold his own in a generation or so." Ju frowned. "Should I make that out as a good comment or not?"

"Up to you. Let's dismount. It will be easier to watch out for any surprises that way."

"Well if Cahal and Jaden have anything to do with it, we will have eyes on us from the start. I will lead us in." Zya tugged gently on the reigns and led Red into the woods.

Immediately the normal countryside sounds ceased.

"Its as if we entered a different world." Ju whispered.

"Nature knows. The creatures of this wood have been disturbed recently. That is why we hear nothing. When your friends leave, they will return. Now be completely quiet when we get closer."

"Lorn, these are our friends we are talking about."

"Zya, how long has it been since you saw them last? Who knows what has happened to them since that parting? All I ask is they you do not go rushing in there. Let us at least have a look first."

With reluctance, Zya nodded her assent. The mere thought that her friends would not be as she left them was beyond comprehension. They proceeded into the copse, following the track until Lorn indicated that they should tie their horses off and continue alone. In the distance, obscured by thickets, there was the unmistakable sound of clashing swords."

"Who do you suppose that is?" Lorn whispered.

"The guards." Zya replied, flatly refusing to believe anything bad about her former family.

"Caution." Tarim whispered, and drew his sword, Lorn doing likewise. Ju readied his bow, but after a quick glance, put the weapon away. "No sense firing arrows in here."

"I doubt you could hit anything." Zya murmured.

They made their way through the thicket as best they could, until it was clear that they were on the edge of a glade. There was a wagon painted in the traditional travellers colours, a symbol in itself of their profession. Around it, people tended horses, or sat talking. Off to one side Zya saw the strangest thing. "That looks like. . . Mavra, *fighting* Gren."

"Well don't times change." Zya did not look back, but she could tell Lorn was smiling. "Well go on then, move forward so we can get a better view."

* * *

148

Cahal parried an overhead blow from Mavra, and the blades slid along each other with the steely rasp of finely honed metal, locking at the cross guards. Normally one swordsman would push the other back at this point and they would disengage, and go at it once more, but this is not what happened. Despite her inferior strength, Mavra twisted the crosspieces so that they locked and kicked him hard in the ankle, causing his leg to buckle. Cahal yelled in pain and Mavra pushed him to the ground as he lost balance. Dropping his sword to one side, he curled his legs and rolled out of harm's way. In doing so he rolled over some of the branches that they had used to mark the boundary of their little arena, and yelped as one particularly springy branch decided to find its way in past his armour and poke him in the ribs. He finally stopped just beyond the circle, sitting up with his hands on the dirt behind his back for support.

"Where in blazes did you come up with that?" He asked, still a little surprised, and that was a lot for him.

Mavra looked down at him for a moment, and then let out a whoop of pure joy, raising her sword so that it caught the sunlight, reflecting like a diamond in the sky. "Why disengage, when you could use the tangle to get a blow in?"

"Why indeed?" Cahal conceded. "Of course, that works both ways if your opponent has the same intention. And do not forget, they may well be much stronger than you."

Mavra flashed him a cheeky grin. "Are you not considerably stronger than me? Would you not have done the same thing?"

"She has you there," Gren noted from his vantage point on the wagon. Zya smiled as she remembered his copious words of wisdom. "Do unto others as you would expect them to do unto you, but do it first."

"And do it harder." Jaden added, grinning as he approached from across the glade. It had been too long since Zya had seen her family. If Lorn had not been holding her arm she would have been up in an instant.

Cahal reached out, letting Mavra help him to his feet. He retrieved his sword, wiping it down with an oiled cloth. "Well done lass." Mavra smiled, "Luck always helps a traveller on a fateful journey. The same could be said for a swordswoman in a battle. I will have to come up with something new against you next time."

Cahal snorted at this remark, bringing her up short. "You are not a swordswoman yet, Mavra." This wiped the smile from her face, which was not his intended goal. "You are doing well, Mother. When you can stand against Jaden and myself together, and keep us at sword's length, then I will call you a swordswoman. But for now rest your arm, girl. Another secret of swordplay is knowing when enough is enough, and in practice never keep at it until your muscles get pulled. No swordsman can fight when these muscles are torn and cannot bear weight." He pointed at the muscles around his upper arm and shoulder behind his neck.

"Some can't fight even when they are fit and able." Jaden joked to his partner. Cahal laughed at this. "Speak for yourself, old man. If you weren't in your dotage, you might even stand a chance against her."

"Tarim? Zya?" Mavra caught them by surprise. She was looking directly at them in their place of concealment.

In an instant, Lorn had them all ducking down, and quietly moving back out of view.

"I swear that I just saw them in the trees." Mavra said from the glade.

Footsteps betrayed the fact that Cahal and Jaden were looking.

"Don't see anything now." Cahal said, his voice quiet.

"You sure you aren't just still caught in the heat of battle, Mother?" Jaden added.

"I saw what I saw." Zya heard the conviction in Mavra's voice.

The guards hesitated, and then turned away.

After a moment, Lorn pointed and led the way, being careful to make no sound at all. Zya followed him until they were well out of earshot of the makeshift encampment.

A whispering breeze caused a slight rustling of leaves, enough to mask the movements of Zya and Ju. Her father and Lorn would have been invisible to her senses had she shut her eyes. The guards were still within hearing distance, and Zya strained to hear their conversation.

"Nuttin.'" Jaden said with an air of discontent. "There's something up here, but I don't know what."

"Agreed," Cahal replied. "Over there. Somebody in the trees."

Hearing this, Zya figured they had seen her, and made to emerge into the glade. Then she saw her two old friends moving with stealth towards the bushes to her right. Ahead Lorn had moved to a position that gave a vantage point over the camp, all but the place the guards were coming from. Zya wanted to call out, but something told her that she should keep quiet, and that Lorn was not in danger. Cahal pointed, and Jaden noticed the gesture. Quietly, they stalked Lorn, closing rapidly on the unsuspecting quarry. Swords ready, they split around either side of the hindmost wagon, and creeping as slowly as a cat before the kill, readied themselves to pounce. Cahal slowed, his sword raised in front of his face. He edged around the front of the bushes, and was met by nothing. Jaden sprang out, and the two guards almost clashed swords. They looked around in confusion.

"If you want to stalk prey friend, I suggest that you do it from downwind, and after you have taken a bath if you want to be successful." A voice said from above. The two guards looked up, and found Lorn crouched comfortably atop a branch, grinning at them with sardonic amusement. "Here are your guards!" He said aloud, to somebody behind him.

Jaden readied himself for a battle, raising his sword and stepping back. "Let's take em."

"No, it is not necessary, old friend." Cahal replied. "They are not here to harm us."

"Well put, old friend." Said a voice, emphasising on the word 'friend'. Tarim walked into view giving Cahal the biggest shock of his life.

"Tarim has returned. Well strike me down where I stand, I never thought we would be seeing you again."

Jaden sheathed his sword and grabbed Tarim by the wrist in a warrior's greeting. "Glad to see you, my friend. There's been dark times behind us, and more to come. Could do with you being here."

"So where is young Zya?" Cahal scanned the foliage, and she decided to make herself known.

"I am here." Zya pushed out through the bushes, to find herself being enfolded in bear hugs by the two guards.

"We have missed you, lass."

"Jaden," Zya gasped, "how about letting me out for air?"

Jaden released her, and she looked to the bushes. "Lorn come down, and bring Ju out with you."

As Lorn emerged, both guards exclaimed curses. "You could be brothers." Cahal said as he looked from Tarim to Lorn and back again.

"Who is to say that we are not?" Lorn replied. "I am called Lorn, son of Hern, of a tribe from the Steppes to the North of here."

"How did you get caught up in this little adventure?" Cahal asked, justified suspicion in his voice.

Lorn related the tale of the fisherman and the tribe as briefly as possible, but it still took a while. Ju joined them during the tale, getting nods of recognition from the two guards.

"So you have ended up here again." Jaden said upon conclusion of Lorn's tale.

"For now." Tarim replied. "We have business in the city, but when it was brought to our attention that you were nearby, we had to come."

"We should take this to the Mistress," Zya interjected, "it is better told that way. How is Anita?"

"Anita is fine, girl. But I suspect that all is not as you have expected to find it. We should take you to the Mistress before any more is said." Jaden led the way back through the glade with not a word more. The sudden reappearance of the travellers deemed lost to the group cause nothing less than an uproar in the camp. The hounds went berserk at the sight of old friends, scaring the horses into trying to run, and causing the wagons to get wedged in amongst the trees. Gren's cook pot got knocked over, ruining the fire, and the cook forgot himself completely and slipped in the mess, swearing profusely. When he saw the cause of the uproar, his anger turned to amazement, plain as daylight on his face. Zya witnessed the change as Gren saw them all.

"Well I never. Of all the things to expect, this was the best. Welcome back, strangers. I see you have new company."

"What's all this commotion?" Called Mavra as she opened the door to her caravan. "You are disturbing Anita."

"Just thought we'd drop in." Zya said with a smile, happy even to see Mavra.

"Really." Mavra was nonplussed. "So you burst into this camp and cause all this havoc. Welcome back, Zya. Get to work tidying the mess up."

"I don't believe it is your place to tell me what to do." Zya drew herself up, indignation on her face. "If Anita wills it, then so shall it be."

"Anita isn't in much of a state to be doing anything right now. If you are in this camp, then you answer to me."

"Not very likely."

"But it is the case nonetheless," said a voice from behind them. "Caught you in a quiet moment?" Asked Layric. He had jumped down from the wagon behind, and had crept up on them as they talked.

Zya turned to see Layric standing there. He had changed since she had seen him last. She jumped to the ground and gave him a hug. Pushing him back to arm's length, Zya studied his face. "You wear many more cares than once you did, Layric Chemani."

"You too have grown, in many ways, Zya S'Vedai. But hearken unto the Mistress of the Caravan when she speaks to you."

Zya's eyes widened, and she turned back to Mavra.

"I did not ask for this, Zya, but it is my burden to bear. I wish things were back to the way that they were. But it is no use wishing is it?"

"Perhaps you should tell me everything that has happened since we left."

"Perhaps later. Suffice it to say that Venla, Gwyn, Jani and Ramaji have been taken, and that Anita lies within after O'Bellah nearly killed her."

"So you are going after them, abandoning everything we stand for?"
Mavra rounded on her. "How dare you accuse us of doing that after you left
us with not a word."

"I have to follow my own path, Mavra. It could not be helped."

"And look where that has led you, right back to where you belong. Zya, you
will never begin to understand what you did by splitting the group like that.
Family stays together. We are family and you took that from us when you
went away. I will go to the next world with a clearer conscience than you
because I know that I am following my heart. We are going to try and rescue
the others because it is the right thing to do, even if it is not the proper course
of action."

"You are doing the right thing," Layric said reassuringly. One of his hounds
came bounding up and he ruffled it behind its ears, sending the hound into an
ecstatic frenzy of leaps and bounds. "Let me tell you what I think of all of this,
mother. If my wife was with us, and one of you went missing, she would move
heaven and earth to get you back. She would do this for two reasons. First
because it was her responsibility as Mistress of the Caravan, and secondly
because she cared, which is a trait that we have seen lacking in too many
people of late. You do not lack that. You care more about our missing than
anybody, and you are only just realising it. Zya, this has all been thrust upon
her with such suddenness that adjusting to all the changes is bound to take
time. Many would have carried on the caravan tradition and continued, or
returned home. Mayhap we are living in momentous times, for surely
something is up when mercenaries kidnap people who want no more than to
make a simple living. You are right in what you have said in the past of
course."

"About the Old Law?"

Layric nodded. "Yes about the Law. It was there for as long as I can remember,
but maybe it is not the way any more."

Zya sat there stunned. "You are losing faith?"

Layric sighed. The normally stolid man, husband to a completely unflappable
woman was finally having doubts. This did not bode well. "How can I have
faith in a code that decrees a way of total peace when we are the only ones
following it? How can a family that is rent apart so violently rely on peace to
bring them back together?"

"Faith is the one thing that will keep us going." Zya said soothingly.

"Zya is right, Layric. Faith is the cornerstone of our society. Venla taught me
that. I have faith that we will find them again, and you have to share in that.

Zya, do you see how things have changed now? This situation could look strange to any passers by. A man pouring his heart out to a girl a third his age. It is not how everybody in the copse sees it. Here is a member of the caravan talking to and being consoled by its leader, and age has no issue to bring to the table. There is always time for change. We have perhaps reached that point. I don't think that living by the way of the Old Law will see us through, do you?"

"How can you say that? It has lasted countless generations."

"Yes Zya, but for countless generations our people did not have mercenaries dogging them, assassins trying to whittle them down, random members deciding that they had to leave with no explanation."

Mavra was clearly losing her temper. Zya did not want to goad her. "I left a note. Layric, you are her husband. Do you not have any sort of an opinion on this?"

Layric chuckled, a slow rumble. "I think that if my wife had suggested all of these ideas, I would have told her that she was being stupid, we would have had an argument and she would have done it anyway. You are a fresh breath of air, Mavra, and I will support whatever you do."

"That is good." Said a voice from behind Mavra, for you will have no choice. I will not take the position, the girl is doing too well." Anita climbed out of the doors and stepped down with Layric's assistance, Mavra looking on all the while.

"How do you feel, daughter?"

"Considering this is the first time that I have been well enough to the point of getting up, I feel fine. There is only so much time a woman can spend cooped up in a wagon while the world goes by. I have missed the steady passing of the countryside. They should make better windows in these things." Anita pointed at the wagon with a skeletal finger, and Zya was shocked to realise how much weight Anita had lost. As if sensing that thought, Anita curled her hand and looked at it, turning it around and then stretching her fingers out. "My, I do have some catching up to do on my food."

"It's nice to see you up and around." Zya reached out to help Anita down from the wagon, but the older woman pulled her arm back.

"I don't know you, girl." Anita gave her a cold glance, as if all the history of their family meant nothing.

"Go help Gren," Mavra suggested. "We have more need of cooking skills than we do of sewing at the moment."

"Your will, mother," Anita replied. "There is only so much sewing a woman can do without a break. I have done nearly a moon's passing worth while abed. If anybody needs anything, it is likely in my finished pile." Anita headed slowly towards the wagon behind them.

"Do you think she will recover?" Zya asked.

Layric stared after Anita, watching her as she made her way carefully and deliberately towards the other wagon. "I think that it would be so much easier if Gwyn were here."

"We all miss her, Layric." Mavra was doing her best to console, a difficult job for one so young, Zya guessed.

She echoed the comments. "I know what you mean. There are times when I feel that I almost cant cope with all that I do, and I just want my mother back." Layric smiled, reaching up and placing a fatherly hand on her shoulder. "Your mother would be proud of you. You have changed in such a little time, and have ever asked only those things of people that you would be prepared to do yourself. That is the mark of a caravan mistress if ever I saw one. But you must remember that Mavra here is in charge, and whatever pulled you away will never be enough to make up for the fact that you left."

"I don't know if I would make a good Caravan Mistress, Layric. I believe my path was always destined elsewhere. Mistress Mavra, you have my support for what it's worth."

"Well I hope that you approve of what I will be deciding next." Mavra replied.

"What do you mean?"

"Let us get set for the day and I will tell you all. For whatever reason you are here, you can help out."

"I know exactly what you are going to do." Zya whispered. "It is why we are here."

"We?"

"My father, Ju, and Lorn."

"Layric, if you would be so kind." Mavra spoke in a tone that clearly said she wanted to be left alone.

Intrigued but respectful of the traditions and who he was now talking to, Layric nodded, and walked away.

"They still leave me to my chores. Granted they are no longer the traditional chores of a caravan mistress." Mavra unhitched the draft horse and rubbed it down, barely able to reach its neck. Securing the placid animal in their makeshift pen, she left it to crop grass while she checked out the state of her wagon.

Zya ran her fingers lightly along the woodwork, a place that had once been the core of her life. The once colourful vehicle had paint chipped off of it and where paint was visible it was faded. This was testament to the amount of time the original caravan had been away from their home to the East. It was a mark of respect for a caravan to return almost stripped. Some caravans were known to operate completely independently, faded with use and inhabited by people that followed the traditions but had never once been to their true home.

"That's seen some days." Zya observed.

"And it will see many more before I give it up. Now what do you know of my plans, and how have you come by this information?"

"One thing Venla always taught us was that actions speak louder than words. You have been making a bee-line for the mercenaries for at least a moon's worth of travel. There are those out there that know this."

"The mercenaries?"

"No, I do not believe so. We had word from tribesmen, related to Lorn." Mavra looked around the camp. "Where is this mysterious man of yours?"

"No doubt keeping an eye out. He has been training Ju as a tracker, and has been doing a pretty good job of it too. It was apparent to just about everybody but me that you were following the mercenaries tracks, but you missed something. They turned off of the road you were following at least a day back. We have been hurrying to catch you."

"Truly? I should have words with Cahal about his tracking."

"Well better now than weeks away when you are wondering where they all went. We marked the place they turned."

"So much the better that we found this woodland then."

"You are going to need help when you go after them. We are here to help." Mavra put down her horse brush, placing it on the wagon. "Zya, whoever said I was going to do that?"

"Like I said, actions speak louder than words."

Walking back to the others, Mavra was silent for but a moment. "Our caravan has been on the road since just before I was born, getting on for a generation. Both my sister and I had never known a different life, nor indeed had you. Like an older sister to me you were. I always knew you were a free spirit, riding a horse and sleeping under the stars."

"We were always different. I just never realised how much."

Mavra snorted out a laugh. "You might consider what I am going to do ironic bearing in mind what I have always thought about that choice of lifestyle."

Zya looked around the copse. Gren had one of his cook fires going, the type that miraculously produced no smoke. Layric and Anita were getting water, while the guards kept an eye on the track. Strangely, Lorn stood with them.

156

"Is that Lorn?" The tone Mavra used made Zya feel somehow uncomfortable. It was how she had always spoken whenever she wanted something.

"It is," Zya replied.

"Well aren't you going to introduce me?" Mavra walked on ahead with a purpose, Zya hurried to keep up.

As Mavra closed like a silent predator, Lorn turned to greet Zya, bypassing the Mistress completely. "They have passed or been passed by any number of strangers up until a fortnight ago, but since then they have been alone."

Mavra was prevented from saying anything by Cahal. "Making our way across central Ciaharr, it had been relatively easy to keep track of where the mercenary band passed, for they had been ungentle to just about every person they had met. Many were the tales told of random beatings, blatant pillaging and the occasional rape. Our tracking skills are passable, but we are warriors, not woodsmen."

"You are lucky that Lorn came along when he did." Mavra now spoke, and everybody listened. "Those chance meetings have only served to strengthen my resolve. I will not allow the rest of the caravan to be tortured or worse by O'Bellah and that crowd of murderers. The time has come to make decisions, lest they become too distant."

And it was with this resolve that Mavra approached the cook fire, where everybody else was gathered.

"Are the horses all okay?" She asked, as Gren handed her a bowl of stew, rich with the smell of herbs.

"They are, and getting fitter with all these leagues you have got us doing." Gren answered as he doled out more.

"Fitter? Or leaner?"

Gren looked over at the horses, contentedly cropping at the grass towards the front of the copse. "Perhaps both. But however hard we drive them, we will never catch up with your parents." Gren had hit the point that everybody had been silently thinking about for days now. "The signs of the mercenaries' passing are growing fainter every day, and the memories of those they have passed will dwindle from righteous outrage to sullen anger."

Mavra nodded her head as she ate. "I know, Gren. That is why I have something to propose. You are not going to like it, which is why I am going to propose it rather than use my privilege as Mistress to command. I want all of your support for this. As you have rightly said Gren, they are getting further and further away, and the further afield they go, the greater the distance we have to cover, and the more time they have to do something terrible to one of our number. My proposal is that as soon as is possible, we lose the wagons and pursue them on horseback."

"No!" It was Anita that claimed the first outburst. "How can you even think of such a thing?"

"I can think it for exactly the reasons that have just been explained, Anita." She replied. "We need speed, not stealth. Only through quicker horses and less baggage can we hope to catch them."

Anita stood, placing her food to the ground. She paced back and forth, finally coming to stop in front of Mavra. She was growing, but Anita was still taller than her, and looked down as she frowned. "I will not agree to this."

"This is only an idea. But it is one we must consider. We all have lost somebody dear to us, but their memory can not be complete while they are still out there. You must consider that as a reason for us to catch them."

"No." Anita was adamant. "You may be the Caravan Mistress and I will neither dispute your title nor your authority, but you will listen to me. This is foolhardy. What happens if you do catch them? How can six of us take on an army of mercenaries? How do you expect to be able to rescue anybody from that mob?"

From the corner of her eye, Zya could see Layric shifting in his place. When she glanced at him, she could see that he was cautioning Mavra to back down, at least for the moment. He was of course right. Anita was far from recovered, and the blow to her head could well have killed her. It was best to step lightly.

"Anita may be right," she conceded with as much humility as she could muster. "Perhaps it is too grand a scheme for six of you. There are those of us that would aid you in this. It was only an idea. Her confidant mien broke Anita's anger, sending it spreading to the four winds like dust. Instantly Anita was back with them, hugging Mavra as if their roles were reversed. Again she had completely ignored Zya.

"Dear child, would that we could do what you ask," she said, holding Mavra tightly. "We will see our loved ones again, I promise you."

While this scene unfolded, Ju had slipped up behind Zya. "There is a man at the border of this wood. He wants to talk to you."

"Take me to him. There is nothing to be done here."

Zya and Ju managed to slip away, but as Lorn followed them, Mavra called out. "Where are you going Lorn? We have to talk."

"There is time for talk later, girl," he called back, and then caught up with Zya. "She likes you. It is easy to perceive."

"That girl is young, and doesn't know what she likes. There are more important issues than the fancies of a child playing follow the leader."

"I'll have you know that she is well entitled to lead that Caravan." Anger made her voice hiss.

"I don't doubt it, but the fact remains that they all wanted you to lead that Caravan. The girl is not ready to do so. Now as we are not here to debate the politics of your people, perhaps we should concentrate on the task at hand."

"They are also your people, son of Hern." A man stepped out from the shadow of a large oak to greet them.

"Judging by appearances I would say we are all related," Lorn replied, studying the man.

"You could almost be brothers." Zya added, but then she noticed differences. The eyes were darker for one, shadowed by hair that was bound in a different style to Lorn. The man was shorter, but only slightly. He was also much thinner. He was as good a match as could be, despite this.

"Peace be with you," Lorn said, offering his hand in friendship.

"And with you," the stranger replied, taking his hand. "Let me introduce myself. I am called Handel, Handel Broadbough of the Merdonese Forest tribe. I know of your travels, Lorn, son of Hern. I had not thought you travelling this way."

"Should I know you?"

"No, I think not. Let us say that it is enough for you to know that we are cousins of a sort. If you would hear more, I humbly ask that you accompany me."

"Where?"

"To my companions. Come." Handel turned and jogged off.

"We have no choice here," Zya said as she ran after the forestman. Handel stretched ahead with long, loping strides. He gained a lot of distance quickly this way, and when he was far enough away from the camp, circled towards the East and back to his companions. They followed as best they could. It took all the strength they could muster to keep up, and even Tarim was stretched. Eventually Handel stopped, and allowed them to catch him. "With me are two of my childhood cohorts, warriors and woodsmen both. We travelled with the portion of the tribe that had left the forest to search for the temple with the three wizards, and have remained on the plains at their bidding, to help survivors."

"Survivors of what?" asked Ju.

"The plague of death that is sweeping the inhabitants of the plains to extinction." After a quick half league to their place of concealment, he approached, and paused, taking time to make the call of a hedge sparrow. The ghostly hoot of an owl echoed back. "It is safe." Handel announced, and led them into the camp. It was small, not more than a few footsteps across, but enough for them to shelter underneath the branches. He was greeted in the tribal manner by a man and a woman, who looked over the intruders warily. "Scarlet Ashenfall, my sister, and by her partner Hawknest, who has forgone his added name."

"Does that matter so much to you all?" Ju's curiosity clearly overcame any fear of the tribesmen.

"It is one of the rare matters of dispute within my tribe." Was all the flame-haired man would say.

When the ritual bows and phrases had been observed, Scarlet brought out some food. "Come, break bread with us in our sanctuary".

"This is a sanctuary?" Ju asked.

Scarlet nodded. "We dwell here, and thus is it our place of sanctuary. You may call it a camp. It serves our purpose."

Tarim took an offered piece of the flatbread. "It is a small camp, well concealed."

"As is our wont," Hawknest replied. "We do not need much, for as forest tribesmen, we know how to live off of the land. What we have is gathered and stored in bedrolls, which can be slung easily about our shoulders. The natural colours help us blend with the surrounding vegetation. We do not want to attract attention."

"These are people, camped not a league from here who are free, and are searching for some taken by the riders." Typically reserved, Handel Broadbough betrayed his excitement in the tone of his voice. "These are the sorts of people we have been asked by the wizards to aid, and keep free from the trouble posed by the mercenaries." Hawknest peered out of their camp, his flaring mass of red hair making him seem much more violent to Zya than the reserved tribesman that he was. He turned to her. "Are they safe to approach?"

"They have had a few bad experiences, and that has put them on their guard, but the six of them are the type to listen before acting, though the guards know how to wield a sword."

"Warriors both," her father agreed.

"You are of them." Hawknest stated.

"We were, but no longer. I heard that people such as yourself were in the region, and also that our friends were in trouble. We have to help them rescue the others."

Hawknest looked less than convinced. "Do we pack and go then?"

Handel considered this. "I have a feeling that this is just the beginning, but of what I can not tell. We go."

"You have made the right decision," Zya replied.

Scarlet reacted by gathering their things. Leaving the shelter as they had found it, they were soon loping out in the stride that devoured ground as if it were but a morsel. They crossed the path of the travellers to the South, taking a different route as they tried to ensure that nobody came across them. Not that anybody would have. The typical tribal woodsman tended to move like a ghost at will, and if they did not want to be seen, then only the sharpest of eyes could spot their passing. They slowed, almost to the point of stopping. The trees were up ahead, the track angling off to the East where it looped around some hills that rose steadily out of the great flat expanse that was this land. Hawknest kept a watch on the camp for any signs of movement, but there was none.

The group did not know it, but Cahal had seen their approach from far off, and made the travellers aware of the situation. Zya led the group through the trees until they found the inhabitants of the copse waiting for them around the wagons.

"Peace be with you," Handel said, bowing."

"And with you," Mavra replied. "It is a pleasure to meet distant friends at last."

Handel introduced himself and Scarlet.

"Damn me." Cahal swore, "your lass is the spitting image of Zya, even more alike than Handel is to Tarim. Well there is a secret revealed." He said. "If Tarim and Zya are not descended from tribal stock, then this is the greatest coincidence I have ever seen, and I do not believe in coincidence. Was there not a third?" He asked.

Hawknest jumped down from the roof of the wagon, landing lightly enough to not make a noise. He bowed. "Well met, my fragrant friend. May the scent of pine hide your odour."

"Well if that's not the strangest tribal greeting I have ever heard. Indeed, may the wisdom of trees teach me to remember all the training that I have received throughout my life."

"Merdonese tribesmen." Jaden said with suspicion. "Are you not far afield for the forest tribe?"

"That is very true, we are far from our home," Handel replied. "But be glad that we met, for you are in a perilous situation, travelling slowly through this country. If you will, let us explain."

"If there is any danger to the caravan, then I want to know about it." Cahal growled.

Mavra inclined her head, bidding the rest of the caravan to silence. "We are following members of our caravan, taken from us by mercenaries. Can you help us?"

"You hold your departed in great esteem," Scarlet observed, and Cahal chuckled. "You even sound similar."

"You make them sound as if they have passed away," Mavra replied. "They are not out of mind, only out of sight. They left us a long while back, and could be anywhere. I am sure that they are coping just fine wherever they are."

Handel strode past them, becoming the centre of attention as he stood before the fire. "We need to discuss our reasons for contacting you. We have news about what is happening in this region, and believe that we could benefit each other. We know where they have taken your companions."

"All of them?" Layric jumped into the conversation. "My wife?"

"We can not say if it is all of them, and would not deem to deceive you into thinking that all are there." Handel was sincere and sympathetic in his reply. "We can tell you that the band of mercenaries rode to the West, and took with them a group of people that did not look like mercenaries, but wore the same garb as you. They were far ahead of you though, and it will take many days for you to catch up with them." He looked around at the travellers gathered listening to him. "I am not sure what you would have done had you caught them. I can tell you that we can help you if that is your aim. We have been charged to protect this region from an atrocity greater than you might believe possible."

"An atrocity?" Mavra asked. "I would say that it is an atrocity that we have had to lose members of my caravan to those thugs."

Handel looked her straight in the eye. "Would you also say that it is an atrocity to see a village full of people that have been forced upon stakes, so that the streets run red with blood, and every house is carnage? That is what we have seen, and we have seen it more than once. Your mercenaries are only a small part of what is happening here, and the evil is growing."

Zya curled up as her stomach clenched. "That is what it is. I dreamed of it happening, but not on such a scale. People are dying right now." To Zya the day suddenly grew that much stiller, and the temperature, even in the protected copse, felt as if it had dropped. Goosebumps prickled up the flesh on her arms as she realised that her life was becoming deadly serious. If there was a natural sound of woodland, then it disappeared as she withdrew into her waking dream.

"What are you talking about?" Mavra asked. "Villages being killed off? I can't believe what I have just heard."

"This is real. There are men being driven by something evil that are slaughtering entire villages of the plains for no other reason than they believe in peace."

"Evil? What do you mean? Where are these villages?"

"There is one a few leagues to the West." Handel spoke quietly, as if the mention of such a macabre topic was an affront to the Gods themselves. "We have passed only one other, and that was enough to convince those that accompanied us that there was more at risk than some random butchering. There is magic at play here."

Zya expected them all to scoff at the reality of magic, but instead they looked at each other.

"That does not surprise me, to be honest." Layric broke the silence. "Zya here is one that has something special about her. I guess that you could call it magic. She had an intuition; I suppose it could be called. Ultimately, that was what led her from us. Maybe she knew this was going to happen and needed to be away from it. I don't know why she is here now"

"She knows magic?" Hawknest asked?"

"No, I do not know magic." Zya stood, straightening her clothes. The feeling was controllable. "I have the power of a seer, the skill used by the wise women of the Steppes tribes. I dream the future. It is not magic *per se*. Nevertheless, I had to find out for myself."

"We would never prevent anybody from following their own path." Mavra interjected. "That is not our way. We follow the Old Law, and so do any that travel with us, for I believe that is what you intend to do."

Mavra had seen straight to the heart of the matter. Zya did not know this wilful young lady, but she knew that Mavra was firmly in charge here, and that she was very perceptive, though only recently so. The girl Zya once knew still looked about for support, but only occasionally.

"That is indeed why we approached you. We have been charged by our companions to seek salvation for those that are in danger of falling to the evil that even now spreads across the land, sowing fear and suffering like seeds in the field. Your companions have been taken by those responsible, and therefore we would help you."

"What good will three of you be?" asked Gren. "Don't get me wrong here, I am sure you are formidable in your own right, but you are still only three."

"That we are," Handel agreed. "But there are more of our tribe spread out in an attempt to save people."

"How many?"

"At last count, there were three score of us that had not gone on with the wizards to search for the Temple of Law."

"As in the Old Law?" Gren asked, suddenly very interested in the change of topic.

"The very same. Three wizards came to our tribe, and spoke words that had been foreordained. They gained access to a temple that had been sealed for generations, and it pointed the way to another place. They each had their own goals, but I can promise you that they would stand by us were they still here."

"And they have told you to guard their backs." Gren sounded less than impressed with the route the story was taking.

"No, that is not how it is," Hawknest butted in, glaring at Gren. "We are trying to help because we have witnessed a horror that you are simply not prepared to comprehend. There are villages out there, whole villages, where the people have been slaughtered, every last man woman and child. Do you hear me? Every last man, woman and child. Nobody was spared."

This outburst left them all quiet. Hawknest's words drilled the truth of the situation home, to both the travellers and his companions. There would be no mercy by the evil force of men out to reduce the countryside to a population that while not great to begin with, would soon be negligible at best.

"Do you know why they are doing this?" Mavra asked.

No answer was forthcoming. "All we have seen are villages and farmsteads ruined." Scarlet volunteered. "They are doing this West of the mountains, through Ardicum and Ciaharr. It is almost as if they are driving us into the sea. Nobody will enter the villages, not any more. Each village is covered by an aura of evil."

"How do you know this?"

Handel answered her. "I was with the wizards when they used their stones to sense the magic. They said that it was all part of a greater scheme, and that only by saving the villagers would it stop, so that is what we do."

Mavra sighed out loud, a disparate sound that seemed to imply that she was giving up. "How are we supposed to get past all of them to rescue the rest? I can't believe that I was going to sacrifice our homes for the sake of speed."

"No, you are not going to do that," Handel replied, "at least not alone. We are going to do it together."

"Find solace in this, Mavra." Zya added. "There is still hope in the world."

"More than hope," Tarim continued. "We will have a chance, but it will take more than we currently have to save your family."

Mavra turned her palms up in a gesture of defeat. "One moment everybody is positive and full of drive, the next plagued with self-doubt and unwilling to see the way forward. This is what we have." She said as she pointed around her.

Handel followed the direction of her hand as she moved around the copse. "What I see you have is a defendable position and camouflage. In fact there is none better within leagues. You have shelter, and you have defence." Handel nodded at the two guards, who inclined their heads in a gesture of acknowledgement. You also have us, and others like us, who will be able to teach you the skills that are needed."

"What skills?"

"Woodsman's skills," Lorn replied.

Cahal grinned with enthusiasm. "I have always wanted to add them to my list."

"It is not easy, but if young Ju can do it, then so too can you."

"You are part of the way there." Handel conceded. "You knew that we were coming didn't you?"

"I saw you when you were still far off, trying to circle us." Cahal admitted, Jaden backing him up with a silent nod.

"Why didn't you tell me?" Mavra demanded.

"Because part of his job as a guard is to judge risks, and he knew that we did not pose a threat." Lorn replied for him. "I am from a tribe that although only a distant relation through some ancient blood, nonetheless values exactly the same view on life as the forestmen. You are as safe here as much as you can be anywhere. Safer, even."

Cahal nodded. "Why scare people when there is no need?"

"Because we have been attacked in the past by tall dark strangers, for one fact." Mavra said angrily. "You remember Zya? Those two that took my sister? The only sister that I have never seen again?"

"I remember, Mavra. I regret in part that we did not take care of them there and then, but should we have done so, we would have broken the most fundamental tenets of the Old Law."

"You would truly have done that?" Handel looked surprised.

"It was not up to us." Mavra offered everybody a drink, pouring liberally. "They were two strangers, one not unlike yourself but with shorter hair, the other covered from head to toe in black. They bewitched Erilee somehow. From the time that they tried to attack our caravan, my sister was never the same."

"They are not like us," Handel promised her sincerely. "Whoever they are." His voice trailed off.

Hawknest took up the tale. "There are stories we had heard in the past. They tell of dark wizards, those who had a different magic to those of the wood and the river. They form part of our upbringing, but only the eldest know them all. I will think upon it some more one of these days."

"Let us compare notes, my forest friend." Gren the cook, until now mostly quiet, spoke up."

"You would help?"

"Nobody can tell a story like Gren can." Zya said, and everybody that knew him smiled or chuckled. "If there is a common factor between your tales, you have a good chance of finding it here."

"How would you say we go about what you have proposed?" Mavra asked. Handel looked around him. "First off, you need to conceal yourselves better than you have so far. You are not going anywhere for a while, and this copse could hide you better."

"Not going anywhere. Are we not going to try and rescue my family?"

"Not in a wagon," Hawknest said. "You can't roll up to these mercenaries and demand your parents back, girl. There are ways and methods."

"We conceal the wagons and the horses, and we go on foot to free them." Handel continued to outline his plan, with help from Lorn and Tarim, who guessed correctly that they were closer than anybody suspected to danger.

"And how will we free them? Fight?"

"If need be," Handel answered honestly, "though it is not the preferred option."

"By the Sun you are right that it is not the preferred option." Layric stepped into the conversation. "We follow the Old Law. We are not butchers or mercenaries!"

"Layric, I have something to tell you all, something that I was told." Handel addressed Layric personally, knowing that the others would listen as well. "The three wizards were from the Order of Law, in a city to the East. One of them was so well versed in the tenets that he lived and breathed them. He once said something akin to what you just said, but with time he came to see that it was only his point of view that was restricting him. The Old Law does not bind a person. It is only a guide. It acknowledges that in order to accomplish certain purposes, other answers must sometimes be sought. Unrestrained violence, vengeance, they are things we must never use. It is intent that rules the method used to accomplish a goal. We will try and save your families, and we may need to fight for them. Ask yourself this: is violence in this case justified? The wizard for one saw that it was. If you go out to rescue your people, and then find that you want to do that little bit more then necessary to get the job done, then you are straying into the Lawless bounds. We have no malice towards these mercenaries, or even those that lead them. Malice would mean that our intent is not true. We do not want to go out and kill for pleasure, but if we must kill to save ourselves, then kill we shall. We have been charged with saving as many of the villagers and farmsteads as we can, and that we shall do."

"That is a fair argument, but I have my doubts." Layric looked at Zya, and from the corner of her eye she saw Mavra tense at being ignored. "What say you, seer?"

"There is nothing to tell me that this is a rash course of action. Handel, you tread a fine line between damning others and damning yourselves." Zya said coolly.

Handel smiled. "Who said anything was easy?"

Chapter Eight

Obrett strained his senses, trying to force as much of his awareness as was humanly possible through the rock beneath his hands. "To the South?" "A little, but also to the East. Do you feel it?"
Obrett changed the direction he was searching. His awareness passed through pure rock as he searched the foundations of Raessa for weaknesses. Over the last passing of the moon from shadow to full and then back again, they had explored every nook and cranny of the foundations of the city. A by-product of this exploration gave him a much better understanding of healing and its relationship to the art of focussing. As he delved ever deeper into the secrets beneath him, so he became healthier. Even the most limited of use provided him with benefits in his weakened state, allowing him to test the limits of the regeneration at both ends of the scale. This was not the only good point about his incarceration. He had learned the art of speaking through a focus, as he now did. "There it is. The tunnel that leads to the focus. I must thank you for your help so far, Brendan."
"It is not I alone that has guided you, my friend. Under your tutelage I have developed skills that supplement my Earth Guild training. This city has so many hidden passageways that it is difficult to keep up."
"Not for general use, I'll bet," Obrett agreed. "This city stinks of paranoia. I think we have a master that is worried about being seen. This city is old. Our records say it has been here in one state or another for as long as anybody could remember, as far back as they go. Somebody had made a home in the lower cliffs of the mountains, and from there the city had expanded. From what I read, it appeared as if Garias has had a part in all of it. Records describe a man with great power who drew people to him as if possessed."
"So where is he?"
"I don't know, and I am glad of his lack of presence. I believe he does not know what to do with us. The man seems to be stewing in self-doubt. The creature visited me again this morning."
"Yes, we noticed. It is hard to not break down when that much evil passes your door."
"The trembling cries of fear and anguish echo through my mind still, and I can not blame you all, but what can I do? It just stood there, looking at me as always. This creature was born of a magic that had been lost for generations untold, and it hungers. Such is the way with evil. It always hungers for more, seeking to devour everything. It will only lead to one end: annihilation. If unchecked, this creature will eventually become too powerful to restrain, and

will consume all life on the continent in its mindless rampage." He knew it was only a matter of time before he was consumed, and to that end, Brendan had been aiding him in searching for routes out of the city.

It was easier than expected, as everybody within the city not willingly serving the Witch Finder was under the sway of the powerful focus that held the entire region in thrall. That too was a work of evil, and Obrett suspected that it was connected to the creature in some manner. For the present, they were sending their consciousnesses through the stone near sewers, and pathways that had not been used in at least ten years.

"I see it." He replied mentally to Brendan's urging. There was a pathway that was almost directly beneath their own cells, and he was willing to bet that it was once used for maintaining the sewerage tunnels, when the city had been a more open place and the air had not stank of fear and compulsion. The only reason that any of them had been able to fight off the geas that desired them to fear everything, leaving most of all, was the mental conditioning that it took to focus. From careful probing, Obrett and Brendan had managed to contact most of the prisoners on their level. A bedraggled lot though they were, they all had power and skills that defied their wretched state. Jacob, of the order of life, a sect that followed the teachings of the High priest of Jettiba, the God of Life, had such skills that Obrett had never heard of before, empathic in nature. He was able to soothe the mind, and he put every living creature before himself. He had admitted that he had been having some reservations about certain beings, which Obrett took as the furthest he would go to siding with them. One other was Ispen, a disciple of the order of Rivers, a derivative of the Order of Panishwa, the sea God. As rocks were initially laid down as sediment, so was he able to draw on the properties of such stone. He was not much help in their present situation, but he was willing to try. The rest, for there were maybe another half dozen at this point in time, were either unwilling or unable to contribute to what was becoming a team effort.

"What do you think?" Came Brendan's thought through the rock.

"I would say that we have ourselves a way out, my friend." Obrett replied, as neutrally as possible.

"Don't get excited, the emotive magic feeds on positive as well as negative energies."

"Objectivity is called for." Obrett repeated their newfound motto. As a result, the four wizards had become dispassionate about everything. The guards tried their very best to scare them, but they refused to be cowed. Beatings led to nothing, as they could heal themselves, and starvation had little effect. They became the ignored prisoners, only those letting their emotions show on their defeated faces got the attention of the guards. The four of them became resolute. Even the creature had ignored them until now, the lack of emotion leaving it no source to hunger for. As they had got to know each other, their places became more defined. As guildsmen, they all shared the same beliefs, and followed to more or less extent, the Old Law. Being from the Order of Law, Obrett became the unofficial leader. He decided what they would do, and when. He in turn taught the other three his knowledge of focussing, thus broadening their skills. They reciprocated, and between them, they built up such knowledge of the arts of focussing as had not been shared in the lifetimes of any of them.

"So when do we make a move?" Brendan's thought wafted through the cell wall like a wraith.

Obrett sent out a mental shrug. "There's no time like the present, but why don't we wait until later tonight? That will give us time to send one little barb into the focus."

A spike of malicious glee was the only response, and was echoed from a couple of places where the other two were 'listening' to the conversation.

"Be mindful of your feelings, my friends. They might draw unwanted attention." Obrett cautioned them all. They had started with subversion. They had sent messages through the focus that kept the city folk and the increasing population outside. At first it had been nothing more than simple things, making them put charms outside their houses. Later on it had become more involved as they tested the limits of the focus by sending subversive messages to the sprawling mass of people outside. Raessa had had to send forth its army to calm the unrest caused when they all suddenly started mooing like cattle. The noise had reached the prison, and caused them to smile in grim satisfaction.

"Tonight's will be the best message: storm the city. The plan is that while the guards are doling out food and changing bedding, we will use the riot that the message will cause to escape down one of the many tunnels that lead out and under the city."

"What about the danger?" Asked Jacob.

They had discovered tunnels leading through the mountain, but there was a danger there. Some life that Jacob could not fathom. Some creature he had never seen before.

"The way East would serve us better, even if it is the more obvious route to take. We do not know anywhere near enough to take the route under the mountain."

"Guards." Came the warning from Ispen, who had a cell across from the corridor. They all broke contact, taking hands away from chosen stone, and sitting with a bored, lifeless look on their faces. The thump of hard-soled boot heels announced that there were more guards than usual, which was strange to Obrett. The reason was apparent, for the cell doors were opened, and each of them dragged out. The four of them, along with the rest were lined up and held by the guards. Down the corridor with soft footsteps came Garias. The Witch Finder looked angry, a cold rage had settled in his eyes, one that was twisted by his lust for power, more specifically theirs. Obrett did not like the look of this, for he had seen that look in too many younger men during his novitiate. They had all turned bad, or been kicked out of the order. They paled into insignificance with what Obrett saw now. He walked up and down the prisoners, his jaw clenching, and the muscles in his forehead twitching as he did so. He stared at them all, one by one. Obrett did not see what the responses were, but when Garias stood opposite him, he faced the man down. Nobody would bully him into submission, and his defiance kept his emotions in check. "You have one last chance to tell me of your three wizards, Obrett Pedern of the Order of Law. Tell me what they were doing, where they were going, and their intentions, and I shall be merciful."

Obrett tried to stay neutral, calm, but his thoughts betrayed him. He felt an emotion for the first time in days, and the emotion was amusement. Obrett tried to hide it, but he broke into a grin, and then chuckled as the irony of that comment hit home. "You? Merciful? I think not, *Witch Finder*." He emphasised the name with such sarcasm that the man was taken aback for a moment, before his eyes blazed with red-hot anger. "You will not take the skills of those three for yourself. You are misguided if you believe that you could coerce any one of them, let alone all three into serving you."

"Think about it while you consider the days you have left." Garias replied, his arms reaching out for the Old Wizard, clutching for something. "They would serve me rightly, if they knew I had you as their guarantee of good conduct. If they are found they will be given a simple message: Serve me, or you will be tortured. Slowly, subtly, until you relish the thought of any lesser torture as a relief. You will not be allowed to die. I have guildsmen that can prolong your life indefinitely. You will undergo agony unlike any this world has ever experienced, and all the while you will service my magic."

Obrett gained control of his emotions once more, becoming unreadable. "Never. You will never find them, and they will never serve you."

"You are wrong. They will serve me." Contradiction was the simplest form of argument, but there was something in the man's voice that hinted at a hidden agenda. "To show you of my intent, I will give you a little demonstration. You there." He pointed at one of the guards, a brutal looking fellow that had been itching to get his hands on one of the prisoners; He used to sit there and talk about what he was going to do to them. "Take one of these prisoners, any one, and show our friend here what we mean."

The guard grinned sadistically, and walked up and down the line, making a show of choosing. He stopped behind Brendan, who did not bat an eyelid as the guard grabbed his shoulder and pushed him towards the cell. One brief glance from Brendan said everything. 'Do not give up.' The look was as plain as daylight. Two others joined the brutal-looking guard in dragging him back into his cell.

"Now, for every day you hold out on telling me everything that you know, one of these will get this treatment." He pointed at the others, lined up between the guards. "They will suffer, and it will all be on your conscience. Can you handle that? Is that acceptable to you?" Obrett just stared forward, into the eyes of a madman. Getting no reply, Garias looked towards the cell. "Guards, do your duty, and the rest of you get back in your cells." Punches and kicks were heard as the prisoners were shoved back. "You will serve me one way or another, wizard." He hissed as a guard shoved Obrett back towards his cell. As he sat down, the sounds of flesh being struck echoed around the prison cells. Wet slaps and thuds, but no cries of pain. Brendan was one tough cookie, but also had the secret of withdrawing into himself so as not to feel pain. Obrett knew that, and he guessed that Garias did not, or the beating would have been worse. In moments it was over, and the guards left at the bidding of the Witch Finder. Obrett would have felt sick for what had happened, had the four of them not made a pact. They all knew the risks involved. They were in perhaps the most dangerous place in the world at this time, and they would do what they had to in order to escape. Obrett's chain of thought was broken suddenly, as a feeling forced itself into his head. Two words formed in his mind: 'Don't stop.' Obrett marvelled at the willpower it must have taken for Brendan to endure a beating and yet send out a message through the stone. "Those earth wizards must have the endurance of granite," he said aloud.

"Enough." Spoke a voice that he had not heard since just before he had been captured. His stomach contracted, and if he had had any food within, he might have vomited. His entire body went cold with a chill as he realised who was talking. Obrett edged towards the door to hear more clearly.

"It will do you no good. He is too stubborn and filled with blind faith as far as his acolytes are concerned. They will not be found by any means as long as you ask him." The voice was dry, as dusty as a sandstorm, and carried the weight of authority. It was a voice that had plagued Obrett since his first days as a novice.

"He will give us the key." Garias maintained.

Obrett searched about his person, finding they key he had discovered long ago in the blackened shell of Belyn's ruined quarters in a hidden pocket. What would they want with that key?

"He will not give you any key, information or otherwise. Any wisdom that you gain from him would be folly to use, I tell you. We have taught them as much as he. Let us find them for you, and we will deliver them unto you for your more delicate ministrations."

Obrett was stunned. For the first time since his capture all those months ago, he was truly genuinely speechless. As if the creature had arrived and sent him reeling with a rock-fisted blow, he was stunned. Looking in at him through the barred window of the cell was Caldar, the head of the guild in Eskenberg. The old man, so often weak and bored looking appeared as if reborn, standing tall and hale. His ragged grey hair had grown to cover the balding spots, giving him an apparently new lease of life. He looked younger than he had in seasons, and glared in with a fire in his eyes. Obrett stood to face him. He was not about to be looked down at by a man that had bullied and cajoled almost every member of his guild.

"So, brought to your true standing at last, as a rat in a cage." Caldar said with more than a hint of triumph.

"Better a rat in a cage than the witless follower of a madman."

Caldar laughed. "From where I am standing, I have definitely got a better lot in life. Your time grows short, and I feel great pleasure in bearing witness to this. I only wish your stinking students were here to witness this with you." Caldar leaned against the bars of the cell. "So morally superior to the rest of the guild. Look where that has gotten you." He said in a voice barely louder than a whisper. "I only wish that upstart Raoul Za were here to share your fate. He thinks he knows the Law. He knows nothing! He would be the ideal man to bear witness to my rewriting of history!"

Obrett had not known that Caldar had borne such a grudge against them, but it came as no surprise. The man was petty to a fault, always scheming when he should have been running the guild. He was the reason that it had become so stale, and his motives were unveiled now. Obrett wanted to leap for the bars, and bring the face outside crashing against it in fury, but he would not. There was now more at stake here than before. "You are the man to do that? A tired old wizard who can do no more than keep himself alive?"

Caldar cackled. "You know nothing, little man. You are nothing. From your cell you will witness the rewriting of the Law."

"I can't believe you are in league with Garias. If the rest of the order knew that you were here, they would expel you without a second thought."

"Would they now?"

Something in Caldar's voice made Obrett take notice. The empty corridors, the apparent forcing of Raoul, Belyn and Keldron from the order, the shadowed whisperings in niches and corners where once the order had been full of vibrancy. "The guild?"

"Are here with me in Raessa." Caldar finished for him. "Well, with the exception of three, almost four *ex* guild members."

"But why?"

Caldar sneered at him, as if it was beneath him to even respond and explain himself. "You have seen the state of our order. The Law is an ass. In cities, the Old Law does not exist. You have to go a dozen leagues into the countryside to find any muck spreader that might try and follow it. We are going to change things. There is a new Law arising, one that bestows riches and power upon those that follow it. We will shape that with anybody who will join our cause. Will you join it?"

"I won't demean myself by answering that. How you ever became head of our order with the blackness festering in your heart I will never know. Rewrite the Law indeed. Only a fool would think such a thing was possible. The Law is bigger than any one person, than any group of people. You could not change things, not forever."

"Yes, forever," Caldar countered. "We are going to make the Gods sit up and take notice. Do you hear? The GODS!"

"Come away from there, you cretin," Garias barked

Caldar stepped back, never taking his eye off of Obrett. "You will bear witness. Mark my words, you will bear witness." With a final hate-filled glance for him, Caldar turned, and was gone. Garias had already left, and the only people that Obrett could see outside of his cell were the guards escorting them, their feet echoing through the corridor. When the sound diminished enough, he turned his back on the scene outside and returned to the stone that he had come to see as his own personal bit of reality in the madness that was this situation. He only wished that he could take it with him, mad though that sounded. He laughed at the thought of an old man digging through mortar to rescue a rock, and then carry it with him for leagues. Obrett poured his will into the crystalline structure of the rock, and sent his enhanced perceptions to the cells around him.

"Brendan?"

After a pause, a voice reached him, dimly. "I am here, barely." The words came muffled as if shouted a long way off on a foggy night. "They worked me over pretty well."

"Can you move?"

A pause in the link meant that Brendan was checking himself over. "I do not think that they broke anything, my friend. But I am going to ache well into the next month. My back is killing me."

"You will be fine." Came the reassuring mental tones of Jacob, who could see any hurt much more clearly as he was attuned to the life force of every living creature that much more.

"I hope to share your optimistic appraisal Jacob," Brendan replied so that they could both hear, "but I think that I shall wait until I get the feeling back in my arms before I start agreeing with you." There was an implied humour in the mental voice that he projected, and both Jacob and Obrett knew that the Earth Guildsman was going to be fine.

"Keep the focus up and you will be fine in no time." The voice of Ispen intruded over all. "If you lot are finished trying to play nursemaid to our poor Earth brother, how about we get ourselves out of here?"

"There's no time like the present. You all know your roles," Obrett replied, and focussed on what he was about to do. Every other message had been intended to do something passive. Hang up a charm, sit around making funny noises. Obrett had misgivings about an actively aggressive intention. Did it go against the very Law that he stood for?

"No it does not, if you follow the logic through," Jacob thought to them all. The link between the four of them was still there, Obrett had just wandered off. "Your intention is self-preservation. This is just a means to an end."

"Perhaps," Obrett thought back to them. "But is it the best way of going about it?"

"It is the *only* way of going about it, Law wizard," Ispen replied.

"Let's do it," Brendan agreed.

Obrett gave a mental assent to the rest of them, and they concentrated their minds on the 'crack' they had formed in the great focus of Raessa. Formed from the very bedrock beneath the city, they wormed their minds down towards the very base, seeking to become one with the compulsion to draw nigh to and remain in the city. Even as they did so, and not for the first time, the force of the focus threatened to draw them in and smother them. It was like a tidal wave assaulting a beach, and they were sat in a rowing boat trying to ride the crest. The magnitude was phenomenal, but they held the secret. It depended on emotion for its power. The fear that the Witch Finder had managed to generate about the region was more than enough to feed the focus, which grew and hungered much like the creature that did Garias' bidding. The secret to riding the wave was the lack of emotion, and their trained minds were more than enough. Their impassivity held them to their course like a rudder, and their training was the wheel. The sail was the message that they now whispered, softly but urgently, so that gradually the entire population would hear their call. *You are not content. Things are bad. Rise up; rise up, against the city. Rise up.* Again and again the four of them spoke the message, and the energy of the focus crackled about them. It took on the message, immersing it within its enormous compulsion. Not only would people be afraid, and yet drawn. They would get angry very quickly, and it would take a lot more control than the Witch Finder presently had to clear this up. All of his resource would be put towards quelling the unrest that would inevitably follow. The focus would have to be dealt with, but if their plan went well, they would be long gone by the time he realised that he was not infallible.

Slowly, they withdrew themselves from the power of the focus. It held onto them with a death-like grip, refusing to part easily with something that had just augmented it. Obrett knew what had happened to Garias. It came as a sudden jolt of realisation. In forming that focus, any power that he had would have been sucked out of him. The essence of the man was contained within the focus for all to see: Anger, spite, jealousy. "You know, the focus is the Witch Finder personified. Just feel the need for domination."

"It must have held onto Garias until the bitter end, rendering him impotent," Brendan agreed.

"It will take a long time for him to be able to bring his mind to bear through a focus once more," Ispen added. "We will have no better chance for this to work. We have no emotion, and there are four of us as opposed to his one."

Obrett withdrew from the focus, and brought his perceptions back into reality. It was always a disappointment when he saw the real world. It was so much less than when his mind was wandering. Maybe it was because he knew that he would be denied the freedom that focussing gave him by means of the cell door in front. His skills meant that he could see everything that much clearer when he focussed, and different realities became possible. Being able to enter through a wall, or contemplate the forming of a rock from within was comparable to nothing when he was sat in his cell. That would change now. All they had to do was wait. He did not even need to focus to become aware of the change in the atmosphere around them. The desire to remain within the sight of the city was still there to trap the unwary, but now there was a more aggressive tone. If Obrett concentrated, he could feel the mounting tension that resulted from the compulsion. He got up and looked out of his cell door. To the left, Brendan stood there grinning through the bars that contained him. "It is working," he mouthed silently, aware that there may have been other prisoners that they could not trust. The mere fact that Brendan was standing meant that he had healed as they had focussed. That was one thing they had never discussed. Obrett had known that the two were linked, but each order had a different interpretation of what focussing actually did for a man. Shortly Ispen appeared, his face filling the gap in the heavy oaken door. Next to him Jacob stood with his head tilted back so that he could see more. It appeared that he was not the tallest of men. After a silent moment where those that could made eye contact with the others, they moved back in to the space of their own cells, to await the results of their work. It did not take long. As the sun set beyond the mountains, noise started to creep up through the windows overlooking the city. It was not much at first, but gradually, the noise increased in volume, carrying an air of discontent through the twilight sky. The wizards listened impassively, gauging the effects of the focus. A few yells became many as more and more people outside the city found reason to become discontent with something or other. Words were indistinct, but the clamour steadily grew. It was about this time that one of the other prisoners started grumbling about being stuck in a cell, with no room to move. Two others joined in. Obrett listened with abject fascination, trying not to become excited by what was happening. Outside the noise had become so loud that it was probably deafening at ground level. If there were not a riot outside the city, there soon would be. Howls of anger now rang through the air, and crash of broken crates indicated that fighting had begun. As the crashes grew in number, so the three prisoners escalated their grumbling, and began yelling, as they banged on the cell doors with their fists. Obrett took one look through his door. His cohorts were all watching in amazement. They had never thought that it would have such a profound effect. Time was suddenly of the essence, and Obrett dove towards the stone that he had been using. "When you hear the guards, join in the clamour," he thought to the other three.

"To what end?" Brendan replied.

"I'll be damned if they aren't going to go in the cells to shut that lot up. What if we can get them in the cells? It will be safer for us than our previous plan."

"Use both," Jacob suggested. "When they open the cells, send a focus to knock them down, or wall them in."

"Whatever you are going to do, decide fast," Came the thought from Ispen. "I can hear guards coming."

Immediately all four jumped up and joined in the noise. It was a glorious counterpoint to the racket coming in from the outside. Their shouting raised the din to the point that it hurt the ears. They yelled about their cells, the food, the mothers of the guards, anything they could think of. The only difference was that they were not angry. Obrett found it therapeutic. He had not had this much fun in years, not since his novitiate, not since before politics had become the primary goal of the order. It was hard for him to keep the grin off of his face as he yelled blistering curses at the approaching guards. He only hoped that his growing excitement was masked by the anger elsewhere.

It worked out even better than he had hoped. Instead of the usual four guards, only two arrived.

One appeared to only just be out of his swaddling, judging by his youthful appearance. "Shut up!" He half yelled, half screamed with the adolescant tones of one whose voice has not reached its final adult pitch. That guard went to look out of the window, turning his back on them.

The other was a bit more wily, and looked as though he might have a bit of a mean streak about him. They all carried on yelling, spewing out curses as fast as they could. "You lot pipe down, or we will be in there to shut you up!"

No effect, and the younger guard was unsure what to do. "Look down there," he shouted above the yells of the prisoners. "There is a full scale riot!"

"The army will deal with those peasants," the older guard responded, spitting out of the window onto the battlements below. "We have our own little chore. This is going to be fun."

"Not half as much fun as your mother had when she dallied with a swine to produce you, I'll bet!" Ispen yelled out at the guards.

"Get that door open!" The guard commanded to the other. "This old man has just earned himself a beating."

Ispen would have retreated from the door after that, for Obrett needed a distraction, and he knew it. Hearing the rattle of keys as the guard unlocked the door, Obrett reached for the stone in the wall. Like an old friend it had become, and he knew its properties. Instead of the subtle nuances that helped him subvert the commons, he fed his intent into the rock and let it build. The power of the stone multiplied his will, and Obrett unleashed the power. His door exploded outwards in heavy wooden shards. At the same time, Brendan and Jacob did the same. The room became a riot of woodchips and confusion. Before the guard in Ispen's cell could act, the water wizard had thrown a shield around him, gagging and binding him on the spot. The younger guard took one look, and ran screaming down the hallway, which pleased Obrett. There was no need to harm the boy. The Witch Finder would probably do as much when he found out what had happened. Ispen had the other guard firmly in hand, and bound him with ropes that had been strewn about the place. A war hammer rested against the far wall, and Obrett lifted it, testing its weight.

"You are committed to a life of peace." Brendan admonished as he hefted the hammer. "Weapons are not your tools. What are you going to do with that?"

"Ensure us a way out of here." He replied. "The guard may have gone, but who knows what else may await us." Taking the hammer, he entered his cell. Swinging with all the strength that he could muster, he hit the mortar to one side of the rock he had focussed with. The mortar began to crumble. He swung again, and again, and several more times. The rock shifted in place, along with copious others. One more swing was all that it took. Obrett raised the hammer over his head, and shattered the stone into fragments. Discarding the hammer to one side, he knelt down, and took for himself a palm-sized shard of the stone. Strangely, the fractures on it left the stone smooth and curved, as if it had been this shape all along. It would do, for it was as good as a weapon in the hands of one that was trained properly. "Get what you can."

Seeing what he had done, the others repeated it, hewing themselves chunks of stone from the walls of their cells. Obrett fretted, as he was sure that the guards would come running at any time. They did not. He looked out upon the plateau that spread out from the city walls. It was alive as people rampaged through the shanties that had grown out from the base of the city. They were out of control, and the city had despatched guards to stop them. It was a right mess. "The only thing that qualms my guilt about this is that we need to escape, and warn others about this."

"The old man speaking to *you*." Implied Jacob.

Obrett grinned at the use of the word 'old'. He was not a young man, old by normal standards, yet years of focussing had left their mark. Caldar had been old when he had been young, and Obrett expected the others could tell of similar cases. "Was the head of my order in Eskenberg," he replied. "It seems that they have taken a side, and the side they have taken I do not agree with. They have sided with the Witch Finder. I thought that they were foolish, and over-political. I never thought that I would see the day my order abandoned reason for madness."

"That is bad news indeed, my friend." Jacob sounded apologetic. "But let us get out of here now. Only by escaping this hive of evil can we hope to affect events without." Ispen and Brendan murmured agreement, and they moved quickly but quietly for the hallway. They encountered no one as they hurried through hallways bejewelled and dazzling. The noise from the city below echoed through the very halls as they sought the passageways that would take them out of the fortress. It was scary for them all; One moment it seemed as if the riot was about to enter a corridor they had just passed, and at other times it was as if they were leagues away, the noise only a distant murmur.

Jacob commented on this. "Are you sure that we are headed the right way? The fighting seems to be in the other direction."

Obrett cracked a smile. "Trust me, Ispen. It is the hidden passages that fool the senses. They make walls thicker and distance the noise." As if to prove his point, Obrett clutched at the fragment of stone he had brought with him, and focussed. "There." He pointed at a section of wall that his perceptions told him had a passage behind it.

Brendan examined the wall for a moment, and then stepped back, pressing a section of the wall as he did so. "Easy." He said as the wall clicked open, revealing a torch-lit passageway behind it. "This is the route we will take. It will lead us straight out of the city."

Ispen looked into the passageway sceptically. "Are you sure of this?"

"As sure as I am that we will be killed if discovered anywhere in Raessa other than our cells." Brendan answered, and then stepped in through the gap. The others followed, and the 'door' closed as Obrett activated the switch, which was an iron lever on the inside of the wall.

"Quiet now, for we do not know how thin the walls are." Obrett followed his accomplices down the passageway.

Jacob stopped. "Oh no."

Obrett felt the evil, coming upon them to rapidly to react. "Run!"

Too late, the wizards stared back at him as the wall crumbled under the creature's onslaught. "Go! I will find you. Get out of the city now."

Brendan gave him a last look as the bulk of the Golem edged its way into the passage. He did not resist. "You found me then." He said as he stared at the black visage. The Golem replied by picking him up with one of its huge paws, and carried him out in to the corridor. Holding him by his tunic, it stared at him as it walked, pulling him closer to it than ever before. He couldn't cringe away, his crawling skin touching the stone. It wanted him, desperately. Only the merest of threads controlled it and kept it from consuming him there and then. While the evil consumed him from without, Obrett did not even notice being put down again.

"Whoever thought you would be capable of such disastrous intent. You are a prize indeed." Garias watched the carnage below unfold with a mixture of anger merged with glee, and fascination. He did not turn away from it, as if addicted to the scenes.

"It will not help you, Garias."

"Why my dear Obrett, it already has. The anger feeds us. You have done more than you could ever comprehend. I do not need to focus any longer."

"Emotions." Obrett said, realising for the first time what was actually occurring. "You couldn't have. That magic was lost in the distant past."

"Not to me. Denial is a simpleton's argument, wizard. I found the keys to using emotions in texts long since forgotten."

"There is no record, or we would have heard of it."

"Where would you look? The Ducal libraries? All their pretty books for show? Even the mightiest storehouse of knowledge on Thiwa does not rival the collection I have amassed. What do you think is going on around you if not magic that draws on emotions? You know already that a focus draws the unwary to this city, but you are far too clever for that. You have it figured out. That is why I have asked you here one more time. Join us. With the powers of the focus and emotive magic combined we will cast out the Gods and place ourselves on their pedestals."

"You think the Gods will just sit by and let you oust them? You have been talking to yourself for too long."

Garias slammed the book he had been holding onto his desk, sending dust flying into the still air. "When I lay my hands on the Tome of Law there will be nobody in your Nine Duchies that can stop me."

To one side, Armen watched the riot and flames with undisguised joy. The man had always tended towards the violent, and this was the epitome. "He started this. Just think what else he could be capable of."

"Armen, get the wizard." Garias commanded.

Armen shot his master a look filled with annoyance at being dragged away from what was surely his ultimate dream. "Yes master," came the dark tones of his voice as he bowed and scurried out of the room. Garias ignored the look. "Killing the man would serve no purpose, and it is much easier for me if the people in the city below believe that Armen was the fabled 'Witch Finder', of who children cried to sleep and even their fathers quailed. It means that I can pass through the city unseen and unchallenged."

Presently, Armen returned, the wizard Caldar behind him.

"What do you require of me, Garias?" Caldar demanded in a voice that announced plain as day that this man expected to be treated as an equal, not a subordinate. Caldar looked around the room and as he saw Obrett his eyes widened. "What is he doing here?"

"I require you to find the source of the disturbance below." Was his short and to the point answer. Garias turned to examine one of the texts he had removed from his library, and found Caldar still standing there. "Go."

The wizard's eyes widened in anger. "How dare you talk to me like that? I am not some menial to be ordered around! I will not move until you answer my question."

Garias did not reply, but closed his eyes. The Golem stumped over towards the wizard, who quailed, shrinking back. "Do not forget your place here. You might be the head of an order where you come from, but here you answer to me. If I give you a command, you will follow it to the letter. If you fail..." Garias indicated the creature looming over him. "Well, there are fates that you could not imagine if you fail me, and I am sure there are plenty waiting to succeed you as head of your order. Maybe even Obrett." He said it so coldly, so quietly, that the rioting echoed in the background like a distant tremor. Caldar's face paled, revealing him for the sneaking coward that Obrett had become used to dealing with, and backed out of the room.

The Golem remained where it had come to stand, still rocking as it absorbed the emotion from the very air. He looked up at it. The blank face was impassive as ever, and the dark eyes reflected the light as if they had been polished.

"I hope you are enjoying this," Garias said, as if it would answer back. "The evil in the air is delicious, no? Of course, had you not hidden her from me, none of this would have been necessary. Now you will absorb it all until she has been found. You are the timer, and the sand will run out all too soon."

The Golem carried on rocking in its trance-like state, ignoring all conversation. "Guards!"

The door opened, and a guard leaned in, his leather helmet covering most of his face. "Sir?"

"I require the remaining prisoners. Accompany me."

The guard straightened, slamming the butt of his spear onto the stone floor with a crack. "Sir!"

"Oh and guard?"

"Yes sir?"

Garias stared at Obrett. "Send word to unleash the army. Send that sorry chattel to their doom."

The guard saluted smartly, and stepped into an antechamber to issue the orders.

"Even the guards do not know who you are."

"Not yet. Just a man to be listened to at all times, and always obeyed without question was what Armen told them, and word filters quickly." The guard appeared, and escorted them through the halls. The trophies and blood-red furnishings looked especially garish in the light of what was going to happen. "You are more creative than I had imagined. Blood will literally run in the streets and I will create another legend. All because of you."

Obrett tried to remain impassive, but the pressure we straining him. He kept a tight grip on his focus stone and looked around as he was led through the treasure-filled halls of this city.

"Legends have been built here in the past, such as the capture of the tribesmen sent against me, and the great focus that had previously been the crowning achievement of my life. I can feel the ability to focus grow within me, and the feeling makes my skin crawl. Ever since I formed the focus that drew in wizards and commoners alike, I have not been able to focus. I abhor your type, relying on instruments to perform."

This made Obrett think; The Witch Finder had lost his ability. Perhaps it was because he put too much of himself into the magic to give it that extra little kick, or perhaps it was because he hated to rely on himself when others would do. He unconsciously rubbed at his arms as he walked, the tingling of the Golem's evil almost making him itch. The mere thought that he would have to focus again was abhorrent given his present situation. He could feel it building within him though.

Garias started again. "I will create another legend on top of the man who sent thousands to a slaughtered death. I will gain the Tome of Law and bend it to my will, shaping the countryside and ridding it of the equalitarian rural folk. Once it is encased upon the dais I have prepared for it, thousands will gaze upon it and marvel at my vision. There is a new world over the horizon, and I am the explorer."

"Exploiter is perhaps a closer word." Was Obrett's glib reply. Even now he could feel the rumble of the gates beneath him, and knew that in mere moments the anger of the rabble below would turn to fear and panic as they were hewn down like wheat at harvest. That thought alone would have revolted him were he not painfully aware of the Golem. He knew how he would have felt. He knew that the Golem would rock in ecstasy when it fed off of the negative emotions only it could feel.

"As it always does, the splendour of this palace becomes plain and utilitarian as the hallways grow. I will not have it that way, and one day will live constantly surrounded by treasure and the oldest, most rare artefacts."

"That is what your new law will gain you? Treasure? That is your grand
scheme, to become rich.

"My plans stretch beyond anything you could imagine, wizard. Guard!"

"Sir," the foremost guard snapped to attention.

"There is something different about this hallway. There is a breeze coming
from the cells. Take yourself ahead and find out the cause." Garias turned to
Obrett. "There should be no way out from there. What have you done?"
Obrett remained silent, defiant.

"Bring him!" Garias commanded the Golem, and the creature shoved him
along. He walked faster, moving tired old limbs long past their best as much
as he could push them. It took an agonisingly long time. No hallway was short
in this city. They were all longer and wider than in any other city he had
visited. Vanity was one thing he had not had to live with in his guild. "If you
can't intimidate with magic then you intimidate with size. There is a word for
you, Witch Finder. Inferior."

They arrived at the prison cells just as the slaughter began to reach its
climax. As swords chopped through flesh and wood, and the screams rose to a
fever pitch, Garias looked around the prison with an utter lack of
comprehension.

"Three of the doors have been forced, evidently from the inside."

"What have you done with the occupants of these cells?" Garias screamed.

"You will never find them. They are beyond your reach now.

"GUARDS!" Garias yelled down the hallway, bringing several running.

"Something is not right." Obrett watched as Garias looked first into the three
cells that had no doors left, and saw the source of the draft. "A wall reduced to
rubble, but the hole is too small for anybody to have escaped."

He looked in the other cells. Three of the other prisoners were curled up in
various parts of their cells, reacting to the Golem's presence. The fourth
prisoner was different. He occupied the cell to the left of that which had been
Obrett's home.

"Who is this?" Garias asked one of the guards.

"This prisoner is one that the Golem took in the forest to the South of the
Nejita range."

Obrett caught a glance of the man; He stood in the centre of his cell, arms
hanging relaxed by his side, as if awaiting them. He was dressed in a rusty
robe, and did not seem the least bit affected. He was calm, and he even smiled
at Garias as he peered down through the bars of his cell. "Why don't you
invite me out?"

184

"I know your type." Garias replied. "That scar down your cheek. I have seen it before. The fire guild, one of the sub-orders that worship Matsandrau the Sun Lord. They are small in number, but great in skill. Anything less than his prize tool would have failed to catch one of your kind. Yet here you stand, smiling slightly as if nothing were wrong. What have you got to smile about?" Garias demanded.

"Look in the cells down my row," the wizard answered. "You might find something that surprises you, and therein lies the answer to your question. What have I got to smile about? Take a look and find out."

Garias shot the man a look of pure annoyance and moved from his cell. Obrett shifted his stone as the focus moved away from him. He was running out of time. Soon the riot could well consume the entire city. A couple of cells down, Garias stopped. "Get this door open." He commanded the guard that had accompanied him, who in turn nodded to one of the guards that had come running. The guard stepped forward with a set of long handled metal keys, using one to unlock the door. The door opened with a click of the lock and the squeal of protesting hinges filled with rust. Garias waited for the guard to step out of the way, and then entered the cell. Obrett tried to get a look without drawing attention to himself. The guard was still bound in the focus. Garias moved closely but cautiously around the guard within, being careful not to touch the man. The trapped guard was breathing, but the strain of trying to move showed on his face. Even his eyes could not move.

"Somebody has been performing a focus, here in the cell." Garias mused as he appraised Obrett yet again.

The guards made warding signs, and moving steadily away. Garias took one more look, and then stalked out of the cell and back to the cell of the fire guildsman.

He was still stood directly in the centre of the cell, annoyingly at ease for his situation. "I can unlock the focus for you, but you must promise me one thing."

"You are not in a position to bargain." Garias sneered.

"The Law Guildsman's life and my freedom." The wizard continued.

"Never!"

"Freedom to serve you." He continued. "All of my order. They will follow my lead. But let me demonstrate my intentions by telling you what has been happening around here first."

"How are you called?" Garias asked, suspicion in his voice.

"My name is Mohin, second wizard of the guild of fire, high servants of Holy Matsandrau, Lord of the Sun."

Garias looked at the man coolly. "You are trying to lead me to believe that I have had the second most powerful wizard of the fire guild in my dungeon for the passing of several months and you have not once tried to escape or raise your hand against anyone?"

"What would I use?" Came the infuriatingly polite reply. "My guild relies on volcanic rock to perform focuses. There are none here, or I would be free." Mohin turned away from him to study the wall. "I bide my time for my own reasons, but I and my guild will aid you. You will need our help, especially if all that you have to rely on are those ancients from the Law guild."

"What do you mean?"

A snort of derision, and Mohin turned back around. "They use their skills for the most basal of motives: to keep themselves alive. They have no more power than what is needed to lift a paperweight. The Law Guild has forgotten more than you could ever hope to learn, and I believe that there are few that know anything about the lost skills. The only one of consequence was in the group that escaped from here, a wizard of considerable skill and immeasurable resource. He stands by you now."

Garias signalled, and the guard with the keys, a bullish, heavyset fellow, unlocked the door.

Mohin stepped over the threshold. He bowed to Garias. "Your master is my master." He said simply, but the look in his eye told Obrett that this Mohin was very dangerous. Mohin had knowledge of much more than he was saying. He then stepped into the cell. One quick look told him all he needed to know. "He is bound up with a water guild shield. A very good one at that. I cannot remove it, but it will dissipate in a couple of days. What you want to know is what happened here, well I can tell you. The four that have escaped altered the focus that drags those dregs you call people here from the wilder lands. They have made it so that the people rise up against you."

"How would you know so much?"

Mohin smiled again, a smile that would make any lesser mortal shudder with discomfort, but had no effect on Garias whatsoever. "I listen, and observe. I have been in worse places than this. When they escaped, three of them blasted their doors open and the fourth did this to the guard. All four of them have power and skills, and I suggest you find the rest. They will be useful."

"How do you know we don't already have the others?"

"Obrett here will not betray his friends." Mohin stepped close to him and it was as if he could almost feel the heat that the man was used to wielding. "He will stay silent, but you should look everywhere nonetheless."

"Do it," Garias ordered the guards.

As the guards marched off, Caldar reappeared with one of his guildsmen, a grossly fat man who had stumps for legs, or so it seemed. It was hard to see the guards go, so big was the body that blocked the hallway. The fat man scowled, as if life had been a continual trial to him and it had the effect of making him look like a rather unfortunate gargoyle with short, curly orange hair. "This is Sandras, a trusted member of the Law guild. He has the answer to your problem."

"We have already found the problem," Mohin replied. "It is unlikely that a fat old fool could grunt his way through such an idea."

"Really," Caldar replied, drawing himself up to look important. "Well why don't you explain just what is going on then, prisoner?"

Mohin did just that, and as Obrett observed the man, he could see that Mohin was as good as his word, revealing their plan almost exactly as they had carried it out.

Caldar went increasingly red as he was put in his place. "Impossible!" He denounced. "Obrett is a gibbering fool and those other wizards would have taken his lead. Sandras has the reason easily explained."

Obrett shrugged. "Just a fool." He agreed.

Sandras stepped forward, grunting and making all manner of ungodly noises as he did so. He cleared his throat, which took several efforts. "I have it on very high authority that the unjust rebellion at your city gates is a direct result of starvation. This has been brought about by the surplus population and their apparent inability to feed themselves."

Sandras carried on and on about food and its lack, walking around the room and ignoring everybody as he began to describe his favourite meals. Obrett lost all interest, since the man had never been able to look beyond his plate. He was torn from his contemplation when a piercing shriek split the air. Obrett looked on in revulsion as he watched Sandras grow fainter and fainter. The Golem shuddered with pleasure as it absorbed the guildsman.

The horror on Caldar's face was plain. The wailing faded, leaving only a trace of an echo against the backdrop of clashing weapons and horrified screams. "What have you done?"

"How dare you present me with this, wizard. If you think that is the best you can come up with, you will be sharing the same fate.

"Your creature feeds well tonight, master," Mohin observed. The
Golem was shuddering with pleasure. "The emotive magic is a rare thing."
Caldar was still in shock, and stared at Mohin with rage in his eyes. "Why?"
"Therein lies your fate unless you prove to be more useful than that morsel."
Garias replied. "I hope that you have more skill with a stone than that waste of
a life had with his voice. Mohin is correct, all you need to do is focus and see
the truth."
Caldar pulled out his stone, and threw his mind into the search. Obrett felt the
focus, a weak affair. Definitely politics made the man and not ability, he
decided.
"True enough, the focus is there as the prisoner describes, and there is also a
message implying rebellion."
Sweat began to bead on Caldar's face.
"You can't let go," Garias whispered in Caldar's ear. The focus has you
trapped, and for every moment you are trapped, you became enmeshed
further."
Obrett began slowly to back away as all attention in the room was taken by his
former guild head. One step at a time, he edged towards the nearest hidden
passage, all the time keeping his eyes fixed on the event in front of him. Caldar
was throwing all of his might into breaking free, but it did him no good.
 "Will he be able to solve it?" Mohin asked.
The corner of Garias' mouth twitched up. "Serves him right if he can't, doesn't
it? Mohin, I want you to go to your guild, and bring them to me."
"To what end?"
"We are going to get the other guilds on side for this. They are going to find
that they have a choice: Join us, or join with my creature."
Mohin broke into a grin, a rictus of sadistic glee. "A simple choice indeed.
What of the escaped wizards?"
"I'm really not concerned about them as a group, but the Law wizard Obrett is
our little prize. We have a lot to get from him."
Obrett saw his chance slipping away, and slammed a focus home using his
stone. The walls bucked and the roof began to crumble in. He struggled to stay
on his feet. Before anybody could react, Obrett three a bolt of force at the
Golem, and then another at the wall behind which was the tunnel that led
directly to the greater focus. The wall exploded, sending stone shrapnel
scattering around the room. A stinging pain bit his arm, and there were yells
from somewhere behind him. He ignored it all as he dashed to the tunnel.

"This is not the end of it, Law wizard!" Came a voice from behind him. "You cannot escape my city! You will be ground into meat before you feel the Golem's touch!"

"So be it." Obrett hurled the words into Garias' head with such animosity that he felt the moment when his adversary dropped unconscious to the floor. For good measure he collapsed the walls behind him. The tower shuddered, and Obrett hurried down the narrow stairway. He never looked back, his purpose was ahead, drawing him on. He crossed hallways, traversing the city as he wound his way deeper into the labyrinth beneath, closer and closer to the greater focus that was the source of all that was wrong about Raessa. He did not need light, so strong was the compulsion that drew him on, and eventually it felt as if he were not alone. Obrett focussed in the darkness, and instantly the light emitted by his stone revealed his companions. They were frozen, looking straight ahead. Obrett knew what was there, and he dared not look. Instead he focussed a barrier of force around them, trusting to his ability to get the focus correct in confined space. As he erected the barrier, Jacob, Ispen and Brendan blinked as one.

"Where are we?" The Earth Wizard asked.

"The focus." Obrett replied, inclining his head to the centre of the room. They all turned. Across the room lay a dais, atop which was set a roughly hacked boulder.

"That is it?" Ispen scoffed. "Any one of us could do better."

"Do you wish to try? Trust me, the Witch Finder seriously neutered his focussing ability creating this focus. In doing so he unlocked what we had feared, only much more so."

"It is not what you have, it is what you do with it." Cautioned Brendan. "That may look like the work of an amateur, but every chiselled mark has a purpose. Before he created this, I would say that Garias Gibden was perhaps the greatest practitioner of focussing there has ever been. Only a true master could create a self-sustaining focus the likes of this."

"We can't do anything about this now, but at least we know where it is." Obrett pointed to his right. "We need to get out of here. I think I knocked him cold with a focus, but he will send his creature after us as soon as he regains consciousness. He has already sent his army against the people."

"We underestimated the man." Jacob sounded cold. "What have we done? Sending innocents to their death so that we can escape."

"It depends how pragmatic you are in looking at it, my friend. They were dead already, they just didn't know it."

"No man lets another suffer and calls himself good." Jacob strode on ahead, disgust ebbing in his wake.

They walked in single file down the passageway, stopping to listen whenever they encountered a turn or steps, which was most of the time. The passageway seemed fairly well used, as was evident by the torches that were burning in the occasional niche. The air belied this fact. It was dank and musty, and had an old feeling to it, as if it had not been breathed in a long, long time. They reached out constantly to steady themselves, for the steps were as slippery as an eel. Moisture clung to everything and pretty soon clung to them, but they did not notice. The clamour of the people outside the city, mobbing in a state of unjustified anger held their attention utterly. The noise seemed so much closer, and as they descended the stairs built within the walls, they four wizards felt as if they were only a hands width away from perilous danger. The riot seeped in between the stones, seeking to paralyse them with its dark potency. Obrett regretted the need for such action now, especially when he heard the screams of women and children as a shrieking counterpoint to the muscle bound anger of their men. Jacob was right. He knew his intent bordered upon the side that he dared not tread, but it was unavoidable. The passageway levelled out, and it appeared that they were at ground level, walking amongst the very roots of Raessa, where the walls thickened and buttressed the great defences of the mountain city. The echoes of the riot subsided as they continued down into the underbelly of the fortress.

"Is the focus losing its effect?" Jacob asked.

Obrett clutched the fragment of stone that he had rescued from his cell, and concentrated. It did not take much, for they had never been closer than they were right now. "The command is still there." His voice was filled with strain as he tried to pull himself away from the clutches of the focus. "It has not been cleansed as of yet."

"Well that is something." Ispen answered.

"I think that the Witch Finder is the only man with knowledge and skill enough to undo our work." Obrett snagged his robe and had to stop to disentangle himself. As he did so, dust fell down from the roof of the tunnel as the riot flared above.

"He might be thinking the same thing about us." Jacob had stopped, turning back to them. "Had you ever considered that?"

"Don't worry, I am sure we will be beyond it all when we end this passage." Obrett tried to cheer them. "It leads to a stable near the outer reaches of the city."

"Won't they have taken all of the horses?" Jacob sounded worried, but strangely hopeful at the same time.

"If they have, they have," Obrett decided out loud. "We will take whatever hand fate deals out. Of course, horses would be a great advantage. The people are rioting against the city, not out from it, so we may be lucky."

They continued down the passage, out under the shanty-like stretches of the city, where those that could not gain entrance were ever hopeful of doing so, even if it was not of their own volition. The noise steadily grew as the fighting and mobbing sent shockwaves and echoes down through the very ground. In fact it got so bad that the roof of the tunnel, though braced, even started to shake loose. "I think it's time to reject stealth," Obrett said as he held his hand over his head. "Run for your lives."

They needed no urging, and ran as best they could through the tunnels. Eventually the tunnel stopped at a set of stairs, and Obrett bade them wait while he checked out the exit with the power of his focus. It only took brief moments, but a smile rapidly spread across his face. "There are horses, and no men. It looks like they have all run towards the city walls, and we are well past them."

Jacob took this as gospel, and surged past them almost throwing himself up the steps. At the top, he shoved hard against the door, and it took the aid of Ispen to help him move it. They spilled out into an empty stable. The door had been hidden behind bales of hay, and it took a moment for them to barge their way past.

"So what was that all about?" Brendan asked of Jacob when they had cleared the exit.

"I hate tunnels," was all the Life Wizard would say.

"I don't understand why."

"That my friend is probably because you are of the Earth guild." Obrett noted with a touch of insight. "Tunnels and underground spaces are second nature to you, but not everybody might share your affiliation."

Jacob nodded at the understanding he had been granted. "I have never liked close spaces, and if there were any other way out, I would have taken it."

"Well don't concern yourself any more about tunnels Jacob," Obrett replied, looking about him. "Worry more about saddle sore. Come on." He led them out into the main stable, a rickety affair, typical of the shabby spread that surrounded the city to the South and East. The horses within the stalls were anything but typical. They were majestic looking beasts, standing taller than any of the wizards, their ears pricked up at the sign of company. "Pay dirt!"

Jacob approached one of the grand beasts, and it snorted once, and lowered its head in greeting. "There is intelligence in these eyes." He said in awe of the horse. "They are truly stupendous."

"And right up to the task," Obrett continued. "They must be guard's steeds, stabled out here for a patrol or some such need I shouldn't doubt. Well they will be getting a patrol all right." He turned to the rest of them. Jacob was stroking the head of one of the patrol horses, while Brendan looked on at the great steeds, and Ispen gazed out through the stable gates for any signs of disturbance. There was none, for everybody had run up to the city walls.

"Have any of you ridden before?" Jacob asked of the others.

"I have," Obrett replied, but the other two shook their heads.

"Never had any cause." Brendan said, looking with trepidation at the great steed in front of him. "There have always been good sturdy carts to carry me."

"Well worry not, I think you will have a time to get used to them. At least as long as the city is distracted. Grab those saddles over there."

With a bit of difficulty, they saddled the horses, which endured their ministrations with the great patience of steeds that were used to being fussed over. Taking a look around, Obrett located blankets and enough food to last them several days. This stable was a lot better stocked than most of the surrounding shacks would be. It was most likely that the stable was usually filled with guards. Obrett felt better at provisioning himself with that knowledge inside him. Had it been the poor and destitute, he would have rather starved. With a bit of effort, and a lot of trial and error, they managed to mount the horses. The two more experienced riders led the two that had never ridden, and they slowly edged their way out into the city for the first time. The muddy tracks that posed as streets were dark and silent. The message had worked well judging from the fires and general mayhem that echoed from the not-too-distant walls. Gradual clashes of metal indicated that at least a token force had gathered about the city gates. It would not be long until whatever army the Witch Finder kept within his fortress would be unleashed. Better for them that they died than became a part of his growing evil. Riding out slowly, they made for the track in front of them, down a winding 'road' to the East.

"Gods, would you look at that," came the awed voice of Ispen.

They halted and turned. In front of them, the darkness of the night sky was blotted out by the mountainous mass of the walls of Raessa. They rose gradually, in subtle tiers, emitting an utter blackness above the city, tapering off to huge towers that split the sky like the clawing fingers of a burned and ruined hand. What made the scene even more grisly was the fact that there were several fires growing with hungry tongues of flame at the base. The light reflected off of the black walls, and smoke coiled about them, oily and thick. "It is a picture we should never forget. It defines for me the evil growing within, in complete contrast to these huts and shacks."

Mostly made of wood, with the occasional dull glint of rusty metal, the hovels were thatched. This was evidence of the type of person that had been drawn in. "Look at this. There are metal smiths, carpenters and thatchers. All country folk that would have been self-reliant, now forced to eek out their existence crammed in because of a compulsion." The city outside appeared as if knelt in supplication to the grand fortress beyond, which was frightening to behold. Even though they were quite far from the base of the walls, perhaps half a league out, they could still feel the warmth that the sooty fires produced. The noise was deafening as well. There were perhaps ten thousand voices clamouring with the false righteousness that they believed to be their own, hammering at the gates to the city proper, and fighting amongst themselves, and with the guards that were engaging them more and more.

"Be thankful that the tunnel did not exit any closer to the city, my friends," Obrett said with thankful relief. "We would have found ourselves in the midst, fighting to get out on foot if we had."

"Why don't we ride now?" Brendan suggested. "Before they find us gone and the guard locked up. The other guard is still at large. Who is to say when he might draw enough courage to admit what happened?"

Obrett nodded in agreement. "We have seen enough of the carnage my friends, and I for one do not wish to see what happens when the army spills out. Nor do I wish to go back into the city as a captive. I have been chained for long enough."

"We have to do something," Jacob urged them.

"We will, my friend, but we have to get away in order to find a way to combat it. We are not strong enough here."

"Ride for Nejait," Ispen suggested. "Our guilds are there, and they will need to know all of this. Guilds should not take sides." The last Ispen muttered to himself in a state of disbelief. Obrett knew what the man meant. He was still having a hard time coming to terms with the fact that his entire guild had turned coat for the most selfish of motives. As they rode to the East, he knew that there were at least three of the Law guild that would agree with him.

Chapter Nine

"The Camp is a series of small settlements in a shallow depression surrounded by gentle hills to the North and South, and a lake and a crevice-like gorge to the West. There is only open Land to the East, all the way to the mountains."

The peaks were ever present on the horizon, though from this point of the countryside they were nothing more than a dark impression in the distance, a purple smudge that spoke of a boundary. It was more than just a physical barrier to Zya, it was psychological as well. Never had she expected to find such wanton cruelty and blatant subjugation. It did not exist on the far side of the mountains, and she had never dreamed that she would witness such a situation. The tribesman, one of many who had arrived through the night, was called Toem Redwood. He paused while Zya sought to control the urge to vent her frustration. "Why would anybody be proud of this?"

"Despite the circumstances, there is evidence that the prisoners have pride in everything they do. It is well organised, and not by the captors. I have watched the camp grow, and there is a woman using her considerable experience to organise the entire area."

Mavra pored over the makeshift map of the area. "So what are we up against?"

"The valley is about three leagues across and two wide, plenty of room for the mercenary bands to be almost independent of each other. From what I have seen, there are several thousand men out there, keeping prisoners camped in various stages of poverty and exposure. The outer camps have been spread concentrically around the valley. There are five of them, and each is guarding a point of access to the village at the centre. One camp is on the route north, blocking the road to distant Bay's Point. Another is near the lake, guarding the crevice that contains the road to Leallyra, the coastal city on a small peninsula to the West. That leaves one camp to the South and two to the East, where a series of obvious but clever fortifications have been built. The central camp consists of an unnamed village surrounded by several communities. These communities are a mix of the growing so-called army, and prisoners that had been gathered from the countryside. The prisoners are kept apart in walled areas for the most part, but others are in houses in the village."

"It's not standard by any means of the imagination. Anybody with a comment on this?" Mavra invited the rest of them into the conversation.

For reasons unknown to Zya, Ju piped up. "O'Bellah is waiting for something."

"What makes you say that?"

"Look at where the camps are. Placed around the valley like that, it's just one big invitation. They might as well have the word 'trap' painted on signs throughout the area. O'Bellah is hoping somebody is going to walk right in there, and then I'll bet that he covers every exit from the valley with mercenaries."

"So we need to be careful then." Mavra arranged piles of small stone on the map where the settlements had been indicated. "Is there anything else?"

Toem looked up from the map. "The strangest fact is that the village appears to be O'Bellah's home."

"How can you be sure?"

"The main village is basically deserted aside from a few of the prisoners. O'Bellah himself lives in the village, but not in the grandest building."

"There is nothing wrong with that. We are used to humble dwellings."

"O'Bellah is not us, Mavra." Zya decided to impart a few home truths. "You never saw what he was capable of."

"And you did?"

"In Hoebridge we visited the council building. O'Bellah had turned it into his own personal hall, complete with spells at the door. He is a braggart, and a bully, and not one known for humility. If he were here as an occupying general, he would be in the biggest building without a shadow of a doubt. If he is not, then it stands to reason that there is someone more important than him here."

Mavra appeared perplexed. "I can't believe that the man is willing to turn his own home into a base of operations for what is conservatively called a war, and at worst a slaughter."

"Well not a slaughter quite yet, Mavra."

"It is not far away, Zya."

"Perhaps. He has an obligation to keep them alive. To whom this obligation is owed I have no idea, but it's clear that commands are coming from elsewhere."

"Why?"

"Because the evil does not flow from here. There is evil in the very ground, seeping through the countryside in the same manner as a tree draws water. There is a wrongness that I can feel and it comes from the East. It surrounds us. If this were the source I would know it." In a moment of anger, Mavra threw a rock at the map. "Damn them," she muttered. "How are we going to get in there and rescue our family?"

"You need an army to conquer an army, mistress, but that is not what we are doing." Tarim had watched for long enough. Zya smiled at how he could not remain in the background for too long. "The camps are spread wide enough apart that we will be able to get in there pretty much unseen. Unless I miss my guess, somebody has been doing some organising behind O'Bellah's back. He is the type of person that would keep all of his eggs in one basket. A hunch tells me that Venla has been playing Mistress. He does not care for these refugees. They soil his very land with their presence."

"Not a nice thing to say about our family, Tarim."

"We aren't talking about your family, Mother, we are talking about O'Bellah's view on the situation. You have to remember what kind of a man he is."

"The camps do look as though they have been given, should I be so bold to say, a woman's touch," Toem affirmed, "but it could be anyone."

"If being in this Caravan was not enough for you Mavra, then just get a feel for the layout of that valley. It has Venla's touch all over it. Perhaps you are too young to have recognised, but this Caravan and that camp are related."

Her father had taken a bit of a gamble in talking down to a young and somewhat insecure Mistress of the Caravan. Mavra could have taken his comments any way, but her reaction surprised Zya. "Maybe one day I shall be remembered as such, Tarim. I have a lot to learn, and I need to rely on those around me. The question is how do we go about getting in there and escaping with Venla and the rest?"

"That trap is waiting to be sprung, Mistress, but I believe that they don't know who is intended to spring it. I have a way in here." Toem pointed to the Northern edge of the map.

"But that is right near one of the encampments. How do you mean for us to get in there?"

"Look at yourself, your weapons, your garb. You look no different to the mercenaries themselves. We will ride straight in without anybody noticing."

"I don't know if I agree with your simplistic solution." Mavra certainly sounded dubious.

"Mercenaries don't give a whit about other mercenaries," Cahal chipped in. "Were we to just ride in there and past them, we would most likely just have to trade a few insults. In the end the decision is yours. It is your caravan, and your family in there."

"I don't see that we have any choice. I don't like having to do it this way, but if there is no way of getting past the guards…"

"Take me prisoner." Zya offered. "Then you can tell them you captured me trying to escape."

"How is that going to get us by the mercenaries? They will hunt us down like wolves, especially when they see you. We can get away with armour, but what are you going in as? Tribal wise woman probably wont be the best of excuses." Wracking her mind for a way to get into the camp, a memory came back to Zya of her childhood. "Mavra, do you remember when we used to bandage Erilee to the point that she could not move?"

At the mention of her sister's name, Mavra's face darkened. "I remember."

"Leprosy. I am going to be a leper that escaped one of the camps. You are bringing me back, wrapped from head to foot for my, and everyone else's protection. They won't want to come within a league of me once you announce what you have. If there is a way into this valley, then it is through superstition and misguided fear, not through force of any kind. The Old Law will not allow you to fight your way in."

"The Old Law might be suspended until we get our family back, Zya." Mavra snapped back immediately. "You do not run this Caravan."

"Don't I know it," Zya shot back. "I am not here to make your decisions, Mavra. I am here to get into that camp. One way or another I need to go. This seems most sensible."

"There is nothing sensible about this. The Caravan left sense behind when my sister went off with those strangers. What we need to decide now is who stays and who goes." A lot of faces suddenly became eager. Whatever the danger, and to Zya that was palpable, there were plenty of volunteers just waiting to be given the opportunity to prove themselves. "More importantly is who stays. The Caravan must be protected at all costs."

"You can leave us, and some of the tribesmen," Tarim offered, indicating himself and Lorn. Lorn threw a desperate look at Zya, but her intuition told her it was the right choice. She remained impassive. "The camp is well hidden, and we know more than enough about tracking and camouflage to see this all safe."

Everybody was now gathered close, and Mavra looked around at them all, uncertainty on her face. "Juatin, you shall remain. I will not be party to you risking yourself." Ju did not appear to take the news well, but he said nothing. "Anita will stay here and run the Caravan in my stead."

"No Mistress you cannot risk yourself." Anita's outburst was as loud as it was quick.

"Yes I can, and I will. Zya will go with me, as will Layric, Jaden and Cahal. Toem too, and Hawknest."

The flame-haired tribesman inclined his head in acknowledgement. "We will see you safely in and out."

198

Toem stayed silent, but Zya could see he was less than impressed. "How far is it to the valley?"

"Several leagues. A good day's ride from here. I suggest riding halfway and then camp, taking it easy with the horses until we reach the valley. That way they are fresh if we need to escape in a hurry."

"We will leave in the morning. That will give us a chance to sort ourselves out. Those of you going, get yourselves ready. If the rest of you could help out in whatever way you can I would be most grateful."

The gathering broke up. Zya remained where she was as did her father, Layric and Mavra. "You look pensive Layric," Mavra observed.

"I am concerned about Venla. She is fragile alone. What if she has not made it?"

"You needn't be worried for your wife, Layric," her father replied, hand on Layric's arm. "If I know Venla, she will have started making offhand comments about the organisation of the place as soon as she got there. She is afraid of nobody, and that will include O'Bellah and his cronies."

"She is still with us," Zya affirmed, "I can feel it. Trust me Layric, everything will be fine."

"Easy for you to say." Was Mavra's grumbling comment.

"Why should I have any reason to doubt my instinct? It has been right so far." Zya could see that Mavra was in no mood to continue this conversation, so she excused herself. Moving away from the camp, Zya found a quiet glade to sit in and gather her thoughts. She closed her eyes and settled on the cool grass, searching her memory for any reason that she would need to go as she suggested. Presently her awareness picked up the presence of others. Ju was in the glade, as was the comforting feeling of her father, and the warm glow of Lorn. They were doing their best to leave her undisturbed. "You don't have to do that, you know. I can sense all three of you."

"I told you, Ju said in Lorn's direction. If embarrassment was hidden on Lorn's face, Zya could feel it beaming out of him.

"In our tribe the wise women are given utmost respect, and a very wide berth." Lorn replied in defence of his actions.

"Well it may surprise you to learn that all the wise women you have been avoiding have known exactly where you were, and precisely what you were doing at the time," Zya replied, opening her eyes and beckoning them all closer. "My men. What am I going to do without you?"

"Look after yourself, that's what Zya." Her father replied as he brushed a wisp of hair back over her ear.

"I won't have any problems in this valley."

"You can't be sure of that," Lorn replied. "I know there's a lot I don't understand about the seers, but you are not yet fully endowed with their gifts. There may be something you miss in interpreting the path of your dreams."

"I am going because I have utmost faith in my feelings. This feels right, Lorn. As much as it felt right to leave the Caravan and end up meeting you, so does this feel right. I have to get in there and see what is going on. I can't tell you how I know I will be safe, but in that valley, O'Bellah holds no threat to me."

"So are you going to help rescue Venla?"

"No, I am not."

"What?" Ju shouted. "Why are you going there if you aren't going to help them?"

"There is something I need to learn in this place, and to go in there and conceal myself is the only method by which I will learn it. If I can help I promise you I will, but it is not my purpose, and it is for Mavra to free her people."

"Not your people?"

"Ju, I don't think they ever were." Zya looked at her father. There were mysteries hidden behind his eyes, and one day she knew he would tall her whether he wanted to or not. "If I think back to my childhood, I was always different. Mavra and Erilee were perfect travellers, happy to stay indoors and do the work. The least I can do is accept that I am different. The Gods only know it is showing." She raised her arms and laughed. Her true family laughed with her. Reaching towards her father, she was pulled to her feet and into a bearhug.

"You be careful, my daughter. You are all I have left in this world. Your mother would be proud of you."

"When I return you are going to tell me about her, father."

"We shall see, Zya."

The night passed quickly for those preparing to stay. For the company headed for the valley, it passed at a crawl as they considered their future and made preparations. For Zya it passed with relative ease. She slept safe in the knowledge that her future was decided for her. She would have no problems in the immediate future. Her dreams were lucid, and she walked through a forest on a steep hillside. Ferns poked out at her, and the brown path, clear of any detritus, wound off up the hillside. She walked, and was not alone. A woman was there, or at least it felt like a woman, for there was a blur whenever Zya looked where she expected her mystery companion to be. Ju was nowhere to be seen, not that it bothered her. Zya walked on, and the apparition maintained its distance, just outside her peripheral vision. "Look

you might as well come where I can see you." Zya's words were suffocated by the foliage. "No echo at all." She reflected on her dream state. "Anything goes I guess." Turning quickly, she tried to catch the blur out, and for a moment, did so. The apparition was about her height, and dark towards the top, but that was all. "I see you now. What do you want?"
There was a reply, just a whisper of a breeze, nothing more.
"You will have to speak up. I cannot hear you."
Again, the slightest of answers, but this time much more urgent.
"It's no good. You are too quiet. Can I help you in any way. Is that you, Ju?"
The ferns around her began to rustle, and then flatten as wind picked up. The apparition no longer evaded her, but instead expanded as the wind increased. Within moments what had been a smudge on Zya's vision had expanded, and coalesced as a whirlwind, black as night. The vortex span wildly, but was rooted to the same spot. It tried to reach her, but huge as it had become, it could not. "Help me, Zya," it cried out in a howl."
"Who are you?" Zya replied, perplexed and not a little frightened. "How can I do this if I don't know who you are?"
"Release me!" The wind shrieked, and purple light spilled out of the vortex and into the sky. Zya closed her eyes, and all went silent. "Dreams." She said aloud to herself. Opening her eyes, the forest was back to normal.
"Release me," hissed a voice, and a great dark creature loomed in front of her.

Zya opened her eyes and jumped up before she realised where she was. Her hands were sticking out in front, in the motion of pushing something away, and she felt sweaty all over.
"Sleep well?" Called her father.
"Not really."
"Nerves probably. It happens to the best of us."
"No, it was not nerves. Something entirely different. I'd rather not talk about it." Zya turned away to see Ju with a questioning look on his face. He hadn't shared her dream and he wondered why. "We'll talk later, Ju. I promise."
The day moved along rapidly from that point onwards. All too soon Zya bade her family farewell and set out upon Red with her six companions armed to the teeth in true mercenary style. Hawknest had been dubbed the unofficial leader as his stature and wild looks were agreed upon as most the most likely quality to get them past the mercenaries should Zya's ruse fail. They rode steadily West until at a predetermined point Toem dismounted and led them to a hollow surrounded by gorse. They spent an uncomfortable night in the cold for fear of giving away their presence. Nobody spoke for the entire night,

and by the time dawn crept over the distant mountains, Zya was chilled to the bone, and fuzzy from lack of sleep.

"Time for your disguise then, Zya," Layric said as he approached her with bandaging. "You are sure about this."

"It's the only way we will get into the valley, Layric."

"Okay then. Remove your outer garments so we can wrap you up. It's too cold to do any more."

Zya allowed them to bandage her as much as possible, enduring the process.

"What are we going to do about her hair?" Layric asked Mavra.

"Tie it back, and put a sack over my head." Zya answered before she risked having her hair chopped off all too soon.

"It's your disguise." Mavra decided. "If you think that will be enough then so be it."

"Trust me, Mavra. The mercenaries will fall over each other trying to get out of the way when you bring me into view."

They got under way, riding much more slowly. "From here on in, absolute silence from the ladies." Toem ordered. "Although there are female companies, mixed bands are rare and will raise suspicion."

"He speaks wisely." Cahal agreed. "I never saw a female mercenary before."

"Well that must mean they don't exist." Came Mavra's sarcastic reply.

"Oh they exist, Mistress, you just don't see them a lot. Now if you will pardon me, shut up and keep quiet. We don't want our façade broken by your sweet murmurings. Just sit there and look fierce."

They rode on while the sun rose to its zenith. About midday Toem halted them. "You cannot see it, but the valley is just around this bend. There may be mercenaries at any point from hereon in. Ride in file, with the prisoner in the middle. The luck of the forest be with us all."

Zya remained silent, cowed, as if she truly had been captured. Bent over in her saddle, she still had a good view of the approaching valley. The ground just dropped away from them and the valley spread out almost like Mavra's map come to life. A little way off was a rude guard post, deserted. They rode quickly past, only to be hailed from behind as they rounded another bend.

"Oi, where you goin?" Yelled a mercenary in muddy leathers wielding a pike. Behind him several others had gotten up from what Zya expected had been a long period of lazing around drinking. The mercenary was unsteady on his feet.

"Prisoner for the village. Escaped with a group of them through the East border." Hawknest yelled back at them.

"Where're the rest?"

Hawknest loosened his sword in its sheath, pulling a foot of the blade out.

"The rest weren't as willing to come along. They made good sport for my men and I." Hawknest flicked his hand up behind his back, and the rest of them laughed at his cue.

The mercenary guard shambled closer. A deliberate move from Hawknest ended with his horse in front of Mavra. "So what's so special about this one?"

"Ever heard of a leper?"

The guard stopped in his tracks, making a sign of warding in front of him. At the word 'leper', the others who had been making their way to their fellow backed off, leaving him to face them alone. "Them as have bits dropping off them? What business do you have with one of those?" He was backing away now. Zya knew her plan would work, but now she could feel events unfolding exactly as she had guessed they would."

"This one works in the village. Somebody very powerful wants this one kept close." This was unexpected, and Zya watched as Toem threatened to become agitated. Hawknest was unpredictable, just as he had said.

"Oh what you mean the boss? Old Dondera?" The guard barked out a laugh, finding something oblivious funny.

"Absolutely. Tell me friend, did you know that lepers can infect those around them? I wouldn't come too close if I were you. Who knows what might start dropping off."

The guard looked down at his midsection and then back at Hawknest, who nodded, his eyes grave. "Go on, get away from me. See that you leave the camp by a different route next time." Without waiting to watch them go, the guard stumbled back to his patrol and whatever pastime was better than guarding the road.

Hawknest led them on around the side of a hill, until they reached a point where the land flattened out. "Good plan," he commented.

"Nearly ruined," Toem admonished him. "You are rash."

"We are in here, aren't we?" Came Hawknest's fiery reply.

"Time for wherefores later," Mavra decided aloud. "We need to get in and out as soon as possible. Zya where do you need to go now?"

"To the main village, which must be those buildings over there."

"This is probably best done overnight, when the prisoners are all gathered together. Toem, why don't you take Zya into the village and the rest of us will find a place to hide until the cover of darkness."

"Sounds like a plan," Toem agreed, and the two of them left the main group.

"They have your mercenaries, they will survive the night."

"And us? In a group the misdirection lasts a lot longer."

"True Zya, but we have to get you to the village, and it is better done in small numbers. We can't find Venla if there is a gang of us banging on every door, so the two of us is best. Now quiet. We don't know what might be watching or listening. You are supposed to be a cowed prisoner. Best thing we can do is find your companions and then decide what to do with you."

As described, the village was a small affair, a few rows of houses strung out along the tracks that led in, with three-tiered buildings in the middle. Toem made for the houses furthest back from the centre.

"How can you be so sure of their location?"

"I have been in and around this village a lot during the passing of the last moon. It is well protected, but not during the day. Only the garrison in the centre of the village is here, and they will be in the inn. O'Bellah likes to keep his home clear of the mercenaries."

"It amazes me that such a tyrant could come from such humble surroundings." Zya said with regret.

"Even the most powerful come from somewhere. Everybody has roots."

"I don't know mine."

"You will. There are reasons for everything. You will find out one day."

They stabled their horses behind the house, and entered through the back.

"Nobody here." Zya said after a cursory look around.

"They are out fishing, hunting, gathering crops and whatnot," Toem replied. "They won't be back until evening, so you had better make yourself comfortable. We are going nowhere else. Make sure you stay away from the windows. We don't know who might walk by."

Zya did just that, secreting herself upstairs in a room with a narrow window that gave her a view over the village. In the silence of the day she could feel Toem moving silently around, both inside and around the house. At one point he appeared in her room. "Are you comfortable?"

"Where is everybody. I thought this village was kept as near to normality as possible."

Toem leaned over and peered out the window. "That I can't answer. The normal populace I have never seen here. It is as though they disappeared completely."

Zya's stomach began to knot. "Something bad happened here. Not the cause of all that is wrong, but an event close to the heart. This village should not be empty."

"It won't be for long. Come downstairs as they will be home soon. It is up to you whether you reveal yourself, but events may unfold a little easier if they do not."

They were waiting in the parlour when the door opened.

"Tarim?" Venla said peering into the gloom at Toem. Zya smiled, safe under her disguise.

Zya took a closer look at Toem as Gwyn was also doing; he wore the typical mercenary garb, and a helmet that concealed most of his face. What it did not conceal was the long dark hair that spilled out from under it, the dark eyes and the serious mien. The armour also did little to hide the fact that this was a true warrior. It was obvious in his bearing, just like her father. "No, not Tarim." He said. Disappointment rang clear in his voice.

Toem removed his helmet, hung it on a chair, and tied his hair back. Only then did he turn and look straight at them. "I am not he of whom you speak." He said in a voice so similar to her father that it brought tears of remembrance to Venla's eyes. "But I do know of the name you mention."

"How? How could you know the name?" Venla demanded. "And what are you doing here? Who are you? Who is that?"

Toem put his hands up in a gesture of placation, seeking to stem her sudden rush of questions. "I am called Toem Redwood, and am of the Merdonese Forest people. I am a companion of Mavra D'Voss, the Mistress of the Caravan. She said that if you know her, you would be able to tell me the name of her sister, and what happened."

Venla looked down to the ground. "All the fateful days that have passed since the chance meeting with two seemingly inept bandits dressed in black, all leading up to the point when the girl had been taken from us. Her name is Erilee. The bandits should have been imprisoned in a village, but were set free by the man who now controls this entire region."

Toem nodded. "That is well then. Judging by your description you are Venla Chemani, wife to Layric." He looked over at Gwyn, who was in the motions of setting down all of the fishing gear. "You would be Gwyn. I have tidings for you. Your wife Anita is well on the road to recovery following the blow given to her by O'Bellah, the tyrant of Ciaharr. She sends her hopes."

"Her hopes? That was an unusual term for her to use." Gwyn replied.

Toem looked around him. "You have a scenic prison, but it is important that you remember that is exactly what it is. A prison. We are coming for you, tomorrow night, in this very village. I have crossed the boundary to give you these tidings. You need to be ready."

"Who exactly are you trying to rescue?" Venla asked. I am unsure that such a feat can be accomplished.

"As many as we can," Toem replied. "Look for us when the moon crosses its zenith. We will ride out of the North." Toem replaced his helmet and went to the door, looking back at them one more time. "There is always hope. Be ready."

"What about your mysterious friend?" Venla called as Toem mounted his horse.

"A leper found near here. He can't speak. He escaped from an outer camp. Was safer to bring him back than let him wander alone in the wilderness. Do with him what you will. Spurring his horse into motion, he bounded away to the South, directly away from them. None too soon, it seemed, for as soon as Toem had gone the thunder of hooves rumbled in from the North. Along the same path that Toem had led them now rode four guards. They were dressed as he had been, but these were real mercenaries. They had weapons clashing all over the place, and made absolutely no secret of their passing. They led two spare horses.

"Up you two layabouts, and get behind these horses." Commanded one particularly surly guard, apparently the leader of the group. There was nothing to discriminate him aside from the fact that he spoke and the others did not.

"What about him?" Venla asked of Zya.

The guard took one brief look in her direction. "What is wrong with him?"

"Leprosy."

The guard stepped back with haste. "Bring him along, but don't get too close, right?"

Gwyn and Venla did their best to obey, keeping their eyes on the job at hand and refusing to let any thought of the imminent rescue attempt betray them was a difficult task in such peril. They handled Zya with the care they had treated her as a girl. It meant a lot that they would do this for someone they had only just met.

On the way into the village, they trailed the mercenaries. The word 'leprosy' was anathema to the guards, who kept them only just in sight for the short journey. Zya listened as Venla spoke to Gwyn. "Thank the Gods that the guards see us as slaves, for I have no mind for fending off blows and insults again." Gwyn did not reply. "Gwyn?" "Mavra has actually been made Mistress of the Caravan. The fact that she has been must coincide with the fact that they were still out there. I worry for my wife."

"I know my husband well, and therefore I know that he would have stuck to the task assigned to him and the others, no matter the cost. This would have meant that the guards must have remained with them too, affording them some element of safety."

Gwyn permitted himself a quiet chuckle. "If only the traveller's council could see us now."

"They would either reward or disband us. My people are spread all over the western side of the Nine Duchies. The largest caravan ever assembled!" Venla took the time to correct herself. "It's not my caravan, it is now Mavra's, and only the girl could give up the position. Nobody would take it from her, especially not me."

Looking across at Gwyn, Zya could see that he too had an air of excitement about him, and it was only when he looked at Venla could she appreciate it. Venla missed her husband, and for this companionship she would be forever grateful, but Zya could now see that Gwyn was as desperate to see his other half as Venla was. Hope was a double-edged sword. It gave one the possibility of joy, but at the same time the disparate chance of failure. If they were going to escape this valley, it would not be easy. Looking ahead, Zya saw the centre of the village. A tower stood above the highest building. It was perfectly square, and made of the kind of rock that only came from the North coast. It had been there when she arrived, but was relatively recently built. It looked so out of place in a rural village, almost as if it had been transported piecemeal from a city wall.

"Have you heard any more about the tower?" Gwyn asked.

"The only rumours of its purpose come from speculation. Nobody I have spoken to has been allowed in, and only O'Bellah seems to have access. Might as well try to gut a stone and use the pieces to halt a horse."

The village gradually came into view as they passed small patches of woodland. A good place for a camp this valley was, for trees were plentiful. Zya felt her companions were safe. There was good potential for hiding and eluding pursuers, but were they already being used to counter that? Zya kept an eye on Venla as they walked. To the guards, stupid to a man, it would appear that she was a suitably cowed prisoner, but in fact she was checking every patch of woodland for exit tracks.

They caught up with the guards, who had now slowed. "Where are we going?" Venla asked.

"Shut it old maid, unless you would like me to silence you for good." The leader of the group menaced her with his sword. They passed the stable, and turned into the courtyard of the inn. The hooves of the horses, shod with iron, made a series of staccato clacks on the cobbles as they were brought to a halt. The guards dismounted and pushed Venla and Gwyn towards the building across from the inn, with the tower standing like a giant over the village to their left. They left Zya well alone, but she followed nonetheless.

"What's in here?" Asked Gwyn of Venla.

"This building is known as the domain of Dondera, the mother of O'Bellah. I know better than to question the guards as to why we are being left here. Keep your eyes open. You too, clothtop. Be careful."

As soon as the guards had put them in a room with several other people they left them alone, retreating as quickly as was possible. Venla breathed out heavily, and sat down, not sure what to make of this strange turn of events.

"What in the name of all seven Gods do they want us in here for? We are just supposed to be captives that hunt for food."

"You know as much as I." Gwyn said in consolation.

Venla got up and walked over to a cabinet, and began quietly rifling through the drawers. The other people in the room watched her and she felt as if she had met them somewhere before, so familiar were their faces.

"It won't do you any good looking in there." A particularly elderly gentleman said with voice that Zya recognised, but could just not place. "We have sought any sharp instruments, blades or otherwise. There are none."

Venla continued looking. "Were you going to fight your way out?" She found a ball of string, and tucked it away in a pocket.

"No," the voice replied, "we were going to kill ourselves."

Venla stopped what she was doing, and looked at the huddled group of figures across the room. "Why would you want to do that? Where there is life, there is hope."

"Not for us. We are damned forever." The speaker stood and approached her. There was something so distinctly familiar about him that it maddened Zya that she could not see the answer that stood before her. He had a shock of white hair, and had not shaved in a month. The most noticeable thing about him though was the haunted look in his eyes, as if the man had tasted such utter despair that he lacked the words to utter a description and left his eyes to speak aloud for him. Instantly Zya knew that there was something very wrong with him.

"What happened to you?" Venla made to touch the old man but he drew back. He trembled as if he would break down and cry but had not the will. "We have been touched by the netherworld creature, the black giant that looms over everything in this world. It has touched us, and it knows us. A word from its master commands us and we must obey utterly. There is no resistance.

There is no hope. There is only infinite suffering and pain. If I could dash my hand through the glass in the window I would, but his command forbids me. I must stagnate in this body instead of being given blissful release, my only option being to join with the creature should I find a way to disobey."

The man was utterly devoid of any positive emotion. "You are typical of a lot of the people I have seen around the camps. They are all missing something, just like the men who had been sent to capture them. Basic human emotions were lacking in all. But you are not alone. The creature Jani and Gwyn had witnessed in that bizarre ceremony, the very same creature that had aided in their capture. It is the key to all of this. What did it do when it touched you?"

The old man would not reply, and sat there staring into space. Zya knew that her only option was one she would never take. She would pick out her own veins before that creature touched her.

"I know who you are," Gwyn said as he looked at them. There were three men in the room altogether. "You are the councillors from the village of Hoebridge, the last place we visited before all of this hubbub started."

"You are right in some respects." The old man broke from his reverie to respond. "My name is Alander, and my two companions are Melgar and Pecifer." He indicated the man with wiry hair and the large man in turn. They looked up, but said nothing, sharing the same haunted view of life as he did. "We were indeed councillors in the village you spoke of, a village that is no more." Alander turned from Venla, and went back to his companions.

Rifling for a few more prizes, Venla joined them shortly as did Gwyn. "What did you mean when you said that we were not entirely correct?"

Alander looked up, his face a display of utter misery confined in a body that could not let go. "This hubbub as you put it so eloquently had started a long time before you were unfortunate enough to arrive in our village. O'Bellah had been in and out for the past four seasons. He brought mercenaries with him each time he came, and the last time, the time after you left, he brought the creature. They did unspeakable things to the women and children, and murdered the men or worse."

"What could be worse than death?" Venla asked.

Melgar put his hand on Alandar's arm. "This is worse." He said. "Enslavement with no will to end it. We are utterly slaves of the creature, and will do its bidding or the bidding of anybody that commands it. We cannot help ourselves. The men were marched into camps like those around this village, and await the command to rise up and decimate the countryside."

This shocked Venla. "Why would anybody want to do this to peace-loving people?"

"He has been searching for a girl, tall and dark," replied Melgar. "He suspects that you know where she is, and he wants us to find out from you. The girl that was with you, called Zya S'Vedai. She fits the description."

This was no surprise to Zya, for she knew she had been sought before this. Nonetheless, she forced herself to remain impassive, overlooked.

"Zya?" Venla laughed. "How would I know that? She left us not long after we left Hoebridge, and the fat oaf knows that well."

"Nevertheless, he does not believe you and desires the truth as he sees it." It was obvious that Melgar had been compelled to ask these questions, and to get a positive clue as to her whereabouts. He tried asking her several times in different ways, but the answer was always the same.

It did not take long for O'Bellah to burst in, red with rage, and this time he was followed by the huge woman that was his mother. "You WILL tell me where she is!" He roared.

"No, I will not," Venla replied calmly. "How many times do I have to say the same thing to you? Zya, if that is who you are truly after left us moons ago. She could be anywhere in the Duchies by now. All this time you have been chasing us, she has not been anywhere near us." Venla was slowly becoming irate, and mindless of the danger to which she presented herself. "She left us in order to protect us, ironically from you."

O'Bellah paced around the room, bringing very obvious flinches from the old men every time he passed them but no such deference from the travellers. Gwyn had nothing to worry about for it was only Venla that O'Bellah had ever focussed upon. "You know where she went, what her aims were. You WILL tell me!"

O'Bellah was now nose to nose. Venla had seen her share of angry intimidators during her life, and stood her ground. "You cannot bully me into telling you, especially when I do not know the answer. I have not seen the girl in ages, but the longer you persist in unbelieving, the further from your flabby clutches she manages to get so that is all right with me. In a season's time you may still be asking me the same thing, but by then you will never find her. Never."

O'Bellah raised his hand to strike her, but a muffled sound came from behind him. He turned to find that it was his mother speaking. "Leave her." Came the words, as though they had been spoken through a bolster. It was the strangest sound Zya had ever heard. Dondera had grown so large that even her voice seemed to strain, the vocal chords fighting to make a sound.

Those simple words were enough to stop O'Bellah in his tracks. He obeyed his mother without question, so it seemed. "Frilzae!" He yelled instead, and with one more venomous look in Venla's direction, he stormed out, paying no attention to the bandage-wrapped figure in the corner. Dondera looked at Venla as well for a moment, and the look was one of pure, undisguised hostility. If the woman could have moved any faster she would have struck out at her, but as it was Dondera shuffled off as fast as she could move, which was not greatly. Stepping in as the lumbering woman struggled up some stairs was a younger man, one with a permanent sneer on his face. His hair was hacked short, in imitation of the mercenaries that were seen about the village and throughout the surrounding countryside, but it was a poor imitation. He had obviously led a privileged life, and it showed. He was no more a mercenary than Venla was a Duke, but he was all the more dangerous for it. Zya remembered Frilzae. He glanced over at Venla, and his sneer turned to a glare. "You. You will both pay for what happened to my friends, mark my words. You and all of your ragged little band."

Alander chuckled at this, and it heartened Zya to see that the man had some spirit left in him. "Friends? Frilzae, whenever did you have time to make friends with people? If I recall, you were too busy being pampered by lackeys and sucking on any morsels handed down to you by your glorious master to actually make friends. Or do you mean those fools who followed you around trying to get close to power, as you did? They were just along for the ride. They were no friends of yours."

Frilzae unleashed a backhand that sent Alander reeling. The old man crashed over a bench and lay still. "Get him up." He said to Melgar, and then looked over at Venla. "You are to go back and remain in your house until called for. Any funny business will result in dire consequences. The master of Raessa will have you dealt with soon enough."

This was no threat. By the gaze with which he followed them out of the room, this was a promise, and one that he intended to keep personally. They could do no more than told, and made their way back to the house. Passing through the courtyard, Venla looked up to see a spear of light come between two of the buildings. Even in such situations, nature could provide wondrous displays of art. This was such an example. The sunlight lit up the western side of the tower, making it seem that much more a part of things. The cobbles and walls were a deep purple in the shade as opposed to the yellow of the striking beam of light, and Zya grieved for the simple life that had been denied these simple folk. She guaranteed that none of them wanted a war where most of the countryside was wiped out of people. In silence they passed the well behind the inn and crossed the field that now lay fallow to reach the houses.

"I have no idea of who else is in the row of houses," Venla said, "but I intend to find out this very night. Our dwelling is right in the middle of the row."

"Difficult to sneak off with guards circling the village so frequently," Gwyn agreed, "so there is no hope of any quick movement. We will have to rely on the darkness. Besides, we need to keep out bandaged friend here out of the wind."

Keeping straight faces and moving slowly, they crossed the track and entered the house, barring the door as best they could.

"Who is this?" Ramaji asked upon seeing Zya dressed up in bandages. She looked Zya over, making Zya feel most uncomfortable. If anybody was going to recognise her, it would be Ramaji.

"A friend of a friend," Venla replied. "Ask no questions. It can wait."

"Yes Mother, Ramaji replied, still using the caravan honorific. Ramaji already had a fire going to ward off the chilly nights and to everybody's surprise, Gwyn pulled a huge fish out of his tunic.

"You kept that under your shirt?" Venla exclaimed in a whisper.

"Only way to give us a decent meal." He replied, also in a whisper. "Better this way than having nothing at all."

They cooked the fish by roasting it in a pot near the fire, and adding what herbs Jani and Ramaji had found on their sojourn into the hills. After they had eaten, Gwyn bade them go upstairs. They took Zya right up into the loft, so that they only had the roof and the floor to worry about privacy over. Even so, nobody dared speak aloud.

"We had a visitor today." Venla whispered, no longer able to contain herself.

"What sort of visitor?" Jani asked. He sat with his wife propped in front of him for it was not warm.

"The sort that brings glad tidings." She replied. Gwyn was checking the roof for holes. They did not want anybody to see the candlelight by which they spoke. As far as any guards were to believe, they were occupying the three bedrooms, and not the loft above.

"He had enough credentials to convince us he was who he said he was, a forest tribesman from across the mountains."

"What was he doing this far across from his home?" Jani asked. By the look on his face it was clear that Jani was as surprised as the rest of them as to the identity of the mysterious stranger Venla was describing.

Venla leaned in, close to them all. "He said he was a recent companion of a caravan, one led by Mavra D'Voss."

"Mavra?" Jani said aloud.

"Oh, my daughter," Ramaji said in relief, tears welling.

"What is Mavra doing leading the caravan?" Jani asked.

"Anita was injured when she was hit by the brute. She is well again, but ceded the responsibility to Mavra, who decided that they are going to come and rescue us."

"They are coming here? Right in the middle of the camp? How exactly are they going to manage that, magic?" It was clear that although he had every faith in his daughter, Jani thought that even this was beyond her, no matter who she had to aid her. Zya felt he would be very surprised in a day or so.

"He did not say. He just told us that when the moon reaches its zenith tomorrow night, they will come out of the North, and take as many as are willing with them. He left our friend here because it's safer with us than in the wild, where he was found."

As the thought struck home, Ramaji spoke the obvious statement. "But we don't know anybody else here, let alone trust them enough to take them with us."

"Well we had better go about making friends tonight and be quick, and very quiet about it." Venla laid out the plans as she saw them, the others listening intently in the quiet room. The rest of the night was split between shifts of watching, sleeping and scouting the surrounding houses. As Venla had explained, they had little or no problem with moving around in the dark between houses for the guards rode patrols along predefined routes outside of sight and sound of the immediate village. There were the occasional watchmen to worry about, but as they rarely travelled beyond the light of the inn a quiet figure in the dark would go unnoticed. One further benefit was that like them, the rest of the captives were assumed cowed by O'Bellah and his mercenaries, for there was no obvious way for them to beat fortifications, guards, and blocked roads on foot. Assumption was to be the mercenaries' worst enemy. Zya waited with patience while her former companions took their turns in scurrying out in search of others. Venla alone made contact with five of the houses, and when she warned them to make ready for a trip the night following they were eager or even excited, but definitely not cowed. Zya's spirits were lifted when Jani and Ramaji returned announcing that all but one of the houses had been accounted for, and they were willing and in most cases able.

The next morning followed all too soon, dawn coming to a cloudy sky and bringing with it the morning chorus as birds sought to greet the arrival of a new day. It was a rousing alarm for Venla, who had hardly dropped off to sleep. "There are more important things for us to think about, including masking the nights activities and spending the day resting as much as possible." She said when Gwyn commented on the state of her appearance. "We face another night with the potential for no sleep, so take what you can." No sooner had they taken what breakfast they could scrape together from the meagre offerings of the guards then the guards turned up at their door. "You two." The leader pointed at Jani and Ramaji. "You are going to work in the inn. The great O'Bellah has developed a taste for fish, and the rest of you are to fish every day from this point on. That includes your leper. Get your things and go." The guard slammed the door on his way out, not waiting to shepherd them again.

Venla looked skyward. "Thank the Gods. The situation could not have turned out any better for us. Jani, will you and Ramaji be able to stay awake over there?"

"We got the most rest, Mother," Jani replied, "so we will be fine."

"Good. Gwyn and I will be able to rest up, sleep and catch food for the impending journey, and hopefully rags here can help."

Zya nodded slowly in agreement. Just because she would not speak, didn't mean she couldn't play a part.

"Excellent. You just let us know if it gets too much. Ramaji, you will need to purloin anything you deem of use from the inn."

"I wouldn't call it purloining," Jani protested. "I would prefer to use the phrase 'obtaining for the greater good'."

"Be careful," Venla warned. "Keep your wits about you. We will see you all later."

They were ferried to their location, Gwyn insisting that they were dropped a little further around the lake than before. They were left near the bank of one of the tributaries running into the lake.

"Why here?" Venla asked when they were finally left alone.

Gwyn looked about him. "Catch a fish, and I shall tell you."

Duly obliging, Venla was fortunate enough to land a beautiful fish almost straight off. "The Gods are with us today Gwyn, I can feel it in the air." She said with a deep breath of the beautiful scent of the valley. Zya was content to remain still and watch the horizon. Such depravity so close by, the peace at the lake was a false security.

"It is a shame that we can't settle down here, drop roots." Gwyn replied. "The land is so brimming with goodness here it will be difficult to leave the place."

"I know," Venla agreed, "But think of all the places we have yet to see, all the villages we may yet still visit. Travellers see those places, settlers do not."

Gwyn smiled. "Spoken like a true Mistress of the Caravan."

Venla nodded. "But one no longer. Not unless Mavra renounces the rights and cedes them to me."

"Will you ask her?"

Venla shook her head. "Never. It is not my place to seek dominion of any form. I would be offered the position, or suffer my place and advise as best I could."

"And offer advice from the sidelines?"

"Gwyn, I could do that about as much as I could lead an army. I heard a story once about a group of travellers that underwent a change in leadership and situation. They had three people trying to run the caravan from behind the scenes, each of them suggesting ways to do things better. In the end, they all left, for their subtle ways were becoming obvious and they were too domineering. The new Mistress took a stand and they left. I would never have that of the people I love. If Mavra is content I will offer advice when asked, but never presume to know better than her. Besides, Layric might enjoy the stress-free life." Venla said the last sentence with a wink and they both laughed. They were looking forward to seeing their loved ones once again. Zya wanted to reveal herself to them, and bask in the warmth, but she had a feeling that it was simply not time.

The cloudy day dragged, for if ever Zya wished a day away it was that one. Venla and Gwyn took turns fishing and sleeping, thus helping them recover from the night before. The fish piled up, more than ever willing to take a bite at an imaginary fly. Once Zya woke up to find herself alone, the rod twitching as a fish was caught. Pulling it out of the ground, she proceeded to land the fish and just as she was removing the hook as she had been taught, Gwyn walked into view.

"Suddenly active, aren't you." He said. "I didn't think you were capable of landing a fish. Not many I know could perform such a feat while completely bandaged up. Most of them would have been taught by me."

He knew. Zya was sure of it. She considered her position of silence and while she did Venla returned.

"Where did you go?" Venla dropped a bunch of fresh herbs to the ground.

"Scouting." Came the brief reply.

"Scouting for what?"

Gwyn smiled mysteriously. "Scouting for some answers." Gwyn glanced at Zya. When he received a scowl that showed Venla wanted a proper answer, he continued. "I was looking for any signs of a ford across the river. There is one about a mile upstream, and it is not obvious so I left a few signs."

"Such as 'This way to the crossing?'"

Venla's sarcasm was an endearing quality. Zya had decided this long ago, and creased up in laughter, forgetting herself. It had the effect of stopping both her companions in their tracks. Zya closed her eyes and took a deep breath. "Remember your place." She whispered.

To their credit, neither Venla nor Gwyn said a thing, though their faces were a picture. Breaking the awkward silence, Gwyn continued his previous conversation. "No, a few woodsman signs; Piled rocks, marks in the ground, twigs bent and snapped in certain directions. I was just thinking an alternative route out would be beneficial." Gwyn then carefully removed certain leaves from a pouch he had been carrying. "I have got something to give O'Bellah and his cronies a bit of a stomach ache as well."

Venla looked carefully at the leaves. "Lypar!" She exclaimed. "Won't that kill them? Oh Gwyn, how could you even think of that?"

"The leaves cooked inside the fish will do nothing more than leave them praying at the holy altar of the jakes God for a while." Gwyn interrupted her outburst. "It will give us more time to escape unnoticed, should the expected come to pass. The leaves are not as potent as the berries, much milder in fact."

Zya recalled how the village of Hoebridge was generally bereft of children, who had all fallen victim to the pretty berries O'Bellah had introduced into the village with his supposedly innocent gesture. As innocent as a murderer was, at any rate. Gwyn tucked a few of the leaves away, but then went about carefully stuffing the rest down the throats of about a dozen of the fish they had caught that day. There were more fish but he left them alone, putting them into a small sack.

"How are we going to hide that?" Venla asked, seeing there was no worldly way of doing so in plain sight.

"You are going to conceal it beneath your skirts." He answered awaiting the explosion. It was about to come when they heard the thunder of horses off in the distance. "Quick!" He said. "Do it now!"

"I'll get you back for this." Venla growled at him as she turned and lifted her outer skirt. "Fish in a sack, under my skirt! What an indignity!" She muttered under her breath. Turning away from him she hitched up the front of her skirt and wedged the top of the sack in where it was caught around her waist. "Okay, satisfied?" She said, but Gwyn was still watching the approaching horsemen. "What is it?" Venla asked.

"Those are not guards." He said quietly. "They are something else."

Zya peered in the same direction, and could see two bands of horsemen. "There they are, behind them!" Now the second group of horsemen were catching up the first, and several members of the first group peeled off and with a distant 'whoop' engaged them. Even from the distance that separated them from the battle, they could see the swords flash as the sun dodged in and out of the clouds above. The leading horsemen did not stop, but the second group had lost, and the victors collected the horses and rode on towards them. Venla and Gwyn had no choice but to pack up their things and wait, for this mercenary band was surely coming their way for a reason. There were between a score and three dozen judging from the noise of hooves, and they varied in size unlike the universal broad shape of the mercenaries. They were not all armed either. As the riders closed in, the reason for this became apparent. There were at least two of the villagers for every armed rider.

"The time for escape has come," Gwyn announced, and picked up his belongings. "I think you can remove the sack now."

Gwyn's comment had two meanings. Venla removed her fish sack, doing so without any further comment.

Zya slowly removed the sack from her head, out of the view of her companions. The lead riders stopped, and one dismounted. He was a large fellow, all decked out in leather armour and wearing a gnarled club hanging from a belt at his waist. There was a certain stance about the man.

"I swear you look familiar." Venla said.

"I think you dropped something." The man said to her, and the voice made Venla's heart stick in her throat.

"That voice. It brings back memories that I felt I had forgotten, of countless ramblings and discreet advice, of love and respect above all."

The guard removed his helmet and there stood her husband, Layric. Venla looked down, standing with legs astride and a sack of fish between them. She could not have looked more ridiculous, but she ran forward and threw her arms around his neck, hugging him tight.

Tears came, and Venla wept with relief. She pushed him back to arm's length and took a look at him. He was dressed mercenary fashion, leather and metal abounded. "What in the name of all that is right and good are you doing here?" She asked, afraid to scold him, but needing to know.

"Doing what is necessary, my dearest." He replied. "There are those out there that need the help of any willing to give it. We are no longer travellers, Venla." She looked him up and down. Zya did not remember seeing Layric wearing such garb before. It was obvious that he was relatively new to the clothing he wore, but it seemed as though it were starting to fit him, like an ill-fitting rug that had just been trampled into place. "Well you shall have to show me what other skills you have picked up during our moons apart." She said coyly, bringing a chuckle from the core of her life.

Layric looked past his wife to Zya. "Did you find what you sought?"

"I believe so." She answered, bringing both Venla and Gwyn swinging around to face her.

"You..? Where..?" Venla said, confused.

"I knew it." Gwyn announced in triumph. "You can't take the fisherman out of the family."

"I couldn't help it." Zya sheepishly admitted.

"Why did you not tell us?" Venla demanded.

"Not now, Venla." Layric replied. There will be time for questions later on. For now just accept that there have been some changes." Layric chucked her robes over, and Zya quickly wrapped them about her.

"Those clothes. Only tribal seers wear that. What are you doing with them." Venla stared at her for a moment. "No."

"We need to leave now." Zya diverted her attention. "We are not safe."

Gwyn looked to the arriving riders.

"Anita is not with us, my friend." Layric said.

Gwyn looked crestfallen. "But the tribesman said. . ."

"I know what he said, for I gave him the message. She remains out of harm's way for now, on the orders of another. You will see her soon enough."

Jani and Ramaji rode up, dismounting as soon as they were able, and leading their horses. Ramaji hugged Venla close. "It is good to see that you are still safe."

"Of course we would be safe." Venla replied. "Whatever do you mean?"

"What my wife means is that when we were working in the inn, they were talking about their orders to go out and despatch the two fishers. Since we know of nobody else out here, we assumed they meant you."

Venla went pale. "It never occurred to me that we were actually in a perfectly isolated position, where nobody would ask questions. What has happened to change that?"

"Mavra has happened." Jani answered proudly, and as if to emphasise his point, three more masked figures rode up to them, the same three that had so coolly dispatched their pursuers. The lead figure reined its horse in and jumped lightly down. Removing the mask, the figure was Mavra but at the same time not. Sunny-haired and fair of complexion she was now tempered with a diamond edge.

"What are you all doing?" Venla asked, almost speechless.

"Saving you, Venla Chemani." Mavra answered in a tone so similar to her own that Venla could not be sure she had not uttered those words once before. "But all this?"

"Questions later," said Mavra. "Mount up and we will talk, but we are not out of the thick of it yet. We have an escape to perform."

"My wife will ride with me, Mother," Layric decided out loud.

Mavra grinned. "You sure that horse can carry you both? You are not the smallest of people Layric."

Layric patted his horse on the flanks. "Old Aroham has pulled many heavier weights in his time, and I want my wife close to me."

"I can understand that." The young mistress replied with sympathy. "Mount up!" She added. When all were mounted she looked back. "Everybody ready, Hawknest?"

The red-haired tribesman stood in his stirrups and laughed out loud. "As ready as they will ever be, mistress Mavra. If we make this escape, your name will be remembered for a hundred generations as a good luck charm!"

They rode to the South, crossing the ford and heading into the gently sloping hills that rimmed that part of the valley. They rode in silence for the most part, but once her curiosity had gotten the better of her, Zya just had to ask a question. "Why now, when you were supposed to be coming at night?"

Mavra pulled her horse in closer so that they could speak. "It was the strangest thing. We were preparing to leave to scout the area, when one of the tribesmen spotted two figures hurtling towards us. We stopped and hid as best we could, and they ran straight by us, oblivious to our presence. It was what they looked like that made us decide to come in early. They were dressed exactly as those two you faced so long ago. That was a bad omen, and I was not prepared to wait a moment longer."

"How did you get all these people out of the village?"

"O'Bellah locked himself in the tower, along with everybody that was already in there." Jani replied from behind them. "It seems that somebody wasn't happy to be stuck in there. The noise was enough to collapse the tower itself."

"We did our bit in keeping them in." Mavra added. "We knocked the wheels off of a cart right in front of the door. That should keep them penned. The only other problem was avoiding the patrols; the one you saw us chasing was the third to find us. They are disorganised though, and it has been easy to slip through their net."

Venla was still in a state of disbelief, and hung on to her husband's broad shoulders for support, her face leaning against his back. "I can't believe that you are all wearing weapons. How could you go so far against the Old Law?"

"We have not gone against it, my wife." Answered Layric from in front of her. "We have made a philosophical choice. It was them, or it was us. We have seen a village where they have impaled *every single* villager on a stake, for no other reason than they believe in and follow the Old Law. That was enough to convince everybody. It certainly convinced the tribesmen, and if they believe it, devout as they are, then so must we."

"What have they done to become so changed?"

"We beheld the three wizards, who revealed the truth to us," Hawknest answered as he rode up. "The Seeker of Truth it was that had the vision. These evil men are concocting dark magic of immense proportions. The Law and the stone wizards both concurred. They laid down the commandment for us to defend the common people of the countryside, and thus do we fulfil our duty. The mercenaries would kill us, and we would save everyone. Therefore we must kill them to prevent them killing more."

Venla was distraught. "I can't believe what I am hearing." She pointed at Mavra accusingly. "You have taken my caravan and turned it into a war band. How dare you?"

"Peace Venla,." came the deep voice of Jaden from a few horses back. "Listen to them."

"Venla, I did not take your caravan. There was no caravan left to take. Layric himself persuaded everybody else that I should be made the Mistress in accordance with our ways. It was also him that agreed with the necessity for us to be able to defend ourselves. We have been hunted, and we have won victories. There are bands like this spread across Ciaharr and even Ardicum. Their mandate is to inform and defend the people. Moreover, it is to teach them to defend themselves. Nobody outside of a city is safe any more."

Venla shuddered at the enormity of what was happening outside of her simple life of the captive. "Everything I believe in has been turned upside down. Even though we are riding on our way to escape, it all feels as bad as when we were first captured. The treks, the previous escapes, they had all been for nothing. The world is on a precipice, and I feel us all sliding a little too close to the edge. There is a word that describes all you have told me." She said quietly. "Genocide."

Mavra looked as determined as once Venla herself had, long ago during her younger days. "We know, Venla. We have chosen this course reluctantly, and with no other option, but there is a word we use in response. That word is *war*."

Chapter Ten

The reunion of Gwyn and Anita was one of the most tear-filled joyous moments of Zya's life. She had cried when Mavra had been bear hugged between her mother and father, but she had suspected they were all okay. Gwyn had told her that his last memory of Anita had been to see her lying in a heap on the ground, unconscious as a result of the cruelty of O'Bellah. Now he embraced her gently while the band looked on. Zya was satisfied with the outcome. Not only had they rescued their family, and locked O'Bellah up in that tower, but also they had released all of the other prisoners from the village, and escaped past the camps of mercenaries into the hills beyond the valley. Against their beliefs Mavra herself had dispatched the only pursuers, along with the help of Cahal and Jaden. Now the band numbered over three score, for the tribesmen had gotten word to their brethren that finally there was somebody else willing to take a stand. All Mavra had wanted was to rescue her family, but now there was something much more that was needed of her. Whether or not Mavra knew this was unclear, but they had to serve the people in a way they had never expected. They had to save them. The camp had been moved from the small copse to a location a bit further away from O'Bellah's mercenary village. This was much more defensible, on a rise and in a deep patch of woods. Not only did the trees muffle any noise they might make, but the space also allowed room for expansion, and that was Mavra's plan. Villages were few and far between, these making easy targets for the marauders. Zya forsaw the villagers making themselves much more difficult options to tackle. The mercenaries were not going to have free reign to murder. Not as long as her *family* drew breath.

Venla walked towards her, away from the main group of rejoicing people. She smiled in that motherly way, but there was also a hint of deference in her stance. "You have come a very long way in such a short space of time." She said, looking pleased at the result.

"I have had little choice in the matter mo. . ." Zya corrected herself just in time. "Venla."

Venla beamed her approval. "My, it's a long time since I have been called that." She did not appear angry at the fact.

"You don't mind?" Zya asked carefully.

"No, I honestly don't think that I do," Venla replied. "When we were taken, and I saw Anita lying there, I was sure that she was ready to pass on into the laps of the Gods. I know my husband, that after wrestling with his conscience would do the honourable thing and ensure continuity. I am just pleased that he did."

"Venla, I am sorry I left you all. I did not want any of this."

Venla embraced her, reminding her subconsciously that although the role was no longer official, she was indeed still the child, and Venla the matriarch. "It is all right, truly it is. Layric explained to me what happened. I can honestly say that I do not know if I would have had the will to follow my path of dreams. Not then, not even now. You have come far in a season, child. A seer. I would never have expected that."

Zya felt relieved at her recent decisions, but still felt a need to try and explain herself. "Venla, what I have done I felt that I was compelled to do. I do not agree with it all, even now. We serve people, but we also serve the Old Law and that states that we can only act in self-defence. I feel that you will be put in a position where you are forced to act out of that same self-defence, and the motive behind it might not be altogether right." She sat down on the edge of the wagon. "By the time that happens we will have gone. I needed to come here and see that you were safe. I am joining the Earth Guild in Bay's Point just as soon as I return. You should hear from the tribesmen about what they have witnessed. It supersedes all other mandates, but I cannot be a part of this in good conscience."

Venla clasped her hand in silence. She was one to know about duty. "Layric has also told me about the villages, and the deaths, and also about some strange wizards that encountered dark magic in the village."

"I do not know much about them, except that there were three, and they are very highly thought of by the tribesmen. It seems that it was one of the wizards that encouraged them to aid the citizens of the plains. They found your band just after we did, and the rest has been one continual rush of planning, practicing and riding."

Venla stepped back to look at the gear Zya now wore. "You are quite the elder for a youngling. What exactly can you see?"

"It's mostly a muddle still. Gut impressions. I dream, and when it happens, which it randomly does, I get a wrenching in my gut, as the future meets the present within me. Still, beats embroidery." Zya added, and they both laughed. "I wonder sometimes how different things would be had I stayed."

"They would have found you," Venla replied, trying not to say too much.

"Had you remained with us, I am certain the consequences would have been much worse for us all. Granted it would have been nice to have Tarim's skills as a warrior, for that was what he undoubtedly once was, but who is to say that we would have continued on this current path had you not gone?"

Zya began to see what Venla was getting at. "Are you saying that you would have preferred things the way they are, despite all that has happened, and all everybody has gone through?"

"Zya," Venla replied sincerely, "I am saying exactly that, because from the experiences you have gained it has made a better person out of you."

Zya looked down at herself. "A better person out of me? Venla, I am still a girl."

Venla shook her head. "No you are not. You are a leader. Maybe not yet, but you have a spark."

"Mavra rescued them. Mavra will be the one they look to for direction, but you are going to have to help decide what happens next." Despite the leather garb, and the sword she held, there was definitely still a lot of the girl left in Mavra. She had obviously been running on nerves as taut as lute strings for a very long time now. She had waited until she felt it appropriate to step into the conversation.

Venla continued speaking to head off any further protest. "It need not be as bad as you think it is, dear. Just because I am no longer the Mistress of the caravan, it does not mean that I will refuse to aid you should you ask it of me."

"Would you not want it back?" Mavra asked, though her eyes already spoke of an immense relief in the knowledge that she was not alone.

"Absolutely not!" Venla exclaimed. "That an ex-Mistress has taken back a caravan while her successor was still around would be a scandal! Besides, I am going to enjoy the freedom, and so is my husband." Venla added a wink after she spoke, to leave Mavra in no uncertain terms with regards to what she meant.

"Well it is good to know that I am not alone." Mavra said with relief.

"You were never alone." Venla replied as she watched Gwyn gently holding his wife, getting immense satisfaction that they were back together again. "As long as there is anybody from your caravan with you, you are not alone. Out there somewhere is a man of your own. One that will defend you till death comes calling, and now all you have to do is find him."

"We have the guards." Mavra replied, unsure of what Venla meant.

"The *guards* won't marry you, girl." Venla replied archly, and suddenly Mavra understood.

"Ohh." She said. "That is going to have to wait. We have started something bigger and more important than that now, and I think that such trivial matters will be left until a time when we can cross the country peacefully and unhindered."

"Maybe," Zya replied, "but know this Mother, you did not start this, not in any way. If you want to finish it, that is up to you.

"Heed caution though," Venla added. "You should know that we witnessed a large gathering of men undergoing a compulsion by a creature of darkest magic. They are out there, maybe in the villages you seek to save awaiting the call of their master. They are men with no hope, and no vision of the future. They have joined what you could loosely call the enemy, and we should all be wary."

Mavra looked around at the other people that had been rescued. There was about an equal proportion of men and women, and even a couple of children. "What about them?"

"Look closely at them, Mother, and you will see a spark in their eyes. They definitely have something to live for, in most cases each other. The men you should be worried about do not have that spark. They have nothing they would call their own worth defending, and no morals worth standing up for. They are the sons of misery, and thus have they willingly been enslaved. They are the worst kind of enemy, one with nothing to lose."

Mavra sighed once more. "If only we could get a hold of the wizards. They would be able to aid us."

"My dear, it is going to take a lot more than a wizard with his useless stone to help us should the struggle really erupt."

"What do you mean?"

Venla shuddered at the memory. "The creature that controls them is a being of stone, twice my height, and emanating so much evil that it makes you cower to look away. It *will* take a lot more than wizards."

"That is a worrying thought."

At the mention of the creature, Zya's stomach tied up completely. She doubled over.

"Zya, what's wrong?" Mavra asked, reaching for her shoulder.

"I have seen the creature in my dreams. It haunts them. I have to get to Bay's Point as soon as I can. I have found the answers I looked for in coming here."

"You will, but for now all you need worry about is what is in front of you."

Zya forced herself back up, taking huge, ragged gasps of air. People were beginning to gather their way, expectant looks on their faces. Everybody that had been a part of the recent episode was there, along with those that had been left guarding the camp. They gathered in a crowd, right in front of the wagon she had been leaning against. Those in front sat down to make it easier for those behind to see. The couples with children brought their fidgeting charges around to where they could see the lady that had helped to rescue them. This was going to be difficult enough for Mavra as it was, but she lacked height. Mavra looked her way, and Zya nodded in encouragement. She climbed up onto the wagon, so that she could look down on them. It was quite a crowd, but they were all hers, and awaited her words. She took a deep breath, unsure what words were going to be spilling out. "We did it," she said humbly, and they all cheered. She raised her hands, and they quietened. "We have been into the spiders nest, past his web of defences, and taken his prize meal: our family. Finally, the Caravan is back together after many heartbreakingly long moons." Mavra looked down at her parents, who smiled on in approval, and Zya saw that behind those smiles lay a couple of people who would never be whole again until they had their other daughter back as well. "We have made new friends, who have a common interest. The forest tribe of Merdon is a very long way from here, but you brave people carry your home with you in your hearts and in your minds. I am glad that we were fortunate enough to meet, and honoured that there is so much we can learn from one another." Zya followed Mavra's gaze to the new faces. They were pleased to be part of such an undertaking, but was that because they were still euphoric about having been rescued? "It would not surprise me if some of you are still a bit baffled as to why complete strangers would take you from your villages and imprison you in the middle of a mercenary camp. Trust me, talk to the tribe, and you will find that your experience has been an easy one compared to some. There are villages that have no living in them, only corpses impaled upon stakes. This was done without mercy, by people who have never known a feeling. It is part of a greater whole, and every village that this happens to makes it worse for us, and for every person on the plains of Ciaharr that still breathes free air. They are being exterminated because they follow a simple set of rules that are supposed to promote goodness and fairness."

"How do you know this?" Shouted one of the recent captives.

"What has the Old Law ever done to them?" Called out another.

Mavra leaned forward, resting her arms on the wagon in front of her. "It seems that sharing and equality is not good enough for some people, and they want a system where few benefit and most go without. This is their way of enforcing it. We know this because people standing around you even now have witnessed the dead villages. They have allies in wizards who are trying to find the answer to this senseless slaughter even as I now speak."

"And what do you expect us to do?" Called out the first, one of the men they had brought out with them.

"What would you do?" Mavra replied.

"I am just a farmer, with a wife and children," the man replied. "What can I do?"

"Look at me," Mavra said in answer. "What do you see?"

The man stared at her for a moment. "I see a warrior who has all the skills necessary to fight a war like this."

"You do not see what I do then. I am a girl, the daughter of two travellers that stand amongst you all."

"Travellers by very definition do not fight!" Denounced another man "What is this?"

"This is a sign that things are changing because they have to." Spoke up Layric from one side of the group. "We did not want this, but it has been forced upon us. Mavra was chosen as the Mistress of the caravan out of tradition and necessity, so that we could continue our journey as should be the case, but she chose instead a more noble cause. The tribesmen and women saw our cause as being similar to their own, and joined us, and we shall fight back."

"But with what skills?" The man argued. "With the girl as a leader? How far do you hope to get with that?"It was clear that the man, despite the euphoria at escaping the encampment, had quickly become despondent.

"I have never wielded a sword until recently, but now I serve the people in a different way." Mavra said. "I do not fight because I want to, that has never been the way of the Old Law, and will not be condoned. I fight to defend people like you, as does every person here. If you do not want to fight, there are a myriad of things that you can do to aid us, for we shall be bringing more people like you out of the bondage imposed by the mercenaries. There are countless villages across the grasslands, and they are all at risk. If the mercenary army can destroy every one, they will do so. We want to ensure that at least some can be saved, and have already seen to the survival of many. There are villages out there that are much more prepared than they would be, and a lot less innocent for it. Mark my words, they are more at risk now for they will appear as a threat to those that seek to destroy you all, but they are willing to take that risk to preserve their way of life. Would you join us and see that you have homes to go back to when this is all over? Or would you live your life out in hiding until one night, not too far from now, somebody puts a spear through your back and leaves you to drip dry." Mavra paused to draw breath. "Mark my words, that will happen."

The man looked a little more convinced, in fact his face paled as the scale of the potential horror washed over him. His wife looked up at Mavra. "What do they want?"

"They want several things at the end of the day." It was Venla that spoke up before Mavra had a chance to answer. "They want you cowed and afraid, they want the pain of your deaths to last an eternity. They also want a former companion of ours, a girl not much older than Mavra here, who would do something about this."

"Why don't you give the girl up?" The man was trembling as he said it.

"We would never do that," Venla answered. "Give up one of our own? To that band of thugs? If we even knew where she was we would never do such a thing. Believe you me, if you thought that giving up one person would serve to end all of this you are sadly mistaken. This is not going to end. That is why we must all make a stand and make a stand now."

Zya ducked back out of direct view. She could still see the crowd, but Mavra had them now and she saw her part ending.

"We have gone against our very tradition, the thing we hold dearest above all else, to make a stand." Mavra said from above them. "Make a stand with us. Join us. The only way to go back to the way of life we so treasure is to do something so abjectly different that they will never see it coming. We have to rid ourselves of these mercenaries. We have to drive them out."

The farmer that had raised his objections now looked a lot less sure of himself. "And can we? Can we make a difference?"

"Anybody can make a difference," Mavra replied. "All you need is the fortitude to start something, the courage to take that first step, and the resilience to see it through. Trust me, you will need resilience, but you are witnessing the start of something phenomenal. You can go if you want, but we would much rather you aided us. For we know, I know, that it will make a difference both to us, and to all those people you will meet in the future that will thank you all for being there to stand up for their way of life."

The farmer looked at his wife, and then down at his children. They were oblivious to the gravity of the situation, playing some obscure game with sticks and dirt. His wife remained mute, but the answer was clear in her eyes. The farmer wrestled with indecision for a moment, and then looked up at Mavra. "What can we do to help?" He said, and everybody cheered loudly in response.

* * *

Tired from the exertions of the previous day, Zya took the moments of peace when she could get them. At the moment, this involved snoozing by a warm fire in the middle of their forest encampment in the early morning.

227

Mavra had convinced the farmers to stand with them, and they had celebrated the rescue in their own muted style. A good feed and a story from Gren was enough to make the people feel like a family. Even the tribesmen sat and listened with appreciation to the old cook, who told the story of the tribesmen that were chased and captured by the Witch finder outside the walls of Raessa. An ominous tale it was indeed, but it had a message of warning and of hope. Those that understood explained to the rest that they were the lucky ones, to have been picked from the viper's nest while the snake was not paying attention. Such a thing rarely happened, and so they all felt blessed. Zya felt little pride in having rescued them, but she was delighted to be back with her father, Ju and especially Lorn. So now she dozed, knowing that as soon as she opened her eyes, she would be asked a dozen questions, and talk of strategy, which she really did not understand. She wished it was all over, but Zya was inexperienced, not naïve. This had only just begun.

"Something to drink?"

Zya reluctantly opened her eyes. Venla stood nearby with a steaming mug.

"Please, Venla." Zya remembered to correct herself once again.

Venla smiled at the near-slip and sat down, producing two mugs. The tribesmen had been kind enough to build a small shelter for Zya out of respect for her tribal status, and now Venla nestled on the bracken next to her underneath fronds of the plant overhead.

Breathing in the aroma, Zya smelled the flavoursome but very bitter drink the tribe had brought with them. She took a quick sip, and the liquid warmed her as she swallowed. "Ahhh, you remembered," she said in appreciation.

"Gren remembered the honey," Venla supplied, unwilling to take the credit for anything that was not of her doing.

Zya leaned back into the shelter. Ahead of her, two of the children ran amongst the ferns and trees, squealing with delight as they swatted at the mist.

"I bet they never knew why they were trapped in that village."

"Probably not," Venla replied as she took a sip of her own drink. She screwed up her face as she swallowed. "How can you drink that?"

"You get used to it, and the honey works wonders on the flavour."

"Maybe I will try it." Venla changed the subject. "You took a great risk coming into that camp, especially knowing who was there."

"I had no say in the matter," Zya replied. "I had answers to find, and the way I went about it was my only choice."

"It is often good to act on instinct. A gut feeling or intuition can often be your unconscious mind's way of telling you something you wouldn't ordinarily think of, but at the same time something you have always known."

"Perhaps," Zya replied. "I would like to think that it is something that I can repeat. I feel that I am going to need that sort of strength in the future if I'm to become a fully-fledged seer, but know this. You have struck a blow with so many consequences. You are going to have to strike again while there is confusion."

Venla looked confused. "You make it sound like we are the aggressors."

"Are we not?"

"That was never my intention. We are trying to prevent an injustice here, not create one."

"The boundary between the two is perilously close," Zya observed as she watched tribesmen ghost in and out of the trees. "The act of rescue makes us all out to be doing the latter in the eyes of our enemy.

"But it exposed you all. Not that I am not grateful for you having done so, never think that of me Zya. The difference is that we were being held for a reason, and they are going to want to continue holding us for that same reason. It seems that the only reason they held onto us and treated us with the respect they did was because they were after you."

This surprised Zya. "Did you not tell them of how we parted ways?"

Venla nodded. "I did, many times, but they refused to listen. The thing you have to understand with these people is that the best of them has a limited imagination. They stick to what they see and know. In our case, since they had captured somebody that had been close to you, they would keep pressuring us not because we would eventually tell them, but because we were the only link. The fact that we had not even seen you in moons never registered. The fact that they had held us for even longer, thus allowing you to move even further away was at the best distant in their minds. Sense does not prevail amongst these people, and O'Bellah is the most pig-headed of the lot. He is nasty, a cruel being, and that gives him the power of command. It begs the question 'Why are you really here?'"

"There were facts I needed to learn. That's why I was there. I now know the source of the evil, Venla. It all comes from Raessa."

"The home of the Witch Finder." Venla whispered. "Are you sure?"

It was at that point that Hawknest approached them. "You had better come and see this." Nothing more the man said, but he turned and beckoned. Zya set her empty mug to one side and jumped up after the man. Venla followed as quickly as she could, but Zya outdistanced her with ease. As Zya approached, there were several of them kneeling around one of the shelters. Layric was there, her father, and Jaden, along with several of the tribe.

"It doesn't look like it was slept in for long." Hawknest observed. "The bracken is not crushed, in fact it is still quite springy."

"I would say this person waited until all had gone quiet and then left." Concluded Layric, who them smiled upon seeing his wife once more. She smiled him a greeting, but remained quiet. This was not the time for banter. "Who was watching the forest during the night?"

"I was, and so was Scarlett," Hawknest replied, "But I have not seen her since we took our posts last night..." Hawknest exuded a sense of urgency, uncommon for one of his tribe, and stood to look in the direction she had been guarding. "There is something amiss!" He pointed. "Footprints in the dirt, trailing off to the edge of the woods." Without another word, he jumped up and walked off in the direction the tracks took him.

Cahal looked down rubbing his chin as he deciphered the marks. "He is good. Almost as good as the person who was here. Somebody intending to use stealth made those tracks. There are hardly any imprints in the ground where they have stepped. I would have missed them had they not been pointed out." Mavra smiled at this frank admission. "It's okay Cahal, we still love you." She said.

"I was hired as a guard, not a tracker," Cahal growled. "You are one fortunate girl to have found this lot. Speaking of that, should we not be following him?" They looked up from the empty shelter and saw the briefest flash of Hawknest's red hair in the woods. Cahal led them, and they followed as quickly as they could. They caught up with the tribesman near the outer boundary of the trees. He knelt with his head down, studying something closely. They approached and he looked up. His face was wet with tears, and his teeth were gritted in anger. In front of him, covered mostly by bracken and grass, lay the still form of Scarlett Ashenfall, his partner. Cahal kneeled down on the other side of her, and touched her ice-cold skin, probing around for clues. He moved his hand around her head feeling around the awkward angles. "Broken," he said without looking up. "Broken and then put back in place of all things."

"To make it look as if she were just lying asleep," Hawknest added, his voice full of grief. "She looks like an angel there, so peaceful, so very peaceful." He touched her face, trailing the tips of his fingers, stained brown with soil across the smooth skin. He did not look up, transfixed by the sight of Scarlett in her death-state. "How could anybody do this?" He asked of them, and of the trees. He beseeched the very forest.

Zya moved away from the grisly sight, having seen enough death in the fight the other day. She beckoned Cahal over. "We will have to let Handel know of this if he does not already. He is going to have to deal with this, but hopefully he is a bit steadier than Hawknest. We also need to find out whom it was that escaped, and what they were doing in the camp in the first place. Ask the people we rescued if they remember anybody who are no longer with us, and ask the rest of the Caravan the same. There has to be somebody that remembers a face that is here no longer."

Mavra broke the news to Handel herself, and instead of a similar reaction, he remained stone-faced, and it was only the look in his eyes that showed he was grieving. "Thank you for telling me of my sister, mistress. It means a lot that you sought me out so quickly. Has Hawknest been told?"

"He found her," Mavra replied tearfully, "covered in bracken and ice-cold to the touch. It appears that whoever did this to her did it very early last night."

Handel said nothing more, but instead went to his people, all of whom gathered around Hawknest to share in his grief. The travellers and the recent captives empathised, but could do nothing other than feel sorry for them. It was a private moment for a very private people. The tribe retreated to the very centre of the woodland, bearing the body of their fallen sister with them. It was at this point that Cahal returned, with the very farmer that had been speaking out against her. "This is Dag, a wheat farmer whom you might remember. He has some information that may help us."

Mavra smiled a greeting, understanding that the farmer might be a bit hesitant after what he had said the night before. "Don't worry about it. You were right to harbour doubts, but I am glad that you stuck with us."

"Don't get me wrong, Mistress, but I still have doubts," Dag replied. "My wife and I just feel that our lot is better cast with you than on our own in a house that might get attacked."

"That is good to know." Mavra said. "How can you help us? Is there anything you can tell us of the person that did this?"

"Aye," he replied, "there is. He was the one that said I would have a chance to speak up and let you all know how difficult things would get. He had been urging me all day during the ride. My wife had given up on me listening to her, as he continually had my ear."

"Who was he?" Mavra asked, beckoning Venla and the others closer with her free hand.

"He was an old man, sort of bent, wearing a great brown cloak. He had little hair, and kept his hood up most of the time. He said his name was Patrick."

"Oh Gods no." It was Venla who had spoken out, and Gwyn and Jani were looking at the ground, muttering and shaking their heads.

"What is the problem?" Asked Cahal, unsure why the information that was so useful had this effect on them.

"When we had been captured at the farmstead, we were taken to a camp in the wilderness. What we have not told you was that when we escaped from that camp, during the ceremony where those aimless men gave themselves to that evil creature, we took with us those that were willing to go. One of them was an old man, stooped and hooded. He caused us no end of difficulties, and in the end he was the one directly responsible for us being recaptured. He was a lieutenant of O'Bellah himself, a man lovingly called Thrasher. He went by the name Patrick when he was with us. He sounds an awful lot like your Patrick."

"And he was with us here, last night?"

Dag nodded. "My wife saw him snooping around the place after you finished speaking. He was acting awfully suspicious, always prodding and peeking into things. At one point I am sure that he tried to get into the wagon there, but something scared him off."

"It makes sense that this was the same man." Zya mused. "How come you didn't see him before, when you were trying to contact everybody the previous night?"

"Did you check every house as we asked you to?" Mavra asked Venla.

"All but one. There was one house on the end of a row that was deserted."

Cahal swore, punching at the side of the wagon. "We got somebody from every one of those houses. It looks as though we have picked up this man with the rest of them, and we didn't know any different."

"And now he has gone, killed one of the tribe and is probably taking our location straight back to O'Bellah," Mavra continued. "So now the question that I put to you is do we stand and fight, or do we escape with our lives and live to fight another day? For surely they will come at us with whatever mercenaries they have now that they know of our location."

"If I may make a suggestion, Mistress," Said Dag, "My village is but ten leagues from here. It is a sizeable community, and if there are any left alive there they will surely be willing to join and aid you."

This brought murmurs of agreement from the rest of the travellers, and Mavra nodded. "Let us give the tribesmen time for whatever rite it is that they hold, and then we shall leave this place." She looked up and around her at the woodland canopy. "So many homes, so little time."

Cahal looked resigned as he said, "that is the way of war."

It took but a day for the tribesmen to commit Scarlett to the earth with a series of simple ceremonies. Zya remained with her father during that time, somehow unable to press him about her mother in this circumstance. So it was the following day that they all packed up and moved out of their camp.

"Are we ready?" Mavra called back to the column. She received nods of approval and cheers from those that made up the 'band', for it was too large to call it a caravan. They moved out in the waning light of the afternoon, trusting to lengthening shadows to hide them from the eyes of any pursuers. Zya rode beside the wagon with her father. She was silent as she watched proceedings unfold She had never seen an army before, for an army was surely what they were becoming.

"It seems so very many people." She said in a whisper as she looked around them.

"Numbers seem less when you are hidden by trees and bushes." Observed Jaden, who was sticking very close to the main wagon, essentially the heart of the column. Cahal had gone ahead with some of the tribesmen who were acting as scouts. The rest of the tribe were busy erasing any clues as to which way they were headed.

That such a feat was even possible considering the number of them moving was astounding, and Mavra chanted a blessing to the Gods as she rode in front. Zya stood up in her stirrups. "How far to the villages?"

"Several leagues, lass." Jaden replied without looking up at her. "We will not see any evidence of them for a good while yet. The villages on the plains are by nature guarded little settlements, not obvious to behold. We might not even see them as we pass should we not be looking in the right place."

"Or should we not have a company of trackers in our midst," Mavra added, and Jaden beamed a grin, white teeth lighting up his dark face. "Perhaps we should be moving further away than our present goal."

"It depends what you wish to accomplish," Venla said. "You will be safer if you decide that we must travel further, but will that help you save the villages that lie in between? Do you sacrifice one set of people in order to preserve another, or do you take a stab at defending them all?"

"The choice was not an easy one. A line must be drawn somewhere," she said quietly, and then an idea came to her. After a moment of contemplation, Mavra looked down at the guard to her right. "Jaden, would you be so kind as to get that farmer, Dag, and bring him back here?"

Jaden complied, and pretty soon, the farmer was riding slowly beside the gently rolling wagon. "I have a proposal for you," Mavra began carefully. "I would send you with your family and a company of the tribesmen to the villages beyond those which we now journey to, in the hope that you can convince them of our needs and ask for aid. You would be out of harms way, you and your family."

Dag considered this for a while, riding along quietly. "That is very considerate of you Mistress Mavra, but I do not think so."

"What is there that you don't like about it? Your family would be safe."

The farmer smiled up at her in appreciation of the gesture. "I know, but I said I would help you and I will. My family I will take with me, but I shall return, with more men to aid you. This is more than the sacking of a few villages, I can see that. This is about you trying to help us survive, and that is a noble cause. I would never be able to forgive myself if you gave me freedom and I could not repay you. Let me ride on ahead with some of your tribesmen, and by the time you reach the village, I will be there with many more men who would see their homes safe."

The counter-proposal surprised everybody but Zya. There was a subtly hidden pride in such people, and it seemed to be surfacing. Dag looked up at Mavra earnestly, old enough to be her father but with the approval seeking glance of a son. She basked in the warmth of the people around her. "So be it. Do what you can. Take ten of the tribe, and ride to the outlying villages. We shall make a stand against them, and they shall come to fear their own spears."

With a whoop of joy, the farmer urged his horse forward to his family, and Mavra indicated that Jaden should seek out Handel. Maybe they would actually have a chance.

This was enough for Zya. "You are on your way," she announced, "and now I must be on mine."

"So that's it? You turn up and then leave?" Mavra was unimpressed.

This did not concern Zya at all. "I don't have to justify myself. I follow the dreams I have, and they lead me elsewhere."

"Bay's Point?" Venla asked.

"I have an appointment with the Earth Guild. I made a promise that I would see you safe then return. I feel I have done that, and I see no reason to believe you cannot go on without me. You are all in a position to do what I cannot. The Old Law guides you, but it compels me. I had facts to learn here, and I understand the source of the evil that now plagues this land. It comes from Raessa. I have to go and learn more about it, and to do that I need guild training. My father, Lorn, Ju and myself, we will see you again. Until that time stay away from the mountain chain, no matter what."

Venla hugged her close. "You be careful now."

Zya glanced at her former family. "I will, Mother."

***

Leagues to the North, two figures clad in black stooped as they made their way through brambles that once had grown around a narrow path but now grew over it. It was a narrow crack in the southern wall of a valley that they were attempting to enter. The brambles had been forced across the gap in an attempt to hide the way through from any that might disturb it, and with the warmer weather, they had grown at a much faster pace. As was typical at this time of the annual cycle of nature, everything else was growing at a frenetic pace as well, and the resulting mass of tangles had become annoying. The bigger of two figures pushed its way through, the smaller following closely like an obedient pet. The brambles did not last for long and soon the two dark figures were winding their way through a narrow gorge that doubled back on itself quite frequently. The top of the gorge could be seen far above, the sky visible only directly overhead, so narrow was the path through. Small lichens and mosses grew on the sharp ledges of the gorge, getting purchase where no greater plant could. The resulting dampness would normally have had travellers slipping on the muddy path, but the two passed quietly and quickly up the gorge, making no noise with their feet and finding purchase where lesser mortals might not have. They approached the point where the gorge opened up into a wider valley, and paused on the rim. It was a near-perfect bowl, just as they had been told that it was. The grass grew all the way up to where trees rimmed the far reaches of the valley, and seemed to stand up and defy the recent winter. The object they had been ordered to observe stuck like the defiance of the earth against the very sky in the middle. An obelisk, huge and jet-black broke the centre of the valley as if the ground had been stabbed from below. The ground was ruptured all around it, as if the event had only recently happened.

"Go look, and tell me what you can learn of it." The taller of the two figures said out loud, and the smaller set off at a jog towards the stone spire. The remaining figure pulled back a black hood to reveal long pale-blonde hair. Maolmordha shook her head as if to clear her thoughts, and her hair drifted in the gentle currents that made it to the valley floor. Her protégé had run the distance now, and was slowly circling the obelisk. Bushes grew at the base, but the dark figure just waded through them as if they were not there.

This stone has a meaning. Came the whispered thoughts of her student.

"How so?"

"It was not originally here. Somebody placed it here and imbued it with magic."

Maolmordha looked down the valley to the obelisk. That it did not belong in this place was obvious, but the fact that it had magical properties showed that her student was learning. *"How can you tell?"*

"I can sense the aura." Came the telepathic reply. She watched as her student poked around the base of the obelisk, and then paused. *"There is something else that you should see, my teacher."*

Maolmordha jogged across the valley to where her student waited patiently. It was obviously safe, for the student had been poking around at the obelisk long enough for any traps to be sprung. Maybe it was just a stone spire, capable of nothing, or maybe her master was actually correct and it had innate properties that they could harvest. She suspected the latter but had learned to trust her instincts, something Maolsechlan had never done. She slowed to a walk when she neared the stone. It was raised up slightly, becoming the focus of the entire valley. This was not by accident. There was a purpose to everything, and the eldritch scent of the valley became compounded the closer she got to the obelisk. "What have you found?"

Silently, her student pointed, pushing aside some of the bushes to reveal a plaque. *"The gates aligned focus the mind to cross the bridge."* Came the whispered thought. She looked at the plaque, trying to understand the meaning behind the words. It was old, but it had been preserved by the fact that it was cut into the base of the obelisk. The same stone with a toughness that defied the seasons.

"What does it mean?" Came the question. Before the apprenticeship, her student had always been full of questions, and although the mightiest of compulsions had been laid upon the student during the dark magic that enabled the reshaping, still certain tendencies could not be curbed.

"It is not for us to decide what it means," Maolmordha replied. "It was for us to come this way to discover perhaps this very line of information." She stood and looked around the bowl-shaped valley. "There is nothing else for us here. We must go to the encampment and learn what transpired here from our allies and their prisoners. You have done well though, my student. I will name you here and now, upon the face of this very stone. You shall be known as Maolnemrhyth, after the questioner that once tortured the answers from our enemies. So do you torture answers from me with your unending questions."

Her student nodded, accepting the name; the spell would ensure that anything was accepted, and that previous memories would be forgotten. In the end, only one thing would matter, a desire to serve their master. Perhaps the spell had not worked so well on Maolsechlan, for he had had a weakness that she was not going to emulate. Already she felt the pull to return to the protective

236

confines of the focus that emanated from Raessa, but she would not return for a great many moons yet. Her master demanded sacrifice, and she would give her life if he asked it. One day, the little brat that they had brought to the Witch Finder would too.

***

Thrasher was in a positively good mood as he rode the stolen horse back to the village from which he had 'escaped' the day before. He had had such a pleasant time of it all, first snapping the neck of that tribal bitch in the darkness and then finding a farmer who was trying to use darkness as cover, and improvising a spear using the spokes of his cart-wheels. The screams had pierced the night, but by then they were nowhere near any dwellings. The screams had only grass and night-creatures for their audience, but Thrasher had watched the man die before he stole the horse. Whatever goods the man had on his cart were forgotten, for Thrasher had a more important mission. The fools led him to their place of concealment once again, and O'Bellah would want to know so that he could obliterate them once and for all. Night had blossomed into morning by the time he rode through the hills that surrounded the valley, and he kicked at the ribs of his mount impatiently. "Trust me to find a horse with ribs stouter than oak poles and less intelligence than my 'friends' in the forest." He moaned out loud. "Still, you are faster then walking, just about." He gave the horse one more kick with his heel and was rewarded with a whinny of pain for his efforts. If he were going to suffer in the delay, then the horse would suffer with him.

He rode down into the valley, and could see the fortifications of the valley entrance to the East, and to the South the ugly square tower that rose like a pillar above the village. He directed the now limping horse towards the nearest mercenary encampment. Guards rode out to greet him.

"Halt and identify yourself," one of the mercenaries ordered as Thrasher dismounted.

Instead of saying anything, he walked calmly towards the guard, and when he was next to the horse pulled the guard to the ground. The horse whinnied and reared, threatening to stomp on the mercenary. The other guard drew his sword.

"Try to strike me and I will see you dead and still riding," Thrasher growled without looking up. "I am taking your horse to ride to my master at the village." He said to the fallen man, "if you do not know of me, then I suggest that this is an object lesson for you." He pulled the man close to him. "I do not like being questioned, and you would do right to understand that, mercenary scum."

The other guard still had his sword out, but now put it away as he recognised true authority. "The other horse?"

"Take it, and kill it for meat," Thrasher said uncaringly. "It is a useless nag, and is lame to boot. It was dragging a cart to the North. Follow the tracks and bring it back for all I care. The previous owner will be able to guide you by his blood trails." He mounted the horse he had taken and it pranced under him, eager to be off. Not sparing another look for the two mercenaries, he rode away from the camp and towards the village in the centre of the valley. The last he had seen of the place was the day before when he had been ushered onto a horse by the girl and her two old bodyguards. They had been doing something outside of the tower, and he was eager to find out what. He rode faster now that he had a decent mount and so became less impatient. Thundering down the track to the village, it was obvious that things had changed somehow. People were milling about around the base of the tower where before they had been confined to the buildings, maintaining the semblance of a normal village. Thrasher grinned as he rode. This was anything but a normal village. Riding in from the North meant that he could not see what was going on in the courtyard of the inn, as everything was blocked by the bulk of the tower, but there was noise enough to show that somebody was not happy, most probably O'Bellah. He was proved right when he reined his horse in by the North well to see his master in a rage, and several bodies lying in a heap at his feet. "No self control whatsoever." He said quietly to himself as he surveyed the carnage. He led the horse into the courtyard, and into the gaze of his master.

The fat man had gone red in the face, which was not unusual, and he was breathing raggedly. "Where have you been, when I needed you?" He demanded angrily.

"Exactly where you asked me to be, master," Thrasher replied without any trace of subservience. To him, they were equals even if O'Bellah was in charge. "You asked me to stay low in case the captives made to escape once more, and once more I escaped with them."

O'Bellah looked as though he was trying to find fault with Thrasher's report, but there was none. His fingers had locked so tightly around the hilt of the sword he carried, even now dripping with the inordinate amount of blood he had managed to spill, that they went white at the knuckles. His eyes were wide in rage, and his teeth were bared.

Thrasher stood there calmly, daring O'Bellah to take a swing at him. It would be the man's crowning mistake. "May I ask what happened here?" He said when no such action was forthcoming.

O'Bellah looked down at the corpses, and kicked one as hard as he could, getting a wet thud and a dull crack for his efforts. "This offal is an object lesson to the rest of you all." O'Bellah announced. "These are the guards that should have stopped the pitiful band of tribesmen from even entering the village, and they were not at their posts." He kicked the closest corpse once more. Blood had started to flow again from the mortal wound the man had been dealt.
It pooled up on the cobbles, seeking the easiest route between the stones. Already there was enough blood to fill half of the courtyard, but it was seemingly not enough. O'Bellah turned on Thrasher. "Tell me why I should not do the same to you for abandoning me to be locked in that tower?" As O'Bellah demanded this, the merest tinge of panic around his eyes betrayed his feelings about that thought. He had given away an extreme weakness to a man who could read others' faces. Thrasher stored the small piece of information away just in case. His master could not abide a locked door with no means of escape. He could not live in a prison. Interesting.

"I have the location of the escaped villagers, and of the tribal scum that aided them. It is but a day ride from here, in woodland to the North East. It looks like they have been planning this for quite a while, but I can lead you back to them. That is what you wanted me to do was it not? It has been done." Thrasher looked around them. Several guards were stood near the tower, and they were visibly shaking. They were obviously the next ones in line for O'Bellah's rage. A waste of manpower if ever there was one. Thrasher felt insulted that it was another man that had chosen him for this. One day he would have that underachiever locked up in a cell, screaming his heart out for release. "Some of them are preparing to leave for Bay's Point: Two men, a girl and a young boy." O'Bellah looked ready to make a comment when a guard rode into the courtyard. It was the very same man Thrasher had dispossessed of a horse.

"Milord, we have strangers approaching from the North." To the man's credit, he did not even blink at the scenes of violence laid out before him like a grisly map.

"Why did you not stop them?" The bullish man demanded, still enraged by his enforced captivity.

"Milord we could not even get close. There was something stopping us."

"What?" He yelled back. "What do you mean there was 'something stopping you'?" O'Bellah had seemingly found a new target for his rage, though this was unwise. The mercenaries would attack even them without the slightest provocation, and murdering one would not make things any easier.

"Milord, stop. Think your way through things." This distracted the man long enough for the mercenary to back out of obvious view.

O'Bellah turned on him, "you presume to tell me my place?"

Thrasher merely grinned. "What, you seek to face me down? I do not think so, Milord. You may be able to quail these poor saps, but I have seen more blood than you could ever dream of. This is the work of a novice compared to the schemes I have hatched in the past."

O'Bellah stopped his advancement. His scathing reply remained unsaid as two figures dressed in black jogged into the courtyard. They commanded the attention of every person there merely by arriving, and others began to lean out of windows and exit out of doors. There was an almost magnetic attraction about them.

"We have come for the captives." The taller figure announced in a cold feminine voice."

"Have you now," O'Bellah replied, anger still vibrant in his voice. "Who are you, two vagabond wanderers, to come into my camp like scrubs from the night and demand that you want to take *my* prisoners?"

The taller figure pulled back her hood to reveal a face of pale beauty framed by the lightest yellow hair imaginable. The only imperfection was the sheer evil that could be seen in the look on her face, bringing a cruel twist to an otherwise stunning visage. Thrasher did not doubt that this woman had a capacity for inflicting pain and misery that bordered on the artistic. He was keen to see where this led, and so remained quiet.

"I am Maolmordha, and I answer only to Garias Gibden, the master of Raessa. Now give me the captives, worm, or face the consequences."

Every man in the courtyard knew the truth: there were no captives. Every last one had been removed the night before. O'Bellah was oblivious to the obvious choice of admitting failure, but seemed intent upon goading this woman in black. "Consequences? If you are who you say you are, then where are my armies? Where is the conquest that has been promised? Why do you run around like masterless slaves when you could be astride great horses? Give me that, and give me your answers, and I will tell you where you can stick your request for my captives. I know you from the village Maolmordha. I had you released when you were but an apprentice. Do not take your sudden rise to mean that you are important. You are nothing more than a whore to our master, and I do not answer to you."

This was obviously the wrong answer, for Maolmordha clapped her hands together, and dropped to one knee, chanting a phrase just too quietly for anybody to be able to hear. The courtyard became much more macabre as everybody dropped quiet, straining to hear the words, the only movement being Maolmordhas mouth and the trickle of slowly-congealing blood around the edges of cobbles. A stray cloud moved in front of the sun, and the shadowed courtyard became cold and dark. Coincidence or not, even Thrasher paled when this happened, for it was a bad omen. He watched O'Bellah, who was refusing to be drawn in by any trickery on the part of Maolmordha. He had no faith in what she was doing. That changed when his comprehension caught up with the situation. He began to twitch with worry as a sense of evil permeated the air around him. It concentrated on a spot only a few steps away from them, and the shadows stretched and lengthened as they coalesced into blackness. The feeling made O'Bellah look away, but Thrasher was fascinated by the imminent arrival of something he was now certain would bring him opportunities that had currently lacked. The shadows formed into a mass that was easily an arm spans worth higher than any man there. It pulsed, as if it were a living form, and Maolmordhas chants reached a crescendo. She yelled something incomprehensible, and the feeling of hopelessness magnified tenfold. Where the shadows had combined into inky blackness, there now stood a being of concentrated darkness. The Golem had grown in stature since Thrasher had last seen the creature. It had gained bulk, and its menacing nature was as silently deadly as ever, perhaps even more so. This creature had certainly feasted on something recently.

"Be sure that my master, the Lord of Raessa watches from through this creature's eyes." Maolmordha warned. "Now would you like to repeat to my master what you said to me?"

This time O'Bellah quailed, looking at the ground, his sword trailing on the cobbles as he sought a way out of answering.

"Well?" Maolmordha pressed.

"They are not here," O'Bellah said ambiguously, stalling for time as he tried to think his way out of the hole he had dug for himself.

The Golem had not moved since it appeared, but now it somehow loomed bigger in front of them all as something behind it's dark eyes balanced control with increasing anger.

"Why not?" Asked Molmordha. "Why have you managed to let a group of mere travellers escape from a fortified village, surrounded with guards?"

O'Bellah stammered, trying to spill out any words to relinquish himself of responsibility, but all that came were a strangled series of noises. The man was not ready to take the fall for his losses, but quite able to blame an underling. This time was different. The Golem was an ally, its evil nature a useful tool in converting the weak-willed. When the malevolence turned upon him, O'Bellah was reminded of how insignificant he really was. By pure coincidence, the commotion caused this to be one of the rare times Dondera issued forth from her house, the noise building up her ire to the point that she could no longer sit around eating. "What is all this commotion?" She demanded of her son, without so much as even noticing the creature, and the two dark figures before him.

"Your son is paying the price of failure." Maolmordha replied, and the Golem reached out. Touching Dondera it began the process of drawing her into it, tapping into her soul and sucking away like the ticks farmers found on their cattle in summer. Thrasher watched with glee as the huge woman comprehended her fate, and screamed with the sure knowledge that she was definitely not going to a better place. He had seen this before, relished the suffering. Dondera began to pale, and eventually her form was as thin as mist. Her screaming reduced to a wail as her life force became as insubstantial as an eddy of wind in a storm. The Golem swelled as it absorbed another life into its matrix, and a funny thing happened. O'Bellah began to smile. More than that, he started to laugh, and soon was throwing his head back in a state of joy, the humour that fuelled it failing to provide comprehension for any other person in the courtyard. He dropped his sword with a clatter as he raised his hands to his face, pausing to wipe tears away from his eyes.

"Oh by the Gods that was a sight to behold!" O'Bellah crowed, and still he made no sense. He stopped laughing and looked around at them all, bringing his attention to bear on Maolmordha. "Was that supposed to cow me? Was that supposed to be some sort of punishment? That was the funniest thing I have seen in years! The look on her face as she became trapped by your spell, the sound of her voice in agony. That was sweet. That was sweet indeed!" O'Bellah indicated Thrasher with one hand. "My man here has the location of the escaped tinkers and the rest. We can go and get them whenever you like. There is nothing to bind me to this place any more, it was only duty to that fat old hag that based my operation from here in the first place."

A rumbling began to issue from what could be construed as the mouth of the Golem, and since this was the first time it had ever made any noise, they all listened intently. "No. Leave them. No use to you. Gather your forces. This is too important to be done piecemeal."

"Your will, master," O'Bellah replied. "What of the party heading for Bay's Point?"

"You will accompany my creature and see to them. Do not fail me." The consciousness behind the dark eyes of the Golem faded once more, to be replaced by the dull longing for life, focussed on O'Bellah. He no longer appeared scared of the creature; in fact he was smiling at it. "That means that we get to take a little trip." O'Bellah grinned at Maolmordha, who was actually looking in surprise at the both of them. "What? You think that you are the only person with the power to summon the Golem? You may be his assassin, but you are no more important in the scheme of things than anybody else. Before you report back to your master by the long route, consider that there is an easier way to reach Raessa." O'Bellah indicated the Golem.

Maolmordha shuddered at the very thought of touching it. Command it she could do easily, but actual contact could result in the will of the creature taking over, and it had become too powerful already. Maybe one day it would take the fat man like it took his mother, but that was of no consequence. She did what her master ordered, and the student was her charge to be taught and compelled, until she too was loyal in every way to the Master of the Mountain fortress. "We will go by the way prepared for us, but we will be taking one other." She lifted a finger and pointed at Thrasher. "That one will join us." Thrasher was intrigued. "This promises to be so much more interesting than riding around spearing farmers."

O'Bellah did not seem to like the idea of his best lieutenant being taken from him, but he shrugged off the notion of losing him. "So be it," he replied. "If you do not want the tinkers then he is of no use to me. I will see them all dead before this is over, and I shall exalt as I deliver the torturous blessing our master decrees for the country folk."

Thrasher opened his mouth to protest. How could loyalty be repaid so suddenly with a dismissal like that? He frowned, but then considered that the possibilities for revenge were endless, and all in all he had gotten the better out of the deal.

For her part, Maolmordha seemed to seethe, her pale eyes turning to ice, and her jaw sticking out as she considered what to do next. "Be careful with this pet," She said, indicating the Golem, "it might turn around and bite you." "Scared, woman? I go to Bay's Point by a much quicker method than you are prepared to take. I will see you at my feet. Bring your mercenaries into the village, and send messengers to the other camps." He ordered of the guard that had arrived with news of the cloaked ones. "We are going to give this magnificent beast something to gnaw on."

The mercenary did his level best to look away from the Golem, such fear did it emanate. "Yes Milord." He replied, scrambling towards his horse just as fast as his feet would take him. With a gesture, O'Bellah drew the Golem off with him towards the tower.

Maolmordha pointed at Thrasher. "We leave, now."

"Whatever you say, lady," he replied, grinning at his new companions.

In response, Maolmordha took one step towards him, and lunged at him, palm up. The heel of her hand connected with his jaw, and he launched across the courtyard, coming to a rest in a stunned heap up against the wall of the inn.

"You will address me only when questioned," She said, still stood in the attacking stance she had taken to hit him, "anything else is your death."

Thrasher trembled as he lurched to unsteady feet. Never had anybody done that to him. It had a profound effect. If a mere woman could generate that much force, then he was willing to learn what he could accomplish. The smug look on his former commanders face would have taunted him once, but now his eyes were open to a bigger truth. Killing a few farmers with spears was childish play. He would be a part of something more.

"Is that understood?" Maolmordha said once more as she relaxed into a stance indicating the ready threat of violence.

Thrasher stood to his full height, a feral gleam in his eyes. "Mistress, I am yours."

Maolmordha nodded in the understanding that all was settled. "This is Maolnemrhyth. If she speaks, be aware she speaks with my voice."

Maolmordha indicated the slight figure at her side, which made no indication that it had not even heard the conversation, nor witnessed his humbling. They turned and ran. Compelled to do so, he followed.

Chapter Eleven

"They are moving out of the valley on horseback."

"What are the chances of them being captured?"

"Not great. They dealt with whomever it was that was chasing them."

"What about the village?"

"There are people alive there, still trapped in a structure of some sort. What it is I cannot see, and they are unfamiliar to me."

A foot scuffed the ground in frustration. "If only there were a way that we could contact them."

Raoul opened his eyes and looked down from his perch on a jutting rock to see Belyn frowning at the ground. "Of course there is a way. You almost got through to them once before, and thank all that is right and good that you tried. Whatever we saw was not friendly, and it passed right by them."

Belyn looked up at him in consternation. "That much. It was no more then an impression. If we could get through with actual messages, maybe we could also pick them up."

Raoul jumped down from the rock. His cloak flared out over the short drop forcing Keldron to step back. "That is your speciality, my friend. I can tell you about any facet of the Old Law, but I cannot make miracles come from rock as you can."

He began the walk back down the short slope to where Malcolm, Joleen and Yerdu were waiting with the horses. "Rubbish. You two are catching up fast. That air cushion you created when Yerdu fell could well have saved her life. I would say that that was a timely miracle of your own, one you know that I am very thankful for." Belyn referred to the one incident when they had accidentally stumbled onto a mercenary camp in the Ciaharrian wilderness. They had been chased for the better part of four days by the mercenary band, and it had only been when they had stumbled on a narrow pass through a valley that they had been able to do something. Keldron threw as strong an air barrier across the gap as he could muster, and then something else unexpected had happened. Belyn tried the focus that produced heat, using the volcanic stone he had once used before. Instead of a heat barrier, the focus produced a lance of fire that shot through the gap and into the faces of the oncoming mercenaries. A side effect of the focus was the bolting of Yerdu's horse. In the panic, she was thrown off, and it was only the fact that Raoul held his own focus stone that had saved the day. He had tried to replicate Keldron's effort for he could see behind the focus, and the barrier under her had formed. There was no way round the blockage, and the mercenaries had not even tried to break through the barrier, for they had seemingly been fried to a crisp.

"I will never be able to understand why that fire broke through the barrier leaving it intact." Belyn murmured as they walked back, hopping down ledges of narrow rock.

"I will never be able to understand how you got a focus so wrong," Raoul retorted. "Maybe the two have a connection?"

Belyn stopped in his tracks, and Keldron saw the wide-eyed stare into nothingness on his friend's face that showed he had just made a breakthrough. His eyes came back into focus, and he walked past Raoul, slapping him on the back. "You may just have a point there old friend, one that definitely bears thinking about."

Aside from the incident with the mercenaries, this had been the most eventful day since they had parted with the tribesmen. True to their word the wizards had kept an eye on their allies through focussing, but until recently they had not even begun to think about anything more. It was Raoul himself that had come up with the idea of an attempt to modify the focus that allowed them to take food from a room that Belyn had paid somebody to keep stocked in Eskenberg. That, coupled with the new skill that they had acquired to be able to see the tribesmen through their very spirits, had afforded them a limited amount of success. They had had nearly two months worth of peaceful riding, to everybody's surprise.

Reaching the horses, Raoul climbed into his saddle.

Everybody was looking at him but as usual it was Yerdu that pre-empted all of them. "Well?" She said, the word implying a total recounting of events.

"They are all safe, as are the people they have met and rescued," he replied. "It looks like they have responded to the sending, but we cannot be sure as to what got through. It also looks like whomever they have met up with has decided to take the fight to the mercenaries. People died just now."

Those four words were enough to bring a sombre mood over them all. It was clear that the fight had truly been taken to the enemy, a situation that they had both hoped for and dreaded.

"There is no turning back now then," Keldron said as he looked ahead to distant Leallyra, not much more than an impression on the horizon from this distance. "They are committed to the preservation of the Old Law by untried means, and therefore so are we. I just hope that we can find a ship to sail us to Caighgard."

"This place is reputed to be a big port," said Belyn. "I don't think we will have a problem finding passage."

Raoul barked out a laugh. "You just need to be more concerned that whatever this madness is that has suddenly gripped the world has not extended to the city. We are a long way from home my friends, and we have no idea what the feelings are to the Old Law and those that follow it in the cities. I can tell you this much. This is a Duchy capital and although the guilds are based here for the sole purpose of the population, you can still expect them to be informed of problems outside. What you cannot expect them to be is supportive of our efforts."

Yerdu sighed. "Overcautious as ever Raoul? Maybe you should keep quiet when we enter the city. We don't want your sense of righteousness damaged by what you might see."

Raoul grinned in response. It was just banter between the two of them, for they had all become like a gang of siblings after so long on the road together. Yerdu had claimed Belyn for her own a long time before, and the natural chemistry between Keldron and Joleen was at times frightening but it had spread to include them all. Only Malcolm was ever distant, and when asked he explained it was his way and that he missed his family. That did not deter them at all, and through persistence he also opened up to their joviality. The horses had become part of the 'family' too, each showing its own character when one was observant enough to watch. Despite the hardship suffered by them all in their private moments, for it was not an easy journey, they had all grown as a result, knowing there would always be five other people that they could always trust. What had heartened Keldron more was the fact that the tribe had made it even this far into the countryside. A great deal of them had left the forest all that time back, and when they had encountered them and told them of what was happening decisions had been made on the spot. Every tribal member felt an affinity for the land, and therefore the people that lived upon it. There was never any dissent when they decided to aid their brothers and sisters across the country. It may have been that there was not a problem in this particular part of the Duchy, but they were made aware and thus prepared against the day they might witness the cruelty that the wizards and their companions had witnessed.

They rode on as ever, slipping into their usual roles. Malcolm rode point, keeping an eye out for danger some hundred paces ahead of the rest. Then followed Belyn in his customary state of concentration, especially with the ideas Raoul had given him. Yerdu had long since given up on trying to bait Belyn during these periods. Instead she dropped back to wind up Raoul, but even he was not having it this time. "I am worried for all the people we have passed by." He said when she pressed him. "They are nothing more than glowing spirits to me, but when I see them and what they are about, I cannot help but wish that I was there with them. If only there was a way to speak to them." He would not give much more than one-word answers to her after that, and baiting suddenly became less important as the gravity of the situation descended over them all. Keldron and Joleen rode at the back of the little column, quietly enjoying the humourous banter in front.

"You two can come forward as well." Yerdu motioned with her free arm. "Not a chance. After what happened to us before, I am best placed to use my shield of air should we get ambushed. We need space. Belyn placed near the front, myself behind. After coming so close to injuring you, Yerdu, I want some open space around me." He also needed time to think while he considered the various focus stones he had secreted about him. At night it was either a case of dipping into Belyn's stores back home or if they were lucky, Malcolm would hunt down game and cook it. The latter did not occur often, for the plains stretched all the way to the coast, and there was rarely enough cover for large game to graze in peace. They had passed several villages in the past couple of days, and if there were a problem the villagers did not show it. Still, Raoul had tried his best to warn them without alarm. It seemed as if they had taken the warning to heart.

At night, when they had settled the horses in a makeshift pen, they settled down in the dark. It was cold but not unpleasantly so, for the weather was much more clement as they neared the coast. The peninsula between the Ardican estuary and the western coast was pleasant enough unless one tried to cross it in the middle of winter. At this point in time they were perhaps five leagues from the city, and shunned a hostel in favour of the rude camp they had become accustomed to. Joleen shivered against Keldron as they lay under their blankets.

"Cold, dear?" He asked, and she snuggled closer.

"Not really," she replied in a sleepy voice. "Just nervous about what I will see tomorrow. I have never been in a city before."

Keldron took a moment to remember that even Malcolm had never visited a city the size of Leallyra. Belyn, Raoul and he would be blasé about the whole affair, having come from Eskenberg. Despite their proximity to the city, none of the others had seen any bigger settlement than the merchant's gathering point in their own forest, and that was not even a permanent affair. "Do not worry overmuch about it," he replied after a moment. "Just stick with us, and everything will be fine. We will only be there for as long as it takes us to secure passage to Rhothamy."

"Rhothamy?" Joleen repeated in a tone that clearly indicated that she had never heard of the place before.

"The main city on Caighgard," Belyn supplied from nearby. "In fact, the only city on Caighgard and that is saying something. The island would probably take as much time to cross as we have taken since we parted from your brethren, but not many people live there.

Joleen turned in his direction. "Do you mean that we are going to travel all that way to try and find a temple in the middle of nowhere?"

"Hopefully not," came the voice out of the darkness. "The temple was the first building on Rhothamy, in fact the island was named after the first high priest of the Order of Law, the man who laid the foundations for our guild. It was rumoured that the city of Caighgard was built at the temple's feet."

"So their magnificently elegant plan is to go to the city and look for the temple once they get there, dear sister," came Yerdu's voice from the direction of Belyn. "Isn't it?" She asked of the men who were all listening.

Silence ensued, an embarrassed silence that was filled with Yerdu's gleeful accusation. The stars glittered overhead where the cloud broke into wisps, and the moon cast an eerie glow over the nightscape. Off to one side, one of the horses snorted in its sleep, and still there was no answer.

"Goodnight boys." Came the satisfied voice of Yerdu. She had hit the nail on the head. While Malcolm contemplated the stars from a distance as he watched over the camp, three very silent and very red-faced wizards warmed the night with their embarrassed reticence.

The next morning dawned to reveal thick banks of fog blanketing the landscape. Fog in Ciaharr was as hesitant to lift as they themselves were to get up, but the fog lingered, where they were forced to be up and about. Keldron looked about him as he watched his friends rise slowly. He had taken over from Malcolm on watch, for he knew all too well what a lack of sleep could do to a man. He himself had missed many nights sleep in his contemplation of the Night of Spears but he maintained that it had given him wisdom, though Joleen complained that all it had done was make him tightly-strung. He smiled as he saw in his mind the truth: She may be closer to him, but she was good for all of them, even Belyn, who had somehow bewitched Yerdu.

"Great, damp firewood again," Belyn grumbled as he got up to check the fire. He went off to relieve himself out of sight and thankfully sound of the camp, and when he returned, his face was alive with thought. "Kel, get up man. Bring your stone to the fire."

Keldron moaned from under his blankets, and then yelped as Joleen elbowed him in the ribs. "What is it, Belyn? Can't a man enjoy a few more moments rest?" Keldron got up with a grumble, his focus stone in hand. "Right. What is it you want of me?"

Belyn squatted near the fire, where the bank of moisture that surrounded them had dampened the once-smouldering wood. "Create a shield down near the fire. Make it weak, and not very big, say the size of a large rock."

Keldron frowned at his friend. "You got me out from under the one and only warm place in this entire Duchy for that?"

"Just do it, please." Belyn urged with forced patience. "I am aware that nobody in his right mind enjoys being pulled from their sheets."

Keldron closed his eyes, raised his stone in front of him and pulled in his concentration. As always they could feel the focus build, though this was a lot tighter than normal. They had been spending so long on creating focuses on a large scale that the menial things had been ignored. "There, it is done."

Belyn closed his eyes and concentrated. Keldron could feel the presence of the focus beginning to dissipate already. Belyn held out the firestone and poured his will into it, becoming one with the once-molten properties. He released the smallest trickle of power from the rock, attempting to create a tiny miasma of heat. That was not what happened. Instead a needle-thin shaft of fire pierced the shield, hitting the wood and causing it to crackle into life. Belyn opened his eyes. "It works!" He crowed in triumph, causing the horses to stir from their morning meal of dew-drenched grass. The once-wet wood had dried out completely, and it blazed with enthusiasm, lighting up the dense fog with a sooty glow.

"I hope that there are no mercenaries nearby," cautioned Malcolm. They looked about them. The fire, as small as it was, had combined with the fog to create a beacon of torchlight in the otherwise gloomy morning.

"Well the sooner we are up and refreshed, the sooner we can be on our way and leave this place to the fog," Yerdu replied.

As they had done on so many mornings before, so they did now. Belyn created his wave of heat, which dried all the blankets, and had the added bonus of drying them all out and warming them at the same time. Malcolm provided breakfast, which in this occasion was a small deer from a distant wood they had seen the night before. The unspoken question on all of their lips refused to be spoken aloud, but they all wondered when he had had the time to go hunting as he was guarding them. Raoul quietened their worries by explaining he had actually been on watch most of the night. They ate a delicious breakfast and then stored the rest of the meat in their packs, burying the remains with a traveller's blessing for good growth. After the horses had been tended to, they set off in the fog.

"So how are we supposed to find our way through this?" Yerdu asked of nobody in particular.

"We remember where we saw things last night, dear sister," Joleen replied with a sunny attitude that belied their surroundings. They all rode closer this morning, so as to not lose themselves in the fog.

"Or we just follow the road," Raoul added. "That seems the best bet as we are on the road to the largest city on the region, it makes sense that we will actually reach that city by following the well-trodden tracks to it."

"A clever and original thought, from a man," Yerdu retorted. "If you weren't already sat astride a horse I swear you would faint from the exertion." That brought a laugh from the others, and another day of Raoul-baiting began.

"Quiet." Malcolm held his arm aloft. "Pull your horses over to the right of the track."

They did so without question, for Malcolm's only spoke at need. Not long after, a muffled series of thuds in the road ahead announced the close presence of a series of horses. In the fog, sound was hidden, and so the party was surprised when a dozen armed horsemen suddenly materialised beside them.

"Halt, and identify yourselves," an officious looking man in a uniform commanded.

Belyn nudged his mount forward. "We are travellers out of the East, seeking passage on a ship from your harbour."

"Bound to where?" The officer asked in a tone that brooked no nonsense.

"That really is our own business, if you don't mind," Belyn replied.

"Not if you want to get into the city of Leallyra it isn't," the officer replied.

"May I ask why?" Belyn enquired patiently.

"All entrants into the city are required to provide proof of their origin and also of their intentions should they wish to be allowed in, on command of my Lord, Duke Jhander of Leallyra." The officer replied.

"So be it," Belyn replied. "We three are members of the Guild of Law in Eskenberg, and our companions are from the forest Tribe of Merdon."

The officer narrowed his eyes, especially when 'Merdon' was mentioned. "Merdonese do not leave their forest," he stated.

Yerdu brought her horse forward. "That is inaccurate captain."

"Lieutenant, Ma'am," the officer replied. "Lieutenant Curtis of the outbound guard. Our mandate is to check all of the roads for incoming travellers, and ward off potential threats. My Lord Duke likes order in his city."

"An impressive title," she commented, "and an impressive task. This must be some city we are travelling to. Anyway, if your historians or whoever taught you about Merdonese got it right, they should have noted that we rarely leave the forest. This is one of the rare times."

"And what, pray tell, are you doing with three wizards?" Curtis continued.

"There was a spot of trouble a while back when we were crossing the mountains. These three aided us and have remained with us as we have the same destination."

"Which brings us back to your purpose. Where are you bound?"

Yerdu looked at Belyn, and he spoke for the group. "We are seeking berths on a ship bound for Caighgard."

Curtis nodded once, satisfied. "Well Gods speed to you all. There are five ships in the harbour bound for the Isle. Three leave today, the other two tomorrow on the morning tide. Mention my name to the captain of the Grotesque, a man called Flynn, and I am sure he will see you safe."

"Our thanks Lieutenant Curtis," responded Belyn. "May the Gods watch over you." He raised his hand in a blessing.

Curtis nodded, and led his riders out into the road, and off into the fog.

Once they were alone, Yerdu turned in her saddle to Belyn. "What sort of man calls a ship 'Grotesque'? It had better be good, for I have no idea how I will react to a sea journey. I have heard that there are monsters at sea that can swallow someone whole."

Belyn laughed as they rode out into the fog, their only point of reference being the road directly in front of them. "You have heard too many tall tales. If the worst that you suffer is a bit of seasickness, then you will be doing well."

"If I suffer any such thing, master wizard, be sure that *you* will be the one paying for it." Before Raoul could add his penny's worth, she looked over at him and said. "All of you."

They rode in silence for the best part of that morning, each of them wishing in silence that the fog would lift. The misty vapour gave Keldron the impression that they had not in fact gotten any further along in their journey. "So is this city a capital?" Yerdu asked.

"It is," Belyn replied. "The inhabitants of the very cosmopolitan Ulecio dispute this title. That particular city guards the straits between the mainland and the Qua'Cliran island chain, close to the Ardican estuary. As a result, the Dukes of old had granted enough favours and titles for the sister city to give itself autonomy. Ulecio had basically become an independent state, governed jointly by the people of the Duchy and the inhabitants of the island chain who had given the city its own makeover. It was reputed that it was the most colourful city in the Nine Duchies. I lament the fact that they are so close and yet at the same time much too far away to visit. As they rode, Malcolm sang softly to himself. Eventually, he joined Keldron at the rear of their little column. He said nothing, but just listened to the words. It was a song of heartbreaking sadness, about a woman that had lost her man in the mist. They had wandered far from home one day and it had caught them unawares, dropping on their hillside like a blanket. The couple had become separated, and spent a lonely and cold night on the hillside. As the song ran on, the woman found her way back to the house, but never saw her man again. She wandered the hillside for a lifetime, never getting over her sense of loss.

When Malcolm quietened, he leaned over and put a hand on Keldron's shoulder. "A sad song. Poignant and also very relevant."

Malcolm looked up and around him at the fog, which was still as dense as it had been when they awoke. "It was a favourite of my wife. It's how I remember that she is out there somewhere, waiting for me to find her. In the mist it makes me feel closer to her than at any other point, for I can imagine she is going to come riding out of the mist to greet me." He looked off into the morning. "We are nearly there."

Keldron peered forward. There was a dip in the road, and the impression that the mist was clearing.

"What's up?" Belyn asked as they rode in closer from behind.

Venla followed this very shortly. "Oh my. Isn't that beautiful."

A gap in the milky fog revealed a city about two miles away from them, down a fairly steep slope. The walls were a uniform height, and looked impenetrable. The rock had been clearly chosen for its uniform colour. Behind them, the city should have sprawled, as was the typical layout. Instead, it was highly regimented. Straight roads crisscrossed the city from end to end.

"When that guard said his Duke liked things tidy and regimented, I didn't think it would extend to the entire city." Observed Raoul.

"I think it is cute," Yerdu replied. "It is like a man has come up here and played with model toys until he has found what he wanted."

Raoul stared at her in silence, and then rode off muttering to himself about toys and perspective."

"Why don't we ride down and find this ship that will take us to your hidden temple then?" Yerdu said without a trace of a smile. Not waiting for an answer, she led her horse after Raoul.

Belyn grimaced in embarrassment at her simple remark. "Do not answer her, and rue it for weeks."

Keldron laughed at the comment. "It is all right for me, old friend. I may share in the embarrassment, but I am not the one with the maps."

They rode down out of the mist to a landscape radically different to the plains. Small meadows were terraced with rock walls where they had been built up to provide more nourishment for the population. Crops had been recently planted, showing that despite the perilous situation, the land around Leallyra was indeed a hale place. It appeared to Keldron that the Duke was obviously as interested in predial matters as he was in matters of order.

The descent remained steep until about a mile out from the city, where it levelled out. There was evidence that this too had been engineered by the city folk, for there were ditches and walls aiding drainage and dividing up the land, and the city lay in a broad bowl down to the fog-covered sea.

Raoul rode on forward. "I'm going on to facilitate our entry into the city. Judging by the experience with the mounted guard, I think we need the time." The rest let their horses walk as they enjoyed this radical difference in the lie of the land.

"You wouldn't expect this from up above," Keldron observed. "The whole shape of the city has been created by somebody. Most unusual"

"What would you have expected?" Joleen asked, interested in what he had to say.

Keldron looked around him. "Cliffs, crags, scree on the slopes right up to the city walls. Maybe a sharp waterfall or two instead of that landscaped effort over there." Keldron pointed and they followed his aim. Way off to their left, a mist appeared on the ground, generated by a waterfall that fell several times the height of the tallest building Keldron had ever seen. The river that was its source obviously came from somewhere inland but the effect of that much water falling so far was glorious, even from the distance they were, even on a foggy day that obscured sight. The sound made it all the more impressive. "Somebody has definitely been busy."

They rode up to the city walls, and met the first cityfolk. Most of them were travelling light.

"Where are you bound?" Belyn asked one man, a tall chap carrying a hoe.

"Just out to the fields, mate. Somebody has to keep this huge garden in order."

"Farmers and hired hands then," Keldron decided.

"Except for them," Belyn pointed. There were perhaps a handful of people setting out to climb the difficult road and leave the city over the land track.

As they rode up to the walls of the city, they spied Raoul leaning in an alcove talking to a pair of guards. They were laughing like old friends, and the apparently jocose nature of the men was a heartening sight.

Raoul turned to wave them on. "Here are my friends." He announced to the guards. "Here are Belyn Stroddick and Keldron Vass of the Guild of Law, and Yerdu, Joleen and Malcolm of the Merdonese."

"You have permission to enter the city." One of the guards, a tall heavyset fellow with a jutting chin, addressed them. "From what we have heard, Captain Curtis has already grilled you enough."

"Captain?" Keldron said in surprise.

"Oh that's just our name for him," the other guard replied. This man was much slighter of build, and shorter with it. The two guards were as mismatched a pair as one could expect to meet. "As you may have seen, he is an officious fellow and he makes no secret that he wants the job of captain when the old man retires." The smaller guard indicated a man back through the gates on a horse. "We just help him along by calling him 'captain'. It makes the low-ranks laugh, and irritates him no end. Saying that, he does it well even if he is a bit stuffy."

"Curtis said that there are ships that would take us where we need to go from your harbour." Keldron said, changing subject.

"Indeed he was right," the guard agreed while his companion watched the road. "There are ships to anywhere from our docks. That is why your arrival here brings a smile to our faces."

Keldron looked confused, to his credit. "I don't understand."

The large guard grinned down at them all. "What my tiny colleague here means is that everybody comes to this city on ship. They all leave by ship. If there is a place you need to get to, there is most likely a ship that can get you there on account of all the major cities being coastal. What probably got Curtis' goat was the sudden appearance of six riders from the landward side. We don't get many people travelling to Leallyra from inland, hence there only being the two of us on guard at the gates." The gates themselves were small, only really big enough for two people on horses to pass side by side. Unlike the reputedly huge gates of other cities, these were defensible by way of their insignificance.

"It would take an army a year to pass through these." Belyn said looking up at the trellis that hung ready to impale an intruder.

"Exactly." The small guard replied. "And should you wish to try your hand at piracy, the harbour is guarded by ballistae and catapults. Our Lord Duke Jhander likes to keep things calm and prosperous."

"With a city halfway between Qua'Clira and Bays Point I can understand why." Belyn agreed.

"Anyway, we mustn't keep you good people," the guard concluded. "Our captain might not be too fussed with the security at the gates, but we will get a real roasting from Curtis if he hears we were doing any more than checking identities."

"One last thing," asked Keldron, "how do we find the harbour?"

The guards both grinned. "Go on through and just follow the road." The large guard said with a bow. "It's the Grotesque that you are after, and you can't miss it. She sails on the morning tide, so take a look around our city should that be your thing. There are inns a plenty down on the harbour side, and some of them are even reputable!"

Keldron waved his thanks, and as he rode through the gate, he saw exactly what had made the guards grin. A road paved with pale yellow stone led as far as the eye could see, until it ended at the seafront, at the very edge of their vision. As it was slightly down slope, it was easy to see that it would still take them most of the rest of the day to reach it.

"Oh my," Yerdu said as she rode through the narrow arch.

"That takes some beating," agreed Raoul from behind. As if on cue, the mist decided to part for the final time that day, and where there had been foggy banks of white moisture, there was now a blue sky that tapered off into distant white, with the sun almost directly overhead. Seagulls danced in the sky, their piercing shrieks combining with the salt air to leave the travellers in no doubt that they had finally reached the coast.

"For your first view of a proper city, it could be much worse," observed Belyn to the tribeswomen.

They rode along the road for a long time. Yerdu and Joleen drank in the sight with obvious gusto, to Keldron's secret amusement. Each house was constructed of the same stone and roofed with slate, therefore providing the distinct colour that emanated from the entire city. Shops were visited, and Keldron found himself dipping into his purse several times before they had even reached halfway. If Joleen and Yerdu had thought the simple city road impressive, all the rest of them were dumbfounded by what they saw at the midsection of the city. Four roads joined, and at this point there was a huge square, wide open and with nothing in it. A simple sign proclaimed its use. 'Festival Square'. At the corners of the square rose four temples, decorated ornately in different colours, with bas-reliefs of faces and figures in marbled dance. They rode towards the temple immediately to their left, stopping a man who was sweeping the steps.

"Can you tell me what temple this is?" Belyn asked of the man, who stopped sweeping, and looked up at him.

"There stands the temple of Holy Yogingi, the bringer of wind." The man said with complete reverence. "The temples across the square belong to the worshippers of Matsandrau the Sun Lord, Ilia the Goddess of Earth, and Panishwa the God of Water."

"What about the others?" Keldron asked the man. "What about the lesser sects? What about Ondulyn and Jettiba? What about the Law?"

The sweeper shrugged his shoulders. "They are present, in a minor capacity. There are chapters in the guild quarter, but the Dukes of old decreed that only the four named would have temples dedicated to them on the square. It has ever been thus, and forever shall be." The man resumed his sweeping.

The party rode away across the square, enjoying the spring air, and the sight of the temples.

"Would they join us, if they had seen what we have seen?" Belyn murmured to Keldron.

Keldron shrugged. "Who knows?" Like us, they are city folk, and may care little for the goings on in the countryside. They are certainly protected well enough from anything that has bearings on other worries than sea travel. To issue an army from here would be madness, and for one to attack would be suicide. This place is just too out of the way."

"I meant the orders."

Keldron looked up at his big, red-haired friend. "Belyn, I think that until we find something significant enough for us to convince the orders that there is more at risk than the lives of rural farmers, they will not lift a finger to aid us. Until we reach the temple on Caighgard, we are on our own."

"I hope there is something we can find on that island to aid the tribe." Belyn prayed out loud.

"There is, old friend. I just have a feeling that we are onto something bigger than we realise. Something bigger than all of us." "I don't know why, Kel, but you have my complete faith."

"I am going in there." Raoul said as he looked up at the Wind Guild Temple.

"Why?" Asked Belyn. "You can't hope to gain anything by going in there."

"They are guildsmen, just like us. They know focussing, just like us. They will see the kinship and help us."

"On your head be it," Keldron said, resigned to the fact that they were not going to dissuade him in this particular mood. "We will wait for you out here."

Raoul stalked off towards the Temple of Wind, which stood bright white in the morning sunshine. He pushed through the door and entered the foyer of the temple, a pristine white affair like he guessed the rest of the guild was. Nobody was there to greet him, so taking it upon himself Raoul bypassed the desk behind which a representative normally sat and entered the guild proper. He had not gotten far when a pair of white-clad acolytes approached him.

"Can we help you?" One of them asked, wrinkling his nose in distaste..

"Yes. My name is Raoul Za, of the Order of Law in Eskenberg. My friends and I have been travelling for a very long time, and seek news of the world and things happening within it."

"Well spring will be here soon enough, Raoul Za," the other acolyte replied smugly, "soon you will be able to air your clothes out properly. Is there anything else we can help you with?"

Raoul frowned. This was not going as planned. "I seek more specific news of a guild nature. Specifically if anything has happened to my own guild since I have been gone. I know that every member of this temple will know of anything happening in the world. It is the Guild way."

"The guild way of vagabonds perhaps," the first acolyte replied disdainfully. "If you are who you say you are, where is your proof? Even if you are of the *Law Guild*, what do we care of a group of stuffy old men that do nothing with their skills except stagnate? Everybody knows the Law Guild of Eskenberg only exists so that a group of living fossils can claim that they have a say in the running of the Duchies. We do not care for such people here, nor do we recognise any representative of that guild."

"But do you know anything? Anything at all."

The pair smiled back at him. "If we know anything and perhaps we do, we would not divulge that information to any wandering beggar off of the street. Now get you gone, before we call upon the power of our God to remove you."

Raoul glared at the two of them. It was clear that they were going to offer no help of any form. The pair of them reached for something under their cloaks and Raoul put his hands up in defeat. "I am going. Take word that there is a great evil afoot in the Duchies. It might reach even here, *if* it has not already."

Shaking his head, he turned from the two acolytes and exited the guild. Once outside he let rip with a stream of blistering curses, enough to turn the faces of the recently appeared temple guards a deep shade of red. As he tired of this, Raoul saw his friends approach him from across the plaza.

"They wouldn't listen," he sighed as they got within earshot.

"We guessed as much," Belyn chuckled, "but you had to try, did you not?"

258

Raoul swore once more for good measure and mounted his horse.

They rode the rest of the way through the city down to the docks. Once they had passed the festival square, the city changed profoundly. Where there had been houses there were now mansions, where there had been shops there were now markets. Housing gave way to the splendour of the guild and merchant quarters, separated from each other by the arrow-straight main road that pointed to the sea like a weathervane in an easterly breeze. The flocks of squawking sea birds increased as the creatures vied for scraps in the waste bins of the merchant houses and inns, but that was as far as mess went.

"This city is unreal. Way too clean." Raoul observed as he watched the passers-by.

"What's the matter, brother?" Belyn chuckled. "Not enough grime and dirt to make you feel at home?"

"Absolutely," Raoul replied. "A city is not right if it does not have a bit of muck in the corners of streets. It adds to the flavour."

"I find it nice to be back amongst people," Yerdu agreed.

To the pleasure of them all even Malcolm cheered up, joining in the general merriment with a song about sun chimes.

As they rode out through a small gate that separated the sea front from the rest of the city, they all looked on in stunned appreciation. Lazy seagulls floated on the breeze while below, on a mass of cerulean infinity, several ships rocked at their moorings. Wavelets lapped up against the small pebbly beach that nestled in against the sea wall, rhythmic in their consistency. Ropes stretched and groaned, and the salty tang of the air mixed with the smell of pitch. Above it all, there was a scent of freshness, of mystery. The six of them sat there on their horses, dumbfounded with a sight they had never before witnessed. Keldron stood up in his stirrups, looking across at the ships that were moored up at the nearest dock. "I wonder which one is the Grotesque." He said aloud.

"Move along please, you are blocking the road," announced a voice from behind them. They turned to see another of the guards that seemed to appear with such efficient regularity to deal with problems of any level.

"Can you tell us which of these ships is bound for Caighgard?" Raoul asked the man.

"Ain't none of them." The guard replied. "Two of those are bound for Ulecio, and the others are headed further off in the wrong direction for you. Those as were leavin' for Rhothamy left already, so I would say yer best bet is to try for the northern dock, along the promenade a ways." The guard pointed off to the northwest, where the city extended as far as the eye could see. In the extreme distance, more ships could be seen.

"What about down there? Could they be going from there?" Keldron looked the other way, and the guard followed his eyes and shook his head.

"Duke's private moorings. Accessible only from the palace. If you would be so kind to move along, we try to keep things easy here as it can get a bit crowded." They began to move off and the guard called again. "If you could lead your horses we would be obliged."

Raoul waved a hand to the guard in thanks as they all dismounted. "Officious fellow, wasn't he?"

"Polite too," Agreed Belyn. "All from the same mould, I bet. This Duke must be powerful to be able to afford his own docks."

"Well you can see his palace from here," Joleen said, and they all turned around. Above the guild quarter rose an imposing building, the only building that looked out of place in the entire city. "I bet that is where your fancy river comes out."

Keldron smiled simply in response. "Maybe, but since we are headed in the other direction, we will never know."

They walked along the promenade, taking in the sights and smells of an ocean-facing city. At one point they stopped to eat a meal of fish that the fisherman claimed had been caught that morning. The meal consisted of a plate of pieces of white and orange striped flesh with a tangy fruit sauce, a meal that Yerdu in particular found to be delicious. It typified their impression of the coast. Fresh and flavoursome with a hint of salt. As they continued their journey with the gently lapping waves for company, the ships at the northern moorings grew larger. One in particular stood out above the rest. It was a galleon with three masts, a true monster of the ocean. As they neared it, the ship proved to be about a half again as big as any other ship at the dock. It had three gangplanks running down from its deck, and these were crowded with sailors loading and unloading cargo. Malcolm made himself useful by asking a passer by the name of the ship, and the mumbled response he got left him smiling.

"Have you ever seen a vessel so fine?" He said to the others.

"What are you getting at?" Belyn asked the tribesman.

"That big ship, that is the Grotesque," Malcolm said.

Belyn let out a roar of a laugh. "But of course it is. It is so grotesquely huge that it could not be identified otherwise!"

Upon reaching the dock, Malcolm and Belyn left the others while they climbed aboard the ship. A short while later they returned, smiling.

"We have passage," Belyn announced triumphantly.

Joleen looked with considerable apprehension at the wooden monstrosity that was supposed to keep her safe across countless stretches of water. "And that has got you smiling?"

Belyn grinned. "Nope. But I would hate to ruin the surprise. We are not going to need the horses, so let's find a nice inn to stay at, and sell them."

Raoul stretched his hands up into the air, exaggerating a comfort that they had not felt in long moons of travelling. "Finally a proper bed beneath my back, and no lumpy ground."

Joleen stuck close to Keldron as they wandered around the promenade. "What surprise?" She said.

"I don't know," he replied.

"Go on Malcolm, what surprise?" Yerdu urged.

"I cant," Malcolm replied with a grin at her persistence. "He made me promise."

Yerdu groaned at his morals and walked on forward, unhappy at not having her curiosity satiated.

They found an inn nearby and managed to sell their horses in exchange for rooms for the night, meals and a small sum of gold on top. When Yerdu saw the look on his face she nudged him. "What's got your face tied up like that?"

He sighed. "Just thinking about the virtues of humility, dear. Money is not exactly a problem, But I was outrageously cheated at the paltry amount I received in exchange for such fine horses."

They ate another meal of fish in an alcove of the busy inn. The alcove chosen by Joleen was most agreeable for it had a large window over the harbour, not to mention deep plush red seats that were the perfect tonic for extensive living from saddle and on the ground. As they ate the sun began to set, turning the sky red and the sea a luminescent reflection of the heavens. The slow but persistent movement of the waves brought the ocean to life, and the ships bobbed on the surface in the evening glow. They watched in fascination, for none of them had ever seen this before.

"It reminds me of home." Keldron said in fond remembrance. "The way the sun used to play over the surface of Lake Eskebeth. It is so much more."

"How so?" Asked Raoul, who had never really seen the advantages of Keldron's eyrie in the Law Guild.

"The movement for one. Eskebeth was huge, but for all that it was, it was only a lake and did not have waves like that. It did have a glorious glow, just before the sun passed beyond the shadow of the mountains. Nothing like that."

Keldron relaxed watching the sunset. There was a brief red flash and then it was gone, leaving just the red trace of its passing on the horizon. All excitement finished with, he turned back to the raucous atmosphere within the inn. Jugglers and acrobats paraded around a stage set up in the middle of the floor, so that everybody could watch. Ale was flowing freely, as the cheering and applause that accompanied every trick became louder and louder. After their meal Raoul stood, leaving his chair in the direction of the innkeeper.

"Where do you think you are going?" Belyn called out.

Raoul turned back. "To get another pint. To sample the local brew before we are taken from it and stuck on the sea for the Gods only know how long."

"I don't think so my friend," Belyn said firmly. "Last time you were let loose in an Inn, you kept us waiting half the next day. None of that this time. We are all to be up early tomorrow, for the tide is at dawn and we can not miss this ship."

Raoul sighed, his shoulders slumped and he sat back down. "It is for my own good, I suppose." He said with great resignation, and closed his eyes. Keldron felt Raoul draw in his concentration.

"Put it back." Belyn said sternly, and they felt the focus dissipate.

Raoul looked up, his eyes bright. "I have never done that before." He said, his face animated with discovery.

"What did you do?" Belyn asked quietly.

Raoul leaned forward. "I had a hold of the flask of Orit, and was bringing it back, when I heard you telling me to put it back, so I did so. Well we have always taken from that room, but never put into it. Who is to say that we cant take an object and put it there? Who is to say that we can't take ourselves and put ourselves into a place?"

Belyn shook his head. "Too risky. You would have to know exactly where you are going."

"But we would in this case," Raoul protested. "We would be going back to Eskenberg."

"It is not as simple as that," Belyn disagreed. "The room I had set aside is guarded from without. Were any of us to appear in there we would surely be dead before we managed an explanation."

"But they know you," Raoul persisted.

"They know *of* me, but they do not know what I look like. The whole set up was through a third party. I know the location of the room, but in order to guarantee the safety of myself and those I was dealing with, we never met. As far as they are concerned, we would just be intruders and trust me my friend, you do not want to be an intruder in that particular place."

Raoul slapped his hands onto his thighs in an outright gesture of defeat. "So much for a good idea."

"Don't give it up just yet, Raoul." Keldron said encouragingly. "There is not much for us in Eskenberg anyway, just a whole bunch of Law wizards who were quite happy to wring our necks, and our rooms which have almost definitely been emptied of anything and everything. We have not come this far just to go back to the start."

"What about Obrett?"

"He can take care of himself, and he would not want us back for our own safety."

Raoul frowned. "I know that we can make this focus work brothers. We just have to have faith."

"And time." Belyn added. "Which is exactly what we will have when we are aboard the ship. We will have time enough to learn every square inch of its hold, and if we can get this to work, we will be able to practice it. All we should worry about now is getting on that ship in the morning. Let us go to our rooms, and get all the rest that we can."

The night passed comfortably for them all. The inn, as was typical in Leallyra, did not stay open late and the patrons had filed out quietly when time had been rung. Order was paramount in the city. The morning dawned, and for once they were all reluctant to rise. It was Belyn that had them all up despite their protests, battering down the doors with huge meaty fists. They ate a hurried breakfast, and with brief thanks to the innkeeper for his hospitality, the six of them were out of the inn and hastening along the promenade towards the berth of the Grotesque. Waves lapped quietly, and the air had a chilly undertone to its salty freshness. Occasionally a bigger wave would surge up, rushing against the pebbles. Few gulls could be heard at this time of the morning, for they were mostly out at sea.

The Grotesque was in an obvious state of readiness, and all that she awaited was her passengers. A few sailors milled around the dock, ready to cast off lines Others were climbing the boarding steps, and there were several passengers also en route. Aside from that, the dock was a quiet place at this time of the morning. The sun had not yet made an appearance, as the hills up behind the city would block any sight of it for some time yet, so it was a clear blue sky that was the most heartening thing for them. It promised good weather, and this was a positive omen. The ship rocked gently, ropes straining with the tide.

"All aboard for Rhothamy!" A man shouted out from the deck as they approached. Belyn led the way onto the ship, the two women holding tightly to the ropes behind him as they climbed the steps.

"A good day for it," Keldron commented to one of the sailors.

"Aye," the man replied as he looked up at the sky. "There be a strong breeze off shore, and we should make good time. You are the last of them. If you'll be getting aboard, we'll be off."

Keldron did as he was asked, and climbed the steps to the main deck of the ship. What he saw when he got there astonished him. At least a score of the tribe were awaiting them on the deck, and Malcolm and the two ladies were already amongst them, bestowing greetings and blessings. "Well I never. So this is your surprise?" he said to Belyn, who was grinning broadly.

"It is. I could not believe that so many had made it this far when I came aboard last night, and to have them all on this ship."

"That is not all," a nearby tribesman added as he overheard the discussion, "there are at least twice this number that have sailed for the Isle already."

"How did you all pay for this?" Raoul asked, still quite stunned.

"We have our means," the man replied, patting his tunic. "Just because we are not merchants, it does not mean we do not have experience at their skills." Raoul nodded, accepting the point. "Well the omens get better and better, don't they?"

"Cast off the ropes! Hoist main sail! You there, up in the rigging!" A man yelled from what must have been the wheel-deck. Suddenly amongst the crowded deck, there was a flurry of activity. Ropes were being coiled; sails dropped and billowed out as they caught the breeze. The ship lurched into action. Every one of the passengers went to the sides of the ship to lean out and watch the city behind as they started on the most momentous journey yet. The ship turned as they left the docks, but it turned to the South.

This caused a moment of panic for Raoul. "We are going the wrong way!" He said aloud.

"Land lubbers," snorted a nearby sailor. The man in question came to stand between him and Belyn, who was content to watch the waves hitting the promenade they had walked up the evening before. "We have to go this way because of the shallows, mate. That's why there are three docks, because shallows are dotted around that will ground those that do not know the routes. This city is safe as houses because only the sailors guild from Leallyra know the proper way through."

"Oh," was Raoul's short reply.

The man clapped him on the shoulder. "Don't worry, matey, we will make a sailor of you yet! We have a huge journey before us."

"I am not doing any of that," Raoul announced, "I am a paying guest."

The sailor looked at Belyn. "You haven't told him yet have you?"

Belyn looked a trifle embarrassed. "No I haven't. I was going to break it to him gently."

Raoul frowned with suspicion at the both of them. "What do you mean?"

"I uh. . . had to sign one proviso to get us on board, my friend. We are part of the crew."

"You what? We are. . . I am not. . ." Raoul was pretty much lost for words at this point.

"It's okay, matey," the sailor said in reply, "we can always send you back to the docks. The swim is not too bad from here."

Raoul looked at them in a state of desperation. "I am cursed, I swear it." He stomped off to somewhere he could be alone.

It was at this point that Malcolm and the two ladies returned from their sightseeing. "Am I right in hearing what I thought I heard?" Malcolm said to Belyn. "Are we all signed onto be sailors?"

Belyn heaved a sigh. "Yes that is the case. It was the only way. If you are not happy?" He left the question hanging.

"On the contrary," Keldron said, his face brightening at the prospect. "They are all looking forward to it." The others murmured comments of agreement.

"That is good then, for you shall all be having plenty of experience of a sailor's life before the end of this journey." A voice spoke to them from behind the cluster of people, a voice accompanied by a rather odd smell. They turned and were mostly surprised to find themselves faced by a pirate who had a pinched little nose, and large eyes, almost making him look a bit like a cat. "Go find that miserable wizard," he ordered the sailor. "Let us see how he finds a watch in the crow's nest."

"Aye Captain," the sailor replied, and moved away.

"Captain Flynn." Belyn offered his hand, which the man took in a firm shake. "Wizard. So these are your companions, are they?" He looked them over one by one.

Yerdu stared defiantly back at the man. "I suspect that the reason for the ship's name stands before us."

The sailor chuckled. "Aye, this is your captain speaking lass. There could be no finer name for such a magnificent ship than that of her master. We could have had 'Flynn's Revenge' or some such name, but at the time my then wife and I were not on the best of terms, and she provided the name when ridiculing my face."

"It is appropriate." Yerdu said.

Flynn let out a bellow of a laugh. "Ye Gods I like this one. She *must* be your wench, wizard." That simple comment stopped Yerdu in her tracks. Her black hair bristled with indignation, and she turned away to look at the sea.

"So what do we do now, captain?" Belyn asked, openly amused that somebody had managed to silence Yerdu for once.

"My first mate, Benson, will show you around the ship, allocate your quarters and such. Once you have all your gear stowed, we will begin to show you a bit more of the life of a sailor. It will make true men, and women out of you."

With a nod the cat-faced pirate left them to their own devices.

"Ooo would you look at that," Joleen said as she looked out over the sea. They turned towards the city, and as they did so the Grotesque passed the tip of the southernmost dock. Directly behind it stood the Ducal Palace. It was a great wide building, built of the same stone as the rest of the city but on a much grander scale. Its magnificence belied the previous view. Great windows abounded, bordered by pillars that looked as if they had been carved where they stood. A blue flag with a white star hung fluttering slightly in the breeze, the flag of the Duke of Ciaharr. A similar pennant had been hoisted on the mast of the Grotesque, thus proclaiming its origins. The city spread up the gentle incline behind the palace, making the view from the deck of the ship all the more imposing. That was not the only reason it appeared so. In front of the palace there were four cutters, armed to the teeth with cannon and archery platforms. Similar positions had been built into the dock itself.

"Nobody is going to gain those docks without a fight," Keldron observed.

"They would be fools to try," said a deep voice from behind them. Joleen and Keldron both turned to find a tall man with dark hair standing a few steps away from them. He wore dark blue clothes more like a uniform than the scrappy rags of the other sailors. "With the defences of the city coupled with the maze-like qualities of the shallows, only those that sail from this city would know how to raid it, and they are all accounted for as members of our sailors guild. Only the foolhardiest of pirates would even attempt it."

"Would you be the First Mate?" Joleen asked him warmly.

He smiled, a big, easy smile that emitted confidence like a master at work. "My name is Benson. You may call me Jared."

"Jared," Joleen replied, a dreamy look on her face.

Keldron did his best to hide his irritation. It was not like him to have such feelings, but the effect the first mate was having on Joleen was quite unnerving. "Are you going to show us to our quarters?"

Benson moved his alluring gaze to Keldron, and the wizard suddenly understood that this was the way the man was with everybody. He was not some hawk out to prey on unwary passengers; he was just a man of supreme confidence. "Indeed I am, master magician. If you will all follow me."

Looking at the way Joleen suddenly followed the man, Keldron felt resigned to a difficult journey ahead. "Roll on Rhothamy," he grumbled under his breath.

Chapter Twelve

Zya marvelled at how her luck seemed such a double-edged blade. Since returning to Bay's Point she had experienced joy and pain in rapid succession. She entered the city life and peace with her family in moments, and just as quick was taken from them by Ralnor Scott, who had known she was returning. She had found the answers that she sought, and yet they only led to hardships. She was not sure which defined her current situation. She looked over at the table in her room, at the seven stones that rested in their stands. They defied her, presenting a challenge that she had just had to take a step back from. Her task was to decide which stone best suited her characteristics as a human being. The trouble was that she did not see any obvious differences in them. They were all grey, dull and had polished surfaces. They were all of a uniform shape, a little larger than an egg. How was she supposed to differentiate? If it wasn't for the fact that it felt right to have accepted the offer of an initiate's post at the Earthen Cleric's Guild, she would have walked out. Her feelings told her she had something to learn here. Feelings were the problem. She was not allowed to do anything by instinct. There had to be proof, and proof that her tutor could see. The infuriatingly polite Ralnor Scott had told her that this task measured her ability beyond all other, and would continue to do so. She thought back to the day that she had met the strange little man. He had a cold handshake, and his eyes looked in different directions. She could not help but stare at them whenever he was in the room with her. He also had a way about him. Quiet, but authoritative from the moment they had met. He had been nearby on guild business when she had collapsed. He had trailed them as far as he could and then just waited until he saw somebody he recognised. That was the way that he put it of course. Zya didn't believe a word of it. When pressed, the man would shut tight like one of the shellfish that were so popular at stalls in the harbour. He had made an eloquent offer. More out of curiosity than anything else she had accepted her place, on the proviso that she could come and go to visit her family. That had rankled him, but he had relented.

The biggest surprise for Zya had been when he led her to a building very close to the kitchen that she had worked in. They entered through a grand opening, all doors and columns decorated in various earthen hues. He had given her a tour of the building, introducing her to many other initiates, and several of the more prominent members of the guild. It had not been what she expected. Everyone was dedicated to the Earth, studying and understanding it. The whole building had an aura of peace, the complete opposite to the manic rush of life outside of the guild walls. That had been the major factor in Zya's decision to remain. What had also convinced her was the feeling that she just belonged in the guild. It was only when they approached the kitchens that she realised they were the exact rooms that she had been working in. She was astonished, as was Ralnor, that she had been under the eaves of the guild for so long and not even known it, and from that point on she had attempted to study under Ralnor's tutelage.

"So here we go again," she said, half in annoyance at herself as she stood over the stones once more. "What would Ralnor say?" She thought for a moment, before breaking into an impression of the little man. *"In all fairness, Zya, you have the tools to find the solution. It's all there, right in front of you. Use them and job done! It's all solved."* This light-hearted moment cheered her, and Zya's heart felt less heavy. Things were definitely different with this problem. When there was something she could not understand, he would not explain, but would sit there and stare at her with the slightest of grins on his face. He knew the answer, but would never tell her unless she became so worked up that she was tying herself in knots. This was such an occasion, but it seemed that he was desperate for her to find the true path herself. She paused in the motions of picking up one of the rocks. That had been the one rule he had set.

"Touch the rocks, and the test is over. Why should I not be allowed to touch them? What is so special about seven little stone eggs that I am not allowed to handle any of them without failing the test?" Banging her fist on the table hurt her hand more than vented her anger. She shoved the chair back, and stomped over to the window. There was not much to see out there, but it proved a sufficient distraction, allowing her to calm and compose herself once more. There was a clear view of the Duke's Tower, from which the monotonous tone of the bell rang away the watches while daylight passed, and there was a distant street that appeared in a small gap between the rooftops of the guild and an adjacent building. Not many people used it, mostly the menial staff of the guild. It had taken her a while to figure out what was so familiar about it, but then she realised that it led to the entrance that she herself had once used. Still, it was nice to be able to see the Ducal Palace without any hindrance. The immense vaulted roof and numerous wings capped what looked almost to be a private city. There were certainly streets in the area surrounding it, but she did not know who lived there, nor was anybody willing to talk about it. The walled enclosure went right up to the sea though. Most odd for an open planned city. Knowing that she was distracting herself, Zya returned to the conundrum of the seven stones. She passed her hand close to one of them and closed her eyes. "Seek what not you can see, but what is hidden behind the veil that obscures sight." She spoke aloud to herself, wondering where the phrase came from. It was either her father or the unnamed woman that had given her the understanding to realise that her dreams meant more to her than to many others. It made sense though, as she was much more able to clear her mind and focus on the problem in front of her. She reached out, seeking the ovular shape ahead, and sensed nothing. Something drew her hand left. On pure instinct, she moved with the sensation, following the unseen path to the source of the feeling. The feeling grew as she hovered her hand over another of the stones. It felt warmer, and there was a notion that she could only describe as right. Testing herself, Zya moved her hand further to the left, and the only response she felt was that she should move her hand back. Doing so, she opened her eyes. The third stone from the left, one off of the middle. It looked no different to the others. It was grey and dull, with the occasional blemish in its polished surface. There was definitely something different about it despite the ordinary exterior. "I touch the stone and it is the end of the test," she said aloud to herself. "Touch the stone.... Touch the stone...." She grinned impishly, and stepped across to the open door. Peering out of the room, it was clear that nobody was around. Ralnor had left her to the test a good long while before, and two bells had rung since then. She closed the door as quietly as was possible, thanking Ilia for her divine guidance in reminding whomever responsible to keep the hinges oiled. The door shut with the barely audible click of the handle as Zya eased it up. She was now ready. There was no other way to test her theory without doing this, so as she prayed that nobody would walk past she tipped the table until the stones fell out of their stands and rolled off the edge. One fell, then another, and another. They all made the dull sounds of stone hitting stone, with neither stone nor floor yielding and breaking. Two more rolled down, which they were she could not see as it took all of her concentration to lift the edge of the table. There was a thud and a crack. The final two stones rolled down, making a total of seven. She dropped the heavy table back to its feet with relief. "I miss the open road," she said to nobody but herself and the four walls surrounding her. Zya was fitter and stronger as a traveller, but there was no call for physical tasks in the confines of a chamber. Anticipation flooded her as she stepped around the table to look at what she had done. Seven stones lay on the floor by the edge of the table, and her joy crumbled into frustration and defeat. Seven stones that looked no different to the seven stones that had been on the table. All grey, all dull and all still in one piece. She sat back onto her chair, legs crossed under her, and contemplated the test. Her instinct told her the stones were different. What it had not shown her was any proof, and that was what Ralnor expected. It was not enough to know that there was a difference, that there was a way around things. He needed to see evidence of that. For him the easiest option was never the best one, and he had let her know that in no uncertain terms. What instinct told her, evidence told him. She decided that this was not a time for evidence, and closed her eyes once more, reaching for the stone that she knew was different. Her feelings guided her to it. It was a red source of warmth beneath her hand, and as she knelt down, she felt herself reach into it. The feeling came in a moment of revelation to Zya, who had never before felt *inside* the structure of the stones, just over the surface. Her stone was different to all the others in one particular way: At its core the stone was hollow. There had indeed been a break as one of the stones hit the floor. She felt through the stone for anything wrong. There was a crack along one edge, a hairline fracture that would reveal the difference to her should she have the nerve to reach for it. She was certain now that this was the stone that needed to be selected, and she kept her eyes closed as she reached for it, lest sight put her off. The stone glowed with invisible warmth as she picked it up, and as she opened her eyes, she could see a crack in the narrow end of the stone. Just a little flick of the wrist, and the top fell off, as if somebody had cracked the top off of an egg. She looked inside, and was instantly ensorcelled by the beauty within. Despite the tiny aperture, Zya could see how the grey of the outer stone faded and became clear as crystals grew out. The clear filaments turned a vivid purple before becoming white at their tips. When she caught the light correctly, the crystals lit up with a violet fire. Reflecting light onto their neighbours, it was enough to stun the senses. This was definitely a different stone. Almost reverently, she picked up the top of the stone, and placed it back so that it formed a whole once more. Strangely enough the top did not fall off, but fit like the final piece of a puzzle.

As Zya contemplated this, the door opened and Ralnor stepped in, a look of satisfaction on his pale face. "I see that you have chosen wisely," he said with a look that showed he was impressed with her choice. "How did you go about it?"

Zya frowned pensively as she thought of the best way to put her answer. She would never jump to words, she had learned that much with the wise woman. There was always time to form an answer. "I felt my way there," she said, and saw his face drop just a fraction.

"That was not the best way to do it. That could be construed as the easiest way out."

"Nevertheless, that is the way that I solved the problem. If it is the easiest way to the answer then there should be no problem with that."

271

Ralnor wasn't fazed by her answer, sticking stubbornly to his point. "Do you not see? The easy way out makes for bad habits. Here at the guild we aim to prove everything that we do. We do that by results."

Her recent triumph seemed almost as hollow as the stone now gripped tightly in the palm of her hand, feeling it as if it were a part of her. "How do you quantify magic?" She demanded. "How do you put a figure to instinct? I closed my eyes and concentrated on the stones, and *felt* the difference in this one. It drew me to it, as a lodestone attracts rust. All of the others gave me nothing. Nothing! This stone was the one I was meant to find. Now if my method is all you are prepared to argue about, then forget the whole thing. I have accomplished the task. I have found my stone."

Ralnor appeared unruffled by her verbal attack. "Pray tell, Zya. How did you end up with all of the stones on the floor when you were told that you could only touch one of them?"

Zya appeared sheepish at this question. "I tipped the table up, so that they rolled off."

Ralnor broke into sudden fit of laughter at this, surprising Zya so much that she jumped, her face coming alive with momentary shock. "Did you indeed?" He said. "That will be noted and written down in the guild history. If you can believe it, never has an initiate passed the test by such a method."

"I have passed it?"

"Why yes." Ralnor seemed surprised that she had not caught on quicker. "You have the correct stone, otherwise you would not feel its pull. I selected stones at random, as I do for every initiate. Most do not make it either because they do not have the skill to focus, or because their stone is not drawn. We believe that there is a reason people join the guilds, and the focus stones are shaped to fulfil that. Ilia in her divine providence has seen to all of our needs, including sorting those that will benefit her from those that would cause nothing but detriment."

Zya missed most of what Ralnor had told her. As soon as he had mentioned the word 'focus', she had withdrawn into herself as if prompted by a command. "I can focus," she said out loud finally, after much thinking about events past and present.

"Yes you can, my dear," Ralnor replied proudly. "Why else do you think that you are here?"

Zya looked up at Ralnor's face. His wandering eye was off in a different direction, but he was still giving her his full attention. "Why here? Why not another guild?"

Ralnor sat down on one of the chairs in the room, bidding Zya to sit in another. "Perhaps luck, perhaps fate. The guilds have different methods of recruiting. Some will hawk their wares, so to put it, in the open, announcing that they are taking on new members. Others will do it in secret. Some are completely secular, only initiating the offspring of guild members."

"How would such a guild continue to exist?"

Ralnor shrugged, as if the question was not really worth an answer. "If one were to say that all of the current members are related by blood, that should suffice for an explanation."

Zya's mouth dropped open in shock at what she was hearing. "Brothers and sisters?" She implied.

Ralnor nodded. "Indeed."

"I hope this guild is not one of those," she replied quickly, seeking the most honest of answers from him.

He smiled in response, finding her statement amusing. "The way we recruit new members of this order is part luck, part guidance. I just happened to be nearby when I felt you attempt to focus your mind through the building."

"Through the *building*?" Zya exclaimed.

Ralnor nodded. "You might not have known what it was that you were doing, in fact I am sure of the fact that you were unaware. You were attempting to use the stone structure of that building to focus, to what ends only you can say. It overwhelmed you, as it should do, because the building is not one single stone, but a collection of thousands. Nobody has ever attempted to focus through so many. To be honest, it is a miracle that you survived, but saw it I did, and sought you out I did. Someone who can survive that magnitude of focus must be worthy of training. It just so happened that on that day, the head of this order had me scouting near the mercenary guild because we do not like the signs that are coming from that place. It is too secretive for that type of guild, and more come in than go out."

"That is what I had heard also," Zya replied. "There is more though. Before I came to Bay's Point, I believe that myself and my companions were being followed, or tracked by a man." Zya took a breath before she continued, for she was unwilling to discuss her traveller past, or the time she had spent with the tribe in Upora. She had to get her thoughts straight. "When I was passing the mercenary guild, I felt the presence of this man, much as I had done in the past. He is part of something spreading westwards. Something bad. I could feel it through the very ground."

"A true Earthen Cleric you are, my dear. Only those in tune with the bounty that Ilia herself provided this world would be able to sense such a thing. It was lucky that we found you before anybody else."

Zya thought that was a strange thing to say. Surely if somebody had certain skills, they entered a certain guild. Her intuition told her that something she had said had affected Ralnor in some way. When she had mentioned 'the man' his face had shadowed, albeit very briefly. Or perhaps the intuition she had gained from the tribe was clouding her ability, and she was meant for another order. Perhaps she had only imagined Ralnor's interest perking up at the mention of the mercenary guild. What had he really been doing so close to the building? Zya kept those thoughts to herself. "I guess," she said out loud, not meaning to sound so unconvinced.

Ralnor picked up on this. "Do you disagree?"

"Well I do not know about fate, or destiny, but perhaps luck has had a role to play in getting me here. I once was advised that perhaps an earth-related guild would benefit me." Zya looked down to her hands, the very same hands that had once stitched under the tutelage of Anita. It was not Anita that had suggested the course of action to her though, it had been Ramaji. Faces phased in and out of her thinking, faces that were so recently familiar, saved from the fate of prisoners. The mothering she had felt from the two women and especially Venla, the mistress. The camaraderie of the two guards. The wit and experience of Gren the cook and the practical and sure handedness of Layric. Gwyn and Jani forever tinkering. Zya even missed Mavra and her new-found power of command. This was a different world she now lived in, one that had remained largely undiscovered. Zya only hoped that she had drawn the danger away from them by returning here. She could not bear to think that her family would ever be in a situation as perilous as she could possibly face.

"What is it?" Ralnor asked, concern written on his face.

"Nothing much," she replied, trying to dismiss the faces in her mind. "I was just reminiscing." She composed herself and sat up straighter, looking into the good eye of her tutor. "Are we done here? Are you convinced that my solution was in fact the best one?"

"That remains to be seen, Zya." Answered the wizard. "There is just one more thing. Can you show me what is so different about your stone?"

Zya held up the dull grey egg between her thumb and middle finger, using the other fingers to spin it around on its axis. She regarded it dispassionately. Her stone had no obvious signs of what was within, not unlike herself in many respects. After gazing at its muddy swirls and flaws beneath the shiny surface, she used her index finger to pry the top loose and caught it in her other hand. She tilted the stone so that Ralnor could get a view of the inside.

His eyes widened and he gasped as he saw what made her stone so special. "That is a wonder indeed. I have never seen its like before. A hollow focus stone filled with a layer of white-tipped purple crystals. Zya, you must come with me at once." Ralnor did not give her time to answer, but stood up, and bade her do the same. He led her out of the room and through the hallways of the guild, until they reached a room she had seen only once before. The central chamber of the head of the order. It was surrounded by columns of stone that looked as if they had grown out of the floor, and joined at their tips all of their own accord. A convenient doorway was filled with light, but no door, for stone could not grow hinges.

Zya peered inside. "Where is he?" She asked. "I can see only light."

"Step inside," Ralnor urged, his bad eye twitching nearly closed with excitement.

Not seeing any problem with doing so, Zya complied. The room grew brighter as she crossed the threshold, and as she stepped towards the middle, the stone in her hand began to grow warm. "I cannot see anybody," she called to the outside.

"Do not worry," came the voice of Ralnor from a distance. "All will become clear soon."

The stone felt as if it were tingling, desiring some kind of release. Zya looked at it, drawing the stone close to her face. She could have sworn at that moment that it was twitching. The white light remained constant and pure, to the extent that all she could now see was herself. "Where is he?" She cried out loud.

"Use the stone to see him, Zya." Came the voice of her tutor in the form of a distant echo.

"Of course." Zya understood why the stone felt as it did. It *needed* the release. It *needed* her to focus. Now that she had to do it consciously, the process was a different matter. How was she supposed to get inside the structure of the stone? She looked at the twitching piece of rock in front of her, and flipped the end off with her thumb, revealing the crystalline structure beneath. In the white light it was dazzling, the crystal points catching the luminescence, and making the inside of the stone look like the night sky, with a million tiny stars contained within it. Zya closed her eyes, to take away the glare of the light. That was a start. She knew from what she had learned during her time in the guild that she needed to work her way into the very fabric of the stone. But there was no way it could be done that she knew of. Beginning to worry, she tried to forcibly enter the stone with her mind, thinking of the crystals and the dull grey rock surrounding them. It did no good. It allowed her to do nothing with it. A sinking feeling in her stomach made her panicky. Her arms tensed and her palms became damp with nervous sweat. In her mounting desperation, Zya opened her eyes to look at the stone and instantly regretted it. White light burned across her senses like a sheet of flame, forcing her to close them. Truly panicking now, and oblivious to the encouraging calls of Ralnor from outside of the chamber, Zya forced herself to take deep breaths. "Think about what I had been doing the times when they said I had focussed." When she had fainted, she had surrendered to the pull of the stones both outside the building and in her chamber. "That is the secret," she whispered in triumph, "not to go against the stone. Not to force myself into it, but to be drawn in." The knots in her stomach disappeared as if they had never been there, and the cold down her neck became the tingle of excitement. She relaxed, releasing her breath slowly, a trickle at a time. She searched the area around her for that warm feeling, and found it. The pull of the stone was there in front of her, enticing, warming her hand. Just as she had done before, Zya moved her attention away from the source, and it vanished. The stone would not suffer violation and the forced entry of a mind, but it would accept a willing soul. She pushed her senses into the stone, letting herself become drawn along into the subtle pull, and suddenly the light changed. Everything went a deep shade of purple, and Zya felt herself scream out loud. It was exactly the same colour as the dream that she had once had. The dream that had made her decide to leave the caravan and pursue the uncertain danger with only her father and Ju. That the stone chose to reveal this exact colour meant only one thing to her. She had found the meaning to the dream. It had told her that she was meant to come here. For a moment longer the colour lingered, and then it deepened to the violet hue of the crystals inside the stone. As she sought her way in, everything took on the same colour. Visions of past events flashed by, all in purple. She felt that she could do anything and everything, that there was nothing not within her power to accomplish. The feeling of being at the very core of her stone gave her such a euphoric kick that it was hard to imagine she would ever be made to leave. As it was, her thought once again coincided with an interruption.

"Open your eyes, my daughter," said a voice so starkly feminine that Zya was convinced for a moment that Venla had somehow found her way to the guild. She did as bidden, and her eyes opened to a completely different type of light. The entire room had turned the same violet hue as her crystalline thoughts. The stone was still nestled in the palm of her hand, fitting snugly between her thumb and little fingers, which held it secure. The room into which she had stepped had disappeared, and the vastness of her mind was opened out around her. The possibilities were infinite, and she had only to stretch out and feel for them. She looked around, seeing tiny points of light floating in front of her. She reached up to touch one, and found that her hand just passed through. Zya looked around, considering the room she had been stood in before, and gazing in awe-struck wonder around her. The contrast was so great it was as if she had stepped into another world. The room was warmer now, as warm as the stone in her hand. There was a pulse beating, sending flashes of brighter purple light around the room, and it took a moment for her to realise it was the beat of her own heart magnified through the crystalline points within the stone. The doorway had disappeared, but from the distant voices beyond, she could tell that it was still there.

"It is beautiful, so very beautiful," she breathed out in a soft echo of her normal voice.

"It is a rare sight," the voice agreed. "Never before has an initiate managed so spectacular an entry into the ranks of the guild. You should feel proud."

"I don't feel anything of the sort. There is no pride to be gained from this, only more wonder into how deep I could go." Zya realised that as of yet she had not seen the source of the voice. "Where are you?"

"I am beside you, in the chamber of the guild, guiding your thoughts through the stone."

"Why must you do that?"

A pause followed, as if consideration was needed before framing a response. Zya could appreciate that, though it made her slightly uneasy. "To keep you on the right track. So that you do not overextend yourself and become lost in the illusion."

Zya reached out, and drew her hand through the purple light surrounding her. "So this is illusion."

"It is," the voice agreed. "It is the first thing initiates can do, and also the easiest. A connection with your own focus stone and an understanding of its nature become juxtaposed with your need to learn more about abilities you doubtlessly have. It still requires a little guidance from their teacher for them to keep the focus steady. I must add that seldom have we had anybody that could maintain conversation while concentrating on their focus."

Zya took that as a complement, but now she had more questions. "Where are you? Can you show yourself?"

"No, but if you withdraw your senses from the stone, the focus will end and you will be able to see me." The voice was gentle and yet carried a tone that was so similar to Venla that it almost broke Zya's heart to hear it. The tone was

277

one of command. Zya took one last look around the room she had created within her mind, and remembered that she had seen this once before in her dreams, and doubtless would again in the future. She closed her eyes once more, and tried to create a gap between her consciousness and the stone's crystalline perfection. It was difficult, having to concentrate, and even more difficult pulling away from the stone, so seductive was the feeling it gave. Eventually, she felt herself distancing from the stone. It was working. Pressure built in the back of her head as she willed herself back, and when it evened out, she knew the focus was over.

"All done?" The voice said beside her, and she opened her eyes. Expecting to see a woman beside her, Zya was startled to find an old man, with a beard that had been plaited so that it dangled like a rope off of his chin, almost down to his knees. His eyes were green and brown, earthen colours both, and were in complete contrast to the white hair that brimmed out from under the hood of his cloak. "That was you?" She exclaimed, still slightly startled at the fact that she was talking to a man.

"It was I," he replied, his voice deeper, but only an octave or two.

"You sound different."

He raised his eyebrows and shrugged his shoulders in a noncommittal gesture of agreement. "Vision is not the only sense affected in a focus, especially for a novice. It may be that you were once close to a person and their voice intruded upon your thoughts."

Zya had not considered that possibility, but then things were so new to her. "You are the head of the guild," she said.

The old man nodded. "My name is Joen Kzell, and I have the honour of heading the Earthen Clerics at this time. Honour in especial when I can be witness to an initial focus the magnitude of what we have just seen."

"My focus was that great?"

"Well Zya, part of the focus comes from the person, and part from the stone. It is a mingling of consciousnesses, a magical mixture of two distinct personalities. I would say that rarely have two such forces ever come together as they appear. I can say in all honesty, to borrow a phrase from your previous teacher, that I have never seen a hollow stone used in a focus, and to such dazzling effect."

Having never seen any other focus as far as she could remember, Zya did not know what to make of such a comment, and instead of saying something meaningless, merely waited, looking about her. The brightness of the white light had faded to the point that she no longer had needed to squint, and she could see the inside structure of the room matched the roughly hewn columns of the outer wall. "How was this room formed?" She asked partly out of interest and partly because she felt he was expecting her to answer with some vacuous comment. She wanted to surprise the man.

In fact Joen seemed delighted that she was answering questions with questions. "Thus was one of our first and greatest achievements created, by the determination and patience of the first Earthen Clerics of this city." His gestures were expansive, and there was an overtone of pride in his voice. "This structure was grown from the very stone of the city, and into it was put the strength of many guildsmen, some say the spirit of Ilia herself. It took nearly a generation in the making, twenty years from base to tip all told. If one meditates for long enough, and has the strength of mind to listen, the distant voice of our Goddess can still be heard, echoing in the heavenly vaults from whence it came." He ended his speech with nearly a whisper, and Zya could see that his flair for oratory was one of the more dominant facets of his personality. Learning from this man meant that this was going to be an interesting time.

"Why are you going to teach me?" His face dropped slightly, so she pressed on, meaning to make herself more understood. "What I mean is that if you are the head of the order, then surely there must be others that could teach." Joen smiled with benevolence. "Do not worry yourself with trifles dear girl. Everybody is capable of teaching in this guild. There is no one person that would not be capable of teaching you to focus, but when we saw the illusion you produced, that marked you as something special. Even more so when we saw what you had been using."

Zya examined the stone in the palm of her hand. The crystals within caught at the light, making them twinkle. The illusion she had been a part of was still there, contained within its own little starry universe. Zya sealed that universe off by replacing the top of the stone. The strangest thing was that the stone clicked together, and once it was whole, it did not appear to have a crack in it. Nonplussed, Zya pocketed the stone and followed Joen out of the room back into the greater gathering hall of the guild. There were roughly two score wizards there watching them, and they bowed in unison. Zya smiled, trying her best to keep an embarrassed flush from spreading up her neck to her face. "Welcome to the guild, Zya S'Vedai, daughter of Tarim," intoned Joen, who then watched with her as the guildsmen stood back up. Whatever her preconceptions were about the guild, they were instantly changed as she saw the faces looking back. Instead of a sea of beards, she saw the faces of all ages. Some were just older than children, and through the age range they grew until old men squinted back. What surprised her most was that there were more than a few women here, dressed in the same garb as the men. It totally rearranged her preconceptions. Instead of looking at the guild as a collection of wizards, she saw from their faces and the way they stood that it was more like a family. This sudden thought made her homesick for her father, Lorn and Ju. "Thank you for the kind welcome." She said out loud. "I hope that I can give back as much as I have already gained."

Joen grinned broadly. "I think I can speak on behalf of everyone when I say that you have already done far more than that, Zya." He then proceeded to lead her away from the gathered mass, and into a side room that turned out to be his study. Decked out with luxuries that seemed sparse in the rest of the guild, Joen bade her sit in one of the high-backed seats to one side of his desk. He took the opposite seat from her, and poured them both a drink.

"Drink up," He said, offering her a glass. At her curious look at the drink he added, "It is fruit juice, imported from the South and iced from the North. Zya took a cautious sip. The flavour blossomed on her tongue, reminding her of the summer morning she once spent looking out over a river. It was a similar instant of joy, and made her pang even more for the company of those familiar to her. She felt quite overcome at that moment, to the point that Joen noticed.

"What is the matter?" He asked, his old eyes full of concern.

Zya laughed in spite of her mood. Everybody was looking out for her. "It is a delicious drink. Excuse me for my frankness, but what do I call you?"

Joen looked up to the ceiling of his study as he thought out loud. "What do you call me? Master? *Sir?* How about Joen, seeing as I am to teach you. Joen it is. Now you can tell me what is the matter."

"I miss my family, Joen. That is the simple truth. I have thought about asking if I may go visit them, or do you have rules about isolation here too?"

"None of the sort," he replied, "in fact it sounds a perfect idea considering what you have been through. That illusion must have tired you beyond measure."

"I am somewhat weary," she agreed, unwilling to let on that she actually felt nothing other than a need to see her family.

"That is settled then. Take your time to go and see your family, and return when you feel up to it. But before you go, let me tell you of the things that await you." Joen leaned forward, looking straight into her eyes. "I would hate to think you would miss out on any of this."

***

If Zya knew Lorn, he would have had carried on with life in the weaponsmiths, only pausing to mope after her in his private moments. So the shock when he saw her walk past the window in the direction of their house brought a satisfied smile to her face. Dropping his work, he excused himself and ran out after her. Already she was disappearing down a side street, staying as unobtrusive as possible. Lorn walked faster to keep up, and eventually gained on her. "You are a welcome sight in a city of strangers." He said as he caught up with her.

Zya stopped, recognising the voice and turned around slowly. "I was homesick." Zya threw her arms around his neck and kissed him firmly on the lips, a lingering kiss that spoke of intimacy. He held her close for a moment as she hugged him tight. She then pushed herself away, smoothing down her robe and laughing sheepishly.

"You are full of surprises."

"I guess that I was more homesick than I thought." Smiling at his confused state, she took his hand. "Come, let us find my father. I would have all that I know to be familiar around me while we catch up. It has been too long."

"He will be pleased to see you," Lorn agreed. "How long have you got away from the guild?"

"Until tomorrow," she replied, implying by the tone of her voice that she did not want to speak any more on that subject.

That made Lorn grin. "Something is always up with you."

"Come on. The walls have ears. These robes mark me out as a guild member of the Earthen Clerics. While they are well respected by most people, they are not universally loved. Every guild has its detractors, and it's clear judging by the faces of some that were I still alone, they would let their feelings out for an airing."

Lorn looked around them. "But we are well within the tribal quarter, where the Gods and Ilia in particular are revered, even loved." Lorn's face and longbow discouraged any attempt at even catcalling, as did the knife that Zya still wore about her waist, yet they did not tarry. They passed quickly and without incident through the couple of streets that separated the weapon smiths from the carpentry and their house. Zya sighed in relief when she spied the open gate that led to the countryside beyond. "Missed the open spaces, haven't you?"

"I have. It is only when I actually see it that I realise how much it means to me. Once a traveller always a traveller, at least at heart."

"Have you got enough time for us to go out there?"

Zya looked at him, and then glanced around at the people about them. "Perhaps."

Lorn's expression betrayed his unease. Zya had more important things on her mind. She crossed the short distance to her father's carpentry, and burst in through the door, leaving it swinging ajar. By the time Lorn arrived she was hugging her father while Darrow looked on with a broad smile. Lorn nodded a greeting to the big pirate, who looked resplendent in bright green velvet with his blue-steeled falchion strapped to his back looking completely out of place. Zya stepped back from her father, and a tear was running down her cheek. "Sorry," she said, embarrassed.

Tarim looked confused. "Why be sorry? I am as glad to see you, as you are to see me. How have things been?"

Zya proceeded to tell the three of them about her experiences thus far in the guild, from the first time she entered and realised where it was she had been taken, up to the illusion she had created and the introduction of the guild master as her new teacher. When asked about the use of a stone by Darrow, Zya produced her focus stone, popping the lid, as she liked to call it, and letting them see the crystals within.

"My, Isn't that a pretty little jewel,." Darrow said as he peered in through the tiny hole at the end of the stone. "How do you use it?"

"Concentration mostly, I think," Zya replied. "Though I do not know how to do anything really with it. The first big test was to try and find the stone from a group of them, and there was no guarantee that I was going to find my stone. Luck has been with me today. The strange thing is that it all doesn't feel quite right. I know what I need to do, and I can use the stone in doing it, but something interferes." Zya thought to herself for a moment, trying to come up with a better analogy. "I suppose it could be different types of training clashing, for I have had several."

Darrow obviously did not know what this meant, but before he could frame a question, Tarim interrupted him.

"Tell me about this Joen Kzell," Tarim asked her. "Is he a man you can trust?"

"I have no reason not to father, they have shown me nothing but kindness and understanding. As it transpires, I had just as much a chance of getting him as a teacher as anything else. My lessons start tomorrow, and continue for three moons. Then comes the Feast of Growth, to celebrate the warming of the North."

"You've been invited to the Ducal Estate?" Darrow looked surprised as he said that. "That's a rare honour."

"Joen said that novices from all the guilds attend. It has become a tradition."

"Looks like you are going to get your wish then, doesn't it?" Lorn said with aplomb. "You always wanted to visit that place."

"Be careful in there, girl," Darrow warned, leaning forward conspiratorially. "Word has it that there are some less than savoury characters behind those walls, and we wouldn't want anything bad to happen to you."

"I am sure I will be able to take care of myself by then." Zya replied with confidence. "Tell me what has happened with you all since I have left you. I must have missed loads."

This question gave Darrow the opportunity to break into his verbal stride. "I have news about Juatin, your young companion, message runner and general sneak. He has been running messages to and from the mercenary guild of all places, for a rival of mine."

"Is that safe?" Lorn asked with a great deal of concern.

"Should be," Darrow replied, not looking the least bit worried. "He is quick on his feet, and keeps his mouth shut. That is all they desire of him, and every day he gets a little more information about our mysterious guild."

"Any news of O'Bellah?" Zya asked, the first pangs of worry coming to her for a very long time."

"That name has half of the mercenaries cussing, and the other half scared into silence." Darrow admitted. "This man that you have claimed is out to ruin the world has to be seriously well connected elsewhere to have such a solid bunch of people acting like that. The strange thing about it is that it seems that they are recruiting, and no longer being secretive about it."

"What has Bays Point to do with him?" Lorn asked of the burly pirate.

"He is connected to Raessa." Zya interrupted.

"Maybe, maybe not. It seems that from what Ju has been hearing the man is not in town at the moment, nor is he for the foreseeable future." Darrow leaned in, as if he did not want anybody else to hear. They all leaned in with him. "They say that does not matter, that he has ways of finding out what is happening from afar. They say that he has wizards aiding him, wizards from guilds all over the land, and that they are turning their fellows to aid him."

Zya found this claim to be slightly incredulous. "Who are '*they*'?" She asked, in tones that plainly echoed her feelings.

"Mercenaries mostly, as far as the boy could tell. It's a seething pot of distrust and anger within the mercenary ranks when there is nobody to keep them in line. That is where your O'Bellah has made a difference." Darrow sat down heavily on one of the polished chairs scattered around the room. "Let me tell you about mercenaries. They are a crude lot, full of bad language and coarse ways, not at all like pirates. Moreover, they usually work in bands, and do not gel well with mercenaries not of their band. Imagine if you will the rivalry that would have existed between the tribes up on the steppes had you not all had that greater purpose that seems to govern you all. Well the worst rivalry you could imagine would be a drop in the ocean compared to the friction that occurs when you put two of these bands in the same region, let alone the same complex."

"That bad, huh?" Zya said.

"You had better believe it, girl," Darrow affirmed. "Now imagine the tension inherent in such men when you have say ten, even twelve of those bands under one roof."

"Volatile wouldn't even begin to describe it," Tarim murmured, setting the tools he had idly been using to shape wood down.

"Right," Darrow agreed. "What you have there is a melting pot ready to be tipped over, and able to consume most everything in its path. Had I not known you better, that one situation alone would convince me that was responsible for the bad feeling not only you, but many of this normally vibrant city have been feeling."

"No, it is not that. It is O'Bellah. We have seen what he is doing in the countryside."

"I believe you lass. The one thing that can seemingly hold them all together. Your mysterious O'Bellah. Imagine what sort of a person is able, despite not even being present in the city, to maintain order and discipline within the ranks of multiple mercenary bands. Remember that this is a group of the roughest individuals that would draw their swords at the slightest provocation. He has regimented them in a way that has never been seen before. Add to that the many that are drawn from the city itself by the apparently easy pickings on offer to those that sign up, and you have all the bad seeds in the entire region packing out a single building. More enter every day, and yet none come out. Ever."

"Maybe I should go in there, and try to find out what is happening." Lorn suggested.

"Not likely," Darrow replied. Not one tribesman has been seen within the vicinity of that place. You are the first to have wandered that street in months, and that was only because you are relatively new here. Trust me when I say that you should never, ever go near the mercenary guild again." Darrow was insistent, but appeared honestly concerned for Lorn.

"Well what about Ju?" Zya demanded. "What if they decide he will make a fine recruit for this army of mercenaries? How are we supposed to rescue him from them?"

"They will not take children. That at least is beneath the mercenary code. They will not have anyone that cannot fight, and that rules children out. Of course that does not mean they will not keep their eyes open for any future potential, but for now, Ju and Nikki are too young."

"Women too?" Lorn was so surprised to hear this that he just blurted the words out.

Zya sidled up to him. "Was that supposed to mean that you think women cannot fight?"

Lorn coughed, trying to hide his embarrassment. "No Zya, I was just surprised to hear it was all."

"It is not so difficult a concept to entertain." Darrow replied, heading off any potential argument. Most women up here are as able to fight as the men. Therefore they are as willing to become mercenaries. It is just a bit less likely. They do not mix with the men, and so there are a few female mercenary bands. Helma's Hellcats is one that I know has joined this freakish union. Mavra's marauders is one other."

"Mavra's?" Both Tarim and Zya exclaimed. When Darrow looked at them in surprise, Tarim elaborated. "Mavra was the name of one of our companions, currently leading what could be called a potential band of her own."

"Well this Mavra isn't her, I can tell you that much. She is as big as me, and most probably as strong. She has also been a mercenary for the past twenty years. Certainly not one you want to mess with. But as for the children, they are safe as long as they keep their noses clean and do what they are paid to do." Darrow rose from his seat. "Look, I must go. It's been nice seeing you all again. I am a sucker for a family reunion, but I have my own people to look after. Do not worry about Ju, he will be ok. But do not go anywhere near the mercenary guild again, not for any reason. It may be that fate saved you when it did last time, but it is a fickle mistress that will rule you should you be drawn under her sway. Me, I never leave things to chance. Too much can go wrong." He shook hands with them all, and then shifted the weight of his falchion to a better position with a grunt.

"You really should stop by the weapon smiths some time." Lorn said critically as he looked at the great curved sword Darrow preferred. "There are perfectly good cutlasses there."

"What? And part with this beauty?" Darrow grinned. "Not a chance in hell." Darrow made his way to the door, but before opening it, looked through the window, and then turned back. "One more thing, Zya. Be careful when you go to that grand ball in the Ducal Palace, there might be more afoot than you think."

"What do you mean?"

"The person that uses Ju to run messages to the guild is based in the palace. There is a tenuous link between the palace and the guild. I would not want you to get caught in anything."

"Darrow, how is it that you know all this about the goings on and yet remain undetected by any of those you watch?" Tarim asked very seriously.

Darrow assumed a tragic expression. "My friend, I would have thought that you had a little more confidence in me than that." Then he grinned. "I am the master of the underworld around here. I know everything that's going on, or didn't anybody tell you?" And with a flourish of his obnoxiously coloured clothes, he was out the door and gone.

Tarim crossed to watch the rapidly repeating form of Darrow as he sauntered off round the bend in the street.

"Has he been here often?" Zya asked as her father continued to peer through the door.

"Now and then." He replied. "He seems to feel the need to keep us informed of what he finds, and what happens within his realm. To be honest it is also good to hear about what Ju is up to as well. He is kept so busy that we hardly see him."

"Is Ju all right?" Zya asked. Her instinct told her he was. She could imagine him sneaking around alleyways with that girl that she had met in the cellars, using his quick feet and quicker tongue to good effect.

As an affirmation of her sudden thought, her father replied. "As far as we can tell. He is here on occasion, but he ends up sleeping in all sorts of places, most of them underground. Still, he has Darrow and Yneris keeping an eye on him, I think he is in no immediate danger." Her father turned back to her. "How are you going to spend the rest of your free time?"

Zya looked down at herself. The robe was nice enough and she enjoyed the play of the earthen colours. "I am going shopping." She decided out loud.

"The needs of the city finally getting to you, are they?" Her father asked, not with disapproval, but a gradual resignation to the ways that were affecting them all.

"Not really." Zya replied. "I still want to run for the hills every time I see the gate, but there are a few things that I need, just modest things."

Tarim smiled, and hugged his daughter. "I am so proud of you, and your mother would be too. You are so very much like her."

Zya looked at her father. He rarely mentioned her mother. "How so?"

"Your committal to values, and your steadfast refusal to abandon them. Your loyalty to those close to you. You even look like her."

Zya smiled, unshed tears in her eyes that would remain so as she would not break down in front of them. "I need to go to the market." At a warning look from Lorn she added, "But not that market, there are others nearby that will suffice. One day you will tell me all, father." With a grateful glance she stepped out into the afternoon, Lorn closely trailing her and leaving her alone with her thoughts. There was another loyal person if ever she had met one. He was even able to split his loyalty between them and his tribe. Zya admitted to herself that there were feelings that she had for Lorn, but feelings that she was not quite ready to come to terms with. She shelved them in the back of her mind, and promised herself that one day, perhaps one day soon, she would deal with that issue.

They walked to a market that had a reputation for quality goods, but provided a little entertainment in the form of travelling performers of every sort. The market was immensely popular as the performer population was as fluid as the river. There were always new acts arriving. It provided light relief in an otherwise crowded and stressful region. For Zya and Lorn it provided the ideal distraction, especially since it was in completely the opposite direction from the guild quarter of the city. They could see the Ducal Palace separated on the hill to the South, and the city wall stretched off to their right, diminishing as it closed towards the ragged cliffs that grew up to the West. The market and entertainment were separated into two adjacent buildings, great warehouses that were built in the least populated quarter. With the denser half of the city across the river, benefiting from the trade and defence that were provided by proximity to trade routes and rock, less people were willing to live further away. This was moderated to a degree by the clever positioning of the palace and the guilds. All in all, it was quite nice not to be jostled around, but Zya soon saw that the situation was not going to remain that way. Bodies bustled in and out of the twin buildings like a colony of ants. "Not more crowds," she moaned.
Lorn chuckled.
"What?" Zya was not in on the joke.
"Somebody has obviously seen a market for a market here," he joked.
Zya groaned and punched him on the arm, laughing all the while.
They entered the building to find row upon row of stalls sectioned off and covered with material roofs. Huge windows let light in; especially bright as the angle of the sun meant that as it began to set it shone directly through, showing up all the motes of dust that swirled without aim through the air above. Zya's attention became riveted on the clothes. Try as she might, she

remained unimpressed by a lot of the gaudy wares that were the norm in this pirate city. Instead, she opted for a wide brown leather belt that could still fit the sheath of her dagger on it. Not even willing to haggle, she paid the asking price and took the belt, wrapping it around her robes. It had the desired effect, and she felt more like a woman. "I have no desire to walk around like a tent, for the robes are enough to announce what I am." Once she had what she came for, the rest of the markets held no more than a marginal interest to her and she wandered, gazing through stalls as much as at their wares. She became one of those frustrating customers that the vendors just could not reach.

"Why don't we go to the other building and see what entertainment they have on offer?" Came Lorn's suggestion through the haze.

Zya smiled in response. "That would be nice, let's do that."

They made their way back through the stalls, ever-more desperate merchants trying with every ounce of persuasion to sell what they could at the end of the day. They walked out into the street separating the two buildings and Zya halted, looking around.

"What's wrong?" Lorn asked as she stared around.

"I know this place," she replied. "I know this street, this very building. I have seen it in my dreams, a long time ago. I have to go in, and if I say something to the man, he will say something back to me."

"Are you sure this is safe?"

Zya turned towards him. "I have no idea, I only know that I need to do this, Lorn. I need to go into this building." Without waiting for him to comment, Zya entered the warehouse. The interior was very different, but no less busy. The difference was in the layout. No packed aisles festooned this hall, but instead, separate areas were put aside for each different type of performer. Stages had been erected for musicians and speakers, while smaller booths lined the sides of the open spaces for the less popular acts. It was towards these that Zya was drawn, bypassing the crowds that pushed and jostled for a better view of a man that was juggling what she perceived to be sticks of fire. It was towards the shadowed far end of the warehouse that Zya began to slow her pace, as she searched for something. Here the booths extended into the depths of the shadows, and were only kept alight by tallow candles and the occasional lantern. Zya looked from booth to booth as she searched for something that only she could see. Suspicious and often greedy eyes peered back at her, but she never once stopped for long enough to become enticed. In the middle of the booths she stopped, peering over the shoulder of a woman who was deeply enmeshed in a game of cards with the small man that was separated by the table between them. The man was nothing special; Dark brown hair that hung loosely and framed his bearded face, dull eyes intent upon the cards in front of him, and nondescript brown clothing. He did not even look up as Zya peered at him.

The woman however, became a bit unsettled by the presence of two people over her shoulder. "Do you mind?" She asked in an acid voice filled with greed and deception.

"Our pardon madam, we were just perusing the games." Lorn apologised.

"Well go *peruse* somewhere else, the both of you. This is my game and I do not want to be disturbed."

While Lorn had distracted the woman's attention, the man behind the table looked up at Zya from between the five cards he had in his hand. He gave her the same odd look of recognition.

"I am the dreamer." She said, not knowing where the words even came from. He smiled curiously, and replied, looking at a slip of paper he had picked up from the table. "The gates aligned focus the mind to cross the bridge."

Chapter Thirteen

The man in the booth leaned forward and placed a small piece of the paper in Zya's outstretched hand. She took the paper, closed her hand, and the whole incident had passed in a matter of moments. As Zya finished speaking the woman ceased to lecture Lorn, and the whole incident was lost to the couple in the booth. She felt not quite herself and yet again found that Lorn, who kept an eye out for any pursuers, was guiding her. When they got outside, he did not lessen the pace, but spoke in a voice that reeked of confusion. "Okay, do you want to tell me what that was all about?"

Zya tried to frame distant memories into words. "I had a dream once that I was outside a building, and that I would enter, and seek out a man. I would say something to him, he would say something to me and hand me an object." As if this triggered a reaction, Zya looked down at the paper in her hand. She unfolded it, and spoke two words, but too quietly for Lorn to hear, even with his tracker's exceptional senses.

"What does it say?"

Instead of speaking, Zya, almost in a daze, handed him the paper. Lorn looked at the curvy, flowing writing. "Wrong Order. Wrong order of what?"

Zya looked at the piece of paper in his hand. "Well, that must be what he handed me. I assume it means that I am a member of the wrong guild. Either that or I have done something before I was supposed to. It could have any number of meanings." As they walked away from the market, Zya tied her hair back with a piece of leather. It exposed a bit more of the warrior in her for the severity of her look.

Lorn noticed the change, not commenting on it. "How long ago did you have the dream?"

Zya considered this for a while. "When I was a lot younger, I think. Not recently."

"And it came true. I think you are more of a seer than anybody understands, even perhaps you yourself."

Zya stopped in the street and looked at him, oblivious of the few people in this district that were winding their way through the detritus left by countless other people. "Is that what you think?"

"It is. I also think that you have had the gift for a lot longer than you care to admit. I think you have had this since you were a child, from what you say, and have kept your dreams hidden from everybody else."

Zya sighed, and started walking, though this time it was more of a trudge. "Perhaps I have, perhaps not. Out in the countryside, little things did not mean so much. It may be that I didn't take any notice of my dreams and for seasons I may have been having them."

"Would you like to know what I think?" Lorn asked her as he walked alongside.

Zya looked sidelong at him, "tell me."

"I think that the closer to whatever destiny fate has in store you get, the more these things matter. Your little episode back there may serve to make you think that you have to leave your guild, but it may mean something completely different. Only you know best what your feelings tell you."

Zya smiled. "Is that the opinion of an objective observer?"

Lorn had the grace to blush, a very rare thing on a man, let alone a tribal chief. "Not entirely, no. Zya I miss you when you are not there. You brighten our days with your presence, and the world seems less futile when you are around."

Zya's eyes roamed into the ever deepening blue of the early-spring sky. "I have to do this, something tells me that I must. There will be time for everything else later, I promise." Zya took his hand, and they walked silently back to the tribal quarter without pause, not allowing any distraction to pull them apart for even a moment.

By the time they returned, the sun had almost set, and Ondulyn was clearly visible in the East. The brightest of the stars had come into view, gradually lighting the heavens with their immortal glow. They entered through the back door, the same way that the wizard Ralnor had found his way into the carpentry. The workshop was quiet, with the slightest trace of candle smoke in the air from a wick that had burned on after the candle had been snuffed. Light crept under the door that separated the workshop from the living quarters above, and they made their way upstairs. Hearing voices speaking yet again, Zya became cautious, and listened carefully. One of the voices was a lot younger than the other, and she instantly knew who it was. Zya looked around at Lorn and he urged her up the stairs, nodding encouragement. She opened the door to find Ju talking to her father. They stopped talking and looked at her, then burst out laughing.

"Did I miss something?" Zya asked, not sure whether to be offended.

"Of course not," her father replied. "Ju was just saying that you would be returning at any moment, probably wearing that look of suspicion you seem to have adopted lately."

"I then said that once you knew it was me, a look of relief would cross your face." Ju added. "It looks as though I was right."

Zya had missed the gentle jesting of her adopted family, and the closeness they had for all of their experiences made her feel home among them. Here in this room was all that she had ever needed of life. As the evening wore on and they ate a meal that Tarim had contrived to prepare with Ju, Zya was reminded of Gren the cook and his culinary delicacies. All of their cooking had stemmed from the man, his countless recipes, and numerous stories of herb lore. Zya found herself yearning for the company of her extended family. The instinct that took over in her from time to time arose and made her feel that they would be together again one day, but it was never soon enough. Then Lorn distracted her with a raucous tale about Darrow and the baker's wife, and she forgot all of her woes for a time. As the night deepened, Zya found herself yawning and sought her bed. She regretted missing a single moment of the joviality that had grabbed a hold of them all, but she knew that whatever training her teacher had in mind for her the following day was likely to be tiring and she needed the rest. She sat on the end of her bed, brushing her hair. "The gates aligned, focus the mind, to cross the bridge, wrong guild." Zya repeated the phrases over and over again.

"The girl said that, in the dream," Ju said, sticking his head around the door. He entered and closed it. The bow still stuck out from behind his shoulder, but it fit him better every day now, and it did not hinder him. "You have grown since I saw you last, at an alarming rate. Do you ever take that bow off?"

Ju looked over his shoulder. "Not often. I forget that it is there most of the time. As I expect you do with the dagger."

"Good point," Zya conceded. "And yes, that phrase was in the dream. I heard it again today, spoken by a man in a card stall at the North Wall Market."

"The one with the players?" Ju brightened up at the mention of the place. "I spend every moment I can there, when I am not running around like a blue-assed fly."

"Such language is unbecoming," Zya reproached him.

"What about the other phrase? The wrong guild?" Ju was becoming adept at turning the conversation, Zya noted.

"I don't know, Ju. It could mean any number of things. It could mean that I am in the wrong guild. It could mean that a different guild is responsible for what may or may not be happening here. It could even mean that the guild that I collapsed outside is not what we think it is."

"Oh, it *is* what you think it is," Ju replied in a quiet voice. "I would not go there were I not getting paid for it. The place is full of brutes and madmen."

"Don't worry about it now, Ju," Zya sought to reassure him. "I have enjoyed this evening, and it has reminded me that there is so much out there that really doesn't deserve our attention. There is nothing more important than family." Ju smiled at the implied compliment. "Goodnight sister," he said, and left her alone as he closed the door.

It did not take very long for Zya to drop off to sleep that night, so comfortable and relaxed as she was. The thick mattress and downy blankets she covered herself with proved more than adequate to send her quickly slumbering into the world where darkness ruled over all, and images came and went as her unconscious mind was left to wander. She had hoped for a night with no dreams, no images for her to remember. She was not an ordinary person though, not by any stretch of the imagination. As Zya had been told in so many words by her tribal tutor, she would one day be able to see the future through her dreams and the paths that she walked would guide her and copious others to safety. That was the one fact that had decided that she would open herself up to whatever experiences had arisen within her head. It was what was guiding her now. The flickering images gradually became one clear vision, that of a market place. It was so familiar to her that she could have pinched herself and found that she was actually there, only she knew that she wasn't. It did not take long before she realised that he was there with her, as he always seemed to be.

"So where are we this time?" Ju asked, unsurprised by the whole turn of events.

"The market that I was supposed to go to the day I collapsed and dreamt of the ships and cat face the pirate." She realised where it was, even though she had never previously reached the place. The uncomfortable feeling of the mercenary guild was magnified tenfold here in her dream, and she could point out its location and distance with her eyes closed. That was definitely not the reason she was here.

"What are we supposed to do?" Ju was ever full of questions, though they were much more direct here in their own private world.

Zya looked over at him. He had his bow ready in one hand, and a quiver of goose-feathered arrows slung over one shoulder. He was also taller here, almost as tall as she. Zya realised with a start that she was dreaming of Ju as she would see him in later life. As much as the fact that Ju was actually there, he was not altogether real. He probably saw himself as he currently was, but to her he was a grown adult. She looked down at her belt, and it was not the belt that she had bought, but the original belt, the one she had attached the dagger to for so long. Her hand rested on the small pommel of the knife. Their connection was unbroken in this place.

"Well?" He said, the impatience of youth shining through the calm and patient adult face that stood before her.

"We wait, and watch," she answered. "This is a dream, not reality. Our path will be shown clearly to us, and all we do is follow it."

Almost as soon as she stopped speaking, a wagon rolled past at a pace that was a bit too slow for the team attached to it. The street was wide open leading up to the market, and despite the people crowding the way the wagon could have moved faster. She followed the wagon without thinking. Moving wide of the route taken by the man at the reins, she looked ahead to see what was keeping the speed down. There was one person loping ahead at a fair pace for somebody that walked, and she recognised him. It was Lorn. He was being followed by the wagon and he didn't even realise it.

"I see him," the adult Ju said from beside her. "Should we interfere?"

"We will know if it is our place to take any action," was all she would say in reply. This was not good enough for Ju and the strain flowed through the link between them. She would not have noticed so intent was she upon the wagon. It was barely loaded, with only a few barrels and items tied down under burlap covers. "This whole set up is too obvious. Lorn would be able to sense any pursuer." As if on cue, he disappeared into the midst of the market, where the streets were too narrow, and filled with stalls. From her position at the side of the street she saw the driver slow the horses and curse out loud, standing up and straining for a glimpse of his mark. Zya smiled. Lorn had known about this all along. Even now she saw him track back and leave from a different part of the market. He did not make his escape quickly enough. The wagon drover spotted him and yanked the reins of his team, driving them into motion. The horses shied from the crowds, and it was only their attachment to the wagon that stopped them bolting for good. This was enough for Lorn to make good his escape, the wagon lagging back as the driver fought for control of the horses, his wagon and the streets in general as crowds began to take notice of what was occurring. Zya and Ju ran past many of the ghost-like faces, for the people in their dream were little more than spectres, or so it seemed. The wagon driver began to pick up speed, and with curses and grunts he wrestled the horses into the right direction. Lorn was now far ahead, moving at a brisk trot towards a path between two three-story houses that would prove too narrow by far for the wagon to pass through. As she watched from her vantage point behind the wagon, she noticed other men closing on him from the direction that the evil emanated. They were coming from the mercenary guild.

Lorn looked like he was close to running a deadly gauntlet. This band of men made no secret of the fact that they were brandishing a variety of weapons, the dull steel heads reflecting light. They were uniform in size, all huge bulking men with faces completely devoid of any human emotion. Lorn would have no chance against them. The wagon drove him towards the narrow street, and now she realised that this was a trap. Judging by his speed, Lorn had still not noticed. She screamed a warning at the top of her voice, forgetting that only Ju and herself were conscious here. "It's not our place to interfere in this scenario," she realised aloud.

"Yeah, right," Ju retorted. He drew and let fly in one smooth motion. His arrow arched up into the air, its mark having not a clue that he was already dead. The arrow plunged down with deadly accuracy, and clattered on the cobbles as it passed right by the foremost mercenary.

Ju looked like a man in shock. "That arrow was as true as any I have fired, and it missed."

"There is nothing we can do." Zya's voice gave away her impending panic. She had been shocked with surprise in previous dreams, but never before had she ever had this sense of mounting nervous tension. She wanted to help, but could do so in no direct way or form. Suddenly Lorn realised what was happening, but instead of turning to fight, he ran straight towards the pathway. The driver let loose, whipping the horses in frenzy while the mercenaries rushed without any pretence of hiding who they were. They yelled, swinging their war hammers as they ran. Lorn however was quicker, and gained the pathway first. Zya ran as fast as she could, despite the benign nature of her presence. The wagon driver got there before her and jumped down, wielding a nasty-looking rusted meat hook. The horses milled about, directionless and without a sure hand to guide them. One tried to bolt, and the pair only succeeded in wedging the wagon across the entrance. There was no easy way for Zya to cross. When she tried to look down the pathway, the noises of close-quartered fighting were accompanied by darkness. There was nothing she could see. "Lorn!" She screamed, desperate for a response but knowing she was not going to get one. Only the signs of fighting reached her as a reply, clashes of metal and screams of pain. Nothing more was she going to get, and well she knew it.

"We must go in there!" Ju yelled.

"No we must not. We can not," she replied, "do you not understand? This could be the future. That is the point of the path of dreams, to show me, us, what may be. It is up to the dreamer to act upon it." She took one more look at the alleyway, with the shadows and the tall buildings, and she remembered no more.

If Zya dreamt again that night, she could not remember it. The details were still vivid in her mind when she awoke, as well as the difference in the dream that had made it all the more real. Never before had she been given independence in a dream. This had been more like a different reality. Its meaning was clear. Lorn could not approach the mercenary guild, or even the area surrounding it without risking his life. Zya decided to tell him after breakfast. When she eventually reached the table in the pantry, it was already laid out for their early morning meal. Zya remembered that she would have been up for a long while already if they were still on the road. She missed that about herself and it added no small measure of guilt. The city ways were habit forming, and not all good. Had she been more of a cynic, Zya would have denounced the city folk as downright lazy, but she had been taught from an early age when to keep her mouth shut and when to voice her opinion. Chewing on a bread roll covered in jam, Zya was lost in her thoughts when Ju entered the pantry. He looked terrible. His brown hair was a mess and his eyes were hollowed, ringed with the dark marks that indicated a prolonged lack of sleep. Still, he looked like his youthful self once more, that child just becoming the man she had seen in the dream. "What happened?" She asked. "What, after the fun and games we were having last night," ee replied angrily. "I couldn't sleep after that, for fear that we had lost Lorn into some abyss of darkness full of hammer wielding madmen." He sat down and started helping himself to food. "I sat there the entire night looking out of the window, praying for the dawn. I don't think I shall ever sleep again, not if I have to endure that." He shifted his shoulders to make the bow move to one side, and then set about his meal.
Midway through their feast, Lorn entered the pantry. Immediately Ju sprung to his feet and poked Lorn in the stomach, causing the fisherman, as he had once been known to double over. "What on earth was that for?" He wheezed. "Just checking you are here and real, sort of in the flesh." Ju answered. "Last time I looked," he answered, and then glanced at the two of them. "What is it?"
Zya took in a breath and told him of the dream that she had shared with Ju the previous night. Lorn listened patiently, looking at both Ju and her as she told him of what she had seen. "Lorn, please do not go there, not to that region of the city. Not after this."

"You are sure that it was the same place? Remember you have not actually been there."

"It was, I know it was. Lorn, I could not stress this any more if I tried. The ill feeling was there, nearby, just like the mercenary guild. It was the same place." Lorn did not look convinced. "I have never known a tribal seer to be wrong, but if you say that I should avoid that place to save my own life, then so be it. But do not think for a second that I would not risk my own life if one of you two happens to go there and end up in trouble. As it happens I was going to suggest a walk there on the way back to your guild, via a different route of course."

Zya breathed out a deep sigh of relief. "Then it is settled. We will definitely *not* go to that market. I really do need to get back to the guild. There are things I need to learn, and right guild or not, I can learn them from the Earthen Clerics. How to properly wield a focus stone is the very least of my needs. Perhaps I can find out more about what is going on in the city from them. If I can discover the cause behind the ill-feeling I have been getting from the mercenaries by means of a focus stone, then perhaps I can make more use of the Feast of Growth."

"You are going there?" Ju exclaimed.

Zya looked at him as if she had explained all of this before. Then she recalled who was actually with her as she had told them; Ju had missed out on nearly all of her experiences. Quickly she outlined them for him, finishing with her invitation as a guild novice to the feast.

Ju's face paled somewhat. "I have heard a lot of this Feast of Growth. People throughout the mercenary guild speak of it, to the point that the name rings around the building while we are running in and out. The people we deliver to harp on about it non-stop."

"Do you know why?"

Ju looked out of the pantry window, as if it would give his memory inspiration. "They are going. I have heard them talk about it. There are many of them attending, for I think they belong there."

"What do you mean, belong there?"

"Well, from what I have heard, they think that it is their right to be there, and they don't need an invitation, nor does anybody else that goes with them."

"Why would they say it is their right to attend, when the only people not invited. . ."

". . .Are the hosts in the Ducal Palace." Lorn finished the sentence for Zya. She looked at them both in stunned silence for a moment. "You cannot mean that the leaders of this city are in league with O'Bellah?"

"Who knows what is possible? The fact is that you are going to be in the same place as some very unsavoury people in a few moons time. You might want to learn all that you can just to be in the position to take a few precautions."

Zya nodded at the wisdom being imparted. "Ju, I need you to listen very carefully when next you go into that place. See if you can find out any more about what they intend. The very fact that such people are going to an event like this worries me, perhaps more than it should. I have a feeling that I cannot shift now. Something is up."

Ju laughed at this. "With you, something is always up."

"True. Tell me Ju, do you agree with the danger inherent in me going to the merchant's guild?"

"Absolutely." He replied without even a moment to reflect on the question. "I may not be a wizard or whatever, but I know what I saw last night. It scared me half to death. Lorn, If Zya says that you shouldn't go near the guild, then listen. What we saw last night showed you in great danger if you go back there."

"I think anybody that crosses anywhere near that place is asking for a certain amount of danger." Lorn continued. "You included, Ju."

"I am safe as houses," Ju replied, fiddling with his breakfast. "They are too busy to notice me, consumed with whatever it is they are hiding from everybody else. I run the messages from the palace to the guild and back, and get paid well to do so."

"Profitable work for one so young."

"Absolutely."

Zya remembered how he had been as a child. Even in the normally reserved tribal society, it had been important to gain approval in whatever way possible. He had done that by hunting his first deer at an incredibly young age.

"It won't last," Ju said as he reached for a cup of milk. "We will be gone from here one day soon, so it is best to do what we can to ensure that things will go well for us."

"And that includes getting money?"

"Yes. I believe it does. How are we supposed to survive otherwise? We have lived on luck and goodwill for a long time now, but one must always be prepared in case the luck runs out."

Zya was surprised at the depths of thinking from the boy, and the foresight he had gained. "I had never considered it that way."

"Well we all do what we can to survive. I may be able to fire an arrow, but in this city that is not of much use. What I can do is use my feet, such as I used to do back home."

Ju had grown up so much in the past few moons that it was difficult to believe that she had only known the boy for a season or so. "Do you miss it? Home, I mean."

"Compared to this?" Ju laughed. "Not for a moment. At home I looked after stabled horses, and spent my nights hiding from those out for an easy target, one who was smaller than they. Since leaving Hoebridge I have learned to ride, shoot, cook and although I am ashamed to admit it, pick a pocket. I have no regrets about leaving that place, though I would have loved to have seen what happened when O'Bellah visited that little village."

"Because he might be after Zya?"

Ju shook his head. "Nope, that's not it. There were several of the councillors that sought O'Bellah's favour. They sucked up to him." Ju appeared confused. "I'm sure that there is a word for that."

"Sycophants." Lorn replied. "Hangers on that curry favour from those in a position of power."

"That's the one. Anyway, they were supposed to keep any outsiders from leaving so that O'Bellah could decide what to do with them. It sounds like the travellers were exactly the type of people they had been told to detain, and they lost them. I would love to have been a fly on the wall when that went down."

"O'Bellah doesn't seem much like a man to accept failure," Zya agreed, "nor one to be told what to do."

Lorn leaned in close, prompting them to do the same. "You be careful when you go back to that place, Ju, and you to the palace Zya. Keep your eyes open, and your ears open wider. If what you say is right, and O'Bellah is related to all that seems to be bubbling just below the surface of this city, then we have landed right in the middle of a hornet's nest, and we had better watch our backs."

"I will do, Lorn." The boy replied.

"And you promise that you will stay away." Zya reminded him. "That dream was too vivid, and there was nothing we could do to help. It might mean all of our lives if you get caught, or worse."

"You have my word," Lorn promised.

"I don't think we would have it any other way Ju, would you?" Tarim said from the doorway.

Zya turned towards him. "Good morning father."

"Good morning and also goodbye, by the looks of it," he replied. "There is a young lady waiting down in the workshop that says she is of your order, and she has arrived to accompany you back for your training."

This was a surprise, for Zya knew the way back to the guild well enough. She raised her eyebrows. "Okay. Why would somebody come to accompany me?" "Better not keep her waiting, and go find out," Lorn replied. "Stay safe." "I will see you both soon," she said, placing a hand on their shoulders, and walked out with her father.

Zya descended the stairs to the workshop with a mixture of trepidation and intrigue. Why would they believe, even for an instant, that there was any need to do such a thing was beyond her. Zya had repeatedly proved that she was committed to the order, and fully intended to remain with them, right guild or not. She left her hair tied back as it had been the night before. The severity of her face might reflect upon the gravity of the situation, and convince whatever high-ranking member of the order was down there that she was serious about the tasks that lay ahead of her. Tarim had preceded her back to the workshop, but had not mentioned anything about her visitor. In fact he had stayed quiet. Before he opened the door he turned, and caught her in a bear hug. Zya squeezed back. Shows of affection were rare from her father, and therefore all the more special. He held her at arm's length for a moment, looking into her eyes; the eyes that he had recently said were so like her mother's. "Be careful, daughter. There are many dangers out there." He exuded the quiet confidence that was typical of both of them. "I will, father." There was nothing more that she could say for reassurance. They both knew the risks that one took when stepping out of the door, especially in a city that was so full of hazards as Bay's Point. The strange thing was that it seemed less of a danger, and more like home. Now that she had been here a while, the city seemed less strange and its people less outlandish and hostile. They were just different, but different in no other way than any other village or town that they had stopped at as travellers. Tarim was evidently satisfied with her simple promise, and took it as written. He turned back to the door and opened it into the workshop. Zya followed through, meek as was expected of a novice, looking down at the floor in respect for whoever was there. "Zya, this is Bethen Duie, of your order." The girl that stood there could not have been any older than she, not at all what Zya had been expecting. Bethen was as sunny and golden as Zya was dark, with pale yellow hair framing her face. She was shorter than Zya, but not by much. Freckles randomly dispersed over her nose and cheeks gave her the disposition of one recently returned from gathering crops in the field. Her inner instinct confirmed that this person would become a friend.

"Hi," was all she said, in a light, lilting voice that was almost musical.

"Hello,." Zya replied. To fend off the awkward silence that would inevitably follow such short greetings, Zya took the first step. "Shall we go?"

"I guess we had better," Bethen replied. This surprised Zya, for it seemed that the girl was not speaking from a position of authority, but more of subservience.

Zya looked back at her father, who was already setting about his work once more. "I will make it back as soon as I can, father."

He beamed a proud smile at her in return. "You will do fine, Zya. I am sure of it. Be well."

With a wave, Zya followed Bethen out of the carpentry, and into the sunny morning. As they walked in initial silence, the early signs of spring were all about them. Birds swooped and chirped, trying to lay claim to the rare trees that popped up around the city streets. The weather was clement, a warm breeze from the South beating off the predominant northerly. As they walked through the rapidly filling streets, Zya just let the city ambience wash over her.

"You like it here," Bethen observed, watching her. It was partly a question, partly a statement.

"I do," Zya admitted, as much to herself as to Bethen. "I never thought that I would, but the city has a certain character, one that I have taken my time getting used to."

They walked on in silence, watching the merchants hurrying to market and the small shops that opened up from the walls of buildings. Dogs chased in the streets, a riotous tussle with children, barking and squeals of delight all round. Zya adored the simple joy people could get out of a bit of fun, and felt better for basking in the all too brief glow that it provided. Her mind turned then to her present company, and the reason for it. "May I ask you a question?"

"You just did," Bethen replied with a completely straight face. Zya gave a scowl of mock-frustration, and Bethen broke into a smile and a laugh. "Please, ask another."

Zya resumed walking, for they had stopped when the children and dogs wrestled past them. "Why did the guild send you to accompany me back?"

Bethen's face lost its glow, and dropped into one of thought, comprehension, and finally shock mixed with understanding. "Oh I am so sorry Zya. I didn't realise that was what you had thought of my being here. I am not here to accompany you, well not in any official capacity."

"Well why did you come?"

Bethen resumed her smile, which Zya found to be infectious and full of good humour. "I had occasion to be visiting one of the tribal boys, and saw you

301

enter the building. I asked said person if he knew anything, and he told me about you. The robes were enough, but it was only when I came calling that I realised what you actually were."

"What I am?" Zya said as she sidestepped a particularly vigorous old woman who seemed hell-bent on shouldering as many people out of the way as possible.

"The illusion you wrought yesterday. I was there in the gathering that witnessed your coming. The like has never been seen before, nor will it again probably. It has already gone into the annals of the guild to be treasured, and all witnesses were called upon to give account."

"I didn't realise that it was such a big deal." Zya said, now slightly overawed about the previous afternoon's events. She had no way of explaining to Bethen that it was not a big deal to her. It seemed best just to ride with the interest, and hope that it dwindled.

"Well consider my own first attempt." Bethen replied. "I managed to create the image of a tree. Not a big image, but a wavering small image just off of the ground. It was called a 'good start' by my tutor, who at the time was in charge of several initiates."

"Ralnor?"

Bethen nodded in agreement. "The very same. He looks after all initiates, and always finds more. Nobody knows how, he just seems to have incredible luck. Anyway, my first focus was about the same size and strength as any others had been, nothing particularly amazing. Then you came along, and lit the whole chamber purple, with stars and swirls of mist and goodness knows what else swirling around in there. Your illusion was so real that even the master could not get through to you at first."

Zya remembered not being able to see the man, at least for a while. She had thought that he was controlling the illusion rather than she herself. Obviously she was wrong. "How long have you been at the guild?" She asked, hoping to change the subject.

Bethen warmed to the question. Talking was apparently one of her strong points. "A little more than half a year, or a season, depending on where in the Duchies you are from. Where are you from?"

Zya shook her head. "I don't know. I have been with travellers all of my life until recently."

"Tinkers?" Bethen replied in surprise. "Oh how wonderful. Think of all the places you must have seen. All the country roads you must have travelled. I lived in a village just out of the city until Ralnor Scott recruited me. I have never been more than ten leagues in any direction from the city walls."

It was at this moment that Zya felt sorry for the bubbly girl. All the things she had missed by the misfortune to live close to all she needed. The girl would never have been able to imagine what it was like to see each sunrise over a different hill, or to follow a river from source to mouth just because it followed the same route. "Maybe one day you will get a chance to travel further." Surprisingly, Bethen shuddered when presented with the scenario. "Oh no, I could never do that Zya. Everything I want and need is right here in this city. I couldn't leave all of that behind, not for anything."

"Not even your order? What if you were commanded to go?"

Bethen blanched. "I don't know what I would do, to be honest. Until I met you, nobody had ever made me entertain the thought that I might leave this city for good."

"Is that not what the orders are for?" Zya posed the question carefully, sure that despite the fact that she was obviously clever, Bethen was naïve to the point that her whims sounded childish. "Are they not to train us to use our skills and go out into the Duchies and aid those that need it?"

"Once, perhaps that was the case. No longer will that ever happen, not since the accursed Law Guild tried to force everybody under their yoke."

"Are you referring to the Old Law?"

Bethen came to some sort of a decision, as if she had overstepped her mark. "It is not for me to say, really. It is just my opinion. I think the Law guild has corrupted the Old Law, and it doesn't mean anything any more."

"Tell that to the countless farms and villages away from the city, who follow its every rule," Zya thought, aware that she was treading painfully close to something the girl did not want to talk about. It was time to change the subject. "Are you looking forward to the Feast?"

Bethen's smile lit up once more, and she instantly forgot that she had ever been talking sedition. "It is going to be the highlight of my life! Introduction to the Duke and the royal family! Oh what a pleasure, what an honour. I have got my best dress ready. It is going to be fantastic. Have you got a dress?"

Zya shook her head, looking around her as they crossed the invisible boundary between the rest of the city and the guild quarter. They passed the great grey monolith of the stonemasons guild, which now stood in a state of disrepair as less and less stone was needed from this side of the river. Many members had taken up alternative careers, or just left the city altogether. Over the road, the building that had once belonged to the woodcutters guild was now being taken over by a band of men in red tunics, what guild they were Zya could not even hope to guess. "I will probably just wear my order colours."

"Oh no, we shall get you a fine ball gown Zya, with ribbons and satin to offset your beautiful dark hair!" Dressing and ostentation seemed to be Bethen's favourite past time, and as they strolled slowly through the morning crowds, Zya was dressed with Bethen's imagination. Zya didn't have the heart to tell her that she cared not for these things, and it didn't hurt to keep quiet. Whatever the outcome of her flights of fancy, it seemed to Zya that Bethen didn't have the slightest care in the world, and that in itself was admirable. To have revealed that there may well be a problem with the Feast of Growth, and the possible but tenuous links to the mercenary guild would probably result in confusion and widespread panic. Zya knew better than to attempt reasoning an argument with somebody more concerned with dress material than what was actually going on in the wide world around her.

Zya found herself paying more and more attention to her surroundings, and less to Bethen. For her part, Bethen seemed not to notice, keeping up her dialogue and mentally dressing Zya like some little girl's doll. The buildings grew in stature as they moved towards the middle of the quarter, each becoming larger and looming ever greater above its neighbours. An ill feeling began to manifest itself within her stomach, and Zya knew that they were approaching the mercenary halls. Subtly, she steered Bethen clear of the streets leading up to the building, though the girl seemed not to notice where she was, leaving Zya to get them there. The ill feeling receded as they bypassed the guild, and the loss of that sensation was welcomed by Zya, The relief in her face was probably not even noticed by her companion, who had moved on to the best type of velvet shoe for dancing. Zya could honestly say that she had never danced a step in her life but instead of voicing this fact she nodded in agreement, and made the appropriate noises when Bethen actually thought to ask her opinion. They had edged through the maze of guild buildings until they were actually on the side of the quarter exposed to the view of the Ducal Palace. From so far off, it dominated the skyline with the palace structure surrounded by what seemed like a small city of its own. Again Zya marvelled at the place, and was truly in awe of the fact that she was going to go there. "Do you know if the Feast is restricted to the palace itself?" She caused Bethen to pause mid-sentence, thus preventing her from completing her monologue on the best frills to add to the hems of dresses.

"The feast is an immense event," Bethen replied. "From what I have been told, it cannot be contained in one building, and so they spread it around the entire complex. Why?"

"I just wondered what else was in there." Zya looked up at the rooftops of the complex as she murmured her response.

"Nothing that they will let you see, any road," Bethen stated. "That is the worst part of the whole affair, the shepherding. They usher you from one room to another, guards everywhere. The Duke values his privacy, you see."

"Sounds a bit more of an ordeal than you have made it out to be," Zya observed.

Bethen laughed, that sunny sound that could not help but lift Zya's spirits. "An ordeal would be the best phrase for it, but it is worth it. No other time will you get to mingle so closely with those in a position of power. No other place will you ever be able to show yourself off, and make an impression."

Zya knew now that there was more to this simple sounding girl than she had first thought. There was a term for what Bethen had just described, and Zya wondered to herself as they walked why such a grand event would be nothing more than a fancy cattle market. She was intending to go there and show herself off, try to find a suitor perhaps. That was not any plan Zya wanted to be a part of, for she felt that only bad would come of it. Shortly, they rounded one of the adjacent guild houses to find their own. Zya recognised the street as the one she could see from her window. She turned, and sure enough, the tower of the palace was visible in the distance. It was nice to see the place she had just started to think of as her home once more. It was strange to her that she could have so many homes, almost wandering from one to another like a drifting hobo.

As they walked nder the shadow of the guild, where the sun was hidden by its bulk, Bethen stopped her. "Listen, I know that I came and found you all of my own accord, but please believe that it was only because I wanted to get to know you. People are in awe of what you did, and I was afraid that I would not have the chance."

"Why not?" Asked Zya, baffled by this sudden change in attitude and demeanour. "Why can't we talk in there?"

"We can't talk in there because of the training you are about to undergo. You could be isolated from everybody else for as long as six months!"

"But I am attending the Feast," Zya replied, a little put out because of what she had already been told. "Joen said so."

"I suppose that will depend upon your training then," Bethen replied. "You have a lot to learn between now and then. If we don't meet until that time, then I wish you well, and try to remember me."

"I will," Zya promised. "It was nice to have met you in the outside world."

The great door creaked open. Zya entered the hall, and Joen stepped out from an antechamber, full of benevolence, full of fatherly love. The expression on his face altered as he saw Bethen. "Bethen, you should be about your studies, should you not?" He asked, composed once more but arching an eyebrow. Bethen flushed under his gaze. "I should, father Kzell," she replied contritely. "I am on my way now."

"See that you work hard, my daughter." He turned his attention to Zya, making her feel the most important person in the guild from the very first moment. "I will tell you now. I am certain that I have found my replacement, the next head of the Order of the Earthen clerics. I have he had trained more and more fresh initiates in the ways of our order, and in the laws that had been handed down by Divine Ilia, all those millennia ago. It is my solemn duty to prepare the children against the day Ilia once more walks the earth, and sets all aright. There is one facet of information passed down only through successive heads of the order: *'The arrival will be preceded by the announcement of stars where there are no stars, and by magic where there is no magic.'* I am convinced that this refers to you, Zya, and that she had a direct hand in both learning from me, and shaping the order for Ilia's impending return. You have a free spirit though, and this must be reigned in. The one that precedes our Goddess must be holy and pure, and I will teach you those ways."

The words began to spill out of his lips as he rambled.

"I never thought I would be the one to witness the return. The second coming of the Ultimate is a dream that masters had lived with for generations, and now it is within our grasp to shape the return."

Joen said 'our', but Zya was sure he meant 'my'.

He would not know what to make of your upbringing. A devout follower of the Old Law as you are, it is generally disregarded in the cities, and the cities are where the power lies in the Duchies. Yet you have also been a tinker, travelling the land with horse and wagon. Trying to continue that dying tradition is admirable, and shows the true spirit of a stubborn breed. Perhaps you do have the strength to do what is necessary to aid the return of my Goddess."

Voices down the hallway caused him to drop his distracted thoughts.

Zya was sure she saw Bethen disappear around the bend of the hallway. Joen continued his talk, in now measured tones. "You are all that the head of an order should be, especially one who would help the Goddess return. Your long dark hair, and earthen eyes are perfect, and you have the natural height and posture of one who would be listened to. I wish that I was fifty years younger right now. In my prime I was tall with golden brown hair that had attracted the women and dazzled my peers alike. I don't remember much of my life before the guild, but that much I will never forget.

The rest was one blur of focussing and theology, as befitted the head of the order. Joen shuddered, and leaned against a wall.

"Are you all right, Joen?" Zya asked in anxious tones.

"Am I. . . Why would I not be?"

"We have been stood here some time now, and though I hate to distract you from your memories, we are supposed to be beginning the training."

Joen bowed his head. "I stand chastised. Times long past, Zya. I was remembering, or attempting to remember what I was doing when I was your age. It might help to give me a little more perspective. It has been quite a while since I have trained somebody as young as you."

Joen turned, and began to shuffle along the hallway.

"Who was he? The one as young as me?"

"I did not say the student was male. That is presumptuous, do you not think?"

Zya grinned, "only if the presumption was not right."

The answer caught Joen off guard, and he laughed a bellyful. Various members of the order stuck their heads out of rooms, ready to complain as the serenity of silence was broken by the noise, but on seeing who was the source, either ducked their heads back in or smiled, sharing in the pleasant atmosphere.

"Ahhh one would have to learn to have a quick mind with you." Joen complemented her. "The other young student that I spoke of is Ralnor, your previous teacher. He has the position of choosing, and that was gained through hard work and a certain intuition, one that you appear to share. How did you know that it was a he that I spoke of?"

Zya did not turn towards him as she said, "I just knew."

"Magic where there is no magic?" Joen mumbled.

They found their way into his study as they talked. The musty smell of parchment was balanced by the freshness of the rock, and damp earthy odour of the loam from which a few plants sprouted.

"My Goddess provides all that I need to exist, and her fingers reach deeper than the surface." The aroma was subtle, but intoxicating to him all the same. Pouring them both a drink, Joen moved around the desk from Zya, and sat silently for a moment, composing his thoughts and sipping the ice-cold fruit juice. "Tell me. What do you know of the Gods and their impact upon the world?"

Zya sat without comment for a moment, remembering all that she had been told in the past. Snatches of information came to mind, but none of them were as substantive as the story Gren had told everybody on a sunny morning, where they had become riveted and almost stopped moving as they had listened to the old storyteller. She repeated the story verbatim, emphasising the interaction of the Gods, and the role of each in creating the world they now lived in. Moreover, she emphasised what she knew of Ilia, for that was what she sensed Joen needed to hear from her.

Joen listened with intent until the end. "I have never heard its like. The perfect recollection of the Gods and how they formed the earth has never been told in such a way. Truly you are a marvel. Never has a student come into the order so fresh-faced and yet so knowledgeable."

"Well it is just a story." Zya replied, unsure of his judgement of her. "It is one that has been handed down through the generations by the story-tellers. I heard it from the man who would profess to being the cook in the group that I travelled with."

"You didn't believe him?"

Zya looked ahead, almost through Joen himself as she sought the words for an appropriate answer. "It was not so much that he was not a cook; he could cook perfectly well, and with so little ingredients could make a feast fit for any Duke in the Duchies. It was more that he possessed an intellect that went so much further than his chosen vocation. He was a cook with the soul of a poet."

"The way you describe people," Joen marvelled. "Your turn of phrase could only be one chosen by Ilia herself. I have never heard anybody speak so eloquently. This must have been fate, for you are the type of person that can speak and everybody will listen. I may be bold in saying so, but I believe you are a prophet for the Goddess, her herald even."

Zya did not know what to make of all this, and sat still.

Suddenly aware that Zya was watching him, Joen formed a reply. "Your cook must be quite a man."

"He would not say that, he is too humble. But he was quite willing to take anybody down a peg or two should the need arise, and neither size nor age mattered to him."

"I can see you hold this man in high esteem. Hold his teachings in your heart. Keep them next to my own, as I will model you after me. It will be my legacy to the world, especially if Ilia shows her divine self once again. I expect you would like to know what it is you will be learning." Joen said, his hands clasped in front of him.

"How to focus, I hope," Zya replied, unconsciously playing with the dagger she wore on the new belt.

Joen's eyes darted over her. Zya remained impassive. This had not been the first time a man looked her over in such a way. It was unnerving because of who it was, and where they were, but Zya always believed in the benefit of the doubt.

"Exactly," Joen replied. "You have shown that you have the capability to learn to focus. Actually I would go so far to say that you have more than capability. You have a talent. If that chatterbox of a girl that came back in with you had said anything, she would have told you that the illusion you created through your first focus was remarkable to say the least. It has already been recorded in the annals of the order, and will be there forever more, showing that you excelled where passing would have been enough. It will also show that the stone you carry is rare, as rare a find as anybody is likely to see, but will always be yours. Nobody will ever be able to take that from you, it was meant for you, otherwise you would never have found it." "Will I still be able to attend the Feast of Growth?" Zya asked, putting on an eager expression.

"I don't see why not," Joen replied. "I have the feeling that you will far exceed all expectations, and the normal six months training will take less than three with you. Of course, that is only a guess, but I have every confidence that between the two of us we will make massive inroads into the work we have ahead.

Zya was less than convinced, though she was relieved at the fact that he had not lied to her about the Feast. What a shame young women were so eager to show themselves off. Little did Joen know she had a completely different motive for attending the event.

"So there is no time like the present for starting then?" Zya was as forthright as she was honest, and once again Joen had to suppress the smile her words seemed to almost always manifest on his face.

"Indeed not, my dear," he replied. "The first rule about focussing is to always work with the stone. Never force yourself into it. That is where many beginners go wrong, and injure their minds or worse. The rest of the rules we will work through as we go along, for they will need gradual introduction. Now take out your stone and hold it in front of you."

Zya removed her focus stone from the pocket in her robe, and flipped the top of the stone off, revealing the tiny purple crystals within. It was truly a dazzling sight. "What now?" She asked.

"Close your eyes, and clear your mind. With the stone aligned we will cross that bridge together."

Zya felt it as soon as Joen spoke the words. They were so similar that she felt the gift of the seer rise up in her almost unbidden. The dream came upon her and she did not even know it.

Chapter Fourteen

Since their escape from Raessa, Obrett and his three companions had maintained a relaxed but nonetheless active vigilance against the possibility of pursuit. Making frugal use of their supplies, they rode due East, crossing one of the tributary rivers that made up the Hotiari, the grand river that cut across the middle of the Nine Duchies, eventually resulting in Lake Eskebeth, the Reedswallower, and the Iscuan Delta far to the South. Obrett only came to realise how far from home he actually was when they crossed the shallow ford. The clear water running with abandon bore none of the trademark sluggishness of the great river at its lower points. Despite his homesickness, he felt a certain joy at crossing the river. It was as if an invisible boundary had passed. In fact, once they were over the second river in their path, almost one month into their escape, they felt a distinct lessening in the compulsion that had managed to subdue almost every individual within its radius into heading for the dark city in the mountains. They passed into a desert; the barren reaches of northernmost Mern where nothing grew except for rocks and weeds. Jumbled boulders were the masters of the waste, the insects and cowering plants their subjects. It was here that they had come upon a ruin that had poked out of the ground like some long forgotten tower, buried up to the neck by rock and soil, and left to its entombed fate, alone. There was something odd about the place, arousing a certain feeling within all of them that spoke of a focus. There was nothing special about the tower by day. It stuck out in stark contrast to the pale rocky desert, the smooth dark walls and domed roof only broken by the iron-framed windows that allowed light in. The unanimous decision was that this would be a place that they could make a stand from. They also decided to send Jacob and Ispen on towards their guild houses in distant Nejait, the city that nestled on the western side of the mountain range to the East. The guilds would need to hear of what was happening, since the joining of other guilds to the madness that was the Witch Finder's cause could not be ignored. Under protest, the two journeying wizards took the extra horses with them, despite vociferous arguments that Obrett and Brendan might need them. And so the Law wizard and the Earth wizard were left standing upon a low circular wall, made of the same dark stone as the tower as they contemplated its existence.

Brendan threw back the hood that he had been wearing, exposing damp hair to the warm breeze. "Were we right to let them go on alone?"

"I think so." Obrett had always been convinced. "Look at the facts. When we were held prisoner, who was interrogated, and who was beaten? Ispen and Jacob were left alone as far as we knew. Aside from having the ability to focus, they seemed to be of no use to anybody there." He looked over at the aging Earth Wizard. "Which was a gross underestimation on their part. It really is remarkable work: there are no seams between stones. It's almost as if the tower was carved out of something, or had been grown from the ground up.

"So you think they will be missed less than us then?" Brendan concluded.

"Exactly," the Law Wizard agreed. "If they look for anybody, it will be you and I rather then Jacob and Ispen. It is better that we make a stand at somewhere that at least looks defendable, rather than ride on with them and risk all four of us."

"That's not all though, is it?"

Obrett looked out to the desert, squinting towards the mountains to the West. In there rested the city fortress from which they had escaped, and the mere sight of mountains gave him a bad feeling. "No it is not. They have full guilds to go to, but you and I are in a different position. You lost your closest brothers when forced to spy on the forest tribe, and nearly all of my order has turned against the Old Law. Were we to go on, we would only be repeating the same words that Ispen and Jacob will tell their orders, and other orders. Better that we stop somewhere and try to figure out what we can do to prevent them gaining ascendancy over every other wizard in the Duchies. Anybody that goes over to him will eventually find themselves victims of that stone monstrosity that follows him like a pet. I mourn for my ex-companions already, for that idiot Caldar has led them astray. They will not survive. Many are old and weak, of no use except as an eldritch snack for that creature."

"I do still have an order despite what happened," Brendan countered. "There may only be a few of us left, but they would heed any warning that is spoken."

"And they will, for Jacob will visit with them and tell them what has befallen you."

Brendan was silent for a moment. "You did not mention this before." He said this with only the slightest of accusations.

"I wasn't sure how you would react, my friend," Obrett admitted, wiping the perspiration from his brow with a handkerchief. "To be utterly truthful with you, I did not think that either of us were as able as the other two to ride so hard and so fast towards the distant city. Better that we stop and make some 'noise' so to speak, to keep Raessa away from our true purpose."

"To align the guilds against the Witch Finder?" Brendan only confirmed out loud what Obrett had been thinking for a long time now. "That is a dangerous course. There are a lot of powerful people out there."

"And the Witch Finder is one of them. At least he will be if he ever regains his ability to focus. We should pray that day never comes. If Garias Gibden does not have to rely on other wizards for focussing, then he will be a force indeed. That is his only problem for now."

Brendan smiled at the irony. "A man who calls himself the Witch Finder, dedicated to removing wizards, is a wizard himself." He shook his head, breaking into a quiet laugh. "Fear is his greatest ally, and I don't think I fear him any longer. If ever I see the man, I think I shall laugh. He is a contradiction in terms. A wizard with no power dedicated to removing wizards indeed."

"Cynicism is a powerful tool when used in the right hands," Obrett agreed. "Beware of his motives my friend. He gathers the guilds for a reason, and that we know all too clearly. His ultimate goal is the obliteration of the Old Law, in some way so profound that we have not considered it yet. I judge that he is intending to remove the Old Law in more than name. I think he is mad enough to want to challenge the very Gods. Trust me my friend, we need every bit of help we can get. Never doubt he has power. Emotive magic is a strong ally. Now shall we stand here looking some more? Or would you like to make this tower into a home?"

Brendan knocked on the immense iron doors that stood at least twice as high as they did. "Is it possible that two frail old men could open a door of such weight and size, even together?"

Obrett pushed at the door, which gave slightly. "There's your answer."

Brendan needed no more prompting, and together they pushed.

The doors yielded grudgingly, many seasons-worth of sand blocking their entrance with a fluid persistence. Yet they opened wide enough to permit entry to the tower. Once inside, Obrett felt the air cool almost to the point of frigidity. In complete contrast to the outside, the air was fresh and sweet with the scent of flowers, yet none were evident. The tower's foyer was clear of anything but a few stone benches, dusty and ancient in their design. The sand did not extend far past the door; it had obviously built up during storms that had managed to push it under the edge of the huge iron doors. Funnily enough, there was no evidence of rust or sand scouring on the exterior. It was as if the doors had resisted any attempt to breach them, until now.

"That is the strangest smell." Brendan walked over to one of the benches and cleared the dust with the edge of his now-removed cloak. He sat down and concentrated. "There are no flowers, or hints of perfume here but when I stand up and move towards the door," he did so as he spoke, "the fragrance gets stronger. Shut the doors. Let us keep unwelcome guests out."

Obrett complied, marvelling at the fact that the hinges were silent despite years of apparent inattention. The doors boomed shut, and a great iron latch locked down without any prompting. The flowery fragrance disappeared. "Strange that." Obrett sniffed at the air, finding only the remotest trace of the flowers.

"It would lead me to believe that this tower is surrounded by meadows in full bloom," Brendan concluded. "Open the door once more."

"It would help if we cleared the sand out of the way first." Obrett kicked at the ripples on the floor. Brendan joined him in clearing the sand, easier by hand as they knelt down amongst it. The sand was as nothing before the immensity of the iron doors, but it was still very clear that it impeded their opening. The task did not take long, and the door opened with ease. The fragrance returned, but when they looked outside the only thing they saw was the low circular wall surrounded by the rocky desert beyond.

"Most strange," concluded Brendan.

"How about we look around the rest of the tower?" Obrett suggested, laying down his pack. Brendan agreed and they went exploring. The ground floor of the tower was a simple layout. Behind the entrance there were two rooms, used for storage as evidenced by the relics that they found. Wooden crates yielded nothing but dried and twisted remnants of what may have been food, and there was the impression that weapons had once been stored by the piles of rust that they found under pegs up against one wall. There may or may not have been the remains of sword hilts in amongst the rubbish, but much had been scavenged a long time ago. Further on from there was a third room, an ancient kitchen. A stone stove dominated the centre of the room, with a table off to one side and shelves protruding from the other wall. Both rooms were lit by windows so small and set to high up in the wall that entrance could never be gained through them. To climb up and jump through would be utmost folly.

"This tower was secure in its day." Obrett poked his fingers around the edges of the windows. "Not a flaw, not a thing wrong with them." He turned to Brendan, who was examining more of the boxes in the forlorn hope that something of use could be found inside. "This tower is suspiciously sound for a ruin, don't you think?"

"Let us see if the upper floors reinforce that suspicion." The Earth wizard replied, leading the way out. They walked back into the entrance to find that the sand had once again built up against the door. This made both men pause. "Strange," Brendan commented as he nudged the sand with a booted foot. "There is definitely something more to this," Obrett observed, much more eager now to see the rest of the tower. He climbed the great set of stone stairs, with Brendan following him. The steps were slick, polished dark by repeated use. They did not reflect the general state of disarray that was prevailed by the rest of the building. At the top was a door, shut in the same way as the iron doors that provided, or denied entrance to the tower itself. This one was not a great door like the entrance, but made just for a man of his size. Obrett twisted at the handle, and pushed. Nothing happened. He reset the handle and then tried once more. Still nothing. "It appears to be locked from the other side." Obrett did not hesitate in pulling his focus stone from its resting place in his robe. Closing his eyes with one hand on the door in front of him, he concentrated on the stone structure around the door. As his will poured through his stone and into the tower, he encountered something strange. It was as if there were two walls around him where he could only see one. The door was simple enough. He concentrated on the iron latch that had jammed on the other side, and freed it using his mind. Releasing his concentration, Obrett opened his eyes to see Brendan staring at him in fascination. "You clearly did not expect to find what you did," he stated. "How could you tell?" Brendan laughed. "The expression on your face. It was as if you had eaten horse dung. There was something you could just not swallow about that focus, was there not?" Obrett reached for the door. "Let's go inside first, and worry about my thoughts later." He opened the door and stepped through, expecting to find something special, and what he found left him gaping in astonishment. His mouth hung open in disbelief as he found yet another dusty old room. "This was clearly not what you were expecting," Brendan observed laconically. "Not in the least. Judging by the look on your face this is something *very* unexpected." The room was huge, and that in itself was impressive. It had six sets of windows, set at equal distances from each other around the walls of the room. They rose too high for any man to be able to see over their bottom ledges, but in several places, small sets of stone stairs led up to the great windows, allowing a view of the surrounding terrain. More worrying was the fact that when they had climbed the stairs, two of the windows provided full view of the mountains that clawed towards the sky in the distant West. From the view that was granted to the wizards, they seemed a lot closer, dangerously close even. The rest of the room was as dusty and as ill used as the ground floor had been. There were a couple of rotting beds to one side, the mattresses once stuffed with straw now only thin shells full of rotted matter. More of interest to Obrett and Brendan was the stone bench in the centre of the room. It was perfectly round, and placed exactly in the middle of the room, as if it were a centrepiece of some description. By looking at it, they could not divine any purpose for its being there. Obrett sighed in frustration.

"So what did you see?" Brendan asked of him.

"It was not so much as something that I saw, but a feeling that I had." Obrett replied, taking a seat on the part of the bench facing the East, the direction in which their companions were riding. There was no trace of their passing in the dust outside, for a steady breeze had obliterated all traces of their passage. "There is something strange about this tower. Something is not quite right here. When I focussed I felt more than one wall, where clearly there is only one wall."

Brendan walked over to the circular wall and poked at it curiously. "Nothing obvious, just cold smooth stone. And yet I agree with you, there is something strange about this tower."

They spent the remainder of the day trying to unlock the secret of the tower, not getting anywhere. Brendan tried repeating Obrett's focus and found that although there was definitely something mysterious about the building they could not find anything more. They explored every inch of the grounds surrounding the tower, and still the flowery scent inside the entrance confused them. They poked and prodded at every wall, and the stone remained dark and shiny. The only inconsistencies the two wizards could find were in the oddities they had already discovered. The sand always reappeared behind the door no matter how many times they swept it away. The scent of flowers was always there when they opened the door, but could never be smelled outside of it. The dust was a blanket over everything, and yet the stairs showed signs of repeated use over the seasons. The tower always remained cool, even when the door had been left open. As the sun began its westward descent, the two wizards sat outside in frustration. Obrett was perched on the circular wall, throwing stones at imaginary targets in the dirt, and Brendan was sat on the sandy ground up against the tower wall opposite. The shadow of the tower stretched over both of them, but they were both warm. If there was such a thing as springtime in this hostile environment, then it had passed them by with merely a fleeting glance.

"What are we missing?" Obrett mused in the company of his friend and the copious rocks. "It feels as if there were a reason that we have stopped here, but I cannot fathom it."

Brendan sipped on his water bottle, and then finished the remainder of the cheese that he had been sparing. "When we were at such an impasse as novices in the Earth Guild, one of our masters gave us a piece of advice that must have been one of the most cherished bits of knowledge one could retain. He said 'When you have lost your way, and know not where to turn, always remember that the realm of Earth is inside of you, and all around you. You are as much a part of it as it is of you.'"

Obrett looked around them. "Well the earth certainly is all around us." He looked about.

"I think what he meant was that we all share similar properties. If you think about it, that is all a focus is, the bringing into alignment of properties within us that are similar with the stones that we use. That is why some stones react better and produce different focuses. In essence, if you had not found that particular stone, who is to say that we would have escaped in the manner that we did? Who is to say that we would have escaped at all?"

"You are on the verge of something here, my friend." Obrett searched around his feet, and selected two rocks that fitted into his palms. The rocks were sandblasted smooth, and were a very pale yellow with a sandy texture. Obrett chucked one over to the older wizard. "See what you can find in common with this."

Brendan observed the stone, turning it over and over in his hands as he sought a clue as to its properties without using his mind.

"I have never seen anybody do that before," Obrett said.

"It is part of being the Earth Order," answered Brendan. "We attempt to divine the properties of stone in order to make the transition of the mind that much easier."

"So what does this rock tell you?"

Brendan peered closely at the stone in his hand. "It tells me that this rock is specific to this tower and the immediate surroundings. Were I to hazard a guess, you would not find this rock within say a half-days walk of here. The larger grains in the fine matrix tell me that subtlety is needed, and finesse, for we are looking to pass through different regions of both the mind and the stone. There are areas of greater resistance here, but they can be gotten around with patience and persistence." He looked up. "This stone could prove difficult, but I believe that once its secret is unlocked it will be a powerful tool."

Obrett peered closely at the stone in his hand. He could now see the larger grains embedded and surrounded by smoother rock. "How does this rock help us unlock whatever mystery surrounds us here?"

"Simple," Brendan replied animatedly. "It shows us that one reality is surrounded by another."

"And I thought I knew all there was to know about focussing." Obrett looked on, forlorn.

"No, you know all you had been taught and had learned about focussing, my friend. I have just learned it in a different way, because my order serves in a different way to yours. Your order formulates Law. We are much more in tune with our stones, and therefore the earth too. My friend, there are things you know that nobody knows."

Obrett spared a thought for his three students, and sent a silent prayer to the heavens in the hope that they had not suffered a similar fate to him. "I feel that I can never know it all."

"That is an admirable trait. It means you will never stop seeking answers. Now shall we have a go? The sun is almost down, and the nights out here are as cold as the days are hot."

Obrett searched the horizon. Beneath the clear blue sky, the distant mountains to the West were stretching forth their shadows like hungry scavengers, seeking to devour the entire desert into chilly darkness. As the men watched, the sun winked out of sight behind a tall peak in the northern range, and a chill descended. Obrett never
felt the cold, for he stood mirroring Brendan, a rock in his left hand and his eyes closed in concentration. Obrett began to focus, but at the same time felt Brendan do the same. This did not disturb him; rather it gave him a sense of clarity.

"*I feel it too.*" Came Brendan's voice in his mind. "*We are on to something here.*"
Obrett felt ready to push his mind into the stone, and at the same time, Brendan sifted his consciousness through his own stone. The effect was instantaneous. Both men felt their minds become linked with the stones, waves of thought finding the easiest path inside. As Brendan had predicted, there were areas of resistance, but these areas promised a resource that once tapped, would provide power the likes of which they had never tasted before. "*Find a fractured grain.*" Obrett thought to the other wizard. "*Let us see if we can't unlock whatever is within.*"

"*Got one.*" Came the reply. Obrett found a grain as well, one that had been crushed long past, one that spoke volumes about how the rock was formed.

But in his mind it was not just a grain. It was a step closer to unlocking something more. It was a pulsating radiance with a weak point that needed to be exploited. Obrett caught himself. It was not exploitation that he required, not dominion of any sort, but a sharing, an enhancement of his own senses that was required. *"Don't force it, or it will ruin everything,"* he cautioned Brendan. *"Why not? Don't we want to release the energy of the crystals?"*
"We do, but think about how we use our focus stones. It is as you have said: a melding, a willing co-operation. The same can be said for the parts that make up our stones. If we force it in any way the results could be unpredictable, but if we can find a way in then we can control the release."
"Got you. Here goes."
Obrett probed at the fracture in the surface of the grain, finding little that could help him. To any casual observer, it might look as though an old man was frowning at a rock in his hand with his eyes closed. They could not however comprehend the energy or the control being exerted. Obrett probed at a different part of the fracture, and this time, the fracture yielded just a little. Eager to go further, his patience was reinforced by years of training. He fed a little more of his consciousness into the fracture, seeking to pour himself into the structure of a single grain, and the gap widened. He had found his way in. Like an hourglass, Obrett poured his mind into the tiny grain at the centre of the stone in his hand, and the mounting sense of mental excitement that emanated from Brendan gave the sense that the Earth wizard had found the way in too. As Obrett's consciousness became one with that tiny fragment in his hand, he began to feel a difference outside of his body. The temperature warmed, the flowery smell that had accompanied them in the foyer of the tower became stronger for the first time outside. His closed eyes registered the darkness falling outside. Even the stone wall upon which he perched felt different underneath him, but he concentrated on the stone. He urged himself into the grain, and power built within him unlike any he had ever felt before. He was ready to burst, his head singing with crystalline-heightened awareness. A blue tinge coloured everything he could see, and then he was there.
Afraid to open his eyes, Obrett remained seated. It was only a hand upon his shoulder that reminded him that he was only focussing on a stone, and not made of one.
"Open your eyes and look, my friend," came the voice of Brendan, but it was a voice that sounded much richer, so very much more vibrant. He opened his eyes, and found himself staring down at the stone in his hand, and beyond that, grass.

"What the?" Obrett looked around, and found that he was sitting on a lawn; the grass trimmed neatly short, several different wildflowers growing through in various patches. The dark tower now rose above them in its midnight splendour, but the circular wall had disappeared entirely, as had all of the desert, sand and all of the rocks except the ones they had held on to. "Are we in the same place?"

"It appears that way, though some things indeed are different." Brendan pointed up into the sky. "It was late afternoon when we started focussing, and now it is deepest night." Brendan continued. The stars were huge in the sky, great white orbs of flaring light, shining down upon the garden, which was now surrounded by a ring of trees, their lush foliage moving gently in a breeze that was barely noticeable. Obrett looked down at the stone in his hand. "What did we do?"

"When we reached our target, we unleashed something a lot greater than we would have imagined. We have changed everything around us."

"Perhaps, but maybe this was always here and what we did revealed it." Obrett moved over to the now chest-high squared-off wall that surrounded what looked to be more like a complex of buildings now as opposed to the single tower that had dominated the desert skyline. "Remember the signs that led us to this. The smell, the stairs, the sand reappearing." He bent and plucked one of the flowers. "Who would imagine that it would lead to all of this?"

"What is that blue glow?" Brendan asked, looking past the tower. "It's everywhere."

Obrett leaned back as far over the wall as he could in order to try and get a better view. "I can't see. It's coming from around the other side of the tower." The two wizards walked through the glade containing the tower to try and see what the source of the blue light was, but when they reached the other side, the foliage of the trees seemed to meld with the top of the wall, blocking any decent view from the ground. The only other thing of significance in the flower-strewn garden was a well that had not been present outside of the 'other' tower, another fact that was not lost on the two wizards. Heading back around to the other side of the tower, they walked slowly around a square building that was formed of the same stone, but was only a fraction of the size. It had a similar domed roof, as if somebody had started to build an imitation of the tower, and then changed their mind.

"Look up there." Brendan pointed at the great windows of the tower. Red light shone from within, just as it did from the smaller windows of the square building behind them.

"Well at least we know we are not alone."

A rustle from behind caused both men to turn from their contemplation of company, but before they could say anything or even move, sacks were pulled down over their heads, and secured about their waists.

"Don't even bother trying to move." A rough voice said. "Not if you want to live to see another day. Ungentle hands turned them around and pushed them in what might have been the direction of the smaller building. They were guided up several flights of steps, almost falling at the top as they tried to step on thin air, and into a warm room. There they were seated and left to wait. A door slammed shut, and Obrett felt sure that they had been left alone. "Well so much for the friendly welcome." He joked, trying to reduce the apparent gravity of their situation. "Can you reach any of your stones?"

He heard some fidgeting as Brendan tried to loosen his bonds. After a short struggle came the defeated answer. "No I cannot, they are deep within my pockets."

Forgetting the use of his focus stone, Obrett tried to extend his perceptions by using the senses that he still had available to him. He tried to smell the air, though the sack defeated most of his efforts. He tried listening, sorting out the sounds in the room from one another. He could hear the struggled breathing of Brendan as he tried and failed to break free of his bonds, but that was not all. Somebody in front of them was trying his best to mask his breathing behind hands. "We are not alone." Obrett stated.

"Truly." Answered Brendan with a hint of sarcasm that expressed his anger at being tied up. "Excuse me, whomever you are, could you possibly scratch my nose? This sack is itching."

"How did you get here?" whispered a quiet voice, so quiet in fact that they almost missed the question.

"We used rock from outside of your tower for focussing." Obrett answered without pause. "It brought us here, wherever here is."

"How did you know to do such a thing?" the voice continued.

"My friend with the itch is of the Order of Earth. I am of the Order of Law. It is part of our training to know such things."

"Wizards?" Scoffed a different voice. "All wizards know what to do is prolong their miserable existences by using their skills to lift pencils."

"Alas that it is so," Obrett agreed. "Whomever you are, your judgement is unjust. There are those of us that have looked beyond the predefined borders set for us by our peers."

"The Law Guild has ever been a hostel for politicians and eloquent speakers." The voice denounced.

"And thus shall it perish," Obrett replied with a note of finality in his voice, as well as a hint of anger and a tinge of regret. "The entire guild from the lake city of Eskenberg has defected to the ranks of Garias Gibden."
Several intakes of breath were heard. "The entire guild?" Said the voice that had been demeaning the Order of Law.
"With the exception of myself, and three of my students." Obrett replied, hoping his honesty was getting them somewhere. "I personally witnessed the head of my order sneering down at me from outside of the cell I had been held in. I feel that there are other orders rallying to his cause too."
"Such as whom?"
"I can not say, but his ambition is without precedent."
There was a pause for a moment, and the near-silent rustle of material indicated to Obrett that the figures that held them captive were discussing this silently, with hand gestures.
"What did Garias Gibden want of you, and how did you escape?" The whispering voice eventually asked.
"What he wanted of me? Who can say?" Obrett paused to recall the time he had spent hung by his arms, asked pointless questions and given demands he was unable to meet by a madman and his servants. "He asked me of the location of my students mostly, but seeing as he had held me captive for several months, I was unable to answer him. How I escaped? With the aid of my friend here, and two more who have ridden on to warn their orders about what is likely to happen. We used stones in our cells to decipher the focus that permeates the entire region, and subverted it to our needs. We added subliminal messages to it in order to cause the citizens he had trapped to riot, and escaped in the confusion."
An indrawn breath caused Obrett to sit up straight. Something he had said had an import of great significance, but what was it?
"It was *you*," the whispered voice said, a little louder this time. "You altered the focus!" A second later, somebody started to loosen his bindings, and he could hear Brendan groan as he stretched. When the sack was pulled from his head, he had to blink for a moment as his eyes adjusted to the eerie blue. He checked on Brendan, and then looked back in front of him where three figures stood. An old man was robed in red in complete contrast to the pervading colour of the light. The younger man had brown hair tied in a tail and wore leather clothes. He had the appearance of one more used to the outside of a building. The woman was dressed in white to match the silver of her hair, but with the light she appeared as an avatar of Holy Jettiba. Obrett was quite stunned by her appearance. This emotion was reciprocated. The old man and

woman had looks of awe upon their faces, and even the younger man looked surprised.

"Clearly you are not what you seem to be," stated the old man with a newfound respect.

"Truly," Obrett answered sarcastically, angered that he had been trussed up for so long. "What about you? Who are you and why are you here?"

The old man took the lead. "We are watchers, inhabitants of the tower in which you sit and defenders of the land against the great evil."

Brendan looked hard at him with a scornful glance that indicated he was less than impressed by their answer.

The old man noticed the look, and expanded his introduction. "I am Endarius, the watcher to the North. My companions are Tani, the watcher to the West and keeper of our records, my younger companion is Irmgard, the watcher to the South."

Obrett picked up on the fact that something was missing, and posed a question. "Endarius, what of the East?"

The old man looked down to the floor sadly, remembering something lost to them all. "Alas we are perhaps no longer worthy for our chosen position. Chandra, the watcher to the East has been lost to us for at least a dozen seasons, maybe more. She was the weaver of illusions, and without her we can do nothing to keep the tower secret."

Obrett grinned over at Brendan. "Told you." He turned back towards the old man. "We would have been living in the desert tower now but for things that were starting to go wrong with your illusions. The steps in the tower show too much use, and the scent of the meadow can be smelled inside the tower but not outside of it. The sand inside the door resets itself as well."

Endarius groaned, "Alas for Chandra!"

Tani looked at him with contempt. "Stop moaning about things long gone, you." The old man quietened, but it was still clear he was having trouble letting go of the thought. "How did you know to use the rock to shift time?" She said as she addressed Obrett.

He heard Brendan gasp at the implication. "Shift time? But I thought that you said we pierced an illusion?"

Obrett looked across at his friend, and then back at the woman. "Please Tani if you would, explain to us just exactly where we are."

Tani settled herself, composing her thoughts. "By focussing the way that you did, you two have taken yourselves outside of time. The concept of time has no meaning here; we exist as always we have. Time passes in the world as you know it, but not here. As a consequence, things appear differently in this reality. Please, if you will." Tani indicated that they should stand up and approach the window. As they did so, it became very clear where the source of the bright blue light came from. It emanated in a solid wave across the horizon. "That is magnificent." Obrett said in awe as he looked on at the spectacle. "But what is it?"

"That is the focus created by the man you know as Garias Gibden. He seeks to enter this reality by pitting forces against one another to cause discord." Brendan cackled. "He is doing that all right."

"Our people have been set here for generations uncounted to observe his creation, and put a stop to it." Said Irmgard, who until now had preferred to keep silent. "We have not made much progress to tell you the truth, but now you have offered us a new way of looking at things. When as you claim you did, you altered the focus, we saw ripples of red within the clear blue light you perceive. This is the first new event we have documented in a long, long time. If it is possible to do such a thing, then we might find a way of countering it permanently. It grows you see, and has been doing so for a very long time now."

"Why is it that you can see the focus in this way?" Obrett asked, genuine curiosity overcoming and previous hesitance.

"You have to understand a bit more about the nature of where you are." Endarius replied, apparently over his brief mourning for the missing Chandra. "You already understand the nature of the focus stone, and the art of calling upon its properties in order to accomplish deeds."

Obrett nodded.

"Consider then that there is a place that the process takes you to that allows for its energies to be converted into use by your mind."

This last sentence confused Obrett, but Brendan seemed to understand the logic. "Are you saying that when we focus with a stone, it is actually taking something from this reality and bringing it back into our own?"

"That is exactly what I am saying. This reality is in essence what you would term 'magic'. When you focus, the process allows you a glimpse into this world, a temporary relocation to put it one way. Furthermore it affords you the ability to use some of its essence to accomplish your desires. Consider us, for we do not look much older than you. Would it surprise you to know that we have been here for what would pass as hundreds of seasons? The mere structure of this reality is a positive one, and encourages healing."

"Hence the restorative and life-preserving properties of focussing!" Obrett exclaimed in growing excitement. "That little window into this reality that wizards get by focussing is enough to heal them and extend their lives!" Obrett glanced at Irmgard. "Which is why you spoke of the Order of Law with such disdain when we were blindfolded."

"That is true," the youngest of the watchers replied. "Before I joined this watch tower, I had experience of the Guild of Law, and watched old men who might have been great and influential become nothing more that dotards extending their lives by focussing once a day. They had no idea why it helped them live for so long, just that it did. You are the first and only Law Wizard that I have encountered who seeks to go beyond his limits. That you are here testifies to your success. You are a unique individual."

"I beg to differ," Obrett countered, "there are three more."

"And what of you, good Earth wizard?" Endarius asked Brendan. "How did you come to be mixed up in all of this?"

"I was captured by the Witch Finder, and forced to do his bidding under pain of something worse than death. He keeps a creature."

"The Golem." Endarius nodded, and his two companions murmured something too quiet to hear.

"It was chance that led to the meeting of Obrett and the two companions we have previously mentioned, for Obrett found a way to communicate through focussing."

"We have heard your conversations from afar." Endarius replied. "They are accessible if one knows how to listen, and we have studied the distant mountain city for a very long time now."

Brendan gazed out of the window. "The Golem has too many people scared to act, and it was not until Obrett convinced me that it could be done that anyone would defy Garias."

Endarius nodded in acceptance of Brendan's words. "We do not see it as you do, for it has a different form in this place. But we do see it as it travels, even from this far. It is as a hole in the fabric of reality, sucking all into it. It is the reason we have lost one of our number." He sat down on a stool that was by the window. "She made a rare journey in the direction you would have come from, to study the focus up close and from within its borders. We felt the Golem reach out to her, and by the time it had taken her, we were helpless to do anything. That was twenty seasons ago, and we have mourned every moment since."

"If I may be so bold as to ask, what are you doing here, and who sent you?" The question posed by Obrett caused the three to go silent as they considered it.

It was Tani that answered, reluctantly, it appeared. "We volunteered to watch here for an artefact that was lost a long time ago. By default we have ended up watching the mountain fortress you call Raessa, though it has been known by a different name once."

"What has Raessa to do with your artefact?"

"We believe that the master of the mountain city desires this object for his own purposes, none of them good. If he gets it, we need to act swiftly to take it from him and to that end we wait and we watch."

Obrett sensed very clearly that they were trying to get around his questions without giving too much away, but he persisted. "Will you know when he has it?"

"We will know, for his great work will be altered immensely by its presence. It is at that time we will take it from him."

"Good luck," said Obrett doubtfully.

"It sounds to me that rather than an illusion slipping, time is almost catching up with you in certain parts of this tower," Brendan observed, "is that how you would see it?"

"Yes, time has been catching up with us all of late," Irmgard confirmed.

"Come, we have kept you in here overlong." Endarius rose and opened the door. "Since you won't be going anywhere for a while, let us show you more of what we do here."

With an oblique look at Brendan that spoke volumes about the sudden evasiveness and change in subject, Obrett followed the ancient wizard out of the door. The two of them would have plenty of time to discuss this, if time were of no moment here. They were in the small square building adjacent to the tower, which appeared to act as living quarters for the three. The blue glare was interspersed with branches, so instead of being bright and consistent to the point of leaving them all with blinding headaches the blue was suffused with green to make the light less invasive. They were ushered into a study that appeared to be a communal room, and sat while Endarius poured drinks for them all. The room was stuffed with books, scrolls and anything that would take ink to it. Where there were not shelves, there were works of art depicting scenery. The whole room spoke of a tremendous amount of patience. "To your very good health, and prosperous beginnings," toasted Endarius. "So you have seen the tower in its other guise? What did you think?"

Obrett took a sip of his drink, and to his delight found it to be sparkling, with a flowery taste. "It passes as a ruin quite successfully. This is wonderful." He held up the glass to admire the liquid in the cerulean glow.

Tani shone with pride. "I make it from the fresh buds of wildflowers. It is a rare taste that must be savoured and appreciated." She eyed Irmgard, who had drained his glass in a swallow.

"It's the way that I drink it," he replied in defence, "I always have."

"Some people have no appreciation for quality," Tani replied.

"I must ask out of respect for your cause, but where did you come from?" Obrett persisted, remembering how they had latched onto his other question and avoided any reference to their origins.

Having been asked directly, Endarius looked at his two companions. "We cannot avoid answers." He said sadly. "It will only hurt us in the long run. Obrett, our people, a clan that lives far to the East in a mountain refuge, have sent us here. We can offer you no more than that, for we have been bound by a covenant more sacred and more binding than anything anybody could use to try and force information out of us. We wait here in this netherworld trying to read signs that will lead us to the whereabouts of an object of such immense value and power that it cannot be revealed even to those that would aid us. We are the few people capable of bringing under control, and if needs be destroying it utterly rather than letting it become subverted." He held up his hands. "You have to believe me when I say that is all any of us can physically tell you, and that is stretching the boundaries."

"I believe you," Obrett replied

Brendan nodded in agreement. "It may be that we can help you somehow."

Endarius shrugged. "There is little enough that we can do, but you are welcome to try."

"Well consider this." Obrett passed the window, and looked outside. "Can we go out to the meadow?"

Intrigued by this, Endarius signalled that they should all accede to Obrett's request, so the five of them walked out into the strange half-twilight.

"You told us that this reality, this world that you inhabit is the place that we visit when we cast a focus. We borrow something of this place when we focus, and that helps us attain our needs."

"That is correct," Endarius replied, unsure of where this was leading.

"So therefore, going by what you have told us, this reality is in all essence magic personified."

"That also is correct. What exactly are you getting at?"

"If focussing provides a conduit, it limits the magic that passes between worlds. Where are the limits on this magic if you are here?" Obrett paced, thinking. Suddenly he stopped, his stomach clenched as if he had suddenly taken ill. The gathered four were all staring at him. "He knows your secret. He knows of this reality."

"He does." Irmgard confirmed.

Obrett looked at Brendan, who had already guessed his logic. The look of despite in the eyes of the Earth wizard that had become his friend was enough to tell him everything. "He is trying to invade this reality of magic, that he will be able to bend it to his will. He is trying to forge a gateway through, trying to remove the limits on our world. To keep it permanently open" The tone in Obrett's voice was enough to chill water to ice, and if it was tempered by anything, then it was the conviction with which he spoke.

"How could you know this?" Asked Tani, who was clearly stunned with the thought that somebody could be seeking to use the reality that she had called home for a very long time for their own selfish purposes.

"Things he said, things he did," Obrett replied vaguely. When he realised that they were watching him in expectation of more of an answer than that, he expanded. "He was repulsed by the notion of focussing. This may have been something to do with the fact that he rendered his mind impotent by creating that massive blue light you see between the trees. He would rather employ somebody else to direct a focus. What if he doesn't need to focus? What if he could just dip into a limitless well of power at whim?"

"Being here would give him no advantage." Irmgard stated.

"Not true, Irmgard. He has the training, that much is obvious. Furthermore, he has a desire for power unlike any man woman or creature you have ever seen before." Obrett pierced their minds with his speech, resulting in the three watchers almost jumping in surprise, and only a grin in response from Brendan."

"You knew," accused Tani.

"I guessed," corrected Obrett. "What could be better for somebody that has no love of focussing than a doorway to the very place it sends us? What better for such a person than to be able to simply reach out and grab magic with his open palm and drain it all in a worthless and selfish cause? I will tell you this now, he is trying to find a way through. I cannot prove this, but I'm sure of it. Did you find out through your studies that he is using emotive magic to try and further his gains?"

"We guessed that had something to do with his plans," Endarius admitted.

"The Golem absorbs negative energy given off by any source. All it needs to be is close by. It feeds on fear, but from time to time I believe it takes more than that. I think that it takes the souls of people in order to satiate its appetite, yet the hunger is growing."

"We have seen that much as it passes," Irmgard admitted. "The black nothingness that marks its movements has become much denser of late."

"Pray that it does not grow too much," Brendan warned, "else there will be nobody left to greet you when you abandon this exile."

"That will never happen, for we cannot leave."

The finality with which Endarius said this made Obrett pause in his striding. It had never occurred to him that the three were trapped here. "Why can you not? The focus is simple"

"We are trapped, as are you." Endarius replied. "The focus to take you out of time cannot be reversed. Once here, it only takes an artefact of great power to return somebody to the normal world. That is the one restriction, and is the price imposed for allowing wizards to draw on this reality. We have studied this extensively."

Obrett held up the stone he had taken from the tower. "Well what about this? It brought us here."

"Exactly. It brought you to a reality where stones are not needed to focus, therefore they will not be able to help you leave. That is the curse if you like that afflicts us all. That is why the loss of Chandra is so great, for we cannot send for another. We cannot even let them know that she is lost. We are isolated here."

The situation that these people believed themselves to be in revealed a lot about what they did not know, and could not do. Perhaps they had never tried to get back, becoming over-comfortable in this reality that had healed all of their ills. "You only believe yourself to be isolated," he countered. Obrett raised his stone and concentrated. Finding the spot in the stone that he had used before, he noticed that it was now a lot easier to cross the threshold. He poured his consciousness through the crystal matrix once more and found himself in the dark. The sand had reappeared beneath his feet, and in the darkness, the only building that loomed near was the ruined tower. Satisfied that all was right, Obrett focussed with his old stone, the stone that helped him subvert the focus in Raessa and consequently escape. *"Are you there, my friend?"* He sent out the thought as a test.

"Are you back there?" Came the ghostly voice of Brendan.

"I am. The focus works just fine. What did it look like?"

Obrett felt a sense of amusement mixed with wonder directed across the focus. *"You became a blaze of crystalline light. It was the most amazing thing I have ever seen. I am standing by you right now, though you would never see me. Endarius says that I can watch you by seeking out your life force, at least he said that after he recovered."*

"Try it, the process might help us." Obrett waited in the dark, and if there was anything to indicate that he was suddenly being watched in a way that he could not conceive, all that he felt was the fluttering whisper of a breeze.

"I can see you. You have never looked more impressive, my friend. You are a figure of bright green light."

Obrett chuckled in the silence of darkness. *"I certainly don't feel like it. Bright green would be preferable to absolute darkness. Even so, this might well be able to help us a bit further afield."* Obrett broke off the contact and entered the tower, pushing on the huge iron door with all of his ebbing strength. Once inside, he made his way through the darkness into the storage room where they had left their packs, and gathered all that they had stored there. Fumbling in his pack, he produced a lantern that he lit with flint and steel taken from the stables back in Raessa. Taking another look around he moved up into the first floor of the tower, finding himself looking out of the windows into the dark beyond. The darkness was absolute beyond the limit of his meagre light, and if there was any light from the very distant city, then he could not see it. A tingling began to make the hairs on the back of his neck stand up and he looked around, trying to locate the source.

"Obrett, get back here now. The Golem is seeking you out!"

The voice was Endarius, and now Obrett understood the strange feeling. Remembering back to more painful days, he could recall the overpowering sense of evil that emanated from the dread creature to the point that it made his skin itch. That was what the tingling was now, the far-off presence of the creature, increasing rapidly as it sped towards him. Wasting no more time on bad memories, Obrett shouldered the packs knowing that they would not make the trip should he not be carrying them. He picked up the stone he had used and as he became more familiar with the focus, he found it a lot easier to make the transition. His mind slipped trough the crystal fragments of the stone and the air shimmered. He found himself in the middle of the tower, and gasped at the view. Raessa's focus was magnified through great sheets of crystal that filled many of the windows, and the resulting beams of intense blue were reflected around the tower in a network. Beneath them various sets of apparatus littered tables, and shelves contained yet more scrolls and books. The room was a veritable workshop. Everybody else had been waiting for him as he materialised, but now their attention was diverted. Irmgard was staring through one of the sheets that appeared to be a normal window, watching as something dark grew larger and larger as it sought out prey.

"How long?" Called Endarius.

"Moments," Irmgard replied without turning. "If you had shown any more lassitude, Law wizard, you would not be here in my auspicious company." Irmgard flashed a grin towards Obrett, and then looked back at the window. "Here it comes. Brace yourselves; try and hold onto something."

Obrett hardly had time to drop the packs before the tower went dark. The tables jumped, the cupboards shuddered, and the very walls shrieked out in protest at the invasion of a force that seemed able to rend mountains to rubble. The tower endured though, and after a moment of pure agony where evil more primal than any force they had encountered had sought to dominate them, the darkness moved on.

"That was the closest yet," Irmgard commented as he checked the walls for cracks.

"There are few ways that we could have gone when escaping from Raessa," Brendan said as he helped right a strange metallic structure that was twisted in impossible directions and housed a crystal in its midst. "The Witch Finder will know that, and direct searches likewise if he considers us to be enough of a prize."

"It seems that he does," Endarius observed. "He will not be able to take you, not as long as you remain in this place, and this reality."

Obrett frowned. "We have commitments, and people we need to inform. There are people dear to us that need to know of the danger they risk."

"If you go back, you only place yourselves in danger," Endarius replied. "Why not stay here with us? There is plenty that you can do from within this tower. You can find anybody from here, and observe their doings. You can also contact anybody. You have proven that you have skills we lack. Perhaps there are other things that we can learn from each other?"

Obrett leaned back against a table, putting his hands behind him for cushioning. "You do have a point. Let me try something."

"Jacob and Ispen?" Brendan asked.

"Exactly."

"Remember, the focus is a focus without a focus," Endarius cautioned, and both men looked up at him in confusion. "It is the same thing but without a stone." He explained. "Just be sure not to do anything different."

Obrett closed his eyes and cleared his mind, seeking two familiar souls moving towards the East. He tried to interpret Endarius' advice as literally as he could, but it was hard to focus without a stone to pass his thoughts through. He stretched out with his mind, and felt a pleasant wash of surprise to find that he had but to think a thing and it was possible.

He felt himself flying over the landscape, searching for his two friends. It was easy to find them for they were but leagues from the tower, riding through a series of deep gullies that scarred the landscape. Jacob was leading, and Ispen was close behind him.

Obrett had no time to be subtle, so he just tried to get through to them. *"Hide."* It had an instant reaction.

"What in blazes was that?" Jacob exclaimed, pulling his horse to a stop. Ispen almost rode into him, and threw curses to the empty horizon.

"Don't ask questions, you fools. HIDE!" Obrett threw the words like a series of punches, emphasising the last. He could feel the darkness approaching from behind him. *"The Golem will be onto you with in moments if you do not hide."*

"Obrett?" Jacob asked to the empty air.

"Let's do what he says, wherever he is he can't help us much more," Ispen decided. The two men scurried under a jutting cliff, where once a river had eroded its way into weak rock underneath. They disappeared from view into the cave, and Obrett watched as the darkness flew past him and onwards to the East.

"It is I. We have discovered something at the tower. Wait there until we have decided what to do. At the very least you will be safe."

"Obrett? What do you mean? We need to get to our guilds to warn them." Jacob sounded confused.

Obrett tried to purvey a sense of calm and confidence. *"There may be a faster way. Hold fast and I will get word to you. If you need me or Brendan, just focus your thoughts towards us."*

"So we just wait in there? In this cave?" Ispen was clearly nonplussed by the whole thing.

"Trust me," Obrett thought with the mental equivalent of a grin. *"I can see you even if you can't see me. You are going to love this."* Leaving the glowing figures, Obrett pulled his consciousness back. He opened his eyes and found that only Endarius and Brendan were with him. The others had gone back to whatever chores filled their lives of contemplation. Obrett grinned, feeling glory in success. "They are safe, but they would be safer if we brought them back here. The Golem passed right by them."

Brendan looked visibly relieved. "Thank the Gods for small mercies."

"What will you do now?" Asked Endarius.

"I am going on a hunt. I have somebody that I have needed to speak to for a very long time." With a nod to his friends, Obrett closed his eyes, and concentrated on three men that had grown in skill and power under his tutelage. They had all developed a keen interest in their chosen vocations within the Guild of Law, and despite the political machinations of the Guild masters had prospered. He thought about their faces, and stepped into a focus to seek their bodies. He sent his mind out as far as he could, and then tried to go further yet. He found himself flying over mountains, speeding faster than any bird in existence. He crossed massive plains following their trails, and hovered over a city by the sea that was full of life, the glowing entities that represented the citizens bright as stars in a moonless sky. Their trail led across water, and even from this point he could sense them specifically. A surge of hope led him to speed faster, to a ship that was way out in the middle of the ocean, heading towards the great island that lay in the vastness beyond. The ship was teeming with life, for it was a busy vessel, but on the deck amidst them, were two of the three forms that he sought. He closed in on one that he knew well beyond all normal means, and spoke the name of the glowing entity next to him.

"Keldron."

Chapter Fifteen

Raoul peered into the distance seeking any sign of the land that was so elusive, yet so temptingly close now. He had stopped using his focus stone to peer long distances as each time that he did he became violently sick. This would have been nothing new, for seeing a landlubber heaving over the ship's rails was not unusual. He had spent most of his time in the crow's nest, and raining sick tended to result in unpleasantness from his crewmates. Since he had to live with them he had to keep his stomach under control, and the stones had been put regretfully away. So he had gained his sea legs relatively quickly, much more quickly than many of the tribesmen. The watch from the nest was one that not many of the sailors preferred, and they were happy to share the watches with him. He ignored the compounded swaying that resulted from being at the most extreme point of the ship's rigging and looked to the distant horizon where blue sky dwindled to grey as it met with the dark expanse of the ocean. It was also the most peaceful place to be on the ship, for Raoul preferred isolation to the constant press of humanity that had nowhere to go. He was accompanied by the occasional gull that chose to perch on the spars of the mast and chatter away at him, but aside from that he had the groan of wood and the grind of tautening ropes for company. It was most peaceful.
"Raoul, get down here!"
Raoul let out a yelp and grabbed for the line that secured him, looking around for whomever had just spoken. There was nobody there. Some sort of commotion was occurring on the deck far below, but from his vantage point he could not quite see what it was.
"Ahoy there, seagull!" called a voice from below his feet.
Raoul looked out over the side of the platform he stood upon. A sailor was climbing up to join him. "Hey there Jenkins," he replied amiably to the sailor that often shared the watch with him.
The stocky sailor flashed a grin underneath the mop of dark hair that constantly strayed loose from the tied-back mass that hung down his back behind the rather smart blue uniform the officers wore. Jenkins was a very junior officer hence the distasteful watches the man often drew. He was good-natured despite this, and took it all in his stride. He accepted it as another rung on the ladder of his career, a necessary duty. The man was good company too, always full of jokes and tales and always willing to debate the Old Law with him. He had a unique perspective for these people; He was once the son of a farmer and steeped in the traditions of the Old Law, but he had joined the crew of the Grotesque on a whim and had remained there ever since.

"You are needed down below, my friend. There is some sort of unholy commotion going on with one of your companions on the deck. I will relieve you for a half-watch, but remember you owe me."

Raoul grinned at the sailor. They all knew that he would stand more than his allotted time in the nest on any given watch, and were already in his debt. It had become a running joke between a few of them to see just how much they could extort from him in deeds and favours. Raoul took it all in his stride, a thing he would once have never done. "Did you just shout up at me, telling me to get down there?"

Jenkins looked back down below him, as if trying to remember any incident where he might have shouted up. "Nope. Wasn't me." The sailor hoisted himself over the wooden guards that were designed to hold a man in rough seas, not really needed in the clement weather they had enjoyed ever since leaving Leallyra. "You had better get down there matey. They were a-clamouring for you enough to send me up here, so you had better join them."

Raoul nodded his thanks, and hoisted himself out into the rigging, continually amazed at the fact that he was okay this high up in the web of ropes and spars that helped keep the ship moving. He had developed the skills of a born-climber since being on board, and the time spent in the crows nest had led him to develop a method to master what were often irrational fears. He understood now that it was not the fear of something that dogged his spirit, trying to drag him down. Rather it was the fear of being afraid that confronted him. Once he was in a situation where he had been forced to face a fear, he had conquered it. Thus climbing down ropes and wood no longer held any challenge for him. Quite the reverse, it had been a benefit. He had a wiry strength to his skinny limbs for the first time in his life, and the pallor was fading from his skin, replaced by a tan. Even his dark hair had flecks of sun-bleached yellow in it. He had taken to wearing sailors' garb, and had carefully stowed his cloak and dark clothes. He was quite at home on this ship. So hand over hand he descended the ladders and ropes that separated the crows nest from the deck, and he even slid part of the way down, slowing before his hands began to chafe and burn. Dropping to the deck with light feet, he made his way towards Belyn, who was bent over something. "You called?" Raoul asked innocently, not willing to let anything cloud his day.

"Belyn turned to regard him, and from the look on his bearded friend's face he could see that something important was happening. "A breakthrough?"

"Of sorts," Belyn replied, and tossed a stone towards him.

Raoul caught the stone with reflexes made quick by the strength he had gained, and looked at it. It was his stone from the village, the very same stone they had used to see the spirits.

"Focus and look around you on the deck." Belyn got his own stone out as he was saying this and made ready to do the same. Raoul spared a look for Keldron, and saw that his friend was already concentrating on the stone in front of him. It had been a while, but Raoul would never forget what he had seen in the village, so the focussing was easy. He concentrated, and then used the focus to look around at the people on the deck. They glowed as they moved, and as Raoul looked around the deck, he noticed a figure that had not been there before. He approached the glowing being, and from the outline deduced that this was a man much older than himself, one wise and learned in the lore of focussing. *"Obrett?"* He thought out loud.

"Greetings, Raoul Za, the Law Wizard," the shape replied, *"you have been busy since last we met."*

Raoul dropped to his knees in shock. *"Master, how are you doing this? What happened to you after we left? Were you injured in the explosion?"*

The glowing figure of Obrett exuded a sense of calm reassurance. *"I am well, my student. A lot has happened to me since we parted."*

"No doubt," agreed Belyn with the mental equivalent of a broad grin on his face. *"The fact that you are doing something that has only been dreamed about for generations tells us that much. Where in blazes are you? And how did you get there?"*

Obrett relayed the events that had thrown his life into turmoil since he had last seen his students. The cell, the focussing, the Golem and the Witch finder all featured heavily. The subliminal messages and the escape to the tower were explained only slightly less so. The three of them expressed outright disgust but little surprise at the fact that their entire guild had turned to Garias Gibden with their loyalty. They had never been favourites at the guild, and the feeling was reciprocated. His fellow wizards quickly agreed Raoul's thought that they should go rot in their own stench. Lastly Obrett covered the discovery at the tower, and the secret that lay behind all focussing.

"So this world that exists behind ours, is it what we are seeing now?" Keldron had kept quiet, so relieved was he to hear from his mentor that he had been overcome by all the good news.

"Not quite in the detail I can see it. What it does give me the chance to explore is the possibility that I can create spells here and help you discover their focus equivalents. The people we have encountered at this tower are not highly skilled in the art, but they are steeped in lore. We dare not leave here for the Golem is trying to track us. It almost

got two of my companions just now. I thought it best to warn you that it might come after you."

"I don't think we have ever encountered this Golem you speak of," Belyn thought to the rest of them. *"How would we know it?"*

"It is a creature of unspeakable evil, though probably not of its own making. You would probably know it from the sense of fear it emits from the aura that surrounds it." They all felt the worry that washed out from Keldron like water through a sieve. It occurred as soon as Obrett mentioned the aura. *"Keldron, are you ill?"*

"I have encountered it twice. Once in the forest home of the tribe we now seek to defend, and then when we were fleeing. It was only the forest spirit that saved us from it, and that was severely damaged when the focus that was its core was attacked."

"I am sorry, for that we had no choice. It was focus or die." This new voice was one they did not recognise.

"See? It is easy." Obrett's thoughts were directed at another. *"My students let me introduce Brendan of the Earth guild in Nejait. He was held captive with me after he was compelled to focus on the forest."*

All three murmured greetings to this unknown spirit they could sense in the infinity of the world that until now had been out of sight.

"Can you contact us again now that you have found us, master?" Belyn asked. *"It is just that we are working on something. We think that we may have found a way to translocate more than just still items from places we know well. We are on the verge of being able to translocate ourselves."*

"Interesting," came the reply. *"Tell you what, why don't you follow me back to where I am. That way you will be able to contact me. Follow me, and try to keep up."* The three wizards sensed more than saw the luminous form of their master take off and shoot into the sky as he recalled to wherever this tower was. They followed in much the same manner, but their tenuous grip on the reality was limited by the focus that intervened. It acted like a barrier of sorts, and several times Obrett had to slow to wait for them. Still, they all felt the rush of soaring over mountains and plains until they saw from their unique perspectives the tower as it truly was, and not the ruin.

"This is where I will be should you need me. The reality I have entered is a place that does not need a stone in order to focus, and I will be able to see you coming as clearly as if you were an albatross in the morning sky. Now tell me what you have been up to, for you have heard enough of an old man's news to last a lifetime."

The three younger wizards relayed their story to a fascinated Obrett. The journey towards the forest, the focus that washed over them and their encounter with the tribe. They went into great detail about their experiences in the cavern. When Keldron spoke of the Tome of Law, Obrett went quiet.

"What is it, master?" Keldron asked.

"I think that you may have given me a clue as to what is going on around here. You are not the only one after this tome. The watchers here and the Witch Finder are after it at the least, unless I miss my guess."

"You are not sure?"

"There are things that these watchers will not tell me, and when I was held captive, Garias Gibden revealed as much to me in his rantings. You lot must be careful. There are some seriously powerful people after this tome. People we should all be wary of, if not worried about them. But anyway, pray continue if you please."

The story continued, the escape from the beautiful bowl-valley and the splitting of the tribe. Keldron's escape northwards and his narrow escapes from the army. The focus wall he threw up, which produced a sense of awe from his mentor. The eventual meeting of them all in Fallmar Pass, and their consequent journey across Ciaharr. The impalings featured heavily, especially when they reached the village. Obrett lamented with them over the needless deaths of an entire village, but when they revealed the forces that had been released, he became fearful.

"What did you conclude from that event?" He asked them.

"Something big is going to be released. That or a store of energy is being saved up."

"What if I told you that the Witch Finder knows of this reality, and is trying to permanently puncture a hole between the two?"

"That would give him an unlimited amount of power," Belyn thought worriedly.

"How close is he to succeeding?"

"I think that he is a way off yet, but the atrocities he is committing in order to build up power will give him a tremendous advantage. For some reason the Tome of Law is the key to things. If he gets it, he will be able to unleash hell."

"We will have to prevent him then." Raoul was adamant. *"We are close to Caighgard, and we hope to find a key to this whole mess in the temple there. The heads of our order have hopefully erred by sending us up here."*

"Good luck finding the temple then, my students. I have heard it was lost along time ago, but do not let that put you off. Be steadfast in your enquiries. Do not let anything disrupt your resolve. Is there anything that I can do for you?"

"Master, you could contact the tribesmen for us. They are on the central plains of Ciaharr dispersed in villages as they seek to hold off the mercenaries, with mixed results. We can see them, but not speak to them. If there were a way we can focus to them, we would learn of it. They have a much more difficult job then we do."

"I will speak to them if I can find them," Obrett promised. *"Fare you well, my students. I am so very proud of you, and my heart is gladdened to find you hale and good of heart. You know where I am if you need me."*

The three wizards left their master in the tower, and flew back over the magical landscape to the ship on which they were sailing. Opening his eyes, Keldron found similar looks of relief on the faces of his two companions. He did not realise until now how much they had missed the reassuring presence of their mentor. The three of them sat there on the deck, revelling in the experience they had just had. Raoul looked down at his stone, while Belyn was content to sit and stare out at the sea. Keldron still had his eyes closed.

"Are you back with us, Kel?" Raoul asked his friend.

"Just think of the possibilities in a world where magic was free and unlimited." Keldron kept his eyes closed, but it was clear that he was addressing them both. "Just think of the wonders we could achieve."

"I would rather not," Belyn replied. "Enticing as it is, can you seriously imagine a world where magic was restricted by nothing? Can you imagine the mess we would be in? Limitless magic available for any purpose?"

Keldron opened his eyes and stared at Belyn, not saying a word.

"My friend, can you seriously tell me that a world where anybody can do anything would be a good one?" Belyn continued. "How would you police it? There would be anarchy. Complete, total and unrestrained anarchy. It would mean the end of law."

"The end of the Old Law?" Raoul looked astonished to even be hearing such a thing.

"The end of any law," was Belyn's dark reply. "Imagine what it would be like. Anybody could reach up and cast a focus, training or not. All they have to do is have imagination enough to comprehend, and the will to make it happen. Intent goes out of the window. Innocence becomes lost in the annals of history. Greed and power would become the new currency. Those who can, do. Those who can't become conquered on a scale never before seen."

"But we can, and therefore we could do," countered Raoul.

At that statement, Keldron shook his head. "That is exactly the point, old friend. Who are we to say that our intentions are the right ones?" As Raoul began to retort, Keldron continued. "We all have good intentions as we are. However, think about this. Are our intentions good because of what we have been compelled to do, or because they are what we should do?"

"That sounds like the same thing," Raoul finally said.

"No, they aren't. On the one hand, we know that we have been told to search out this temple but for no good reason than somebody wanted us out of the way. On the other, we know that we might find answers to our questions there, and therefore we seek to help those around us that would benefit. How do we know that they are the only ones to benefit?"

Raoul looked from one of his friends to the other, and then back again. "What are you talking about, Kel?"

"I think what our esteemed brother is trying to get across is the somewhat jumbled though that although we are seeking to do this despite all that was said to us by the order, they may have sent us on this errand with a purpose in mind. We must be very careful when we get to Rhothamy. All might not be as it seems."

As the others got up to resume their duties, Raoul sat for a moment longer as he considered all that had transpired in a matter of moments. To be given a glimpse into the ultimate gift and to have it taken away by his own reasoning and logic was a bittersweet blow. He could hear Belyn already discussing with Keldron the theory that each stone was not for a different mindset, but that the properties of each allowed a different aspect of exposure to the alternate reality. That the focus stones were now looked at as the more important part of the process was somewhat disconcerting. He had always thought that the person was what mattered most. He realised as he was thinking this that he was right, in a way. The person was still the initiator, and it was their intentions that ruled the overall objective. Nothing had really changed, just perceptions of what was essentially still the same. The sooner they got to the distant isle, the sooner they could hunt for clues that might unravel the whole thing.

* * *

Blood dripped, falling in a crimson descent to the floor with the wet noise of a thick liquid. Not quite a drop, and not quite a splat. The former guard was unrecognisable. His face had been beaten to a bloody pulp, any features rearranged and left broken by his former master. The young man had endured mind-numbing agony for the mistake of deserting his post outside the prison cells, and had hidden in the city as the riots were quelled, skirting from hovel to hovel. Then the guard had found him as he attempted to leave Raessa. He had never known how they had found him, and now he never would. He struggled to lift his head, for he could see his mother beyond the light, beckoning him towards her. That smile he had remembered since childhood was all he knew of comfort and love. He moved to the light, forgoing the bloody mass that was his body, and with the gurgle of blood-filled lungs the body gave up its place in the world. It settled to the floor, and grew rapidly cold on the chilly cobbles beneath.

Garias kicked the offending corpse in the ribs. "Damn him for dying. He did not suffer nearly enough."

Caldar looked on in fascination, his crooked old body hunched up beneath robes that did little to keep the chill out of his bones. "Would that one could being the dead back to life, then one could kill them again."

Garias glared at the Law wizard. "Why don't you try and find a way to do that? It might mean that you and your precious guild are finally of some use to me."

Caldar shrugged, dismissing the ire. "Our time will come, and when you find the Tome of Law you will need our aid."

"So you keep saying." Garias raised a finger in warning. "You had better hope that I do, for a worse fate than this awaits you if you are wrong." The threat failed to intimidate Caldar, and that wound Garias up more than the ineffectual 'questioning' of the sap that let his prize captive get away. He could see now that the real power and skill in the Law guild had lain with Obrett. These clowns postured and made out that they were knowledgeable in the Old Law, but they were politicians. Those types he had dealt with before, and harshly so. Their time would come. If they lacked use, then they would suffer to the end of time.

"With the riots long-ago quelled and the focus back to normal, you can once again resume the search." Caldar offered by way of compensation, that being a poor veil for changing the subject. Garias was about to mention as much when Caldar continued. "Why concentrate your search for just the one man? It is true that he is the head of the snake, but there are other ways to catch it."

"Go on." His curiosity now piqued, Garias was suddenly eager to listen. He stepped out of the way of the rivulet of blood striking a line for his feet.

"Well you have been after Obrett as the primary source of information. He would not know of where exactly his students have gone, but I can tell you where they are planning to end up."

"Go on." Garias stared at the man, impatient for a clue that would lead him towards the Tome.

"Their destination is Caighgard. We banished them to the island to repair and resurrect the ancient Temple of Law."

"And you think that they will go there?"

"We know so. They might not have gone there directly, but that will be their eventual goal. If nothing else, the three simpletons will do what they are told." Garias stared at the man with flat eyes, not believing that he had granted any sort of boon the man. "And what do you suggest that we do to find them?"

"There are only three places that they could cross to the island. Ulecio, Leallyra and Bays Point. I am sure that you know of somebody that can look in these places to find out whether they have passed."

What Caldar was implying was that he knew of the spies that Garias had in place across the West. How he knew was something he would have to be questioned about at a later date. "You have a point," Garias conceded, "and you are very well informed."

"One does what one can," Caldar said with heavy obeisance, and the very act churned Garias' stomach. This man was a source of focussing, and nothing more. He would learn that soon enough. He waved the fawning wizard away, and left the lifeless husk that bled on the cobbles to his servants. At times of stress, he was most eased by his tower and the feeling he got from sitting with a glass of wine. It helped him to think and he needed that now. Hurrying back to his lair, he ordered that Armen be sent to him. Once back there he poured a goblet of Ardican red and gazed out upon the ruined outer city. It had taken extreme violence to make the peasants obey his soldiers, so strong was the focus that compelled them. He cursed the day that he had been released of his ability to focus, the day that he had created the massive compulsion. It had been a bittersweet blow to create a spell that protected him, guaranteed him slaves and sources of magic from the cursed tribes to the North but at the same time robbed him of any ability to concentrate his mind and focus. It was like a barrier. Every time he tried his mind was swept away in a tide of dizziness. In the end he had come to despise focussing to the point that he could not touch even a stone. The disgust had come to rule him, and even though he accepted this fact readily, still he wanted rid of it. "One day I will use the Tome of Law to rewrite everything that is. It shall be formed anew, all mine to control and the girl will serve me and call me master."

"And she will relish every moment." Garias turned in a rare moment of surprise. Had it been anybody else, he would have ordered them thrown from the window, but he knew that Armen shared his view to the point of zeal. His advisor and the false Witch Finder, Armen would forever have the look of a chained maniac, with his bulging eyes and grimacing smile.

"I have a task for you."

"You have but to name it, master." Armen did not bow, would not bow to every statement. Unlike the fawning wizards who believed themselves to be paramount to his plans, Armen undertook every task with the same dedication, the same thoroughness that had brought him to the attention of Garias in the first place. A common slave, he showed initiative and prospects beyond his station when dealing with rivals. It had been the Golem sniffing around that had caught him in the process of strangling a superior, the fear and pain drawing the Golem like a bloodhound. From that point on, Garias had confided in the man, something he had never done before. Now he trusted Armen with both his personality and his spies. "Send word to look for the three renegade wizards and report on their movements. You can get accurate descriptions from those pathetic Law cronies, if they have the brains left to do more than normal bodily functions. Try Caldar. He seems to detest them, that should leave a pretty accurate imprint of their faces in his mind." Negative emotions were always ambrosia to him. He would choose a person full of hate over one at peace every time. Peaceful happy people were hazy and indistinct, but hateful people remembered every little detail. Vengeance was a powerful tool and for some reason he had not bothered to ask about, Caldar needed to exact revenge on the three of them. Armen knew his job, and left Garias to contemplate his plans. He was drinking and mulling for quite a while before he was disturbed once again by Armen. Instead of the usual zeal and fanaticism, this time his face was filled with glee and cunning. "What is it?" he asked.

"We have word, master. Several guilds have heard your offers and seek to join you."

Garias rubbed his hands together ecstatically and poured two goblets of wine. "Tell me more." As Armen sat down opposite, Garias was filled with the rarest of emotions, excitement. The tide had just turned.

* * *

Ispen glared out at the sky that was gradually turning pink with the first slivers of morning light. He hated waiting here. It was against his nature to hide from an enemy and yet he had no other choice. Jacob had submitted to Obrett's recommendation quite willingly, and they had felt the moment when evil washed over them like a tide that had never touched this part of the world. That had been nearly two days now; two days when they could have been closer to their city, two days that may have seen them encounter somebody that could aid them. But instead they waited. What chafed him even more than the saddle sores was the fact that they were only a couple of leagues away from the tower. They could have ridden out under cover of darkness but for the treacherous footing. Ispen was all for riding out in the day but Jacob was being stubborn. He insisted that they wait it out. As if on cue, Jacob stirred back in the cave. It had proved a surprising boon that the cave opened out into a chamber where subterranean water still flowed. They had rations enough to survive, but water was always a problem. The horses stamped impatiently, echoing Ispen's feelings. They knew that something was up with the human that stood by the entrance night and day.

"Still nothing?" The wizard of the Life Order asked as he stretched muscles cramped from sleeping on a hard floor.

"The evil has not passed over us again, therefore I maintain that the Witch Finder's creature is in another part of the world." Ispen shifted his position against the wall, trying to get a better view of the sky without exposing himself.

"Patience my friend. Obrett will tell us when it is safe. He will have good reason for us to stay here."

Ispen grunted in reply, and went back to daydreaming of the great river that crossed the countryside from his mountain city to the sea.

It was not until much later that day that they finally got word. Ispen had given up watching, and gone to sleep, and Jacob was wandering aimlessly around the cavern.

"Time to go." Came words that originated from only one source, though something was different.

"Obrett?" Jacob thought as Ispen jumped up and started coaxing the horses out of the cavern.

"Brendan." Came the reply. "The creature has been scouring the region, but has now moved West of the mountains. They must have given up. Ride like the wind, my friends, and when you get to the ruin, pick up a stone from the outside, and bring everything with you into the tower."

"About bloody time," Ispen growled.

Going out into strong daylight after residing in the dim cave for so long resulted in a lot of squinting for both men and horses, but eventually they got used to it enough to ride as fast as possible up out of the gully and West towards the ruin. The staccato clack of the iron-shod hooves on the hardpan raised enough noise to waken the dead, but they encountered nobody as they fled to the questionable safety of the tower. They had yet to experience the wonders Obrett said were there. The land smoothed out rapidly, becoming the familiar dry rocky desert as the horses galloped. The wizards urged them on in a frenzy, for both were aware of how exposed they were. Trails of dust marked their passing, and with no breeze to get rid of it the trails just hung in the air like marker signs, great brown arrows pointing towards the two galloping horses. They trusted to Brendan though, and did his bidding. Ispen once again managed to question the reasoning behind riding the wrong way, but even as he was doing so the ruined tower became visible in the distance. The monolith rose from the ground like a saviour, offers of its protection spurring them on. Time seemed to slow as they watched around them for any signs of company. The horses breathing became laboured, not just because they were tired after such a dead run, but because every moment became stretched with expectation and a latent fear. The sound of their hooves hitting the floor appeared to slow, and the growing ruin in front of them did not appear to get any larger. Ispen imagined that he could see specks of dust floating in the breeze that was created by their passing. Movements became languid, the horses slowed to a crawl and he could hear the pounding of blood in his own ears, a muffled thud drowning out all other noise.

And then they were there, the illusion of lassitude broken. Both men jumped down from their horses as quickly as they could manage, and while Ispen held the horses, Jacob scoured the terrain for some suitable stones. Once they would have never considered any rock other than their own personal focus stones, but Obrett had shown them a wider world, a world in which the skills of the caster were much more important than the properties of a rock. Suitable rocks in hand, Jacob held onto the horses while Ispen, a man much more physically imposing, opened the doors. Forcing the sand that had blocked up behind out of the way, he widened the doors to let the barrelled bodies of the horses through. The horses were skittish at the prospect of another dark entrance, but they were eventually cajoled inside. The doors shut with a boom, and the wizards and their horses were left with a cool darkness and the slightest hint of flowers for company.

"So what happens now?" Jacob asked.

"You sit on your horses and focus through the stones." Came the instant reply as if from right beside them.

"That simple eh?" Jacob raised the stone to look at it, and closed his eyes.

"Not quite. There is a method to my madness." Obrett described in great detail what they needed to do, and led them through the process. It was a focus unlike one they had ever performed, and it left them feeling somewhat surreal.

"You can open your eyes now," Obrett said in a friendly voice, and the two wizards found themselves looking down at the smiling faces of Obrett, Brendan and three other people.

"Wow, that was a hell of a thing," Jacob grinned.

"You ain't seen anything yet," Brendan said as he helped them calm the extremely confused horses. If the wizards were left bemused, the horses had no idea. Introductions were made, and the two newcomers were taken up to the main floor of the tower to view the world that although the same, was emphatically different.

"So you focussed to speak to us, but did not use a stone?" Jacob asked as he stared at the enormity of the compulsion focus emanating from Raessa. "Indeed. There is no need for the stones here. Try it for yourself."
"Is there a limit?"
Obrett shook his head slightly. "I spoke to my three students yesterday. They are alive and well, on a ship bound for Caighgard. There is no limit to distance. Just make sure you have an image and a memory of the person to cling to when you focus. It will make it much easier for you."
"The reason you brought us back," Jacob murmured. "A good thing, too. We would have probably starved or killed the horses before we got anywhere near our city."
Ispen had already closed his eyes in concentration, and in this reality they could feel the focus much more acutely. It was like a tangled web reaching out towards the East, and it was being reciprocated. "They are with us. They will start travelling here at once."
"What, some friends of yours?"
"The entire order. They recognise the danger inherent in what I have told them, and are acting to prevent it. It seems that I was not the first person to approach them regarding this. Discreet enquiries have been made by another party, one looking to test the water, if you will pardon the pun. The river guild will be subjects to nobody but themselves, but in this they will act as one body."
Immense relief filled the room. "Thank the Gods," Obrett proclaimed.
"You do so, my friend. I will thank Panishwa for granting my order the wisdom to listen to sage advice." Ispen was not joking.
Obrett turned to ask Jacob's opinion, but he too had gone into the trance-like state of the focus. As different stones had separate qualities, so did the focussing practice of people. Obrett could feel the focus piercing the sky around them, and gradually settling on a point in roughly the same direction as Ispen. A startled look crossed Jacob's face, and then the Life wizard opened his eyes wide and looked down at them. "My order is already halfway here, and have been attacked by wizards wielding fire." He sat down on the stone steps, thanking good Jettiba for his capture in quiet words. "Several have been killed, burned alive by some dread conjuring." Jacob did not look up as he spoke. "Had I not been captured, I might have been one of them. Anyway, they have heard of the unrest in the Duchies, and where possible, they have warned other orders against it."
"How is that possible for one order to know so much?" Tani asked as she handed out goblets of her spring wine.

"My lady, the order of Life is part of a greater good that is smaller than the rest of the orders, as a result of having fewer sects. My personal guild is in primacy, meaning that we are the chief guild of Life. This affords us certain insights into the balance of this world. Unrest, discord, they all drive us to maintain the balance by committing acts of good, all within the Old Law of course. My order has reacted to the waves of evil that radiate from the central duchies. They will do their best to arrest the discord."

"Will they fight?" Asked Ispen, who was personally unsure of what his own guild would actually do.

"If need be they will fight. Corner a badger, and it is most dangerous." Jacob meant that his guild would not attack, but they would aggressively defend themselves. How they would go about it was a matter for each person there to try and second-guess, for Jacob was saying nothing. All there knew the tenets of the Old Law however, and they understood that a certain moral flexibility could easily turn defence into something akin to attack. It seemed that some had already crossed that threshold.

"I am glad for you, friend Jacob," Brendan vocally applauded the Life Wizard. "Your guild seems to have made it through the initial attack. I daresay it will be not the last. Will they stand to the end?"

"My friend, the Guild of Life will always stand. As long as there is life, then the God Jettiba has a priority on this world, and as long as Jettiba graces us with her benevolence we will always have a guild."

Brendan sighed. I remember the exhausted state of my fellows even before the backlash of the scrying focus that sent many of them sprawling to the feet of Divine Ilia. Would that our Gods watched over us a little more actively."

Jacob laid a consoling arm on Brendan's shoulder. "My friend, it has ever been thus. The gods created this world, but it is for us to decide its fate. They do not see us as right or wrong. We just are. We just exist. There is no one person on this planet that is so important that the Gods will renounce their exile and come down from the heavens to do more than observe."

"No," Obrett disagreed, "there is one person. Whoever finds the Tome of Law had better hope that the Gods are on his side, for they will have plenty of enemies. If the Tome is important enough to make the Witch Finder try and bribe the Orders to engage in battle with innocent people, for him to build a whole temple dedicated to something he only hopes to have, and to engage all manner of arcane arts in order to find a person he does not know, then this person is in great danger already. There is only one answer that should occupy our minds in this place. We should be looking, as Garias is, to locate the person who is destined to find the Tome of Law, for only in the hands of that person is anything possible."

"Well where do we start?"

Obrett looked up at the walls of the tower, lit by the eerie blue glow of the Raessan focus. It was never going to be easy, but then nothing worthwhile was ever easy to accomplish in his opinion. Not that simple things needed to be full of worthless toil, but it seemed that it always worked out that way. "We start with what we know," He said finally, "we start with what we know, with those that we know best. From there we will have to tread unknown paths, but have faith. We have been put here for a reason, and we must believe that what we do is for the best."

Ispen grinned at the prospect, while Jacob gazed at the blue glow to the West. Brendan looked at his friend, a twinkle in his eye. "Well you couldn't have picked a prettier place to start from."

* * *

"Watch there, the crest of the ridge."

Mavra squinted as she peered into the distance. The ridge in question was over a mile off, and hid the movements of mercenaries out for one reason: to hunt them down. She was being taught a lesson in observation by one of the tribesman, a dour-faced man called Hawkeye, in no way a relation to the grieving Hawknest. Hawkeye was the best of the scouts in the ever-growing group of tribesman that had seemingly congregated out of nowhere. Mavra had been constantly surprised. She had heard that a great many of them had escaped their forest home when it was attacked by an army, the steep sides to the valley, the only saving grace as the entire attacking force had to come down a path only wide enough for one man at a time. By the time the army had assembled at the foot of the valley, they were long gone, those that were going. That army had not been heard of since. Mavra wondered what had happened to it.

"There it is, once more."

As Mavra watched, a flock of birds flew into the air, coming into view as they crested the ridge. "What does that tell us?"

Hawkeye did not look at her as he spoke, but remained focussed upon the distant horizon. "The birds scattered in all directions as they flew. Something disturbed them. They would not normally fly in such a way."

"What if it was something like a fox?"

"No, a fox wouldn't cause such a havoc, and not repeatedly. That is the third time we have seen birds fly like that since we have been watching."

Mavra would only admit it to herself, but that had only been the first time she had seen such an occurrence, but then she did not profess to having anywhere near the eyesight that Hawkeye possessed. "And you are sure of what you see?"

"Lady, that many disturbances could only be caused by something big," the scout replied. "We knew that they were going to move eventually, and they are at least trying to be careful in their movements."

"Not careful enough though," she observed, and Hawkeye gave her a nod of agreement. Reading her face as he read the signs in the distance, he knew that she had seen enough, and began to crawl slowly back through the grass, lest they cause exactly the same disturbance and let any mercenary scouts discover their location. Mavra appreciated the scout's judgement, and followed him out of the tall grass. Mingled with low bushes, it made ideal camouflage, and they wormed their way back through the bushy gorse without being caught by too many of the non-lethal but still very painful barbs that grew on it. The only problem would have been the snagging of swords, but Hawkeye had prevented that with the simple statement that they would leave any weapons near the entrance to their hiding place. The less metal they wore, the less likely a beam of sunlight would catch upon it. As luck would have it, it was a cloudy day, though the visibility was poorer for it.

When they escaped the gorse and retrieved their weapons, they jogged lightly away down the hill where they had lain for a long time while they watched for signs. It was one side of a gentle valley, the other side also a ridge of hills, those being the hills now traversed by the mercenaries in an attempt to hide their numbers and tactics from any prying eyes. From there they kept up a steady jog, only pausing when it became apparent that they were likely to cause startled birds to fly squawking in all directions. Mavra was again astounded at the changes in her own body. No longer was there a young girl without strength who dreamt of nothing more than sewing in a wagon. Now she had lost all puppy fat, and was lean to the point of gauntness. Were she not filling out with muscle as well as the normal transition from girl to young adult, then one might consider her underfed. She jogged beside the ultra fit tribesman with no concern whatsoever, knowing that even when they got back to the village she would still have enough energy left to fight. The leather she now wore as armour was light and supple; treated with various resins it was still able to deflect most blows even if it hurt to take them. But it was light, and she could run in it so it was usable. Worries tore at her. Concerns plagued her.

There was an army of mercenaries scouring the countryside for her people and as she ran Mavra fretted that all she had done to date, the warning of villages and the liberation of her family would not benefit her one iota. She would not voice her worries; they seemed to be the things that a leader would worry about and keep to herself, and Mavra could guarantee that everybody else had the same concerns. They themselves were a force to be reckoned with, that much was proven by the way the mercenaries were moving. A more reckless crew would have come thundering in at them with no regard for what might be lying in wait. She voiced her concerns as she jogged along.

"That might be interpreted two ways, Mistress," Hawkeye replied, his mind as analytical as any of his fellows. "Respect, or caution."

"Are not both the same thing?"

"Maybe. They could respect you for the bold tactics you employed in releasing their prisoners and be acting like this because they expect you to do the same thing again, or they could be cautious not out of regard for you but because it is their way."

"A mercenary band that sneak? That is most unusual, is it not?"

"Very much so, and for that we should be wary. You should assign somebody to get closer and find out what it is that they are doing sneaking around countryside that as good as belongs to them." It was clear that Hawkeye was volunteering right now for the job, so eager was he to try and put to rights the murder of his kinswoman. Such dedication was admirable, but Mavra knew that she had more to worry about with those left alive rather than with those that had passed on. As long as they were willing to follow her lead, then she was going to keep them out of danger for as long as possible. "We will worry about that when we reach the encampment," she said, and left it at that.

'The encampment' was a stretch of grassland that sat neatly between two villages. It was about a mile wide at its narrowest point, and had ample room for manoeuvres. Many of the tribe slept under the stars, seasons of camping that way not an easily dispatched habit. Some of the former prisoners had lodged with villagers, the kind-hearted people doing whatever they could to aid the folk that had appeared from nowhere to warn them about what was coming. Many were scared, some had fled, but most rallied to the cause. The men of the two villages all jumped to defend what was theirs, as did many of the women. Those that couldn't helped in other ways, sharpening their gardening implements to the point that they were only recognisable as tools of war, cooking food, preparing bandages against the worse of two outcomes for there was definitely going to be a reckoning. The encampment was also where Mavra made her home, with the tribes that had become her family. Cahal and

Jaden had remained with her, as had her parents. She did not worry that
Gwyn, Anita, Layric and Venla had all taken rooms in houses, for they were
there at the dawn of every day, and stayed with her until the end of every
evening. This was a concerted effort on everybody's behalf. They passed the
nearest building, getting waves of greeting from any of the villagers that
happened to be nearby and headed for the wagon that had become the hub of
everything that occurred between them. There was a crowd of tribesmen
around one edge, and Mavra had to forcibly push her way through to get to
the centre of them. At the entrance to the wagon Aynel and Arden stood
guard, two dark-haired monoliths, stern faced and grim.

"What has happened here?" Mavra asked, worried suddenly that her concerns
had manifested themselves in the guise of some disaster or other.

"Mistress, Handel awaits you inside," Aynel said solemnly, and beckoned her
forward.

Eager to see what had befallen one of the foremost amongst the Merdonese,
Mavra almost jumped up into the wagon, catching her shin on the wooden
steps, and remembering at the last moment to conduct herself properly. She
opened the doors of the caravan slowly. Inside, Venla was sat opposite
Handel, who looked up at her with reverence in his eyes. "Mistress, I have
been visited."

Mavra frowned. "What do you mean?"

"The three wizards, the ones that gave the responsibility for saving the
innocents over into our hands. They have spoken to me."

"I don't understand. How could they do that?"

"We don't know," answered Venla, "but all of a sudden Handel came over all
strange, and then collapsed to the ground. After a second he was back up, but
smiling as if he had just been touched by a divinity."

Mavra looked hard at Handel, who just looked back under the intense
scrutiny. "Are you sure it was them?"

Handel nodded eagerly. "I am, Mistress. They were there, right beside me on
the grass. I could see them all."

"And did they say anything?"

Handel looked distant as he remembered the words spoken to him. "They
asked about former companions of yours, and told us all to be strong. They
said that eventually, wizards like themselves might join us to try and spare the
villagers from a fate such as they had witnessed before, but not yet."

"They asked about former companions?"

"Yes. They wanted to know about those that had left you in the past. I told
them all that I knew of your past. That others had left you a long while back,

and that you had lost and then rescued others. I feel that it was those that had left you first that they wanted to know about."

"It's a shame that you did not know more, or that they could not ask somebody who knew them."

"They did say that the situation might change, but for now they could only contact those that they knew well."

Mavra accepted this at face value, for no member of the tribe would lie for any reason. She was not as sure about the wizards, but then as of this moment they were only mysterious figures that had been described to her in tales. She would need something more of them before she would talk about members of her caravan, present or former. "Well it is good to know that we aren't alone," she said wistfully, never feeling more alone than she did at this moment.

* * *

"Are you sure that he understood?"

Belyn looked up at Raoul, who stood over him in an almost vulture like pose. "My brother, we have known few of the tribesmen longer or better than Handel. Trust in the fact that he understood our intentions. He knows that we would be there if we could. He also knows that help will be on its way eventually. To be perfectly honest, the young lady that is leading them all around the countryside is moulding them into a much better force than any of us could have done."

The word 'force' brought a slight frown to Raoul's face, his eyes darkening. "They are not an army."

"Not in every sense of the word, no they are not an army. They are spying on the movements of the mercenaries, and they are forming a more than adequate defence. Should they be attacked, they will have a pretty fair chance of surviving. Should the mercenaries find them and then be as bold as to attack, they are going to draw them into the middle of the two villages between which they are hiding. From there they are going to surround them and slaughter them."

"That is horrible!" Raoul shouted. "We do not condone slaughter!"

Belyn raised his hands patiently in order to make a point. "We do not condone people seeking out and attacking the innocent. The Old Law forbids such. However, it does condone the defence, and force as a representative of such."

Raoul stared at his friend, knowing that in every sense he was right. It was a rare defeat in an argument over the Law, in which he was amongst the foremost dedicates. He stood down, and showed that he did have humility. He slumped to the deck, not taking his eyes off of Belyn. "Are you sure that there is no other way?"

"There is not. If those mercenaries attack, then their lives will be forfeit."

"That is barbaric."

"My friend, they have undertaken the most barbaric plan in over two decades. How can you compare the lives of murderers against those of innocents impaled in their own homes?"

"I can't. All life should be sacrosanct, regardless of the nature of the individual. Life is a precious thing, and the Old Law reflects that."

"It is more pragmatic than you make it out to be. Whomever created the Old Law at least accepted that there might be cause to defend one's self should the need arise."

Raoul toyed with the end of a coil of rope, flicking it from side to side. "Perhaps, but I will never be content with needless killing."

"I doubt the mercenaries would disagree with you, should they come to know of what lies ahead. Were they to learn of the precise location of the camp, they would be merciless. They do not care for life, but for getting paid. Money is their Law."

"Any joy?" called Keldron as he hurried over to them. He had been discussing ways of using focussing to aid the ship with the captain.

The two other wizards waited until he had joined them before Belyn replied for the both of them. "We have had some interesting developments." As Keldron's eyebrows rose in interest, he continued. "It seems that the Merdonese are readying themselves for battle, under the leadership of the travellers, of all people."

Keldron's face fell. "That is not right. How can they do such a thing?" The fact that Keldron to some degree echoed exactly what Raoul had said was not lost on either of his friends.

"They do it in order to defend two villages against servants of the enemy, whoever that may be. They do it because they are honourable and understand that people who could be speared through the guts do not have much of a future, and that their future should be fought for. Mostly, they do it because we have asked for them to do it, because they believe in what we are doing." Belyn looked around at the various tribesmen, mingling with the sailors like they were born to be part of the Grotesque's crew. They were climbing the rigging, scrubbing the decks, generally being treated just like anybody else on the ship. Even Joleen and Yerdu could occasionally be seen aloft, though Malcolm kept himself busy in the cook's pantry. He was one man that could not wait to see dry land again.

"You are right," Keldron admitted, "we did get them all into this mess with us. Now we can only do for them the best that we can, and try to find a way of keeping them all alive. Did you learn anything else?"

"Not a great deal. I learned that they once had companions that would be considered unusual, one of whom had prescience as a gift. The tribe did not know much more, for they have not had reason to ask. Something has got me intrigued about this person, but they had left a long time before all of this really started. So unless we speak to the travellers, I don't think that there is any more we can learn. I asked them to be careful, and promised them that soon we would find a way to get somebody there to help them."

"You think that Obrett will find a solution?"

Belyn bit his bottom lip, nodding slightly as he considered his answer. "I think that he will find something, but I hope that we find it sooner. This whole 'being behind the scenes' worries me. It seems like an easy answer to learning, almost cheating in a way. If we are just supplied with the answers to all of our problems, then it is like an empty promise, it has a hollow ring to it."

"But what if in learning the answers, we can save lives as a result?" Keldron countered.

"That is why I feel so bad about knowing more so quickly," Belyn visibly slumped. "We have spent our lives searching for the knowledge of focussing, and now it is all open to us. It is as though there has been a book written about it for decades, and now all we are doing is reading the first chapter after struggling along for donkeys years."

"But that's exactly what had happened when you discovered that text on focussing in the guild library." Raoul challenged Belyn's morose mood with his argument. "How does that differ to this? In this case we will be able to aid more people, from any point in the Duchies. It is the biggest discovery in the existence of the Order! How can you refuse to take answers when given, especially by our teacher?"

"You are right Raoul, but it still does not feel right. I had hoped that I might be the one to discover the answers. I am so close to it all, I can feel it in the air." Surprisingly, Raoul burst out laughing. "The reason you are being so sheepish is because you wanted to be the one to find all of the answers?"

"In part." Belyn admitted as he played with the stone that had aided them in the village. "I just have a feeling that I should be disagreeing with the whole process of quick answers. It seems to me that we have to focus for a reason. Can you even begin to comprehend the troubles that could face us should others discover what our master has? Can you imagine what would happen to all of us if that creature got into that realm? Or the Witch Finder? We would be wiped out in a heartbeat!"

"Belyn, my brother, I think we have been over this before, but you should look at it this way." Keldron perched on the pile of rope by the railing. "Our master is fine, and in a place that is much safer than our current position. He has access to magic that will aid us almost infinitely in our pursuit of the troubles behind all that we have witnessed. We might even find the Tome of Law, and discover why those poor people were butchered as a result. I think that it was fate that has had a hand in our fortune so far."

Belyn opened his mouth to argue his case further, but his voice was drowned out by two simultaneous shouts.

"Land ho!" Yelled a voice high up in the rigging.

"Monsters!" Screamed Joleen from further down the side of the ship.

The three wizards did not know where to look first. The captain solved their problem. "Where away?" He bellowed.

"Two points to starboard!" The sailor yelled back. They could see a smile of satisfaction on the captain's face, as if that was exactly where he had expected it to be. Ignoring the land now that they knew it was there, they ran along the wooden walkway to find Joleen pale faced and frozen to the railing, staring in terror out at the sea.

"What is it?" Keldron asked, not seeing the source of her scare anywhere in front of them.

"Watch," she said in a timid voice, looking out at a point not a hundred paces from the side of the ship.

They watched in silence, looking into the dark blue of the ocean for the nightmarish creatures that had so scared Joleen. Soon enough bubbles rose to the surface, and a wondrous sight rose to behold them. Several sleek dark shapes cut the surface, blowing air from holes toward the front of their immense heads. The mass that cut the surface was easily several paces across, and the shapes continued to move with a grace that belied their bulk. Arching slowly, the bodies passed by until the part above the surface diminished, becoming much narrower. At the last, when the creatures had appeared to diminish to almost nothing, great tail fins emerged, black edged at the back end with rippled white. The fins hung in the air for a moment, and then slapped the water hard enough to cause water to splash as far as the ship. The three wizards whooped in amazement, enthralled by something that appeared truly magical. Joleen however, ignored their joy and gripped the railings as if her life depended on it.

"That shows that we miss too much by being stuck in a city." Belyn laughed as he watched the creatures alongside the ship. What in the world are they?"

"The Leviathain," called Benson from a few paces away as he looked on with immense respect. "They are creatures that breathe air but live in the deep, true children of Panishwa." Benson inclined his head as he mentioned the name of the God of water. "It is good luck to behold them. They are definitely not monsters."

Joleen did not look convinced, but watched in stark terror as the creatures slowly swam off to wards the open ocean to the West. To their right, a faint smudge on the horizon represented land. She noticed this gradually, and her face brightened. Clearly Joleen had not been at ease on the ship, but she had hidden it well from the rest of them. "How long until we reach the end of the journey?" She eagerly asked the first mate, still warm towards the man despite his obvious inattention. Keldron did not mind. He had spoken with Jared on many occasions during the night watches, and had established the beginnings of a warm friendship. The first mate was married, his young wife living in relative opulence back in Leallyra. He doted on her to the point that he ignored most other women. If truth were told, the man was too humble to accept any advances due his station on the ship, but his knowledge of the seas and his forthright authority coupled with the agile skills of a swordsman meant that he was an ideal choice for the position of first mate. It was Benson as much as Flynn that ran this ship, and none of the sailors would have it any other way. He looked out at the horizon, seemingly judging distances. "Anything between ten days and a full cycle of the moon, depending on prevailing winds and the tides around the isle." As he watched her face drop, he continued. "The city of Rhothamy lies in an inlet to the North-West of the island. We are just seeing its southern tip. We will be seeing land for quite some time before we can stop." This did not seem to do the trick, and Benson well knew it. It was all that he could offer though, and he bowed curtly to the group of them and moved off to resume his duties. The Leviathain were a distant feature now, their location only given away by the flocks of seagulls that encircled them wherever they swam. Keldron put his arm around Joleen; It had been far too long since they had really had a private moment as there was just about nowhere on the ship that they could be alone. She pulled his arm tight, as if seeking all the comfort that he could give. It was enough to have a private moment together in public. It did not last very long. "Back to work, you loafers! What do you think this is? A pleasure cruise?" Captain Flynn yelled in a pleasant enough voice. The cat-faced captain had come to like his guests well enough for their unusual skills and willingness to do even the most degrading chores, but he was never one to allow people to hang around in his field of vision. He received a chorus of smiles for his yelling, and watched with satisfaction as the several robed figures hurried off to their tasks. "Ah what it would be like to have a wizard on every ship." He sighed out loud and looked at his helmsman, who was manning the massive oak wheel. He had arms that looked as if they were made out of the same stuff as the wheel, so knotted with muscle were they. "Would they truly be of any use?" The massive man said, possibly not sharing his captain's view.

"Perhaps, perhaps not," he replied. "They certainly make it a more interesting journey, with their stones and their mysticism. They are also the best damned sailors I have ever had outside of the crew."

"You might want to think about how it is not wizards that do that, but men instead. They are secular, and do not get this chance often."

"What do you know about wizards?" Flynn asked his enigmatic helmsman. A shrug was all that his helmsman initially gave him. The man looked out at the land on the distant horizon, recalling a distant memory. "I was going to be one." He said, lamenting for his past.

Flynn looked on in disbelief. His helmsman a wizard? He shook his head and looked out to the sea, forever his companion, and nearly always the one person that could confound him. Nearly.

Chapter Sixteen

Seclusion was such a damnable thing. Unfortunately it also seemed to be a crucial part of Zya's training. Meditation and contemplation were two words that were almost constantly on the lips of her teacher. If ever there was a new focus that she attempted to perfect, she was ordered to think it through for hours. Even if she had a question, she was first asked to contemplate all possible outcomes before her tutor would reply. It was an abstract difference from the way things had been before, but if nothing else it fortified her perception of what patience actually was. These people took nothing to chance. Zya leaned back on the chair in her study, flipping the focus stone up in the air and catching it as it fell. The top of the stone stayed intact. This was the cause of her latest question: Why did the stone not come apart unless she really needed it to? The answer seemed simple: concentration and the power of the mind. However, her tutor would not take that as a simple answer and commended her to a day of meditation on the subject. Zya found that her 'meditation' often took her to unusual situations. She concentrated as she focussed on an area of land across the street. It was a rare area of park in amongst the buildings of the guild district. Zya returned to a previous study she had been given, the contemplation of life at a level of existence far beneath her own. She pushed her mind out to try and capture some sense of the life that lay below the surface of the soil. At first it had been difficult, but she had learned to sense the tiny sparks of life that existed within that small plot of land. Mostly insects, they struggled for an existence that did not even take into account wizards and Gods and stones that could be harnessed for power. Worms struggled through the soil, swallowing and depositing, as was their wont. Bugs crawled through the grass above and up in the trees. Zya let herself go once she found the tiny life forms, her very essence following them as they scurried about their busy but altogether too brief lives. It was a lesson that taught students of the Earth to put things into perspective. They were not the centre of all things; in fact their lives as individuals were not important. What they served was what mattered, and that was the very stuff from which their buildings were made and their tools were shaped. It all came from the Earth. Zya was sure that all the lessons she had been taught were interconnected, and it was this comprehension that caused her to jump up from her concentration. She put her hands on the window ledge, leaning out to breathe in air that suddenly smelled fresher, cleaner with the realisation of what she had discovered. That she had come so far so quickly had been noted with great interest by just about everybody, except for Zya herself. She took it all in her stride, her gut instincts guiding her every step of the way. Never once did she pause to consider that nobody else had ever been like this. To her it was always about learning the next focus, reading the next tome.

The door to her room opened, and in walked Joen Kzell. The master of the Earth Guild was an old man with long white hair, but he still maintained an energy that belied the years that hung on him. 'Seasoned with seasons' was one way he had described himself, and it certainly showed. He always appeared at exactly the same time every day, to talk about her studies, and to assign new tasks to his tutee. "Good morning, and how are we today?" He asked pleasantly. He had never been anything other then kind and loving to her, much like her father in many ways although Joen could never replace him. The thought reminded her of the fact that she had not seen any of them in a long time, almost the turning of a moon. The festival of growth was almost upon them and unless she was lucky, it would pass by with her isolated. Zya put that out of her mind as she arranged herself on the chair opposite her teacher. Even loneliness could not dampen the discovery she had just realised. "I am well, Joen. I have solved the task that you set before me."

Joen did not move so much as a muscle. "And pray tell, what answer would you give me?"

"That we do not control the stones when we focus."

"That is known," Joen countered. He would not take such a straightforward answer, and he knew that she had more up her sleeve to offer.

"Is it also known then, that further than us not controlling the stones, that we are actually surrendering part of ourselves to them? Is it common knowledge that when we focus, we give of ourselves to animate the stones that we hold so dearly? That to accomplish so much as lifting a feather, we need to put ourselves partly into another place, from where we can draw power, and by doing so, allow the stones to become conduits for something so much more? What I am saying is that I believe we are entreating the stones to let us into another place, a place from where we can draw power. It is neither us nor the stones that have the power, but the combination of the two that give rise to the window from which we can draw it."

Joen did not move, but instead sat there looking at her, observing her. "How came you by this theory, and what has it to do with your stone?"

"It was a hunch," Zya admitted uncomfortably, "a feeling that sometimes I get, one that is usually right even if I do say so myself." She had no other way of expressing what she knew to be right, and she knew Joen would not accept 'a hunch' as a reasonable explanation. It was more of an excuse.

"Zya, you disappoint me." Joen expelled breath in a wheezy sigh. "I expected so much of you, and all that you can give me is that you have a hunch."
"What if I proved it? What if here and now, I proved this very hunch of mine to you?"
"How would you go about that?"
Zya stood, not caring where her teacher stared. She knew he was going to follow her every movement, despite his apparent disappointment with her.
"You know when anybody in this guild is focussing."
"Do I?" Joen asked innocently.
"Well I do, so you must do too." She answered, and his face softened, though he said nothing more. "If I focus and you follow me with your mind, you will see what I am attempting to do. The top will not open any way now other than by the use of a focus, pulling the energy back through the stone." To prove her point, Zya intentionally dropped her focus stone. It hit the floor with a crack, but there was no damage. "It was meant to be found by me you say. I say that it was only meant to be broken once, and never again." The ominous tones she used as she said this finally convinced Joen that she was serious. It was the recollection of a village many leagues away that struck through her mind, when several young men were trying to assault the boy that had become as close to her as any brother. It was the same voice that was to put it succinctly 'not her' that spoke for her now. If it was a voice of prophecy she did not know, but when it left her she was grasping the small but sturdy hilt of the dagger her father had given her. She was suddenly reminded that there was something unusual about the dagger. Cursed, it had once been called, but she was suddenly ever so certain that it was so much more. Aware that she was becoming distracted, she pressed on, also aware that Joen had sensed the difference in her at that moment. "I will focus, and you will watch." Zya closed her eyes and breathed slowly as she had been taught. She visualised the stone as she wanted to see it, a matrix of crystalline beauty. Into it she poured her awareness, her very soul. If there was any resistance she shied away from it, empathic in the knowledge that power could never be forced. She aimed to do something little, for she was never one to impress or be impressed by gaudy displays of grandeur. She elected to use the power of the focus to lift Joen from his seat. A simple display, but easily enough to show her intent. Pushing herself through the matrix of the stone, she felt the power pulsing just out of reach. Her mind in tune with it, she knew that she could harness that power whenever she needed to now. It begged to flow back through the conduit and be melded into the focus, to be used by her mind. Embracing it tenderly, Zya sent forth tendrils of power to wrap themselves gently around the old man's

body. Though she kept her eyes closed she could see him for the pure form that he was, a glowing entity surrounded by the vastness of Earth. She willed more of the tendrils under him, and eventually gravity gave way. With a startled yelp of surprise Joen floated off of his seat, rising to the height of the chair-back. Zya opened her eyes, finding the mortal image of Joen mixing with the crystalline overtures of the focus. He looked strangely angular where the facets of her hollow stone accentuated his features.

Joen saw a different sight. As Zya opened her eyes he looked down at her and saw a person filled to the brim with power. Her eyes reflected it, possessing a calm quality that spoke of a firm command and a will that was unmasterable. She literally bled power from every pore and her mind was unreadable, despite his trying to reach her as he had done countless other students. Zya raised her hand, and he felt as much as saw the surge of energy though it was miniscule. The top of the stone flipped up and amethyst light flooded the room, much as it had when Zya had revealed her talent for focussing.

"Point proven?" Zya asked calmly, as if nothing in existence could possibly gainsay her at this point in time.

"You have mastered much in the relatively brief time that you have been with us, Zya. In my lifetime I have never heard of anybody excelling so convincingly in every aspect of the focussing arts. The initial cantrips should take any normal student years to master, and the fact that you have learned them in what could not be more than a few days has not gone unnoticed. How you have come to the point of being able to levitate objects is nothing less than remarkable. That should take a good decade of studying and calming of the mind. Yes, I will concede the point, and add that maybe I should be the student and you the teacher from now on." Joen felt himself back in his chair; He had not even noticed her settling him back down. "You are subtle as well as powerful. I think your hunches need listening to. I have to say, my dear that I am tempted to introduce you to the Guild as an adept, but there is one thing that cautions my mind against it."

Zya sat back down opposite her teacher, closing the top of her stone carefully. The click was still audible, and there was no line as she put it away. She looked sincerely into his face. "Is the one thing important?"

"Well yes, I would say so. Zya, you only wanted to show me something simple." He arched one eyebrow as he spoke. "That much was obvious for you wielded enough power then to level the city. That focus however was one never before employed by the Order of Earth. You lifted me off of my seat using power. That clearly shows that you must be an adept of Yogingi at the very least."

Zya studied his face, searching for some sign he could not fathom. "Is that so very bad?"

"That I can not tell you. It is true that you have mastered several of the skills that are key to the practices of an Earth Adept, but you also show aptitude in many other skills. I saw the day when you tried juggling fire, using earth to cover your failed efforts."

Zya blushed, not aware that anybody had been watching her midnight studies of the land opposite her window.

Joen waved any excuses away. "I am not concerned about things like that. I am more concerned about you personally. I need to know if you feel right here." This was the most forthcoming Joen had ever been with her, and Zya was not sure what to make of it. Something inside her told her that if she voiced her feelings about being in the wrong guild now, that she would miss out on something very important. "I am unsure as to whether or not I am in the right guild, but at this time, I feel that I would be unsuited elsewhere. This is where I should be."

"Indicating that it might not always be so?"

Zya looked into herself, trying to search her mind for some premonition that would answer her teacher's question. There was nothing. "I cannot answer that, for I honestly do not know. It may be that one day I travel the Duchies as a representative of Ilia, or it may come to pass that I find a different path to follow. Whatever it is, my destiny seems to be in my own hands." This worried her greatly, for Zya had rarely been in a position to admit that, even to herself. For his part, Joen accepted her comments with good grace, smiling, as he knew that he would have her for company for the foreseeable future. "All is well then. I pronounce you to be an adept in this order. I think that we should let the rest of the order know." With a new energy that belied his even usually energetic stance, Joen hopped up and led her from the room. They passed the chambers of other members, some doors open in welcome and others shut, their occupants engaged in study or sleep. Hurrying down the corridors they bypassed the kitchen section where Zya was certain that people she had known would be preparing food even as she walked by. She was not certain that they would recognise her now. Her change in station would make any recollection impossible. As they were about to enter the central chamber of the order, Joen stopped. Backing out of his own study was a small form, hunched and bent and covered by one of the brown robes of the order. In its arms were many tomes, all belonging to Joen by the look on his face. The figure looked up and only the most acute hearing could pick up the tiny hiss of breath taken in by the person. "Who is there?" It called in a dry voice, accented with the homeland twang of the Northern peoples.

Joen stepped into the light, and Zya decided to follow him rather than remain concealed. The face that belonged to Ralnor Scott paled slightly, and then he smiled. "Master, Zya." She felt sure that he said her name with a bit less of the forced pleasure with which he greeted Joen, but she smiled and nodded silently, giving respect to her former teacher. That her greeting was underlain by a feeling of confusion as to what all of this meant did not pass either of the men by. "Care to tell me what you were doing sneaking out of my chamber?" Joen asked lightly.

"I. . .uh. . .master?" Ralnor indicated that he would rather not speak in front of Zya, but Joen waved his uneasiness aside as if it did not matter all of a sudden. "Anything you say to me you can also say to my former student, Ralnor." The small man looked at her for a second, eyes wide and pupils unusually straight for once. He glimpsed back at his master who was now frowning, and something passed between the men. All of a sudden, a feeling hit Zya. This man was now a danger to her. She dismissed the idea out of hand. Ralnor had never been anything but patient and kind to her, but the feeling persisted. If anything changed in his countenance, it did not show. "Very well," he said, "I was removing certain texts that I wished to show a particularly promising young student, one with *much* potential." There was an avaricious look in his eyes as he said this, and Zya felt herself becoming very uncomfortable. She remained in her place. Not knowing why, she felt the need to speak out. "Who is this student?" Was all that she could manage to say.

Ralnor stared at her, and she didn't know why, but felt that she was soon to understand this sudden change in her former tutor. His attitude seemed to be one of a rival rather than a superior. "The student is called Bethen Duie. I believe that she is an acquaintance of yours. She shows *great* promise."

The leery quality in his voice suddenly awoke Zya to a now non-existent future of her own. She was shocked to see the man act that way, but at the same time it felt right to see the different side of him. "Well you had better not keep her waiting." She said dismissively, and Ralnor actually bowed to her before leaving. She was sure that there was a stare formed purely from the coastal glacier to the North concealed under that bow, but she was still unsure as to why he would ever show her subservience.

"Strange, that," commented Joen as he watched the rapidly retreating form of Ralnor, "he has never needed anything from my study for his own personal lessons." Joen noticed the look that was plain as day on Zya's face: it spoke of a sudden distaste for the man. "Do not worry over it, Zya. I am sure that he will return the books. Bethen must indeed be promising if he needs such diverse subjects to cover with her as a novice. Let us go from here." Joen led the way, with Zya not believing what she had just heard. Joen had dismissed what sounded like a poorly veiled excuse at best, and even more worrying was what Ralnor might do to poor Bethen if he had not done so already. Zya felt that her time at the Guild might suddenly be coming to an abrupt end.

They entered the central complex of the guild with no more incident than a couple of curious guildsmen wondering what was happening. Joen bade them wait until the answer was clear for all, so they lingered in the hope of a march on the others. At the central chamber, Joen paused. "Wait here for now. Please do not enter the chamber." The look on his face was one of excitement and relief. It seemed that he was glad he had made it this far. Joen disappeared out of sight, and Zya was left standing alone outside the chamber. A couple of the guildsmen stood nearby wondering what they were about to witness, but they had no more idea than Zya. The air stirred, and Zya looked down to her feet. A green mist was forming about her. It appeared to emanate from her, though she could not find the source. Whenever she turned, it just seemed to waft out from her robe, an iridescent green mist that clung to the ground and seeped off down the passageway. Pretty soon the mist had started to reach chambers, permeating even the most airtight of rooms. That much was evident by the excited noise that rose from the hallways. Something momentous was occurring, but she did not know what. Gradually, members of the guild gathered in the central hall, packing closely to the walls as they observed Zya with respect that seemed to be aimed at her. There was nothing that she could do about the mist that was now spilling from her robes, and she stood there helplessly. Faces she knew peeked out at her from the increasing crowd: Families whose acquaintance she had made, children at once shy and giggling. Young men whose juvenile attempts at flattery had provoked no response from a young lady who was not in the guild for romance, older members of the guild who had wise but mysterious smiles on their faces. Zya reached back self-consciously to tidy her hair, and the green mist spilled even from her raven locks. The object of so much scrutiny, she was steadily becoming unnerved. She looked about her. Few of the guild were not there, most worryingly of all the faces of Bethen and Ralnor were absent. That would not have worried her, but for the recent exchange. The crowd quietened, and Zya looked down once more. The green mist had almost disappeared from her robes, its purpose obviously fulfilled. She stood apart from them, the chamber containing Joen at her back. And then she was not alone. The most elder member of the guild stood beside her, smiling proudly. "You all know why we are here," Joen looked at Zya for a moment before he continued, "well most of you do at any rate. We are here because a discovery has been made, and we will join in celebration. For the next guild master, or should I say mistress has been revealed to us by Divine Ilia."

As he pronounced this, everybody cheered. They had been waiting for this moment for quite a while, and that was no secret. The noise was deafening, and it showed the profound relief of every guild member. At last there was a future where there had previously only been Joen, and though they all loved him as children do their fathers, there had come a time when the guild would eventually outgrow him. Zya suspected that time was now, but she suspected more. She knew that even if she was this future leader of the guild, she could not stay. She had something to witness elsewhere.

"Now is a time of consolidation, the time for teaching and study," Joen announced solemnly. "Later will come the time for celebration, for the Festival of growth is almost at hand. Let word go out that our newest shall go to the Feast as has always been. We shall celebrate here privately at that time, as always we have done."

Zya did not appreciate the enormity of the burden being placed upon her shoulders, but then she did not expect to. She knew that she was going to the Feast of Growth, and that was what mattered. Maybe she could steal a moment alone with Bethen while they were there, for surely she would be attending as well. Such thoughts were washed away as members of the guild closed in to offer their congratulations. The kindness and warmth shown by all was sincere, but they were not really received for Zya's mind was elsewhere. She glanced around the room, and at last saw Bethen. The girl's hair was bedraggled, and she had a look on her face that should have belonged to a trapped animal. Zya knew that she should help the girl, for behind her she caught a glimpse of Ralnor, his face a picture of triumph. Something needed to be done about what was occurring under everybody's noses. It seemed that fate had a hand in all things, much as she had seen so many times in the past. Just as she mustered the courage to raise her voice above the animated chatter of the crowd, they began to disperse back to their own individual pursuits and the chance was lost. Ralnor and Bethen disappeared amongst the hubbub, and Zya sensed that there was little she could do about that episode of guild life, but nonetheless she would try.

The people around her became fewer and fewer, until only a handful remained. Joen was amongst them. "I suppose you would like an explanation," he asked.

"We would too." Said one of the people who remained. "What proof have you that this *girl* is to be the next head of the order?" The person that asked was an older member of the guild that Zya had never seen before. Judging by the travel-worn clothes and mud-stained boots, he had travelled far and quickly to get there. It was no wonder she had never met him. He fumed at the fact that somebody other than him was being honoured so, or so it seemed.

"You know the rules as well as any, Sparan," Joen replied defensively. "Only one who knows our innermost secrets can tell, and those secrets remain property of the successive heads of the order. Ilia herself has decreed that Zya will head or order next. Who are you to dispute the approval of the Goddess?"

"Bah! That green mist is a cheap illusion." Sparan concentrated, and Zya felt rather than saw him direct his concentration into a focus, though he did it in the most dreadful of manners. Zya could feel the crude force, as could Joen. Eventually a wispy green vapour flowed from around the newcomer, though it was a pale imitation of the lush green fog that had called everybody to the hall. Sparan's lack of strength was such that the mist did not even manage it as far as the hallways, fading into nothingness as did his will.

"Why don't you go back to selling your stones to merchants and tricksters, Sparan? It seemed that you always had a much greater aptitude for the less respectful side of guild life."

"You had better count your days, old man, for you will not last much longer as head of this guild," Sparan nodded in her direction, "and your little puppet even less." The stranger stormed past them, leaving only a group of stunned people in his wake. Nobody had ever spoken like that to the head of an order.

"Why did he speak so?" Zya asked Joen.

"He has a great deal of distrust and resentment, but at heart he was once a good man." Joen obviously spoke from the perspective of one that was honouring a past memory. "You are right in thinking that perhaps I should have banned him a long time ago, but we all make mistakes and I am as always, prepared to give a person a second chance. Still, if Sparan does not come round, then I will have no choice but to excommunicate him from the order. His words are hollow and there is nothing he can do within these walls to harm anybody. But do not let that worry, my dear. Events have overtaken you much too quickly. Our discussion today showed that you understand more of this Order than anybody has in a long time. Do not share the knowledge you have unlocked, not for selfish reasons but because of the consequences should somebody of malicious intent breach the 'window' as you so aptly put it. I know this has been one long trial of a day. Go, get some rest, and find diversion. It will probably be the last chance that you get." Joen waved her away before she could argue. Despite the certainty that she was not going to remain in the guild no matter what Joen or anybody else said, her gentle nature and good heart made her feel obliged to try and sort out the problems that she now saw in the order. But were those problems truly hers if she was not going to stay?

"My thanks, Joen Kzell." Zya intoned formally, and turned without looking back so that her eyes could not betray the fact that she would never be the head of this order to Joen, or to any of the others that were still gathered in Sparan's wake.

Zya wandered without aim around the halls of the guild. She let her feet guide her through openings and down corridors as she thought about all that had happened. Eventually, something distracted her. She came back to herself, realising just exactly where it was that her feet had led her. She looked about, wondering if she had been followed but there was no sign and no sound, not even the presence of anyone to her blossoming mind. No, that was not right, she corrected herself. There was one person. Zya crept into the kitchens, the place she had once worked, certain that there was somebody up ahead.

Stepping with care as Lorn had taught her to do, and thankful that the soles of her tribal shoes were soft and whispering compared to the occasional clack on the floor up ahead, she followed. Not getting any closer to the person ahead, Zya made sure that there was at least one corner between her and him for only a man could make so much noise when trying to be stealthy, and a good route of escape behind. She was sure of outrunning any pursuer in this place, for she knew the kitchen area well and was much more in shape than any wizard that had never been closer to a kitchen than his servant. She neared the door that she had once used to enter her life as a menial, and paused. Whoever was up ahead was not leaving, despite having the door ajar. It seemed as if they were waiting for somebody. Zya crouched behind one of the large wooden tables used in preparing the great quantities of food consumed by the guild every day, and waited for events to unfold.

For a while nothing happened. The silence in the kitchens brooded, like a menacing creature building up malice enough to cause it to strike. The kitchens still carried the faintest scent of a meal prepared during the afternoon, but they had been empty for a while. The only current occupants aside from Zya and her quarry were the lengthening shadows thrown in by the cobweb-filled windows. As they stretched across the kitchens to make the suite of rooms their own, still Zya waited. What had her interest was the identity of the person that waited by the exit. She imagined him peeking around the edge of the heavy oaken door that was the symbolic barrier between the acolytes of

Ilia, and the normal world outside. She sifted through the myriad of sounds that she could hear, the noise of the dwindling crowds in the guild quarter, the mice fighting over a scrap in an adjacent storeroom, even the faint whistling of the wind through a loose pane of glass in an adjacent guild until she managed to identify the breathing of the man she was sure she had followed. It was faint and surprisingly light, but it was hurried and obviously nervous. Whoever it was knew that somebody would be coming, and they wanted this over with. Anybody could come wandering into the kitchens, for they were not sacrosanct. If anything, that would buy Zya time to try and see whom it was she had followed on nothing more than instinct. She knew that the person was so nervous that they were as likely to bolt through the door as cower and hide should they be disturbed.

Then something changed. A feeling that Zya had not felt in a long time began to surface. It began as a twitch at the base of her spine, but grew with alarming rapidity until it was a hole in the pit of her stomach. She was already crouched, so she could not curl over any more. Her shoulders tensed, her arms pressing into her sides and her hands bent up at the wrists as she struggled to deal with the feeling that had her trapped. She knew not who was nearby, waiting by the door, but she knew exactly who was coming to meet them: O'Bellah.

Had she possessed the level of control that she had upon entering the city, Zya would have crumbled in a second. However, in the brief time that she had spent at the guild Zya had awakened a skill that she seemed born to. The power of her mind was such that although she was very aware of who approached the guild, it did not paralyse her with fear as once it had. This time she reacted with intrigue. What was a man responsible for spreading an evil far to the East doing in one of the westernmost cities of the Nine Duchies? That question helped her focus her thoughts and master her will. It was a blessed relief. The knot of fear was still there, but it was manageable. From the throb of it, she knew that O'Bellah was in the alley outside of the kitchens. She itched to get up and take a look at the man, to see if he was worth all the worry he seemed to generate in her, but for the moment she waited. A waft of city air indicated that the door had been opened wider and then he was there, in the next room from her. Zya was itching to get up, but something warned her that such a move would be no less than fatal. Thankful for the prescience that she now relied on she edged nearer to the room, getting as close as she could without giving her hiding place away.

"Were you followed?" Asked a bullish voice that could only be O'Bellah.

"I was not," replied a voice that was startlingly feminine, "because the kitchens were empty this afternoon. Apparently something of great import has happened and the menials were given the afternoon to themselves."

"What has happened?" He demanded.

"I do not know." The feminine voice was terrifyingly familiar. "I was kept busy this afternoon with studies." The word 'studies' came out in such a way that it could have meant one of many things. It certainly did not mean research. Where had Zya heard that voice before? She racked her memory to try and recall it, but could not concentrate on both that, and keeping the fear quelled within her. There would be a way around the latter; Zya was sure of the fact that this nimbus of fear was projected, and not something that occurred naturally. That alone aided her in her own personal battle with the fear. Her thoughts were invaded by the sound of a strong hand hitting flesh, and a stumble into boxes. "Foolish wench," spat the male voice, "I do not come here for suppositions and excuses by yellow haired village girls. Where is he?" A sob was stifled, and then the female voice replied. "My teacher is predisposed with new information that may help you subvert many of the guild. He bade me beg forgiveness on his part, but he told me to tell you that by the time of the Feast, he will be in a position to give you not just an answer, but the guild as well."

"With him as its head and that merchant Sparan as heir to the title, I don't doubt." O'Bellah replied sarcastically. "Well if that is the way the merchants want it, then they will have to live with the consequences once their 'prince' holds sway over the wizards." Zya knew not what the man was talking about, but she listened closely. There was something momentous afoot here, involving just about everybody she seemed to know. She knew the identity of the person speaking to O'Bellah, but did not want to admit it to herself until she laid her eyes on her.

"Is there anything else? What of your fellow novices? Are any of them looking like they can be persuaded, or are they still singing the guild song?"

"Most are nondescript, studying as I am. Some show more promise than others, and a couple have been singled out for special treatment." The detached, almost analytical side to the person surprised Zya. She had not seen that side to them in the time she had known them. Maybe she was not meant to, but now the cover was blown.

"Tell me of them," he demanded.

"You are looking at one, and the other was recruited after a fainting spell outside the mercenary guild. My teacher witnessed it and tracked her to her house in the Tribal Quarter."

369

"Wandering scum," O'Bellah spat. "What was she doing there?"

"I do not know why, but her father has a carpentry there, and evidently one of the nomads lives with them. One who is well positioned within the clans. My teacher attempted to get information, but none was forthcoming."

"Information of their movements dries up quicker than a worm in the desert when they feel threatened. Tell your master that he should be more careful when dealing with their kind. You haven't said what is so special about this girl. A faint does not do much to impress."

Zya sat in the dark with growing anger as her only company. Her entire guild history was recalled, from the moment she had been invited in to the point that she had discovered her own focus stone. Only things entirely private to her were left out such as the actual reasoning behind her discovery, a thing she would never have revealed before and certainly would tell nobody of within the guild now. Who was she able to trust? Two people that she had judged to be sound of character were now revealed as false. Zya suddenly could not see herself remaining in the order, whatever might happen. The only blessing was that there was little or no information given about her time in the order after she cast the focus that alerted the guild to her potential. Evidently Joen had no knowledge of this, though that would change if Zya could help it.

The information had animated O'Bellah in some way that Zya could not see. "I want you to do me a favour. Get to know this girl. Find out about her roots. I am after a girl of tinker origin, not tribal. She once wandered much as the tribe do, but with a purpose. I need her for something."

"Would I not do?" There was a cattish hint of jealousy in the girl's voice, as if she considered herself to be the centre of everybody's attention. Nothing had changed there.

"You are a comely wench, to be sure, but this one thing you could never hope to do." There was lust, dripping thick in his voice, but he was determined. "Find out about her, but do not tell even your teacher. If I hear so much as one whisper about this from anybody but you, I shall have you given to a lover whose embrace is eternity and whose clutches are torment personified. Do NOT fail me. You can get information to me by sending a runner to the mercenary guild. Now go."

"What if she is not the one you seek? How can I win?" The voice was timid now, very much afraid.

"My dear girl," O'Bellah replied, "who ever said anything about winning? You serve. Remember that and never question me again."

This obvious dismissal was as embarrassing as it was terrifying. Zya kept her gaze on the door from her hiding place as much louder footsteps echoed through the kitchens. A light flickered, and Zya saw tears running down Bethen's face as she half stumbled, half ran around the obstacles in the dark. The bumps and yelps went on for some while as the girl navigated her way out of the labyrinth in the dark, but the ill-feeling that O'Bellah caused Zya never went away. He was still waiting there for something. She considered herself fortunate that she had served in the rooms, for she knew her way about with her eyes closed. She felt compelled to see the man's face, and to that end edged her way around the silent kitchen to a window that was the other side of the doorway, and would give her a perfect view. The window in question was obscured by one of the very rare curtains, which was ideal. Zya found herself an ideal spot from which she could observe the alleyway, looking out from the edge of the window around the curtain. She looked out at the man that had evidently been trying to hunt her down, maybe from as early as the visit to Hoebridge. He was big, with a flabby neck, and piggy-little eyes that seemed to reflect a spoiled childhood in the candle's glow. He had a sneer that was part of his face as much as an ear or nose, and he gave off an air of contempt for everything that was obviously the cause for the ill feeling. Never had she seen anybody that hated everything so much. As she watched, another form materialised out of the shadows. "What do you think?" The dusty voice of Ralnor grated.

"She will do just fine. Are you sure she is up to it?"

"Young women are malleable. She will do her job at the Feast, and the Duke will be putty in *her* and therefore *our* hands. It is well documented that he takes a new concubine from the guilds to ensure their good will. This will backfire on him, and we shall get him to accede to our plans, or he shall die."

"She mentioned your other student. Was it wise to take a second pupil?"

"My first had no knowledge of our plans. She progressed too quickly for her own good. Do not worry. Guild politics will have her bogged down for years to come, especially with Sparan to stir things up. If she ever came to primacy that would be bad, but the guild will be forced to war or disbanded long before that ever happens."

"Then she is a force to be reckoned with?" The eagerness in his voice alerted Zya to the fact that this was a very, very dangerous place to be, not just the Guild, but also the entire city. She suddenly wished that she were not here, but something was forcing her to witness all of these events and she could not help but follow the path laid out for her.

"She is strong, but too independently minded for our needs. She has a streak of self-righteousness a league wide, and believes strongly in the Old Law."

"Old Law!" O'Bellah spat. "Their time is at an end, Ralnor. They will be part of the new order, the merchant order, or they will cease to exist. Sparan will see to that."

Zya had decided that she had heard enough, and silently left her perch behind the window. Making her way back to her room through the dark kitchens and dimly lit hallways, she avoided sound wherever she thought that she heard it. She did not want to be explaining herself to anybody at this time of the evening. Fortunately, Zya reached her room without incident and quietly let herself in, locking the door behind her. She had so much to think about, but the events of the day caught up with her and before she knew it she was fighting to keep her eyes open. Curling up on her bed with her dagger in her hand for comfort, she fell quickly asleep.

It did not end there. Zya found herself suddenly wandering through a deep valley, the path surrounded on both sides by thick, dense pine trees going up as far as the eye could see. The path sloped down in front of her, and she followed it without knowing why. She never once looked back, mainly because she knew that in this dream, she was destined to go ever forward, deeper and deeper. The forest was not cold, moreover the density of the trees made it comforting. The comfort took away some of the underlying chill created by the knowledge that this forest was in fact extremely dangerous. What made it so was not apparent, but she kept going forwards and down. It was gradually getting darker, much as it had in the kitchens. This did not seem relevant somehow for there was a subtle, unearthly glow coming from somewhere ahead. Down she went, and in the distance she could see her path crossing with another path to her right. The ground was firm, and the steep descent was easy for her in her tribal shoes. The path suddenly bottomed out, and Zya found herself at the join of the two paths in the gloom. In front of her, there was a high fence resting on a raised wall of dirt. It made a statement that said as pure as the driven snow, 'Do not cross here'. She looked around, and noticed a small figure walking down the path. It was a boy just on the edge of becoming a man, an impressive bow slung across his back in such a way as to almost render it invisible. He wore the nondescript brown clothing she had last seen him in, a little more soiled in the real world, she presumed. For his part the boy grinned back, and jauntily strolled down the remainder of the path through the dimness of the trees. The sky above did not seem real, so far away was it, and more of a lid on the bowl of the valley than the deepening infinity that it actually was. There was a glow from above, beyond the trees, but it was as indescribable as it was indiscriminate, shining through in dim patches where the trees thinned. She reassessed her perceptions of the valley. It was not so much as the trees thinned, but more that they allowed light to pass through their branches. He finished his walk down the path, ending up to her left as she looked up at the two paths.

"Ju." She said simply in greeting. They had never had a need for useless chatter, not in this place.

He responded by hugging her as a brother would his sister. "I have missed you."

"It has been a while," she admitted.

"Wizards keeping you busy?" He asked as he too looked around at the valley as if seeing it for the first time.

"You could say that. It all helps though." Zya sat down, leaning against the earthen barrier behind her.

Ju joined her after one more glance up the path from which she had come. "There's something up there," he warned.

She followed his gaze certain that whatever it was had been the cause for her uncertainty. All she could see was the bank of trees though. "I can't see anything."

"Still, there is something there, further up the path."

"Is it coming our way?"

Ju strained to see. "It has no interest in us, for the moment."

Zya had not asked that, but took his answer as a positive one. "So what have been you doing in the moons since I have seen you?"

"A little this, a little that." He replied, not being specific on purpose for some reason. "In fact since you have been away, things have been fairly quiet. Lorn has been making bows and arrows as if he were single-handedly outfitting the city for war. Your father has been keeping his head down in the tribal community while doing his woodwork, and I have been delivering messages and making a healthy profit. When are we going to see you again?" Ju sat down next to her on the earthen bank. Like the air around them it was warm, an ambient temperature that was as comforting as the rest of this reality. It was relaxing to not have to worry about looking over your shoulder, she thought.

"Soon, I think. Sooner than many would expect, perhaps. They have decided that I am to be the next head of the Order of Earth in Bay's Point. There are some who are happy about this, and others who are much less so."

"That's great!" Ju was obviously still caught up in her apparently good fortune.

"Not really," Zya replied sourly, "I am not staying. The time has come for us to go elsewhere. There are few things keeping us here now, and there are bad omens. I saw O'Bellah this evening."

"You what?" Ju exclaimed. "What do you mean you saw him?"

"He came to my guild and spoke to a couple of people. Who they were does not have much meaning for you, but what they said was dreadfully important." Ju was all ears, not saying a thing, so she continued. "O'Bellah may be onto me, or not, but he is seeking to throw down the guilds just after the Feast of Growth. He is going to try and poison the Duke and then blackmail him with the antidote from what I can gather. His intention will be to create instability between the guilds, and shut them all down outright if he can get a Ducal decree. Somehow we need to stop this. I need you to get somebody into the mercenary guild and find out what and why, anything you can that will aid us."

"I will go myself, for they trust me," Ju replied. "I take a lot of messages to and from that place, but I have never tried to get deep inside it. Perhaps now is such a time to try." The enthusiasm and solemnity of his response moved her. Zya tried to remember that this was not much more than a child, but the weight of responsibility that he tried to carry should have been a mantle for somebody much greater. She doubted that he would let anybody else take the challenge. "You know that if anybody even suspects what you are up to, they will kill you without a second thought. Mercenaries are loyal only to money, and especially not to people."

"No, mercenaries also treat those that do them favours with a bit of respect, and I have been doing that while I have been busy." Zya suspected that whatever it was he had been doing, she was about to find out. "The mercenaries I have seen are bound by some rule or other to remain in the confines of the guild. They are a rowdy lot, bullies all, but they have needs. I have made it my job to supply them with those things."

"What things?" Zya asked warily, not sure that she wanted to hear the answer.

"Bottles of drink, tobacco, things that they sniff and then sit there looking like grinning fools. Those are the favourites. One time I even managed to sneak in a woman."

"Why, was she the wife of one of them?"

Ju smirked at the innocent suggestion. "Not quite, Zya. Let us just say that when on the street, she is known to provide a certain. . . service to gentlemen." Zya's eyes widened. "Ju!"

The boy shrugged simply. "It is that or get beaten, and I prefer to run around without the benefit of broken bones. Besides, that particular man owes me a

huge favour now, and he is not one to break his word. I will get into the guild
for you, and we shall see what we shall see."

"Thank you, Ju." Zya put an affectionate arm around her 'brother', and the
two of them sat enjoying the peace of the strange dream they shared.

After a while, Ju turned to her. "What is it that you are going to do?"

"I don't know," she admitted. "I think that it might be my place to prevent
whatever is going to occur at the Ducal Palace. I had hoped that my training
would go well enough to allow me to attend the feast, and for a while I was
not sure that I would do it. Now I know that I must at least attend, though
anything beyond that is not clear."

Ju stood up and walked around them. "Maybe we are fated to come to a
strange forest with an eerie glow and trees dense as walls, where strange
creatures thump and rumble through the distant undergrowth." As flippantly
as he said this Ju was deadly accurate in his prediction, for the first footfall
sounded with a thump. They both looked up in silence, not afraid despite the
feeling in the air that had accompanied both of them as soon as they had first
set foot on the path. The thumping noise soon reverberated around the valley
as others joined the procession. Both Zya and Ju gradually sank into a pit of
fear, holding hands at the bottom of the valley but the creatures paid them no
mind. The forms, when they became visible, were immense. Great shaggy
affairs with slow lumbering movements all, the creatures were about a third of
the way up the valley using a path that the two of them had obviously missed.
"What is it that we are supposed to take from this dream?" Whispered Ju in as
quiet a voice as he could muster, but before Zya could answer, one of the
creatures let out a bellow. It was more of a series of grunts, but it was loud
enough to shatter bone. It reverberated around the valley, and was met by a
fresh series of grunts from way off to their left. There were obviously two sets
of the creatures ploughing their way through the trees above them. The
grunting continued, and the two of them were able to see through their fear
and comprehend that it was a method of speech. The pitch and speed of the
grunts varied if one was so inclined to risk permanent hearing problems, and
both of them could hear it well enough though their hands covered their ears.
As well as the different sounds, they were also able to tell that the group off to
the left were further up the hill than the first group, though what significance
this meant was not clear. At some point, the grunting began to trail off even
though they could see the shambling bodies still passing in a line above them.
What was odd was that they never once crossed the path, but appeared in
amongst the trees only.

"What if that is not a line of creatures?" Ju said quietly. "What if that is something trapped by the trees, unable to escape, and what we are seeing is frustration made visible?"

"Whatever they are, they do not sound distressed, "Zya replied, "they sound like it is a chant or nothing more than a conversation, but I do not sense any distress."

"Then why does the air still tingle with an uneasy fear?" Ju looked around him. "You feel it, I know that you do. There is something not right here."

That made Zya chuckle. "When is there ever anything right in a dream that I have? There is always something chasing us, or jumping out on us, or yelling in strange voices at us. It is only a dream Ju, and I say that this one is going to end peacefully with nothing attacking us and us walking up our respective paths." Zya was adamant, and before Ju could interrupt her, she continued. "I am fed up of my dreams ruling me. I am going to rule my dreams. They say that I am a seer. Well I am going to see what really needs to be seen, and not let petty nightmares rule my sleep. We are going to walk up out of this valley now, because the noise is going to stop NOW!"

As Zya yelled this, the grunting ceased. The trees quivered with the power of her command, and the beasts melted slowly back into the shadows. "Thank you," she said to the air around her, and the sense of foreboding lessened somewhat. It was almost easier for them to breathe as the trees around them became still, and the only sound came from their own boots on the loamy path. Zya turned to Ju, knowing that the time had come for them to part. "You might not see me for a while yet, but remember what you have to do."

"I will, and have no fear Zya, I will find out anything there is to know and get out of there before they even notice me." Ju turned to leave, but Zya held him by the shoulder. "What is it?" He asked, but she had a far away look in her eye.

"Tell my father and Lorn that the time will be upon us to leave, very soon. The avatar is here, but the evil that spreads through the land has not quite arrived. We need to be on a ship when it does. To that end, have them contact Darrow and Yneris, and tell them we will keep our pact with the underground pirates, and join them on their ships. Advise them that they would do best to leave en masse, for I believe this city will not be habitable within a season."

"What if they do not want to leave? And where are we going to find you?"

"If they do not want to leave then it is their own choice to make. They may know best. But as for myself, tell Darrow to look for me on the spit that guards the Duke's private harbour. He will know where that is." Zya shook her head as if coming back to herself. "We must leave, now. This place is dangerous."

Ju grinned. "But you said it was nothing to worry about," he said easily. "No, I was wrong. I would not say such a thing. We must go! Remember all I have said. Go!" Zya gave Ju an urgent hug and pushed him in the direction of his path. Not one to ever take a warning lightly, he shot her a parting glance and left. Zya was on her way back up her path before he had turned his head again.

Zya knew not what had prompted her precipitous change of heart, but her command to the trees and the beasts within clearly altered something. She climbed the path without looking back, moving slowly against the steep incline. Suddenly the footholds were that much slipperier, making her less sure of her ability to get out of the valley. There was a loud crack behind her, and she knew that the fences had burst asunder. A hint of purple light shone from deep down within the valley, and then she was knocked flat by a wind so strong it tore at the very breath in her lungs.

Zya blinked, gasping for breath and realised that she was on her bed. The candle on her table had burned down to a stub, and yet there was no sign of light outside. The birds were awake despite the darkness; their merry chorus announcing that dawn would soon be here. The raucous chirps were mingled with the early sounds and smells of the city industry, bakeries cooking the first batch of bread, and merchants hauling teams of horses through the cobbled streets of the guild quarter.

"Another dream, another night used up," Zya said to herself. She was glad in part that nobody else here could spy in on she skill that only she of the whole guild possessed. It would take a lot of time to understand what she had seen. Perhaps the actual physical reality of the dream was coincidence, and the dream was meant for her to see her way forward. She did not know why the spit was so important, and yet she knew that on the night of the Feast of Growth, she would be there or face unenviable consequences elsewhere. She also had a strong feeling that her words on the pirates were true, that some would stay behind and forfeit their freedom and perhaps even their lives as a result. She had done what she could, and was sure Darrow and Yneris could lead as many of their people as possible away from the rising danger. She sat on her bed pondering the fates of others, and watched the sky brighten. It was a good while later that Zya realised she was not alone. Through the tiny gap that separated her door from the floor, she saw something blocking the light, and perceived it to be a person. Moments later, there was a light knock on the door.

"I'll be there in a moment," Zya called, and hastily arranged her clothes and brushed her hair. She had not had a chance to change from the night before; she would have to do so later. Her mirror showed less than satisfactory results, but that would suffice for now. She had never been one for appearances. Crossing her room quietly, she opened the door and stepped back. As expected, Bethen crossed the threshold, a sunny smile spread like a lie across her face. If she had known that Zya had witnessed her every word, she would not have been smiling. Still Zya had decided to play along, for now.

"Good morning," Bethen said in a voice that seemed happy to behold the dawn of another day, "did you sleep well?"

Zya suppressed a shudder. "I slept like the forest in winter last night," she answered, and Bethen took a second to register her understanding of the metaphor.

"That is well then. We all need our sleep before the upcoming feast."

"Oh I disagree," Zya countered, "there is so much we can do and learn before then, do you not think?"

"Surely you need time to find that dress you have always talked about?" Bethen asked innocently.

"You mean the dress you have always talked about." Zya answered severely, and then silently reprimanded herself as confusion and hurt showed on Bethen's face at her acid tone. Zya took a moment to remind herself not to be too short with Bethen, as the girl did not know yet that she was being played from every possible angle. "I will be wearing my guild dress. As representative of the guild, I feel that it is my right and duty."

Bethen shook her head in defeat. "There is more than just being a part of the guild, Zya. This is a chance to show that you are not just a nameless face, but also a beautiful woman. I am sure that your parents would be very proud of you." The question was left hanging, as if Bethen expected an answer. None was forthcoming.

"Whoever is proud of me is none of my concern, Bethen. I am here to learn. If I have the honour of understanding that bit more it is by my doing, not by any of my forefathers." If Bethen wanted a story, she would surely have one. Zya decided to confuse the girl more with facts contrary to what Bethen had already witnessed first hand with her own eyes. She would go away with an impression of discord in Zya's life. "I certainly do not wish any of my family to be here, the money-grabbing thieves that they are."

"Thieves?" Bethen's vapid look was enhanced by her mouth dropping open at the thought of Zya coming from a les than reputable background.

"Merchants, but canny ones at that. They have been swindling the Ardican wine market for generations." Zya had only recently heard of Ardican Red, and although she refused to touch the drink, she knew of its importance all over the Duchies. There were some very rich merchants in Ardicum. She put on her most innocent look, and huddled closer, apparently confiding in Bethen. "I could not bear to witness the avarice any more, and that is when I left on my travels. It was fate that brought me here, for I can use the Old Law to make things better down in the Southern Duchies." It was no secret that Zya was a firm believer in the tenets of the Old Law, for she had made no secret of the fact since being in the guild. It was better for Bethen to believe that Zya was intending to go back South to 'teach her people a lesson', for it was as far from the truth as was possible. Once again Zya had to hide the guilt that she felt at her deception. The Law would frown upon it were she not only trying to react to the scene she had witnessed the night before. It was at this point that Zya came to a realisation. She had found the skills of several orders under this one roof, but she had never looked into the possibilities of studying at the Guild of Law.

"When will you go?" Bethen asked innocently, though Zya now knew her for the spy that she was.

"Not for a while yet. There is too much to learn, too many things that need doing here. If I am to be given this order there are things here that will need to change, but everybody will learn that in due course. Life has taught me that study and contemplation are a means to an end. In order to save this guild, we are going to have to go out and preach our word to the masses. But that will not happen for a while yet. People have to be converted to the idea." Zya looked up, her eyes wide as she spoke with a voice that was aggressively zealous. She shook her long black hair and it flared out like the wings of a raven. Fixing her stare on Bethen's face, she made sure that the girl understood that she was deadly serious. There was only one way to treat her immediate future, and that was to confuse as many of them as possible. She knew that word would never make it back to Joen: these people were far too secretive, and she had nearly had enough of them.

Bethen had completely taken the bait, and a look of shock rested permanently on her face as she realised that a life spent in the guild would not be one of leisure and contemplation. It suddenly seemed as though she could not be more eager to leave this room, and the unpleasant situation that Zya proscribed for everybody. Zya knew that eventually, politics would dictate that her 'plan' would surface, but by that time she would be long gone. She was too caught up in the thoughts of finding the Order of Law that she barely noticed Bethen making her excuses to leave.

"By all means," Zya replied, "but mention this to nobody. It will not happen for a while, and I need those that I can trust at my back."

Bethen actually bowed to her, before leaving. The thought would have been laughable but for the severity of the situation. Bethen would probably be even closer to her now that her masters would realise that she apparently had a hold over her, but that did not matter. Zya was too keen to escape the rapidly closing trap with her life, and the jaws would close on the night of the Feast of Growth. Maybe she could still make a difference.

Chapter Seventeen

Abad Santos was excited. He rarely got so in his position. A minor member of the order of light, a fractious little group that had once worshipped both Matsandrau and Ondulyn but now tended towards the Sun God, he rarely got involved in anything that did not include a healthy bribe of some sort. That had changed with the appearance of the stranger, a wiry little man that had spoken in prophetic tones about 'the time that would soon be here', the uprising when only the strong guilds would remain. That the man had come to him in particular marked him out for special treatment in his own mind, and so it had gone with his guild. He had spoken in dark corners, whisperings of what was to come, and unbelievably people had begun to listen. It seemed that the thirst for power and riches was not his alone and that it was a drink many were willing to sell themselves out for. The city of Bay's Point was not a poor one, far from it. But it was a rabble of paupers compared to the great southern coastal cities. Still, such opportunities arose rarely and he was going to take full advantage of this one. He had consulted most of the order. Of the score that inhabited the guild house, the only dissent came from the top two ranking wizards. Everybody else saw opportunity in the chaos ahead. The order would unite, he had said, and it would unite behind him. He was the man with the means to seek out answers amidst the apparent serenity of the guild, and his peers respected that. A man of middle age, he approached the sleeping chamber of his master on silent feet. The knife with which he intended to end the guild master's life tucked up one sleeve. It was cumbersome and very heavy, but the ceremonial knife that once had hung in a place of honour in the shrine of Matsandrau was still a weapon, and one with significant meaning at that. It was the weapon of their God, which he would sanctify once more with the blood of his highest-ranked worshipper. The shrine would be born anew as a temple dedicated to more than just their God. It would be dedicated to him. He, Abad Santos, would extend his reach beyond the small guild house that occupied a dusty corner of the guild quarter. He would take one of the bigger guilds, for he was assured many would fall. Perhaps he would take the Earth guild, or the guild of those pathetic wind wizards who spent all their time imagining that Yogingi was sitting by them. He would make the first move, and others would follow his lead. He would be the man in charge of the city when the Duke succumbed to whatever mysterious fate had been ordained for him, he would make sure of that. Waiting outside the door for a long, silent moment he ensured that there

was nobody near him by way of a miniscule searching focus. His stone carefully concealed, he lurked in the shadows as the tracer searched for others. When it fizzled out without streaking down the corridors, he knew his chance had come. He was still nervous, his hands slick with excitement. It was not enough to do this act alone. He must ensure that he was unseen. Though respect might come from his act, they would just as well turn him into the authorities for murder. Power came from acts of strength, and if they knew he would do this they knew he could do it to anybody. He opened the door as slowly as he could, taking every precaution to make no noise. Slipping inside, he closed the door, and then considered opening it once more as the rank smell of stale breath almost overpowered him. The guild master was fond of spicy foods, and it left him with the worst case of dog breath Abad had ever witnessed. It was almost too much for him to approach the man, who lay snoring with his mouth open, a trail of saliva dribbling down from one corner of his mouth to the coverlet beneath. Abad could imagine a green vapour arising from his nearly former master. He stood for a while over the man, leering at him and imagining the robes of leadership about his own treacherous shoulders. Removing the blade from the sleeve of his own robe, he carefully put the garment on a nearby chair. There would be no way that his own robes would suffer the touch of blood this night. He looked around the room, eyeing with distaste the lack of furnishings. That would change with this singular act. Resplendent in his dark hose and jerkin, Abad glared down at his victim as he raised the blade. He could not help it. He had to intone a ritual, as often he did at any gathering. It had earned him ridicule, but he persisted. "Great Matsandrau, I beseech thee. Bless your blade as I sanctify this chamber with the blood of a holy man. Grant us the wisdom to see the path through the difficult days to come, and see us through to the glory that awaits."
"What do you think you are doing in here?" Asked a voice from beneath him. He opened his eyes and saw the face of his master awake and trying to focus on what he held above him. "How dare you disturb me?"
"I dare because you do not. Now is the time of the new order, and you are not part of it."
So saying, Abad drove the massive blade of his God through the chest of his former master, and into the mattress beneath him. He clamped one hand over the mouth of the struggling man, and used the other to keep a blanket secure around the wound that was spewing blood. He wanted to sanctify the blade, but he did not want to cover himself in the lifeblood of this filthy man. The struggling subsided as the man quickly weakened. Blood began to seep

through the blanket and Abad moved away. A gurgling was the only noise
being made by the near-corpse.

"Well at least I didn't use a stake!" Abad said to the body, his lips drawn back
in a leer. Re-robing himself, he exited the room as quietly as he entered it,
triumphant in the knowledge that when everybody awoke they would do so to
a new style of Guild. One that was going to war.

* * *

"I, Joachimedes have called you all here to discuss the conflicting views we
have been presented by our far-seers. To get straight to the point, we have
been offered a part in the 'new order', so to speak, and a part in the defence
against it. Tonight we shall discuss these options, and shall not leave until we
have reached a decision that can only be seen as momentous." The high priest
of the Order of Weavers walked past the members of his order, and locked the
door shut using a focus of air that was the sole providence of the high priest to
seal them in. The weavers were followers of Yogingi, the God of air. They sat
on seats or floated on simple cushions of air, as was their wont. An immense
grey stone flecked with many different colours dominated the debating
chamber, around which it was said Yogingi himself had woven clasps of air
that he could watch his worshippers. It was this that led so many to create the
cushions of air that so easily sapped their energy; they wanted their God to
notice them, and they so rarely got the chance. Joachimedes preferred to think
upon his feet, and although he could feel the focuses all around him and
identify every strand of air that had been woven in the guild house he
remained apart from the shows of ostentation. He had risen through the ranks
as a result of dedicated study, not by showing off. It was naturally one of the
younger members of the order that flipped a focus into the air, indicating her
wish to begin the deliberations. Impetuous to a fault, every one of them
challenged the old ways. How they had ever been drawn from so far to the city
of Nejait was beyond him, but he was thankful for it. His order had found
continuation. He did the young lady the courtesy of addressing her directly.
"Before you start Rozmin, let every member of the order here present bear
witness to the fact that we will not act rashly upon any single opinion. What
we decide is not just for our personal glory, but could very well affect the fate
of all who dwell on this world. As our God touches every living being outside
the province of Panishwa, so does our decision affect them. Perhaps only
indirectly, but in the end if we chose poorly it will be to our own detriment,
and the detriment of those around us."

As if to emphasise the point, cloud whipped over the opening that granted them closer access to the flows created by their god. Power kept the rain out, but streaks of grey mingled with white as the storm clouds hurtled past. Nobody was in any doubt that this was as important an occasion as the ordaining of any high priest. Their God would judge them on what they did this day.

"I thank the high priest for his words of wisdom, and echo that we should all caution ourselves before this goes too far." Rozmin stood, her guild robes of light blue and white falling gracefully beneath her long brown hair as she bowed formally to her master. He was pleased that she would get in the first words, for she was a magnificent orator and more clever by half than many of the lesser wizards that inhabited his halls. What made her stand out especially was the fact that her eyes were completely white, filmed over with cataracts. Despite this, she moved with the grace of a dancer, all due to the air weaved about her. She had discovered a means by which she could see just by the touch of air, viewing the world around her differently but more than effectively. If a blind girl could see, then it showed more than adequately that miracles were possible. She was an example of them all, and proved herself again. "I would like to begin with a brief recounting of how we heard of the two offers, just to that we all know for good or ill. On the one hand we have the word of a mercenary dressed in leathers and armed for battle, come to the door of our halls and demand entrance. He tells those within earshot of a pact with Raessa, in order to release us all from the disharmony that has stood between the two mountain ranges for so long. He warns that we have the chance to become part of a new way of life, and have a say in how things are run when the other guilds fall." There was a slight murmur of disagreement, with one or two mumbling phrases along the lines of 'lies', and 'false witness'. Rozmin picked up on this. "False witness? I beg to differ. I was at the gate when the mercenary came to the guild. I listened to what he had to say, and Wisam and Walid can testify to that." Rozmin approached the twin weavers who were unnseperable since birth, and sat side by side with equal expressions of dismay at being the centre of such attention.

Walid stood up, towering over Rozmin. Joachimedes knew that Walid was the lynch pin in Romzin's testimony to the guild, and despite his natural shyness, he did not disappoint her. "We can confirm that Rozmin was with us at the gate, for we all shared duty that day." That did enough to quieten all of the dissent in the room.

Rozmin looked around the chamber, eyeing up those who would most likely be her opposition today. She spoke now in a hushed voice, so that everybody would be forced to listen hard and hang upon her every word. "The other message we received was from two sources. Firstly a message given directly to our high wizard himself by somebody called Obrett Pedern, of the now defunct Law Guild in Eskenberg, telling us of how the Witch finder is planning war. War! Against our kind, against people who are being drawn even now into a focus that radiates out from his city like a deadly spider's web. We know exactly what this pertains to, for we ourselves have lost brothers and sisters to that place. Where this man is we do not know, for he would not reveal his location. What we do know is that he was held hostage in Raessa, and escaped amidst confusion he created. One thing more this man claimed: That Raessa has found a way to utilise emotive magic, one that has long been unused."

"Rubbish! You are talking rubbish!" One older man with a distinct lack of hair anywhere on his face called out from his nest of air.

"Am I, Olmsted?" Rozmin stared straight back at the man, undaunted by his place in the guild, or his own personal attempt at interrupting proceedings. "If I am talking rubbish, then why do we have the same message but from two other sources? Sources that are completely different." A rumble of interest mingled with not a little surprise reverberated about the room. Nobody had had a chance to learn of this, so preoccupied had they been with preparing themselves for the gathering. "We have had messages from both the Order of Life and the Order of Water, saying exactly the same thing. They both believe that there is trouble brewing across the plains, and that we would be wise to oppose it. Not for our own personal glory, but because in the western Duchies innocent people are being slaughtered in order to increase the use of emotive magic by Garias Gibden. They have both forewarned that should one of us receive a message in unusual circumstance, we should pay a great deal of attention to it."

"That in itself implies that they have reason to be behind the messages," called an elderly lady from her place near the back of the hall.

Romzin bowed in acknowledgement; She was nothing if not polite and courteous. "That is exactly my point, elder Keturah. Two *different* sources giving the same message. But yes, in answer to your point the guilds *are* related in this matter. High priest?"

Joachimedes stepped down, a smile suppressed. He was very impressed by the youngster, and her control of the debate was solid. "Your supposition is indeed correct, Romzin." He addressed the rest of the gathered guild. "It was mentioned to me by Obrett Pedern that he was with two other wizards, both of different guilds. Their names are Ispen Demuth, and Jacob Manh. They were going to contact their own orders and spread the word."

Romzin looked around as she thought about something. "If I am not mistaken, those two names are affiliated with the Water and Life guilds, being prominent members are they not?" A few people nodded their heads, but most remained silent. "Your reticence brings up a good point. We are too secular by half. I propose that not only do we support this, but we also spread the word, and try our best to get other guilds on board."

"I propose that we do no such thing," shouted a voice from amidst the crowd. It was a dark-haired wizard by the simple name of Fleck. He was outspoken in his opinions, and never shy of trying to enforce his will upon others. He was as good a speaker as Romzin, and from the look of determination on his face he intended to prove it. He rose and walked to the centre of the floor, where there were no people and everybody could see him. He literally drew the guild member's gaze towards himself with his posture, one of supreme confidence. "I propose as an alternative that we consider peace with Raessa, rather than stirring up what is already a volatile pot." At his suggestion, the gathered wizards clucked and muttered in anger. It was clear that many had already made up their minds. Fleck pressed on. "We are talking about the survival of the guild here!" He boomed, and the animation subsided. "Whereas we may go into a war that we may or may not win against a foe with who knows what on his side, we also have the chance for peace. Peace!" He looked around the room, seemingly catching the eye of every single person therein. "I tell you, is that not worth consideration? Is that not worth choosing for the preservation of the Old Law, the very premise we strive to keep alive and find so difficult to do? Surely you all can see the sense of it. We are obligated to give peace every possible chance."

"Peace is an interesting term when applied to the treacherous master of Raessa, do you not think Fleck?" Romzin approached the part of the room Fleck had seemingly marked out as his own personal territory, and stood beside him. The Old Law has many facets, but above it all stands the notion of intent. Do you for a moment believe that if we willingly stand with the Witch Finder, we will have a moment's peace? Of all the outcomes that are possible, do you actually think that Raessa will honour any that mean we just sit by and do nothing? That is the worst course of action, for it means that other orders will falter and the people will suffer even more. You cannot fail to have read the reports that come in daily about the depopulation of the headwater regions East of Raessa. It has long been a fact that he is using a focus to draw people in, especially those that have the focussing ability. Do you think that there are any guarantees that this will stop should we side with them? Do you take the word of a mercenary armed for war above that of three wizards who have been to Raessa and escaped with their lives?"

"Here indeed is a point for everybody to consider, "Fleck interrupted Romzin, causing no end of irritation to the gathered crowd, "where are these wizards? How do we know that they are not already working for Raessa? We receive words of warning, but who can say where these words originate?"

"Fleck, that is really a rather stupid thing to say." Romzin stopped him in his tracks. "If they were working for Raessa, why would they warn us against the Witch Finder and his allies? What could they gain by asking us to stand against them?"

"They would ask us to do such a thing in order to draw us out of Nejait and toward Raessa, where they could take us." Fleck was already on the defensive. Romzin was like a bird of prey in flight, swooping in elusive circles while her prey appeared to run blindly in panic. Fleck was in no way evil by any means of the word. He was just contrary to the point of fussiness. "That is exactly what we do not need to do, my friend. The countryside is massive, and Raessa is but a little part of it. There are countless villages and towns that we can help with that lie nowhere near the source of the focus. Do you believe that the Witch Finder would be in any way satisfied with keeping people within his own boundaries? That man is looking to expand until Raessa is the one authority under which the Nine Duchies exists. We cannot let that happen. Nor can we stand around and watch it happen from afar. We *need* to get out there and spread Yogingi's word, and preserve the Old Law. If you pause to consider it for but a moment, you will realise that defending the people and the country is the most honourable course of action in this event. Intent is everything. If we intend to sit by and watch Gibden and his cronies unleash war on the innocent people of this land, then the intent is just as bad as siding with him. The only way that we can save our souls is by taking an active stance against all of this. I tell you now, as you believe war advances towards us, by this method I assure you peace is closer. High priest Joachimedes, I have nothing more to say."

The high priest was impressed. "Thank you, Romzin. Fleck, have you anything more to add?"

Fleck scowled at Romzin; He did not like to lose a debate, but she had beaten him thoroughly. "I have represented the cautious approach high priest, for I think this is the way forward. I do not condone war in any sense of the word, and that is what we do if we side with or against Raessa." Fleck turned towards the gathered men and women. "Let the guild make its choice."

Joachimedes raised his hands in a gesture of invitation. "Two bells there are at the back of the room. The light bell for yes, and the dark bell for no." He turned and pointed. Revealed to the order were two bells that shimmered into existence from behind a wall of air, used only for deciding such a weighty matter. One was a bright polished brass, magnificent in its appearance. The other was almost black, but equally impressive. "Make your choice. Shall we go to war, or stay out of the way and leave others to direct the future of the Duchies?" Each member of the order focussed, and sent a force of solid air towards one of the bells. The dark bell toned low to start with, and then the light bell responded with its shimmering ring. As each wizard decided they sent their focus towards one or the other. Occasionally the dark bell tolled, but it was the shimmering brass of the light bell that rang out more often.

The order had been stirred into restlessness by Romzin's words, and Joachimedes approved. He personally would never have stood by and watched others reduce his country to ruins, but the forms of the guild had to be observed. The next part he dreaded, for he had no idea what his guild was thinking. "As decisive as the previous question was, it needs to be clarified. It has been decided by us all that we will take action of one form or another. Here is the choice: For Raessa, or against Raessa. Choose the dark bell for and the light bell against." Joachimedes made the conscious choice of giving the dark bell for Raessa, as it was a path that saw no good. The answer was swift and sudden. The light bell rang out in magnificent song, with not a single dark tone to offset it. "The choice is made," the high priest rang out as the bell still hummed with vibration, "we will see this through to the bitter end if need be. Gather your strength my kinsmen, for we go out as soon as we may to join those that would fight this oppressor and his allies. We will seek out those orders that will stand by us, and the wizards of Nejait will put an end to the Witch Finder once and for all!" The guild cheered their leader, even the dark-faced Fleck yelling out in support. The weavers were as one; they would do their utmost to preserve the Law by which everybody once lived, and hopefully would live by once more.

***

Gregoriades rued the day so many members of his guild had left on the pilgrimage downriver to the larger cities. It had meant the decimation of his order, and the end of the good that they did in Nejait. No longer could they range far and wide in search of villages to aid. No longer could they even sustain an active temple. The grand temple dedicated to Ilia stood barren and disused. There was not a lot that three of them could do. For a place so large, there was little more that the three of them could do than keep the 'home fires burning', and keep looters out. The latter was not hard: simple cantrips and a focus that guarded the entire building saw to its protection. The former was the problem. The guild was so empty without the rest of the members.

He looked down at the floor miserably as he shuffled out of the main hall. "Nothing to be done."

"Nothing," agreed a voice as downtrodden as his own.

He looked up and almost bumped into Bortcosh, another of the surviving trio. "What can we do, Bort? We keep the halls clean and polish the windows until the crystal gleams in the sunshine, but it will not bring back the others. We keep stores of food until they go rotten, but still we have no more mouths to feed."

Bortcosh leaned into the crutches that he had used since a child to compensate for the leg that was stunted at the knee, and moved along beside him, the only noise that any of them made for a while being the tap of wood on stone. "We exist, my friend. That is what we do. Perhaps an answer will present itself if we just look in the right place."

"I wish I shared your optimism," Gregoriades replied, defeated by the great walls of stone around him.

A door slammed. "I thought that I would find you two moping around somewhere." A high-pitched voice assaulted the silence. Teresita, the final member of the surviving trio was definitely not going to become overwhelmed by the circumstances, and had been trying to take what advantage the situation provided. She was a severe-looking woman with her grey hair tied back tightly and her clothes as grey as the walls, but she had a heart of gold and both men were fond of her finicky ways.

Bortcosh smiled. "What would you have us do, o great lady?" He bowed, intentionally just missing Gregoriades with one crutch and making him jump out of his way, and out of his sour mood.

"I would have you both accompany me to the former master's room. There are things that we must discuss, and they can only be spoken of in that room.

Intrigued, both men followed with not a word. When they all walked together, the guild felt less lonely. It was not uncommon to wander the halls alone, or in pairs or trios but when alone in a place they knew would never be filled again the company was more than welcome. All three had developed close bonds that would never have had time to form in normal guild life. They relied on each other in their different ways. Gregoriades was of a very practical nature when he was not moping. Bortcosh was massively intelligent and good with focuses. Teresita was a real find, as she was a miracle with documents, administration and research. She was most determined to keep the guild alive, and whenever she had a point to raise both men listened. Ushering them into the office of their former master, Teresita motioned for them all to sit down. Pulling up a chair for Bortcosh, Gregoriades eventually eased into an immense leather-bound chair across the desk from the other two. "What have you found?"

Teresita unfolded a huge leather tome that she had produced from one of the drawers. Since they had waited so long, they had only recently begun to respectfully delve into documents that they would normally have had nothing to do with. As it had dawned on them that they were now the only members of the guild, they had lost their timidity and looked deeper and deeper into the secrets of the Order of Earth. Thus had the network of chambers surrounding the high-priest's become their own mini-guild. They rarely journeyed far beyond the rooms that they really needed. "This is a tome that will raise your eyebrows. If you concentrate, you will see that it is surrounded by a focus, a most unusual focus."

Bortcosh leaned forward, his cloak spilling over the side of his chair, and dipping one of his crutches to the floor as he did so. Squinting at the tome in the dim light, he proceeded to probe at it with a focus of his own. "It is not all there," he said after a moments' consideration.

"How can a focus not be all there?" Gregoriades asked.

"Not sure," came the reply, "but it appears that the focus is part here, and part somewhere else. What is inside it?"

Teresita flipped the book open. "Messages, some written quite recently. It appears that this is some type of communiqué between all Earth guild heads." All three of them poured through secrets that were only known to the principal worshippers of the Earth goddess, staring in awe as they did so. Not a word was spoken until they had read all the covered pages within, and then they looked up at each other in silence.

"I had no idea that all of the guilds were so intertwined," Bortcosh almost breathed, "we are not as alone as we think."

"So it is a simple case of writing in this tome and then the other guild heads will pick up the message?" Gregoriades asked rhetorically.

"Perhaps," Teresita agreed as she eyed up the page that was mostly blank, "but something tells me that this script was not written with ink and a quill, but by a method much more subtle."

It was at that point that the room became suddenly chilly. It was instantly noticeable, and all three guildsmen shifted their clothes around them. They suddenly felt as though they were not alone.

"Who are you and what are you doing here?" A voice hissed out of nowhere. "Answer!"

All three of them gave their names and guild ranks, adding the reasons why they did not accompany the pilgrimage, though they did not need to.

"Gregoriades, Bortcosh, Teresita." The voice repeated out loud, more human now it had been mollified somewhat. "I remember those names. You were away from the guild at the time of the pilgrimage. You were expected back but did not make it. Lucky for you that you did not."

"Listen, I don't mean to be rude whomever you are, but you ask a lot and know a lot for somebody that stands behind us and offers little. Who are you?" Bortcosh was nothing less than forthright, and the hissing voice had his eyes flashing in anger. He risked much, but then he had always figured that he had little to lose.

"It is Brendan. That is my name." The announcement made them all turn around at once.

"Where are you Brendan, for we knew each other well." Teresita stood up and walked towards the source of the voice.

"I remember you now, Teresita. It has been too long."

"I'll say," she replied as she searched the shadows, "we thought you were all dead."

"I might well have been." He answered. "We were captured by the Witch Finder's forces and taken to Raessa where we were held and forced to use our skills in focussing to aid him. Unfortunately he had no care for our skills, and many of our brethren were killed when a particularly powerful scrying recoiled on us. I am the only one that is left of the pilgrimage as far as I am aware."

"Where are you?" Teresita persisted.

"I am all around you, inside of you, in the wood and in the stone." Brendan replied with an amused tilt to his voice. "I am in a place that cannot be reached by yourselves, but I have some powerful allies. Ispen of the Water guild and Jacob of the Order of Life are with me, as is a Law Wizard called Obrett Pedern. It was he that taught us the methods by which we freed ourselves from Raessa. I cannot tell you of our current location, for the knowledge would put you in danger. What I can tell you though is that we can relay messages just about anywhere, and that is needed especially now. There is war coming, a war involving all of the guilds, a war started by the tyrant in Raessa."

Shock ran up the spine of all three presenting the room. "War? Brendan, are you sure?"

"I have seen it with my own eyes, heard it with my own ears. He is after something, and he is going to use any means to get it. He has already unleashed emotive magic in the form of a Golem."

This brought sharp intakes of breath from all of the three; they knew of emotive magic only from ancient tales. "Brendan, can you tell us any more?"

After a pause, Brendan continued. "As we have all learned in our novitiates, emotive magic was a dark and very powerful magic that utilised the energy given off by the negative aspects of the human psyche. Fear, anger, pain, they all serve to feed any given sink. The Golem is such a sink, and the level of suffering being stirred up by Garias Gibden and all those he rules over is something that can no longer be measured. There is something really wrong with this world, and it only makes his creature stronger."

All three looked at each other in stony silence, and then looked down at the ground as they wondered what had caused the world to go so wrong. As usual, Teresita took control of the conversation. "What is it he is after?"

"An ancient relic, with the potential for more power than you could ever imagine. Again, I will not reveal too much for your own safety. I am sorry that I cannot be with you, my brethren, but were we to reveal where we are then it would put you all in danger. Pray, tell me what you have been doing since we abandoned you so."

Brendan listened as the three told him of their attempts to keep the guild on its feet, their growing numbness at being left alone, and finally their discoveries, most importantly the book.

"I had thought there must be a way for them to keep in touch. They seemed to get messages across to each other just a bit too quickly at times." Brendan's invisible form said out loud, half in thought.

"You knew of such a thing?" Gregoriades asked.

"I suspected," Brendan replied. "I mean no disrespect to you all, but I was higher up in the guild than you and therefore privy to more of its secrets. Several of us suspected that such a thing might exist, but only the head of the guild could know it all."

"And are we supposed to use this now?" Gregoriades looked at the tome doubtfully.

"You must," Brendan replied, "because you have to warn all of the other head wizards about the problems that we face. It may be too late for many of them. They may have already chosen the path down which they will travel, and it might not be the same path as yours. But any who still truly represent Divine

Ilia will read your words. Leave nothing out. Use all the detail that you can. Perhaps we will all get out of this alive."

The three of them looked at each other. "Who are we to chose the user of this book?" Bortcosh sighed.

"You are the Earth Guild of Nejait, that's who." Brendan answered with a grave tone. "I am in a place that cannot be revealed, not for perhaps a long time. But I am always with you. Guilds often started out with so few members, quite often with one alone. In time things change. Have faith in yourselves, for I do not see three minor members of a guild. I see the head wizard and two assistants to help run the Order of Earth."

It was so simple. Gregoriades locked eyes with Bortcosh and they understood. "Brendan, please welcome Teresita, the head of the Earth guild and the keeper of the Nejita range." He intoned this carefully, using the honorific bestowed upon the traditional guardian of the mountains. Teresita's face paled, and she looked both men in the eyes. "Are you sure about this?"

"You are the most capable of the three of us in mind, body and spirit." Bortcosh answered her.

Gregoriades nodded eagerly. "We will aid you as well as we may, head wizard."

Teresita, obviously never having ever thought of herself as the head of a guild let alone such a traditionally powerful one, kept a straight face. But the tears were shining in the candlelight. "Thank you, you dear, dear people. We have much work to do. What else can we do to help?"

Together with Brendan's advice, they discussed the strategy of their 'guild' from that point onwards. It was clear that they simply could not function without replacements despite Brendan's encouragement, so it was agreed that they would ask for any volunteers from other guilds to boost their numbers. It was a desperate play by an honoured guild that had nowhere left to turn. It was also agreed that they would try to convince the surrounding guilds in Nejait of the danger. They further decided to encourage the other guild heads to do the same. At the end of what had amounted to more than a half of a day in discussion, the revitalised if somewhat smaller Earth Guild of Nejait felt a great sense of accomplishment.

"Are you not tired from the focus you are casting?" asked the new head of the order to the empty space that they had all agreed contained Brendan.

"Not at all. There may come a time when I can divulge to you the great secret that I must keep, but until then let me leave you with this knowledge to suffice." There was a pause, and Gregoriades felt as if they were alone once more. Then Brendan's voice returned. "Ask the other guild heads to send forth wizards to the plains of Ciaharr and northern Ardicum. There has been a great battle fought there this day, one which we have won but at a great cost to those fighting. This cannot continue to happen. People are being slaughtered out there, whole villages put to the stake."

A gasp of shock left the mouths of all three wizards. "Put to the stake? But that has not happened in over twenty years."

"Well trust me it is happening now. Act swiftly."

"How do we contact you?" Gregoriades asked, feeling isolated at not being able to contact this knowledgeable source.

"Do not worry for I am keeping a watch on you, on all Nejait. The time is coming when we shall all have to band together. We shall speak anon." The voice of Brendan disappeared, and left alone were three people who, geed up with ideas and a desire to dig a hole in the easy trail towards destruction that emanated from Raessa, left their seats to go out and speak the word to those in the city around them.

Brendan closed his eyes and willed himself back to the tower. When he opened them once more the familiar blue glow was on the horizon, the tower dark and shiny with a subtle red glow from the windows within. He was under one of the huge trees in the courtyard, though he could have conceivably just remained where he was in Nejait. He now had the knowledge to transfer himself entirely to the city, but once there he would have to make his way back to the ruin in order to activate the focus that would shift reality and allow him to enter this state Ispen called 'out of time'. It was Jacob that waited for him when he came back to himself, his face eager and yet frantic at the same time. "Any more news?"

"Not much, save that casualties to the tribe and travellers were less than previously assumed." As a member of the Order of Life, Jacob was very finely attuned to the goings on in the normal world. In the enhanced state of the tower's reality it sometimes became too much for him, and it had been Jacob crying out that had caused Brendan to break contact with the brave souls that were all that remained of his guild. "What about your findings?"

Brendan took off at a stroll, finding immense contentment in the various shades of blue around him. What he realised was odd was that the leaves on the trees still thrived without proper sunlight. "I think the guilds are starting to take sides. We know that the Earth guilds will come behind us, especially after the discovery of the message tome. We have your guild and Ispen's guild, and between them much of Nejait. It is basically up to those guilds to go about contacting others. If they have similar methods to my order, then we can hope for a good showing. If not, then we will just have to hope fate is on our side."

"It is hard to gauge how many orders may have been influenced by Raessa," Jacob agreed.

"It will be the coastal cities that will be the key to it all, my friend," Brendan continued as they headed back towards the tower. "If money is the reason the mercenaries march, then you can bet your right hand that there are merchant princes behind it all. They control many of the coastal cities, with their bribes keeping the Dukes happy. They have no love at all for the Old Law, and less for wizards. The only guildsmen they care about are those that can make a profit, and there is very little of that in focussing. I just hope that the coastal guilds believe in the Gods as we do, and then we might prevail. Otherwise we are going to find ourselves surrounded with enemies and only this tower to find refuge in."

"Not a lot we can do from here though," Jacob admitted, seemingly mourning for their inactivity.

"Well we are going to have to change that, my friend. We are in a unique position here, with access to magics unparalleled by anything in the normal world. We will make use of it and we shall prevail."

"*If* we ever manage to get anything out of our hosts." Jacob looked up at the tower they were about to enter. "They seem to be less than willing to share whatever it is they have learned during their tenure here. We have made all of the discoveries."

"I am beginning to think that there is a reason they are here and unable to do anything. I think we are on the verge of finding out why." Brendan moved his hand in front of him and the huge door opened silently. "See? They do not even do that. They are watching for something my friend, and it has nothing to do with focussing."

The two wizards climbed the great stairs that led to the main chamber and entered. Inside, Endarius, Irmgard and Tani sat in awe, looking up at Obrett, who held in his arms a wisp of a girl clad in leather, a sword hanging half out of a scabbard.

"I never did believe in the ways of magic," Irmgard said reverently, "but I'm beginning to wonder why it is you can do such amazing things."

"It is because I believe," Obrett replied, and put the girl down onto the ground. "The only way to save her was to power a focus through her, something that has never been done."

"Was one girl worth the personal risk?" Tani asked gently. "Obrett, you could have killed yourself."

"This girl is special. She represents something, an ideal for lack of a better term. She has given hope and direction to those that lacked it."

"Is she the one you seek?" Endarius had spoken to Obrett in the past of his thoughts on Raessa, and knew of the theory that there was somebody special they were all after.

"No, she is something different, but equally special. She has cast off the life of a traveller, and become something more."

"A warrior?" Endarius challenged. "That is hardly noble."

"It is not her choice, and therefore she is innocent of any ill that has happened. What she *has* done though is lead a group of people into the heart of a bear pit to rescue her family. She has led people through the wilderness and kept them safe from the true enemy. Now she has nearly died protecting them and I will save her."

Brendan approached his friend, and found that the girl in his arms was bleeding onto the floor. As if to confirm the grisly state, Jacob spoke up. "If you are going to do something, do it quickly for the girl is almost one with my God. Her life force ebbs."

In response Obrett concentrated, drawing in his will and sending it snaking out in the form of pure magic. Instead of ranging afar, as so many of their spells had, the spell dove into the girl in Obrett's arms. The wizards beheld a miracle as the spell emerged in a different form, causing a breeze to manifest in the chamber. The breeze quickly became a gale, whipping pages and tomes around and forcing the three watching wizards and the three guardians to jump to it and save the paperwork. The gale howled around the edges of the chamber, reaching maelstrom proportions. Lightning flickered and the room went dark. Tables started to shift, along with their contents. Streaks of vapour raced around them and the wind began to howl as well as rush. At the centre of it all the warrior girl lifted from Obrett's arms and rose into the air, lifted by so much wind pressure. The body was inert as if defying the terrible forces about it, but it was rapidly healing as the focus that had been sent through it worked its own magic. The blood that dripped stopped and a hale colour returned to her face, or appeared to for as much as the wizards could actually see what was happening, they were sparing at least as much concentration avoiding flying objects. At the height of the storm in the tower, Obrett sent forth a different type of focus, and the girl disappeared. The winds dropped, and suddenly the only noise was that of paper sifting back through the air to land wherever gravity determined. The room was a complete shambles, but

Obrett stood there, a strange smile on his face. "It worked," he said before anybody had a chance to berate him for almost single-handedly destroying everything in the chamber. "The girl is back with her loved ones, and I can see that she is alive and well."

"I thought that you could not move people around," Irmgard said, his face a thunderous reflection of the recent vortex.

"She wasn't all there when I did it. She was not conscious, and so could not comprehend what was going on around her. Maybe that was the difference, but I tell you now we are almost there. We can nearly move a person with their own knowledge and wits intact."

"Well perhaps you had better come down from your little cloud and help us get this chamber back in order, so that we can use it once more."

"Do you not see? This is exactly the sort of thing that this room was designed for!" Obrett's face was animated with the truth as he now saw it.

"They would not see, my friend," Brendan answered, "for they cannot see. They have no concept of magic whatsoever. That is why whoever it was put them here, because they had no knowledge at all. They have never focussed, and perhaps never will despite the magic that is all around them. They are ignorant of any of our ways, of perhaps anything except the Old Law. They are a people unlike us, and they would probably not recognise the world as it is now, a world full of merchants and mercenaries, a world ruled by gold.

The three stood there dumbstruck. "How could you know what we are?" Tani asked, her voice quivering.

"I know because my intuition tells me so," he replied. "You are so far removed from the normal world that you can only be from a completely different people. You watch for an item or an event, and I would bet that you have been watching for a very long time. A *very* long time. If I was a betting man and sometimes I *am*, I would say that you are connected with whatever it is you are looking for in some way, and that what stops you from leaving here is your knowledge that it is out there calling to you. But you have been so long looking that you forgot how you got here in the first place. Help us learn, and we can help you in return. Give us your knowledge, and we will help you find this item, and you can do with it what you will."

Tears of gratitude ran down the faces of both Endaruis, and Tani. Even the normally stolid Irmgard was looking emotional. "We want to help you, but we don't even know where to begin." She said, looking at the results of the paper blizzard. "We can't even get out of here, we have no knowledge of magic."

"Well then," said Obrett as he balanced a sphere of pure white light on his palm, "we are going to have to see what we can do about that, aren't we?

* * *

The village was sombre despite the victory. They had watched the mercenaries filter quietly into the village, great bundles of stakes carried between them. Then the trap had been sprung. The tribal men and women had fired a hail of arrows into the group, and then the villagers and the rest had waded in with swords, axes, and various farming implements. Victory had been certain even against better-trained foes, but the cost had been immeasurable. As Mavra had raised her sword in the air, a mercenary that had been missed had jumped up behind her and run her through, gurgling with insane laughter as he had done so. The man had been slaughtered on the spot, but it was not enough. Ramaji had fainted at the sight of her daughter unconscious and dying, and Jani could only stare and cry. Both parents were inconsolable. They sat there crying, not talking, not even acknowledging each other. Then the ultimate desecration had happened. When they had finally been persuaded to leave the body of their dying daughter to the ministrations of one of the village elders, somebody had taken the body of their dying daughter. The villagers tried to keep it from them, and it had only led to Ramaji fainting at the news and Jani settling down into an icy silence.

It was just as the former Mistress of the caravan and her husband, not sure if they would be called upon to resume their duties, were trying to break through to them that a wind manifested itself. Jani and Ramaji paid it no heed, but the rest of the villagers had dived for cover. It was not just a wind but a tornado, a whirling vortex of immensely powerful winds. The vortex appeared over the barn where they had held Mavra's body, and ripped it asunder. Wood flew everywhere, and the whirlwind was so dark that nobody could see what was going on at its centre. On the plains of Ciaharr, this type of phenomenon was never seen, and so nobody had ever before witnessed it. One innocent child went as far as to walk right up to the edge of the vortex, where eddying winds ripped at anything within reach. Playing with the currents for a moment, the child was snatched to safety by her terrified father. The vortex eventually blew itself out, and after the wood had crashed in a rain of splinters to the ground, the villagers, tribes' people and travellers gradually emerged from various hiding places to view the ultimate desecration of their fallen heroine.

The man who had owned the barn was the first to look at it. "It is not the cost of the barn, but rather that it was such a good, solid building," he lamented to his wife, who just stared ahead at the dust cloud that was still settling around them.

"Yes dear," she replied, numb to all that had happened around her on this strangest of days and yet proud that her husband had never given in to the will of the merchants that passed through, preaching their ways of money. "Well would you look at that," he observed, "there appears to still be something undisturbed amidst all of this." The dust was clearing, and shapes began to resolve in the dusty air.

"It's a shame that it is not the body of that poor girl who gave her life up for the likes of us." She replied, not really seeing what was in front of her.

"Look," Her husband exclaimed, "Everybody, come look!" He called to the people that had witnessed the maelstrom. Upon hearing his voice, people began to drift over and see what he had managed to salvage.

It was only then that his wife registered the scene with her own eyes. "Oh dear Gods above, how can it be so?" In front of them on the floor of the wrecked barn, as if nothing had ever happened to her, lay the body of Mavra. She was still, composed, and there was no sign of the blood that had stained every inch of her clothing. Her sword lay at her side, and there was a slight smile on the face of the still form. Strangest of all, and it was something that no person in that village would ever forget, was that the young lady in front of them was breathing.

One look from Gren, himself badly injured with a broken arm and a gash down the other was enough to send him yelling for his companions. "Venla," He cried out loud, "bring Jani here at once! There is something that he must witness!"

Normally one to let grief take its course, Venla did not want to disturb the parents of the late mistress, but something in Gren's voice was enough to send her running. In moments she was leading a still-shocked Jani back to the scene of what had been a dastardly crime. The man was still shell-shocked by the events of the day. He had fought as fiercely as anyone, weeping with tears as he had been forced to kill mercenaries that had been trying to kill him. It would have stood against everything he had ever known as a traveller, but for the fact that he was saving his daughter. All for nothing it seemed. When Jani saw Mavra lying there amidst the rubble, he ran to her. "It is good seeing her back, and looking so calm." He gently brushed the cheek of his eldest, and then pulled his hand away as if he had burned it.

"What is it, Jani?" Venla asked, confused by his reaction.

"Her face, it is warm." Jani looked up at them. "What sort of devilry is this? First my daughter takes up the sword, something which no traveller let alone a girl has ever done. Then when we battle she gets killed, and in the middle of our grief she is stolen from us only to be returned and bewitched. I do not want my daughter's warm corpse! I want all of this to have never happened. I want my daughter back!"

"And you have her," said a weak voice from behind him.

Jani's eyes widened, and the villagers gasped. He turned back around to see his daughter looking up at him, and struggling to rise. "Oh my Mavra!" Jani swept her up in an embrace that left both of them weeping, tears streaming down their faces. More than one of the villagers joined in seeing the raw emotion on the face of the traveller. "I thought you had gone for good. I have no idea what happened."

"I do." Mavra did not disengage herself from her father's arms, but instead gave herself a little room to breathe. "I was taken from here to a place that was inhabited by beings of supreme power and skill. There I was healed and sent back with a message: 'Be strong, the darkest days are not yet upon us'."

"Healed by who?" Her father asked.

"Mavra! Oh my sweet daughter how can this be?" Ramaji, very much out of her stupor hurtled through the press of people and hugged her daughter tight. Tears flowed freely once again as everybody celebrated, and it was some time before the standing question could be answered.

Finally pushing her mother to arm's length so that she had some space, Mavra answered. "Who else could it have been? The beautiful light, the magic that healed me. It could only have been the Gods that have touched me."

"Truly?" Asked one of the villagers, a farmer named Ralf. "You were truly touched by the Gods?"

"What other reason could there possibly be?" Mavra replied. "Who else could have done this?"

"The wizards, who are our allies," answered Handel. "They are responsible for this, as I have just been told."

"Told by whom?" Demanded Ramaji, who was willing to counter the word of any who spoke against her daughter, only recently returned. Passion ruled reason and she was far from reasonable. It was understandable though, and Handel took no umbrage from her tone.

"By the wizard that healed you."

"And how is it that he cannot speak to the rest of us?"

"It is difficult to speak, and easier to observe," said a voice out of thin air, "but perhaps the time has come for me to reveal a little of what is happening to you all."

The villagers looked around, seeking the source of the voice. "Please, be still," it said. "My name is Obrett Pedern and I am a wizard. I am in a place you cannot reach but where near miracles can be performed. You have to trust that I am watching over you all, as there is a great deal at stake. Please listen as this is taxing. The mercenaries you defeated are as nothing. The army that will rise would dwarf this like a tree to a blade of grass. They will be armed not only with warriors, but possibly wizards of their own."

"What are we going to do against magic?" Cried out one woman.

"We also have wizards lending aid to our cause." Obrett replied. "They are hastening towards the plains even as we speak. There is always hope my friends. Look towards Mavra D'Voss, for she is a special hope. She was worth risking attention. Follow her example, and serve the Old Law in the way it needs you best at the moment. Defend your homeland until aid arrives. Seek out the villages that have yet been spared, and defend them too. A darkness arises even as I speak, and too soon it will hang over us like a stifling blanket. This is where the fight to defend what is good and right begins. Always remember that. Individual villages and farmsteads are alone no more. You are a rare breed, that of a free people. Tyranny will hunt you like a wolf and you must elude it. My friends and I will do what we can, but until then look to the tribe for aid. They know of our wishes. I bid you farewell. I am watching over you." The last sentence faded out as an entire village of stunned people stood amidst the wreckage of the barn.

"Well, you heard the man," said Ralf, "this is not over yet. I suggest that we go get ourselves some swords."

"Perhaps not," Handel intervened, "for a lot of the success was from the long-reaching weapons that you made from your farming tools. The mercenaries could not get near you long enough to do any damage."

"That will not always be the case my friend." Jaden looked at the motley crew of would-be warriors. "These mercenaries are driven by a force that we cannot underestimate. The moment that we do, we will lose." He looked around at the gathered villagers. "Have any of you ever fired an arrow from a bow?"

Initially nobody replied, but then a couple of men stepped forward. "We hunted a couple of times," said one, and received gasps of shock and outrage for his candidness. "What? It was only a couple of times, and these men need to know the truth."

"That is right," Handel agreed. "The time for secrecy and dishonesty is long past. If we are to survive we need to know of every skill you have, legal or not, moral or not. In order to preserve the Old Law, we might have to go as far against its tenets as any apparent follower has ever done, but in the end we shall prevail.

"Will we, truly?" Asked one slight doubter.

"Truly, we will, "Handel stood tall and smiled, something he had never done before, "For ours is a noble cause, and we have powers beyond that of the enemy. We have hope, and we have faith. We have a reason to stand against anything, and we have magic on our side to back us up."

"If it ever gets here." One person was heard to mutter, but the rest of the villagers cheered, reinforced in their beliefs by the tale of the invisible wizard.

Maolmordha watched the distant crowd, scanning it for any sign of the wizard that had escaped her master. She was sure the filthy rat was amidst them. She had heard his voice, witnessed his magic as he had stirred up the wind. Any fool for leagues around would be able to taste the tang of a focus in the air, and it seeped into her through every pore. Maolmordha shared her master's distaste for focussing. Maolnemrhyth on the other hand had never acquired such a distaste, and observed the gathering dispassionately. This was the student's first test. To be placed yet again within proximity of those that had once been most loved, and to see how she would react. So far nothing adverse had shown. Perhaps the magic of the Golem was as strong as it had once been for her.

"What do you feel?" She sent the thought into the minds of both people, but the question was obviously intended for her student.

"I feel nothing," was the reply. "If there is a wizard down there, then he is shielding himself, or is too subtle to be sensed by others." That was not what Maolmordha had meant, but she took that as a positive answer. She had been testing for any sign of an emotive memory driven by the proximity of those that had once been very dear to the figure clad in black beside her. It appeared that the focus was doing its work well. Glancing over at the man who called himself Thrasher, a stupid name at best, she caught him leering at her once more. She glanced down at herself as she looked away. It was true that she had blossomed into what many would call a beautiful woman, but she cared not for the shape of her body. It was the will of her master that dominated her, and the magic of the Golem that gave her such power and control. "You," she said aloud, "what do you think?"

Thrasher turned his attention from her and looked to the distant crowd; they were hidden behind bushes on the crest of a hill that was close enough for them to observe unnoticed, for that was their way. "I think, mistress, that those idiots down there killed a lot of my men and should be sent on their merry way just as soon as we can get down there and run spears through their chests."

"Fool, this is about more than your useless mercenary bands running into a trap."

"Is it? Well if O'Bellah had sent the bands I asked for this would not have happened."

"Silence," Maolmordha hissed in what came as close to anger as her subdued emotions could muster.

"No woman, I don't think so. You asked for my opinion, well you got it. We need decent bands doing this sort of work, not some ragtag group of. . ." Thrasher broke off into a fit of choking. Maolnemrhyth watched as her teacher released a thread of emotive magic, causing his throat to lock up in fear. In an instant the man became so terrified, so desperate to continue his own miserable existence that he dropped to his knees, supplicant and obedient.

"You will witness your vision if you wait patiently. If you burst out when we should be observing again, I will not cease this flow." In saying that, the thread of magic stopped. Maolnemrhyth knew that her teacher had paid a terrible price to cast even that tiny spell, losing a bit more of herself to the Golem. The price to pay must have been worth it, for suddenly the big man seemed that much smaller. "I will do as you wish, mistress," he replied, his eyes full of a fear that was dreadful to behold, for his fear should have remained private but instead it was written on his face for all to see. That was the kind of hold evil had over anybody. Too easily were they ensnared.

"Yes, you shall do as I wish," she replied, her eyes flashing at him in the light of the day. "You shall have your army of mercenaries, but you shall not lead them. Your path lies with us now. You shall be known as Maolgatot, and be the third of our group. In that way we will be able to travel faster. We are no longer needed here. Our master has other plans for us."

If any further outburst was forthcoming, Thrasher hid it well. Only a slight tightening of his eyes gave anything away. He would not take any of this lying down. Maolnemrhyth looked at her teacher, and a simple meaning was conveyed between the two. *"This is dangerous. I am aware that I had a life before this, but I am also aware that magic will change me, make me stronger. This man has no such preconceptions."*

In a rare moment of agreement, Maolmordha looked at the darkened hood of her student and agreed with her. *"You have a valuable insight, my student. And you are right, but we have no choice. Our master commands this and through the Golem he controls us, therefore letting us know his needs. This man thinks with a man's thoughts, has a man's urges. If he cannot be controlled, he will be killed and we shall find another third."*

The fact that they had been communicating without sound was not lost on Thrasher. He was a shrewd man despite his bulk and rough exterior, and he knew that he had a better chance of survival with this woman and her child than he did with the failing camp of O'Bellah. Always one to take a chance, he knew that he had made the right choice but this lack of inclusion annoyed him. "When are you going to include me in your silent speech?"

"When you are able, and willing," came the short reply.

"I am willing now, and more than able to listen to a few silent words."

"ARE YOU? ARE YOU SURE?" The words exploded into his mind with the force of an anvil, sending pain searing through his head. Thrasher, or Maolgatot threw out an ear-piercing scream as the words echoed around his mind. He had not been prepared for that. He dropped to his knees and vomited, tears streaming down his face as he emptied his stomach. He grabbed onto his head to stop it from exploding, for that was surely what it was about to do.

"You are not ready for our communion yet, you primitive excuse for a man. See how those few words almost render you unconscious. You had better learn that when I speak to you, then you reply. Otherwise you will suffer the same agony."

Maolgatot looked up into the face of fear, the source of pain, and nodded weakly. He was suddenly a lot less sure of himself, and the failing mercenary camp suddenly seemed a better choice. He could not go back though; something was keeping him here, something magnetic. He looked up and saw the power behind the beautiful woman in front of him, and the cruelty that gave it a jagged edge. Of all the places he had been, finally here on this grassy hill had he found the kindred spirit he had never before sought. She would be his. He would find a way to make her his own, and then the world would tremble at their passing. He had no idea who her master was except that he was in some way related to what O'Bellah was doing, but at this moment he did not care.

Noise alerted him, and he stood next to this remarkable woman, this new obsession. "They come."

"They will not catch us," she replied, "we run now. Nothing can stop that. We go where we are needed. We go to hunt us a wizard." Her words were true, for by the time any of the villagers reached their hiding place, all that was left were a few imprints in the ground, and no tracks. Unknowingly, the villagers turned away, oblivious to the fact that for a moment, they had stood on the brink of death under a cloud of utter sorrow.

Chapter Eighteen

Every springtime the city of Bay's Point erupted in a display of gaudy appreciation of the season's changing. The latitude meant that the festival was held much nearer to the longest day than it would have been had the city been down nearer the southern coasts. The temperature did not detract from the lavish displays put on by all in the city. There was colour on every street. Would-be criminals danced and mingled with their intended victims as all crime was put on hold for this one day, and food was distributed wherever possible. Much of the gaiety was paid for by a fund called the 'Duke's Levy', which came from the city taxes. It was a magnanimous gesture by a rare Duke named Beswetheric, some time in the past. Aside from being a pirate, he knew the value of loyal men and his gesture had been returned in kind. From that point onwards the gesture had become as traditional as the festival. Only once had a Duke tried to withhold the money given out so generously, and the carnage that had followed had threatened to reduce the city to the state those once vengeance-seeking flotillas of ships had done. So it was that Ju found himself strolling through streets clogged with banners and ribbons. A city normally so bleak and dark had erupted into a bloom to rival the best of flowers. He reasoned that they must have warehouses full of the stuff. What it did do was provide him all manner of places in which to pass unobserved, especially in the guild area, which seemed over-decorated. Barely was there a single part of any building visible. "Such is their wealth." He said to himself. Ju appreciated the accumulation of wealth. As he had done much accumulating himself, he had begun to appreciate it even more. Then the dream came with Zya, and he remembered his promise and how temporary this actually was. He had cast off any trappings that would make him stick out, and except for his bow he carried not a thing. The ostentation around him drove Zya's point home. These people did not appreciate the difference outside of their walls. Whoever it was that O'Bellah was working for would reduce the world outside to nothing and these people would probably live on in ignorant bliss. Thus was he charged with getting into the mercenary guild to try and find out what was going on. The message had been delivered to Tarim, Lorn and Darrow, the latter uncharacteristically subdued when he heard that he would finally get his wish. It seemed that the warning he had received to save his fellows had been taken very seriously, and now he knew that the time was almost at hand. Lorn and Tarim had simply closed the carpentry, leaving it to passers-by to witness a shop boarded up and nothing more. It was not uncommon in a city of this size; the nomads respected privacy. On hearing what Zya had asked Ju to do, Tarim had said one thing.

"Be careful," he had said with one hand laid atop the young boy's shoulder.

"Know that we sail on the evening tide boy, and we cannot wait for anybody," Darrow had added. "There is more afoot here than anybody can guess perhaps, and we are leaving. You know the place from which we sail. The tide will turn one hour after sunset, and we shall sail at that time and no later. We shall only make one stop before we leave Bay's Point."

"I will be there," Ju had replied, and that was the last timet he had seen his foster family. They all knew enough about what was going on to act swiftly and decisively, but they did not know, could not know as much as he had shared with Zya during their dreams. Thinking about it distracted him from the chore at hand, and he almost found himself wandering in front of a party of well-armed men. If they saw him they did not notice, for they were swaying with the awkward gait of those already too far in their cups. A chime sounded, and it was the ringing of the bell. From the count he had been keeping, it was four watches until sunset, five until the ships sailed from the underground refuge of the pirates. He had to get busy.

Stepping out boldly behind another crowd of people in the guild quarter he found himself blending in wit ease as there were as many children, all of differing ages, as there were adults. Even better for him was the fact that they seemed to be heading near to the great grey monolith of the mercenary guild. He loitered around the back of the group, looking for all intensive purposes like the bedraggled elder child who just could not be bothered to keep up. He studied the children in front of him. Some were quiet, others eager. Several had tears streaming down their faces but none were speaking. The adults were all grim-faced, even the women though they tried to maintain the party atmosphere. It was obviously false to Ju, but there were enough drunks around to make it look convincing. As they approached the mercenary guild they made a beeline for the great entrance doors. The only concession to the gaiety of the day had been to put a few maroon ribbons up around the door, but the fact that it stood wide open was fact enough that something was different. Pleased enough that his job had been made easy, he stayed close to the group.

"Remember, if you are to get anything out of your lives you should be like the people within these walls," one particularly grizzled man said to a couple of the children.

"But papa, what if we don't want to go?" Asked one small boy.

"Don't speak nonsense boy!" The man replied, half-moving to cuff his son around the head. This was met with a huge flinch from the child, obviously the recipient of more of those in the past. "These are the best fighting men in the Duchy, and they are taking comers of all ages to train in their ways. It is a better life that you can live once you have discipline and training to back you up. It made me the man I am today." If this man who was so full of himself impressed the children, they did not show it. Ju certainly did not like him. A bully he was, and Ju had seen his type time and again back as far as he could remember. This man had nothing but personal gain on his mind. The plot thickened. Ju remained close as he passed doors that he had previously never been allowed through, even as a trusted message carrier. None of the usual guards were evident, and certainly none of the challenges from boisterous mercenaries. In fact the further Ju walked, the more he was certain that something was up. The guild had been positively bulging with mercenaries to the point that certain rooms were packed wall to wall with particular mercenary bands. There was space now, and a sort of serene tranquillity about the place. That lasted until they reached what Ju assumed was the core of the guild. Doors bigger than the main entrance stood slightly ajar, impressive in their decoration, covered from top to toe with beaten gold. From within came martial chants and shouts of varying degrees. It was through the crack in the doors that they were all headed. Ju was intrigued and instead of breaking off and hiding as he had thought to do, he stayed with them, for this room was obviously the focal point of whatever was occurring. The family entered the room and Ju tucked in behind the father. When he peeked around the side of the family he could see that they were not alone. There were between two and three score of them watching a group of men in the square at the centre of the room. The group he recognised immediately. They were called Gnang's Black Marauders, and were amongst the more well known of the mercenary bands. Gnang himself stood off to one side, a broad-shouldered man with a love for chain mail. He wore it on his head and had it draped about his body, almost forming a dress as it dropped to the floor. He carried it easily for all of the weight, and would have dwarfed Darrow had he stood next to him. The band was dressed in identical uniforms, the only difference being in the marks of grade and experience, ribbons pinned to one shoulder. Word had it that many of the marauders had been in the band for twenty seasons or more, and had become vastly rich on the spoils of war. It was not enough though, and it was evident. Many a hungry gleam came from the men in the middle of the room. They were not done yet with their warring.

"Square! Break!" Bellowed Gnang in his Kimarullian accent, a musical voice that sounded deceptively meek for all that it was shouted out. The men responded swiftly, breaking formation and reordering themselves into a phalanx with shields slung impossibly quick and razor-sharp swords whisked out with a chorus of steely rasps. It was an imposing sight, and many of the younger children stepped back behind their parents at being presented with the tips of swords. Ju chose this moment to step around the hall a bit to try and get a better view. He carefully wove his way through the crowd, working his way back to a rise where he could see.

"Come now my friends," entreated a particularly smooth and melodic voice, "do not be afraid of men such as this. They are what we all aspire to become, the pinnacle of training and education, of war and of peace. These men would not harm a hair on a boy's head, but for the battles they fight so righteously. Come see for yourselves."

Ju climbed up the base of a column with good footholds to see who was speaking. A large man stood from the table at the front of the hall, and from the connection he shared with Zya, he knew immediately that it was O'Bellah. This was not the man described to him though. Instead of the bully in armour stood a man in robes doing his best to appear kind and reassuring. It was obvious from his bearing that he was neither, but the forced façade was fooling just about everybody else. There was something in the air, something dark. Magic was being used; Ju would have put money on it. Hesitantly, one and then a few more of the children walked forward, to push at a sword or touch a shield. The marauders held themselves rigidly straight, only making sure the children did not cut their fingers. In Ju's opinion they *looked* like they wanted to cut the children to ribbons, but he was sure that he was the only person noticing this. While the sword-feel was going on, O'Bellah had turned from the crowd and was conferring with Gnang, another man, and a buxom blonde lady who looked as though she would rather be somewhere else. In fact she was dressed more for court than for a mercenary guild. Ju thought he recognised her, but he could not make out her face from so far away. What did stand out was that she played with a blue jewel around her neck constantly. She seemed afraid to let go of it.

"If you would be kind enough to stand off to one side, we shall show you more of the things you will be learning as part of the guild of educated warriors." O'Bellah announced grandly. Ju decided to move, but found that the spot he had vacated had now been filled as many more families brought their children into the hall. The chamber was packed with them, and Ju had no idea where they had come from. They looked like the dregs of humanity, and as he watched the parents he realised that he had seen some of them before. A man with one arm and no hair caught his attention, and he realised that he had seen the man begging on street corners. The man had two boys with him, both younger than Ju by appearances. "He has a family?" Ju whispered to himself. As he looked around now he recognised more of them from his street capers. They had all brought children with them, all sharing the gaunt, half-starved look that they portrayed. Ju was moved almost to tears that their begging was the only means of providing welfare for their young. The people around him did not share his moment of emotion; their attention was fixed on the unfolding spectacle in front of them. A variety of men entered from a side door, each bowing ritually and intoning a different phrase. The murmur was such that Ju could not hear the words properly but some sounded like 'Raessa', or 'Ciaharr', if they had been spoken strangely. What did vary was their size, which varied from huge men, almost giants to small men, boyish in appearance but for their scraggly beards and shoulders that were too broad for any child. It appeared that all had been considered for this band, which was unlike any Ju had ever seen before.

"The men in front of you will now perform the Stance of Life, a series of moves designed to protect." O'Bellah's voice rang false with every word that dripped from his acid tongue, and Ju wanted none of it. The rest of the crowd was totally taken in by the spectacle, and murmured in amazement as the gathered men in front of them shifted into different patterns of sinuous movements. Each time they moved it was in direct response to a word shouted by a leather-clad man with his hair tied in braids. He was obviously related to the men, partway between the biggest and smallest, but showing the traits of both. These were not a local people. The hall was silent in response to the strange shouts and smoothly flowing responses. The commands were less recognisable than the shouts by the fighters, and only understandable by just those people. As he watched them, it became obvious to Ju that these were no longer just another brand of mercenaries. This was a closely-knit group of deadly killers who did not even have to use weapons to kill. The families observed from all sides, but it was not the loudly voiced man that Ju found himself watching, but another man that sat quietly in the midst of O'Bellah and the various mercenary leaders. He raised his hand and the braided man called in the unintelligible language an order that must have meant 'stop'.

"Now is the time for you to come and try my friends." O'Bellah said invitingly as he forced a warm smile to his lips of ice. "For you too can be one of these magnificent warriors, that dance across the floor to protect their friends from their enemies. You will one day be able to dance the dance, and save the city. Come now, and try."

This time the children did not need asking. It was obvious that from whatever bewitchment O'Bellah had used before, the spell had been magnified. The robed man next to him had not moved, but under his clothes his hands gripped something spherical, and his mouth moved in near-silent whispers under his tightly fitting hood. Ju leaned back against the wall, and his bow got in the way for once. Reaching back to adjust it, as soon as his hand came in contact with the wood Ju was given an electrifying contact. His awareness magnified, and he felt and almost saw the power coming from the shadowed man and surrounding the families, the children especially. He tried to shrink down in case anybody else could feel him sensing the wizard, but everybody was looking at the children and their awkward attempts at the fighting stances of the foreigners. Removing his hand from his bow, Ju took another look around. Nothing had changed, and the class went on. He tried it once more, and without the element of surprise he watched as the power spread out from what was surely a focus stone. The object was clear in the eldritch vision that was granted him, a focus stone that was tiny but powerful in the hands of the wizard at the front of the hall. Ju recalled what Zya had told him in the almost-distant past. His bow and her dagger had a connection, but what it was they did not know. Zya had been rid of the compulsion that had been lain upon her when she received the weapon, but no such magics had been performed on Ju. He wore the bow that once he had used to kill a deer as if it were a part of his body, another limb perhaps, but this was the first time that it had been of any use to him since that day. On an impulse he removed the bow from his shoulder, feeling a keen pang of loss at doing so. This was too important. He looked at the weapon. It was still shiny as if brand new, with its recurved wood and horned tips gently holding the string taut. He had never unstrung it, nor had he any inclination to do so now. Something told him that it would make no difference and he liked to be prepared. All the time he held it he witnessed the world through different eyes, and wondered if this was how Zya saw it when she was focussing. In the distance a bell tolled, and this brought Ju back to his senses. How was he to escape from the middle of a great hall of warriors without being seen? The bell tolling must have been at least one watch since the last, and the time he had left to find out for Zya what was actually going on here was running short. He had to get information and get out, and then make it all the way across town to the underground wharf, and that was *before* the ships sailed. Shifting in his place near the column, Ju decided to make for the door and trust to luck.

411

It was at that time the well-dressed blonde-haired woman stood up. "Come call out to me, my children. Show me how you would shout at those that tried to get your mothers and fathers." Oddly, Ju found himself turning around and wanting to call out, just as more and more children did. Ju retained enough concentration and self-possession to reach behind and touch his bow once more. The air cleared, and he saw a vastly different sight. It was not the beautiful duchess that stood before him but a woman whose clothes fit too tightly around her over-ample frame, causing her midriff to stick out in several places where fat rippled through. Her chin hung in several loose jowls, and she had put much too much make up on. Ju was amazed, but he could see the magic being directed from the wizard. He was the source to it all but she was the one encouraging the children to reciprocate, and he could see something going out of them and towards the wizard. To make things worse the fighters returned, and added their howling to the noise. Even the parents of the children that had stepped forward were adding their yells to the cacophony. Ju was afraid to put his hands over his ears, as he did not want to lose the only thing keeping his mind clear. He saw this time as the best opportunity to make a break as the attention of all the other people were focussed on the scene in front. He backed away from the family he had followed in and edged his way around the hall, his back to the wall and his eyes fixed on the howling mass in front of him. He reached a point in the hall where the people ahead of him were no longer visible, hidden as they were by all of the columns and buttresses. Ju breathed a sigh of relief, and wiped the perspiration from his young forehead with his free hand. Before he knew what was occurring, he felt himself being yanked backwards. A bony hand clamped over his mouth and he could feel the bones in the narrow fingers keeping his yells in. He gave up struggling very quickly when it became apparent that he was getting nowhere, and found that he had been drawn into another room. This did not match the splendour of the rest of the inner guild, and was instead lit by a series of smoky candles. The wooden walls were rough and uneven, and there were crates scattered about, gnawed into splinters by generations of flea-infested vermin. It was onto one of these crates that Ju was carefully placed. Ensuring that he was still quiet, his captor manoeuvred around him so that his face was visible in the flickering shadows. Making a motion with his free hand that implied caution, he warned the young boy. When he saw who it was, he nodded his head, and the man removed his hand. Moving his head in several different directions to check that his neck had not been injured in the event, Ju took stock of his surroundings. "Foster, what are you doing in here? In fact where is here?"

The man known as Foster sat down on a crate against the opposite wall. Foster the guard had once been one of the few fellows within the mercenary guild that Ju had almost gone as far as to be fond of. A member of a small band of mercenaries known as Torquil's McDougalls, he had been one of an elite few that had actually guarded the guild itself. Normally a man with a barrel chest and a hearty laugh, he looked as gaunt as Ju had ever remembered him. It was clear that he had not eaten in quite a while. His face was unshaven and patchy, his eyes hollow with fatigue and worry. He had lost his smile.

Foster leaned forward to minimise the sound he would make, and Ju leaned in also. "You have seen with your own eyes what is going on out there, boy. It ain't right I tell you, it ain't right not at all, boy. Have you seen all that they have to show you boy? They got monsters running around this place. Flipping MONSTERS!"

"Are you sure that is what you saw?" Ju was normally one to take a man at his word, but he had seen no such creatures.

"They have got men the size of boys who fight like demons, boy. They have got men twice the size of normal men who can pick you up and crush you with their bare hands. They have got wizards, boy. It ain't natural. Ain't natural at all. Worst off, they got some great hulking creature that prowls the halls, well the halls it can fit through at any rate. I have been safe in here as it can't fit inside."

"Why are you in here at all?" Ju asked, as this was the question that perplexed him most of all. "What happened to your band of mercenaries?"

"They have gone. Gone to some place through some kind of doorway. They touched the creature and went through. I wasn't going to have none of that, but they was hunting down all the mercenaries as wasn't going along with the plan and forcing them to go or outright killing them. It all came down to what the man who led them wanted, the one as calls himself 'O'Bellah'. Boy, I have been a mercenary for more years than you have lived, and I have never seen nothing like this." Foster leaned back, clearly miserable.

Ju had not moved an inch. This was what he supposed Zya had sent him to the guild for. "I would like to hear what happened, Foster."

Foster smiled. "I bet you would at that, boy. Back in the day, me and Boulter joined up for the chance to make a decent wage, the type of wage that someone without many hopes could only earn by stealing. Me and Boulter, we had standards. We had dreams. One day we would both retire and run farms next door to each other in a village someplace. Oh we found many villages that looked just right for us, full of comely wenches." As he said this, he looked at Ju and cut himself short. Ju wondered what it was about comely wenches that he did not already know that Foster would not speak about, but he did not press it. "Anyway, we had found many a place as would suit us, and plenty of gold to buy the rest of our lives comfortably when we were taken off of the road and given the honour of guarding the guild. Now you have been here as much as any person not of the guild, so I am guessing you knows your way about. Eighteen months we been guarding this place, and the stories we heard would keep you from sleeping, lad. Very nearly has had me awake for days on end. Stories we heard about people losing their souls and such. Terrible stories where the bands as have passed through here have been rapin' and stealin', and murdering people by staking them. Just like the bloody Night of Spears and everything boy! Like a bloody nightmare come true. Well the worst starts to happen when this here O'Bellah turns up out of nowhere. Now we've been told from up on high that we got to be real accommodating and the like to him, so we let him have the run of the mill, so to speak. He comes and goes, sometimes not appearing for ages. He is nothing special to us. But then all of a sudden things changed. He starts appearing with other mercenaries, men and bands that we have never heard of, savages from far away. Except they got the look of military men. There are those as are clearly in command, and they won't speak to any but their men. We might as well not exist as far as they are concerned. They bring other bands of mercenaries in here as I have heard of, but we never get to come into here, into the heart of our guild. Now I have seen why. One day, they call us in, into the very room I dragged you from."

Ju looked over at the wall. There was a door there, but there had been no sign of a door on the other side.

"How did I get here? Well I shall tell you that in a while, lad." Foster reached down to pull at something and chew on it. "Rat," he said around a mouthful, "not nice, but I've eaten far worse in my time, boy."

"That's disgusting," answered Ju, and he rummaged around in a pocket, bringing out a small flask he kept and a dried cake wrapped in paper. "Take these, Foster. I think you need them more than I."

The big guard looked down at the morsels in Ju's hands, and took them carefully. Then he wept. "You don't know what this means, boy. I'm gratefuller than I have ever been for anything."

Ju sat and watched while Foster carefully devoured the cake, swallowing every last crumb. Then he took a few sips of water. "That's the first time in days I felt less than starving." Ju listened for the howling cries of the families beyond the wall. They were still there but they had changed somewhat, becoming shriller in pitch, and also further removed though that could have been because of the wall.

"Anyway we got brought to that room and that there O'Bellah, he says things to us. 'You all got a choice,' he says to us, 'to join us voluntarily, or to suffer the consequences.' Now Boulter and me, we follow orders as well as the next man but the tone in his voice, it was like we had no choice anyway and he was just amusing himself. Well as it happens, me and Boulter be at the back of the room when this is going on. We watched as some of our band 'volunteered'. They stepped up and this Gods-awful great hulking creature turns up out of nowhere. They touch its skin, if it can be called such; looked more like rock to me. Anyway, they touch it, and start screaming! Screaming in such pain as has never been described before. They calm down and the rest of us are practically soiling ourselves about what might happen next. We look towards them, and they just stare back, all blank like. Then O'Bellah whispers something and the creature makes a movement, and suddenly them as have all touched it suddenly come at us, and the fighters block the doorway. Well me and Boulter, we know the guild inside and out, like. We knew of these here tunnels. Makes the place right like a rabbit's warren it does. We slipped into a hidey-hole that we knew of, and waited for the commotion to die down. 'Slip into the tunnels', he says, 'and I'll hide the way'. Well Boulter was always senior to me, so I took his orders without question and just as I was out of the way and hidden they came into the hole and got him. I watched from the darkness. They took him right up to the creature and threw him against it. He screamed as if there were no tomorrow, almost split the walls and shattered the windows. Well there was nothing that I could do to help him. He was a lost soul to be sure, and he had ordered me to hide. I was only following orders."

As he said this, Ju realised that it was the one truth that he was clinging to. It was the one thing allaying his guilt at not helping his friend. Beyond it all was the overpowering stench of evil coming from the creature nearby. The evil, the darkness that had been ever encroaching from the East, it was now here. Ju could feel the presence of it under his very feet. It was not just the evil that had arrived, but a sense of loss, of hopelessness, of utter desolation. The time had come to leave the mercenary guild, certainly for good. "Is there any way out of these tunnels?"

"Sure there is, if you got the guts to take the long walk outta here." Foster showed no sign of the inner fear that had blighted him since he had taken Ju from the hall. "Problem occurs when you cross one of the main corridors, the place where most of these fighters and monsters gather close to the black creature. These tunnels are a maze if you get disoriented but to the canny man they are much, much easier. Just don't turn off the path no matter what, and you shall reach the hallway. If you can get across without being seen, get into the tunnel on the other side and you are home free. It runs parallel to another tunnel that the Duchess uses."

"That's where I have seen her before!" Ju exclaimed. "She is the Duchess Deborah, formerly the Lady Langley, mistress of one of the biggest brothels in the city."

"How do you know of brothels, boy?" Foster asked with a disapproving stare.

Ju grinned cheekily. "The people I have been running messages and errands for do not always live in palaces and guilds. I have been all over this city. I know that the Duke spied Lady Langley when returning from a hunting trip, and word has it that she bewitched him with her umm. . . skills."

Foster shook his head in disbelief. "In my day, children were innocent. It is sad that is no longer the case."

"When you have lived most of your life in the courtyard of an inn, innocence is an overrated thing." Ju replied, wise beyond his years, and still fuelled by the contact with his bow, and by default Zya's essence.

"Perhaps you are right, boy," Foster conceded. "But anyways, that Duchess. Right strange creature she is, always traipsing in and out of here like she owns the place and only ever talking to that O'Bellah. Foul as they are they make a fouler couple, for I am sure that words are not all they are exchanging." Foster had evidently taken Ju at his word with regards to his lack of innocence, and spoke to him man to man instead of man to boy. "She has her own agenda though. If I were to think long and hard I would probably say that she is trying to do away with her husband and get someone else in there. I don't wish the tunnel to the palace on anybody though."

"Why not?"

"Coz they are bound to have it guarded tonight of all nights, what with the feast and all. You would be foolish to go there, boy."

"Maybe," Ju replied, "but it is there that I have to go. I have a friend there, a friend who will need me to help her tonight of all nights. Will you come with me?"

Foster chuckled. "Why would you want the help of an over-the-hill guard who sells himself for gold?"

"Because you are worth more than that. You have a sense of honour in what you do, and intent rules a man even if the outcome doesn't."

Foster stared at him hard for a moment, as if deciding something. "Boy, you got a real strange way with words," he said finally, "but they are most often the right words. Ol' Boulter would never forgive me if I were to sit here and rot like a rat in a trap without trying to carry on." He stood, and motioned Ju behind him as he grabbed at a torch. Walking into the gloom of the tunnels Ju at first became wary, listening hard for the screaming which had died away so suddenly. His fear was quelled by two things at once. First came the realisation that he had no other choice but to reach Zya, for the hour was too late and he would never have reached the other side of the city let alone the underground wharves of the pirates. The second source of calm came from Foster himself, as he sang in a low, mournful voice:

> *Legends from the fields afar*
> *Speak of battles fought*
> *With death our foe and honour our quest*
> *And gold the prize most sought.*
>
> *Bravery and scars abounding*
> *Our quests are long and cold*
> *With hearts so full yet minds so empty*
> *Our journeys become tall stories told.*
>
> *Hail the Golden Grail of Freedom*
> *It is to you we sing this dirge*
> *Though our lives are forfeit to the quest*
> *We cannot resist its urge.*
>
> *A vein of rock to blind our eyes -*
> *A wealth of metal to trade and store*
> *In blood-soaked earth our prize awaits us*
> *Beneath the weeping fields of war.*
>
> *Hail the Golden Grail of Freedom*
> *Hear our songs of mind and heart*
> *While into myth our journeys fade -*
> *A time when man and gold must part.*

They rounded a corner to a long tunnel as Foster finished. He stopped for a moment, smiling. "The hymn of our Mercenary band." He said aloud, answering the unprompted question. "Me and Boulter used to sing it so loud before we would go out. It always inspired the rest, and now I am all that's left of a once-proud band of mercenaries."

"It was a good song," Ju replied, not knowing what else to say.

"It was the best," Foster agreed, "but it shall be sung no more. Let us go."
Foster led Ju out through the tunnel, and then looked behind him and paused.
"Run, boy!" He whispered urgently. "Run, and don't look back!"
Ju did not need telling twice in this dark and forbidding place, and ran as fast
as his legs would carry him. He heard the footfalls of Foster behind him, but
the malnourished man gradually started to drop back as he weakened. Much
further back, a roar of anger erupted from a side tunnel as a knot of the
fighters Ju had seen in the hall caught sight of them. Pausing for nothing more
than a bizarre-sounding war cry, they gave chase. For all their fighting skills
and vocal prowess, they did not run very fast or very well. The simple motion
of running did not seem to fit in with the delicate balances they had attained
when showing off their skills, and they fell behind even Foster's ragged flight.
As he saw this, Foster began to jeer at them and they yelled back. The language
may have been different, but the inflections and gestures were the same. Ju bet
that the fighters were saying some very unsavoury things about them. One
thing this did not serve was to make the fighters run any faster. They simply
could not keep up.
"Quick, down here!" Foster whispered, and pulled Ju down a side passage.
Not stopping, Ju looked over at the guard. "I thought that you said the way
was straight there?"
"It is, but I would say that we have a better chance of reaching it by another
route, would you not agree, boy?"
Ju looked back, down the hallway that was now dark, with only their fleeting
torchlight to guide them. The brand began to splutter and Foster simply
reached into the darkness and pulled a fresh torch from somewhere. "I think
you know best, Foster," he agreed.
Foster grunted an acknowledgement. "When we reach the end of this tunnel,
there is a courtyard of sorts, and the doorway we will exit through will lead
outside of the guild. It is as likely to be guarded as the route we would have
taken, but we have no choice now. All we have left to us is the hope that they
think we are still fleeing down the main passage. When we get outside, cross
the courtyard towards the Ducal Palace, and look behind the loosely stacked
pile of crates. There is a little rat-hole that a skinny youngster such as yourself
should squeeze into easily. I might be a bit more of a problem, but we shall just
have to risk it. I might even make it through if your feast hasn't given me my
gut back."
Ju looked up and saw that Foster was smiling. There was still a bit of the
kindly mercenary he had once known left there. "What if you can't get
through?" he asked, scared to be alone.

"Well, I have been hunting gold all of my life, lad. Maybe it is time I hunted honour as well. My sword has been ever sharp in service, and a guard's duty has not dulled my blade. Quiet yourself now, young Ju, for we are nearly there."

The two fugitives crept forward silently now, listening for any sign that they were not alone. The tension pressed around them as much as the darkness threatened to, and both were only held back by the light of the torch. They reached a dead end and Foster looked back, maintaining a silent vigil. Eventually he decided that nobody was following them, and turned to Ju. "This is the door to the outside, boy. From here we will need to cross the courtyard and get to the crates on the other side. Walk quickly, but do not run. We may well get away with this yet."

Foster swung open a door that protested at its use with the shriek of rusty hinges, and Foster cursed. "Bittersweet luck, boy. We are on the wrong side of the guild. Let us pray to those good Gods above that it has helped us more than hindered, for surely it has done both."

"Be careful out here, Foster," Ju warned in reply, "there is something nearby that is too wrong for words." When the mercenary looked at him in puzzlement, he shrugged his shoulders. "I know some things that maybe I should not."

Foster accepted him at his word and led the way out. They were behind a neatly stacked pile of wood in a side alley. With his finger to his lips, Foster led them out into the street. The party was just getting into full swing as merchants hurried home to dress in their finery, and people wandered already intoxicated through the streets of the guild quarter. They emerged in front of the guild a mere stones throw from the spot Zya had collapsed at, judging by Lorn's description. Ju spared a thought for the fisherman, and hoped he was safely on board. Listening to the talk, there was nothing about a flotilla of escaping ships so it seemed that everything had gone without a hitch. Ju brought his mind back to the present, and his stomach dropped. He was walking in exactly the same place he had once dreamed of. The people stood to one side were exactly the same, and the merchants arguing up ahead were identical to his dream. An intense feeling of prophecy came over him, as he knew that he was being swept up in events that may yet be beyond his control. For his part, Foster had noticed the change in the boy's demeanour. He had slowed, and had paled visibly. "Come on, boy. This is not gonna help us."

Ju came back to himself and nodded, following the mercenary up the street. He dreaded to look back, but as he changed direction and glanced behind him

Ju saw the horses and cart, driven by the very same moustached man he had seen before. What made Ju the most scared was that he was in front of the cart, whereas he had been behind in the dream. They walked out into the market square, and Ju looked off to his right. There was a gathering by the side of a market stall that led off down the road. A group of perhaps ten men with swords at their sides stood, blank faces aimed towards the middle of the square. It was from them that the uncomfortable feeling nagged Ju. He looked off to his left, and there was the alleyway. "Foster, this is a trap," Ju warned quietly.

"What do you mean boy? We are free!"

"No, we are not," Ju contradicted. "Look around you here. There are men off to the right, and they are about to intercept us. Behind us is a man on a cart, and he is going to try and herd us towards that alleyway off to our left."

As they continued walking across the square, the men moved as if on cue, controlled by something else. Foster turned around and looked straight at the man in the cart, who instantly assumed a pose of indifference. Foster grinned at the man, and then at the blank-faced mercenaries approaching them from across the square. "Boy, listen very carefully. When I tell you, run straight across the square, and then double back around behind those men."

Ju looked up at the guard. His face had melted from the excitement of the escape to a calm, almost serene look. He had obviously come to some inner decision as to his fate. "Foster, what are you going to do?"

"Spring your trap, boy. Remember the hole behind the crates lad. Now go!" Foster pushed Ju into a run, and an instant after yelled out at the top of his voice, "COME GET ME YOU WIZARD SPAWN, YOU SCUM!"

Ju did not look back, but instead did as he was told and sprinted across the square as fast as his feet would take him. Once he reached the obscurity of an alleyway to gather his breath, he looked back. It was his dream, but from a different angle. The man on the cart had indeed angled his team after Foster, abandoning all pretence of being an innocent merchant. The blank-faced mercenaries had broken into a shambling run, some of them attempting to draw swords as they did so. Ju watched in fear as Foster slowed and turned around. He said something quietly, and then shouted it out loud.

"Boulter, what have they done to you?" The words were shouted, but the tone made them sound so quiet that the astonishment in the guard's voice made them sound like a whisper. The mercenaries did not respond with words, but instead increased their run at him. Not for a second did they look towards Ju. Foster did, for just a moment, and his face spoke of an impending battle, one that he might not live through. It was something that Ju could only do one thing about. People around the square were gradually becoming aware that something was going on. A large amount of shouting on a festival night was not unusual, but the present of a troupe of armed mercenaries and a near out of control team of horses and cart in the same place at the same time caused more than a little unrest. People began dodging out of the way of the mercenaries, fleeing the square in all directions. It was exactly what Ju needed. Reaching over his shoulder, Ju grasped his bow with the intention of firing it for the first time in many moons. His quiver slid into view and he notched an arrow without thinking. Just as in his dream he fired at the lead mercenary, who seemed impossibly large as soon as Ju drew a bead on the man. He loosed the arrow, which soared through the air bypassing several fleeing partygoers, who did not even notice the arrow in flight. The arrow arced, and plunged into the back of the lead mercenary. A look of relief passed over Foster's face, and he mouthed the words 'Thank you' at Ju. This served only to give the boy more confidence, and in a moment of inspiration he loosed two more arrows. One hit the man on the cart, causing him to lose control and tip it as the horses tried to bolt. The other hit the front mercenary in the leg causing him to stumble and roll, consequently knocking several of the others down as well. There were only a few mercenaries still running, and Foster led these few into the alleyway with a cry of defiance. Moments later, amidst the screams of confusion and panic throughout the rapidly-emptying square, the clash of sword upon sword rang out from the alley. Ju used this time to make his escape in the direction Foster had indicated. He dodged left and right, running around the fleeing people and using his fast feet to make sure he wasn't pursued. Pretty soon he had rounded the guild, and found himself walking with urgency towards a pile of crates up against a wall. The people around him were either not aware of what had happened back at the square, or had not reached the scene yet so Ju felt fairly safe. Most had fled down other paths, and nobody had noticed a boy dodging in and out of the crowd. He walked around the crates looking for the hole as it had been described, but to his dismay, none was there. Beginning to panic, Ju hurried out and around the crates to the other side. He almost bumped into several people, but by the time they had noticed someone walking a little too close he had made it round there. Again, there was no obvious place for a hole to be concealed. Ju leaned against the wall and reconsidered Foster's words. 'Look behind the loosely packed stack of crates,' the man had said, and he was doing that now. This stack was not loosely piled though; it was just a messy dumping ground for rubbish. Looking askance, he spied another set of crates a bit further down the path. "These must be the wrong ones," he whispered to nobody but himself, and dodged out into the flow of people. Taking no more than a couple of dozen steps made his feet feel as if they were leaden. It was the longest walk of his life. He was afraid to turn around lest the mercenaries be there, but he made the pile of crates with no mishap. Moving carefully around to the side farthest from the square, he examined the wall. There appeared to be a small gap behind one of them, but it involved moving the crate. The large wooden boxes were cumbersome things, and Ju knew that he would have difficulty moving it. Still, he had no choice but to try, and so he shoved himself against the crate. It groaned in protest, much louder than Ju would have wished for in such a public place, and a few people glanced in his direction. He shoved again, and the crate shrieked as wood and metal ground together.

"Here boy, what do you think you are doing?" A loud voice demanded, and a hand clamped down around the back of his neck.

Ju was unable to turn around, but had a good grip on the crate that was only a whisker away from overbalancing. "I dropped something down the back of these crates. It was a coin for my mother on this special night." He tried his most innocent voice and attempted to look around at the man who held him as he tried to look convincing with a face of anguish.

The hand that held him did not relent. "Yeah right you dropped your coin. Guards!! We have a dirty little-sneak thief here! We will sort you out, my boy. Here they come now."

The man turned Ju's head enough so that he could see the guards coming to intercept them. He must have been new to the city; otherwise he would have known that there was a general amnesty on this night of celebration. The 'guards' wore faces with no expression, and marched stiffly towards them. One of them bore an arrow protruding out of his middle, blood seeping down his leg from the wound. There was not even time to panic; the mercenaries would be on them in seconds. Ju did the only thing that he could do. He shifted his weight and toppled the pile of crates. The man holding him released his grip and moved to dive out of the way, and for a split second Ju saw his goal. There was a dark hole low down, at ground level in the wall. He saw his chance and he took it, diving for the hole even as crates began to fall down in every direction. He spared the briefest of moments to peer back at the man who even now was rolling out of the way. The man was dressed in gaudy attire, bright blue finery that was perfectly suited to the festival, but would have been even too much for Darrow. That was all that Ju saw as he dived towards the hole and a temporary freedom. Landing on his front, he slid most of the way along the dirty ground in through the hole. By some miracle his bow did not catch and he made it through easily. Luckily for him the hole was just big enough to allow him to crawl the rest of the way as the rest of the crates toppled and smashed behind him. From the scream of pain, it was obvious that his recent captor had been caught in the collapse. Inside the tunnel there was a faint light, both from the hole he had crawled through, although it was mostly packed with broken wood and metal, and from a source far off to his right where the tunnel seemed to dip. Ju pressed himself up against the far wall, breathing quickly as he sought to calm down after the recent shock. Outside, he could hear the voice of the man in blue.

"Thank the Gods you got here quickly. He was under the pile of wood, a dirty little thief who had stolen my purse. He. . ....." The voice of the man was cut off by a slicing sound, similar to a butcher cleaving meat. A low groaning was all that followed, and then Ju saw blood begin to drip into the hole, flowing with increasing volume. It was all too clear what had happened. The man had sentenced himself to death by naivety. His lack of knowledge had killed him for being a busybody and a liar. Ju did not know whether to feel sorry or feel vindicated. He did know that his time here was limited, and looked toward the other light. As he did so, the rubble that blocked most of the hole began to shift where somebody attempted to move it. Ju started away from the hole, staying to one side of the tunnel where the dirt was dry and packed. The tunnel was relatively clear, with only the occasional scrap of rag decorating the walls. It had been maintained to the point that there had at least been an attempt at cleaning the floor. Brush strokes in the sodden earth gave that away. There was a very narrow path through the dirt, and Ju found himself following this. The roof rounded as the path descended below the level of the streets, and the temperature dropped. Periodically there was a torch wedged without care in an iron rung, and every one of these was alight. Somebody else was using this tunnel. Far behind him there was a crash as wood fell down, and this reminded Ju what he was actually trying to do. He hurried down the path, and felt the air get colder as he did so. Looking back up the slope, he realised how far down he had come. Ahead of him the tunnel levelled out, and despite the clear path it was considerably messier, with dripping moss sending up fizzes and steam from the torches. In the distance another light bobbed out of sight around a corner. Ju forgot about the problems behind him and concentrated on catching the person in front in the hope of finding a way out. He was forced to keep off of the clear trail in order to mask his footfalls, which sounded unbearably loud. It was not hard for him to sneak up upon the person in front of him. As he reached the corner, he heard a shuffle and the rustle of robes. Risking himself as he peered around the grimy wall, he caught a glimpse of two people caught in a tight embrace. One was a big man, fat and gristly in appearance. The head of the woman in front of him blocked his face, but it was clear who both people were.

"We must hurry, if we are not to be missed," Duchess Deborah said as she sought to regain her breath. The kiss they had shared seemed to have sucked something from her.

"Patience, Duchess," replied the vicious O'Bellah, "we will only be missed if my men make it so. I can guarantee that your husband will be having the time of his life, however brief that may be."

"Are you sure that the poison will work?" The Duchess seemed unsure of herself. Perhaps the step up from running a whorehouse to cold-blooded murder of the most despicable degree was too much for her.

"And they are the type of people trying to take over the world," Ju whispered aloud in disgust. It just reinforced to him the reason why Zya was so adamant about saving people from these types.

"The poison will work," O'Bellah replied, as a hand moved around the clothes of the Duchess. "The Duke will feel so good later tonight, he won't care that his blood will begin to boil. He will be in the throes of passion, at least within his mind." O'Bellah laughed at this, the thought of someone in agonising pain obviously amusing to him.

"Who are you going to get to administer it?" The Duchess was a nosy type, as Ju had often seen with his dealings in her former career and it was clear that her penchant for asking questions had not diminished. She had no idea what sort of person she was dealing, or in fact dallying with.

"Why who better to administer the poison than somebody unexpected, somebody trusted, somebody undeniably close to the Duke?"

Ju caught the look on her face as the blood drained with the realisation that it was meant to be her. The amusement in O'Bellah's eyes caused them to twinkle viciously.

"Surely you don't mean?"

"Absolutely, dearest Deborah. That is *exactly* what I mean. We had considered using another, in fact we still might. Depends on how you do. And now I think that we should head on up to the feast before you truly are missed, or before you miss your opportunity."

The Duchess, now clearly less excited about the night's work ahead of her did not make a move, but O'Bellah grabbed her by the arm, squeezing cruelly.

"How dare you handle me so? I am a Duchess!"

"You are a snivelling whore who got a lucky break. Well guess what, your luck has taken a considerable turn and is on a knife-edge. Falter just a bit, and I think that you will find out just how little I care for your station. Do as I say, and the city and perhaps the entire Duchy will be yours." The Duchess still looked scared out of her wits, but the greedy aspect had returned to her face. She moved a little more easily with the thought of untold riches. The two of them walked a little way down the tunnel and then disappeared through what must have been a side tunnel, so sudden was their departure. Ju waited for a short while, and then crept up the tunnel in their footsteps. The side-tunnel was no bigger than a crevice and Ju was amazed that the Duchess could fit in there, let alone the hulking O'Bellah. He stepped forward to the side and realised that the crevice was actually an angled tunnel designed to stay hidden. A noise in the distance disturbed him, and he looked back down the tunnel. He stepped quietly back towards the corner and peered around. The blank-faced mercenaries were no more than a dozen paces back down the tunnel, striding slowly towards him. He did not know if they saw or heard him, nor did he care. He bolted for the side tunnel, missing it momentarily as his wits escaped him. It was only by looking back that he saw it and as he ran into the darkness, he saw the flash of metal in the torchlight. He heard rather than felt a sword deflect off of his bow, but by then he was running and did not care. This tunnel was much smaller, and he nearly ran into several walls as the passage twisted and dodged. It also sloped rapidly uphill, and Ju prayed that there was going to be a favourable reception for him at the top. It was certainly preferable to the sharp and painful ending behind him. He jumped up steps still full of energy from his fright, not looking behind him for the fear that the mercenaries had caught him despite his lucky escape, and cursing himself repeatedly for taking so long. In a flash of clarity he realised that he was probably trapped anyway as he was running from death straight into the hands of something worse. It had not been that long since O'Bellah and the Duchess had gone ahead of him, and they surely could not move as fast as he. They must have taken a different route. In a panic he began to look about him, but saw nothing. He swallowed down the fear that arose from the thought that they had taken the proper route and him the wrong one, and carried on running up stairs. The path evened out and the temperature warmed, the air becoming drier. The walls became cleaner, in fact markedly so. Ju burst out of the passageway and into a huge cellar. Looking behind him, he saw that a thick wooden door that had been reinforced with metal could seal the passageway. Pushing on the door with all the strength he possessed, he gradually closed the passageway. As soon as the door closed, he threw the huge iron bolt with an audible 'thunk'. For the first time in a long while, he felt a tiny bit safer. Turning around he began to explore the cellar into which he had entered, and found it to be stocked from floor to ceiling with glass bottles.

He had found his way into a wine cellar, one that was obviously cared for judging by the lack of the usual dust on the glass. If it had been any other time he would have stayed and looked around the room, but he knew that the pirates would be sailing by now and would only wait for so long to minimise the risk of discovery. He had to get out of the cellars, into the main palace, find Zya and get her out of there and all within the space of one or two watches. As luck would have it, the opportunity presented itself to him there and then. Ju found himself with nowhere to hide as a door creaked open in the next room. The racks of bottles were up against the walls and so there was only one way back out. He was not going to risk the gauntlet of the mercenaries, and so he tried the bolder approach.

"What have we been told to get?" One voice asked, simple in its tones.

"We have to get some of the Duke's special brew, the one only him and his wives drink. He wants a couple of bottles to celebrate the end of the night's festivities."

"Where is it?" The first voice asked.

"Through in the second cellar, but not near the doorway." Replied the first. "Be sure to pick the bottles three rows up as we have already *taken care* of the other bottles below that."

A shadow loomed across the doorway and without a moment's hesitation Ju reached over and picked up two bottles of wine from exactly the place specified.

"Ere, what're you doing down here, boy?" The voice asked slowly. The man who looked down at him was almost a giant, and built like a fortress to match his granite tones.

"Why, I was told to come down here and fetch two bottles of the special vintage for my Lord Duke." Ju replied without missing a beat.

"Oh yeah?" The hulking man replied after giving his reply some thought. "And who was it as sent you down 'ere?"

Ju did not have a chance to answer before the other man popped his head through the gap. "He was sent down by the Duke, being one of his page boys weren't you lad?"

Something told Ju that contradicting the man was not a good idea. "Yes, that is right. I was told to hurry down and get two bottles. Who told you to get them?"

"Nobody, lad. We were thinking on our feet. Still, now that you are here we do not need to think on our feet, and can think on our backsides. But you had best get up there with the wine, had you not boy. And you had best be forgetting you ever saw us, because we would not want the guards to find the Duke's special wine turning up in his page's quarters would we?"

"Umm, no sir we would not. I had best be on my way now." Ju hurried past the two men, who even now were in the process of uncorking a couple of bottles of the special vintage.

"Make sure you forget this boy. There will be wine enough there come tomorrow. Just never take any lower than three rows up, else you might be in for a nasty surprise." The smaller man grabbed his arm just as he passed through the doorway. "You ain't seen us, right?"

"Seen who, sir? I was alone down here fetching wine."

The man chuckled. "Clever lad. We might meet up for a bottle or two yet."

Ju nodded and hurried through into the next cellar, which was twice as big, and much more used. He did not stop, for he knew how close to peril he still was. He had to restrain himself from breaking into a run when he heard the distant comments of the smaller of the two men.

"Open that cellar door, and let the breeze through here. I hate the musty stink of these cellars. Make for bad drinkin' time."

Ju carried on up through the passageways, certain that he had but to follow the press of people to make his way towards the main feast and consequently the Duke. The halls he passed through he barely noticed, for he felt safe in his anonymity. The mercenaries would never find him now. Following the crowds through the passages he was a lost soul, an invisible being, another small servant beneath everybody's important eyes. But he carried something that would gain him access to the most important man in the city, and possibly save his life. The bustle increased, and he felt as if he was almost swept along with it until he reached a passageway full of guards. Although something was nagging at him that this was the right way to go, he knew that he would be halted. Sure enough, his turn came.

"You there," one guard signalled to him to step off to one side, "what is that you carry?"

"Wine for the Duke, his special vintage from the deepest cellar," Ju replied, using all the information he had gained in passing to sound more convincing. If he looked as scared as he felt, he would surely be found out.

"You aren't the usual scullion that does this. Where are those two other fellows, the hulk and the skinny runt?"

Ju broke into a grin. "They are the ones who ordered me out of the cellar, sir. They said they were going to help themselves to a good portion of my Lord Duke's wine, and were into their cups before I even left."

"And I suppose you were not thinking of doing the same?"

Ju bowed his head piously. "I serve my Lord Duke, and do not dream of such things, sir."

"Perhaps," the guard replied. "but make sure you present yourself at the guard's gate come sunrise. If we find these men down there, you will have to identify them. You three, come with me!" The guard took three of his fellows, who grabbed their pikes and marched through the crowd like a battering ram through wool.

Ju was directed through the passageway and found himself in the entrance to the most lavish feast he had ever witnessed. Nowhere else had he ever seen roasting carcasses all up and down one side of the hall, table after table of vegetables and sweetmeats, and more wine than a man could drown in. His two bottles must have been very important indeed. His instincts told him to press on, and the dais was the obvious place to go. He hoped that this drama might soon play itself out. He had his foster sister to find.

Chapter Nineteen

The late afternoon always brought flocks of sea birds haunting the Grotesque as she made her way through the waters off of the coast of Caighgard. Ever since the sight of land had buoyed everybody's hopes, they had risen each day to see more rocky coastland slipping by. It was somewhat of a relief to see even the stony cliffs, as it was more to look at than the endless expanse of ocean. All of the Law Wizards had come to have a profound respect for the great blue deep, as the captain liked to call it. The way the currents would shift in the water as much as in the air was a skill it took a lifetime to learn, and they had barely scratched the surface. Here in the relative shallows, the blue turned to greens as the sea floor rose up to greet them, and groups of dark-skinned sea mammals barked out greetings from small coves on the shore. Raoul maintained his watch in the crow's nest, the only place he could truly be alone. At least that was what he had once believed. Ever since the discovery of communication by stone, the Law Wizards had rarely been apart in their discussions. He watched the rocky horizon go by, but his concentration was turned elsewhere. *"Just because you managed to move an inanimate object, it does not mean that you can move a living breathing being by sheer force of will."*
"I think you should let me try, Raoul," Belyn replied, his thoughts drifting up from a cabin deep within the belly of the ship that he shared with Yerdu. *"We will never know until one of us tries it."*
"And what if we lose you? What then?"
Amusement flowed from the consciousness far beneath. *"Then you will finally stand a chance of winning an argument against me."*
"Would you two just give it a rest?" Keldron split their conversation in two as he hammered his distress into the both of them. *"It is a moot point, Belyn. We agreed that only if we all did agree then would we let you use yourself as an experiment. Until that time comes, you will not."*
"That is exactly what I am doing, Kel, bringing us to a point where I can see agreement."
"By arguing the same case over and over again? Belyn, we are as brothers and we love you dearly as one, but give it until we reach the island to start arguing again. Once we reach the temple there may be something more to aid us in our decision, but Raoul is right. If we lose you then we lose the strongest of the three in the art of focussing. Should we get attacked, we would stand a much better chance of survival were you with us rather than off stuck in limbo with a demon and your own thoughts for company." Keldron was at the prow of the ship. Raoul needed no focus to sense that. His friend was visible in his own unique blend of Order garb and sailors

uniform, making him look decidedly half-dressed. It suited him strangely enough. *"Belyn's thoughts might be the worse of the two."* Raoul thought to himself, forgetting that he was mind-linked with his two friends, earning him a mental slap from Belyn and a chuckle from Keldron.

"It has been decided, Bel, stop trying to convince us. Give it until the temple and then we can worry about losing you."

"That might be sooner then you think, Raoul," Keldron advised, *"look to starboard."* Raoul did as he was bid, and saw that the land was receding rapidly. "Where is the land going?" He asked out loud rather than merely voice the thought. His friend's thoughts were lost in the nothingness as a sailor in the rigging yelled out a reply. "Them's the straits of Rhothamy, wizard. We sail up them to the city at their head, the capital of Caighgard."

The sailor went back to his work in the rigging, and shortly the bellow of the captain rang out all over the ship. "TWO POINTS TO STARBOARD, CHANGE WATCH! CROW COME DOWN!" Raoul took this to mean that his time was up. Captain Curtis was pretty lenient in Raoul's case, as the wizard had perfected the focus of far-sight and often took several shifts at a time. It had its uses, giving him a lot of time for contemplation of the Law, his favourite pastime, but had also earned him the nickname 'crow' from the rest of the crew. He did not really mind all that much, but he scowled when called it to give the others something to laugh about. At heart Raoul had a wicked sense of humour, but was loathe to acknowledge this fact to others around him. Let them keep guessing, that was his motto. This of course gave him what he wanted, but he still obeyed the orders of the captain. Climbing out of the crows nest into the top spar above the main mast, he descended the rigging on feet calloused with several months worth of climbing experience. Raoul did not get in the spirit as much as his friends, but he had removed his boots quite early on after slipping on a rope and nearly falling from halfway up the mast. Now he hopped down the ropes and knots that were his road to the deck. In moments he had dropped to the wooden planking and found that there was a small gathering on the deck below the captain. Several of the sailors were muttering about ill omens, and the tribesmen stared off to the North.

"We want your opinion, wizard, and those of your friends. There are strange things afoot at this hour." The cat-faced captain said nothing more, striding from side to side of the deck as he waited for Belyn to arrive. When the third of them finally arrived accompanied by the small and unusually jolly Yerdu, the captain turned to address them.

"There are things that are wrong, and as learned men we would like your opinions."

"Anything that we can do to help captain, you know that," Belyn replied with a smile.

Curtis nodded in thanks. "You can see that we have turned towards land."

"At long last," Belyn answered.

"All is not well, wizard. We do not turn for the coast this soon. Not for another watch do we turn, riding straight up the middle of the passage as we do. The currents have shifted, and it is they that are taking us in towards the straits. The breeze is wrong, and has changed direction. The winds are such that you can set your direction by them here, and this is not right."

At this official proclamation by their captain many of the sailors experienced in seasons of sailing began to make wards against evil, brandishing various charms and waving them around. Raoul gaped, not having realised that the sailors were such a superstitious group of men. The tribesmen and women stayed on the deck or in the nearby rigging, stoic and impassive, accepting whatever fate threw in their path. They all knew that they were treading the right road, and they accepted it all.

"What I am saying wizard, is that we are at the mercy of the elements here. Is there anything you can do to help us?"

"Perhaps," Belyn replied, "there are some focuses we could use to aid but we would have to understand more of what we are up against."

"Captain! We are becalmed!" cried the helmsman, and several of the sailors yelled in alarm. It was true, in open water, the ship had stopped moving completely. The land was distant, but not out of reach.

Curtis wet a finger in his mouth and held it up. "No breeze," he cursed.

"Captain!" Yelled another crewman. "To the South!"

They turned to look and saw two smudges of inky darkness off in the distance, flickering with lightning.

Curtis climbed down to the deck most of the crew were stood on, and approached them. Raouln held his breath, as he knew the captain was fond of the strangest smelling foods.

"Wizard, whatever you are going to do," he pleaded, "do it now."

* * *

"No, it's okay, I am fine." Zya replied, brushing off the gentle advances of the courtier trying to steady her as well as impress her with his charm and not inconsiderable wit.

"You do not look well, darling lady," the man persisted. "Perhaps a walk in the fresh air would do us both some good."

"It might do you some good," she retorted, "why don't you go and find out?"
The courtier stood back, surprised and not a little offended by her words. His
dark eyes and oiled ringlets were wasted on someone like her, and it was
about time he knew it. The man had been preying on Zya since the moment
she had walked into the focal point of the Duchy, the Duke's great hall.
"You guild girls are all alike. You and that blonde one."
"I think that you will find 'that blonde one' a much easier target for one of
your pursuasion. Why don't you go and bother her?"
 Now the courtier's eyes flashed as Zya dismissed him, his court-practised
manners preventing him from using the curse that she was sure was hovering
just behind his lips. Zya turned away, looking up at the gaudy festival
decorations. She had a lot to consider. Nearby, events were unfolding as she
had foreseen. She had felt Ju witness the chasing of Lorn into the alleyway, and
the thought that he may well have been killed nearly broke her heart. It was all
that she could do to stay standing. Now, far to the West another dream was
becoming reality, and something told her that in this very palace were one or
possibly two forces that could affect the outcome. Her gut feeling was that she
would end up meeting both of them before this night was through. To distract
herself, she looked around some more as she twined a ribbon around her
fingers.
"Impressive, isn't it?" Asked another male voice.
"Not really," Zya replied without bothering to turn around to give satisfaction
to the whims of another whiny man who couldn't hold the sword at his side
for any more than a moment before nearly fainting from the weight. She so
wished Lorn was here with her. "It is a gaudy display of wealth that
sometimes offends the eyes, nearly blinding one with the offensive riot of
colour. The money that has been spent on this has been wasted when it could
have gone to people outside and around the city who are nearly starving."
"Very well put," the voice agreed, "but it would mean my head on a spike if I
became the second Duke to not allow my city this celebration."
Zya's head shot around, and she beheld a man who although not overly
impressive in stature and looks, had a bearing about him that spoke of
command and instant obedience. He was her match in height, and he wore his
sword like a warrior, not a popinjay. From under brown hair bleached blonde
by seasons on the waves, the Duke smiled back at her. The feeling intensified,
and Zya was sure for an instant that one of the powers was facing her right
now.
"My Lord, it is an honour," she said, her throat trembling as she forced the
words out.

"No, I think the honour is mine, young Zya S'Vedai. Rarely have we had the honour to meet somebody who rises so quickly amongst their respective ranks. If I were to perform as you, I would be overlord of the Nine Duchies before the year is out. Tell me, how is it that you have learned in a matter of months what it takes some a lifetime to accomplish."

"My Lord I could not say. I do not know. It just comes to me."

"Marvellous!" The Duke exclaimed, and the feeling became stronger, much more potent, "a natural! I have never met the like before!"

Zya bowed her head at the complement. "Neither have I, my Lord. But I have heard about your many accomplishments."

The Duke puffed up at her compliment, not taking it the way Zya knew that she meant it, but still the feeling grew and it was not a bad feeling.

"Splendid! We shall dine together then, just you and I, and talk about other things than gaudy festivals."

"I would be honoured, my Lord, but I have responsibilities. I am. . ." Zya looked down to the floor, and caught sight of someone she recognised. "Ju?" The bottom edge of a curved bow more stylish than any piece of tat in the whole hall called to her through her dagger, and she realised that the converging weapons knew each other somehow.

"You are due?" The Duke replied, waiting on her answer as he misheard what she had said.

Zya realised that she was not going back to the guild, no matter what her excuse was to be, so she gave in to temptation and it felt right. "I am due to go back to my guild very soon, but I do not see why we can't have some food beforehand."

"Perfect," replied the Duke with a winning smile, "let us adjourn to the privacy of my table." And he led her to the table on top of the dais. 'Private' might not have been quite the word Zya would have chosen to represent this situation, but there was a distinct separation between the lavish spread on the dais and the crowd beyond. Even now, Zya had begun to doubt what she had heard about this man. Was this straightforward and polite gentleman the head of an army of mercenary-backed merchants, who took concubines as often as the day changed? She could not be sure. Many courtiers and the like tried to follow, but were rebuffed by subtly dressed warriors in deerskin and leather, weapons concealed beneath cloaks. The Duke strolled through with Zya beside him, not even noticing the difference and blithely ignoring the guards as if they were but commoners beneath him. The look in his eye betrayed his demeanour though, and Zya read him in an instant as a man who was prepared for much more than a party. It was as clear to her as the wine in her goblet that this Duke aimed to be prepared for any eventuality.

"And what is this?" The Duke said as he mounted the dais. Zya leaned around him to see a partially hidden boy.

"Your wine, my Lord Duke," came a voice that was achingly familiar, and a blessed relief to Zya.

"I did not order any wine brought up, young man." the Duke replied, a stern edge creeping into his voice. Obviously being prepared was the result of a slight case of paranoia in a younger man.

"Well I was asked by two men to bring you up a couple of bottles of your private wine, and to be double quick about it, my Lord. I serve my Duke as best I can, and thus am I here."

The Duke although not satisfied was nonetheless mollified, and sat down at the table. Zya sat demurely beside him before looking up and winking at the broadly smiling Ju.

"I know you," she said, "you used to be a message runner in the city. You came to my guild once, and I have seen you about the place."

"You know this rapscallion?" The Duke asked, impressed with her knowledge.

"Yes, you could say that I do, after a fashion. His name is Juatin, and he is as good a servant as could be asked for, taking into account his quick feet and forgetting his quick mouth."

The Duke laughed at this, and patted Ju on the shoulder. "Well then my lad, let me approve the bottles and you can pour us both a glass of wine."

Ju passed the bottles over, and after a moment's scrutiny received them back from the Duke with a nod of approval.

"A mark known only by me and my vintner protects the bottles from tampering. One can never be too careful."

"What about the vintner?" Zya asked innocently.

"Well let us say that he is more trusted by me than just about any person alive." The Duke replied as he watched Ju uncork a bottle with consummate ease. "Very well done, lad." He complemented as Ju eased the cork out in one fluid motion.

"Thank you my Lord, benefits of spending time in and around an inn." Ju replied with a bow. "Would you like me to pour, my Lord?"

"I will do the honours, lad." the Duke replied, taking the bottle from him. "Only one person has ever poured this wine, and that has been me."

"Take some advice, and make sure that is ever the case." Ju cautioned under his breath.

Taking a goblet of the heady wine, Zya breathed in its aroma. It smelled of earth mixed with numerous fruits. The earthy taste appealed to her, and Zya found that she was quite relaxed within next to no time. The feeling that her dreams were unfolding as prophecy became actuality never diminished, and she knew that she had things to do. After eating a delicious but altogether too brief meal, Zya pushed back her plate and goblet. The crowd noise had increased as things got more festive and more wine was consumed, but the private cordon created by the guards remained. "My Lord Duke, I must beg your forgiveness to take my leave from you now. There are things that I must do. Things that cannot wait."

Ju looked mutely at Zya, appeal in his eyes. It was clear that he wanted to say something, but was hesitant as to whether he should do so. Zya felt that anything unsaid now would be for the worse. "Would you consent to a little advice yourself, my Lord? I always take advice when it is offered. For even if it is not heeded, it can often be of great use later on."

"I would be a fool not to listen to one who rises so rapidly in rank from such a well-established guild, dear Zya. Say on."

The Duke looked around in surprise as Ju spoke up. "My Lord, we are aware of how you seek to oust the Guilds using the merchants gold and the mercenaries force. We are also aware of your tradition whereby you take a concubine at the end of every festival. I must warn you, Zya shall not be she. Despite all this, despite all reservations, you must hearken to my words. My Lord, there is a plot against you, one to take your life."

"What foolishness is this?" The Duke asked, looking from Zya to Ju and back again. "Concubines? Merchants replacing guilds? Plots against me? I have never heard such a collection of ridiculous statements! What is your part in this, boy?"

"My Lord, I came here to seek you out, and I arrived through the tunnels that lead here directly from your mercenary guild. They lead to the wine cellar, where I met two men that told me to take wine to you."

The Duke looked down at the bottle of wine, and then slowly back at Ju. "Say on."

Ju swallowed, nervous at being the source of such intense scrutiny. "They said to take two bottles of this special brew to you, as it was the only one that you drank."

"So they gave you the bottles of wine to bring to me?" The Duke turned around, to shout for the guards, but in a flash Zya stuck her hand in her pocket and called on the power of her focus stone. A moment's concentration and the voice of the Duke had been muted to a whisper, and his body held rigid in the chair. To all eyes below the dais, it appeared as if he had just turned slightly to look across the hall.

"Please my Lord, listen to all this boy has to say. He is only trying to help you, and before you jump to any conclusion you must hear him out."

The Duke continued to try and shout, but his mouth just made the normal shapes of conversation.

"I will release you once he has finished, but until then you will hear only his voice." Zya focussed again, and built into her original spell a weave of what Joen had called 'air', to block out all sound but that immediately around them. Nobody would know any different.

"My Lord, the men did not give me bottles of wine to bring to you. They were too intent upon helping themselves. I overheard their conversation about where your wine is kept and took two bottles myself as a cover story. I was on my way with information and needed a reason to get close to you."

"There are much worse things afoot this evening than a young man with good intentions, my Lord Duke." Zya affirmed.

"This is not the first plot against you that has tried to bear its fruit tonight, my Lord. The first failed only by the apparent fact that one of my soon to be ex-colleagues did not manage to find her way here in time. Somebody else will come to you this evening, unwillingly, and offer you a taste of one of your bottles of wine. I suggest that you let her taste it first. Her, or somebody close to her that you can stand to lose, for that will be poisoned. I first saw the lady in question a while back when running messages. She owned a particularly successful gentleman's establishment, one where I was forced to avert my eyes more than once." Ju grinned as he said this. Zya frowned at the image. "She had blonde hair and a full figure, and an eye for any man that could give her a decent advance in her station. I hear she got that." The Duke had ceased shouting, but his face was red with rage. He knew exactly what Ju was getting at. "Her name was Lady Langley during the time I knew her. I saw her for the last time over a month ago. That is until today. I had been asked by a very close friend to look into what was happening in the mercenary guild, another place I had worked. We had heard some strange things about it, and it needed confirmation. I followed some people in there for it was open today, and witnessed some very strange men fighting. There were none of the mercenaries that had been filling the halls like ants for days uncounted, just these giants and dwarves that could kill without weapons. They impressed all of the children, trying to make them join them in something. Sat at a table, next to an evil man known as O'Bellah, was the Lady Langley, except now she was all dressed up in a blue gown and jewels, looking right out of place. She spent most of the time playing with a large blue jewel at her throat." As Ju said this, the Duke's face paled. "She was very close to this man, and several others, one of whom I think was a wizard. I followed her when she left with O'Bellah, and I am sorry to say my Lord, but I saw her kissing him in the tunnels beneath the palace." The colour drained out of the Duke's face as Zya watched him. It was as if somebody had driven a barrel-tap into his chin and turned it on. "I was as close to them as one end of this table is to the other, my Lord. While I watched, they spoke of poisoning you, and when she asked eagerly who was to do it, he told her that she was. The Duchess was not happy, but complied."

Something in the Duke's eyes gave Zya hope, and on instinct she released the focuses thus freeing him.

"She will be called the Duchess no longer, boy. Not if what you say is true. If the lady that you speak of is she whom I have married, then the blue jewel was my mother's gift to her. However, if you are lying, then I will personally cut out your tongue and feed it to you. I will find out who sent you to me, and I shall do the same to them."

"If you doubt the boy, Lord Duke, then I suggest that you check your bottle if and when she brings one. Wait, and check the wine, and we will go nowhere." The Duke looked at her, picking up on the change of reference. "We? Who is the 'we' now?

"The 'we' consists of Ju and myself, my Duke. I sent him to the mercenary guild to find out what was happening because I myself could not venture there. He was supposed to get out and leave the city but has obviously been waylaid. His next best hope lies with me. We are kin by way of fostering, and I will vouch that Ju has nothing but good intentions in his heart. As a member of the Order of Earth and their future high wizard, I pronounce that to be true. Trust me, my Lord, and trust him. If you drink of the wine that your *wife* brings to the table, you will know no more."

During this exchange, Ju had been nodding fervently to everything Zya had said. The Duke eyed him now. "Why did you come here when you could have escaped the city?"

"Because this was the only way left to me." Ju stood as close to the Duke as was possible, and poured more of the wine. "I was stuck in a tunnel with mercenaries all around, and one man showed me the way out."

"Where is this man? Why is he not with you now?"

Ju sighed, wiping a tear from his eye in memory of Foster's brave but suicidal act. "He led a group of mercenaries that were under some sort of spell away from me in an attempt to let me go free."

"It obviously succeeded then, for here you are."

"Barely, my Lord Duke. There were men close behind me to the point that one of them nearly tagged me while I was watching the Lady Langley and O'Bellah."

"Pah!" The Duke spat out loud. "That man infests our lives like maggots to rotten meat."

"More than you could know," Zya agreed while she picked at a sweetbread in front of her. "He has been the root cause of discord throughout the Duchy for the entire time I have been here. You are dealing with a very dangerous man with some deadly connections, my Lord."

"If anybody was behind these merchant rumours then my bet is on him. I personally have heard nothing, but since when is that a surprise. But how are you going to leave now, if these mercenaries are all around us? This complex is on a headland."

Zya looked at Ju, and then back at the Duke. Honesty was all that they had.

"At the change of the second watch from now, there will be a ship waiting for us outside of your Grace's private docks. My Lord, this might be difficult to believe after so long, but the pirates of Bay's Point have sailed, and as it stands they do not intend on returning."

"What?" The Duke exclaimed. "What pirates? There have been no pirates per sé in generations!"

Zya shook her head. "You have been much too closeted, my Lord. The pirates run the city, in fact the city is pretty much populated by pirates. I fear from what has been said here that you only see what people let you see, and that is a shame. There is evil spreading here, I can feel it in the bones of the Earth. It is here now, enclosing us. The only way to beat it is to fight back, to defy it. The pirates are what have kept this city going for generations while the nobility that once were pirates themselves became distant. You really need to take control of your city, my Lord."

The Duke slammed his goblet down on the table, sending a shower of ruby tears over everybody. "How am I supposed to do that surrounded by mercenaries who are supposedly hunting you down?"

"Not just us," Zya corrected, "but yourself also. O'Bellah plans to take over the city, probably with your wife as a figurehead but not necessarily. He will have the backing of the mercenary guild, and who knows however many wizards of copious orders. Plus, he brings a darkness to this city unlike anything you have ever seen."

"And I suppose you can tell me that you can stop this in exchange for my help?" The Duke asked sarcastically. It was obvious that the potential stress of the situation was getting to him.

"No, my Lord, we only wish to escape it. There are commitments we have elsewhere."

"Dammit, if you are living under the protection of my city then you have an obligation to me too!" The Duke stormed. "I need those pirates. My own guard numbers barely four score men and some household staff. There must be something you can do?"

"Let us get to the ship and I might be able to persuade some of them to. . ." Zya broke off as her stomach clenched and she convulsed forward, narrowly missing the table. "It is getting worse."

"What is?" The Duke nearly yelled, clearly frightened."

"The dream we shared," Ju answered for her, "Zya sees things in dreams, and I share her visions. We had a dream once about a ship being swamped by unnatural storms, storms whipped up by the misuse of power. That dream is unfolding as we sit here and do nothing."

"Balderdash!" Scoffed the Duke. "Such things do not happen!"

Zya nodded weakly and looked up. "Yes, they do. Another dream unfolded as you were speaking to me earlier this evening. Ju witnessed it. The mercenary turned protector, his plight was the cause for some great worry a while back for us. Aah."

Zya clenched again, and the Duke looked at Ju. "How come you do not suffer?"

"Who said that I don't suffer?" The boy countered. "Your wife, has she had anybody of note in her quarters?"

"She is always dallying with wizards, trying to beg their focus stones off of them. Maybe she has had merchants in there too. It is not uncommon for her to have strangers in my palace. Who knows what she might have stored in her rooms."

"Do your wife's rooms face the sea?" Zya asked between gritted teeth. "These wizards will need that."

"They do." The Duke leaned back in his chair. "Look, you have both asked me to take a lot on faith here, with the only certainty being that I am more confused now than I was when I got out of bed this morning. I will show you to my wife's quarters in the West wing."

Zya gasped, a slow intake of breath becoming a rush. "*That* is where they are. I can feel them now, sending out the focus to the western Isle. We must go quickly. We are running out of time." Zya's pleading look made the Duke stand immediately to assist her, but as he did so, a fracas at the back of the hall caused him to stop and stare as his wife barged through a knot of half-drunk guests. His face slipped from panic to icy hate as O'Bellah stepped into the room behind her. "It would be best if you two were not here to witness this. Ju, help your foster sister through the curtain behind the dais. You will find an alcove leading to a passage. Wait there and I shall send a guard."

"May providence guide you, my Lord." Zya blessed him prophetically.

"That or a quick sword hand," he answered.

Aided by Ju, Zya made her way down to the alcove at the back of the dais. If anybody noted her departure, it was well masked by the now raucous crowd filling the hall. They opened the curtains and sat down on a cushioned seat of stone in the shadows.

"Leave the curtain open, Ju. I want to see what happens."

Zya peered through the narrow gap, and Ju made it larger for her. "How do you feel?" He asked.

She smiled. "Better for the moment. Ju if I should pass out or some thing worse happen to me, you have to stop those wizards. What they are doing is unnatural and I swear the Gods themselves are frowning upon us all. They are working in waves, sending out focuses once they have recharged their minds. That is why it feels worse from time to time. The waves are getting closer now, and if we do not do something soon, I feel it might be too late. They are building up to an immense release of energy."

"But against who?"

"I do not know, but whomever we dreamed about on that ship is in perilous danger, and we must save them."

Ju pulled back the curtain so that it provided an oblique view of the dais, a view from which nobody could see them but the Duke, who gave her a short but very grave glance. Up in front of the gathered crowd the Duchess approached her husband. She had obviously gone to great lengths to make herself appear relaxed and attractive, but to Zya's trained eye she was nothing more than a fat wench in too much make-up with clothes several sizes too small. She could hardly breathe in the corset she was wearing, and Zya knew that only carefully placed pins stopped the rolls of fat from poking out. By the time she reached the dais with her escort consisting of O'Bellah and two guards, she was nearly fainting from the effort.

"It is a joy to see you looking so fine on this special evening." The Duke spoke warmly, but Zya could feel the disgust in the Duke's words from her seat.

"It is an honour to be received as so, my husband," Duchess Deborah replied. "This is a companion of mine who I have the pleasure of introducing. O'Bellah is a merchant from the interior of the Duchy,"

O'Bellah nodded his head, smirking as he did so.

"Quite," the Duke replied, not even attempting to hide the insult implied in his short reply. "A merchant indeed. How is it that you come to me now when you should have been by my side all of the evening so far?" By now, most of the gathered gentry and assorted guests had quietened enough to pay attention to the exchange on the dais, though quite a few were still very noisily making merry. The din was enough not to distract the people they had come to gawk at.

"I have been busy in the city, my husband. I have been greeting the populace on this joyous day." That much was technically true, thought Zya, and Ju grinned as he had the same thought. "If I have been overlong in my preparation, it was only because I did not want to disappoint you. Here, I have had some of your special wine brought from the cellars."

The Duke looked at the bottle, eyeing the neck for a moment. "Oh, you have not disappointed me, my wife," he replied with the tone of an adder about to strike, "you have just confirmed my faith in you."

Deborah glowed at this perceived complement, though it was anything but. "Would you like a glass of wine?" She asked as innocently as a small girl begging for sweets from a candy maker.

"Do you know what, I believe that I shall. Come sit beside me, my wife, and we shall toast this evening together."

The Duchess looked less than pleased at that proposal to Zya's eye, but gave no outward sign of any distress to the Duke. O'Bellah seemed to look on in mild disinterest, his attention elsewhere. "May the good merchant join us?"

"The good merchant," the Duke replied sarcastically. "Is that such a good idea? Think of our privacy." The Duke believed them, that much was very clear.

The Duchess frowned. "But you were entertaining as we arrived, I saw you. It should only be right that I am afforded the same privilege."

The Duke nodded at his wife's knowledge of court ways. The Duke and Duchess were equals. What one did, the other was obliged to do in most cases. Unfortunately for him, this was one of those times when his wife left her petty pursuits behind and invoked her rights. "You are of course correct, my dear. Seat the good merchant beside you and he can regale us with tales of creaky wheels and dodgy deals."

Zya cringed. Although his words were lost on his wife, who was too busy being smug about having got her way, O'Bellah had mottled at the insult. It was as she was watching the scene unfold that a sharp pain bit into her stomach and she nearly rolled forward off of her seat.

"What is it?" Ju nearly yelled, kneeling down on the floor to stop her from falling through the curtain.

"It is time," she whispered in reply, "the forces are gathering. One more wave like that and they are done for. Our only chance of saving that ship from being sunk before its time is to stop them and we have to act." She looked up to see the Duke uncorking the bottle of poisoned wine. Had he listened to her after all?

Pouring two goblets of wine, the Duke set them before his wife and their guest. "Please, do not wait on me on a night like this."

The Duchess looked warily at her goblet. "Will you not be joining us?"

"Oh for certain, but since I have already got a full goblet of wine, there is no point me overfilling my cup is there?" The Duke raised his goblet to the crowd that watched them. "I charge you all to raise a toast to the springtime!"

"THE SPRINGTIME!" Yelled back the crowd, and downed what drinks they had to hand. The Duchess and O'Bellah held their goblets, but did not taste the wine within.

"What is this?" The Duke said loudly, turning from the crowd to the couple beside him. "You did not drink the toast! You dare insult my table? You had better do so now."

"I do not feel well, my husband," Deborah replied. "My stomach is not what it once was, and I feel that should I drink any more wine then I might not recover." She looked mutely to O'Bellah for support, but he ignored her.

"To the feast," O'Bellah said with a sneer, and drank his wine. It had the desired affect. As she saw O'Bellah drink the wine, the Duchess came to the realisation that it could well be a hoax. "I think I could manage a sip or two," she said sheepishly.

"You do that," the Duke replied.

The Duchess looked over to O'Bellah for reassurance, and he nodded gently. The Duke, who flicked a hand behind his back and motioned his guards into readiness, did not miss this gesture. They changed their stances, loosening whatever weapons they held beneath their cloaks. The crowd, oblivious to the potential for savage violence, looked on, talking amongst themselves when the pause became unbearable. The Duchess, buoyed with confidence from her paramour, tentatively took a sip from the goblet, and when nothing happened drank more deeply. She looked from man to man, and then stood up. Her legs wobbled, and she had to lean on the table for support. "Would you like some now?" She asked the Duke, and then clutched at her stomach as she convulsed in pain, letting out a scream that drowned out any other noise in the hall.

"Thus do those who conspire against the Duchy perish." The Duke said coldly. "My own wife brought poisoned wine to my table this very evening, this special evening. The proof lies open for all to see, the penalty for treason has already been dealt by her own hand." The Duke turned to look at O'Bellah. "The only thing now is for her conspirator to join her."

O'Bellah ignored the Duke's threat. He was focussed on the suffering of yet another human being. "Antidote, Deborah, that is what you lack. I however was dosed with enough for me to have finished off that bottle myself."

The Duchess whimpered as her eyes became unfocussed, and she tried to make a grab for him. O'Bellah pushed her to the ground with satisfaction, relishing every painful moment. Aware that the Duke approached him from the other side of the dais, he raised his hand, which contained a bottle of antidote. "Stand fast! She will die without this!" It was too late already. The poison, which was supposed to have been pleasurable, was actually constricting her windpipe, and her face had nearly turned black.

"I think the woman is beyond help already. But you we shall have a wonderful time dealing with, whoever you are."

"I think not." O'Bellah countered. "Now!"

At his command, several of the onlookers threw their cloaks off and bellowed war cries. Brandishing swords, they rushed the dais, cutting down several revellers who did not even know what hit them. Women screamed, and several men attempted to actually use the rapiers they wore, but were cut down. The hall erupted into chaos as more mercenaries attempted to enter through the hallways. In the middle of it all, O'Bellah drew a sword of his own, one that had been hidden about his person. The Duke grinned in response, and leaving the mercenaries to his guards drew his own blade. It sang out in rapturous joy as it was unsheathed, and at that point both Zya and Ju stood up. It was a weapon from the same source as their own. Ju put his hand to his bow, and Zya held her dagger, and for a moment the three of them were locked as one mind. It confused the Duke, who dropped his guard, and O'Bellah sliced along his arm.

Without thinking, Zya hurled a focus of pure force against O'Bellah, and it threw him across the line of guards and back into the midst of his own mercenaries. Shaking his head as he stood, he tried to see who was responsible. "KILL THE DUKE! A THOUSAND CROWNS TO THE MAN WHO BRINGS ME HIS COLD, DEAD HEART!"

The mercenaries roared in blood lust and threw themselves against the Duke's guard, who were backed up by the Duke himself. The room was nearly empty of guests now, with several brave men throwing aid to the Duke's guard. They were overwhelmed by the mercenaries, but fought with skill, wounding and maiming rather than killing outright. Soon enough the fallen mercenaries were starting to get in the way of their comrades, but the flow of mercenaries into the hall did not lessen as more and more answered the call of their leader. For his part, O'Bellah was actually still dazed, despite his orders, and he had no idea of what had hit him. He started beyond the slaughter, though his eyes did linger at all of the blood. "Bring in the stakes!" He commanded. "Let them see the means by which their miserable lives will end!" There would be suffering for any survivors of this fight, enough that the Golem would be satiated for a while. "Press the flanks! You!" He pointed at a squad of mercenaries that had not been touched by the Golem and therefore were more than halfwits. "Close the right flank. Make it past the dais and earn a month's wages for the head of the Duke!"

Behind his guard, the Duke was still overcome by the sharing of thoughts for that brief moment with Zya and Ju. He dropped back, and turned towards the alcove. Closing on it, he stopped short of going through. "Are you still there?" He asked.

"We are," Zya replied, "are you well?"

"You know the answer to that as well as I, Zya S'Vedai, daughter of Tarim, tribal seer and wizard of one order but spell caster of many. What happened there?"

Zya peeked around the curtain, flicking a focus out that incapacitated one of the mercenaries long enough for the defending guard to avoid a killing stroke and deliver one of his own.

"From what I seem to know of you now, you should not even be here."

"Correct," Zya agreed, "but Ju said he was going to save your life, and that is behind what we do now. Motive is everything, my Lord Duke."

The Duke looked over at the blackened corpse of his late wife. "Hester, my name is Hester. Please stop calling me 'My Lord Duke'; it gets tedious, even in situations such as this. We need to get you to her rooms, and then maybe we can sort this mind-linking trick of yours out."

"It has to do with the weapons, Hester. They are linked somehow. LOOK OUT!" Zya jumped past the Duke, her eyes ablaze as three mercenaries broke through the left flank. Ignoring the cries of protest, she sent a focus of lightning speeding towards them that left them roasting where they stood. At the same time Zya spotted a familiar face peeking into the hall. Bethen had finally found her way to the feast. She looked across the hall to the dais, and locked eyes with Zya. For an instant there was recognition and understanding. A wave of hate emanated from the girl. This wave was cut off as Bethen was run through from behind by one of the mercenaries. Her eyes filmed over and she dropped to the floor, surrounded by only her shredded dress and a pool of blood. Zya's action had not been missed by O'Bellah, who came face to face with the adversary that had handled him like a rat in a trap. Something else nagged at him about her, but he only caught a glimpse of her – tall and long dark hair. The reason he recognised that was forgotten in the heat of battle. "CATCH THE GIRL! FORGET THE DUKE! SHE IS ALL THAT MATTERS!" He roared. The mercenaries shifted with the change of orders, and the Duke called back two of his guards. "Take these two to the apartments of my ex wife and do whatever they command. They act with my authority." That was enough for the guards, and to plug the gap in his line, the Duke himself jumped to the fore, his sword flashing like a crimson spectre in the blood and flame. "For Ciaharr, the Duchy!" he cried, and as Zya turned to look, she caught the glance of O'Bellah. Finally he had seen the prey he had been unknowingly chasing for so many moons.

* * *

The ship lurched to one side as the waves caught the Grotesque in a crossfire of violent shudders. The two great waterspouts that joined the seething sea to the maelstrom above were less than a league off, and despite the fact that the ship was moving with all the combined efforts of the wizards thus far, still the unnatural current prevailed against them.
"It is no use," Keldron gasped as he held onto the railing at the stern of the ship, "we cannot move the ship far enough to catch the wind again."
Raoul nodded in agreement, but panted instead of speaking. Only Belyn continued to try.
"Give it up, Bel," Raoul urged his larger friend, "you will only tire yourself out by continuing this alone. We need to harbour our strength against what is to come." He looked up at the towers of water, columns of spiralling darkness more ominous than anything he had ever witnessed. This was not how his existence was meant to end, not in a watery grave, not if he could help it. "If we can find a way to avoid them at all." He added quietly.
"We need to make a decision about the rest of the crew, "Keldron urged, as he looked out at the crew standing fascinated by what could possibly be their final hurrah, "they can reach the shore in the boats attached to the side of the ship."

"Not everybody on here is going to fit into those boats, wizard." Curtis disagreed, his violent breath providing a welcome distraction to the finality of the situation.

"I know, captain. That is why we have to decide who goes, and who stays." Curtis looked around at his immediate crew. Some hard decisions had to be made. "I am staying!" He announced. "I want volunteers for a skeleton crew to keep the ship afloat. Who is with me?!"

The entire crew of the Grotesque raised their hands in yells of 'ME!' or 'I WILL!', and Curtis smiled his feline grin. "That decides it men. I commend you all, and by the Gods we will have a celebration when we reach Rhothamy! Current watch! You will stay. The rest of you, get our passengers safely ashore. Man the boats, lads. You got some rowing ahead of you. You know what to take, and what to do." Curtis turned now to the three wizards. "What will you do? You can go with the rest if you wish."

"We will be staying, and perhaps we can get us all out of this mess yet." Belyn decided for them all. Raoul looked about to say something, but Keldron's icy stare shut him up and finally he nodded in rueful agreement.

"If you are staying, then so are we," Yerdu announced from the steps to the deck below. A flash of gold showed that Joleen was with her also. "You will not cast us aside when it suits you all to play the hero, Kel."

"I can, actually," he disagreed, "and I will. Captain, these ladies will be going with the rest of the tribe, willing or otherwise. If we have to bind them then so be it, but they are not to be left on this ship."

"You would not dare!" Yerdu erupted, her outrage filling the decks and making many of the sailors grin.

"If they would not, I would." It was Malcolm, who had crept silently on his huge feet up the stairs behind them. "I know what you mean to everybody here, especially these wizards you profess to love. I know what it is to lose somebody Yerdu, and I will not let you be lost to them, not if there is a chance to survive."

"What if they are lost to us?" she asked in a tiny voice, one that truly showed how small she could become.

"You will have to have faith that we will not, dearest." Belyn spoke with emotion that he seldom showed, proof of how serious he thought the situation to be.

In response, Yerdu ran to him, and hugged into him, kissing him deeply. "I will pray for you, Belyn Stroddick. Get out of this alive."

Joleen and Keldron were of a similar, if more bashful parting. A lingering kiss out of sight of the rest. "Come back to me," was all she said, but the unshed tears spoke volumes more than words alone.

"Always," Keldron replied, and then she was gone. He turned his attention back to the spiralling columns that were almost within touching distance.

"Are you two finished?" Raoul said with a grin. "We still have to figure out a way to save ourselves from this mess."

"Patience was never one of your virtues." Belyn replied, shaking his head despite the infectious grin on Raoul's face causing one on his own.

"I prefer to think of it as 'There's no time like the present'. Now what are we going to do about that?"

Keldron retrieved the focus stone he had used to sense his master, the spirits, and all manner of things since they had figured out the use of it. He closed his eyes, pushing through with his consciousness. What he saw astounded him. A force was holding the columns together similar to the focus that he had used to create a barrier of air. Bright blue ropes of focussed energy twisted the seawater until it touched the cloud. "This is not natural." He announced to the two glowing forms beside him.

"You don't say?" Raoul replied sarcastically.

Keldron ignored the jibe. "The source of the focus is incredibly far off, but there is a source for sure. It is feeding the water, keeping it moving towards us. There is more. A different focus is doing the same thing to the clouds above. Wizards are working in tandem on this, and it looks like they were not selecting a random target. A pulse has just hit the columns this way."

"We see it," Raoul replied, they are moving faster." One of the glowing forms moved away for a moment. "The boats are being lowered."

"Good. The sooner they are away the sooner we can try something more drastic." Keldron was already having ideas.

"Like what?" Belyn asked.

"Like attacking the towers of water about to swallow us, or perhaps the people behind them."

"Try contacting Obrett," Belyn suggested, "perhaps he can shed some light on what is happening here."

Keldron sent his thoughts out through the focus, heading in the direction his master had come from. It seemed as if he had travelled over half a continent before he was shaken by something. Any lesser man would have collapsed in mind-numbing agony as being disturbed so, but Keldron was well versed in the ways of the mind and mentally shrugged it off. Raoul stood beside him, a hand on his shoulder. "What happened?"

447

"You were searching too long, my friend. Any of us could have reached Obrett in that time. We have to face the fact that we are on our own for this one."

"I could have searched a little longer…"

"No you could not have, my brother. Look behind you."

Keldron turned around. "What the..?" The towers of water were only half as far away as when he had started his focus, and now they could see the twisting columns moving visibly towards them. The water churned frothy white around the darkness of water mixed with black cloud, twisting in unnatural ropes, internal currents threatening to rip the columns apart.

"It is as if a whirlpool had been turned inside out." Curtis murmured. "All hands secure the decks! I want lines rigged everywhere. These things aren't gonna suck the Grotesque to a watery grave, not if I can help it!"

The remaining sailors jumped to it, carrying out the orders of their captain with not even the whiff of fear amongst them. "That won't help us if we can't do something quickly."

Curtis turned to Raoul, who had spoken the words everybody knew, but was afraid to admit. "I know that, you know that." He pointed at his scurrying crew. "They know that. The only thing keeping them from jumping ship and swimming like rats for the shore is the fact that we have three wizards on here who might be able to get us out of this situation, so I suggest that you keep trying."

"Okay, here is what we are going to do." Belyn had evidently made up his mind and decided to take charge. "Raoul, you and Keldron create as grand a focus as you can manage, and try anything to divert those columns. Take one column each. I am going to try and move the ship closer to the shore."

"Are the boats far enough away that this will not affect them?" Keldron asked. Raoul looked off towards the shore where the boats were moments from landing. "They are safe. Worry more about us, brother.

Keldron nodded and set his mind to the task. He picked his favourite stone, the focus stone first given to him as an apprentice. He knew every facet of the golden marble, every nick, every flaw within the rock. Pouring his concentration into it, he used more passion, more sheer guts than he had ever done before. The world became a different colour for him as he looked through his mind's eye, viewing the potential catastrophe before him as one who was not really there. The energy within the twin columns before him surged as another focus churned up two elements that were not really meant to mix. To one side he felt Raoul doing the same, and beyond that Belyn was concentrating on forcing the ship ahead of the current, with little success. "I think we can help you there, Belyn." He said directly into the mind of his friend. "Raoul, you take the left column, but whatever you do, push against it as well."

He received a mental nod from his tall friend, and together they released the twin focuses against the might of enraged nature. Keldron pushed against the columns of water, and his focus dissipated along the lines of power used to contain the churning elements. He tried to fight the other focus, to break the bands of force, but he found that his efforts had no effect. "Try twisting the water the other way." He called out, hoping that Raoul could hear him. If there was any acknowledgement, it was masked by the sheer immensity of the power being wielded by the three wizards.

"We are moving," Belyn announced, "slowly at first, but with your efforts a bit faster over time. It is doing no good though, the columns have moved even closer."

Keldron nodded, and ploughed into the other focus with his own, hoping to reverse the bands of power and destroy the water spouts. For a moment the churning water slowed, but as soon as it looked as though they had made a breakthrough, the water span around even faster, the counter-focus knocking both Keldron and Raoul off of their feet. Dazed for a moment, both men took a few breaths before they opened their eyes. What they saw astounded them. The waterspouts had moved alongside the ship, one either side. They looked up into the yawning maw of eternity twisted amongst coils of watery wrath. It was pitch black, for the cloud was so close to the surface of the sea that the darkness blotted out any possible light. In addition, rain had started to fall amidst forks of lightning that blasted from one spout to the other, almost concussing the sailors with each rapport. The surface of the sea nearly boiled with the currents created by the twin vortices, and the ship began to list heavily to one side.

"HOLD TIGHT, LADS!" Curtis called to his men. "If one of those spouts touches my ship, we will all be drawn into a watery grave." He said this to the wizards, with only his helmsman also in hearing distance. "Do something."

"Belyn, how fast can we get this ship moving if we all try what you are doing?" Keldron called to his friend.

"Doubt we can go much faster, but we can try." Came the shouted answer above the roar of the twisted water churning up to the sky.

"Raoul, join with us!" Keldron ordered, and the three wizards combined their efforts. Forcing the ship against the suction that threatened to pull the Grotesque under, they managed to break if not totally, then partially free of the watery death that awaited them. The ship forced itself ahead of the waterspouts, appearing to the people on shore as if it had been squeezed out ahead of them. On the ship, the sailor's cheered encouragement as the focus appeared to be working. The ship was moving steadier, and listing less. The shore seemed as close as the twisting towers of water behind them, but it was still at least a half a league too far away. They could see the rest of the crew and passengers gathered on the shore out of reach of the surging tide created by the focus.

"It is working!" Raoul cheered as he looked up, but then something stirred up in the cloud hit him, and he lost his concentration. Raoul dropped like a stone, the plank of wood next to him obviously responsible for the welt on his forehead. The response was instantaneous. The speed of the ship dropped to nearly nothing with only two wizards focussing, and the twisters began to close once again.

"We cannot maintain this, not between the two of us!" Belyn yelled across through the sheets of rain.

"We have to!" Keldron roared back. "We have to save ourselves, we have to save Raoul!"

"Not this way!" Belyn roared back, and Keldron felt his friend release the focus. Completely unsure of what Belyn was doing, Keldron poured his heart and soul into the focus to keep the ship ahead of the destructive force behind them. "What are you doing?" He yelled as loud as he could but Belyn had crouched down, seemingly lost to the world.

All sound and exterior feeling was lost to Belyn as he drew within himself to concentrate on a focus that had been denied him for far too long. The rain and the wind was but a distraction for the living, and if he did not pull this off he was as good as dead anyway, so what harm could it do to try? He remembered all of the times he had moved inanimate objects from one place to another, and the feeling he had known as he performed the focus. He thought also of his conversations with his mentor, and the way they had travelled across country with their minds. Most of all, he remembered what it was like to move his casks of spiced Brandy from a place he knew well back to his own body. Those feelings combined were surely the source of what he intended to do now. "Intent is the paramount cause. Everything we do now serves our intentions, and the intentions of others."

"What?" Shouted Keldron. "Get the focus going, we may yet save this ship!"

"Too late for that, my friend." Belyn replied, and sank into the depths of his mind, searching for the key.

And there it was, stretched out in front of him like a map. The fundamentals by which the world was governed, a law older and more basic than any that they had ever heard of, had ever dreamed about. As he swam within the depths of his own perceptions, he saw that which had been clouded until now. It had taken a situation where he faced his own death to find the answer. The whole world served a basic law of existence, with everything interconnected. From here he could move wherever he liked, touch the souls of infinite people should he have the will to do so. It would still take energy though, and a lot of effort, but Belyn knew that all he had to do was will it, and through his focus stone it would be so. He looked at the beings surrounding him on the ship, and considered the wrongness of the waterspouts. They were an affront to the basic law, and their violence was a direct result of the natural order of things trying to assert itself. He knew how it had been done now, could sense the focus that held the water in sync with the storm clouds, but was powerless to fight it. His intent had provided him with a window to a different world, but it seemed there was little more than that. What he could do he would, even should it cost him his life. At least Raoul and Keldron would be spared. Gathering his concentration, Belyn linked all of the beings aboard the ship, and cast his mind towards the shore where others waited. Linking the others to that point through himself, he sent them to the point he had chosen and his mind shrieked in pain. Too much! He was straining himself to the point of self-annihilation. He had gotten half of them to the shore, and felt as if he had but moments left. Belyn dug deeper, and found reserves he never knew that he possessed. Life around him discoloured as the manifestations of energy that were the spouts drew within touching distance of the ship. They screamed at him, hungry to swallow him and end their painful existence for that was surely what they wanted. He did not know, but he had dropped to his knees as he passed yet more of the sailors to the shore. Had he but looked, he would have seen his two friends stood on each side of his corporeal form supporting him, pale with fear in the rain that plastered their hair to their faces and stung their eyes almost to blindness. His stomach churned as the ship lurched, but he never knew. He stopped breathing as he concentrated so much on his task, and he never recognised the pain coming from the lack of fresh air in his lungs. It was so close, so very close. Hoping against hope that his friends were still battling the elements, he waited until the very last to send them on their way, and then he was alone. The ship was his sapling in the storm, and the storm closed in. The mountainous towers of water and lightning bent towards him gleefully, hoping to swallow their prey, but he had one last trick left. The vortices would claim no prey today. He thought he heard the sound of breaking wood as he forced himself along the same line that he had sent the others. The impression of land speeding by as he travelled through this nightmare was only relieved by the blackness that opened up to swallow him into dark, blissful eternity. His energy was spent. No longer would Raoul argue with him.

Chapter Twenty

"This way, quickly." Hurried the guard named Cameron, who had been assigned to Zya and Ju as guide and guardian by Duke Hester. The Duke was oblivious to the personal peril that he placed himself in, or he judged Zya's needs equal to or above his own.

Zya clutched her stomach as another pulse was forced along the focus. Combined with the prescient feeling that one of the more worrying dreams was imminent reality, she was barely able to stand. "Are we near?" She spoke out of the back of her throat, a weak, whispery sound.

"It is not far now, a hallway or two, ma'am." Cameron replied as he scanned the walkways for any more mercenaries.

Ju had his bow in hand and an arrow notched. "The sooner we get there the better."

Zya struggled to move, aided in part by the guard. "Whatever happens, let me try and deal with them first."

"Are you sure the ones that you seek are in there?" Cameron was still shaken from the events in the hall, betrayed by his trembling hands.

"I am sure." Ju and Zya replied simultaneously, their unconscious connection through the weapons still linking them together.

As an afterthought, Ju added, "Your Duke fights on, but is sorely pressed. I suggest we get this over with quickly that we can get back to the hall and aid him." The feeling of the third weapon was still so new that its spell was magnified and they almost felt every parry and thrust used by the Duke.

In reply, Cameron hushed them silently. "These are the quarters of the Duchess, and have been so ever since this city was built. Have respect for them, for the rooms are almost as precious as the title of 'Duke'." Cameron had great respect for the history of the Duchy, and it shone from his face, a beacon of sincerity.

"We will be careful," Zya replied, "but let me go in first."

Cameron opened the door, which squealed in protest. "Sea air." He said in disgust, implying that the salt in the air had corroded the hinges. "These rooms are unkempt."

"I doubt the late owner had much use for them." Ju muttered.

"Stone me!" Cameron exclaimed as the door opened wider, admitting them to the suite of rooms. They had been stripped bare of any decoration, the cold stone all that graced them as they entered.

"Sold it all, I bet." Ju observed.

A cold look had settled over Cameron's face. "I curse the day that woman ever set foot in this palace."

"It is the wizards that are within who require the cursing, Cameron," Zya replied, her face calmer as inner resolve took over, "they are about to kill somebody a hundred leagues away and we have to stop them."

The three silent figures crossed the floor of what had once been the opulent personal abode of the Duchess to the suite of smaller chambers that faced out towards the sea. Both Zya and Ju could feel the pressure of imminent disaster. Things were about to get out of control.

"They are in the room beyond this one." She said quietly.

"That is the balcony over what remains of the estate before the ocean." Cameron replied without hesitation.

"That is the best place to work a focus from."

They opened the door, a polished affair with none of the roughness associated with many of the heavy tarred doors belonging to this region. In fact it was the one thing in the entire room that would remind them of the softer nature of the Duchesses from the past. The next room was smaller, and the door to the room beyond was ajar. This room showed signs of recent use. Scraps of food covered a small table, and blankets were evidence that people had been sleeping rough. There was other evidence too, but Zya averted her eyes. It was to this room that she had been drawn, to save some unknown people from a dream. The path that she trod was a strange one indeed. They stayed close to the wall that hid them from the next room. If there was anyone watching then surprise needed to be as important an element to them as the power Zya could focus or the weapons that they bore.

There was no sound from the balcony aside from the wind whistling in the early evening. Zya risked a glance out to sea, and was relieved to see nothing on the horizon to make any wizards change their spells. Zya pulled Ju back when it appeared he was going to step through, and it took the briefest of explanations to placate her angst. "No ships."

Zya looked confused for a moment, and then indicated her understanding with the briefest of nods. The communication passed right by Cameron, who concentrated on the door.

"Draw your sword, Cameron." Zya said slowly, and withdrew a stone from her robes. She did nothing with it for a time, but closed her eyes in concentration. "They are far away from here, concentrating on their target. Their loss. They are putting themselves heart and soul into the storm, which will presently sink the ship. Now is the time."

Zya stepped into the doorway of the room, her robes flying out behind her as she did so, and instantly Ju and Cameron sprang to either side. The reaction was not what they expected. Three wizards stood on the balcony, outstretched and partially withered hands clutching focus stones. They wore different robes, and from this Zya deduced their origins. "One wizard of the air, one of the water and one of life. That shocks me most of all, that a dedicate of Jettiba could be involved with this but it also explains much."

"Zya, I think we need to do something quick," Ju warned, "for these strangers on the ship will be gone while we ponder over links between crusty old men."

"Indeed, we must do something, but not quite what I thought." Zya replied. "Stand back you two." Zya closed her eyes, and Ju felt rather than watched a sharp gust of air knock the focus stones out of the hands of the three wizards. Nothing happened for a moment, but then Ju had a momentary vision of somebody hurtling backwards at uncharted speeds. Two of the wizards let out piercing screams, forcing Ju and Cameron to drop their weapons and cover their ears. Zya seemed unaffected, and drew her dagger. The third wizard just dropped to the ground. After but a moment, he was joined by the other two. As they did so something not so far off screamed as well, a mental projection that reeked of madness, and of unspeakable evil.

"Oh dear," Zya said quietly, "I think we may be in trouble."

Cameron bent down over the still forms of the ancient-looking men. Dropping to one knee, he tested the pulse of the air wizard. "They are dead! What happened to them?"

Zya was surprised to find a pang of sympathy for the three wizards. Or was it empathy? "They committed themselves to their cause so much that they were almost completely crossing over into the focuses they had created. It required so much power and control from all three of them that when I knocked the stones clear of their hands, they were ripped from the focuses and torn between returning to their own bodies and remaining there. What actually happened was the equivalent of slicing them to ribbons, just without the blood."

"Where did that happen?" Cameron appeared to be having a hard time adjusting.

"Wherever they were," Zya replied, "which could have been right here in this very room, or a hundred leagues away where they were trying to kill somebody with their power, a damnable act at best."

"It was better done this way than despoiling these quarters with needless blood." Ju added.

"It's not proper. Not big and it's not clever." Cameron muttered.

"No, but it was necessary."

"Has it worked? I cannot feel it." Ju looked into the distance, where the sky was fading from the reds and yellows of late afternoon into the purples and dark blues of early twilight.

"The feeling has gone, though I cannot tell whether or not we have succeeded. We might have been too late, There is only one way to find out, and that is to go there. We need to go to Caighgard, across the sea. To that end, we need to get back to the main hall. The Duke is sorely pressed."

"You want to just leave these dead man here?" Cameron was still fighting to deal with the unnatural way the wizards had died.

"If you want to save your Duke, then the time to leave is now." Zya replied with no hint of emotion. "Wait here and deal with this, and risk losing him. Come now, and we might yet save him."

Cameron looked up at her, his sunken eyes haunted by all that he had seen. "How do you know all of this?"

"Look at her robes, man. She is a wizard too."

"No, she is but a girl." He said, a strange kind of longing in his voice.

"We will go." Zya announced. "Cameron, you can come with us, or stay to deal with this chattel as you desire. We have other methods of finding the Duke."

"No, I will not stay here. We will go back and deal with the mercenaries, and save my Lord Duke." His priorities seemingly reasserted, Cameron led them off of the balcony without a single glance back.

"What was the 'Oh Dear' about?" Ju quietly asked as Cameron stalked ahead of them in pursuit of some invisible enemy that perhaps he could use a sword on.

"You sure you want to know?"

"I think that I should, Zya. I get all the feelings that you do because of these damned weapons."

"You are right, of course," Zya agreed, "but do not let our trusty guard get word that anything is wrong. There were two sources of danger in the palace. We have faced down one, but the more deadly peril still lies ahead of us. The dark and dismal feeling that spread throughout the land? Well the source is a few rooms away. Ju be very careful, and absolutely do not approach it."

"You have no need to fear me doing that. I have heard of it, and what it has done. A man saved me this very afternoon and it was mercenaries that had been touched by it that he was protecting me from." Ju shuddered at the memory of the blank-faced mercenaries, Foster, and the flight through the dimly lit tunnels with invisible foes pursuing him.

The sounds of fighting began to manifest themselves in the form of the occasional clink and crash. As the three neared the hall, the sounds became more defined. Jeers and yells accompanied the screams of pain and the clash of swords. Behind it all, the bellows and threats of O'Bellah provided a very poignant reminder that there were foes of a source less ethereal but just as deadly. A man that was willing to drive others to their death was somebody to fear for they would lose nothing to send a friend or foe to oblivion for a personal goal, and that was exactly O'Bellah's aim.

They passed up the hallway that led to the alcove, and Cameron bade them wait. "This is too dangerous for you."

"My foot," Zya replied and shoved her way past him, focus stone in hand.

"What about you?" Cameron said defeatedly, looking at Ju.

"I go where my sister goes." He said with a grim smile.

Cameron shook his head. "I give up, lad. Where you kids get your balls from I will never know, but most guards in this Duchy would learn a thing or two from you."

"We do what we must." Ju replied, and unslung his bow. The instant contact with the weapon gave the clear feeling that the Duke was fatigued, but the contact also registered with the Duke, and hope replaced fear. Ju followed quickly almost on Cameron's heels. The very fact that they had returned cheered the guards that were left, but Ju found it hard not to gawk at the room, which had changed considerably. It was carnage. The lines of fighting had shifted but a little, and the remaining guards were ringed in front of them around the dais. Beyond that was a wall of chopped flesh. At some point reinforcements had entered the palace, most probably by one of the tunnels underneath the building, and the face of those opposing them had changed. O'Bellah remained behind his forces, but now he threw rank after rank of the numb-faced mercenaries at the guards. There were a few of his 'conscious' mercenaries on guard around him, but it was the slaughter by the Duke that drew the eye. The dead and dying were several deep, and the blood was flowing freely on the floor around the dais. It had pooled so deep that it splashed up when yet another body fell down. Tables had been chopped to kindling in the fighting, and hardly any of the festive banners remained. If there was a courtier within hearing distance, Zya doubted they would even move to assist. It was the immediate sight that had such an impact on a boy who was not yet a man. Zya shook her head. The slaughter was senseless, but it was unending. The Duke was clearly tired, and even the addition of Cameron to the ranks did not make much difference. For his part, Cameron threw himself into the fighting so forcibly that at least a couple of the other guards were able to take a breather. The mercenaries he faced attacked, but they tried to do it in formation and with no passion. They used no intelligence, and just attacked whatever was in front of them. The creature that had done this to them had no concept of tactics, or strategy. It only had want, and a desire to spread its corruption about like a tree shedding leaves. It was getting what it needed.

"The girl and the whelp! Get them! There they are, behind the guard!" O'Bellah had noted them the second that they had returned, and Zya felt that this was no time to be scared. The duty that the Duke felt echoed to him through his bow. He climbed atop a column behind the dais and found a perch to fire from. He would save the Duke the only way that he could. The mercenaries that had surrounded their foe now joined the attack, and O'Bellah closed behind them. "Join Me!" He commanded, and with a roar the unarmed fighting men burst in on the hall. With a lust for battle that had been missing in the catatonic mercenaries, they lit up the hall with their animation and obvious hunger for blood. As a unit they charged towards the dwindling force of the Duke and his guards, and as a unit they crashed into an unseen barrier.

Ju smiled. "Fight that, why don't you?" He called out, and sent an arrow into the arm of a mercenary about to chop down the Duke himself.

Zya stood in front of the great table, her eyes ablaze as she conjured a focus that had encircled the outlanders. "I will not permit you to do this, O'Bellah. You serve an abomination, defying the very Law by which we live, and you shall fail."

O'Bellah laughed evilly at her denouncement. "Will I, girl?" He shouted across the din of fighting, "I think not. You do not have the tricks to stop everybody in this room. I know you for what you are and you will not escape me again. You will be taken to the proper place and I think you will find that you are not the only one with tricks up your. . .AAH!"

"Yes!!" Ju crowed from his perch as he readied another arrow. "I don't think you will find much more up that sleeve than fat and bone!"

O'Bellah crouched down and with a gesture that spoke of anger as much as it did of insanity, pulled the arrow straight through his arm. "Kill them! Kill them all! Keep the girl and slay that archer!"

The fighters bellowed and attacked the focus to little avail, but the other mercenaries heeded his command and attacked with renewed ferocity. Ju sent arrow after arrow into the enemy, only felling them where they were about to take out one of the guard. "We are going to have to get out of here, Zya. There is no more time left. Zya! Watch out!"

One of the mercenaries rushed the line, feinted and then dodged past two of the guards wearied by the extensive fighting. He ran straight for Zya, who froze to the spot. She had her focus stone glinting in one hand, but no other weapon. Closing her eyes, she apparently prepared for the inevitable, but she was recalling a memory that was recent, although it seemed a world away from this death and violence.

'"Is the dagger bad?"
"The dagger has a type of magic that you will come to understand, child. You shall have it back, so do not worry yourself. But you shall have a different outlook on life when you wield that weapon once again."'

The old woman had been right in her assessment. Ju was too young to appreciate the compulsion that wielding the weapons gave to a person, but she understood the words now. The magic linked a select few, granting them the one thing that so many people lacked in their solitary private lives, a sense of companionship that bordered on the preternatural. A sense of solidarity that meant she was never truly alone. She felt it now, in the young hands that protected her, in the sure hands that wielded the sword mere steps to her left. Knowing that there was no other choice, she stepped to one side and brought the dagger up and around in an arc.

The dagger plunged straight for the heart of the man that rushed her, and he stopped in his tracks. Saliva dripped off of his quivering bottom lip as he sought to comprehend what had just happened, but this turned quickly to blood as he fell back off of the blade. With a questioning look he dropped to the ground, shuddered once, and then died.

"Oh my, what have I done?" Zya looked at the blood on her hands, on the blade of the dagger that had seemed for so very long an object of comfort. Now it was an object of revulsion. She could not drop it though, and knew exactly what the woman had meant. She had often imagined herself defending valiantly as she was attacked, but now the dagger showed her exactly what it was. The release of life to a different plane of existence, to forever be denied a body. There was more to it as she considered her feelings. The mercenary that had rushed her had been one of those in the front ranks, wooden in movement numb in intelligence. The change had happened suddenly, the man getting released from his stupor for a reason perhaps. Zya turned away from his corpse to consider her options and found Ju facing her, no longer perched above the massing ranks of mercenaries.

"We must go now if we are to reach the ship in time."

"I. . .Yes you are right. I will follow you Ju."

"Look!" Exclaimed one of the Duke's guards. "We are pushing them back! See now as the coward flees!"

Zya peered through a gap in the mass of bodies. It was true. O'Bellah was backing out of the door behind the ranks of mercenaries. He had an evil smile on his face that spoke of bad things to come, and Zya felt them. "This is not played out yet, Ju. O'Bellah has one card left to deal."

Zya felt the evil, the sheer malevolence of the thing before it even entered the hall. It had dogged her dreams, filled her unoccupied moments with thoughts of terror, and the very land on which she stood recoiled from its passing. Darkness preceded it, and the lanterns in the hall dimmed as it crossed the threshold. In the twilight of the day, the Golem had come at last. The mercenaries that were currently unaffected by its touch stepped quickly back, the rest just dropped their swords and turned towards the thing that had taken part of their very souls in payment for their services. The Duke's guard remained defiant, but it was obvious to all that they would run given the chance. That none of them was looking any higher than the floor was understandable. The creature had rendered many stronger men with a glance. Zya looked the creature over for the first time. It was bulky and black, seemingly created from the darkest stone. It had no features to speak of, but the impression of eyes under that overgrown rocky brow was definitely there. It grumbled and groaned as if rock moved against rock as it walked towards her, slowly, unemotionally. There was an air of expectation mixed in with the evil that made her so tempted to look away, and Zya realised that O'Bellah had returned.

"Your time is at an end, girl. Come with me now. Release my warriors, or you shall all perish in a land of torment and pain, where you shall exist forever." The statement made Zya laugh in defiance, despite the situation. "You stupid man. How can we perish if we are going to exist forever? That is a contradiction in terms. Maybe you should write down your petty speeches before you reel them out. And to think I have been running and keeping ahead of you ever since Hoebridge."

This last sentence registered with O'Bellah. "You are without doubt the girl we have been after, the very person that Garias Gibden needs to grab ultimate power. My search is at an end. You are all I need to gain favour over any of my rivals in the Nine Duchies. Oh the riches that will be mine when I present you to him. I would look around you, girl," he said slowly, "you are outnumbered, outmatched and about to pass into a world where all you will know is pain. Smart comments are the last stand for a fallen people. This Duchy is about to have its head chopped off, the start of the end for the Duchies. You will be responsible for the new order coming in, whether you like it or not."

The Golem approached her, and the guards parted like fat around a dagger straight from the fire. The Duke managed a glance, and then stood back with the rest. Zya felt the horror through her dagger, and realised that the joined weapons were the only source. She looked up at the Golem as it rumbled closer, and realised that she had accepted her fate. There was no dream to equal the feeling she was experiencing. If her end was now, then so be it. She stood defiantly on the middle of the dais, and waited for eternity to overtake her. The Golem mounted the platform in one easy stride, and the Duke and his guards cowered back, shivering with fear, unable to look up. Zya sent a reassuring thought through her dagger. The only person to remain anywhere near was Ju, who held tightly onto his bow as if he could still do damage to this creature of stone. The Golem hulked over her, and Zya tensed for the blow that would surely flatten her, but nothing happened. Zya tipped her head up to look into the face of darkness, the pit of oblivion seething behind the unreadable 'eyes'. The creature stood immobile, seemingly ready to move, but something held it back.

As this strangest of confrontations was taking place, a man entered unseen by the mercenaries and whispered something to the Duke. Breaking the spell of the Golem's evil, the Duke got the attention of his guard. "Fall back," he whispered, and motioned to Ju with his hand indicating that he too should come.

"I stay." Ju replied, and with that decision, the Duke remained with them. "We make a stand together for my realm, and all that would oppose you." O'Bellah pouted, trying to look sad. "Such a noble statement. Shame it is wasted on ears of stone. Golem, take them, they are yours!"

The Golem shifted as if to move forward, but remained otherwise immobile, tensed as if waiting for something.

"Golem, Take them!" O'Bellah raised his voice. The creature did not stir in response as always it had. Zya looked up at it as she had done in a dream. It was waiting for something, but not from O'Bellah.

"TAKE THEM!" He ordered, but still no movement.

"Zya, the shield around those outlanders is weakening." Ju whispered loud enough for her to hear, and she glanced across. It was true. Oblivious to the tense standoff happening in front of them, the warriors were working up a frenzy as they beat against the focus that surrounded them, and they were having success. The raw energy in their voices was getting louder.

"It is the Golem, it is draining the focus. That is why it hasn't taken us." Zya felt the focus being absorbed, felt the redirection of her will being sucked into the Golem by its presence. Looking into the face of darkness, Zya remembered a phrase, the simplest phrase, a phrase that was used commonly a million times a day in a million different places. In her dream it had been a bizarre phrase that uttered in a nightmare, but it made sense to try it. Looking into the face of the creature, she uttered three simple words. "I love you."

Everything stopped. The Golem froze, and the drawing of Zya's focus halted. The air seemed to shudder around them.

"Now! Let us get out of here!" The Duke yelled, and grabbed Zya by the arm. They ran through the alcove, Ju close behind as he fired a volley of arrows into the mercenaries who now swarmed after them. The Duke locked the heavy wooden door as they ran down a different passageway, and then Zya remembered where they were supposed to go.

"We need to leave, don't we Ju?"

"Absolutely." The boy agreed.

"Wait. First you need to tell me why my sword suddenly acts as if it were alive whenever you two are around." Duke Hester was insistent. "They will come through soon enough, and we shall be ready." He indicated the two ranks of archers lined up along verandas on either side of the hallway. The room was a semi-circle, focussed on the doorway through which they had come.

"You are going to slaughter them? That's monstrous."

"Zya, they would do the same to us."

"Intent is everything, Zya," Ju reminded her, "and it is the only way to save them."

Zya smiled grimly. "We all use the Law to our advantage, whoever we are. The sword that you carry is enchanted somehow. I cannot tell you much more than that, and also the fact that it is linked to my dagger, and Ju's bow. We were given these weapons by my father, but as to where your sword came from I cannot tell."

"It is an heirloom." Hester replied, as he looked down its engraved surface. Double edged, it was gleaming and looked brand new. "I would make a supposition and say that it came from the same source. Judging by my ancestors deeds, it is probably safe to say that they stole it from someone while on a raid."

"Why they are linked remains a mystery," Zya continued, "but perhaps there are others." "Different weapons meant all for some grand purpose?" Hester mused out loud.

"Perhaps." Zya agreed.

A resounding boom came from the door, making them jump.

"They are coming! Places, men. Shoot anything that comes through that door, man or otherwise!" Hester turned to his two guests. "Now is the time you should go, is it not?"

Ju nodded urgently. "If we do not leave, we will be stuck here. Our chance is now. We must take it."

"Go then, and the God's speed to you both. I pray we shall meet again. Cameron, Joshua, accompany my guests to the dock, and see that no harm comes to them."

The two named guards stepped forward to lead them away, but Zya stood as if in a trance. "We will meet again, Duke Hester. You can count on it. Pray also that we meet in better circumstances."

The mysterious look in her eyes was enough to convince him that the words she spoke were sincere. "Go then, and I look forward to our next encounter." The guards nodded to their Lord, and led the two out to safety. It was only moments later that the door splintered with another boom, and finally burst inwards. Hester peered through the dust, and for a moment saw O'Bellah stood there with something in his hand. Then the fighters poured through. Yelling with fury, the outlanders were silenced just as quickly as they were mown down with arrows. But it was not enough. Warriors and mercenaries ran through quicker than archers could aim and fire, and soon there was a knot of resistance.

"Through the door! Follow the girl!" O'Bellah bellowed to his men. More of the numb-faced mercenaries stood there taking arrows while the conscious ones ducked behind. Because they had no concept of pain, it took many more arrows to fell them, and by the time Hester led a counter attack, the mercenaries were through and gone. The dead piled several deep, as was intended when one Duke built this particular hall, but it was no good. O'Bellah had still made it through with a sizeable force.

"What do we do now, my Lord?" Asked one of his captains.

"There are rats loose in my palace, captain," he replied as he held his sword up to his face, "we have to go and catch them."

Zya did not even bother to look behind her as she ran through courtyards and under the sturdy wooden bridges that made up the Duke's coastal estates. The heavy footfalls and shouts they had been hearing had grown steadily louder. It was obvious that they were being chased, being hunted down by a pack that would show them not an ounce of mercy. She hated to admit it to herself, but she was struggling with the pace. The two guards were hardy and fit, and could run for days on end so it seemed. Ju as well had been running from one end of the city to the other, and found the pace easy. Zya did not want to believe the fact but the secular existence while she had learned about focussing, even for a couple of moons, had robbed her of the fitness she used to enjoy. Breathing heavily, she managed to gasp out a sentence. "I cannot keep this up. Go on ahead."

"No, we will stop." It was Ju that had replied.

The guards looked around them. "Through here." Indicated Joshua, and they ran through a narrow side-passage and out into a different road. Shouts and footfalls went past the other end of the passage. They had been so lucky, and they all knew it.

Holding onto her stomach, Zya heaved in great gulps of air. When she had recovered enough to look up, she was presented with a sight that puzzled her. They were stood so it seemed halfway up a street of shops. In the twilight there were dark shadows where signs hung, and glinting reflections of the early moon above. "What is this place?" She asked.

"The Duke's private town, called Dukestown by many." Cameron whispered as he watched the passage for any pursuers.

"But who lives here?"

"The household staff, the private army." Came the whispered reply.

"But where are they?"

"You may have forgotten in the excitement Zya, but it *is* the Festival of Growth today." Ju grinned as ever he did when he was able to get a dig in. "They are not here because they are out celebrating. The one day they have to get away from their daily life was today."

"Through here! Voices!" Came the deep cry from the other side of the passageway.

"Run!" Zya cried, and bolted towards the darkness. What possessed her to run so fast so suddenly she never knew, but before any of the others could react several mercenaries beset the two guards. Flowing into action, they defended while Ju did his best to incapacitate. The mercenaries were as confused by the sudden change of scenery as Zya was, and it was their undoing. Even though they were outnumbered, it was easy work for Cameron and Joshua. After they had dragged the bodies out of the way, they stood quietly drawing breath, listening for any others. There were none.

"Did either of you see where Zya went?" Asked Ju. There was no sign of her.

"Sorry lad, we were concentrating on the enemy." Joshua replied as he checked his blade for nicks.

Cameron looked at his brother guard, a stare that Ju could not entirely make out in the darkness. "Why don't we split up and see if we can find her? Either road leads down to the dock."

Joshua nodded and moved silently off down the main road of Dukestown. "Come on lad, let us see if we can't find her ourselves." The tone in Cameron's voice gave Ju no reassurance at all, and he remained silent as he followed the guard into the darkness.

The deepest shadows became a blur for Zya, flying by with the speed of the swiftest bird, a collection of deep colours mixed with deeper shades. She ran without thought, without any conscious decision. If there were buildings along the path, she did not notice them. She stared straight ahead at all times, and did not feel it when the stone beneath her feet began to shift and change. If she had looked down she would have seen the road fall away beneath her opening up as a great void filled with distant stars. She ran on, drawn deep into herself by the shock of the mercenaries, her eyes drawn to the beautiful but very distant light. It was silver, and nebulous. Gradually, her fright over the mercenaries subsided and she became more aware of the gleaming expanse in front of her. The stars, the darkness had disappeared from beneath her and now Zya was running on a bed of silver sand that shifted with a wind that she could not feel. Her footsteps erased by the strange surface as soon as she passed, Zya did not look back. There was no way back to where she had come from. The sand rippled and beams of pure white light shot out at her, but she was not afraid, did not look away. The horizon began to turn a light shade of blue, and azure glow at the farthest point that the eye could see. Above her, the stars gathered, closer and closer until they appeared to fill the entire sky before her. Something bade her slow down, reassured her that she was safe. Zya fretted silently that somehow the sand would not bear her weight.

"Do not let that worry you, daughter of Ilia. I would not let that happen, not in this place."

The words somehow boomed, and yet were spoken inside her mind as the tiniest of whispers. It took much for Zya to concentrate on one aspect of the voice, so elusive was it. "Where am I?" Zya asked simply, giving up on trying to get her bearings in this vast desert of the night.

"You have been brought to my place of eternal residence, where I spend forever casting my eye over all who care to look up at me." The voice now came to Zya as one so beautifully feminine that only the perfect woman could have spoken it. The lilt was so musical and distant, yet warming and close. Zya felt instantly comforted by it, at ease in the very depths of her troubled soul.

"Fear and angst are feelings for another time, another place," the voice soothed, welcomed, and instantly all thoughts were banished from her mind. Zya stared into the light, trying to seek out the source of the voice. There was no obvious reason for her to look this way other than the light, but she led her hand up trying to see past the dazzling brightness. "Who *are* you?" She wondered aloud.

"You know the answer already, deep within yourself, Zya S'Vedai. I have brought you before me to tell you this. The dreams you have had were but the beginning. They have significance, but significance unlike any of those who have gone before you would realise. Your dreams cover a wider vision, and it is up to you to realise that vision before it is too late. Time continues to pass you by, and you are but one of a few that will need to survive the coming darkness. Remember Zya, the gates aligned focus the mind to cross the bridge. Seek out the gates, and use the knowledge that you gain to open or close them as you see fit."

"But where shall I look?" Zya squinted. There was a humanoid form behind the light, but it was encompassed in the eldritch glow, far too bright for the eyes of a mere human.

"You are already looking in the right places. Seek within yourself for the final answer. You shall have seven dreams. Over the course of the seven you will learn certain truths if you have the fortitude to withstand and survive. It will not be easy."

"I don't understand the relevance."

"One seeks to change your world at a level more profound than most could understand. Your world cannot take this. At the end, you must destroy it all if you cannot preserve it. The world was not meant for this."

"Not meant for what?"

The glowing being ignored her question, and continued. "Your dreams, Seer of the Law, shall be the seven dreams of the Gods." The light faded just enough that Zya could make out the form in front of her. Robed only in a silver glow, the lithe body gleamed in the light. The silver hair matched the colour of the skin, the only difference being the reflection of the face in the silvered chest that marked the being as female, if such a distinction was possible. There was one difference, that being the eyes. They were completely blue, and looked into Zya's soul. She knew exactly who she was seeing. "Go now, make your way to my brothers domain, for it is the only route to safety." The light dimmed just enough for her to have one better glimpse of the glowing being in front of her, and then it brightened to the point she had to close her eyes in pain.

"Zya? Can you hear me?"

In the darkness Zya's senses began to return to her. The pain remained.

"Ondulyn? Moon Goddess?"

"She knocked herself out good and proper," another voice observed, "let us get her to her feet. We need to get away from here."

In the distance came the distinct ring of sword against sword. Zya opened her eyes slowly, trying to see who held her in the near-darkness. "Ju? Is that you?"

"It's certainly no Moon goddess. She resides up there." Ju pointed, and Zya followed his gaze. A great white moon hung low in the sky.

"What happened to me?"

"Feel your forehead. That might answer your question."

Zya touched tentative fingers to her face, and winced at the pain.

"Best guess we can give is you ran flat into something during your little moment of panic." The voice was Cameron, the guard that had been with her since the great hall.

"How long have I been out?"

"Not a great deal of time. We were attacked and fought them off, and then came after you. I think we should best be getting to the dock though. If the ship is still there, then time is wasting." Ju turned to walk on towards the sea, and the next moment he was lying flat on his back. Cameron turned round to her, and for a moment Zya thought that he had run the boy through. Dropping the cudgel he had hidden from them both until now, Cameron approached her warily, stalking her like a cat would stalk vermin. "Oh I don't think you need to worry about the fighting. They are a world away from here, from you and I."

Cameron closed on her, and Zya came to realise very quickly that he was a very dangerous man. Even in the dark there was a gleam to his eyes that equalled the cunning of O'Bellah, and perhaps the viciousness as well. He reached for her, and she batted his hand away. "Leave me alone, I'm warning you."

In response Cameron hit her with a backhand of such ferocity that she flew backwards into the front of a shop and crumpled in a dazed heap to the ground. "You do not tell me what to do, woman. You are no wizard, nor any sort of important person. I know you for what you are, just as I knew that whore that married my Duke. You would supplant him, bitch. I will not let you do that. I will show you what you should face should you ever come here again." Zya felt hands reaching over her, but fortunately she was barely aware of what was happening. She did not feel the hand between her legs, seeking out her most private parts, trying to separate her robes. She could not see the lust in Cameron's eyes, the flecks of spittle that hung from his chin as he tried to molest her in the dark. She wondered instead about Ju. Zya could not reach him.

"Step away from the girl." A voice spoke out of the darkness.

The hands removed themselves from her, just inches away from their goal, and the moon's reflection intruded itself upon her confused eyes. "What are you? Some kind of mercenary with scruples?" Cameron's much harsher voice, thick with lust and annoyed at being interrupted, growled.

"Perhaps I am," the voice replied, "but at least I can attest to the fact as I have never raped a girl."

"Well you can swear that before the Gods, when I am finished with you!" Cameron shouted, and drew his sword. The clash of swords and resulting sparks indicated that the newcomer was ready for this, and the battle that ensued did a lot to wake Zya from the stupor that had come over her. The din made her ears ring, but she managed to gather her wits enough to look around her. Ju was on his side, blood seeping from what surely must have been a nasty cut to his head. Zya reached over to him, and pulled his inert body closer to her.

He groaned in response. "Mother?"

"You wish," she replied, "call me sister maybe."

"Zya? What happened?"

"Cameron has lost his wits. He is very dangerous, tried to kill you, rape me, and only the intervention of one man has saved us."

"Ju tried to look round, but groaned and nearly collapsed. He shivered from the shock of the assault, but stared out into the shadows where the two men fought. It was a ferocious battle, both of the men very competent swordsmen. Even in the moonlight there was no clear advantage. One would strike low, and the other would parry low. Thrusts were met with counter thrusts, chops angled off by the opponent's blade. In the moonlight they fought like avatars of the Goddess that Zya had seen or thought she had seen only moments ago, silvery monarchs in their world of white light and darkest shadow.

"Zya, we have to get out of here." Ju insisted.

"Can you walk?" She asked.

"I could probably fly if it would get me to the ship. It is late though. They may have left without us already. We may be stranded here."

"We will have to take our chances." Injured and dazed as they were, Zya and Ju managed to get to their feet and make achingly slow progress down the street towards the dock. The key was to not let anybody know they had gone. Zya knew as soon as Cameron spotted them, he would move in for the kill.

Even now she could hear his battle roars as he tried to unsettle the mysterious opponent. They eventually made it to a point where they were nearly out of sight of the combatants when Ju turned to her. "We should help that stranger. He is doing us a favour." Without pausing for breath, Ju unslung his bow from its accustomed resting place on his shoulder and notched an arrow.

"Ju wait. You don't know who is who."

Ju looked up at her and nodded grudgingly. "You are right of course. I could hit the other man and Cameron would hunt us down. But not before he had a few arrows sticking out of him."

"Intent rules everything Ju. Were you to shoot the other man just because you hoped to stop someone who might have killed us, that is as bad as cold-blooded murder. You have to understand that we are out of harms way for now, and with no idea of who is whom in the darkness you have no right to try. Any intention of helping is cancelled out by blind chance."

Ju lowered his bow. "We should try to get to the docks as quickly as we can then." Reshouldering his weapon, Ju turned to look down the gentle gradient of the road to the sea. It was a clear night now, the moon reflecting the sun's light as well as a mirror and the sea shone back at the sky. There were occasional patches of darkness in the distance, probably waves. As the sea shifted in its graceful dance, shapes materialised in the darkness. Shadows topped with white crests that could have been waves out to sea toppling over in the wind. Except that the crests never plunged. Zya realised what she was seeing. "Ju, look out to sea."

Ju turned and looked down to the waves, and at that point the moon chose to highlight the bay as far West as she could see. "Oh my."

"You see them too." Ju said with renewed energy.

"That is a welcome sight to behold. Let us get down there." What the two had witnessed was the unveiling of the entire pirate flotilla. Nearly a hundred ships floated in the bay, most of them far out to sea. Several were closer, but none were in range. This was disheartening to the two of them, but they persisted in their attempt to reach the dock. Behind them a piercing scream split the night, making Ju jump and Zya tremble. The two of them looked at each other, and without a word hurried on. The shops became closer and more crowded as befitted any dockside wharf. There were many more places for a mercenary to spring out on them, but their only concern was getting to the expanse of the sea.

"There they are!" Shouted someone from across to their left. Down a side street Joshua pointed towards them, and then ran. Behind him another man with a sword already unsheathed followed closely. Ju grabbed his bow and Zya managed to find her focus stone. They readied themselves for the hopeless battle so close to freedom. A rush of wind and noise prevented their fate from reaching out and taking them as a shadow erupted into motion. They stood there mere moments from death, and watched in amazement as a man with a dented helm and a notched sword attacked the two guards at a blistering pace. Time seemed to slow for them. As Zya breathed she felt each particle of air pass through her lungs, felt the slow steady thump of her blood as it rushed through her ears. The men in front of her slowed, to the point that the fighting became a graceful dance of death. She could see every move as if it had been scripted a generation ago, and for some reason everything else became more and more remote. It was only the slowly waving form of Ju shouting into her face that brought her back to her senses. She shook her head, and suddenly the fight was at full tilt once more. "Our would-be saviour is certainly taking the fight to those guards. Damn my trusting nature to think that any of them were not thinking of themselves on a night like this."

"The Duke? Is he like that too? You know what everybody said about him. Darrow and Yneris spoke about the Merchant Duke, hoarding his gold. Even things that Jenni said to me about rumours of him. He is thought of as selfish, a womaniser, and a lecher of the highest degree. I cannot feel that."

Zya reached for her dagger. Through it she felt the contact with Duke Hester, felt the very sincerity of his words as he had last spoken to them, reached into the depths of his soul. "No, he is not. His men might be a little more wayward than he believes them to be, but he is doing the right thing. He is hunting O'Bellah and his mercenaries, defending his Duchy to the hilt. He is not the man made out to be so bad. We have seen the true source of the lies."

"A little more wayward?" Ju looked off into the alleyway where the stranger was finally getting pressed back. "Can we do something now? It is clear enough to see who is blocking the way, and if that were Cameron, I think there would be three of them and two of us, and not the other way around."

Zya watched the fight momentarily. "He is hurt, bleeding all over the place. It's a miracle he is still standing. Ju if you can help save his life and ours, then the time to act is now."

Ju flashed her a grateful smile and took aim, relieved that he could finally do something useful. The fact that he was going to end a life did not even register. Zya lamented for the innocence lost from such a young person, but accepted the fact that at least he understood that his intentions had to be right before he could commit to such an act of violence. The bow had moulded to him and he had adapted to his weapon. He had not accepted the addiction of such power as Zya had. That was a task she would face in the future. For now, Zya pulled her own focus stone from her pocket and poured her thought into its crystalline perfection. Her thoughts melded with the lattice of crystals and she waited, her mind invigorated by the focus that was a moment away from release, her body filled with the energy that spilled back from the focus and made her whole again. As she stood there in the semi-transparent overlay of the crystalline world to the real world, she realised that was one question she had never asked Joen. Then the thought arose that she was still angry at the betrayal of that bug-eyed little weasel Ralnor, and her mind was brought back to the present.

Their shadowed saviour was definitely weakening from blood loss. His arm heavy, it became harder and harder to fend off the two guards, both fitter and stronger than he. The moment had worn off and now only the cold reality that he was going to die remained.

Joshua feinted, and then ducked for the other man to lunge over his shoulder, but nothing happened. Looking back, he saw an arrow sticking out of the mercenary's neck, the wound gushing blood as he clutched at it. The moment cost him, for the stranger angled his sword straight up through his ribs. Joshua's last moment of dimming sight was of a man pulling his sword free.

The stranger turned towards them. "Thank you both. Your arrow was timely, lad. Only an expert could have shot like that." He appeared to be smiling, but he took no more than a couple of steps before he collapsed to the ground at the end of the alleyway.

Ju ran to the man, still very wary of the mercenary and the guard beyond, and rolled him over. "Foster!" He exclaimed.

"The man who saved you?" Zya hurried to the man. He bled from a dozen wounds, staining the shadowed street darker with his blood. "Ju, he is dying, look at his wounds. Stand back, I am going to try something." Zya repeated the focus that she was going to use, and it flowed as easily through her as the breeze from the sea did around her. Extending the focus to include both Ju and Foster, Zya changed the intention of the focus to search the ground for other people. Her stomach dropped when she realised that there were a great many, only a couple of streets away. Obviously the hunt did not go well.

Withdrawing the focus, Zya looked down at her companions. Ju stood ready and alert, while Foster glowed back at her.

"Lady, I don't know what it was as you did just then, but I owe you my life and I shall follow you anywhere." His voice throbbed with sincerity and his face was a beacon of gratitude.

"It was levelling the scores as far as I was concerned." She replied. "You have saved me twice, and Ju more times than I believe I know of.

Foster stood up. "Blow me, that magic of yours is potent stuff. You wizards are a force, that's to be sure. But what are you doing down here? You are surrounded."

"If we have to, we will swim, Foster." Ju replied before Zya was forced into a dangerous explanation that anybody could have overheard. "Care to join us?"

"Right now I feel as if I could take on the ocean myself, and everything in it." Foster replied as he bent to pick up his sword. "I'm game."

Leaving the alleyway, the three walked down the remaining slope to the dock. It consisted of a series of huts on the stone jetty, and a boulder spit into the sea. Both Zya and Ju looked around in desperation as they sought out the ship they had hoped was still close by. As one their stomachs sank when they realised that they were truly stranded. There was barely a ship in sight, but Foster saw the ships in the distance.

"You are not going to be able to swim that far, not if you were even a fish, lad. You were thinking as one of them might have been a bit closer and you could have rowed out. Good idea, bad luck." Zya looked at Foster, who looked down at the sea glumly while the gentle waves lapped against the dock in the silence of the night. A silence that was broken from behind them by the scrape of metal on metal. The three turned to find themselves face to face with at least a score of mercenaries, all of them heavily armed. Surrounded by them was the corpulent form of O'Bellah. "It seems that you have lost your way, you little green witch. Nowhere left for you to run. Nowhere left for you to hide."

"You will not kill any of us, not while I draw breath." Zya stood on the brink of rage, determined to focus the very fabric of life around her to defend them all.

O'Bellah laughed, and many of the mercenaries joined in the moment, chuckling, though the smile never reached their eyes. It created a very dark scene in the evening. "Who said I was going to kill you? I have plans for you, bitch. There is one man just dying to make your acquaintance, and I shall take you to him. It will be my pleasure." O'Bellah said the word 'pleasure' with a sick lilt to his voice. Whatever the experience, it was unlikely to involve pleasure of any sort.

In response to this, Zya threw up a protective wall around the end of the dock on which they stood. The mercenaries tried to break through, but O'Bellah just stood there, smiling insanely. He pulled a focus stone from somewhere around his wide girth.

"Would you care to go one on one with me?" Zya challenged him. "Do you think you have the strength of will to overpower me with a focus?" Stalling for time was her last ploy. She could not kill any of them with a blast of power no matter how desperate the situation became, not if they did not attack.

"I think, young lady, that your time has come. You know my allies, and I can bet for certain that if we stand here long enough your focus will drain away to nothing." He leered at her, and Zya searched the focus. Truly enough it was seeping away. The creature still remained apparently immobile in the palace, but its influence was being felt everywhere. The very ground sucked at her focus, drawing the energy to the Golem. She shook her head. "You stupid man. That creature will draw from you as much as it would from me. You, and every one of those idiotic fools that follows you."

"Then you have only one choice." He replied to Zya's shock, Ju's amazement and Foster's complete outrage. "You must submit yourself to me and end it."

"Don't listen to him, Zya," Ju warned, "he is playing you false."

"O'Bellah, ever since the foothills of the mountains we have seen and heard of your treachery. Nobody would be stupid enough to listen to you." Hope welled up in Zya. Premonitions were coming to pass, premonitions she had only just felt.

The comment only angered O'Bellah all the more. "Pathetic whore! I will bind you and take you screaming to my master!" O'Bellah closed his eyes and concentrated, and Zya felt the smallest of pushes against her wall of air. The only consequence was to distract O'Bellah, and for that he missed the trap being sprung.

"Have at 'em, men!" Roared Duke Hester of Kimarul, and a similar number of guards roared down the road to the mercenaries who now backed up against the air barrier in surprise.

O'Bellah's face registered shock. "This cannot be! Take them!"

From behind her barrier, Zya watched with fear-streaked relief as Duke Hester came to rescue them.

"At least we will have a way out of this." Ju said with thanks clear in his voice.

"No, we cannot go backup to the palace." Zya replied.

"Why not?"

"Yes lass, why not? Added Foster. "It seems as being the right course of action."

"The creature is still up there, and I cannot risk facing it."

"Ahh it's only being a moving statue." Foster said cheerfully.

"No, it is so much more than that. It is evil. A manifestation more malevolent than any other being on this continent." Zya looked at Foster with deadly seriousness as she said this.

He glanced down at Ju, who nodded in agreement. "This creature will end us all, Foster. If Zya believes it, then it is true."

"I'm sorry but my only option is to swim out." Zya continued. "We must get out to the end of the spit, as near to those ships as is possible."

Foster sighed. "I have gone through fire and brimstone to reach you lad. How I survived I don't know. I must have had the God's luck on me tonight. I will fight them if you want to leave. It is the least I can do."

"I don't think things need get that desperate." Said a voice from behind Zya, and she turned around to look into the raven hair and midnight eyes of Lorn.

"Lorn!" Zya shouted, and hurtled into his arms, kissing him forcefully. She had not realised how much she had missed him."

Lorn put up with her ministrations for a moment, and the looked past her to the battling guards and mercenaries. "You can drop that now, we are ready to go."

"Lorn, if I remove this focus they will kill us!"

"I think not." Lorn moved aside, and now Zya saw what had not been revealed before. A ship pulled into view on the dockside, its beautiful sails eerie in the full moonlight, its rigging full of men wielding bows.

"You *have* been busy." She admitted.

"Come, you do not need to stand on the spit now. The tide is turning, and we must make haste." Lorn guided Zya to the steps to the jetty, where she descended with almost a jig in her steps. She had never been this relieved in all her life, and Ju was just speechless.

Foster remained standing on the dock. "I will do what I can from here, my Lady. Maybe get one or two of the bastards before I meet my fate."

"Come with us." Zya urged him.

"Yes Foster, come with us?"

He shook his head. "What use would one turncoat mercenary be to you? How could anybody trust me, knowing that I am associated with them?" He pointed at the band of mercenaries now fully engaged with the Duke's remaining guard.

"You have proven yourself to Ju, and that counts for much Foster." Zya climbed back a couple of steps, trying to reassure the man. "You have saved my life at least twice, and that is proof enough to me."

"You have also proven that you are as blockheaded as ever, Foster, and were your mate Boulter here too he would be laughing at you!" Roared Darrow, who had climbed the steps behind her."

"Captain Darrow?" Foster asked?

"Aye, the same. You know me, mercenary, and if these kids trust you then I do too. Now get aboard my bloody ship before you get pinned like a seamstresses cushion!"

It appeared that the former mercenary needed no more urging, and followed them quickly down to the ship. As asked, Zya released the focus and suddenly several mercenaries found themselves off-balance. They turned, and howling war cries ran after their fleeing quarry.

"Archers!" Roared Darrow, who lit up the night in his gaudy blues and yellows, "fire"

A hail of arrows slammed into the mercenaries, and they melted to the ground. The arrows ranged further up the dock, and everyone dropped as they were drawn into that fatal wave.

Zya climbed aboard the ship, and after a brief embrace with her father ran to the side of the deck to see what had happened. The mercenaries had been felled to a man, and the guards were celebrating. One man had run toward them, and the archers were readying arrows. "No!" She cried, and with a nod from their captain, they relaxed. It was Duke Hester.

"I am alone now!" He yelled at the departing ship.

"You will never be alone!" Zya shouted back. "I will make sure. I made a promise."

"The Gods bless you, girl." Hester yelled back. "Find a safe port and return some day!"

"I will, I promised you that too. Keep fighting the good fight! One day we shall prevail!"

"We already are!" Came the faint cry of the Duke from the dock, and behind him a roar of victory reinforced his words. "Until next time, Zya S'Vedai."

Zya turned to Lorn, who held her from behind. We have stories to be told, but I must keep a promise to the Duke. Tell Darrow to send some of them back. The Duke needs a new army, one Loyal to the city of Bays Point. More importantly one loyal to its people.

Lorn went in search of the captain, leaving Zya and Ju standing on the deck together.

"Will we see him again?" He asked.

Zya flashed him a smile. "That man is stronger then the steel he wields. The next time we see the mainland it will be a changed place. He will be better for it, and the Old Law will have taken a great step to being preserved. We have a long way to go Ju, a long way before this will ever be finished."

"Will it? Will it ever be finished?"

Zya looked out, not answering, and Ju joined her in her contemplation. They looked out on the rapidly retreating landmass. The moonlight turned the cliffs into silver daggers of stone, and the city and palace into beacons of metaphorical hope. In the darkness they said their goodbyes to Bays point. Under the watchful eye of Ondulyn, the fugitives caught the last glance of defiance against the tide of evil. A man with a sword raised aloft, reflecting the moonlight from his blade. After a moment he passed out of sight as the ship turned to join its fellows in saying farewell to Bays Point for perhaps the last time. They were leaving, and not even the Gods themselves would stop Zya from following her Path of Dreams.

Epilogue

The water lapped gently against the side of the dock, rippling and trickling as it found its way into nooks and cracks worn away by the generations of tide. All had fallen quiet since the battle. Dried blood caked the steps, limbs and corpses began the slow process of rotting up on the road. The moon had passed over to the point that its light no longer bleached the nightscape white, but instead cast long, deep shadows.
A hand reached up out of the sea, grasping for a hold on the slick surface. Finding purchase between two of the cobbles it tensed, and up out of the water slid O'Bellah, rising from the depths like one of the behemoths that inhabited the dark deep. He dragged his battered body out of the water, smearing the blood onto himself as seawater poured off of him and onto the congealed mess beneath. He knew that his own would mix with the blood on the steps, and even in this predicament that gave him cause for excitement. Lying there, he did not risk looking up to see who might be watching. The pain of the arrows biting into his huge frame had now subsided to a dull ache, but still the arrows were there, in his arm, his side and his legs. He felt weak, light headed from loss of blood, but he was alive. In his opinion he had won, because the cursed Duke had not finished him off, and that meant he could wreak revenge. His only cause for alarm was that he had lost his focus stone, the prized possession that was his only means of survival.

After resting, he looked up as he tried to gauge the easiest way out of this mess. The sky to the East gradually got paler and paler as he tried to crawl up the flight of steps to the road. As morning threatened to break the only cover he had. It was darker at the top of the steps, and it took a moment for him to realise why. He managed to raise his head enough to see what passed for huge stone feet, and then dropped to the ground in exhaustion.
"Thank the Gods."
"Oh I think that the Gods will have little to say to you when you meet." Said a voice, and something kicked O'Bellah over onto his back. He was presented with a view of all that was bad for him at this time. Ralnor, and the wizard known as Sparan stood there grinning. The Golem blocked out the sky, but in front of him stood a much smaller figure. "You have failed me for the last time, O'Bellah."
He reached his hand up, a last desperate move. "I can find her," he croaked, "I have seen her, I can find her again. Please Garias, help me, master." His hand slumped down as his last energy left him. "Give me a stone."

"No, a stone would be an easy way out. You will be serving penance for this, to remind you whom you serve. You shall live, but you will heal naturally. By the time you are well once again, you will have learnt what it truly means to serve. Pick him up."

"What about the Duke?" O'Bellah's eyes blurred with the pain as he was forced to his feet.

"This Duchy is as good as dead. We go now to the central plains, where we will annihilate every man, woman and child until your quarry comes seeking us out. We will have both the girl, and the Tome of Law."

With a mental nod, the Golem surrounded them all. As he was taken to another place to begin his convalescence, O'Bellah swore that Duke Hester would one day bleed for his victory. He would bleed slowly, and O'Bellah would be there to watch.

About the Author

Matthew W Harrill lives in the idyllic South-West of England,
nestled snugly in a village in the foothills of the Cotswolds. By
day he plies his trade as a Business Analyst currently for
Hewlett Packard, but who knows for how long? By night he
spends his time with his wife and four children, playing Guild Wars
and GTA4, enjoying the odd movie or three.